WILDCAT

Text and Design Copyright © 2019 by Rebecca Hutto

All rights reserved. No part of this publication may be reproduced, distributed, or transmitted in any form or by any means, including photocopying, recording, or other electronic or mechanical methods, without the prior written permission of the publisher, except in the case of brief quotations embodied in critical reviews and certain other noncommercial uses permitted by copyright law. For information regarding permission, send an email to RHPublishingHouse@gmail.com.

This book is a work of fiction. Names, characters, places, and incidents are either the product of the author's imagination, or are used fictitiously, and any resemblance to actual persons, living or dead, business establishments, events, or locals is entirely (most likely) coincidental.

ISBN 978-1-7330034-1-4
10 9 8 7 6 5 4 3 2 1

Printed in the United States of America
First Printing, June 2019

For my family, and all the
maple orange moments you've given me.

The Great Unknown

Nameless Creek

Murky Rapids

Starcross's Gorge

Fernburrow Falls

The Kivyress

Silver P

The Glade

Western Territory

The Valley Creek

The Cliffs

The Lowlands

The Fields

Coyote Rock

Wolf Trail

The Great Unknown

The Great Unknown

Eastern Territory

The Rift

Stone Ridge

ARC Facilities

ond

Fire Creek

Gale Springs

N
W E
S

The Great Unknown

THE CATS OF
DARK'S VALLEY
WESTERN COLONY

Commander

- Aspen – a ruddy brown agouti tom with a half white face, one yellow eye and one blue eye.

Chief Advisor

- Cloud – a grey tom with patches of white on his face, a white stripe on his chest and orange eyes.

Senior Historian

- Whitehaze – a silvery agouti tom with yellow eyes.

Colony Cats

- Ember – a sable brown molly with three white paws and orange eyes.
- Songbird – a sable brown molly with a white blaze on her face and yellow eyes.
- Kivyress (Kai-vee-ress) – a greyish-blue mink furred molly with yellow eyes.
- Hyrees (High-reese) – an overweight fawn agouti tom with green eyes.
- Wren – a ruddy agouti tom with three deep scars across one of his green eyes.
- Farlight – a white tom with patches of agouti fur and orange eyes.
- Tainu (Tay-new) – a black and white molly with yellow-green eyes.
- Lupine – A dark brown agouti tom with yellow eyes.
- Fern – a torbie molly with yellow eyes.
- Fledge – a silver smoke molly with yellow eyes.
- Silentstream – a grey and white molly with yellow eyes.
- Rowan – a dark brown tabby tom with yellow eyes.
- Redwater – a sable tom with orange eyes.
- Sumac – a light tan agouti tom with orange eyes.
- Trout – a silver smoke tom with yellow eyes.

EASTERN COLONY

Commander

- Jade – a brown tabby molly with milky green eyes.

Chief Advisor

- Falcon – a dark grey tabby tom with bright green eyes.

Colony Cats

- Shard – a lynx point tom with bluish-green eyes.
- Echo – a lynx point molly with bluish-green eyes.
- Boreal – a brown tabby with a white underside and leaf green eyes.
- Crow – a black cat with flecks of white in his fur and green eyes.
- Sunshine – a creamy orange tabby molly with light green eyes and a twisted paw.
- Brook – a silver lynx point molly with blue eyes.
- Thunder – a grey smoke tom with a white underside and yellow-green eyes.
- Kite – a fawn tabby tom with sharp green eyes.

OUTSIDERS AND ROGUES

- Eclan (Ee-clan) – a black and white tom with mottled yellow and brown eyes.
- Starcross – a black molly with a white cross-shaped marking on her forehead and golden yellow eyes.
- Bracken – a fawn tabby tom with soft green eyes.
- Buck – an orange and white tabby tom with a stubby tail and dark brown eyes.
- Vixen – a ruddy agouti molly with white-furred burn scars covering her body, one yellow-green eye, and one blind, blued-over eye.
- Galax – a black and white tom with white, pupiless eyes.

CHAPTER 1
EMBER

'*Am I going to die today?*' Ember thought. Her breathing became shallow and irregular. Wind cut through her sable brown fur, rustling leafless trees and making her shiver. She rubbed her white forepaw against the maple branch supporting her. '*And why do I do this? This job?*'

Glistening silver, the color of morning fog, lingered in her head. It was also the color of uncertainty, and it came every morning; though it wasn't so much a color as it was the feeling of a color.

'*Then again, why do Outsiders sneak in? And why—*'

"Ember, it's time to go," a voice said, snapping her away from her thoughts.

She opened her eyes. Searing white flashed, scorching her vision. She blinked until the sky faded back to its usual painful blue. "Coming, Dad. One more moment."

"That sounds familiar," he said.

Ember squinted and looked out across Dark's Valley. The rounded slope of the Eastern Mountain, with its bare trees and clusters of conifers, made up what she could see of the horizon. Far below, a murky lake of morning fog shrouded the Lowlands. A smaller, thinner cloud of mist covered the Western Forest around her.

"Hey, we've got a job to do, Sparky. Let's do it."

"I know. Y-yes, sir," she said. Her white-tipped tail twitched anxiously. *'He's right, Ember. We really do need to go.'*

She peered down through the mist. A silver-furred tomcat looked back up at her, eyes glistening. They were the same shade of faded orange as her own. His expression was unreadable, but she'd recognize his white-patched face anywhere—her father, Cloud.

He stood in a little crook between the roots of the maple tree and propped himself up against its trunk with a forepaw. The rising sun hit his long, silky fur, giving him a fringe of gold. Ember smiled at the familiar sight, one she'd seen almost every day since joining the guard.

"So, are you coming or not?" he asked. "Because if not, I'm leaving without you."

She sighed again. Her breath swirled away in a wispy puff of condensation as she rubbed her muzzle against the branch below her. Frosty bits of ice flaked off and clung to her whiskers. *'You stay here,'* she commanded it. She stood up, then arched her back. "Coming."

As she climbed down, the breeze picked up. A mechanical hum filled the air, whirring and buzzing like an army of bees going to war.

'Oh no. Again?'

Ember flattened her ears. Her heart thudded against her chest as the noise grew louder. Vivid cyan flared in her head. She looked up. A human-made contraption appeared in the western sky. It was sleek, white, oval-shaped and huge. The six spinning blades set in its sides created a tempest. Ember jumped to the ground and covered her ears with her paws. She bit her tongue and trembled as the machine passed overhead, thundering, snarling at her.

'Please stop. Please stop. Please stop.' The words echoed through her mind. All other thoughts disintegrated into swirling grey static.

The noise faded. The craft rumbled over the Lowlands, churning up mist, then disappeared behind the Eastern Mountain. Ember got up. She stared blankly at the horizon. In the silence, her ears rung. Her jaw quivered. She forced it to stop.

'Calm down, Em. You're okay.' She breathed out slowly. "Why do they do

that?"

"I don't know. But as long as they stay in the sky, they can fly around all they want. Better than coming after us," Cloud said.

"Do you think they know we're still here?" she asked.

"Again, I don't know." He licked her cheek. "It's been so many winters, they've probably forgotten about us. I think we're safe."

Ember shuddered. According to the History Tree, the same creatures that made the silver sky machines had also made the first Colony Cats. They'd tried to imprison and experiment on them until Commander Dark led an escape, freeing them all. It was the most terrifying and exciting story on the Tree. The first time she'd read it, she'd had a nightmare about long-legged monsters hunting her and her kin down. She shook her head, trying to clear the thought from her mind.

Cloud walked back onto the border trail. "Now come on, we have a job to do. Let's go do it."

She followed after him, head lowered in respect. "Yes, sir."

He smiled.

'Why are you smiling? If you're trying to tell me something, well, you know I don't know what it means. Kivy would, but she's with Mom, so I can't get her to translate. At least you're smiling, though, so that's good, I guess. Oh well. You know, I'm glad you can't read my thoughts; you'd be so confused.' She stopped walking and tilted her head. 'Or maybe not.'

She chuffed to herself and kept going. Her eyes followed the ground. As she walked, her mind raced; subconsciously calculating the exact places each paw should land for maximum comfort and silence. After mooncycles of tripping over roots and stepping on thorns, the habit had been clawed into her.

Morning sunshine streamed through the mist, creating light beams that stung her eyes. As they walked, birds fluttered and chirped around them. A soft warble joined in the chorus. At the bottom of the ravine beside her, the Kivyress sang with rocks and water. She looked down. The nervousness went away, silver replacing itself with a bright, happy orange. The creek, her sister's namesake, flowed over and around time-smoothed stones. The deepness of the ravine hid it from the sun, cloaking it in a soft blue shadow. Frost still covered most of the ground leading to it.

Ember sucked in a long, slow breath. Scents of dead leaves, dried berries, and trees rubbed free of bark filled her nose. The frigid air made her muzzle burn. Little sparks of sky blue flickered through her mind.

"Hey, Ember," Cloud said, breaking the ambience, "just to let you know, I have to head back to the Glade early today."

Her tail drooped. "Oh, right. The Meeting."

"Commander Aspen wanted to discuss some of the things he plans on bringing up tomorrow. Needs a final opinion, I guess."

"So, er, how early are you suggesting we turn back?" Ember asked.

She bit her tongue. Being the commander's chief advisor, he got summoned away often, and it happened even more frequently near the seasonal meetings. She liked knowing he helped make things work, but it didn't make his absences any easier.

He chuffed. "We can turn around when we—"

"Wait," Ember said. She stopped and lifted her nose to the breeze. The air stung her nostrils again, but the tangy stench that followed made her wince. "Someone's here," she whispered.

Cloud stopped. He stared at the ravine, ears perked forward. He sank into a fighting stance. "Good nose. Stay close and hold position."

Ember obeyed. She bent her legs, pointed her toes outward, and lowered her head to shield her neck from throat grabs. Her heartbeat echoed in her ears, and her nostrils flared as she dissected the smell.

'Not a Colony Cat. Definitely not a Colony Cat. Adult tom. Middle-aged. Outsider or Rogue. Not a wildcat. There's blood in there. Did he fight with Wren and Hyrees earlier and not leave for some reason? No, they wouldn't let him go like that, and he's not dead yet.'

"You have entered Western territory," Cloud said. "Show yourself."

A mottled black and white head popped up. His eyes looked like dying birch leaves: gold with patches of deep brown. Both of his ears were torn, and a recently-dried cut arced above one of his eyes. He vaulted himself out of the ravine and glared at Cloud. Scars covered his body.

"I've shown myself," he said. His gruff Lowland accent made Ember tense. "You happy now?"

He watched them, looking from Cloud to Ember, then back.

"Who are you, and why are you here?" Cloud asked.

Ember kept her eyes trained on the tom's scruffy torso, subconsciously watching for signs of an attack. Meanwhile, her active conscious analyzed every scar and scrape she could make out on his body. Her vision blurred.

'Those scars aren't normal for an Outsider, so definitely a Rogue. Then again, most Rogues aren't that scratched up. Maybe he is a wildcat.' She bit her tongue again. The silver came back, making a knot form in her throat. *'Tahg,'* she mentally cursed, *'he's a mercenary, isn't he?'*

"If you'd like to live, you'll answer my questions," Cloud said.

Ember shook her head and blinked until her eyes regained their focus. Cloud looked the cat over, waiting for a response. Getting none, he shoved a paw against the cat's throat, claws unsheathed.

The cat grinned up at him. He pushed Cloud's paw away and wavered as he stood. "Eclan. What's it to you?"

Mint wafted off his breath. Ember wrinkled her nose and coughed, trying to rid herself of the mind-numbing plant's scent.

"Alright then, Eclan," Cloud said. "Why are you here?"

Eclan glared at him. "S'pose I don't tell you. What'll you do, then? And if I do, do I get to finish what I was doing?"

Cloud growled. "Oh, another wiseacre. About our luck. Better than some kinds of outsiders, I suppose. That's enough questions for you. Time to leave."

He pushed his paws against Eclan's side. Eclan staggered backward, and Cloud clamped his teeth over his scruff. Eclan hissed but didn't struggle.

'Okay, that's not right.' She bit her tongue again. *'This is not good. This is really, really not good. Oh, he's leaving.'*

Cloud dragged him down the slope of the ravine. He walked across over a path of rocks, Eclan's lower body sliding along the creek bottom. Still, he remained limp. Cloud stepped onto the opposite bank, then started up the other side.

Ember half ran, half skidded to catch up with them. When she reached the creek, she leaped across the stones. "Dad, wait!"

Her paws hit a slick patch of algae. They slid out from under her. Ember squeaked in surprise as she stumbled into the creek. Near-freezing water splashed her underside, covering her legs. Prickling, searing pain stabbed at her paws, creating blue polka dots in her head. She tried to climb back onto the rock, but her claws couldn't find traction. She slid back into the water. "D-D-Dad?"

Cloud reached the top of the ravine. He dropped Eclan and spun around. "Oh! Are you okay?" He ran back to her and helped her out of the water. "You've got to be careful on those rocks."

"I kn-kn-kn-know."

"I know you know, but knowing you need to be careful only helps if you *are* careful. I guess now we know when we'll be heading back."

When they reached the opposite bank, Ember shook herself off. She shivered as they climbed to the top.

Ember lifted a forepaw and wiggled her toes. "I c-can't feel my paws."

"Th-that's what happens when you fall in the creek in the winter, kitten. Be glad it h-hasn't snowed yet," Eclan said. He twisted around to groom the wet fur on his haunches, then transitioned to his feet.

Ember tensed her jaw to keep her teeth from chattering. *'Oh, right, him.'*

Somewhere in the back of her mind, she realized this was the farthest she'd ever been beyond Western borders.

Cloud nudged Eclan's flank with the back of a forepaw. "Leave. Now. You'll have plenty of time to groom when you make it back to the Lowlands where you belong."

Eclan stopped grooming mid-lick. His tongue hung limply out of his mouth for a moment. He stood up and looked Cloud over. "You don't say. Well, I hate to break it to you, but this here's outta your territory. You can't make me leave land you don't own."

"I also can't leave you here to slink back in the moment we're out of sight, and I certainly can't sit here watching you all day. I have more important things to do."

He stretched and yawned, then walked in front of Cloud. As he passed by, the tip of his tail thwacked Cloud's nose.

Cloud growled. "You know what? Maybe I should kill you. Or take you to Aspen and let him figure out what to do with you."

Ember swallowed hard. *'Kill him? You aren't going to make me help with that, right?'*

Eclan sniffed a few times. He sharpened his claws on a young tree, then turned around and sprayed it. "No authority, ol' tom. You're in my territory now."

Cloud growled again.

Ember bit her tongue. *'Go away, silver. You're not helping. This is not going to end well. Come on, Em, do something.'* She sucked in a deep breath and stepped closer to her father.

"Okay, can we decide on something, please?" she asked. "I'm cold. This is taking too long. Dad, I, uhm, I think he might be a mercenary. So maybe we should take him in for questioning?"

They stared at her for a few moments. Eclan sniffed again. "Sounds reasonable. Let's do that."

A faint smile flashed on his face, then he pounced. Yellow flared in her head. His paws slammed into Ember's side, knocking her over. They hit the bank of the ravine and momentum sent them into a roll. The world somersaulted around her. Pebbles and debris scraped at her sides.

"Ember!" Cloud shouted.

His voice was muffled by the sound of crunching leaves and her own heartbeat.

'What's going on? What just happened? I'm falling—that's what. Come on, Ember; there are rocks down there. Do something or you're going to get hurt!'

7

Ember tucked her head in. She closed her eyes hard, sunk her claws into Eclan's fur, then yanked him in front of her as a shield. They crashed into the creek together. The stream sucked her under like thick mud. Icy water seeped into her nose. She tried to cough, but got a mouthful of liquid. For a split moment, she couldn't tell down from up nor up from down. Her side hit the creek bed. Ember pushed off to get her head above the water. The landscape spun in and out of focus as she burst through the surface. She staggered against the current and almost fell back under. She gasped for breath, stabilized herself against a stone, then exploded into a fit of coughing and uncontrollable trembling. Eclan splashed up beside her, shivering and sputtering.

'Out the water. Out the water! OUT THE WATER!'

"Ember!" Cloud yowled. "Ember, are you okay?"

He ran down the ravine. Ember climbed onto the creek bank, back in her own territory. Eclan bounded toward her again.

She lowered herself into a fighting stance. *'Ohhh tahg, what am I doing? I'm going to fight a Rogue. I'm about to die.'*

"Be careful. I'm coming, okay?" Cloud called. "Try to hold him there."

Eclan leaped out of the creek. He swiped at her flank. Ember jumped a clawlength out of reach. Before all four of his paws hit the ground, she sank her teeth into his hind leg. Eclan hissed and spun to bite her. She pounced out of the way again, still shaking. Her heart pounded in her throat. Adrenaline pulsed through her veins like lightning bolts of energy.

'Why is he attacking me? Why is he attacking me? Oh, I'm so cold.'

His claws ripped her shoulder. Sky blue; pain blue. Ember squeaked and staggered back. *'Why are you worrying about why? Focus on how you're going to stop him, or you're definitely-probably going to die.'* She ducked beneath a swat. Wind tore through her fur. *'Oh, the fire pits would be nice right about n—FOCUS!'*

Ember faked a lunge for his throat. When he moved to counter it, she adjusted her course and shoved him off-balance. He stumbled. Before he could right himself, she darted up the ravine. He caught his balance as Cloud ran to scruff him. Eclan jumped out of reach and charged after her.

The ground leveled off. Ember spun to face him. He pounced on her. She landed hard on her back, air leaving her lungs in a painful *huff*, and he took the opportunity to shove a paw against her neck. Ember bit her tongue. Her breath dissolved into shaky puffs of steam. Cyan and yellow.

"Shouldn't 'a stopped, kitten," he said. His claws dug pinpricks into her skin. "See, when you turn, it has to be in a direction your attacker isn't coming fr—"

She kicked him in the chest. He staggered backward. His hind paws slipped on a patch of damp leaves, and he plummeted down the ravine. Ember rolled back to her paws and watched in silence as he tumbled past Cloud.

'*It actually worked. Hum, maybe I'm not so crazy after all.*'

Eclan's head struck a rock on the creek bank, and he stopped sliding with his lower half submerged in the shallows. He didn't get up. Ember's throat tightened.

"H-h-h-hey, um, he's s-still breathing, right?" Ember asked. A gust of wind tore through her fur. She shivered harder.

Cloud walked down to him. "Yes, he is." He looked up at her, face unreadable again—this time without the smile. "I . . . I told you to keep him there, Ember. That was dangerous. I could've helped you."

She lowered her head. "S-s-sorry."

"It's okay. I'm just glad you're alright. You are okay, right? Those cuts look bad," he said.

'*Cuts?*' She craned her neck to look at the wounds. Four stripes of bloody fur lined her shoulder. "Oh, yeah, I-I-I'm fine. Just a little c-cold."

"I know," Cloud said. "Hold on; we'll go back to the Glade. I just have to get Mintbreath here and take him back for Aspen to deal with."

Cloud dragged Eclan up the ravine. He set him down at Ember's paws, then licked her forehead. "Let's get you warmed up."

"Th-thanks, Dad."

He nodded once, picked Eclan back up, and they started down the mountain. As they walked, Ember studied the Rogue's soaked form.

"So d-do you think he's a m-mercenary?"

"Maybe," he replied through a mouthful of fur.

He looked away. They moved in relative silence, the only sounds being the forest's ambience. Birds chirped. Branches rustled. The ever-present breeze hissed. Ember pulled her head and tail as close to her body as she could. Every change in the wind cut through her fur and bit her skin.

'I messed up again, didn't I? I wish you'd tell me what I'm doing that's so wrong. At least I stopped him. Isn't that good enough?'

Ember sighed. It turned into a shudder halfway through. *'When I become the new historian, you'll see that I can do something. I can recite every passage and law I've read in any order you want. I can do it, and that's my place. It has to be. Because if I don't have a place, I'll be just another Outsider to chase off.'* She shook her head. *'Tagh,'* she thought, *'I wish I could just say it. But come on, Ember; even if you could get every word out without stuttering, or switching something up, it'd only make things worse. So be quiet. Focus on not freezing to death.'*

Cloud pressed closer to her. His warmth offered some refuge from the frigid air; not much, but enough to ease her wandering mind. An image appeared in her subconscious: her as a kitten, falling asleep in her parents' paws. It came encased in a halo of dark blue, maple orange, and a tired, distant mountain green.

'They love me. Calm down, Em. He's just worried. He's doing the best he can. And he knows I've got a place here. Everything's going to be okay.'

"You okay?" he asked, voice still muffled.

She kept her eyes on the ground ahead. It flickered in and out of focus as she fought to keep herself awake. Already the effects of the adrenaline rush were gone. "I guess so."

Cloud set Eclan down. "You guess so? Don't you think that's a little indefinite for a yes or no question?"

"Maybe. I don't kn-know. It's n-n-nothing, really."

The tip of his tail twitched back and forth. Ember watched it move; it gave her something predictable to focus on.

"One thing life's taught me is that it's never nothing," he said. "If something's wrong, or if you have any problems with anything at all, you really should tell me. I can help, or at least I can try to. It is my job to fix things, after all."

'I just want to go to sleep. And if the dreams I have are nice, I don't want to wake up. I don't think you can help with that. Besides, I'm an adult now. I need to start fixing my own problems.'

"I'll b-be fine, but thanks," Ember said. "Let's j-j-j-just hurry before I fr-freeze to death. Then I-I won't be fine, because I'll be dead."

He sighed. "Okay. You know me; I like to worry. I hope this fluffhead doesn't wake up before we get back."

Ember yawned. *'And I hope I don't pass out.'*

He grabbed Eclan's scruff, then they went back to walking. Ember sucked in a noseful of burning, freezing air. She closed her eyes a moment to savor the quiet bustle of Dark's Valley before burrowing back into the world within her own windstorm of a mind.

———

The smell of smoke drifted through the forest, filling Ember's nose with the savory scent of home. She smiled softly as a broken ring of sharpened sticks came into view. Some of the sticks were coated in flame-hardened clay, and others were exposed; still others were rotting. Each one had a name marked into it, letting observers know which cats had done the carving. Ember searched the lake of sticks for the one with her own name. She didn't have to read it to find it, because it stuck out at a skewed angle near the Glade's side of the abatis wall. She chuffed gently as they passed by.

For the most part, gatherers were the ones who maintained the wall. However, every trainee was expected to contribute to it at least once, and how competent they were determined how much they would be trusted with when they became apprentices.

They walked through the Northern Entrance, a break in the wall lined with a young ash and a birch. Ember's eyes locked onto the nearest of the fire pits. Cloud nudged her toward it.

'Fire. Finally!' She nodded her thanks, then ran to the glowing pit of warmth. She stopped a paw-length away from the clay spires surrounding and guarding the dancing flames. They'd once supported a platform on which clayworkers could harden their bowls and bijoux, preparing them for sale on market days. Many winters of wear, tear, and exposure, however, had made the platform crumble long before anyone still alive had been born. Instead of repairing the old structure, clayworkers had made a separate pit just for their work about twenty winters back.

Ember leaned as close as she dared and let the heat of the flames engulf her. It would never compare to curling up beside her parents in the old family den, but it would be more than enough to keep her from freezing.

As the fire crackled, radiating with welcoming warmth, she peered past the pit to study her home. Huge, slanted boulders connected by a rise of dirt formed a second, south-facing wall which blocked the breeze from entering the Glade. With multiple natural and feline-made crevices and caves, it housed several family dens. In the trees nearby, sleeping cats lounged: seven of them. They were night guards, resting up for another evening of protecting their colony. Across the Glade, two mothers watched over their playing kittens. Squeals and faint snores hit her ears, along with playful paws on frozen ground, chirping birds, and the mothers talking about hunting. She bit her tongue.

'You'll need to learn it someday, Em. Being able to hunt well can mean the difference between life and death,' her cousin's voice scolded. Tainu was a group hunter who had become obsessed with her craft; so much so that she seemed to think everyone else should share her obsession.

The mothers noticed her and stared for a few moments. Why they stared, Ember didn't know, so she looked away and lay down. Her ears rung. She'd asked Fern, her aunt and one of the healers, why they did it sometimes. Fern hadn't known. It seemed some mysteries were never meant to be solved.

She let out a gentle sigh. Burning wood crackled and snapped, giving her something constant to focus on, so she closed her eyes and tried to use the flames to burn out the noise.

"Commander Aspen," Cloud said from somewhere across the Glade, dragging her tired mind away from the fire.

Ember bent around to watch them. A ruddy brown tom with a half-white face walked over to her father. His right ear twitched. It had been torn during the Battle of Stone Ridge, along with much of the right side of his head. The damage caused his ear to spasm any time he got nervous or felt uneasy. Ember liked it in the sense that she could physically see anytime he got aggravated.

"You're back early," he said. "Earlier than I had in mind, but better than being late." His eyes, one blue and one yellow, caught the light and appeared to glow. He stopped and sniffed at Eclan. "Who is this?"

"That would be Eclan. He attacked us, so we brought him here for questioning. Ember seems to think he's a mercenary. What do you make of him?" Cloud asked.

Aspen looked the Rogue over. "You've nearly drowned him. He's soaked through his skin. Get him by the fire. Mercenary or not, you can't question a dead Outsider."

Cloud helped Aspen drag Eclan closer to the fire. Ember edged away from his cold, silent body as disgust, a bright pink, tinted her thoughts. She pulled her tail closer to her side. The tip of it flicked in unease.

'Go away, please. You look like a dead cat, and I don't like sitting next to dead cats. Okay, focus Ember. Think about fire. Hopefully this time it'll distract you.'

Her mother had once suggested that she try to find a focal point anytime things started to overwhelm her. It didn't usually work, but she'd made a habit of it nonetheless.

Aspen walked over to Ember's side. "You're wet too. What happened? Were you the one who fought with him?"

'Why am I being included in this conversation?' Ember lowered her head.

13

"Yes, sir. I'm pretty sure he was trying to kill me. I, uhm, did what I had to do."

'Think about fire. I like fire. It's warm . . . it's warm. And nice. And what else? It's, uhm . . .'

Aspen groomed a mat of blood from her shoulder. "Impressive work. I can tell you stood your ground well."

Ember flinched with each lick. *'Please don't do that. I don't want to be touched. Oh, it gives us light. There you go; there's something you can work with. Yes, it helps us see where to go when it's too dark to find things on our own. That's good.'*

He stopped grooming. "Once you get warm enough, go get a healer to take care of that shoulder. It looks painful."

'It protects us from predators. It keeps food fresh longer. Bites if you get too close.'

Ember nodded once, but tried to ignore the implications of his words. The ambience of the Glade continued to batter her ears. "Yes, sir."

'Nope. Still not working.'

Aspen inspected her for a few more moments, then turned his attention elsewhere, apparently losing interest in Ember's waterlogged fur. "Cloud, why do you think this cat is here?"

"I'm not sure," Cloud said. "Worst-case scenario, he could be a spy—or an assassin. If he is, he's not a very good one. He could also be a stubborn Outsider who doesn't know when to quit, which is the most likely option. We'll have to wait until he wakes up to get anything close to definite. In the meantime, we can discuss those points you said you wanted to bring up."

'I'm done here,' she thought. *'Have fun talking about the Meeting. I'm going to the other fire pit to continue getting warm. Alone this time, not that you can hear me.'*

Ember crept away across the Glade, head and tail low. Her fur wasn't dripping anymore. Instead, it stuck out in damp spikes, as if she'd been dipped in tree sap, then licked by a herd of deer. She got the urge to find a puddle to see her reflection in, but it hadn't rained all mooncycle, so she ignored it.

A giant oak tree sat in the middle of the Glade. Its branches were covered in the clawmarks of Dark himself, along with the carved words of generations of historians. It beckoned her to take shelter in its massive branches and read all morning—and maybe even add a few marks of her own one day. Ember sighed.

'I'll be back for you,' she thought. 'My training is almost over. I'm getting close; I know I am. But I really should get dried off. Then I guess I'll go back to patrolling, with or without Dad. Because I have to start taking control of myself, or I'm never going to achieve anything. And, of course, I have a routine to keep up, otherwise I'll be all antsy for the rest of the day, and that's never fun. I'll be back tonight. With Hyrees. I'll be back. Hopefully.'

As she lay by the second fire pit, sparks flickered around her, flashing like the last fireflies of the year.

'How is Hyrees doing?' she wondered. 'What will he think of Minty Murderface the Rogue? If he's still around when they get back, obviously. He'll probably just talk to him. It's what he's best at. Or ignore him completely. I guess that would be just as Hyrees-y.'

She chuffed gently to herself. The thought of her best friend, and now mate, sent a little blossom of orange fluttering through her mind. It was the color of family; the color that reminded her she was never truly alone.

Ember rested her chin on her forelegs, ears flicking around at every sound. She tried to catch bits of Cloud and Aspen's conversation, but they were too quiet and too far away, so instead their words meshed with the rest of the ambient symphony, creating a gentle, unfilterable murmur. She half-smiled. It wasn't the most calming of lullabies, but it was home.

When she could leave the fireside without shivering, she loped toward the northern entrance. As she neared the abatis, she shot a look in Cloud's direction. He and Aspen sat on either side of an awake Eclan.

'Guess he's not coming. It's okay, Ember. You can do this. You're an adult, and it's an easy patrol. You can do this alone.'

"Where are you going?" Aspen asked.

'Is he talking to me?' Ember stopped, heart pounding. She turned to face him, eyes studying the scars along his neck. "To patrol again. I don't want to leave a gap in the border for too long."

Cloud flicked back his ears. "Ember, you don't have t—"

"Has your shoulder been looked at?" Aspen asked, cutting him off.

Ember lowered her head. "N-no sir."

"Then go to the healers' den," he replied.

"Who's in right now?" Ember asked. A prickly lump formed in her chest. Her lower jaw started to tremble. Faint blotches of cyan appeared in her head; swirling, pressing and relentless.

'Not this again. Calm down. Now is not the time to panic.'

Aspen sighed. "That would be Silentstream."

Ember let a tiny huff of air escape her mouth. "I, uhm, I think I'll take my chances with infection. Now, I have a border to guard, so—"

"Ember," Cloud said.

"What?" she asked.

Cloud slow-blinked. "You don't have to patrol today. You're free. Take some time to rest, or study for when Whitehaze gets back, if you want to."

'This is a test, isn't it? Some kind of evaluation. Right? Because you don't usually bring Whitehaze into these conversations. Not unless you know something I don't, in which case what are you trying to tell me?'

Ember sighed. "I really should go. I'm already breaking routine enough with the meeting tomorrow. I don't need to mess myself up for today too."

"No, wait," Cloud said, "I can get you some mash once we've finished up here. We need to get your shoulder cleaned. Just give me a few moments."

Eclan pawed at the ground. Ember squinted to get a better look. *'Is he clawmarking?'*

"Cloud," Aspen said. His gaze drifted to whatever Eclan was drawing. "Let her g—"

Aspen jumped to his paws, eyes wide. Eclan wiped away whatever he'd written.

"Oh," Aspen said softly. "Eclan, was it? You're, ah, you're free to go. Come back tomorrow, after the meeting. Meet me by the log on the Northern Border, just after the sun peaks. We can talk more there. Is that . . . acceptable?"

"I'm a patient cat, 'n so is she," Eclan replied.

'She? He works for Commander Jade?'

"Thank you. Now I have a meeting to prepare for, so you may leave now," Aspen said.

"C-can I, uh, go too?" Ember asked.

"Yes, leave. Go patrol. And while you're at it, escort him out. He won't hurt you."

Cloud stood and pinned back his ears. "Wait, how do you know that? What did he tell you? Sir, you can't just send my daughter away with a Rogue."

Aspen placed a paw in the dust in front of him. "That's not important. I gave an order, and I expect it to be followed through. Remember your place, Cloud. Your insubordination is beginning to wear on me." He turned to Ember. "Be careful out there."

Ember stepped back. *'Oh, so now I don't actually have a choice, and I'm stuck with Eclan. That's wonderful. Absolutely wonderful.'*

"Th-thank you, sir?" She turned to face the northern entrance. Her stomach grew tighter. More silver appeared in the back of her mind. "Come on, Eclan. Let's get you to the border, I guess. You aren't too upset about me kicking you into the creek, right?"

Eclan chuffed and loped over to her. "I don't hold grudges, kitten. I just do my job."

'A Rogue with a job that might not be mercenary or assassin. That's interesting. Maybe he's just a messenger or something like that. As long as he doesn't hurt me, I guess it doesn't really matter. Now come on, Em. You've got your own job to do.'

She sucked in a deep breath, and together they left the Glade.

CHAPTER 2
EMBER

Ember slunk through the woods toward the Glade. Her ears swiveled to catch any sound within range. As Aspen had foretold, Eclan had left the territory without resistance or complaint. He hadn't even spoken to her during the walk out. He'd simply crossed the creek without once looking back, and after he'd left, the day had been quiet—too quiet for comfort in the solitude.

'Come on, Ember. You're almost done. Almost done.' Her mind played the thoughts on loop as she walked, and silver swarmed with them.

The sun hid behind the Western Mountain, casting a dreary purple shadow on the world around her. Sunlight caught the tip of the Eastern Mountain, setting it ablaze with golden light. A soft mist crept up from the Lowlands, making the forest look 'fuzzy,' as Hyrees would say. Wind pushed against her side. Her long-dried fur blocked it, or at least most of it. She bit her tongue. Rotting leaves crunched beneath her paws. Every now and then, a bird chirped or fluttered around in the trees or underbrush.

Her eyes and nose stung from the cold. She coughed twice. With every step, her shoulder throbbed a little more, but every step brought her a little closer to safety—to home.

'Why am I doing this? Why did I think this was a good idea. I should've just accepted Dad's offer. Almost no one crosses the Northern Border *anyway.'*

Leaves rustled. A twig snapped. Ember's ears perked up.

'Oh tahg, what now?'

Her heart pounded, pumping a burst of adrenaline through her system. She lowered herself into a fighting stance and sniffed the air. An involuntary chuff escaped her throat as she straightened up. A flash of white and tan leaped out at her. Ember stepped out of the way. The cat tripped over its own paws, then tumbled onto a pile of leaves. The silver in her mind disappeared altogether, maple orange replacing it.

"Ow," the cat moaned. "Border guard down. How dare you defeat me, you wildcat!"

Ember smiled. "I didn't touch you, Kivy. I think you defeated yourself this time."

"Okay, fine, point made," Kivyress said. She rolled onto her stomach. "But remember when we used to play that? You were always the outsider for some reason."

"Eh, I'm always the outsider," Ember replied, her voice emotionless.

Kivyress jumped to her paws and padded over to Ember. Despite being born a winter apart, they were already almost eye-level with each other, Kivyress being only a few clawlengths shorter. "No, you're not. You're the historian in training. You're going to be a high-rank, like Dad. The first molly high-rank in the West, too. There's nothing outsider about that."

She batted at Ember's side. Ember winced as her sister's paw hit the wounds on her shoulder.

Kivyress stepped back. "Oh! Sorry about that. I didn't realize you got cut there. Ouch, that looks painful. What happened?"

"I fought with a rogue this morning. That was, uhm, an experience. So, where's Mom? Did you escape her again?"

Kivyress laughed. "Yeah. She was training me and Farlight for a while. Then Lupine came, and he took Farlight back for his private commander lessons. After that, Mom and I played a game of 'where's Kivy.' I think I won. Then I found you. Anyways, while we're asking about parent locations,

19

where's Dad?"

"Last time I saw him, he was at the Glade, talking with Commander Aspen again."

"Important meeting business, right. Oh, hey, it looks like Mom found me after all."

A reddish-brown cat trotted toward them. A blaze of white ran up her muzzle and down her neck. She pushed her way through a tangle of dead leaves, then stopped in front of them.

"Kivy, we were supposed to be hunting for rabbits, not you," she said.

Kivyress looked away. "I know. Sorry, Mom."

"Then why did I spend half the day—" She glanced at Ember. Her wildflower-yellow eyes widened. "What happened to your shoulder? And where's Cloud? Is he back at the Glade again?"

"Yes, ma'am." Ember rubbed her paw against a patch of dirt. "I got into a fight with a rogue. It's just a scratch. I'll be fine."

Her mother, Songbird, examined the wound on her shoulder. As she did, a red bird landed on a branch overhead and chirped a few times, bringing the forest back to life for a moment. Then it flew away toward the Lowlands.

"He let you come out here, all alone, with a wound like this?" she asked. "You didn't even get it cleaned."

Ember grimaced, her tail thrashing. "It's a long story, but Dad didn't exactly have a say in it."

"It might get infected now," Songbird mewed.

"Silentstream was the only healer available. Then Commander Aspen sent me to bring the rogue out, so at that point I couldn't get it cleaned, even if I wanted to."

Her tail twitched. "Oh. Er, I see. That's . . . Uhm, I'll admit that's a little strange for the commander, but whatever he was thinking, we should get you back to the Glade. Both of you."

"Oh, hey, there they are," a voice said from behind them.

Two ruddy agouti tomcats walked toward them along the time-worn border trail. The gathering mist shrouded their shadowy figures, but she could recognize them from anywhere.

"Hyrees!" Ember smiled. She ran to greet the one in the lead: a plump young cat with sage-colored eyes. They touched noses. She rubbed her muzzle against his shoulder and breathed in his familiar scent. *'Finally. It's about time you showed up.'*

Wren, the older tom, stopped beside them. His fur was a darker orangy-red. Three deep-seated scars crossed his right eye, which had blued over many winters before. "Is everythin' okay over 'ere?" Wren asked in a thick Eastern accent. His oddly pronounced vowels and lilting, almost melodic way of speaking never ceased to fascinate her.

Ember pressed herself closer to Hyrees and sighed with contentment. As she did, the maple oranges of family burned brighter in her thoughts.

"We're fine, Wren," Songbird replied, "thank you for checking on us."

He nodded his head once. "Not a problem, ma'am."

Hyrees licked Ember's forehead and flicked back his ears. "So, how are you doing?"

Hyrees, being born in the West, had never picked up his father's accent. Accent or no accent, however, he was still Hyrees, and that was good enough for Ember.

Ember chuffed. She pulled away from his warmth and paced in a loose circle. "I'm continuing to do by continuing to live. How about you? You look alive too, which is always nice."

He smiled and gave her a squinty-eyed look. "Heh. I'm doing fine. But no, really, what happened to . . ."

"My shoulder," Ember finished for him. "Rogue. I'm fine. Doesn't matter."

'Will everyone please stop asking about my shoulder? It's a scratch. I'm aware I have a scratch. And I'm a border guard, so it can't be too hard to figure out where it came from.'

"You're doing it again," Hyrees said.

She stopped pacing and looked up at him. "Doing what?"

"Making weird faces."

"I've never made a face before, much less a weird one. Unless you're talking about my only face, in which case I can't help if it's weird."

Kivyress giggled.

Hyrees huffed. "No, I mean, sometimes when we aren't talking, you'll start going through a bunch of different expressions. It's almost like you're having a very passionate one-sided conversation about something."

'And this is important why?' Ember tilted her head. "Oh. Astute observation."

"Come on, moggies, let's get ourselves back to the Glade. It's gettin' late," Wren said.

"He's right," Songbird said. "Daylight is fading. We really should get going."

Ember's stomach growled. She pranced toward her mother. "Then let's go. I'm starting to feel meat-pink."

Songbird pinned back her ears. She shook her head slightly. Ember scrunched up her nose, trying to figure out what she was saying.

"Colors," Songbird whispered.

'Oh.' Ember coughed. "Uhm, er, I meant I'm hungry."

It had taken a lot of courage for her, as a kitten, to explain to her parents the colors she felt through her emotions. It was a hard thing to explain, especially to cats who couldn't imagine being able to feel with colors. After she told them, however, they'd instructed her not to tell anyone else. They'd said it might get her into trouble, but they never specified what kind or why. The three other cats she'd told didn't seem to mind.

Kivyress pranced down the mountain slope. "Come on!"

Ember sighed and moved to follow her. They all walked together through the haze and toward the Glade. Hyrees placed himself beside Ember.

He leaned closer and whispered in her ear, "It's getting worse."

She hesitated mid-step. Her body tensed. "What? A-are you sure?"

"Yes. And I mean noticeably worse," he replied.

'Oh no. It really is going to happen, isn't it? But why to you, of all cats?'

He looked at her and grimaced. The centers of his pupils were a faded blue, like toned-down versions of Wren's injury. "Your face is just a smudge now. I want to see it like I saw it as a kitten. I think I remember how you look, but I'm not sure."

She nuzzled his cheek. "At least you can use your imagination."

"Yeah, but at this rate I probably won't be able to see anything by next spring," he said. "Not even color. Which is why I'm thinking about leaving the guards."

Ember flinched. His mention of springtime sent a shiver up her spine, but she tried to ignore it. The bright pink and silver in her mind made it harder. She glanced at him. *'Wait, leaving?'*

"If I can't see," he continued, "I won't be able to fight well enough to be any kind of help. It's already hard enough as it is, and at that point I'd just be in the way."

She bit her tongue. "So what will you do?"

He stared at the ground. "I don't know yet. I've been thinking about it a lot today. I may become a clayworker. I can apprentice under Fledge now, while I can still sort of see. Then, when I lose my vision all the way, I'll already know what to do and I can just feel my way around the job. What do you think?"

"It'll work, but is it something you actually want to do?"

"I . . . don't know. I do know that I don't want to be a blind border guard."

Ember flattened her ears. *'What if we could trade eyes? Trade them for a mooncycle or two. Not forever. Maybe we could change them out every mooncycle. That would work. Well, it wouldn't actually work, but in this hypothetical scenario it would be the best solution. Or we could each trade one eye. That might be better. Then we'd all be like Wren.'*

Ember chuffed, picturing her, Hyrees, and Wren with matching eyes. She shook her head. *'That's not funny, Ember. He's going blind. Now is not the time to laugh.'*

Instead she tried to imagine how the world looked to him, and would look by the time the forest turned green again. If he was right, he might never see the color green again, or at least not the green of sunlight shining through a million tiny leaves. Just a giant green smudge, or possibly nothing at all.

She shivered. *'What does nothing look like? Does it have a color? Is it darkness? Or would darkness still be something? I can't see from behind my head. Would it be that kind of nothing, where there's just nothing at all?'*

"What is it? What are you thinking about?"

Ember looked up at him. "How you're the bravest cat I know," she whispered. "I was trying to imagine what the world would look like without any detail, then what it would look like without any light or colors at all. It's . . . well, it's terrifying. And yet here you are, calmly making plans."

"Calm?" he asked. "Well, I certainly don't feel calm. Or brave." He chuffed. "At least I look like I know what I'm doing. But thanks for being quiet about it."

"You really should tell them," she said. "Your dad, your brother; they care about you. They deserve to know."

"I know, I know. I just don't know how, okay? I'll try to figure out something."

They kept walking through the woods, side by side. While talking, they'd fallen behind. Up ahead, Songbird and Wren chatted about the day's events and what kinds of meats would be available during the meeting feast. Kivyress tried to join the conversation every now and then, but they kept speaking over her. Eventually she gave up and fell back to walk with Ember and Hyrees.

"They really like talking about turkey, I guess," she mewed.

Ember looked around at the forest. Soft purple shadows and the gentle blues of mist painted the woods. The delicate beauty of moss and leaves beneath their paws covered the ground with intricate detail. Blue-green fungi blossomed like flowers from rotting logs. Bark clung to the living trees, making the most precious and random of all patterns. She sighed, realizing he probably couldn't see most of it.

"Ember? Emm-ber. Are you in there?"

Hyrees's voice jerked her out of her thoughts. Her stomach growled again. As if in response, Hyrees's stomach growled louder and longer.

He laughed. "I'm such a show-off, aren't I? Now, where were we before you zoned out and my stomach so rudely interrupted?"

Ember nodded to the forest behind them. "Back there."

Hyrees chuckled. "Oh, that's right, we were discussing what I should do with myself."

'What does—oh, you meant where we were in the conversation. Okay. Makes sense. Stupid, fluffhead, Ember. Think! Think before you say anything. Anything at all.' She groaned softly. Her insides sank like stones, and her face burned as blue and white lights seared into her thoughts. *'Stop being a fluffhead.'*

Ember sighed and shook herself off. *'Sleep. I need sleep. Everything will be better tomorrow. Better once you get some sleep. Need sleep. Just need to forget for a little while. Put everything back in line. Nice, even perspective.'*

"Are you okay?" Hyrees asked as they neared the Glade.

"I'm okay enough."

He looked away, head low. "So what should I do?"

"Do like I said: tell someone who might actually be able to help. It's not a good idea to keep a life-changing development a secret from your own family. Especially not your brother. He is the future commander, after all. And really, it's only a matter of time before it becomes obvious. I can already see the blue if I look hard enough."

"Farlight doesn't even know?" Kivyress asked.

Hyrees sighed. "No, he doesn't, and I know I need to tell them, but once they know, almost everyone in the Colony's going to know. It's hard enough being one of the only half-Eastern cats in the valley, and it's even harder being the only fat one. If cats found out I'm going blind too, that'd be it for me."

"But it's the only way to get help," Ember replied. Faint shimmers of cyan and fang yellow appeared in her mind as hints of panic and anger nipped at her chest.

Hyrees hung his head. "No one can cure blindness, Ember."

They approached the Glade and padded toward the Western Entrance. Ember yawned, then shuddered as a strong gust of wind ruffled her fur.

"You know, you could just tell Fern," she said. "She doesn't mind keeping secrets. She knows about my colors and hasn't told anyone. Who knows? She may even surprise you with some kind of cure."

"No," he growled. "I'm not ready yet. Stop trying to make me do something I'm not ready to do. I'll tell who I want to tell when I want to tell them. End of story."

She shrunk away from him and shivered again as they entered the Glade. Unlike the gentle, ambient lull of that morning, the spacious, rocky clearing now bustled with life and noise. Cats surrounded both fire pits. All around, Westerners lounged, or sat, or groomed themselves or their kin. Two young trainees, about four mooncycles old, sat in the History Tree with Whitehaze, the senior historian. Ember's eyes narrowed. An iridescent, oily shimmer appeared in her mind's eye.

'Better not scratch those marks, little creatures of mass destruction.'

Whitehaze nodded to her as they walked past. The breeze, now blowing from the north, riffled his long, greyish fur. Ember recognized his greeting and nodded in reply.

"Look, sorry I growled at you," Hyrees said. He wrinkled his muzzle. "I'll think about it, okay?"

She offered what she hoped was a tiny smile. "Okay. And I shouldn't keep pushing you. Sorry about that."

He nuzzled her cheek. "Apology accepted."

Her stomach growled again. *'Oh, right, I'm hungry.'*

Hyrees's ears perked up. "Heh, I feel you, Emmy. Let's go get some food." He started off for the storage cave.

Her smile faded as the oily shimmer reappeared. *'Why do you keep calling me that? Do you think it's cute to have a nickname for me that I don't like? It's not like I haven't asked you to stop using it.'*

She sighed and followed behind him. Her gaze wandered the Glade. Songbird and Cloud sat in front of their den, talking. They never once looked in her direction. Kivyress was already deep in conversation with another trainee. Wren had wandered into the bustle and disappeared. Aspen was nowhere to be seen. They were alone in the crowd.

They stopped at the storage den, where a group of hunters were dividing up a deer they'd taken down. Its leg still dripped with blood from where one cat had landed the killing strike, severing the creature's iliac artery. Ember tilted her head, wondering who'd felled it. Only highly skilled hunters aimed for leg bites.

Cats crowded around the doe and its hunters, all waiting to get their evening rations. Ember bit her tongue as their voices hit her hears.

'This is too many cats. Too many cats.'

A tall black and white molly got up from slicing a slab of rib meat. Blood covered her mouth and paws. She spat out the sharpened stone she'd been cutting with and raised her tail in greeting. "Hungry again, Hyrees?" she asked.

She clawed out the slice of rib meat, then set it down in front of him.

"Yes. Yes, I am. Thanks, Tainu," Hyrees replied.

He tore into his meal with the etiquette of a rabid coyote. Several cats glared at him in disgust.

"As if he needs more food," one cat growled.

"Oh, leave him alone," Tainu said.

"You guard your mouth, Outsider," the cat replied.

Tainu showed her teeth but said nothing. She'd been born in the Lowlands, but her parents had left her in Western territory when she was only a mooncycle old. Fern, Songbird's sister, had taken her in and, with help from Fledge, raised her as their only daughter. Ember only ever saw her as a cousin, a friend, and at times a guiding figure, yet most Colony Cats considered her Outsider blood to be inferior in some way.

Tainu snorted and shook her head, then cut out another piece. "And for you, my weird little cousin."

'Okay, we're adults now; you can stop calling me that. Even if I am strange, smaller than you, and your adopted cousin, there's really no need to keep bringing these things up. Everyone knows.'

Tainu placed the meat at Ember's paws. "I'm taking a break," she called over her shoulder. "Be back in a moment."

"You'd better hurry up, young'un. We've still got mouths to feed," the hunter beside her said.

"Yeah, sure. I will, old tom."

Ember pinned back her ears. *'Should I eat? Or does she expect me to talk to her first? Well, she's still sitting there, so try talking?'*

"So," she said, "a deer. You must've had quite a day."

"Oh, it *was* a day," Tainu replied. "We caught more than this, of course, but they're flaming it for tomorrow. How was your day?"

"Long and mostly boring," Ember said.

"Really?" She examined her injured shoulder. "'Cause this doesn't look all that boring to me, and I know it wasn't there this morning."

"You do?"

Tainu hesitated a moment, then twitched her tail and chuffed. "Yes. Because it's too fresh to have happened yesterday. Em, this is completely unrelated, but I've been meaning to ask if you wanted some more hunting lessons. After we go catch more food for the Meeting, I should be free tomorrow. Y'know, if you're interested. Aaand even if you're not."

'What? No. No, no, no.' Ember shuddered slightly. *'Definitely no hunting lessons. You know that's not my thing.'*

"Ember, hey, you listening?"

'Oh, right, you can't read my mind.'

"Ah!" Ember squeaked. She groaned internally. "Uh, I mean no. Maybe?" Her fur bristled as the stares of her colonymates shifted onto her. "I don't know. Could we talk about it tomorrow? I don't want to back myself into a corner. A metaphorical corner, of course. No real corner-backing, please."

'Nope. Bad idea. Very bad idea. Do not go hunting tomorrow, Ember. Tahg, why can't you ever just say 'no'? Maybe it's because she's right.'

Tainu stared at her for a few moments. She smiled again. "I'll make sure to track you down tomorrow, then. Back you into a corner myself if I have to." She chuckled and bent down to nudge Ember's cheek. "You're going hunting with me one of these days. I know you don't like it, but you have to be able to take care of yourself. And I'm not just saying that because I want you to say I was right, and that hunting is fun and easy. I'm also saying it because I love you and don't want you to starve. You know, if things ever get bad."

'If things get bad? Why would things get bad? What are you trying to say?'

"You need practice," Tainu continued. "No telling when you'll need to catch yourself a rabbit. That rabbit could save your life."

"I said 'maybe,' " Ember replied. "If you push me too hard, you'll only make it a definite 'no.' It'll probably still be 'no,' but at least give me time to think, okay?"

'Oh, wait, that sounds an awful lot like what Hyrees said. Sorry again, Hyrees.'

"I will, I will." Tainu pawed the top of Ember's head, ruffling her fur. "Stay safe, you two. Oh, and Ember, get that shoulder taken care of. Now I have work to do, so if you'll excuse me."

She trotted back to her place beside the ever-diminishing doe carcass. The ambience of the Glade grew louder. Ember sighed. Her stomach twisted into a knot. "Let's go somewhere else to eat. It's too loud and cat-dense here."

Hyrees stood up. "Anywhere you had in mind?"

"Nowhere in particular, so long as it's comfortable and relatively quiet. You can choose the specifics."

"Alright. I'll find us a place."

He picked up what remained of his meal, and Ember did the same with hers. Her stomach felt like two arguing kittens; one kitten wanted food, and the other hated the sight of it. She couldn't decide whose side she was on, so she tried to shake the imagery away. They loped over to the far edge of the Glade, away from most of the Colony.

Hyrees dropped the meat and smiled. "How's this?"

'Thank you.' She sighed. "Good enough."

Ember lay down and licked her piece. Her stomach growled again, but she wasn't hungry. *'You really should eat, Ember. You need food. But you also don't need to hack up your ration, eating when you can't. Why is this, of all things, difficult?'*

"Are you okay?" Hyrees asked. "Be honest."

"Not really."

His ears flicked back against his head. He sat down beside her and wrapped his tail around her haunches. "What's wrong?"

'What? What is the problem?' Ember looked away, trying to find something that might give her the answer. *'What's wrong with my life? Why am I not okay right now? Why am I not okay?'* Her thought voice grew louder. *'There is absolutely nothing—'*

Ember sprang to her paws. "That's just it. I don't know what's wrong." She closed her eyes and let her head droop. "I don't understand. I've got the best family in the forest, the future job I want; all my basic needs are taken care of, and yet I'm not happy. All logic and reason says I should be, but I get scared for no reason, I can't focus, I don't ever sleep well, and I . . . never mind."

Bright pink mixed with the duller shades of hunger. She sat down and wrapped her tail around her paws. "What is wrong with me? I'm missing something. Part of me is missing. Hyrees, tell me what I'm doing wrong. How do I make myself better than this? How do I find the rest of me?"

He sighed. "I don't know. Hey, maybe it's already there somewhere."

She shook her head. "No, it's more than that. I feel . . . empty. Like I'm missing something important that everyone but me has."

"Food?"

She growled. "Food is not—know what? It doesn't matter. We should eat."

Throughout the meal, her mind drifted, trying to find the reasons behind her problems and fears. Yet each fault had a root cause that was entirely different from the complications it created. The more she thought, the more vividly she imagined herself as a wingless fly, caught in an abandoned spider's web and suspended over a void. Some of the silk strands ensnaring her also supported her. Without them, she risked falling into the silvery nothingness lurking below.

Ember pushed her half-eaten food away. "I'm done. I can't eat anymore.

You can have it."

Beside her, Hyrees was grooming himself. He stopped and looked at her. "But Em, you need more than that. I don't want you starving on me. Besides, look at me; I don't need any more."

"If I eat any more, I'll make myself sick. If you don't want it, I'll give it to someone else."

He shook his head. "No, you should eat it. You already feel a little too thin. You need to eat more."

"I'd eat better if they would split the meals up more. I can't eat a lot when I'm nervous, even when I'm nervous for no reason."

"I'll take it, if you don't want it," a new voice said.

A white kitten with patches of ruddy brown walked over to them.

"Hey, Far," Hyrees mewed.

Farlight butted heads with Hyrees, and they purred gentle greetings to one another. Farlight was younger by several mooncycles but already bigger than his brother.

"Hey, Hyrees," Farlight said. He turned to look at Ember. "So, you're sure you don't want it?"

She pushed the meat to his paws. "Yeah. You can take it."

He pulled the extra ration closer. "Kivy, wanna split this with me?" he mewed.

Kivyress appeared from behind a tree. "Sure."

Ember tilted her head. "What were you doing back there?"

"Sneaking up to pounce on you. But then I was told there was food to be had."

She trotted over to Farlight and they devoured the meal together. When they finished, Farlight lay down. He rolled onto his back and placed a paw against his stomach. "That was good. I'm full now."

Kivyress curled up near his head to groom his face. Farlight swatted at her. She nipped him and they transitioned into play-fighting. Hyrees chuffed and jumped in. He caught Farlight in his paws. They tumbled to the ground, with Hyrees on top.

"Oh, you think you can beat me, do you?" Farlight said in a mock snarl. "Kivy, now!"

Kivyress leaped onto Hyrees's back, knocking him off of Farlight.

Ember watched in silence. She imagined herself as a spirit, watching her loved ones being happy together after her physical form had left them. She smiled. Some unseen force calmed her racing heart.

'Maybe this is all I need; just to know they're still okay, with or without me.'

"You all did well today," Cloud's voice said.

She became a mortal again and spun around. Cloud and Songbird walked over to them. Hyrees and the trainees stopped playing.

"Except for you, Kivy," Cloud said. "Did you really spend half of the day hiding from your mother?"

"Maybe," she replied.

"Maybe, huh?" he asked.

Songbird stepped closer and nuzzled Ember's chin. "I'm proud of you for going on that patrol alone." She pulled back. "But next time you get cut like that, go to the healers' den first. If you need one of us to go with you, you know we can. Just don't leave a wound uncleaned like that. Okay?"

Ember dipped her head. "Yes, ma'am."

'I wish it were that easy. And I think, at this point, I can face Silentstream alone. I just really don't want to.'

"Hey, Sparky, I need to tell you something Aspen and I discussed today," Cloud said.

Ember's ears perked up. "Okay."

"Aspen thinks, with how well you've been performing, you might be ready to record your first clawmarks on the History Tree. Now, I told him you probably wouldn't be interested, but you know Aspen. He wouldn't take 'no' for an answer. He insisted you'd want to do it, so tomorrow morning, Whitehaze is going to give you your historian's trial. If you pass it, you get to be the historian this meeting."

Her entire face lit up. Orange, bright, joyous orange, filled her head. *'I can*

do it. I can become a historian. Because that's where I belong; I can feel it.'
Her smile shrunk. *'Oh tahg, what would Dark think of me? Would he like me putting clawmarks on his tree? Calm down, Ember. If you'd been born in his time, he probably would've trained you himself.'*

Cloud chuckled. "See? I knew you wouldn't want a promotion. I don't know why he didn't listen to me."

'Wait a moment, I'm not ready. I can't become a historian yet. I'm not good enough. I need more practice.' The orange faded as her ears drooped She looked at her paws. "So what happens if I fail?"

"Then you try again next time." He groomed her forehead. "Don't worry, you'll do fine."

'But what if I don't?'

"And if not, you'll at least have more experience and know what to expect next time," he said.

She laughed and nuzzled her father's neck. "Thanks, Dad."

He chuffed. "For what?"

"Everything." Ember moved over to Songbird. Her soft, thick fur engulfed her, like it had many a night before, during the times when, as a kitten, the fear and the uncertainty were too much for one young cat to bear alone. "You too, Mom. I love y'all."

Songbird groomed her neck. "Love you too, my little furball."

When Ember pulled away, she noticed Hyrees watching them. He wasn't smiling. *'They're here for you too, you know—not just me.'*

Songbird extended a paw toward where he stood alongside Kivyress and Farlight. "I love you all, my big-little family."

No one moved. Her paw lowered. She shook her head and chuffed awkwardly. "Oh, come on. Hyrees, Farlight, Kivy, come here."

Farlight and Kivyress exchanged a look, then tackled Songbird to the ground. They rolled around in a ball of laughter until Songbird went quiet.

She craned her neck to look back at where Hyrees still stood. "Hyrees, why don't you come join the fun. Don't you want to help them beat me up?"

Hyrees remained in place, tail twitching. "S-sorry, ma'am. I'm . . . I'm not ready for that. You can be a mom to my brother, but with all due respect, I'd like it if you stopped trying to be one to me."

Their mother, Light, had died during kittenbirth last spring. Songbird, who'd had Kivyress not long before, had taken Farlight in and raised him as her own. She'd tried many times to extend the role to Hyrees, but he always turned her down, and with each attempt to reconcile, they drifted further apart.

Songbird eased the two trainees off of her, then got up. "I understand. I miss her too."

"Yeah," Hyrees said.

Ember rubbed her left forepaw, the only brown one. *'If I could see your colors, or anyone else's, things would be so much easier, wouldn't they? What are you not saying, Hyrees?'*

Cloud stretched and yawned. "Well, it's getting late. We've got a big day tomorrow. Let's go get some sleep. Come on, Kivy. Far, you too. You want to stay with us or your dad tonight?"

Farlight looked at Kivyress for a moment. He sighed. "Thanks for the offer, but I really should be with Dad. He gets lonely at night, and with the Meeting tomorrow, he'll definitely want someone with him. I'll see you all in the morning, though."

"There's a good tom," Cloud said. "Go find him. Tell him I said we ought to go do something after the meeting. It's been a while since we've really done anything together."

"That's because last time I left you two together alone, you ended up in the healers' den with a snake bite," Songbird said.

Cloud shook his head. "Excuses, excuses."

"I will, sir," Farlight replied. "Bye, Kivy! See you in the morning."

"Bye, Far," Kivyress mewed, a content smile on her face.

They parted ways, Cloud, Songbird, and Kivyress leaving for their den, and Farlight heading toward his.

"He's the one, Song. What did I tell you?" Cloud mewed as they walked away. "He's going to make a great commander when the time comes."

Songbird replied, but it was too quiet to make out over the casual chaos of the Glade. It was probably something about how much an intelligent, half-Eastern commander could do to improve inter-colony relationships, which was why Aspen had chosen him in the first place rather than training up any of his closer kin.

Ember sighed. She nuzzled Hyrees before they padded to the History Tree. The two studious trainees, along with Whitehaze, were long gone.

After a moment of hesitation, Hyrees climbed up. He sat down in the cozy cleft made by the massive oak's diverging branches. Ember went up after him. Words greeted her—so many words. They were words she recognized, words she loved. Words she loved so much, Aspen allowed them to sleep among them. She curled up beside her mate and skimmed over the story of the division. It began with the most intense opening line of any account carved into the tree:

DARK DIED IN THE TENTH WINTER.

No matter how many times she tried to read over it, it still managed to jump out at her, and it never failed to send a tiny chill across her neck. Both the words and the elegance with which they were carved were each inspirational enough on their own to motivate her. She wanted to be there—not in the tenth winter, but in her clawmarking ability.

'I could do that too. One day. Tahg, I don't think I'm ready. Not yet. One thing's for sure—I'm not fast enough. That could be a problem.'

"So tomorrow you get to put some on here, don't you?" Hyrees asked.

"If I pass the test. Which I probably won't," Ember replied.

Hyrees lay down and slipped a paw over her back. "I'm pretty sure you will. But hey, if you don't, you get to be free tomorrow. We could do whatever we wanted, just like the good old times."

Ember shuddered and nudged his side playfully. "We're not even two winters old yet. Don't start talking about good old times, you big furball."

He chuckled. "Well, my point still stands. No matter what happens tomorrow, we win."

"Until you start asking yourself 'what's the worst that could happen?' Then you'll find plenty of ways tomorrow could be terrible."

Hyrees shoved his wet nose into her ear. "Hush," he whispered. "Don't ruin it."

Ember jerked away. Her ear flicked as she tried to rid it of the damp spot inside. "Oh, come on. Don't you try to pretend you haven't already come up with at least ten worst-case scenarios."

Hyrees snorted. "Actually, I've discovered seventeen. How dare you underestimate me. Out of curiosity, how many have you thought of?"

"Hmm, let me count," she said. Her mind wandered, trying to calculate every problem they could possibly face before the next sunset. A few extra ones popped up as she organized and counted. "Forty-three, I guess. If you count the ones that aren't exactly probable, it'd be a lot more. Around a hundred. But hey, you never know what could happen. Let's just say the odds of tomorrow being perfect are not in our favor."

His ears drooped. "Oh. Wow, okay. So, should we try to go to sleep tonight? Or do you want to stay up snickering about nothing until the moon sets like we did last night?"

'Oh, we did, didn't we? Maybe that's part of why I have such a hard time sleeping. I know at least part of that was your fault.'

"I'd like to get some sleep tonight. I'll need to be as awake as I can be if I want to pass tomorrow," she said. "So sleep well. And quietly, please. No snoring."

Hyrees chuffed. He rested his head against her neck. "I'll try. You too, Em."

As he closed his eyes, a soft purr rumbled up his throat. Ember let a few tiny purrs escape her own, then she quieted down and tried to drift away. Yet her mind refused to be silent. She lay awake long after the night guards had taken up their posts, long after Hyrees began snoring, thinking about anything and everything.

She thought of worst-case scenarios, best-case scenarios, what secrets the near future might hold, and the true definition of nothingness. She even imagined several creative ways she could get Hyrees to stop snoring, and how she would most definitely scold him about it in the morning. She thought about whatever came to mind until sleep finally took over even her agitated sense of hearing and sent her into a dreamless bliss.

CHAPTER 3
EMBER

"So, are you planning on getting up any time soon?" Hyrees asked.

Ember groaned and forced her eyes open. Light flickered and blurred. The morning chill sent tiny shivers down her neck and back. On top of that, her shoulder still ached from the fight, aggravated even more by the night's usual tossing and turning.

'Too cold. Need more sleep. Pain. Can't walk.' She closed her eyes again and yawned. "No."

"Come on, Em. It's time to get going. The meeting is today, remember?"

Ember covered her face with her paws. She scrunched herself into a tighter ball of fluff. "Wonderful. Let me know how it went."

Hyrees leaned toward her. His cold, wet nose touched her ear. He snorted.

'Send a fox on you, Hyrees! What are you doing?' Ember sprang up with enough force to go airborne for a moment. Her paws slipped as she landed. She scrabbled at the tree, trying to keep from falling, but her claws refused to find traction.

'Oh tahg! What is going on? Just grab the tree!'

Her claws snagged on a rough patch of bark. She jerked to a stop. Her heart pounded in her throat as she cast a wary look at the ground beneath her. "Well, at least I'm awake now."

Hyrees stared down at her, eyes wide. "Uhm, yeah, sorry about that. Wow, that was not the reaction I was expecting."

She jumped to the ground. "I can tell. But I'd say this does not bode well for the rest of the day. When I came up with that list of what might go wrong, falling out of the Tree because you put your nose in my ear wasn't even on it."

'Well, that's certainly one way to wake up. So, the meeting, and the test, and a day off. Anything else going on I should be aware of?' she wondered.

Ember looked around the Glade. Cats littered the cramped clearing, making her feel even more claustrophobic, so she backed up against the Tree.

'Okay, yep, too many cats. I wish I could go back to sleep.' She shook her head. *'No. First off, you know you'll never get back to sleep in the middle of all this noise. Second, you need to get ready. Commander Aspen will want to get the trial over with as soon as he can. And come on, you know you do, too.'*

She sucked in a deep breath of air, imagining it contained some form of confidence she could absorb. Morning sunlight poured through the trees around her. It bounced off the frost-covered rocks and abatis wall. Both fire pits had fresh wood, and several cats congregated around them. Smoke from the flames rose beyond the treetops and filtered the light into pristine rays. The brightness stabbed her pupils. Spots flickered and lingered in her vision, so she closed her eyes until they faded.

'You know, Ember, you don't have problems like this when you don't oversleep. Or at least, not as many problems. So don't oversleep. As if I can actually control when I wake up. I can't even have dreams consistently. Though being able to wake up at exactly the right time would be nice.'

She shivered as another gust of wind cut across the Glade. Hyrees pounced out of the History Tree. As he landed, his paws caught on a root, and he tumbled to a stop beside her.

"And now I'm awake, too," he said, staggering to his feet. "Remind me why we sleep up there again? We could have a nice den on the ground, and you could come up here every morning and evening, or whenever you wanted to read." He sat down and scratched an ear with his hind paw. "I mean, why not? You know, we wouldn't have this falling out of trees every morning

39

problem if we had a proper den. And there'd be actual shelter from things like rain, and snow, and bird poop. This whole traditional setup really makes no sense."

Ember smiled. "You know, we could get a new sleeping place after the test, if I pass, because then I would be a real historian, and I wouldn't have to study as much."

"I don't understand why Whitehaze isn't the one who has to sleep in the tree. Why does it have to be us?"

Ember chuffed. "Because I *like* sleeping in the History Tree."

Hyrees grumbled to himself. "That is a terrible explanation, but okay, as long as you're happy."

Ember shook herself off. Around the Glade, clayworkers busied themselves with setting out their work to sell for credits. She sucked in another deep breath as she watched them. Her chest was tight, but her mind was alert for the first time in days. There was a special lightness to the air that only came around during special occasions: days with especially exciting ceremonies, like the Mid-Winter Apprentice Initiation, or the seasonal meetings, where everyone got time off, extra food, played games, and held sparring competitions.

In addition to providing much-needed entertainment, the festivities also added another level of security between colonies. Without peace, there would be no point in holding a meeting, which would mean no day off or extra food for either colony. In the spring and fall, the Western high-ranks would travel to the East for a similar celebration.

The soft crunch of paws on leaves made Ember spin to face the noise. "Oh, hi, Commander Aspen. We were just getting down."

His tail twitched. "Good. Get yourself ready."

A tiny shiver crept up her spine. "So, er, when am I supposed to be taking the test?"

"As soon as you're ready. Get some food, then meet me and Whitehaze at the Cliffs. You will take your test there."

Ember's ears flattened. *'The Cliffs? What? Oh no.'* "Uhm, y-yes sir. I will.

Thank you."

He nodded once. "Do well."

Aspen trotted away toward the Southern Entrance, where Whitehaze waited for him by the abatis. He stood up to join him, then they disappeared together into the forest.

Ember shuddered. She hated the Cliffs, but not because they were dangerous. At one point, many mooncycles ago, she'd actually enjoyed standing near the edge and looking down at the Wolf Trail, which ran beneath it far below. It used to be a thrill to exist so close to the human-carrying machines following along it, especially since she'd always known she'd be safe.

However, one day, two days after Light had died, Hyrees had attempted to take his own life there. He was going to throw himself over the edge, hoping he could be with his mother again or at least stop the pain of losing her. She'd managed to find him in time to plead him out of it, but the place had been scarred with memories of fear and desperation.

"So . . . food?" Hyrees asked, pulling her away from her thoughts.

Ember forced a smile. "Yes. Let's go get some."

As she said it, the tightness in her chest formed a cold lump. Cliffs or not, if she failed today, she would have to wait six mooncycles for the Summer Meeting. If she passed, there was always the chance of failing during the Meeting itself. Even easygoing Aspen wouldn't tolerate mistakes permanently etched into the History Tree.

Hyrees led the way toward a group of cats crowding around the food storage, where a few of the hunters gave out morning rations. Songbird padded toward them, carrying an uncooked rabbit. She dropped it on the ground beside her daughter. Ember fought back a gag as the stench of long-dead flesh filled her nose.

"Good morning, Em. You've got a big day today, huh?" Songbird touched noses with Ember. She nodded once to Hyrees. "And good morning to you too, Hyrees." She chuckled. "Did you sleep okay, Farlight?"

"Not that well, ma'am," replied a voice behind them, "but I'll be okay. It's

Dad I'm worried about. I don't think he got almost any."

Ember and Hyrees turned around in unison.

"Farlight! How long have you been standing there?" Hyrees asked.

"I followed you from the Tree. You know, practicing stealth. I think it worked."

Hyrees chuffed. He groomed Farlight's neck. "Yeah, it did. You know, if you weren't going to be our next commander, you would make a great full-time hunter. Or anything you wanted to be, really. You're incredible at everything you do. Don't you ever forget that."

As he said it, he ruffled Farlight's fur with a forepaw, making it stick up like a red bird's crest.

"Hey!" Farlight batted him away, then bent around to straighten himself out. "Don't touch my fur. You'll make me look weird in front of the East. I need to make a good first impression. They've never met me as commander-in-training before."

"Oh, you don't need me to make you look weird, Far," Hyrees said.

Farlight laughed. "What happened to me being incredible at everything?"

Hyrees swatted at his whiskers. "You still are, in your own special way. That doesn't mean you aren't weird." He touched his nose to Farlight's. "Don't ever change, you little furball."

"Oh, uhm," Songbird muttered. She nudged the rabbit carcass to Ember's paws. "You know, speaking of hunting, I caught this rabbit yesterday morning and saved it for you. It might not be fresh, but you know. It's food."

Ember licked Songbird's cheek. "Thanks, Mom."

"You're very welcome." Songbird pulled away and smiled narrowly. "I, uh, I probably won't be here when you get back from the test, because, you know, I have to work, but when I do get back, tell me how it went. Okay?"

Ember sighed. "Okay."

"You'll do fine, Ember. Don't worry about it."

'Thanks, Mom. Your faith in my ability to succeed is definitely lowering the pressure I've been feeling to pass this thing.'

She stepped back. The shadow she'd been standing in didn't. Sunlight exploded from the eastern horizon, flew between the trees, and hit her in the eyes.

"Ack!"

She ducked her head between her forelegs and closed her eyes as tightly as they would close. When she did, the sounds of the Glade amplified: muffled speech, kittens' joyful shrieks, claws being sharpened on wood; it distracted her for a moment, dragging her attention away from the colorful spots dancing in her vision.

Songbird nudged her cheek. "No, no, calm down. It's going to be okay," she said. "It's just a little test. You can handle it."

Ember's ears perked up. She looked up at her, careful to position herself away from the sunlight as embarrassed blue and grey stripes burned in her mind's eye. "What? Oh! No. No, no, no, it's not that. I've grown out of that. No more panics. It was just, uhm, yeah. I'm fine. I mean, no, I'm not exactly the, uh, ideal of self-confidence right now, but it wasn't that that made me . . . You know what? I should probably get ready. I'll go take this rabbit somewhere and eat. Thanks for that, by the way."

Back when she was still a kitten, things like loud noises and bright lights had caused her to see-feel cyan and panic. When it happened she'd sometimes hurt herself or others. Even the thought of losing control again made her uneasy.

Songbird gave her the half-squinty look everyone always gave her when she stumbled over her own words, yet she smiled a moment later. "Okay, then. You already thanked me, but you are definitely welcome. Oh, hey, Farlight, I just remembered—Kivyress was looking for you earlier. Since you've both got a day away from training, I'm guessing she'll want to chase you around the Pine Grove with needles again. Just remember to be back for the Meeting. We can watch it together if I get back in time. I can even show you how to get your own opinions in there without breaking any rules."

Farlight's fluffy tail stuck straight up in the air. "Oh! Thanks, Mom—er, Songbird. I'd love that. For now, I think I'll go find Kivy."

Farlight trotted away. Not knowing his true mother never seemed to bother him. He'd spent the first few mooncycles of his life calling Songbird his mom, even though he'd almost always known she wasn't. He only tried to correct himself when Hyrees was around.

"Wait! She's on the *other* side of the Glade," Songbird called. She shook her head. "He didn't hear a word I meowed, did he? Aaand yep, he's gone. Excuse me."

Hyrees flattened his ears as she ran after the wayward trainee. "Come on. Let's find somewhere quiet to eat."

He picked up Ember's rabbit, then without waiting for a reply, walked away. Ember sighed and followed. *'Why can't they just get along? Mom's just trying to help. There's no reason to get all defensive about it.'*

She ran to catch up with him. The chill in the air sent a tiny shiver down her spine and made her fur raise.

'Calm down, Em. Today is going to be good. You will make it good, Ember. Right? Right. Make this be a nice day to remember. Please.'

Hyrees set the rabbit down in the same place they'd eaten the night before. "Are you hungry now?"

An energy beyond her anxieties filled her body, charging it up for whatever the day might bring. Her tail thrashed like that of an excited wolf pup. "Yes, I'm hungry, and that rabbit is mine. I'm also nervous, er, *still* because of how important today may be for the entire rest of my life. But any day could be important, so is it really all that big of a deal? I mean maybe. It might not be. I don't know. What do you think?"

"I think we should eat," he said.

"Oh. Right. Okay, that's not what I wanted to know, but at least you're being honest. I won't be able to finish the whole thing anyway, so I guess we can share."

They tore into the rabbit, dividing it more or less evenly between them. As usual, Hyrees devoured the tendons, organs, and any other squishy or crunchy pieces Ember disliked. When they finished, Hyrees sat up and licked his muzzle a few times.

"I'm still hungry," he said. "Heh, I'm pretty sure that rabbit was just meant to be for you, Emmy."

"Hey, you haven't actually gotten your rations yet. You might be able to sneak a little extra. You should clean your mouth a little more, though. And speaking of cleaning up, I need to hurry. I'll have to stop by the Kivyress first. Not my sister, obviously; the other Kivyress. I'm thirsty."

He cocked an ear and stood up. "I really, really shouldn't." He sighed. "But fox it, I want to. I'll, um, I'll see you later, Em. Fly through that test, and find me when you're done."

Ember chuckled emotionlessly. The colors in her head changed to a dull note of grey. "Yeah, sure. And you have fun with, er, that."

He didn't even hear her. Or if he did, he didn't acknowledge it. As he raced away toward his second meal, the ever-present wind picked up speed, tousling her fur and beating against the backs of her ears. Ember shivered. Her throat burned, longing for hydration.

'I wonder where Dad is. Shouldn't he have shown up at some point to at least say good morning? Or good luck? Or good something? Maybe he's gone out for a quick patrol. Okay, Ember, that doesn't matter right now. No more procrastinating. Time to do this. You can go to the Cliffs.'

As she loped out of the Glade, birds sang their usual morning songs. Branches and the needles of evergreens rustled together. Scents of wood, moss, and rotting plants all swirled around her nose, mixing with the occasional woodland creature. It only took a few moments for the whispering warble of the Kivyress to join the chorus. With every step forward, it grew louder.

She walked at an angle down the steep slope of the ravine. The creek, wide and rushing, greeted her with a friendly trill.

'Good morning to you, too.'

She lapped at the frigid water until her stomach felt bloated and her mouth became numb from the cold, then she headed up and out for the Cliffs. She trembled as her stomach tightened and cramped. She tucked her tail and willed her body not to ruin anything. Faint, light green flickered in her mind. She coughed once, then twice.

'Oh great. Now? We're doing this now?'

She ducked her head low and speed-walked to the nearest tree, where she coughed out a lump of fur, along with part of her morning meal. Ember rubbed her tongue against the roof of her mouth in an attempt to get rid of some of the taste. After a few rubs, she gave up, buried the furball in leaves, then continued on her way.

Sunbeams and songbirds agitated her senses as she moved. Unnerving or not, she missed the darkness and silence of evening time; in the nothingness of dusk, she could breathe properly and release some of the tension in her everything.

As she neared the Cliffs, the rocks got bigger: rocks of all shapes, covered with moss like huge, tiny-leafed bushes. It was the largest collection of green still in the forest, even compared to the clusters of evergreens dotting the mountain. Here, every tree still seemed alive, blooming with mosses and blue lichens.

Her mind wandered back to Hyrees's suicide attempt. She shook the thought away. To calm her nerves, she imagined winter as a giant white cat trying desperately to take over the Cliffs. The trees and rocks fought him back with the power of moss. They won every battle until winter attacked with snow, its secret weapon. When that happened, the war came to a draw, and anyone who wandered onto the Cliffs during the aftermath would be greeted by a brand new season: wummer.

'Or sinter. But I like wummer better. Sinter sounds scary for some reason. Not sure why. Come on, Em, back to mentally preparing yourself. You can do this, Ember. There. Now I'm fully prepared for anything that could possibly happen today.' She stopped and chewed on her tongue. *'Not anything. I'm definitely not ready for kittens. And I don't think I'm quite ready to die. Wait, does that mean I'm slightly more okay with dying than I am with becoming a mother? What in the forest is wrong with me? Then again, if I died, I wouldn't have to worry about being a mother, but if I became a mother, I'd definitely have to worry about dying. Maybe that's why.'*

"There you are," Aspen's voice said.

Ember looked up. He peered down at her from atop a boulder, Whitehaze crouched over beside him.

"Er, will I be taking the test up there, or should I stay down here?" she asked.

Whitehaze stood up. "You will be taking it up here. We," he mewed as he pounced off the stone, then landed beside her, "will be down here. You have to be able to clawmark above the conversation. As highly as the East thinks of themselves, they still can't fly, so the Meeting will be held below the History Tree, and by extension, below you."

"I know, sir," Ember said, trying to focus on warding off the color of panic. "I, uh, you let me watch you during the Summer Meeting. I remember how it works."

"Good. You've got a piece of leaf in your fur." He groomed her cheek. "There. Now, up you go. Your carving stick has already been prepared for you."

Aspen jumped down beside him and touched noses with her. "When you were a kitten, I didn't know what kind of cat you'd become. I want to let you know that, so far, you've surpassed almost all my expectations."

Ember tried to smile. "Thank you?"

She examined the rock and the drop-off beside it. Roughly a leap below, the dirt and shale beneath her boulder had been eroded away by winters of weather patterns. Small trees and dying ferns masked some of the deadly jagged boulders and the Wolf Trail waiting far below, but not enough for her to pretend she might land softly if she fell. "So, I don't mean to be rude, but why here? Why can't I do it in a tree somewhere?"

"I know." Whitehaze leaned closer and whispered, "I don't trust it either, but the commander insisted your trial be held here. It isn't my place to say, but I'm beginning to fear for his sanity. Try to jump lightly, Ember. Be careful."

"I wanted to test her tenacity, Whitehaze," Aspen said. "Willpower and the ability to perform under stress are extremely important traits which every historian must possess. But as you could see, Ember, Whitehaze and I waited for you from atop it. The rock is stable. You'll be fine."

Ember sucked in a deep breath, then pounced onto the rock with as much grace as she could muster. She sniffed her carving branch, examining it, and sat to await her instructions.

"So, what do I do?"

Aspen's tail twitched. He cocked back his ears. "We will begin to discuss some things you might expect to hear during a meeting. You must pick out the important parts and summarize them in the clearest way possible. Also, even though the History Tree is always growing, there is still a limited amount of space on it, so your clawmarks must be small and clear. No mistakes or cross-outs. Do what you've been trained to do."

'Okay, I can do that. You can do it. You can do it. You've got this, Ember. No need to panic. Noooo need to panic. Ignore where you are, and focus on what you're trying to do.'

"And when do I start?" she asked.

He chuckled. "Right now."

Then he began the most forced-sounding discussion in all recorded Western history . . . by asking Whitehaze about the weather. She knew because she had every clawmark of recorded Western history memorized. As they spoke, the topic shifted to things they could do to improve inter-colony relationships. It wasn't hard to pick out what needed marking down, as they kept emphasizing the important things. It wasn't enough to be insulting, but rather with subtle cues: a little louder, a little longer, a little softer, or a little lighter.

Ember bit her tongue. Her clawmarks refused to be nice and pretty, but if she wanted them to look good enough for even the lowest standard, she needed to slow down. They needed to slow down.

'Come on. Just take a moment to breathe. A moment to breathe. How can you possibly be able to talk so long? Don't your throats hurt? Please. I'm not fast enough. I don't know if I can do this. But I want to—I want to so badly.'

"Whitehaze, do you think colonies should trade clawmark tablets?" Aspen asked.

Whitehaze hesitated. "Hmm. On the one side, there's something to be said for exchanging knowledge, but those tablets are extremely hard to craft. We only have a few good ones, molded by history's greatest historians and clayworkers. I'm sure the East would value their tablets even more, considering they don't even have a history tree."

"But does that mean they would value *our* tablets even more?"

Whitehaze chuffed. "Hah! They might not even read them. And how in the forest do you figure we'll get them across the Valley to make the exchange? No matter how careful anyone was, they'd break before they even left the territory. No, I say we leave them where they are and allow them to be read by anyone, Eastern or Western, who wishes to learn."

"But what if . . ."

She wanted to wait and let the discussion sink in. Their words weren't forced now; they were real thoughts coming from some of the biggest authority figures in her life. All hints stopped. The conversation became a debate. Jumbled nothingness mixed with a few good quotes scattered here and there, and she couldn't decide if they were worth mentioning or not, as some of it was still nothingness, but more poetic.

Thoughts backed up. Her paw refused to move quickly enough. Her mind refused to discriminate between the important and the superfluous-but-beautiful. She took a moment to evaluate her work and found the marks were getting bigger and more lopsided with every word. She growled, clamped her teeth over her tongue, and forced herself back on track. Somewhere at the edge of her mind she registered tasting blood, but she refused to acknowledge it.

'Come on, Ember! Paws, work! Work! Come on, this is what you want. Be a good molly, and do it! You can do this, Ember. Please don't fall, rock. I don't want to die today. Just calm down. Calm down and focus. OW!'

A searing pain cut through her mouth. Bitter liquid coated her throat. Ember stopped and released her own tongue. She wiggled it around her mouth and winced. Her stomach tightened.

'Wait, did I just bite through my tongue? I just bit through my tongue.' Her eyes widened. Light green gripped her insides and twisted them into knots. 'I just bit through my tongue! What am I doing? I have no clue what I'm doing. I can't do this. I can't do this. I literally can't do this.'

The world spun around her, bouncing in and out of focus. She shivered all over and glared down at her work. 'Stupid. It looks stupid. Why did I agree to do this? My clawmarks have always looked like carrion. And now my mouth is full of blood, and my tongue hurts. My shoulder. My shoulder. My everything. Why do I feel like this? Am I dying?'

Darkness crept along the edges of her vision. Her conscience was wide awake, but her body felt like it was drifting away. She jumped off the rock and stumbled, but regained her balance a moment later. Ember searched the mossy forest for Aspen, or Whitehaze, or anyone at all.

'What's going on? Why can't I see? Am I going blind? No, that doesn't make sense. My tongue isn't attached to my eyes. Oh my mouth tastes terrible. Commander Aspen. Whitehaze? Where are you? Come on, say something, Ember!'

"I, uh, I don't feel very good. I don't wanna do this anymore."

Then it became so much easier to just let go. So she did; not caring if she passed, or failed, or died, or lived. She heard voices, distant voices calling her. She thought they might be calling her name, but she couldn't decide for sure. They didn't matter. Something similar to running pawsteps echoed in her ears, too muffled to make out from the soft hum of the breeze.

She realized she was still inside her own body and shook her head. Something wasn't right. Something sharp tugged at her neck. She opened her eyes. A little spot of color flickered in her vision—green, then brown. Something rough and cold rubbed against her forepaws and hindquarters.

"W-what happened?" she asked.

She felt herself being lowered, but she couldn't quite secure the connection between her mind and her body to confirm the sensation.

"You passed out," Aspen said. "Ember, listen to me; are you well enough to walk? I don't think I can carry you all the way back to the Glade on my own."

'That's strange. I don't remember passing out. It feels like I've been awake the whole time. I don't feel all that sleepy. Actually, on second thought, could I just stay here? The dirt is surprisingly comfortable. never mind the bad taste in my mouth. I'll deal with it. Maybe if I concentrate hard enough on what a failure I am right now, I'll pass out again and skip forward a few days.'

Still, instinct said she needed to get moving, so she tried to blink the vision back into her eyes. "Can't Whitehaze help?"

"Whitehaze went to tell the healers what happened so they can be ready when we get you back. Come on, Ember. Please try to get up."

Ember closed her eyes and forced her body to obey her. It took almost five times longer than it should have, but when she opened her eyes again, she was standing. She blinked twice. The shadows creeping along the edges of her vision faded, but not all the way.

She coughed out blood, then felt queasy all over again. Her stomach lurched and she dry-heaved.

"Can you walk?" Aspen asked. "Come on, we need to get you back."

"I can walk," Ember said. She coughed again. "I'm—I'm fine. I don't need the healers."

Aspen nudged her into motion. "Ember, there's blood dripping out of your mouth. You passed out. You yourself said you aren't feeling well. It could be something serious. You need the healers."

She tried to focus on placing one paw in front of the other instead of the end destination. "Actually, there's a reason for all that. I, uhm, I wasn't exactly paying attention to what my mouth was doing and bit through my tongue. Hence the bleeding and such. I guess everything happening at once overwhelmed, well, not really me, but my body definitely didn't like it for some reason, so it just kind of . . . stopped working. I don't know why."

Aspen didn't reply right away. He grimaced and shook his head. "You will still be visiting the healers' den."

She sighed. At least the darkness was gone. Her gaze wandered off into the forest. Without the moss, everything looked dead again, and the wind pushing against her fur didn't help. "I'm guessing I didn't pass."

Aspen watched her for a moment, then looked away. "No, Ember."

Ember grated her teeth together, careful to avoid her still stinging tongue. "That's fine. I wouldn't make a good historian anyway."

He stopped. "Don't say that, Ember. Anyone can be good at anything with enough time and determination. You just need more practice."

Her legs felt like they might give out at any moment. She growled internally at how pathetic and weak her body was being, but she sat down anyway. "Ever try flying?"

Aspen sighed. "You know that's not what I meant. When I was your age, I was a terrible hunter. So I practiced every day, and eventually, after a few winters had passed, I could even catch birds."

'And after that, you caused a mass murder.' Ember shivered. She closed her eyes and played with the little swirls of indigo and grey light that appeared.

"I'm trying. Maybe I'm not meant to be a historian," she said quietly, her tongue stinging with every word.

Aspen nudged her side. "Maybe you are, maybe you aren't. Either way, we have to keep moving."

She opened her eyes and obliged. As they walked, the swirls of grey in her mind got brighter, so she imagined them turning into a ghostly figure who weaved in and out of the trees, following them, protecting them.

'I have to be a historian. I've studied the Tree since the day I learned to read. I spent mooncycles upon mooncycles memorizing every line of law, tradition, and documentation I could find. If I can't be a historian, what was it all for? What am I supposed to be? Who am I?' She mewed quiet gibberish to herself. It helped calm her aching chest. *'I messed up so bad. What am I going to do? What are Mom and Dad going to think?'*

Ember shook her head and lifted it. As she did, a soft, sorrowful misty orange joined the grey. *'It doesn't matter. I can try studying harder. Practicing more. Once I get better control of myself, I can do better, and Ember, if you can't find yourself a place, you can always try your best to* make one. What you can't do is give up. If you give up, you'll never know if you would've passed the next test, so you have to keep going. Try. For Mom and Dad, if not yourself.'

Her vision blurred. She blinked furiously, trying to keep herself from crying. 'Don't cry, Ember. This is not the time or place for all these emotions. Save it for tonight, after Hyrees has gone to sleep. Or, preferably, don't cry at all. This is nothing. Nothing worth crying over, at least.'

She growled at herself as the tears escaped. Ember let out an aggravated huff and gave up. They continued to fall, making her cheeks cold and wet. 'Thanks, me. Way to listen to yourself.'

"Don't be hard on yourself," Aspen said. "You'll get another chance next summer. I suggest practicing on your own time. Have your friends talk about something and try to mark down the basics of what they say on a young tree or stick. It will help you improve your speed."

"I . . . I might try that," she whispered.

"You should," he said. "You'll know you've passed when they can read your marks and remember almost everything they spoke about."

She stopped for a moment to wipe her eyes. 'I'll try to remember that.'

As they neared the Glade, the silvers in her mind grabbed her by the throat. She coughed. 'Right. Silentstream.'

Before she'd even passed through the southern entrance, Cloud ran to meet her. Instead of touching noses, he walked around her, sniffing her all over. "Ember, are you okay? *Are* you okay? Whitehaze said you passed out. Are you okay?"

'Alright, Ember. Say "yes." You're fine. Everything is okay and will have gone back to normal by tomorrow. You're okay.'

"No." She pressed her head against his neck, her tears dampening his fur.

'Why would you say that? I'm fine, right? Who am I trying to fool? I'm not. Nothing is okay.'

"Oh, Ember," Cloud whispered.

The next few moments passed in a blur. She felt herself being ushered to the healers' den. She opened her mouth to let Fern, Silentstream, and the other healers examine her tongue. Hyrees and Tainu appeared for a moment before being walked out by Fern's partner and mate, Fledge. Meanwhile, Ember was in a whole other world, trying to figure out what went wrong. Cats whispered outside the den, most too quietly to make out coherent speech, but plenty loud enough to know they were all talking about her. Words like 'failure,' 'disappointing,' and 'defect' pounded at her ears. Two of the voices belonged to Cloud and Aspen.

"So how did all this come about?" Silentstream asked, breaking her dazed concentration.

"I bit my tongue," Ember replied.

"I can see that. You know what I meant. Don't you play fluffhead with me."

Her mind locked up again as a sickly green filled her head. She shivered and clamped her jaws shut, trying to keep herself from throwing up. "I, urm, I," she stammered.

Fern wrapped her tail around Ember's haunches. "You're alright. Calm down, okay? She wants to know why you bit your tongue."

Her mind loosened up enough to flicker with creamy white indignation, but couldn't quite form a coherent verbal thought. Instead, Fern's quiet meows made a little mouse appear in her head. Ember closed her eyes. She let the mouse scurry around a blank void until the nothingness got boring. She threw it into a lush fern patch and watched it nibble on grass seeds.

"I'm waiting," Silentstream said.

Ember flinched. "Uhm . . . I, uh, I bite it sometimes when I, er, get nervous. It usually helps me feel better. Unless I bite through it."

Silentstream shook her head. "You need to stop doing this. These silly little habits of yours seem to be causing you more problems than anything you could possibly be gaining from them. Find something more productive to calm yourself down."

A coyote appeared in Ember's fern patch. Before the mouse could run away, the coyote snatched it up in its jaws, then swallowed it whole. Ember mewled quietly and opened her eyes. Tears threatened to betray her again.

Silentstream sat down and nudged her into an uncomfortably upright position. "Ember, my little maimed fawn, you must realize your actions have consequences. What you do reflects on your parents' reputations, just as Cloud's choices have had an impact on mine." She placed a paw under Ember's chin and lifted her head to face her. "When you do anything of importance, you carry your heritage with you. Be strong and confident. Bear yourself with pride, and soar through your next trial. Okay?"

"Why?" Ember asked.

She winced. Alarming yellow lightning flashed through her mind, startling the coyote into taking shelter in the ferns.

Fern nudged Silentstream's side. "Maybe you should let me handle this. Go take a nap if you need to. I'm sure it will help that headache of yours."

The mouse reappeared in front of the half-hidden coyote. Both imaginary creatures stared at each other in confusion. Ember sighed, and they vanished together as she wiped her mind's eye clean.

Silentstream stood. "Don't touch me, Fern. I can move on my own, thank you. And you know what? I think I will go. You kittens are going to kill me with all this stress one day, I swear."

She left the healers' den, still muttering to herself. Fern sighed. She bent over to examine Ember's shoulder. "This isn't fresh, but it hasn't been treated. Ember, does she really bother you that much?"

The coyote in Ember's mind reappeared. It chased its own tail around, snarling as it spun. Ember clenched her teeth, causing it to disappear again with a soft *pop*.

Ember lowered her head. Habit sent her tongue between her teeth and pain sent it back. Her throat burned for water. Her tail thrashed. "I don't know . . . what to say."

Fern sighed again. "Then you don't have to say anything. I'm sure—oh, please keep your tail still. You might spill the medicine. This supply has to last all winter. And speaking of medicine, here, let me get something for your tongue."

She separated out a few well-cleaned root pieces into a tiny clay bowl with a rock at its center. She pawed at them a few times, crushing the cluster of roots into a flat lump with the stone, then dumped the bowl's contents into Ember's mouth. Ember fought the urge to gag. The sharp, bitter taste itself numbed her tongue.

"Don't swallow it, if you can help it," Fern said. "It'll give your stomach a bad time."

The pain dulled, but didn't disappear completely. She slackened her jaw and let the wet lump fall to the compacted dirt floor.

"Agh, that tasted terrible," Ember mewed. "Are you sure that was safe to put in my mouth?"

"Well, usually it's used for cuts in the skin, not the tongue, but it shouldn't give you any problems. Just make sure you let someone know if you start feeling weird."

She tried to drool out the flavor. The tension in her head loosened. *So I shouldn't die from it, but I might?* Ember sighed. "I always feel weird."

Fern chuffed. "Oh, you and me both. But we're all a little weird, aren't we? Even the great Silentstream."

"Hey, whoa! What happened, Fern?" Fledge, a smoky grey molly, stepped into the healers' den. She touched noses with Fern. "Not-so-Silentstream just stormed past me, mumbling about ungrateful youngsters, or something like that. Just wanted to make sure everything was still okay down here," Fledge said.

Fern nuzzled Fledge's cheek. "We're fine. Thanks for checking though. Just finishing up, right Ember?"

Ember looked at her paws. *I certainly hope we're done. I'm not sucking on any more roots.*

"Yes, ma'am," she whispered.

"Alright then," Fern said. She licked Ember's forehead. "You're all fixed up and ready to go. Have fun at the meeting. If Tainu tries to force you to go hunting with her again, you tell her I said not to. She should know better than to keep pushing you like that."

Ember got to her paws. "I will. Thanks, Fern."

She trotted out of the den without looking back. Hyrees sat outside, waiting for her.

"So, how did it go?" he asked.

She kept walking. "I don't want to talk about it."

"Oh," he said. "Did you want to go do something then?"

"Yes. Alone."

"Oh," he said again. "Later then?"

"Maybe." She turned toward the Western Entrance and almost ran into Cloud. Ember jumped backward to avoid colliding with his chest. "Ah! S-sorry, Dad."

He smiled weakly. "No, no; it's okay. How's your tongue doing?"

"It hates me, and probably Fern, too. Me for biting it and talking, and Fern for putting lobelia roots on it."

Cloud stared at her in silence. Ember examined his tight expression, trying to figure out what it meant. She gave up and lowered her head. "I meant sorry for ruining everything."

"You didn't ruin anything. Everything's . . . going to be okay."

She glanced up at her father. Her mind tore itself away from him, and Hyrees, and everyone else. *'You're keeping secrets again. Why can't you just tell me when I'm causing a problem? I'm not a dead leaf. I'm not going to crumble and fall apart if you put a little extra weight on me.'*

She stepped back and bit down on the other side of her tongue. Her ears flicked against her neck. *'Then again, isn't that exactly what just happened? Tahg, I need to think. Your presence is preventing me from thinking. I need to be alone.'*

He sighed. "I'm going to have to leave with the welcoming group in a little while. After the Meeting, though, I'd like to talk to you about some things. Okay? There are some things I need to tell you that I really should have told you a long time ago, and—"

"Cloud! We're going now, with or without you," Aspen called from across the Glade.

Cloud stretched his neck to look at his commander. "Coming!" he shouted, hurting Ember's ears. "Sorry, I have to leave. I'll see you later, I guess."

Ember rubbed her brown paw. "I'm going to the Falls," she said. "You can get me when the Meeting is over."

Without waiting for a reply, she strode past him, left the Glade, and made her way toward Fernburrow Falls.

CHAPTER 4
CLOUD

'I hope this meeting goes well,' Cloud thought. *'Ever since that Outsider showed up, Aspen's been more tense than usual. It's one thing when he won't tell me why he makes the decisions he makes. It's another thing entirely when there's something obviously important going on and he won't tell anyone about it. If it's bothering him, as the commander, maybe it should bother the rest of us. Or at least me. Doesn't he trust me?'*

He sighed as he walked, dead leaves rustling beneath the paws of the high-ranks and border guards around him. The welcoming group reached the Eastern Border and came to a halt. Trees, tall and ancient hardwoods, surrounded them, providing shade from the morning sun. Storm clouds gathered overhead, possible precursors of the winter's first snow. He drew a quiet breath of air, and wondered how an early snowfall might affect the Meeting.

Cloud sat down beside Aspen. He'd spent most of the morning in the Fields, helping prepare the camp for the East. The simple fire pit was cleaned, the dead grass around it was pulled and set aside for kindling, and the firewood was kept dry from possible rains beneath the protective snout of Coyote Rock. With a few generous rations of meat, their guests would want for nothing that night.

'It's a good thing Jade doesn't take these things personally. If what I've

heard about the Battle of Stone Ridge is true, she could use anything we do as a declaration of war and make it justified. I wouldn't even blame her if I weren't stuck in the middle of it all.'

The wind picked up, sending a lone leaf fluttering down. It smacked against his muzzle, then landed to rest at his feet. *'Then again,'* he lifted the leaf to his face with a forepaw, *'I still don't understand why it happened the way it did. We were clearly in the wrong. He was clearly in the wrong.'*

He curled his toes, causing the leaf to crumble apart.

"Cloud," Aspen whispered, "when the East has left, I'd like to speak with you about Ember."

Cloud flinched. He'd tried to forget about Ember's trial the moment they left the Glade. It hadn't worked during the tedious trip to the edge of the Lowlands, but another reminder didn't help. "Yes, of course, sir," he replied under his breath. "What about her, if you don't mind me asking? I know what happened earlier, but I can almost guarantee it won't happen again."

"Can you?"

A sinking feeling caught him in the chest. He lowered his head and shook it. "No, sir."

"Don't be upset. You've done your best, and surpassed every expectation I had. You both have. However, I'm undecided on what the best course of action will be, going from here. We already aren't performing by the rules, so what comes next will need a lot of forethought if we try to follow through with this experiment."

Cloud sighed with relief and straightened up to face Aspen. "Sir, let her have a say in this. She deserves to know the truth. I'm going to tell her today, and you are not going to stop me."

Aspen huffed. "You know it will change the way she sees you, and almost everything else. The truth may well break her."

"I'm willing to take that risk. She's not a kitten anymore. She can deal with it," Cloud replied. A growl edged into his voice.

"No. She's not ready for it. As long as I'm commander, no one is to tell her Dark's final decree. If you so much as mention the Commander's Tablet, I'll have you removed from the Council, and put an end to your experiment myself."

His heart lurched. "Sir, no, you're not—"

"Look sharp, everyone," Aspen shouted, cutting him off. "The East will be here soon. We'd better be ready for them."

"Sorry to jump in, but I smell cats approachin', sir," Wren said.

Cloud grimaced and silently willed for his heart rate to return to normal. *'Fine. We'll discuss this later.'* His nostrils flared as he scanned the forest for new scents. He couldn't find any, but his sense of smell had never been good.

Wren growled and stood up. "They aren't Eastern, though. I'd know Outsider stench from the next valley over."

"Stand together and hold your ground," Aspen commanded. The cats obeyed, forming a semi-circle with Aspen in the middle. "Wren, about how many are there?"

Wren lifted his nose to the breeze. "I'd say five. Not more than six."

"We can take them. Be ready," Aspen replied.

In the ensuing silence, the never-ending wind howled. It whipped their fur and bent their whiskers. The stench of decay churned and mixed with sweet water, dead flowers, and sun-dried blackberries.

A few birds fluttered around the trees above them, chirping too loudly to ignore. A plump, bluish-brown bird landed in a bush a leap away. Cloud curled back his lips and stepped closer. The bird fluttered away, trilling as it went. He watched it flap up to a nearby tree. When it landed, it stared down at him with emotionless black eyes. He growled quietly.

Near-worthless as food or not, birds weren't just annoying; they were vermin. They caused so many problems, he occasionally killed them as pests and left them for ants and flies to eat. The noises and messes they made were only surface issues. Large, unafraid flocks attracted more predators into the territory. Eagles would fly in looking for a blackbird, then fly out with a beloved kitten. A beloved kitten whose parents mistakenly thought the Glade was safe and decided to look away for a moment. In addition to eagles, Outsiders and other Lowland creatures would risk their lives to sneak in for an easy hunt. Occasionally they would take his fellow border guards' lives in their desperation for a quick meal. Birds got good cats killed.

A breaking twig snapped him to attention. *'Right. Outsiders.'*

Flashes of white fur moved toward them through the underbrush. He lowered himself as a cat emerged from the bramble. Four others followed. All five outsiders were tabbies with white patches, or white with tabby patches, and all of them had strange, fur-lined objects strapped to their necks or sides: containers of some kind. The Outsiders stopped and watched the band of Westerners with wary eyes.

Cloud stared at the containers. *'What are those things?'*

The first cat stepped forward. He boasted impressive patches of ginger, a shade typically found in the occasional Easterner, or outsiders descended from Easterners. Half of his tail was missing. Aspen closed his eyes for a moment, seeming almost relieved.

"Ah. So you do send your guards to greet the East. Perfect," the ginger tom said.

Aspen curled back his lips, bearing his fangs. "Go back to the Lowlands. You don't belong here."

"What if we want to talk to you?" the tom asked.

"Then you're out of luck. Our guests will be coming soon. We need to be ready," Aspen said.

"Wait, hear us out. We would like to come to the Meeting. We represent the—"

"Listen, cat," Cloud said, "we don't have time for this. Get out of here before I hurt you."

Aspen pawed his side. Cloud spun to face his commander. Aspen jerked his head toward the empty space beside him. He sighed, backed into place, and sat down.

Aspen had been commanding the West for a few years when Cloud was born. Four and a half winters had passed since then, but as much as he'd seen and learned in those four and a half winters, he still felt underprepared. Every now and then he found himself wondering if Aspen felt the same way.

Aspen nudged the nervous, brown smoke-furred tom sitting at his other side. "Lupine, you may be better suited for this. Go speak with them."

Lupine turned to look at his brother. "W-what? Me? Why? You-you're the commander, Aspen. Not me."

Lupine was only younger by a matter of moments, but he submitted to Aspen like he would to Whitehaze, his former mentor, or any other high-ranking elder. Cloud had heard rumors that Lupine hadn't always been so skittish or submissive. Some said he'd once been the most outgoing cat in the Colony. However, that was before Aspen became commander and tried to unite the East and the West by force. It had been the bloodiest battle in all of recorded history. No survivor returned as the same cat they'd been when they left. Most hadn't returned at all.

"Yes," Aspen said, "but if anything happens to me before Farlight is ready, you will be the one to take my place. I'd like to see how you choose to handle this."

Cloud fought back a growl as Aspen spoke.

"Well, ideally, I-I won't be needing to, uh, take your place, but I'll do my best to-to speak with them." Lupine walked over to the ginger tom. "Y-you said you wanted to come to the Meeting, right? Why?"

The tom raised his half-tail in a polite greeting. "Oh, finally. Yes, we do. My name is Buck, and these are my kin. We aren't Outsiders, sir; we've come to represent the recently formed Midbrook Colony. Our leader isn't present right now, but he trusts us to speak for him. We have our own food, and don't plan to stay for any festivities. We'd only like to stay long enough to discuss a three-way peace treaty during the meeting itself."

Lupine swallowed and glanced over his shoulder. Cloud followed his gaze to silver-furred Whitehaze, who offered an encouraging smile.

"I, ah, honestly don't know what to tell you," Lupine said. "This is a . . . a little short-notice. Maybe we could set aside a different time and place. Our relationship w-w-with the East isn't the best right now. I'm not sure how they'd take to us inviting a, uhm, third Colony without their consent."

"We could wait for them to get here, and you can decide together," Buck replied.

Wren moved to sit at Cloud's other side. "East's getting close," he whispered.

"Fight a fox," Cloud growled under his breath. He leaned over to Aspen. "Wren says the East is almost here. These Outsiders have to go."

Aspen grimaced. "Agreed."

He nudged Lupine's flank, and Lupine stepped out of the way. Aspen moved to take his place. "There will be no waiting for you. Take your kin and leave. The Western Mountain is no place for Outsiders."

Buck flattened his ears. His eyes narrowed. "Pardon my correction, sir, but we're not Outsiders. We are from the Midbrook Colony, and our leader—"

"Will be lucky if his band of rogues lasts until spring. Your kind is not welcome here," Aspen said.

"Our kind? I'm as much a Colony Cat as you are. Me, and all of my kin, we aren't bobcats or foxes to be chased away. I promise you we're just as capable of the kind of trust and teamwork it takes to stand together."

"Then stand together somewhere else. Go, or we will hurt you."

Buck scoffed. "Will? You already have. *Your kind* already has. My mother was sent into exile when Commander Sunflare found out she was pregnant with her third litter. With *me*. You know, I used to not believe all the stories my elders would tell me about you and the East. Now I do. Now I understand why so many of my kin want you dead. In fact, the only reason you're not yet, *sir*, is because of Br—"

"That is quite enough," a sharp, authoritative voice said.

A large, tanish-grey tabby stalked toward them. She carried herself with stoic dignity. Her soft, green eyes retained an icy chill as she glared at the Outsiders. The Eastern Council followed behind her, moving with the silent power of well-trained soldiers.

Buck growled. Without another word, he turned and ran off into the Lowlands. The Outsiders with him followed suit, and they disappeared in the underbrush.

"Well, that was easy," Aspen said, raising his tail in greeting. The strain on his face lessened, but it didn't disappear. "You've always had good timing, Commander Jade, but I think this downs the buck. Hah. Almost literally. Someone was about to get hurt."

Jade chuffed and lifted her tail in reply. "Those fluffheads came to us last autumn. We sent them scampering away like squirrels. If they ever try to force their way into a meeting, they will find out very quickly why the other Outsider groups leave us alone."

"Outsiders never change, do they?" Aspen said.

"No, they do not." She cast a glare in Wren's direction. The familiar look of betrayal she gave him told a story different from her passive body language.

Wren had left the East shortly after the Battle of Stone Ridge. He'd grown tired of their rigidity and wanted some personal freedom. With this new freedom, he'd wandered the Valley for a few mooncycles before getting attacked by a coyote. He'd managed to make his way to the West, where he'd recovered and fallen in love with Light, the young border guard who had taken pity on him and helped save his life.

Jade and Aspen walked in a circle, sniffing under each other's tails. Cloud examined his paws. Scenting was a normal part of greeting someone, but watching someone else doing it was considered rude.

When the circle broke apart, Aspen groomed a foreleg. His eyes darted around the forest, as if at any moment, someone or something would jump out and grab him. "So, how have you been, Commander Jade?"

"We've been operational," Jade replied.

In the two and a half winters following the creation of the Dark's Valley Treaty, Cloud had been exposed to Eastern culture multiple times. Their militarized social structure, while strict, always seemed to be more efficient and straightforward than that of the West. Their Colony was always going, working in shifts during both day and night. Even their main settlement was a strategic stronghold. They lived in a massive rift in the Eastern Mountain, a fortress easy to defend and difficult to penetrate.

For a split second, Jade's gaze flashed directly into Aspen's eyes. Aspen caught her glare and looked away, tail drooping.

'She's tense, too,' Cloud thought. 'And more hostile than usual. Did I miss something last Meeting, or does this have to do with that Outsider we found? I wish you'd just tell me what's going on, Aspen. I might be able to help.'

A dark grey tabby walked up to Jade's side. He brushed against her shoulder. "Come along, then. There's no use in standing around like this," he said. "There's a meeting to be had. And I believe I can speak for everyone when I say we're all feeling a bit bitey, aren't we, love?"

"You're always feeling a little bitey, Falcon," she purred, nuzzling the tabby's cheek, then glanced back at Aspen, another threat clawmarked on her face. This time, if he even noticed, he ignored it.

"Aye, that is true," he mewed with a chuff.

Jade smiled at him, but turned her attention to the gathering of Westerners. "That said, I do believe we should be leaving for the Glade now. Why are we all standing around like useless elk?" she asked. "Lead on then, Commander Aspen."

Aspen nodded toward the Glade. His ears lowered, cocked to the sides of his face in a display of caution. "With pleasure."

The Eastern-Western mass followed Aspen away from the border, laughing, teasing, and comparing work, as they did every meeting. As if the cats each party was joking with hadn't killed dear friends or beloved family members. As if Aspen had never once caused the unwarranted slaughter of tens of good Colony Cats. Cloud stood still and watched as everyone left for the heart of the Western Colony; he wanted no part in the insincerity.

Wren's ears flicked in his direction a moment before Wren himself turned around. He padded back to where Cloud waited. "What's wrong? Somethin' botherin' you?"

Cloud sat down and stared, eyes unfocused, into the Lowlands. "I'm worried about Aspen. There's something going on, and he's not telling me what."

"Well, you're only his advisor," Wren said. "He isn't going to tell you all his secrets. He may not need advice on what's botherin' him."

Cloud grimaced. "Yes, but I'm starting to wonder if the pressure is getting to him. He's been taking more risks than usual lately, and Whitehaze said he put Ember on an unstable rock for her trial." He sighed. "He's getting to be as anxious and paranoid as Lupine. If there's something real threatening our Colony, everyone in the West deserves to know about it. I don't care if he's trying to prevent a panic. If something is coming, we need to prepare. If it's a personal problem, he needs to see the healers. We can't afford to have a delusional or otherwise unfit leader right now."

Wren nudged his side. "Don't worry, Cloud. Give him some credit. He'll let you know if it's important."

He let his gaze wander past Wren, into the great unknown of the Lowlands. His life in the Colony was one most cats longed for; he was a high-rank with respect, authority, and a family he cared about. His mate still wanted to be with him after they'd had their two litters.

Many cats had kittens together not because of love, but because of the social and credit-related benefits of being a parent. Every molly was expected to have at least one litter, but no more than two to prevent overcrowding. Songbird was a rare exception; she didn't care about status. She'd loved him for who he was before he was anyone important, and he loved her.

Yet even with such a seemingly perfect life, he couldn't shake the feeling that he was missing out on something. There was something more beyond his well-marked boundaries; something beyond Dark's shadowy reach, where no long-dead cats would ever threaten him or his family again.

"Rather be off on your own again, wouldn't you?" Wren asked.

Cloud sighed. There was a whole world out there, and he hadn't even seen half a valley of it.

'What would happen to the Colony if I stepped down from being chief advisor? I could still do that. I could leave.'

His gaze trailed farther into the distance, still not focusing on anything in particular. *'For now I guess I'm stuck here, in this mundane little life of mine, serving the Colony and my family with every bit of life I have. But Song, as long as you're just a few leaps up that mountain, I'll be okay with mundane. For now. I can't stay here, though. You know I can't. I just hope I can convince you to come with me when the time comes.'*

Cloud huffed out a pent-up breath of air.

"Alright, that's the third sigh you've sighed," Wren said. "Is there something botherin' you? Anything you'd want to talk about?"

"Not really."

"Understood," he replied.

Cloud almost smiled. Wren was one of only two cats he could count on to not force him to answer questions he'd rather leave unanswered. The other cat was Songbird. In the back of his mind, he wondered if Aspen felt the same way about whatever secret he was keeping.

He spun to face Wren. "Thanks. And you're right. If he doesn't want to tell me something, I guess I'll just have to trust it's not my place to know. We should get back with the group. Aspen will be looking for us."

Wren snorted. "You mean he'll be lookin' for you. He doesn't care about me," he said, voice devoid of emotion. "But I do agree. We should return to the Glade."

Cloud gave a slight nod and they started toward the Glade. They walked back up the mountain in silence side by side. Up ahead, an Easterner caterwauled at some joke that may or may not have been funny. Life continued on.

"So, how have you been with the patrols lately?" Wren asked.

"You heard about the rogue Ember fought with, huh?" Cloud said.

Wren chuffed. "Oh yeah, but did you hear about the bobcat Hyrees took on yesterday? Big as a fox-fightin' boulder, it was—and a feisty one, too. Hyrees took him on like a cougar."

Cloud smiled. "Ahah, so that's why you asked. You just wanted to brag."

"Maybe. But I might also be wantin' to get my mind off the death looks Jade keeps giving me. But mostly because I wanted to brag. Hyrees is a good cat to brag about. He claims he doesn't enjoy fightin', but tahg, when he does he gives it his all. Not a cat alive would think he was going blind if they couldn't see the fog in his eyes. Poor tom. I can't help but wonder when he's going to tell me about it, or what I'll tell him when he does." Wren looked away. "I'm gonna miss havin' him as a partner when the fog takes over. He might well prefer a quieter job, but it still doesn't change how much I'll miss his company."

"I can imagine. So how's Farlight doing?"

"You know how he's been. He's almost your son at this point."

"This is true. I guess that means we can both brag about him. He's going to make a good commander when the time comes."

"Aye," Wren said. His ears and tail drooped. "It's times like this when I wish Light were here to see the young tomcats her sons have grown into."

"She'd be proud of them, I'm sure," Cloud replied.

Wren sighed softly. They walked the rest of the way to the Glade in silence and came to a stop inside the Eastern Entrance.

"I should go track Hyrees down," Wren said. "Promised I'd help him look for something. I'll find you later, okay? Farlight told me you'd wanted to do something after the Meeting. Is that still the plan?"

"Actually, I may not have the time." Cloud lowered his voice. "Commander wants to have a word about Ember after they leave."

Wren's tail threshed. "Ah. Well, I'd best be off." He loped into the throng, leaving Cloud alone.

A few leaps away, the Easterners and Western escorts chatted and scented among each other. The cat at the back of the group, a large, ruffled-looking lynx point, sat apart from them. He looked up at him, then shied away. The similarly colored, yet fluffier cat beside him smiled. She licked the tom's side. He relaxed and smiled at her. They were Jade's son and daughter, Shard and Echo; he recognized them, though he'd never actually spoken to them. Jade always forbid them from saying anything during the actual meeting, and after those they often wandered off with their Western friends.

"Cloud! There you are," Songbird's familiar voice called over the din.

His ears perked up. Songbird appeared from within the crowd. A patch of red stained her cheek.

Cloud broke into a run. "Song! What happened? Are you okay?"

69

"I'm okay," she replied. "The turkey we chased down today really didn't want us to take it. I can't blame it for putting up a fight, but feeling sorry for prey doesn't feed hungry Easterners."

They touched noses, breathing in each other's scents.

He sniffed the two puncture wounds piercing her face. "Ow, that must've hurt. It just missed your eye. You group hunters don't get enough credit."

It wasn't until a deer kicked, and ultimately killed, one of Songbird's closest hunting companions that he'd realized the brutal reality of being a group hunter. As it was with guarding borders, the rule of hunting was kill or be killed, and sometimes the creek would flow backward.

"I'm fine," she said, "but where were you this morning? I couldn't find you anywhere. You were supposed to be here for the trial. And speaking of the trial, where's Ember? I've searched the whole Glade looking for her. Kivyress told me what happened. She said she hasn't seen her since this morning when she went into the healers' den for her tongue."

"Ember said something about going to the Falls," Cloud replied. "She's probably still there. And as for this morning, I was helping everyone get the camp set up. I meant to come back before they left for the Cliffs, but there was a lot more that needed to be done than we'd expected, so—"

She walked in a circle. "The Cliffs? The Falls? The camp? Why? Why is all of this like this?"

Cloud twitched his tail in confusion.

She hesitated. "Look, I know I'm not explaining myself well, but you know what I'm trying to say. The camp is not important. The Easterners could've set it up themselves."

He lowered his head. "Look, I'm sorry, but they needed my help. I had to go."

She walked around him, tail snapping against his sides. "You *volunteered*. Volunteer work is not required work. Now come on—think for a moment." She did a graceful skip, then slowed to a stop. "The Cliffs are dangerous, and he knows they make her nervous."

He looked away, mind trying to rationalize Aspen's decisions. "Song, every historian's trial is set up to be stressful. To pass, she has to confront that stress and discomfort and learn to focus on doing her job. I had to do something similar when I went through the advisor's trial, remember? It's not easy, but not just anyone can become a high-rank. The position carries a lot of weight."

"But you weren't in actual danger." She sighed and lifted her nose to the breeze. "Smell the wind, Cloud; there's something wrong with it. It's going to snow soon. She can't be out in the middle of a storm."

"She'll come back when the weather starts to look bad," he replied.

"That's not what I meant. Something isn't right with the commanders. We should all stay near the Glade. Outside isn't safe. And you should guard yourself around Jade. She's not safe, either."

"Oh, so you noticed too. I guess that means I'm not going crazy."

Songbird looked at her paws. "Good. I'll get Ember," she whispered. She leaned over and licked his cheek. "Tainu is already out looking for her, but I don't think I trust those two enough to come back on their own. At least not in time. I told Farlight I'd show him how to become an honorary council member, but I may or may not be back in time, either. Don't bother waiting for me. Oh, the commander wants you. Have fun and be careful."

He couldn't tell if she was joking or not. It sounded like she couldn't figure it out either. She leaped past him and darted toward the Northern Entrance.

"Wait, don't you want to . . ." he called after her.

She usually watched Meetings and subtly gestured her thoughts to him. On occasion, he gave those gestures a voice. She was almost an eighth council member. It involved a lot of rule-bending for her to participate, but there was no denying she had a knack for diplomacy, so no one ever brought it up. Without her nearby, he felt lost.

"Cloud!" Aspen shouted. He stood with Jade beneath the History Tree. "We're waiting."

"I know. I'm coming, sir." He watched longingly as Songbird's ruddy brown tail vanished behind the abatis wall. Cloud shook himself off, then walked over to the Tree. He took his usual place beside Aspen, who sat on a root lump near the tree's massive trunk. Above them, Whitehaze waited, gaze fixed on the gathering below. Jade sat directly opposite of Aspen on a smooth stone barely two claws higher than everyone else in the Eastern half of the circle. It was nothing compared to the massive boulders they met on in the Rift, but it served its purpose well enough.

Aspen took a moment to groom his face. His torn ear twitched uncontrollably. He lifted his head and drew a deep breath. "Thank you, Commander Jade, for coming to the West in peace, and for bringing your most trusted council members with you to negotiate with us today."

Cloud sighed and straightened himself up. *'Let the meeting begin.'*

CHAPTER 5
EMBER

Ember gazed up at the sky. It was silver and murky, kind of like her mind. The light filtering through the clouds stung her eyes, but she didn't care enough to look away. Rushing water drowned out some of the background noise, but every now and then a falling branch or a string of bird chirps broke through.

The cool, refreshing scents of moss and dying ferns filled her nose. They mixed with smells of unkempt fur, rotting plants, and an oncoming storm. Despite the chill in the air and the frigid water droplets covering her fur, she smiled. She tried her best to ignore the coolness of the stone against her back. It reminded her how easily she could roll off and fall into the death pit below. The icy sting of her own thoughts and color-feelings were harder to ignore.

Fernburrow Falls cascaded around her, rushing into the ravine below. The mossy rock she lay on divided the water into two streams. Mist wafted up from where the creek collided with time-smoothed stones. Ember flicked back her ears. A tiny flame of anxiety burned in her chest, making her see-feel silver yet again. Ember pulled her paws closer to her body.

'At least the sky is perfect today. Grey. Silver. Little patches where it's darker or lighter.'

The wind picked up. Ember winced as a hovercraft rumbled across the sky. Its massive propellers sent twigs and dead leaves flying through the forest.

She shuddered as it disappeared into the mist. Faint hints of green and cyan fluttered through her mind. Mimicking the machine, they faded into silvery unease.

'If Dark modeled clawmarking after their marked language, they must have some kind of history tree of their own. There has to be at least one of them who cares about it and knows we're still out here.'

Cloud, Whitehaze, and many others had reassured her that the humans were no longer threats, but in quiet times, when no one thought she was awake or listening, she had heard fearful whispers about their mysterious, long-legged kind. Everyone in the Colony knew better than to dismiss them as harmless. Even visiting Easterners seemed to fear them. However, the ways they spoke about humankind made them seem not just wary of them, but terrified.

'Why does all this have to be so complicated? It wasn't like this last winter. At least not for me. Tahg. I'm not ready for real life, or growing up. There's so much fog, I can't see in front of me. And to think I used to look forward to becoming a border guard and starting my historian training. I used to love that fog. It was exciting back when I thought I'd never die.'

A hint of thunder grumbled through the air, so faint she almost mistook it for wind against her ears. She lifted a forepaw to her face and examined it.

'What am I going to do with myself? Wait, I know. I'm going to find that part of me I'm missing. If I can fix myself, I can—'

"Hey, Ember! Are you up there, or am I talking to myself?" a distant voice called.

Ember rolled onto her stomach and looked down. Her trail of thought came to a dead end. Tainu's soft yellow-green eyes peered back up at her.

She tensed. "I'm a figment of your imagination. Pretend I'm not here."

"What?" Tainu said. "I can't hear you over the water. Could you come down?"

"I said—" She bit the less sore part of her tongue. *'She can't hear you, you know.'*

Ember stood up. She leaped across the rushing water, then hiked down the mountain slope to join her. Tainu raised her tail in greeting.

"Sorry, I couldn't hear what you were saying," Tainu said.

"It wasn't important," Ember replied.

"Ah, okay."

They circled each other for a few moments, scenting. When they finished, Ember broke free from the circle. She padded over to a nearby tree and sharpened her claws. Tainu followed.

"Look," she said, "I'm really sorry, but I don't think we'll be able to go hunting today. The weather's looking pretty bad, and your mom is looking for you. Also, some things have come up for me that'll probably keep me busy most of the day."

"It's okay. I didn't really want to hunt, anyway," Ember replied. She flinched as her tongue reminded her to be nicer to it.

Tainu's tail thrashed. "I know, but I feel terrible having to leave you like this. You have to be a strong hunter, otherwise . . ."

Ember cocked her head. "Otherwise what? And what do you mean 'leave'? Where are you going?"

"Hah, funny." Tainu placed a paw on Ember's forehead and ruffled her fur. "I meant leaving you without hunting skills, silly. Never mind. We should go back. Echo will probably be looking for me soon."

Thunder growled again. It would have been perfect timing if she'd said something more dramatic.

Ember stepped back. She shook herself off and glared at her cousin. "Okay, that's enough. Will you stop this?"

"Stop what?"

"For this past mooncycle you've been obsessed with hunting and trying to get me to do it. And it's not even how I am with learning history either; it's been more like 'I have to teach you how to hunt now, or you're going to die.' You're scaring me, so please stop."

"I am *not* obsessed with—" She looked away and sighed. "Okay, maybe I have been a *tiny* bit obsessive."

Lightning flared across the sky. Thunder roared like an angry bear. Ember jumped back from the tree.

Tainu nudged her side. "Come on, weird little cousin. We really should get going. "

"Agreed." Ember flattened her ears. As she said it, she felt a sense of loss. Some incredible thought might get left unthought and unexplored. She was on the verge of something; she could feel it. However, she had also told Hyrees she might do something with him, and Cloud had wanted to talk with her after the Meeting.

'Alright, Ember. Enough alone time. This is what matters right now. Okay? Okay.'

They made their way toward the Glade. As they walked, wind rustled the branches of trees and howled through the forest. It cut through their fur, making them both shiver. Tainu kept her head and tail low as they walked. She paused for a moment, then sighed.

"Don't tell this to anyone, not even if they ask," Tainu said.

"Don't tell anyone what?"

"That I've been going into the Lowlands," she replied.

Ember stopped mid-step. "What? But that's ag—"

"Wait! I know it's illegal, but let me explain. I've been trying to find my parents. My real parents. I mean, Fern is great, and Fledge is nice too, but I want to know who I came from, and maybe why they abandoned me. I wish I could remember them better, but all the memories are so blurry. I can't make them out."

"Why are you telling me this?" Ember asked. She continued walking. "I mean, you know I'm not going to tell anyone, but why? And if you don't remember your parents, how will you know when you've found them?"

"I think some part of me still does remember, and I'm hoping, if I ever find them, that maybe just smelling them again will bring everything back. You've had smells remind you of things, right?"

"Yes, but I still don't understand why you're telling me this."

"Because while I've been in the Lowlands, I've seen the realities of being an Outsider," she said. "I've . . . met cats who *are* Outsiders and such. It's really amazing how any of them survive at all. If you were to ever find yourself alone down there, in the Great Unknown, you'd have to be able to hunt. Otherwise, there's not even a chance you'd survive it."

Ember snorted. "I don't plan on being in the Lowlands any time soon. Except maybe to go to a Meeting as a historian. And I especially don't plan on going there alone. The Valley is nice to look at from above, but it's too silver and misty for me. Besides, I have everything I need here." She put her teeth over her tongue and pressed down until it stung. "I think."

More lightning flashed. A bird in a nearby tree chirped twice, then flitted away.

Misty orange and navy blue danced in her mind's eye. *'But I'm still missing something. I can find it here, though, so I don't need to hunt. Ever. I will never, ever become a monster, or a wildcat. I will be calm, and peaceful, and helpful to my kin. I will be better than this. And after I find the rest of me, I can teach myself to hunt.'*

"So," Tainu said, bringing her back to the present. She stopped and lowered her forequarters, as if about to pounce on something. "Race you back?"

"Sure." Ember placed her paws against a nearby tree. "Just as a warning, I won't go easy on you this time."

"Yeah, sure, you were going easy on me last time, were you?" Tainu asked.

"Unfortunately, it's been so long I can't remember. But I do remember you defeating me. Logically, that must mean I was holding back in some way. But not today."

"Oh, logically, huh? It can't possibly be because I'm faster than you."

Ember chuffed. "Of course not."

"Wait a moment, you're having a race without me?"

Ember and Tainu jerked to attention. Songbird emerged from the mist and trotted toward them.

"Hi, Mom," Ember mewed. She ran to touch noses and scent with her mother. "I guess we aren't now that you're here. What happened to your face?"

"I call it 'turkey's revenge.' " Songbird said.

"Sounds painful."

"I'll be fine. Mind if I join you?" Songbird asked.

"I needed some real competition anyway, so you might as well," Tainu said with a laugh.

"Hey!" Ember said. She batted at Tainu's shoulder.

Another flash of lightning arced across the sky. All three cats jumped as a resounding clap of thunder filled the air.

Songbird chuffed. Her fur stood on end. "We're running back to the Glade, I hope. I don't want to get stuck out here if it snows, and especially not if it rains."

"Yep, that's where we're heading," Tainu replied. "So, are we ready?"

"I am," Ember said.

"Let's run, then," Songbird mewed.

Ember lunged forward. Swift as a squirrel, she scrambled up the nearest tree. She scurried from branch to branch. Her movement became a rhythm. Her body became the lyrics as trees creaked and limbs bent. The forest itself seemed to be moving around her. One branch, then another; one branch, then another; one branch, then . . . nothing? She slowed to a stop. The closest limb of the next tree was gone. A light-colored spot of ragged wood rested in its place, still wet with sap.

Far below, as Tainu and Songbird raced past on the ground, she spotted the fallen branch. Parts of it had shattered on impact.

'I guess you'll have to take the long way after all. But at least you didn't jump on a rotting limb and fall to your death, so that's good.'

Another roll of thunder rattled the air as she scaled down the tree. She didn't run at her fastest pace. There was no catching up to them, so she was only running for pride. Any faster and her stamina would fail her too. She slowed to a walk a few leaps away from the Glade, panting. Her heart pounded in her ears. Her sides ached for water. She walked past Songbird and Tainu, who stood in the entrance waiting for her.

"So what's the excuse this time?" Tainu asked.

"Branch," she said between pants. "Broken branch. Had to . . . had to climb down. Hooohhhh, I need water."

She padded over to one of the clay water bowls scattered around the Glade. They were mainly for kittens, who weren't allowed to visit the Kivyress without supervision, but extremely thirsty adults weren't strangers to using them. Under normal circumstances, she would never so much as touch one of the bowls, unless she accidentally knocked one over, then had to go refill it. They sometimes went days without being dumped and freshened with new water. More than once during her kittenhood she'd found little wiggly things swimming around in them. There was also the taste of other cats' tongues, which never ceased to disgust her.

When she lapped at the water, her mouth stung, but she ignored the pain and freezing cold. Everything else was freezing cold already, so it was the easiest part to overlook.

A drop of water fell on her nose. She snorted and shook herself off. Another drop landed on her back. The wind picked up, howling like a wolf. A hiss echoed across the mountainside.

"Ember, Tainu," Songbird said. "We really should get under something."

As she said it, the sky fell. Rain stabbed her back, head, and sides like a thousand thorns falling from the clouds. The other end of the Glade disappeared in the downpour. She charged for the nearest overhanging rock. Songbird and Tainu, though they'd started from farther away, were right beside her. They reached the stone at the same time, and almost collided with Echo. Ember slid to a stop a clawlength away from the Easterner's nose. She shivered.

"H-h-hi, Echo," Ember said.

"Hello there, Ember," Shard, Echo's brother, said.

"No need to stay in my face," Echo growled. "Your tail's still in the rain. So go on, get in all the way or you'll freeze."

"Oh!" Tainu said. She shook herself off. "Echo! There you are. T-t-tahg, I'm c-cold. You two think you could help a f-f-few freezing cats out?"

Echo pushed past Ember and placed herself next to Tainu. "I'd help you out anytime, Nu. Even if you ended up making me colder, which you are, being wet like that."

Tainu leaned against her side. "S-sorry. Not like I can help it."

Echo groomed her between her ears. "I know, I know."

"I'm here too, you know," Hyrees said from somewhere behind Shard.

With Hyrees being smaller than average and Shard being larger, Ember hadn't even seen him. Shard got to his paws and placed himself between Tainu and Songbird.

"Excuse me," he said as he sat down. "Wow, you weren't joking, were you? You *are* cold. I hope all this rain lets up soon. I could do with a nice warm fire right about now, I could."

Hyrees moved to sit next to Ember. They touched noses. She sneezed, causing Hyrees to jerk back, and shivered harder.

He chuffed. "Ugh, hey, watch where you spray."

"S-sorry," she whispered.

"Hey, it's okay. I was trying to be funny, but as usual, it didn't work." He leaned closer to her, his warmth engulfing her freezing side. "You okay?"

"Better."

"So, Sh-Sh-Shard. Echo. How have y'all been?" Songbird asked.

Shard's ears perked up. "Not bad, Ma'am. Just, you know, the usual," he said. He flattened his ears. "Uhm, ah, well, you probably don't know, actually. But all the same. Hmm, oh! I'm not making you uncomfortable, am I? Being so close. Oh, I do hope not. Just-just let me know, if, ah, at any time, you know, you no longer want my help. Just say the meow."

"No, you're okay," Songbird replied. "And you know what? You're warm. You can get closer, if you don't mind m-my wetness."

"Ah, okay, good," Shard said.

As the cats settled down beneath the overhang, a third-person image of the arrangement appeared in Ember's head. *'It's like a caterpillar of warmth,'* she thought. She smiled and leaned closer to Hyrees. Shaky purrs rumbled up her throat. *'Yes. Warmth. Warmth is good. It's also good she came and got you when she did. You would've frozen to death if you stayed out there much longer.'*

They sat in silence, watching the rain and keeping each other warm. Ember played with her breath, blowing different-sized steam clouds. Shard joined in. For several moments, all six cats snorted and sighed clouds of mist. Ember chuffed. A moment later everyone fell silent as lumps of icy sludge replaced the rain.

Shard leaned forward to get a better look. A clump of ice-goo landed on his nose. He jerked his head back and shook himself off. "Ack! Oh, that's cold! So bloody cold. Agh, it stings."

Echo reached across Tainu and swatted what remained of the ice off of his face. Shard sneezed, then snorted. "Ugh. Thank you, Echo. Oh, I hate—er, *strongly dislike* all this cold weather, I do. And I suppose it'll snow tonight too. Wouldn't that be bloody wonderful? Gotta walk all the way back, through the snow, through the cold, all day, for two, bloody, days. Why couldn't we have the winter meetings at our place?"

Echo leaned over to lick his cheek. "I don't know, Shard, but it seems we're stuck here for now. You know, you're starting to sound like me. Should I be worried?"

Tainu laughed. "Oh, I-I don't know about that. He's s-so adorable when he gets all ind-d-dignant. Just like you. I need more angry Echo and Shard in my life." She nosed Echo's cheek. "Especially angry Echoes."

Ember snickered. A lake of snarling Echoes appeared in her mind, each Echo duplicate in the same position as the others. She brushed aside her discomfort and held back a giggle.

"So, any idea how the Meeting went before all this started?" Hyrees asked, changing the subject.

"Not a bloody clue," Echo said.

He cocked an ear. "And what is it with you Easterners and the word 'bloody?' "

"Not a bloody clue," she said again. "No, actually I do know. In a sense. Hunters like me say it a lot more than your typical Easterner. It's usually used in long-winded complaints about prey that refuses to die, if that gives you any ideas on the origin."

"Ah, lovely," he replied.

The awkward silence following lasted until the downpour stopped. The rain ended like it began: suddenly and gracelessly. They waited under the ledge for a few moments more to make sure it wasn't just a break in the storm. Tainu got up. She padded away from the sheltering protection of the ledge and sniffed the sludge coating the ground.

"Ew," she said, "l-looks like the sky decided to give us some half-frozen slime mold today. Thanks, sky. Cold, wet, *and* icy paws? What is this? The Meeti—oh wait, it is. N-never mind."

She turned back toward the ledge. "You harehearts c-can come out now. I already see some blue up there, and it's getting bigger. And by bigger, I mean the clouds are going away. Let's just hope your dad d-doesn't leave with them, huh, Ember?"

Ember sighed. *'Tainu, I love you, but your jokes are still terrible. Hyrees does better.'*

"Is everyone okay?" Aspen's voice asked from across the Glade. "Are we all here? All safe? Is there anyone who wasn't able to get to shelter before the rain? If so, there are cats working on replacing the firewood right now. Anyone with wet fur gets access to the fire pits first."

Ember searched the sudden outpouring of cats for her family. Cloud walked toward one of the fire pits several leaps away, fur slightly damp. He dragged a branch beside him with his mouth. Songbird went to help him.

Ember sighed again. *'He got caught in the rain, yet he's helping out. Yes, he has slightly longer fur than you, and isn't nearly as wet, but he's still in a similar situation doing something more worthwhile than you. And I'll bet he'd still help if he were in my exact situation. And Mom definitely is. Also, the more cats that help out, the faster you get to dry. Oh, and the faster everyone else who got wet gets to dry too. Don't wanna forget them, Em.'*

She stood up. "I-I'm going to go help them."

"Ember, wait. It's colder out in the open," Hyrees said.

"I know," she replied. "F-faster fire. Ring o-of warmth."

"Oh. True."

"You understood that?" Echo asked. "Does she always talk like this?"

Hyrees slunk out of his warm spot. "Yep, and sometimes. I'll see you two later. For now I guess I'm going to help build a ring of warmth."

Hyrees loped over to where Ember waited, shivering. Before he could react, she bumped her nose against his, then trotted toward the wood storage —a long-abandoned fox den set in a tiny hill. It had been expanded on by some of the earliest Colony Cats.

Beneath her paws, the ice goo melted and clung to her pads and fur. The chill sent a bolt of light blue running through her mind. The light blue became a snowy landscape, which then faded into a pristine silver that made her stomach churn.

When she reached the storage, she selected a decent-sized branch and picked it up in her mouth. The rough wood rubbed against her tongue, but she ignored the pain. She carried it over to the nearest fire pit, then set it down within the ring of broken clay spires.

When enough firewood was in place, Lupine struck the sparkstones against each other. The sparks landed on a pile of dried leaves and ignited. Ember watched in awe and longing as the baby fire ate and grew, spreading to the twigs and branches above it. Her namesakes swirled into the air in a delicate-yet-deadly display of power.

Ember huffed. *'Is that what I am? Delicate and deadly? I hope not. Anything delicate gets crushed, and anyone deadly gets chased out or killed. And I'd personally rather not get crushed, chased out, or killed. Maybe I can be like a real ember some other way. Maybe I could save lives and keep everyone warm. Then again, that sounds kind of crowded, everyone huddling together around me.'*

She imagined herself at the center of a lake of cats she didn't know. She shivered.

'Instead of trying to be like my name in some way, I should probably just be me. It'd make things easier.'

Cloud and Hyrees sat down beside her, and Songbird leaned against

Cloud. As they waited by the fire, Ember's shivering slowed, then stopped altogether. When her fur had dried, Songbird left to help the other hunters prepare for the feast.

"Ember, you know how I wanted to talk with you when you got back?" Cloud asked.

She nodded, too tired to bother speaking.

"Well, I don't know if we'll be able to have that just yet. Some things have come up, and well, uh, we probably won't be able to do it."

The fur along her back rose. Dark purples filled her head. "What do you mean?"

"Ember," he said.

She waited for him to finish his sentence, but apparently it was over. "What? What's wrong? Am I doing something wrong? I mean, I know I messed up, but I don't understand."

Out the edge of her vision, she spotted Tainu loping out the Eastern Entrance. Echo followed moments later. Ember looked around the Glade. Shard was nowhere to be seen. More dreary purple broke through the grey static, along with tiny flickers of oak leaf green and dark orange. She shook her head. The static returned.

"Did you hear anything I just said?" Cloud asked.

Ember's ears perked up. "Purple! That's not—oh, er, sorry. No, sorry. What were you saying?"

He sighed, and leaned close enough for his whiskers to brush her ear. "I don't know when we'll be able to discuss what needs to be discussed, but one of these days we need to have a talk about life, and reality, and not getting distracted by your thoughts, or fears, or those colors of yours."

"Will it be a good talk?" she asked.

He stared into the fire. "It will make you uncomfortable, that much I know. But sometimes you need to be made uncomfortable. Sometimes you need to know the truth. It's a part of growing up."

She rested her ears back in their usual half-cocked positions, and lowered her head closer to the flames. "Yeah."

He sighed again and leaned closer to her. "Listen, I'll be having a talk with Aspen when he gets back. I'll ask him about it again. For now, you take a break. Okay?"

'Again? Wait, when he gets back?' she wondered. "Where did he go?"

"To meet that Rogue from yesterday," he replied. "I'm guessing that Eclan cat doesn't work for Jade after all, but that's where he went. And oh, there he is now. I'll go see if I can catch him. You'll be okay here?"

Aspen walked through the Northern Entrance, heading toward his den. Ember glanced at her commander and nodded. Cloud got up, then padded after him. She crouched down on her forelegs. The grey haze in her head cleared a little more. Her thoughts drifted back to the flames.

'I'm glad fire exists.' A creamy, deja vu gold swirled in her subconscious. *'Wait a moment. I guess there's a reason this feels so familiar.'*

She leaned back against Hyrees and burst into tiredness-induced giggles. Hyrees chuckled.

"Why are we laughing?" he asked.

"I don't know why you're laughing. I'm laughing because I think it's funny how I've been drenched two days in a row. I can't wait to see what happens tomorrow. Will someone dump a water bowl over my head? That'll be fun."

Hyrees curled up beside her, smiling. "Oh, Ember." He licked her cheek. "You and that mind of yours. Don't ever become normal. If you do, uhm . . . I'm not sure what I'd do, but I'd have to do something."

"Sneeze a bee?" Ember suggested, using the first arbitrary thought that came to mind.

He laughed and tapped her nose. "Sure; I'll sneeze a bee. Which sounds really painful, by the way."

Ember shook her head in an attempt to rid herself of the itch he'd placed on her nose. She swatted at his whiskers. He closed his eyes and laughed even more, filling her thoughts with the sweet oranges of family.

"Which is why I'll try not to let it happen," she mewed, smiling. Just hearing his laugh made all the pain and discomfort of that morning worth it.

As they huddled beside the fire, the 'fun' part of the Meeting happened around them. Tomcats, and even a few mollies, wrestled in two-cat sparring competitions. Each of the winners would receive extra food, and the cat who won the most matches would get even more food, medicine, or a finely crafted bijou to take home with them.

In other parts of the Glade, kittens and trainees mimicked the adults' competitions, chased each other around, or interrogated Easterners. Off to one side, three littermates played with a clay ball their mother had just bought them.

All around the Glade, clayworkers had various items scattered around near their dens. Cats could use work credits or precious tradestones, usually obtained from the East, to get them. Credits and tradestones were mostly for luxury, as the only things they actually bought were accessories, toys, highly-valued clay clawmark tablets, and extra food. Everyone got daily rations to eat, water to drink, and somewhere to live. High-ranks earned more credits than most other cats—three a day—so many of them wore intricately modeled clayvines around their necks or decorated bands around their tails.

Ember closed her eyes. Beside her, Hyrees rolled onto his back and batted at her whiskers. She ignored him. Her temporary giddiness, brought on by her own imagination, was gone.

"Oh, come on, Emmy. You don't want to play? It's the Meeting," he said.

"Not really." She yawned. "I just want to sleep, and play with my dreams, if I have any good ones. Though if I have a really good one, you might be there. I could play with you that way."

Farlight pranced over to them. "I can play with you, Hyrees. I'm done with all my commander-in-training duties for today. A little sparring contest might be fun, don't you think? Though as a warning, I'm bigger than you now; I might actually be able to win this time."

As he passed Ember, he smiled in her direction and nodded his head.

Hyrees chuffed and rolled to his paws. "You probably will, but I won't be defeated easily. We should probably go have it somewhere away from the fire though." He nuzzled Ember's cheek. "And don't you worry; once I'm through with him, I'm coming for you. Be ready."

He licked her muzzle, then trotted away with his brother. Ember licked a paw and tried to groom away the wet patch he'd given her.

"Rough day?"

Ember looked up to find Kivyress standing in front of her. She sighed and let herself go limp, Her head flopped against her forelegs. "Everything hurts."

Kivyress moved to lay beside her. "At least you've got tomorrow."

"Assuming I don't die between now and tomorrow. But in truth, I'm starting to worry tomorrow won't be much better. Apparently Dad wants to talk to me about something important, but he's not able to for some reason. I'm not sure I want to know the whats or whys. The way he keeps talking about it is making me see-feel silver, so it probably won't be anything good."

"Maybe he's trying to pretend it's something serious so you'll be relieved when it's something little. Messing with your expectations. If it makes you feel any better, I don't know of anything anyone might be trying to hide from you specifically, so it'll probably just be some boring lecture."

Ember groomed her sister's neck. She almost laughed. There wasn't much in the Glade she didn't know about. The only benefits to having insomnia and hearing everything was how many secrets she'd picked up. She knew hidden things about cats whose names she couldn't even remember. "You may be right. Or at least partially right. I hope you are."

"Yeah." Kivyress purred softly. She leaned over to return the favor, grooming Ember's side. "Oh, you weren't here when it happened, but the Meeting today was really weird. I don't really remember the Spring Meeting well enough to compare, so this could be normal, but the Easterners seemed really tense when they were talking. I don't think Commander Jade likes Commander Aspen very much."

"If you consider what he did to them, that sounds normal," Ember said.

"I guess so, but it seemed like a lot more than just Jade disliking him. She looked like she wanted to hurt him, and he looked really scared when he walked back in here earlier. I'm kind of starting to worry."

"I'll try to find out what's going on tomorrow. I'm too tired to worry about the commanders right now. Besides, the Meetings exist to keep the peace. If there were any real problems between our colonies, Dad would know about them and figure out how to fix them before anyone got hurt."

Rays of sunlight broke through the clouds. They formed soft beams caught in the ever-shifting smoke that filled the air.

Kivyress sighed. "I guess you're right. Everything'll work out eventually. Hey, look, even the sun's come back, and the sky is pretty again."

Ember smiled and half-closed her eyes. *'Well, if today's been anything to go by, I might never become a historian, forever crushing my one and only current ambition. I've also finally decided I really should end that tongue-biting habit. But all things considered, it wasn't terrible. Or maybe it was. At least after the feast I might actually be able to get a decent night of sleep. If I can, it'll be close enough to decent. Maybe even a success.'*

"What do you think, Kivy?" Ember asked.

Kivyress hesitated for a moment, then smiled. "That we should catch up with Hyrees and Far."

'Might as well try to make it enjoyable.' She got to her paws and shook herself off. "I concur. Enough grey for today. Let's go!"

CHAPTER 6
CLOUD

"Commander Aspen," Cloud said, "you wanted to speak with me?"

"Hmm?" Aspen asked. He sat on the rocky rise over his den, watching the more frivolous side of the meeting unfold.

Cloud straightened himself up, careful to look his commander in the face but not the eyes. He focused on Aspen's still-twitching right ear.

"You wanted to have a word with me about Ember?"

"Ah, yes, the talk," Aspen said, never taking his gaze off of his colony. "Today has been rather . . . eventful. It can wait."

"Oh. Okay. So can I tell her the truth, then? She deserves to know."

Aspen flicked his ears intentionally. "No." He slow-blinked. "I already told you my stance on this, and I stand by my word. Besides, she looks like she's finally enjoying herself. I'd hate for you to spoil the mood."

Cloud growled under his breath and looked over his shoulder to where Hyrees, Farlight, and Kivyress assaulted a squirming, flailing Ember. He breathed out slowly. It was just a play fight, yes, but she could do better. She wasn't even trying to fight back. At least she seemed to be having fun.

"Cloud," Aspen said. "Come up here, would you, son?"

'Son?' Cloud snapped to attention. *'Did you just call me 'son'? You've never called me 'son.' Not even once until now. What's bothering you, Aspen? Because something has definitely been bothering you.'*

"Yes, sir," he said.

He ascended the hill, then sat by Aspen's side. "Is there something wrong? I know it didn't go as smoothly as you'd hoped, but I'm not sure there's much we can do at this point. Aside from keeping everyone from killing each other, of course. But I think we can straighten everything out in the spring."

"Have you ever felt as though you aren't ready for something, and no matter how long or hard you try to prepare for it, you will never be ready?"

Cloud's eyes narrowed. A sinking feeling snagged in his chest. "Uhm, yeah, yes sir. I think everyone has at some point in their lives. Commander, is there something wrong?" he asked.

Aspen closed his eyes and swallowed, ear twitching more violently. "I'm afraid so, son. I fear I may die soon."

The fur along Cloud's spine rose. "Sir . . ."

His mind traveled winters into the past. He was a trainee again, helpless as his father went off to fight a war he would never win. Though his father hadn't been the most fatherly of fathers, he was the only dad he'd ever had. He'd pleaded over and over for him to stay as the adults prepared for that fateful battle. Every time, he'd been shaken off, shoved away, and told to go play like some ignorant kitten. He never saw him again.

He shook the memory away. "Wait, sir, are you sure? How do you know? Are you sick?"

"No. But I have a feeling somewhere inside me that my past crimes may get punished soon," Aspen replied.

"With all due respect, sir, a feeling is not enough evidence to convince me you're about to die."

"Cloud," Aspen said. "I don't expect you to believe me, but there are forces at work right now that are beyond the control of any of us. Forces you, and I, and everyone else here cannot stop. If you try to stop them, or save me, you will only be putting both yourself and the Western Colony in danger. I want you to listen closely, son. If I die before Farlight can finish his training, I've already told Lupine he will command until Farlight is ready."

Cloud's eyes narrowed in rancor. *'Oh. Yes. Lupine, of course. Not the one who's put in any actual effort to keep these cats alive. I had to work to get this rank, and what did he do? Get born a few moments after you? We'll see how that works out.'*

"If that happens," Aspen continued, "You will finish Farlight's training, and be an advisor to my brother. Keep them both safe, Farlight especially. Defend them with your life, if you must. Don't let the forces of shadow take them."

Cloud's tail flicked. Below them, Farlight and Kivyress continued wrestling while Ember and Hyrees cuddled together once again by the fire.

"I will protect him, sir. I'll protect both of them. But hopefully we won't have to worry about any of this." He flattened his ears. *'Because you're being delusional,'* he mentally added.

Aspen smiled. "Hopefully not, but ever since Stone Ridge, I . . . I like to plan ahead. We must make sure the Colony gets cared for, no matter what happens. You never know what the future hides. Do you?"

"With all due respect, sir, I'm not sure how to answer that question," Cloud said.

Aspen pawed Cloud's side, tousling his fur in the process. It was the same way his father used to do it on those rare occasions Cloud managed to impress him. Though it'd only happened twice, he remembered it as if it were a daily routine.

"Stop being so formal," Aspen said. He chuckled. "Don't worry about me. Go enjoy yourself for a change. Your kittens aren't the only ones who need a break."

"Are you sure? I can stay if you need my help."

"No, you go on. I only told you about all this because I know I can't hide these things from you. I don't need or want your sympathy. I also don't want you telling anyone about this. No need to cause a panic, especially if it turns out to be over nothing. What I do want is to sit here, and watch my kin enjoying themselves; all of them, which includes you."

"If you're sure you'll be okay. I am worried about you."

Aspen groomed him behind an ear. "I'll be as fine as I can be. Now go on, son. You deserve to have some fun."

Cloud dipped his head. "Thank you, sir."

He climbed down the hill. When he reached the bottom, he looked back at Aspen, who flicked his muzzle toward the Glade, urging him on.

'I guess the stress finally broke him. He's becoming paranoid, isn't he? He's still got ten or so more winters to live. I don't know what kind of feeling he's feeling, but it must be fairly significant if he thinks he'll only get to live half of his life.'

He pushed through the cats around him as if they were mere objects obstructing his path. They glared at him in disgust, but he ignored their looks and growls.

'If, on the off-chance he does die, and Farlight becomes Commander, it would be hard, leaving this behind. It would also be one less thing holding me down. I can work with that. Even if the circumstances wouldn't be ideal, but fox it—if he dies, they might need me more. Why did I let myself get here? I should've said no when he offered me a place on the Council. Now, if I leave for four days with the Council to visit the East, everything nearly falls apart.'

"I guess I should find Wren now. Looks like we'll be able to do something together after all," he muttered to himself.

Cloud padded out of the Glade. Wren always hid in the Pine Grove during meetings to avoid the glares of his condescending kin. When he reached the Grove, instead of calling out Wren's name, he sniffed the air.

'Come on, pick it up for once,' he thought.

His nose refused to isolate Wren's scent. The ever-shifting wind only made the task harder. He growled at himself. *'Useless little—'*

He pressed his head against a pine, then clawed at it as if it had personally offended him.

"I never liked that tree much, either."

Cloud whirled around to find Wren standing behind him. "Oh, there you are. Did you want to do something? We're waiting until tomorrow to have the talk. Everyone's too exhausted to take in anything else," he said.

Wren hesitated, then sighed. "I'm afraid I can't think of anythin' at the moment. A walk, perhaps?"

"A walk?" Cloud asked. *'Why am I hiding out here? I could be doing something actually useful right now. I can't afford to waste my time meandering around the forest.'*

"Unless you have a better idea, of course," Wren said, smiling bittersweetly.

Cloud turned back toward the Glade. "Yes, I do. I could go help prepare for the feast. I need to make sure Aspen's paranoia doesn't ruin the Meeting any more than it's already been ruined."

"Wait, I thought you wanted to do something together. It has been a while."

Cloud ignored him. Work—he needed to work. There was no enjoyment to be found in kittens' games or aimless strolls.

'When I get back, I'll have to have a word with Fern. We'll need a cure before his worrying escalates and he becomes too paranoid to function. I can find a cure, I just need enough time.'

Someone tackled him from behind. Cloud rolled, toppling over his assailant. "What are you doing?"

"I'd like to know the same of you." Wren replied. "I thought you wanted to have a bit of fun for a change."

Cloud grimaced as he got back to his paws. He shook himself off, then helped Wren up. "We aren't kittens anymore, Wren. That time is over. Now I have a lot to get done, and a very difficult speech to prepare, so if you'll excuse me—"

"You're not excused," Wren said.

He jumped between Cloud and his destination. Cloud tried to walk around, but Wren sidestepped to stop him.

Cloud held back a hiss. "Would you let me through? This isn't funny."

Wren chuffed. "It's not meant to be funny, you big fluffhead. Come on, you know you want to fight me."

"Yes, but for reasons you didn't intend."

"Go on, then. Get me." Wren batted at his face, claws tucked safely in their sheaths. "I'll not have you go around breakin' your promises. A cat as important as you needs a reputation for reliability."

Cloud sighed. *'Okay, Wren. You win. One quick spar. Keep myself from being a liar.'*

He feigned a jump to the left. As Wren moved to block him, he sprang right instead, then shoved Wren onto his back.

Wren laughed. "There's the Cloud I know. Show me whatcha got, tomcat."

Cloud half-smiled. *'Okay, that did feel good.'*

Before Wren could get up, Cloud tackled him. Wren snapped his teeth a clawlength away from Cloud's shoulder. Cloud whipped his paw around and ran it across his neck. Wren faked an agonized yowl.

"You know, in a real fight, I could've leaned in and killed you like that. You'd better watch yourself," Cloud said.

"You'd best watch yourself, you big coyote," Wren replied.

Cloud jumped back, and Wren's hind legs kicked air. Wren sprung to his paws. They circled each other for a moment. A tiny burst of adrenaline entered Cloud's bloodstream, providing a high he hadn't even realized he'd been missing. More satisfying than mint and ten times more invigorating. The reason he'd become a border guard. He smiled.

As they fought, his mind raced, calculating Wren's moves moments before he made them, then working out the best way to deflect him a split moment later. Wren reacted just as quickly. They swatted, jumped, and spun around the Pine Grove, each cat fighting to get the other back on the ground, and neither one succeeding. Despite his blinded eye, Wren matched Cloud nearly blow for blow.

In the branches above them, an owl called out, signaling nightfall. Cloud stopped, panting like a coyote. "Oh, it's getting late. We should get back to the Glade."

Wren pushed him off balance and he toppled over onto his back.

"Hey! Fight's over," Cloud said.

Wren collapsed beside him, chuckling like a trainee after an intense game of chase. "Now it is. See? You can have fun, you big tomkitten. It's not the end of the world."

Cloud stood up. He shook himself off, yet he couldn't help but smile. "Yeah, sure."

"Admit it; you're not the best anymore," Wren said.

"I never said I was the best."

"Oh, you and that ego 'a yours."

"First, what ego? And second, what does this have to do with anything we just did or said?" He pawed Wren's side. "And get up, would you? I'd rather not keep everyone waiting."

"You're proving my point." Wren rolled back to his paws. He bumped his shoulder against Cloud's. "I'm afraid the Commander's not going to make everyone wait to eat on your behalf."

'Right. Aspen,' Cloud thought. *'And I guess he has a point.'* He sighed. "Probably not. Let's go before the food freezes."

Wren smiled narrowly. "Assumin' there's any food left at all."

EMBER

Ember stared blankly at the dying fire. She'd left its side several times that day, but she always seemed to find her way back to it. It was the only place in the Glade outside of her parents' den and the History Tree where she felt at home. The sun was sinking, and the temperature was dropping with it. Hyrees was out getting more wood. As she waited for him, she blew softly into the cinders, sending sparks and ash fluttering through the air.

Several leaps away, Tainu and Echo slunk into the Glade.

Ember forced herself to get up, then loped over to them. "Hey, where were you?" she asked.

They exchanged a look. Echo growled. "Watch your own rabbit, would you?"

"Echo, be nice," Tainu hissed. "I told her I'm looking for my mom."

"Ah, okay. So we're sharing secrets with her, are we?" Echo said.

"Some of them," Tainu replied. "She usually finds things out anyway, so we might as well."

'Okay, that's not suspicious at all,' Ember thought. "So that wasn't the only thing you were doing."

Both cats' eyes darted around as if something would jump out and attack them at any moment. Even Ember recognized the fear in their expressions.

Tainu touched her nose to Ember's. "Let's not talk about this here, Em. I just really wish we could've done those hunting lessons this morning. I probably won't be able to do them with you for a while."

Ember pinned back her ears. *'Alright, now you're really scaring me.'* She stepped closer to Tainu and sniffed. "So who were you meeting with?"

"Ember, I said don't talk about it here," Tainu snapped. She stepped away from her. "Look, I need some time to think, little cousin. Okay? So please just leave me alone."

Tainu pushed past her and walked into the bustle of the Meeting.

"Wait!" Ember called. "I'm sorry, I didn't—"

"Leave it, kitten," Echo said. She trotted after Tainu. "You've done enough already."

Ember pawed at the ground. Dark and misty oranges shrouded her thoughts. "Okay. Sorry," she whispered.

Behind her, near the fire pit, Hyrees struggled with an oddly twisted stick. She walked over to him and nudged the dangling end of the branch over one of the spires. "Need some help?" she asked.

Hyrees hefted the other end up and into the fire. "Thanks. I guess I did. I don't know how much good it'll do, but it may help get it burning again."

Ember's eyes locked onto a clayvine dangling from his jaw. Hanging from the woody loop was a clay bijou in the shape of a maple leaf. Her eyes widened. "Oh, you didn't."

He smiled. "What do you think of my new clayvine?"

"Hyrees!" she mewed as he slipped it over her head.

"What? Don't you want it? If you don't, I can see if someone else would like it."

"No," Ember said. She rested the maple trinket in a forepaw and lifted it closer to her face. Even the shade of clay was perfect—a flaming orange-red, the color of autumn leaves; her favorite color out of all the colors in the forest and all the colors in her mind. "It's beautiful. Thank you. Tahg, it must've cost all your work credits. I-I hope it didn't."

He nuzzled her cheek. "Don't worry about it, Ember. It's yours now. Just don't break it, and we'll call it even. Okay?"

She laughed. "I'll try my best. Might not wear it much, though, just to keep it safe. It's not exactly something to take to work."

"True," he replied.

They settled down once again beside the fire pit. Together, they stoked the flames back into existence. As the shadow engulfing the Western Mountain darkened, the Meeting died down. After a light-hearted feast, which Cloud briefly appeared for, the Easterners gathered together at the Southern Entrance. With a few Western escorts, they made their way to the Fields. Ember and Hyrees climbed the History Tree full and, for the most part, happy. Hyrees curled up in his usual spot near the sturdiest branch in the fork. Ember lay on her side in front of him, watching stars through the branches and clouds.

Hyrees licked his lips, then yawned. "That was some meal, huh? The turkey was delicious."

"I know," Ember said, still watching the sky. "Mom helped catch it. It was the one who gave her that bite."

"Oh. You know, when you mention how our food bit someone earlier, it makes it a lot less delicious."

"Sorry."

Hyrees chuffed. "No, it's o—"

"Hyrees, look," Ember mewed, cutting him off.

A single snowflake fluttered down from the sky, barely visible through the darkness. It missed the History Tree, flew toward the ground, then disappeared into the shadows. A few more tiny particles of white followed.

'Snow is terrible to work in, but at least it's pretty to look at,' she thought with a smile.

A flake landed on her nose. She wiped it off with her paw instead of her tongue. She'd learned better than to lick snow last winter; it didn't taste pretty.

Ember shuffled closer to Hyrees. They would need each other's warmth to survive a snowstorm, no matter how lightly it came. Hyrees shivered and curled into a tighter ball. Within a few moments he was snoring. Ember sighed. Yet again, she couldn't bring herself to sleep, but unlike most nights, not even the cool blue-greens of drowsiness would come to her.

Her heart wanted her to run and chase snowflakes as they fell. Her mind wanted to leave entirely to try to find the missing part of her. Instead of listening to either side of her, she stayed and looked for the moon through the few cloudless patches of sky. Tomorrow morning, she and the rest of her family would toss up snow at each other like they did last winter. The Kivyress would start to freeze over, and Fernburrow Falls would sparkle with tiny icicles. Winter was a time of hardship, yes, but it was also beautiful.

"Beautiful hardship," she whispered. "Sounds poetic."

'I think today worked out pretty well, all things considered. Dad didn't say anything else about that talk he wanted to have, so I guess that's something I'll have to do tomorrow. But how bad could it be? No worse than what you just survived today, that's for sure. Whatever happens, you can take it. I hope.'

She looked down at her new bijou, which hung dangling from a nearby branch. *'You can do it. Wear your leaf and think of Hyrees anytime you start feeling overwhelmed. That'll work.'*

Paws tapped against the icy ground. Ember's ears perked up. A shadow of a cat padded across the Glade toward the tiny hill and rock mound housing the commander's den. She sniffed the air. Nothing smelled out of the ordinary. There were too many scents strewn around the Glade for her to make out which cat so urgently needed to see Aspen, but it didn't matter.

'Lupine, probably. Anyway, what was I doing? Oh, right. Look for the moon, Em. Then tonight will be not-terrible.'

An ear-piercing yowl filled the air. Ember jumped to her paws, heart racing. The shadow cat darted out of the commander's den and raced out of the Glade.

Her head locked up, but pictures of the shadow cat hurting Aspen in various ways managed to get through. Before she could even process what was happening, Ember charged down the History Tree and out the Southern Entrance.

"Help!" she called out. "Someone please help!"

She tried her best to ignore the chaos behind her. Voices meowed and caterwauled in an agonising uproar. As she ran, they faded into the sounds of the forest and paws on slippery leaves. Snow flew against her face and stuck to her fur.

"Hey!" she called between breaths. "Stop! What did you do? Who . . . who are you?"

The cat ignored her. Ember sniffed the wind, but it wouldn't carry the cat's scent to her nose. The moon refused to show itself or reveal the perpetrator. Grey and shimmering silver swirled through her mind. She couldn't bring herself to think about Aspen, or what could've happened to him. She also couldn't bring herself to think about what might happen to her if she caught this cat, or how she would catch him or her in the first place. Another image entered her mind: one of the Fields. She saw herself and the mystery cat running in the tall grass and to the Eastern camp. A flash of yellow followed.

'Oh no.'

The cat made a series of sharp turns, jumping off tree roots and pouncing over logs. Still, Ember continued onward, ducking and leaping like her life depended on it. Wind blew at her tail. Snow flew in her face. Behind her, she thought she heard the sounds of more paws, but she couldn't make them out over the pounding of her own heartbeat.

"Ember, stop! Go back to the Glade—this isn't your fight," a muffled voice called. It sounded like Cloud.

The forest thinned out. Up ahead, dead grass waved her on. Ember bit down hard on her tongue and ignored her father's faint orders. The cat wouldn't be able to hide its identity once it entered the Fields; thick underbrush held more scent.

Moonlight appeared through the clouds a second before the cat vanished into the grass. Black and white. Another round of adrenaline hit her body. She felt both exhausted and ready to fight. Her teeth felt warm, but she didn't have time to wonder how that was possible. She dove, face first, for the same grass the cat disappeared in. She slid to a near stop as shock took over.

'Tainu?'

Pictures of confusion and fear, stained with purple and green, filled her mind. She shook her head, numbed her non-verbal thoughts, and kept going.

"Tainu! Wait! Please stop! What are you doing? What's going on? Please tell me something!"

Her vision blurred as her body threatened to fail her yet again. She did her best to ignore it. Tainu's scent veered to the right. Ember turned and found herself in the middle of the Eastern camp, yet before they could even react, she followed the scent back to the Fields. Ember's heart caught in her throat.

'Oh.'

The grass shrunk to a less obstructive size. Up ahead, a human-made barrier separated the Upper Field from the Wolf Trail. The Wolf Trail, a path made of solid stone and two metal strips, carried sleek machines along them at speeds no cat could outrun. Crossing at the wrong time meant getting crushed to death.

Ember slowed, panting, as she neared the Trail. "Please stop! Please! I don't know . . . what you just did . . . but please . . . don't run from me."

Tainu complied and came to a halt by the barrier. She turned to face her. Ember inhaled a frigid breath of air and stopped, frozen in shock. Blood coated Tainu's muzzle. The spatter extended to her neck—a spatter that could only be produced by a torn artery.

Aspen was dead, and Tainu had killed him.

Ember's jaw quivered. "W-what did you do?"

"Ember?" Tainu asked. "No, no, no, this wasn't supposed to happen. It wasn't supposed to be you! Go back to the Glade. Let someone else chase me.

You have to!"

Green, the brightest green she could imagine, filled her head. "You k-killed him. W-w-why would you do that? Why would you ever d-do that?"

Tainu trembled. "It's not what you think it is. I did what I had to do. I'm sorry, I really am. If I'd had a choice, I promise you things would be different. Listen, I don't want you getting caught up in this, so you have to leave."

"You just killed our commander," Ember said. Her paws and face grew warm. Her teeth and muzzle burned. She imagined herself sinking her fangs into Tainu's throat. For the first time in over a year, she didn't shove aside the thought of violence. A painful ringing filled her ears. Her field of vision narrowed until Tainu became all she could see.

"Go back to the Glade," Tainu said. "Go! Run! No one needs a little kitten on a battlefield. You'll just get in the way. Because that's all you are, Ember— a little foxing kitten in an oversized body. NOW GO!"

Ember winced. All the terrible things she'd heard whispered about herself in the past came back. She wanted to run away from it all, but one word stood out, sending a yellow shock through her mind. *'Battlefield?'*

The ringing became louder. Beyond it, yowls of cats in pain echoed in her head. She couldn't tell if she was imagining them or if they were real. Her ears went numb. Ember snarled. "You killed Commander Aspen *and* led us into an ambush?"

"I said 'go,' you stupid kitten. I never . . . I never liked you, okay? You're weak. A little coward—that's what you are. And you never listen to anyone. So go already." Tainu spat. She was crying.

Ember yowled. Without thinking, she hurled herself forward and tackled her cousin to the ground. Ember raked her claws across Tainu's neck. "You brought them here to die! You brought *me* here to die!"

"It's not my fault you followed me," Tainu growled.

She kicked Ember in the stomach. Ember staggered backward, then lowered herself to fight. The world seemed to spin around them. Her legs threatened to give out. Ember panted for breath. She wanted to hide, but part of her was paralysed. The other part of her wanted to take away the threat by force. "You k-killed him," she said.

"Okay, so screaming at you doesn't work," Tainu said, getting back to her paws. "Not that I expected it to. Ember, I don't want to fight you. I want you out of this, and I want you to stay out of this. Go back to the Glade. I'll leave, and you won't have to ever see me again. Please, just go already."

"I can't," she whispered. "I want to, but I-I can't. I c-can't move."

"Then let me help you," Tainu said.

She swiped at Ember's face. Ember jumped back. Tainu's claws tore through her cheek, missing her eye by a clawlength. Ember hissed and stumbled backward.

"Stop fighting me, Ember," Tainu said. "I don't want to hurt you, but I will if I have to. You know what I can do to you."

'She killed him. She betrayed you, and everyone else.' The thoughts echoed through her mind until they became all she could think. Her head became a thunderstorm, and she struggled with it for self-control.

"Get out of here, Ember. Now!" Tainu spat.

'She killed him. She killed him!' Something in her mind snapped. Ember's eyes narrowed. She leaped at her cousin. Tainu swatted at her shoulder. Ember ducked and slashed Tainu's chest. Tainu came down hard on top of her. Claws cut into Ember's back. She held back a yowl.

The snow picked up around them, muting the area into a deafening silence. Ember rolled under the barrier, free of Tainu's grasp. Patches of fur tore from her skin. Tainu dove under behind her and lashed out again. Instead of jumping out of the way, Ember pounced at her. She sank her teeth into Tainu's leg. The scream that followed rang louder and sharper than her ears.

Her heart leaped into her throat. Her mouth filled with blood.

"Tainu!" a distant voice called.

Ember released her cousin's leg. Blood pulsed out of the wound. Something grabbed her scruff. Before she could react, or even think, a bright light, like a midnight sun, flared in her face. Her side hit stone. Her legs hit metal. Her mind cleared just enough to think again.

102

'Oh tahg, I'm about to die.'

A split-second later, the light disappeared. A surge of pain took hold of her, then elapsed into nothingness.

Before her vision faded out completely, her mind choked out one final thought: *'Please . . . Please, someone, let me die.'*

CHAPTER 7
CLOUD

Commander Aspen was dead, and fighting cats were everywhere. Cloud shoved a snarling Easterner off of Hyrees. He leaped over them both, then caught the attacker in a scruff-hold. There was no time to think about the guilt or pain. Not now, when lives were still on the line.

"Get help," he growled through clenched teeth.

Hyrees stood up, eyes wide with terror. He stepped back, but didn't move any farther. The fat reserves on his sides quivered. "S-sir, m-my dad and Ember—"

"Will be dead if we don't get backup soon. Go!"

Hyrees sucked in a deep breath and nodded. "Yes, sir." He turned and ran back into the forest.

'And in Dark's name, hurry.' His gaze searched the fields. Grass blocked him from seeing more than a leap ahead. *'Come on, Ember. Where are you? Why wouldn't you listen to me? Please be okay.'*

The cat he'd been holding tore free, leaving fur stuck in his teeth. Cloud sunk into a fighting stance. The cat, a small brown tabby, did the same.

He hesitated. *'She's a molly. A young one, too. How did you get here? I can't help but wonder. Are you a mastermind too, or just the daughter of someone important?'*

"Why are you fighting us? I don't understand. What did we do?" she asked.

Her fur stood on end, making her appear bigger, but still not large.

"Someone just murdered Commander Aspen." He shoved aside the shock and sadness still tugging at his mind. "We followed the cat back here and got attacked. If none of you sent the assassin, why did your Colony ambush us?"

"But we didn't do anything. We were sitting by the fire, talking, when *you* started attacking *us*," she said.

He pinned back his ears. Out the corner of his eye, lights flickered along the Wolf Trail. "You should choose your words carefully, young molly. Trying to shift the blame on us only makes you sound more like a liar. Now listen, you're still a youth, so I'd feel bad about hurting you. How about you go back to—"

An ear-piercing yowl filled the air. *'Tainu?'* A sharp yelp followed. His eyes widened. *'Ember?'*

Cloud charged past the molly, toward the source of the scream. The cat didn't follow. *'Come on, come on, come on, come on.'*

A sickening, crunching thud hit his ears. His heart skipped a beat. He shivered all over. "Ember!"

As he tore free of the grass, a high-pitched noise sliced the air. On instinct, he stopped and sunk to the ground, paws over his ears. His eyes remained open and searching. Shard and Echo leaned over a body a few leaps away, both cats also covering their ears.

'Blood, I smell blood. Come on, Ember, please be okay.'

Ignoring the noise, he lunged forward. "Ember! Where is Ember?"

"I-I-I," Shard stuttered. "I'm sorry. I'm really, really sorry. I didn't mean to, but she was . . . she was . . ."

The sound faded. The ringing in his ears didn't. Panic gripped his chest. "Where is she?" he demanded.

"Come on, Tainu. Stay with me! Stay with me!" Echo yowled. She cradled Tainu's head in her paws. "Stay with me, or I will bloody murder someone. Come on!"

Tainu didn't reply. She lifted a paw toward Echo's face, then fell limp.

"Tainu!" Echo screeched.

Shard uncovered his ears. He was crying. "W-Wolf Trail," he said.

'Oh no.'

He dove under the barrier, ignoring the stopped pod on the nearest rail. And there she was. Cloud didn't have a weak stomach, but he threw up anyway. His daughter lay in a puddle of her own blood. Her legs were crushed against the indented metal strip, twisted at angles so unnatural they didn't even look real.

The rest of the world faded into nothingness. He took a single, shaky step forward.

"Ember."

He wanted to call out to her, to see her get up and limp it off like she always did, but he knew she wouldn't. Not this time. Something inside of him crumbled and fell away, vanishing into oblivion. It left behind a void nothing could ever refill.

Her side moved. At first, he thought it was his eyes playing tricks on him. He stepped closer. Her rib cage shifted up and down in rhythm; slow and subtle, but there. She was still breathing, barely breathing, but breathing nonetheless.

His chest tightened. The realization that she wasn't quite gone hurt more than he'd expected. Even though she was alive, the best healers in the Valley wouldn't be able to keep her that way for more than a day. Yet, if he left her, it could take hours for her to pass. In that time she could regain consciousness and suffer every moment of it. She would fade slowly, like some common, senseless animal who had wandered onto the Trail at the wrong time. It would be a painful death without honor.

'I have to do it.' he thought. *'For mercy's sake, I have to kill her.'*

His heartbeat became the only unmuted sound he could hear. He couldn't move. He was stuck in his tracks, transfixed on his daughter's broken body.

Movement caught the edge of his vision. He looked up. A slender-legged creature stood over Ember's limp form; a bipedal thing with a flattened, mostly furless, misty-pale face. It crouched down to look at Ember, eyes wide.

He stepped back, panting with fear. Everything inside of him screamed for him to run, but he didn't. "Get away from her, you monster," he spat.

In that moment he hated humanity. He hated their machines. He hated their oh-so-able hands that only seemed capable of causing pain and destruction. He hated that they'd made him sentient, given him a soul, made him care. He hated that this particular human even existed.

The human slid its upper appendages under Ember's body and hefted her into the air.

"What are you doing to her? Stop!" he growled.

He lunged forward. The creature spotted him, and with expert balance, it lifted a leg to block him. He hissed, but he knew better than to attack. One wrong move and Ember would get dropped, or he would get kicked to death.

'But I need her down here. I can make a clean bite. She could go peacefully if I'm fast enough.'

Yet something about this human stopped him. The creature made noises as it lowered its leg; soft, slightly melodic noises his muffled hearing almost missed. Its gaze shifted to the Upper Field, then to him, then to Ember, then back to him. This human wanted to help.

'But how? How can you help her? There's no helping this. You can't.'

"Let her die," he said. He stepped closer. "Just let her die and leave her be. Leave! Haven't you done enough already?" He blinked away the tears forming in his eyes. "Go on. Leave and let me do this. I have to do this! You're only making it worse."

The human ignored him. It backed into the pod it had stepped out of, carrying Ember with it. It spoke again as he ran after it, then a sliding door covered them both. The pod whirred back to life.

"No! No, wait!" he yowled as it started to move.

With a steady growl, it pulled away. Every moment, the white sphere shrunk a little more. It rounded the mountain slope and disappeared altogether, taking Ember with it. He stopped, and he let go. The tears he'd fought back so valiantly broke free, rolling down his cheeks and trickling into his fur.

"Take care of her," he whispered. "Please."

'I'm sorry, Ember. I am truly, truly sorry. I've failed. I was weak, I hesitated, and I failed you. I failed you. If they can help you, if they can work a wonder, please come back. Whatever it takes, please come back and let me know I did the right thing.'

His heart nearly stopped as reality sunk in. *'What am I going to tell Songbird? What am I going to tell Hyrees? Fox it! Fox it! Fight a fox! I've lost her. And now she's—'*

He caterwauled in frustration. His hearing returned. A cat cried out in the distance. *'I have to keep fighting. Cats are going to die if I don't get my priorities straight. They are going to die. There's nothing I can do for her now. I'm of no use here. My colony needs me. I'll fight now and cry over it all later.'*

He pawed the tears from his eyes and forced himself to run back to the Upper Field. He sniffed the air but couldn't smell Hyrees or any additional cats. Heatwaves of anger burned in his face. *'Where are you, you harehearted tomcat? We need more cats. Even three more good ones, and we'll have the area secure. Come on, Hyrees, where are you?'*

"Cloud! A little help?" Wren called.

Cloud pushed through the grass to where Wren wrestled with a tabby tom. He scruffed the tomcat and jerked him off of Wren's stomach. Wren jumped up and ran his claws across one of the tom's eyes. The cat howled in agony. Cloud let go. The cat ran into the grass and disappeared. Cloud glanced at Wren warily.

"I knew him, back when I lived in the East," Wren said. "Never liked him much."

Cloud only shook his head. He didn't have time to worry about grudges. Wren's ears flicked back. "What's wrong?"

He forced the renewed guilt and sadness back into an irrelevant corner where it belonged. "It doesn't matter right now. We have a battle to fight."

"If you're sure it can wait," Wren replied.

"It can."

They positioned themselves next to each other, each cat facing opposite the other. Grass moved around them. At least two Easterners were stalking them. He watched the grass waves, readying himself for the next attack.

No matter how hard he tried to focus on the present, however, his mind kept drifting back to Ember's broken body and the human who had carried her away. Every time he mentally shoved them away, they came back stronger and more painful than before.

A younger cat, the molly he'd refused to fight, leaped out at them. She landed hard against Cloud's side. He stumbled back and swung at her. He missed. She dove into the grass, then reappeared next to Wren. She sank her teeth into his flank. He growled and swatted at her face. She let go and jumped back. His claws dug into her shoulder. She squeaked and staggered into the overgrowth.

A second Easterner, Falcon himself, lunged at Cloud. Cloud leaped out of range, then shoved him off-balance. Falcon landed on his back, paws and claws extended. In his mind, Falcon morphed into Ember's broken body.

He shook his head. "Call them off, now. We've had enough bloodshed for one night."

Falcon got back to his paws. "You and I both know telling them to stop won't do anything. Some Easterners still feel as though your colony should be punished; even among the few with us tonight. They aren't going to miss this opportunity to deliver what they consider justice."

"Desire for revenge shouldn't stop us from trying."

The molly pounced back out of the grass, knocking Wren onto his side. She sunk her claws into the flesh between his ribs. Wren bent to snap his teeth in her throat. She reared back on her hind paws, then used the momentum to lunge for his neck.

Cloud leaped toward them. "Wren!"

Falcon shoved Cloud onto the frozen ground. He caught him by the scruff, rendering him helpless. "Don't take this personally."

Instead of a scream, there was only a choked, sputtering meow. Cloud trembled as Wren tried to yowl. Fury burned in his chest. He ripped himself free and snapped his teeth around the closest thing he could grab: Falcon's muzzle. He bit down as hard as his jaw would allow. Blood coated his tongue. Falcon tried to shake him off, but his teeth only sank in deeper. Falcon jerked his head away. Cloud's jaw snapped shut. One of his upper fangs snapped off, still embedded in Falcon's muzzle.

Cloud growled at the pain and forced it aside. Behind Falcon, the young tabby stared down at Wren, eyes wide and mouth gaping. He yowled in frustration and clawed Falcon out of the way. He charged. The cat's eyes locked onto him. She lowered her head and ran into the grass.

He ran to his friend's side. Wren coughed twice, then went still.

"No," Cloud whispered. *I could have saved him. This is my fault; I could've saved him. My fault,'* his eyes locked onto Falcon, who pawed the tooth from his muzzle, *'and yours.'*

They pounced at the same time. Cloud adjusted his aim. His claws cut into Falcon's neck. Falcon swatted at his face. He whirled his head to the side and braced for impact. Claws ripped through his lower cheek and jaw. A moment later, they hit the ground.

"Stop! Everyone, stop fighting! Have y-you lost your minds?" a voice, faint, but distinctly Lupine's, called out. "Jade! Jade, call them off! I-I-I don't know what happened, but please s-stop this madness."

"Easterners, stop fighting and group under Coyote Rock, *now*!" Jade yowled.

Cloud and Falcon stood up and glared at each other.

'Now they finally decide to come. You're late, Hyrees. Too late.'

He walked back to Wren's now lifeless body. The wound didn't look like much, just four small puncture holes in his throat, but they'd been enough to sever an artery and bleed him out. Cloud didn't touch the body, or say anything to it. Instead, he lowered his head and said his goodbyes in silence.

'You deserved more than this, my friend. I'm sorry I wasn't able to reach you in time.'

"No hard feelings?" Falcon asked.

Cloud opened his eyes, staring at the bloodstained ground. "If it weren't an act of war, I'd kill you now."

When he spoke, his torn cheek and snapped tooth burned. The anger and bitterness that came alongside the physical pain tore at him from the inside.

"Can't say I blame you. But that's what happens when we fight. Let's go have a word with Jade. If she thinks I'm dead, war will be inevitable," Falcon replied.

"All it took was a few words, and now the fight is over. You wouldn't even try to stop it," Cloud hissed.

"What did you do to stop it?"

He grimaced. "Advisor or not, you're just a cat. You aren't worth starting a war over. No one is worth starting a war over, no matter how important they may be."

Falcon's tail twitched. "Her logic, not mine. I'm jealous of your colony's laws, Cloud. Only toms allowed to lead. Yes, Jade makes a wonderful commander in times of peace, but she doesn't do so well in times of war. The stress gets to her, irrationalizes her decisions."

Cloud spun to face him. "You only say that because if those laws existed in the East, you might have become commander."

Falcon snorted. "No. I'm not kin of anyone important enough for that. Though really, I'm just as content with how things are now. So long as our second discussion goes well, at least. We currently have the disadvantage. For our own sake, I hope it all works out. Shall we?"

Cloud let out a long, slow breath. His heart still wanted to fight; it pounded in his ears like chants of war. For his colony's sake, he ignored it, and walked beside Falcon back to the shelter of Coyote Rock. Cold sorrow and bitter anger filled his heart. As they moved, they passed the bodies of their slain comrades. The snow fell in drifts around them, coating the field, the forest, and the fallen with white, and hushing the world. The silence might've felt eerie to a less rational mind.

Beneath the rock, Lupine, Whitehaze, and several other Westerners waited. Lupine and Jade both visibly loosened when they saw them approaching, but Lupine was still trembling. Shard, Echo, and the tabby were nowhere to be seen, yet Jade didn't seem concerned for their safety.

"Cloud," Lupine said, "there you are. I w-was so worried we'd lost you too. So far everyone seems more or less okay. I-I think a few are missing, though," Lupine said.

Cloud looked around, taking note of the cats present. "At least two are dead. Several others are unaccounted for. Where's Hyrees?"

The calmness of his own voice startled him. *'Huh. I sound like a wildcat. Probably look like one, too. What would Songbird think if she'd heard me just then?'*

"Oh," Lupine said. He sniffled. "Oh no. I-I hoped I had gotten here in-in time to prevent any more deaths, but . . . I guess I was too late after all."

"Where is Hyrees?" Cloud asked again.

Lupine shrunk back, ears pinned. "He ran himself too hard. P-p-passed out moments after he made it to the Glade."

Cloud closed his eyes as he sat down. Inside he'd already known it wasn't Hyrees's fault, but Lupine confirming it sent another wave of guilt crashing down on him.

"S-so Jade, could you explain what happened?" Lupine asked.

His adrenaline high faded. With the intensity of the fight over, nothing could distract him, or his thoughts, from reality. He struggled against the tears still vying to form in his eyes.

"We were all getting ready for sleep when cats started running through our camp," Jade said. "Some of your cats attacked us, and we had no choice but to defend ourselves. After all these winters of peace, I can't even begin to comprehend why any of you would want to start this up again."

"Which cats attacked you?" Lupine asked. "I w-will be sure to punish them."

"I can't remember."

His eyes narrowed. "I-I-I find that unlikely."

Cloud gave up on fighting his emotions. He stood. "I'm sorry, Lupine, I can't do this right now."

"Oh. Wren?" Lupine asked.

He nodded softly. "And Ember."

"Tahg, I-I'm really sorry, Cloud. You can go. I'll try my best to settle this without you or, uh, Songbird."

Cloud lowered his head in thanks, then padded back toward the forest. He cried silently as he walked. Each tear left a patch of ice in his fur. When he pushed through the last blades of dried grass, he stopped. The woods loomed ahead, cold and unforgiving. And empty—too empty. When he reached the Glade, Aspen wouldn't be there, at least not alive. Ember wouldn't be there either, and Wren certainly wouldn't be there, but forty-odd questioning faces would be; faces who would sob, mourn, ask questions, and make an emotional racket. Songbird would be there too. How could he tell her the daughter they'd fought so hard to keep was gone?

'What would she think if I had killed Ember? Would she say it was the right thing to do? Or is this way better for everyone? Who am I trying to fool? She's with the humans. She'd be better off dead. I failed her. I failed Aspen. I failed Wren. I failed them all.'

Instead of going to the Glade, he wandered west along the mountain slope. Moonlight reappeared from behind the clouds and illuminated the patch of white-speckled green in front of him: the Cliffs. He jumped onto a rock that smelled like Ember, then sat facing the sunken mountainside and the Wolf Trail far below.

Another mechanical pod zipped past on its railing, its whirring distant and haunting. He shuddered and sighed. *'I didn't even get to tell her. I should have. I should have let her know the truth about Dark, and Aspen, and me. Maybe if I had, she'd still be here. She wouldn't have ran or fought, that's for sure. And Aspen wouldn't be able to follow through with his threats.'* He wrapped his paws over his muzzle. *'What are we going to do now? What am I going to do? I can advise during peace, but if there's going to be a war I don't know what to do. I'm just as lost as everyone else. Everyone is depending on me, but I don't know if I can keep doing this. I'm not a leader. After Farlight becomes commander, I have to leave. For too long I've given this colony everything only to get hurt by it over and over again. I'm not putting up with this anymore. I can't.'*

He got to his paws. *'Enough hesitating. Time to tell them. The sooner they know, the sooner . . . How am I even supposed to finish that thought? The sooner the pain will go away? The sooner things will go back to normal? The sooner we can all forget they even existed? I don't know, but I do need to tell them. They deserve to know the truth. Even if they don't deserve what the truth is. This time I will tell them.'*

Cloud jumped off the rock. When he did, the ledge it sat on crumbled. Both boulder and ground tumbled down the cliffside with a series of crashes. He stared back at the now empty patch of air.

'Huh.'

For once, he couldn't think of anything else to think. He walked back to the Glade in silence. When he got there, cats ran to him. Several voices at once asked about the fight, or about loved ones who may or may not have survived it. The voices became a muffled blur. He pushed past them. Songbird, Kivyress, and Farlight sat outside the healers' den, where Fern and Fledge were helping an exhausted Hyrees regain his strength. Songbird's eyes lit up when she saw him, but only for a moment; she knew something was wrong, and he was about to confirm it.

She approached him slowly, cautiously, as if he might attack her but might also give her a big nuzzle and say everything would be okay. Cloud trembled. Tears were already forming in her eyes.

"Cloud," she said, "is she . . ."

He pressed his forehead against hers. "She's gone, Song. I'm . . . I'm sorry. The humans have her now. She was on the Wolf Trail, and they took her. Even if they were trying to help, she was . . . she was in pretty bad shape."

"Ember," Kivyress whispered, shivering.

Songbird sat down and cried into his fur. She didn't say anything, because nothing else needed to be said; loss was a given, and no amount of yowling, or even whimpering, would ever change it. So she spoke nothing and sobbed against his shoulder.

"What did you say?" Hyrees asked. He appeared in the den's entrance, eyes wide and shaking all over. "What did you say, Cloud? Tell me, please."

Cloud swallowed hard. *'Only one more. This is almost over. Just a few more words and it'll be over.'*

He sucked in a deep breath. "Hyrees, Farlight; your father is dead, and Ember may be as well. They're both gone."

Hyrees staggered forward. He lay down to keep himself from falling. "Oh my . . . my, they," he stammered.

Farlight and Kivyress looked at each other, both searching for comfort. They walked closer to where Songbird and Cloud sat. Songbird's gaze landed on Hyrees. She sniffed a few times, then extended a paw. He limped to her, welcoming her embrace. They remained in silence until Fern urged them to get some sleep. He suspected she just wanted the chance to mourn her traitor of a daughter alone. Yet she was still his sister-in-law, and she'd just lost her only kitten. She deserved a chance to grieve, so they gave it to her.

"Last night, five courageous cats gave their lives after the assassination of Commander Aspen, my beloved brother, and the unwarranted ambush that took place following it," Lupine said. He was shaking all over and speaking through tears, but his voice was strong and more clear than usual. "Whitehaze spent all night carving a memorial into the-the History Tree for them. Those five brave souls w-will be remembered for generations, thanks to him. They have left us in body and soul, but may their courage and strength live on forever; especially i-i-in the hearts of those closest to them, whom they've left behind. May their spirits heal and strengthen us through these difficult times as w-we prepare for war, and for the battles yet to come."

A few hours earlier, before they'd all gone out to the Fields to burn away what bodies they could, Lupine had officially announced that the post-fight meeting was a failure. Jade had refused to take credit for Aspen's death, or the ambush. Any attempts he'd made to apologize or amend their relationship were met with hostility and bitterness. Finally, Jade agreed to camp elsewhere, and Lupine agreed to let her leave, but not before a state of war was declared.

Peace was over.

Cloud glanced over at Fern, who had her head buried in Fledge's chest. As much as he tried to avoid them and their less-than-presentable ways, another pang of sympathy stirred in his head. Tainu would not get a memorial; she wouldn't be allowed to get mentioned in speeches. Yet that was the fate of a traitor: to be remembered as nothing more.

"D-Dad?" Kivyress whispered in his ear. Her jaw trembled. "You don't think she's alive, do you?"

He hesitated. He didn't want to run through all the worst-case scenarios again, but his mind acted without instruction, showing him visions of pain and suffering he couldn't even imagine feeling. "I . . . I don't know. If not, I hope she went quickly."

"Will you be saying something for her?" she asked.

"I don't know. Probably not. I'm going to be honest with you, Kivyress; part of me still thinks she's alive. I don't know if she really is, or if it's just me being hopeful. I guess I'm afraid that, if I say something for her, she'll really be gone, and we'll never get to see her again. It's illogical, and fluffheaded, and stupid, and any other word you can think of, but . . . I don't want to lose her yet."

She'd already been given a memorial stone. It rested beside the ash-covered stones of all the others they'd lost. Since her body had been taken, others' ashes had been scattered around her marker. She would never get a proper send-off. Part of him hated the ambiguity, but the more imaginative side of him preferred it

"I think it makes sense," Kivyress said through tears. "You don't want to say anything because . . . once you do, that'll be it. She'll be gone, and everything will be over."

He pulled her closer. "I guess so."

Songbird leaned closer to them, engulfing Kivyress in warmth. On the other side of them, Hyrees cried softly beside his brother.

"I never did tell Dad about my eyes," Hyrees whispered. "Why didn't I tell him? Why didn't I ever talk to him about anything? He wanted me to talk to him. He just wanted a decent conversation, and I never gave him one. I-I spent every day with him. How could I have never told him?"

'He needs to know.'

Cloud edged closer. Kivyress and Farlight moved out of the way. He rested his head against his son-in-law's neck, trying to offer any emotional support he could. "He already knew. He didn't want to make you uncomfortable by bringing it up at the wrong time, so he never brought it up at all."

Hyrees opened his eyes, but they didn't focus on anything. His breathing became louder and more panicked.

"He was always proud of you, you know," Cloud said.

Hyrees pulled away, breath rate stabilizing. "He was?"

"I was talking to him yesterday, before the Meeting. He was bragging about you. He was *bragging.* Bragging and going on about how much he'd miss you when you became a clayworker. But he knew it would make you happier. He wanted you to be happy."

Hyrees's eyes lost focus again.

'I hope that was the right thing to say.'

"You know what? You should give Ember a speech," Hyrees whispered. He stood up, then slunk away from the gathering.

"Cloud," Lupine said. "Would you like to s-say anything?"

He realized he'd missed the rest of Lupine's homage.

Cloud stood. "Yes, sir."

As he walked over to the rise on which Lupine waited, he rehearsed the eulogies he'd prepared for Aspen and Wren during the burning. As he'd gathered wood, he'd also composed his thoughts and stomped out the last of his tears. He'd never been one for crying, or for displaying his emotions at all. Emotions made him vulnerable, easier to take advantage of, so he suppressed them whenever he could—even at his best friend's memorial gathering. If it meant he was the only one not crying, so be it. For now, this was his colony. They needed someone to be strong for them, and being strong for others was part of his job.

"I am proud to have called Wren my friend. He was one of the best cats I've ever met, and probably ever will meet. When I found him at the border back on my first day of apprenticeship, I couldn't understand why Commander Aspen would let an Easterner join our colony. But he let him in. He let him stay because he saw something in him no one else could."

Cloud swallowed. "He saw his heart. His spirit. His courage and bravery. Someone who deserved a chance. Someone who would prove himself over and over, through his work as a border guard, and last night, in his death, when he laid down his life for us."

His paws still stung from scraping up ashes to pour over the memorial stones, so he sat down. "For a cat who'd lost so much, he never managed to lose that spirit. He had the heart of a cougar and the gentleness of a fawn. He was one of the strongest cats I've ever known. He will be missed."

'I just wish I could've saved him. He didn't deserve to die. It should've been me.'

He moved on to his next speech. "Commander Aspen was one of the best leaders the West has ever seen. It was an honor to serve under him."

He'd intentionally composed the two speeches to open with similar statements of gratitude. He loved them equally, Wren like a brother, and Aspen like a father. They'd been more his family than the cats he was born to.

"Yes, he had his misgivings, but he never stopped moving forward. Not even when the forest seemed to be against him. Not even when his own colony hated him. He used those times of heartache, those times of sorrow and pain, to improve himself and the West. He took his old thoughts, his old beliefs, and he threw them over the Cliffs. He changed rules that have existed since the time of Dark. It is because of his generosity that my daughter, Ember, was able to grow up. It's because of him that I met Wren."

Cloud paused for a moment to lick the feeling back into one of his forepaws. "Without Aspen's guidance, we would've never held the first Meeting. We would've never made all those wonderful memories, or had those celebrations, those feasts, and those games. He gave us an era of prosperity like no other. This era was short-lived, but that is the way of all beautiful things. As we ready ourselves for the less beautiful side of life, for this time of war, may his strength continue with us."

For a moment, he considered making something up on the spot for Ember, but he couldn't bring himself to even begin thinking about it.

"The pain of loss, it will never fully go away, but it can heal. It can teach us. Though there will be scars, we have been made better because of the lives of these cats, who sacrificed themselves so we could move onward. We must continue our fight without them. We must continue to be strong. May their sacrifices not be in vain."

He stepped down from the rock. "Thank you."

"Cloud, wait," Lupine said. "What about Ember? I-I know what you said, but I think it's safe to say she's probably—"

"I'm not giving a speech for Ember."

"A-a-are you sure?"

Cloud glared at him and growled. "Yes."

He padded back to where the remnants of his family sat. A few others gave speeches, but he didn't hear them. He sat in numb silence, trying to force his mind to be silent too.

After the gathering, he climbed the History Tree to look at the memorials Whitehaze had carved into a young branch. In terms of words, it was simple, but the carving itself was a masterpiece. No one name got more attention or detail than the other. They were all equally beautiful, and each name had leaves carved into either side of it: aspen leaves for Aspen, maple for Ember, and creeping ivy, complete with flowers, for Wren. He smiled softly. Wren loved ivy. It had been Light's favorite plant, which he'd adopted as his own favorite after she'd passed. Now he would be immortalized with it.

He glanced over the rest of the names. The list was small when compared to the Stone Ridge memorial carving a few branches away, but there hadn't been nearly as many involved in the fight. Five was a tremendous loss when the ratios of participants to deaths were compared. It meant over half of the first few cats to chase Tainu had perished.

'What does this mean for the future? If we keep this ratio up for a few

more battles, we'll kill ourselves off. Granted, the attack was an ambush, and an ambush will typically have a higher death rate than a more standard battle, but all things considered, it won't be giving anyone here a confidence boost.'

"Cloud?" Songbird asked.

"What is it, Song?" He jumped out of the Tree to greet her, then butted his head against hers.

She pulled away. "Stop, please." Her voice wavered. "It's Hyrees. He hasn't come back yet, and he skipped his morning rations. Farlight is afraid he might try to do it again. And fox it, Cloud, I think he might be right. If that's the case, you know I can't go after him, and Farlight is busy with Commander Lupine."

Cloud growled. "Why do I—"

"Cloud!" she snapped. "Not everything is about you. This is not about you. This is about Hyrees, a heartbroken, scared, *kitten*. Your best friend's son. You know he can't think rationally right now. Go—save him before he does something we'll all regret." Songbird coughed a few times, then her pained expression dissolved into tears. "Please. We can't afford to lose anyone else. *I can't lose anyone else. Not now.*"

'What have I done? What am I doing? What's wrong with me? Come on, Cloud, get your priorities straight. Hyrees, I hope you're still there, tomcat.'

Cloud pinned back his ears. He licked her cheek. "Sorry, that . . . came out wrong. I'll find him, okay?"

Songbird tucked her head under his chin. "Be careful."

"I will. I'll go easy on him. You get some rest. We'll be back soon."

She nodded once, then they parted ways. As he loped out of the Glade, Cloud examined the tracks in the thin layer of snow. They fanned out in different directions. He sniffed the ground, then the air, but couldn't make his nose pick up the correct scent.

'I guess I'll have to use logic then. Those go in the general direction of the Cliffs, and I know for a fact that they aren't mine, so I suppose I should start there. I hope I'm not too late. That'd be the fourth death to rest on my

conscience in the span of less than a day, and I don't want to deal with that level of guilt.'

Moss replaced compacted dirt and dead grass as he neared the Cliffs. He lifted his snout to the breeze, yet it still refused to work properly. "Hyrees, are you here?"

"W-what are you doing here?" a voice asked. It sounded panicked.

'So he is considering it. He really is unstable. And impulsive. And none of these thoughts are going to help him.' Cloud quickened his pace. "Making sure you're okay. What are you doing?"

Hyrees stood near where the boulder had been, tail tucked between his legs. He backed away from the edge and sat down. He was shaking. He was scared. "E-enjoying the view."

Cloud sat beside him. "It's a good one, but not such a good last view."

His eyes widened. "Sir, p-please don't tell anyone. I wasn't actually considering it. N-not really. It was just a-a stupid thought. I'm-I'm too much of a hareheart t-t-to pull it off anyway."

"I won't tell a soul as long as you stay alive. But the moment you die, well, the meows get meowed. What would Ember think if she came back to find out you threw yourself over the Cliffs? She may still be out there, you know."

"I'm sorry," Hyrees choked out. "I-I don't know what-what came over me, I just . . . I wanted the pain to be over. I couldn't think. I couldn't think about a-anything but how much, how much less dying would hurt, but-but like I said: I'm a coward."

"Songbird was the one who sent me. Her and Farlight. They're worried about you, you know. Especially Farlight. You've gotta pull through this for him. Your brother, he needs you, just like you need him."

Hyrees dropped to his stomach and wrapped his paws around his face. "Oh tahg. Oh tahg, what was I thinking?"

"Calm down, Hyrees. We'll get through this. It may not be okay, but we can deal with it. I know you can deal with it, because you are a strong, capable tomcat, and you will make it through this."

Hyrees didn't reply. He remained on the ground, shivering and mewing little whimpers to himself. Cloud groomed the top of his head and whispered comforts.

'This was a lot more than a passing thought, and you know it, Hyrees. I guess I'm going to have to watch out for you for a while. Well, I can do that for you. I'm a border guard and advisor. It's part of my job.'

At long last, Hyrees sat back up. "Please d-don't make me go back to the Glade yet."

"I'm not going to."

He coughed up a lump of mucus. "Ugh. Th-thank you, sir."

Cloud nuzzled his side. "Don't get yourself so worked up."

Hyrees nodded.

'Should I ask him? Is it too soon?' He sighed. *'It's not like we have anything else to talk about or do.'*

"You know, until Ember gets back, I'm going to need someone to patrol with me. The border won't guard itself. If you like, we could take a walk to the ravine to calm down, and perhaps think of some nicer things than jumping off of cliffs. Maybe see how well we work together. If not, we could just sit here and admire the view. For real this time."

"But sir, I'm going blind."

"You'd only be doing it for a little while. Just until you finished your clayworking apprenticeship. It'd be nice to have some company for the time being."

His ears perked up. "You mean it?"

Cloud forced a smile. "Every word."

Hyrees drew a deep breath. "Just until Ember comes back."

Cloud nodded. "Just until Ember comes back," he echoed.

'If she ever does.'

CHAPTER 8
EMBER

[Thai 3.1_boot sequence initiated]

[boot sequence successful]

[autotest results: system is stable]

[network setup required]

'Huh?' Ember thought. *'What was that? Who's there? Anyone else here? Inside my head? Hello? No?'*

The words lingered in her subconscious, then faded. She wondered if she'd imagined the little voice and symbols. She could bring them back with her memory if she concentrated enough, but they looked and sounded like passing muses.

Beyond the confines of her head, she heard something. No, she heard multiple somethings: the soft, distant murmur of voices she didn't recognize, clanks, thumps, and a faint rush of air. It was warm air with a burnt smell that mixed with the scents of urine, scat, and something strong and bitter. She couldn't ignore it, or tune it out, but she could listen and let the strange new ambience welcome her.

Blue and yellow appeared. The colors formed little dots and swarmed around her mind. Nothing hurt, and there was nothing to be alarmed about, but a sense of dread came with them. Beyond the dots lay a backdrop of black. Tiny stars of indigo purple joined the jumble of color and sense. She contorted it all into a quad-toned picture of the Glade. The image morphed into one of full-color, which she then placed her family in.

Something barked. A canine of some kind. She opened her eyes enough to get a blurry line of white—everything was white.

'Bright! Bright! Bright! Ow.'

She closed her eyes again.

'What was that thing? Am I—I don't think I'm in the Glade. Doesn't smell like the Glade. It smells like . . . I don't even know what, but it's burning my nose. So if you aren't there, where are you, Ember? Are you dead? Unlikely. You wouldn't be this tired if you were dead. And I don't think there would be any coyotes, or wolves, or anything like that nearby. Or, at least, I certainly hope not. If that's the case, though, can I go back to living? This is mildly terrifying.'

"HELP! Let me out," a voice called.

Her eyes snapped open. Her replica of the Glade exploded into solid yellow. She blinked furiously until her eyes adjusted to the brightness, then stared at the alien scene in front of her. It was so unlike anything she'd imagined, all of her mind colors disappeared.

Directly in front of her, a clear panel with paw-sized holes in it separated her from the outside world. Beyond it, several more metallic dens sat in two horizontal rows against a wall. Some of the dens contained other cats, but these cats all looked tiny and out of proportion, even for young cats. Their legs were too thin, their tails were too short, their heads were too narrow, and their paws were too stubby. None of them had oily fur or leaf debris in their pelts. A few of them had coats so short they wouldn't last a day in the snow.

Something clicked in the back of her hazy mind and sent bright green flaring through her subconscious. These weren't even her own kind; they were her less-developed relatives: domestic cats. The humans had her, and she was at their mercy.

'Oh no. Oh no, oh no, oh no. Am I dreaming? Please, please, please be dreaming.' She tried to lift her head. Pain shot up and down her spine, giving

her a headache. A quiet mew escaped her throat. *I'm not dreaming. That hurts. Why am I here? They must be so angry at us for escaping. What are they going to do to me? They're going to punish me, and experiment on me, and hurt me, and I'm going to die, and—oh tahg, what did they do to him?'*

The cat across from her snapped his head in her direction. He was the fattest creature she'd ever seen, so obese he looked more like a lump of clay with legs than a living thing.

"Who are you?" he asked. "Can you get me out of here? I need to get outta here. Help!"

Ember's eyes watered as the pain faded. *'He needs help escaping? That means I really am stuck here. They really do have me, and I really am going to die.'*

"Please! Please help me," the fat cat said.

"I can't . . . help you," she replied. The words came out so raspy and slurred, she didn't recognize her own voice. Each meow made the back of her head ache even more. "Where . . . are . . . we?"

"Don't know. Don't know. Gotta get out!"

'Oh, I really need water. I need to get up. I need to get away from here before the humans come back, but I can't. I can't move.'

She stuck her tongue out and bit down on the tip. It drew away some of the pain from her back, but not enough to get comfortable. Ember mewed a dull, barely audible note to herself in an attempt to keep herself calm. The tone raised and lowered, loosely following a series of two-dimensional mountains and valleys in her head. With each thump, or meow, or bark, the tune changed. Like the creek, it flowed with the landscape and never repeated itself.

"Oh, hey, the new cat's finally awake. And for real, this time," a voice said.

Ember's ears perked up. Her eyes searched the cubes in front of her, but none of the domestic cats visible were the speaker.

The overweight cat backed into a corner. "Ohhh, not him!"

A big, fluffy face popped in front of her. Ember jerked her head back. She squeaked in surprise, then moaned in agony. Her eyes watered from the sudden surge of pain.

"Don't . . . do that," she whispered. "What do you mean 'awake for real'?"

The cat, a brown and white tabby, smiled. His paws were latched onto the holes in the clear panel. The piece of blue metal dangling from his neck clinked against her enclosure. "Sorry," he said. "Didn't mean to scare you. Last night you started yowling about how much you miss the leaves, or something like that, but I don't think you were actually awake. Those painkillers are pretty strong, huh? Anyway, I'm Yegor, the Center's resident feline therapist. You are?"

The purple stars came back, along with flashes of silver. Some of his words didn't sound like Felid. "Ember. What happened?"

"You got hit, remember? And you almost died. I honestly didn't think you were going to make it, but here you are, all alive and—whoopsie!"

His claws slipped, and he fell back to the ground. Four soft thuds indicated he'd more or less landed on his paws. Ember snorted. He'd flopped back so casually, as if he'd done it a hundred times a day. She imagined him jumping in front of the other cats at random. No wonder they didn't like him.

"Hit?" she asked. "What does . . . oh."

A cold, hard lump settled in her stomach. Every muscle in her body tightened at once. Her heartbeat echoed in her ears. Breathing. She needed to breathe. She couldn't breathe. *'I killed her. Oh tahg, I killed her, didn't I? And, oh, Commander Aspen is dead too. Oh, tahg, the ambush! Are they all dead? What if they all died? Is everyone gone? And what if they're not? There's gonna be a war.'*

A battle played out in her head. Every last Westerner fought hard, but Jade and her forces kept coming. One by one, everyone she knew got picked off, or left to suffer with fatal wounds. Those closest to her suffered the most, and all she could do was watch, helpless, stupid, cowardly. An overgrown kitten—like everyone always said when they thought she couldn't hear.

She shuddered. *'But I really did kill her, didn't I? She's dead, and it's all my fault. I lost control and killed her. That wasn't supposed to happen. How did this happen?'*

"Ember? Are you still there?" Yegor asked, momentarily dragging her away from the violence of her own thoughts.

She ignored him.

'I have to go back. Unless this is a dream. Please let this be a dream. A really, really bad dream with a lot of very real-feeling pain. Go away, please, go away! Let me wake up in the Tree; let everything be okay.'

Loud, slow pawsteps tapped against the ground. Ember flicked back her ears. Even they hurt to move. She clenched her jaw more tightly to keep her teeth from chattering. A new scent entered the chamber, or rather, a stronger version of a scent that was already present. She shuddered all over.

"You aren't tormenting our patient, are you, Yegor?"

The voice spoke in Felid, but the voice itself wasn't feline.

"No, no, I was just performing my therapist duties," Yegor replied. "All is fine."

She shivered harder, closed her eyes, and rested her head on the den's floor. *'Play dead, play dead, play dead.'*

"I see. How about you step out and tell Mrs. Castell she can come in?"

"She's here?" Yegor mewed.

"Just got here. I told her our special patient might wake up today."

Before the new voice even finished speaking, Yegor's pawsteps were fading.

When they disappeared altogether, Ember closed her eyes tighter. *'I'm dead. I'm dead. I'm dead. Please think I'm dead.'*

"Don't be scared," the voice said.

A tiny whimper escaped her throat as the speaker's footsteps drew closer. She opened her eyes. A creature looked back at her, taller than a stag and standing on two slender legs. Flappy things the color of pain draped his body. His furless skin was the tone of wet sand, and his undersized eyes were almost black. The patch of fur covering the top and back of his head was also black.

He closed his eyes slowly and tilted his head away, a gesture she'd learned to be non-threatening. "Ember, was it?" he asked. "I'm Doctor Hye-sung

Sagong. You can call me Hye. Welcome to the National Center of Veterinary Science and Animal Research. N-C-V-S-A-R for short. Or, more simply put, 'the Center.' "

Ember blinked a few times. Each time she reopened her eyes, she expected him to disappear, but he didn't. Her vision lost focus for a moment, so she blinked again to bring it back.

Ember swallowed hard. "I don't . . . know what that means."

Her tail thrashed, as if it wanted to detach itself and wiggle away like the tail of a desperate lizard. Part of it felt cold against the metal of her den.

"I know," he replied. "Most of it's in my language, because Felid, unsurprisingly, doesn't have the right words. Basically, all it means is this is a place where people help creatures of other species. In other words, you're safe here."

"Why am I here?" she asked, eyes narrowed. "I sh- . . . I should've died. I think. I don't understand. W-what did you do?"

His lined brows raised. He opened his mouth, then closed it. Ember bit her tongue again, ignoring the taste of blood coating her mouth.

'Not supposed to bite yourself. Not important right now.'

He lifted an elongated paw, a hand, to his chin. "You know, I kind of suspected, given your size and features, that you were an appala, but . . . hmm."

Another human entered the room, speaking in some strange human language. 'Appala,' the word he'd used to describe her, came up again. She leaned her head forward as gradually as she could. It still hurt, but not as much as before, and it didn't add to her headache.

The second human also had black hair, but unlike Hye's lighter tone, her skin was the same shade of brown as Ember's fur. The flappy things on her were less flappy, and made of two different colors: red on her top half, and grey for the rest. Two black rectangles framed her eyes.

Ember lowered her chin to rest once again between her paws. Her head felt heavy. Out the edges of her peripheral vision she noticed the tips of her toes. Both sides were dark, instead of just one. And discolored. She swallowed hard, then moved them closer. Her legs *hissed*. Her heart sank to her stomach. Both of her paws were furless and segmented, with a dark grey coating on each piece resembling cooked skin. She moved the toes on one of her forepaws, each one in turn, creating a little toe wave. A series of whirs followed the motions.

"GA-AAAAAH!" Ember shrieked.

She jumped into a stand, hyperventilating, then yowled again. Her head and torso throbbed. A sharp ringing filled her ears, clogging her senses. She closed her eyes and bit the tip of her tongue harder.

'Stop! Stop! Stop! Stop!'

The word repeated itself, echoing for what felt like an eternity.

"My gosh, cat! Calm down. You're okay," Hye said. "Look, calm down, and lay down, and we'll tell you what's going on. Ember? Ember, hey! Listen to me. You've got to calm down. You'll hurt yourself if you don't."

His voice was so muffled and distant she almost didn't hear it. The second human said something, but she couldn't make it out at all. Her eyes watered. Her ears went numb. Grey and blue swirled around her head, snuffing out any additional verbal thoughts before they could form. Only a few patches of yellow escaped the fog. Somewhere behind it all, her mind formed an image of a sleek, cat-like contraption with glowing eyes. She closed her eyes more tightly and clenched her teeth as hard as she could.

These humans, they'd turned her into a machine. She wasn't even real anymore, or at least her legs weren't. She didn't know about the rest of herself, and she didn't know if she wanted to.

There was a faint *click*. Something pulled at her legs. Her front end lowered with another ear-grating whir. Her back end lowered too as her hind legs were bent by someone stronger than her. The voice spoke again, but she couldn't hear what it said, or even if it was speaking Felid. Everything still hurt. Her jaw trembled.

"Take it easy, Ember," Hye said. His voice was so close, it almost sounded like it was coming from inside her own mind. "Calm down. I'll explain everything."

But she couldn't calm down. Not now, not with this. Not with Tainu murdered by claws she no longer controlled. Not with a human telling her to be calm in her own language. She opened her eyes. A familiar darkness crept along the edges of her vision. She tried to focus on breathing.

'*Stop thinking about it. Stop! Don't pass out. Not now. Oh tahg, what did they do? What am I?*'

Hye held his hands up, as if their presence might somehow comfort her. "It's going to be okay. I promise."

Yegor's scent re-entered the chamber. "Treats?" he asked.

The second human replied in her own language.

"Oh, sorry," Yegor said.

Ember covered her face with her robotic paws. They felt cold, even through her fur. She yanked them away and trembled harder. "W-w-w-what d-d-did y-you do to m-m-me?"

Some kind of canine barked. Another replied. Things *clicked* and *thudded* from everywhere. Voices, terrified meows, human laughter, and a screeching series of *clangs* as countless objects fell to the ground—the noises attacked her. Ringing, her ears were ringing.

"First, could you tell me if anything still hurts?" Hye asked. "I may need to get Michelle here to run a diagnostic on you to make sure everything is still working properly."

She bared her teeth and growled. "D-don't touch me! W-w-what did you d-do?"

Hye and the other human, Michelle, exchanged a glance. Michelle spoke something in her own language. Hye ran a hand through his fur, sighed, then replied. Michelle walked away. Ember's ears perked up when she returned carrying a flat, shiny thing. Michelle held it up for her to see. Ember leaned closer, trying to make sense of the image. It took a moment for her to realize it was her own reflection.

Pain forgotten, she stared at herself in shock. All four of her legs were coated in artificial, blackish-grey skin. The material extended all the way up to her shoulders and hips, where it joined again with her real skin. One of her ears was cut off almost entirely. She moved her tail closer to see its reflection, and felt sick all over again. The white-furred tip was gone, along with a third of the rest of it. Part of what remained was almost furless. Much of her torso was also furless.

The grey fog lifted. *'That's me. This is what I am now? No. No, no, no.'*

Michelle pulled back the reflective thing, but Ember kept staring. Her eyes widened as the darkness came back. The noises around her deadened to a muffled growl.

'Ohhh, I don't feel good.'

Hye crouched closer to her. His lips moved, but she couldn't comprehend the garbled noises that came out. Ember lifted her head to look at him. These two creatures—these humans, of all things—had taken the time to learn her language, make these machines, and both save and ruin her life. Nothing made sense anymore. The greens and yellows of fear and shock faded. All that remained was a shimmery, surreal turquoise.

"Why? W-why would you do this?" she asked.

"It was either this, or letting you die," Hye replied. "I'm sorry we couldn't save more of you."

"No, no. You . . . you gave me new legs after my other ones got crushed. That's not easy. It can't be. Why? Why would you help me? You don't even know me. Tahg, we're not even the same species."

Ember gazed down at the paw that used to be white and flexed her toes. Even when splayed apart all the way, no claws came out. She clenched her jaw tighter and tried to ignore the nausea nipping at her insides.

'Guess I won't be clawmarking anymore. Not that I could clawmark right now anyway, even if I still had my claws.'

Michelle tapped on a thing wrapped around her wrist, then spoke. The wristband spoke after her, "We helped you because that's what people do here. They help animals in need. Not usually me specifically, but you were a special case."

Hye stepped closer to Michelle. "Also, I don't mean to sound dark, but that procedure you just underwent involved entirely new medical technology. We needed an example of how effective it could be. Then you came along with near flawless timing. I'll admit, I got pretty excited."

Ember's eyes narrowed. "Oh. So you just needed me to experiment on."

"No, that's not what I meant," he said. "The timing just happened to be beneficial for everyone."

"Dark was right," Ember whispered. Her throat still burned for water. "You're only in it for yourselves."

Hye and Michelle exchanged a glance. Hye said something in his own language. Another human called out. He turned to Ember. "Sorry, I have to get back to work. Michelle will finish setting everything up for you," he said.

Hye strode away, farther into the Center.

Michelle watched him leave for a few moments, then slow-blinked. "We all have our reasons, sweetie," she said through her translation device. "Not all of them are selfish. Dr. Sagong's are not, and I don't consider mine to be either. That tech inside your body right now is going to save lives of every species, and you've just proven it works. I wouldn't have spent two years making it if others didn't need it. To see it finally doing what it was meant for after all those late nights, to see you alive against all odds, it *is* exciting."

Ember sighed. She covered her nose with a paw and breathed out through her nostrils. The prosthetic not only felt the skin of her nose and the fur around it, but the warmth of her own breath, and it did so with a precision she couldn't remember her old limbs having.

"This only took two years to make?" she asked.

Michelle chuckled. "Your bionic skin? No, that was easy to make eighty years ago. My challenge was to create almost an entire body that could be printed to order, and do everything someone's original parts could. Then, if anyone were to lose or badly damage any part of themselves, someone could fix them right up, and even make improvements."

Ember lowered her paw. "H . . . how long has it been?"

"Since what?"

"Wolf Trail."

"Sorry, I don't understand what that means," Michelle replied.

Ember closed her eyes. "Hit. Since I got hit by the thing."

"Oh. It's been five days. You've been out a while. Now, before you ask anything else, how about I get you set up? Did Thai boot and autotest?"

'Thai? What?' Her mind wandered back to the strange voice she'd woken up to. 'Oh. So I didn't imagine it.'

"I think so."

"Good," Michelle said.

She tapped the black band around her wrist. A glowing square appeared in the air a few clawlengths away. Ember's eyes widened as she touched a tiny circle on the projection. The glowing square changed colors.

"Thai will be your new assistant and monitoring program," Michelle continued. "She will help control and customize your prosthetics. She can also answer questions, check weather, and I-M anyone with a connection. That means you can more or less talk to anyone else, no matter where they are, so long as they have a device or A-I implant of some kind. Think 'Thai, link with device.' "

Ember licked her lips nervously. 'Thai, link with device?'

[syncing]

[sync successful]

[You are now connected to "Chell's Glowy Wrist Phone." To disconnect at any time, say "disconnect."]

The voice spoke inside her head. It seemed to be everywhere at once—pure sound without a source. "Whoa, okay. So, er, it says I'm connected with your glowy wrist thing."

Michelle laughed. "I know. I honestly forgot I'd named it that. Wait a bit while I get this ready."

Like subconscious thoughts, images appeared in her head, images matching those displayed on Chell's Glowy Wrist Phone. Most of the images were symbols she couldn't understand, and they kept coming as Michelle pressed her fingers against the light.

"So those are like clawmarks, right?" Ember asked.

"Clawmarks?" Michelle said. "It would depend on what clawmarks are."

"They're symbols that mean different words or sounds. I know your kind has them, because Dark took a lot of inspiration from humans."

Michelle stopped touching the light projection. Her hands dropped to her sides. She said something too quietly for her phone to translate, then covered her mouth. "You have a written language," she said, more loudly this time. "So how do you . . . how do you know about Dark? Word of mouth? These clawmark things? Is he somehow still alive?"

"He died eighty-four winters ago. I learned about him by studying history, and it's very interesting. I could recite some, if you want. Wait, what does it matter to you?"

"History? You keep records of history? Oh. Oh, this is big. It matters because people have made some mistakes. Big mistakes that will affect you and any appala anyone finds after you." She stood up straight and closed the clear panel. "I . . . I have to go. I'll be back soon."

Without waiting for a reply, Michelle ran off in the same direction Hye had gone. The screen at the back of her mind disappeared.

[device disconnected]

Ember couldn't stop a tiny twinge of disappointment from creeping in. She liked the little symbols. They were familiar and comforting, yet new and strange at the same time. Even though they had only been present for a minute at most, her head felt empty without them.

'Okay, that's not important right now. These new legs seem to work about the same as the old ones, so if I can just figure out how to get out of here, I should be able to go home. This can't be too far from it. And once I make it back, everything will be okay.'

Yegor's face popped in front of her.

"ACK!" Ember jerked back, then groaned. "Ow. Why do you keep doing that?"

His paws were hooked into the holes in the moving panel again. Ember felt the urge to shove them out and watch him fall, but it would hurt her to do so, and he might be able to answer some of her questions.

He smiled. "Sorry again. So, how does it feel to be part robot?"

"Purple," she said.

"Oh, okay. I've never felt purple. Wait until you get an ETAg. I'm sure they'll give you one. I've got one. Watch this. Thai, what will the weather be like tomorrow?"

"Tomorrow will be partly cloudy with a twenty-five percent chance of scattered snow drifts," the piece of metal hanging from his neck replied.

"Oh. So that's what it does."

"That's just one of the things she can do. You can ask her almost anything."

"How about 'why did that human leave after I brought up the History Tree?' And 'should I be concerned?' "

"She can't answer those questions, but I can," he replied. "See, you're special, like me. Only you're even more special, because you're a purebred appala. I'm only half. Because of what you are, the bad people might try to take you if they find you. I think she wants to use your mentions of keeping history and such to try to prove you shouldn't be taken away."

"Bad people?"

Yegor frowned. "You really don't know what's going on, do you?"

"No, because no one will explain it to me."

"The humans that created the Appala Cats are all long gone, but the place, ARC, is still around. The people who work there want us back."

"What do they want to do with me?"

"Sell you to a celebrity. Make you a war spy. Study you. Have a celebrity study you, then train you to be a war spy. You never can tell what they want, but it's never good. They probably won't kill you, though. It'd be a waste of money. Fortunately, you're with the good people right now. Unfortunately, the good people get paid by people helping the bad people, and if they don't let them know you're here, there will be some big problems."

Her stomach tightened. "So they can't bring me back home?"

"Bring you back like this? You can barely even stand up."

She clenched her teeth. "What does a resident feline therapist do?"

"Uhm, I, uh, talk to patients and keep them calm. Why?"

"You're not very good at it. If that was your real job, you'd have been dropped already. Why are you really here?"

Yegor flattened his ears. "Because if I weren't here pretending, I'd probably be dead. Look, I might not be as smart as a purebred, but even I can figure out these guys don't want another species running around, being equals with them on their own planet. These humans might be good, but in the end they're not all that different. You think those neat big hands of theirs are clean? Michelle hasn't, but Hye and the other doctors have killed domestics. Out of mercy, yes, but they do it. Call it 'putting to sleep.' "

Ember winced. The colors of shock and fear came back.

"Hey," he said, "don't worry about it too much, my genetically enhanced friend. They won't kill us, but in their eyes, we'll always be mistakes, so we all have to be fixed. No more appala kittens for you."

He snorted. The panel fogged up around his nose. "My paws are starting to hurt. I should go."

Yegor dropped back to the ground. As his pawsteps faded, he growled. "Wouldn't want to scare the patient."

CHAPTER 9
EMBER

While Michelle attended her strange humanly business, Ember examined her cage. It wasn't large, about the size of her parents' den, but without anyone else to share it with, the space didn't feel cramped. In one corner, she discovered a large, rectangular bowl filled with tiny white rocks. Nearby, closer to the moving panel, a second, smaller bowl greeted her with water. She managed to drag herself closer without too much pain. It wasn't the Kivyress, but it quenched her thirst all the same.

As she lapped her fill, she tried not to think too deeply about Yegor's foreboding mews. Too much speculating without enough facts could send her into another panic. Yet she couldn't help but wonder what it all meant.

'No more Appala kittens? If he's telling the truth, and I can't have kittens anymore, what will that mean if I do go back?'

Ember licked the odd grey skin of her foreleg. Grooming tickled now that she could feel each little spike of her tongue.

'Hyrees will obviously be disappointed. Will he want me still? The Colony would shun him even more if we stayed together. Especially now that I'm whatever this is. What if he—oh no. What if he tries it again? I can't stop him this time. What am I going to do? What is he going to do? He promised he'd never do it again, but he's broken promises before, and that's the problem with him. Why is he so unpredictable?'

She gave up on grooming, and instead rested her chin on the cold metal supporting her. *'Calm down, Em. It's probably selfish of me to think he'd kill himself because of this. He knows it was stupid the first time. He won't do it again. At least, I hope not. Of course, if he were to die, I wouldn't have to worry about—Ember, stop! What is wrong with you? What is wrong with me?'*

She sighed. She couldn't even force herself to feel guilty, or to imagine the shade of dark orange that usually came with it. Her insides felt numb and detached, as if nothing beyond her own head mattered. As if the uncertainty of her family's fate didn't matter. As if she could sleep soundly never knowing who lived or who died. Yet, if she never saw them again, how would their deaths affect her? She could keep them alive in her imagination, or kill them all and move on, but without them, what was there to move on to?

She snorted. *'That Yegor cat was probably just trying to mess with me. And Hyrees is probably fine. Now, find something more interesting and less heartless to think about.'*

After what felt like an eternity of letting her mind wander, Michelle returned to finish Thai's setup. She relinked Thai to her wrist phone, then gave Ember words or sentences to repeat in her head until the AI consistently recognized her thoughts.

[setup complete]
[Hello, Ember. I am Thai, your new personal assistant. Is there anything you would like me to do for you?]

'This is creepy. I know you're inside of me, but do you really have to sound like it? Then again, it would probably be even more unsettling if you sounded like you were somewhere in front of me. Or behind me. Wait, why do I need an assistant? When I'm not trapped by the creatures of my nightmares, I can usually tell what the weather is without asking someone. Or, in this case, the voice inside my head.'

"There. That should be it. Now that that's done, I can send the scan over, and your prosthetics should take on your original colors," Michelle said.

"What do you mean?" Ember asked.

"To print everything to fit you, I needed to scan you with a special machine. It looks at you and sees everything about you that needs fixing, even the damaged parts inside of you. Then it sends the information to something called a computer, which figures out how to put you back together. It also caught your fur colors. Those are important to do this."

Michelle tapped at the light square again, and Ember's legs changed colors. Ember stared in awe as her toes morphed from their bland dark grey to a familiar brown and white.

"Oh. They changed colors. How did they do that?" Ember asked. She examined the new tones of her prosthetics with analytical eyes. They weren't perfect; the browns were too dark and the whites too bright. Without fur, the color transitions looked blurry and unnatural, but when she imagined the dull grey they'd been moments before, she almost smiled.

"Using technology modeled after lizard skin," Michelle replied. "Now, how about you ask Thai something? We might as well make sure she, uhm, *it* works."

'Okay then. Thai, are there any mountains nearby?'

[Yes, you appear to be within the Appalachian Mountain Range. The nearest named peak is that of Little Toad Mountain.]

"That mountain is actually where you were found," Michelle said.

Ember grimaced. *'Oh, right, you're still connected, aren't you? Can you read my thoughts? I don't want you to read my thoughts. Thai, disconnect.'*

[device disconnected]

"So you do know where I'm from," Ember said. *'Wait, if they know where I'm from, they can find the Colony. What if they attack the Glade? Did I just get everyone taken? If I did, what am I going to do now? Calm down,*

Ember. That's what you're going to do. Maybe these humans really are nice. Calm down, and pretend like it's nothing.'

"This means you can bring me back, right?" she chanced. "Also, Little Toad Mountain? You humans couldn't have come up with anything better than that?"

Michelle swiped away her phone screen and straightened herself up. "There's probably a really interesting story behind why someone chose that name, but what that story is, I don't know. History was never my area of study."

"But you *can* bring me back, right?"

Michelle sighed and shook her head. "I'm sorry, sweetie."

Cyan flashed through her mind. "What? Why?"

"I don't think I can explain it in a way you'd understand. Just know that I want to help you, but things aren't always that simple."

Her heart thumped against her chest. Ember splayed, then curled her right paw over and over. The hisses and whirs of the robotics created a tune only she could control, with every note calculated to sound random. It offered some comfort, but not much. "Y-you're not going to look for my family, are you? Don't take them, please. I couldn't live with myself if I found out they'd all gotten captured and experimented on because of me."

Michelle tilted her head. "Captured and experimented on? You really do keep records, don't you? But no, I'm not going to look for your family."

"Are the bad people going to?" Ember asked.

"Oh, I get it. You've been talking with Yegor, haven't you? What did he tell you?"

"Uhm . . ." She hesitated. Michelle didn't seem like the type that would hurt or yell at someone if they didn't do or say what they were supposed to, but her judgments weren't always the most accurate. *'Truth, Ember,'* she thought. "Well, he kind of implied I couldn't have kittens, I think, but the way he said it was vague and weird, so I don't know for sure." She bit her tongue. "He also said there were bad people who wanted to have a celery train me to be a spy. Or something. It didn't sound good."

"A celery, huh? Well, he was right about some things. You can't have kittens anymore, but that may be your way out of here. There are people, the ones Yegor likes to refer to as 'the bad guys,' who might come for you in a few days. Because of your condition though, they probably won't need you. If that's the case, you can come home with me and finish recovering."

"But do I get to go back to my real home?"

"I don't know, sweetie. I don't know. Like I said, it's not that simple." Something beeped on her wrist phone. She looked at it for a moment, then swiped the screen away. "Sorry, I have to go. If you have any questions, you can either call me using Thai, or you can ask Dr. Sagong if you see him. Okay?"

Ember nodded.

"Did you just—" She shook her head. "Never mind. Goodbye, Ember. I'll see you in a day or two. Get some rest, okay?"

Michelle strode down the chamber without another word. As her footsteps faded, Ember sighed and glared at her paws again. *'What am I, now? Am I becoming something I'm not, or is this what I really am? A wildcat? A creature? A monster? A machine? Maybe I'm all of them at once. Or something else entirely. If I can't go back home, what am I going to do? Even if I do go back home, what will I do? I don't look like me anymore. They might not even recognize me.'* She wrapped her paws over her eyes, trying to find some comfort in the darkness. *'Everything I've worked for is gone. My family, my apprenticeship, my colony. I know for a fact that Commander Aspen and Tainu are gone. At least one Westerner probably died in the ambush. And even the ones who did survive I'm probably never going to see again. What am I going to do now?'*

Most times, when the misty oranges of sorrow crept into her thoughts, she tried to push them away to prevent herself from crying. Yet here, in the keep of the enemy, she had nothing left to lose. The domestics wouldn't judge her, and the humans didn't care, so she let the tears fall. It felt refreshing to cry in the darkness, and to not have to worry about hiding it from the world.

After a while, Hye's scent re-entered the chamber. "Hey, are you okay?"

Ember didn't move.

"Michelle said you might have some questions. I've still got a little break time left to burn, so I thought I'd try to answer them."

"Why is it so important to you that I stay here?" she whispered. "Michelle said the bad people probably wouldn't need me, so why can't I leave?"

"Oh boy. That's quite a question, and one I'm not sure how to answer in a way you'll understand. I'll try my best, though."

Ember lifted a mechanical paw and peered up at him with one eye. "Okay."

He drew a deep breath, then let it out in a sigh. "To start with, I'm something called a 'veterinarian.' I help injured animals heal. That's my job. If I don't do my job, I can't feed my family, and I'll lose my home. How I get my food is through something called 'money.' I use it for pretty much everything I and my family want or need. The people who give me this money have rules I have to follow. If I let you go against their instruction, I could lose everything. Please understand that I don't necessarily agree with all of these rules, but I can't change them, or break them. I'd be putting myself and my family at risk."

"What if those people decide they don't want me?" Ember asked.

Hye held up a hand. "Wait, let me finish. In addition to all this, you and your prosthetics represent a large amount of this money, and given how you're the first creature to have this procedure done, and at this scale, you also represent a significant technological breakthrough. We need you to show the world what can be done. You being here could help improve and save lives, especially now with so many war veterans coming back permanently wounded."

'War veterans? You're at war too?' Ember covered her face again to hide her tears. "You don't understand. I have to go back."

"Ember, listen to me, the parts we put inside you are self-healing, but only to an extent. They need to be monitored, otherwise they might break, and if that happened out in the woods, you'd be stuck. Chances are, we wouldn't be able to get to you, and you'd die. If you leave, you'd probably only have a few years to live, if that."

"But if I stay, I'll be a prisoner. That's not living. This isn't living. I can't be your example of life if I'm not living. I have to go back."

Hye sighed. "We can talk about this more, later. If this really is that important to you, I'll see if I can work something out. For now, my break is over. I should get back to work. Before I do, you're probably hungry, so let me go get you something to eat. We had nutrients running to you while you were under, but when it comes down to it, there's nothing like real food."

Since she'd woken up, the thought of food had never once crossed her mind. Now, with even a chance at going home, she could relax enough to listen to her stomach. It growled at her.

"I guess I am hungry. Don't give me anything too big, please. I'll make myself sick if I try to eat it all. Maybe just a mouse."

Hye had already ventured farther into the chamber and out of earshot. After a few moments of waiting, he returned with another bowl, similar to the one containing her water. A strong, fishy scent filled the area. The domestics nearby perked up. A few of them yowled for him to give it to them. He opened the panel, set the dish in front of her, then closed it again, as if she might try to escape.

Ember squinted and leaned back as the nauseating smell clogged her nose. She coughed, then peered into the bowl. Little flakes of what appeared to be cooked meat filled the bottom, and a thick brown goo coated them.

"Er, what is this?" she asked.

"Food," Hye replied. "Give it a try. If you don't like it, I'll find something else."

That's not very specific,' she thought, fighting back a gag. "Food? Did someone else eat it already? Or is it rotten?"

Hye raised a hand to scratch the back of his head. "No, and no. Most domestics love strong-smelling food, so it's made to smell strong. Just try it, okay? It might surprise you."

'Come on, Em. Give it a chance. Food is food, and food is valuable, and you should be grateful for it.' Ember held her breath and licked her meal. She licked it again, then ate a meat flake.

143

"Not bad," she said. "Thank you."

"Okay, great. I need to get back to work now. Enjoy your meal."

'I mean, it's not good either, but it'll keep me from starving, so I should eat it.'

Ember stared down at the slime-covered food. Another canid of some kind barked in the distance. More foreign clanking and tapping noises came from somewhere nearby. The sounds of unseen footsteps meandered the alien structure. They made her heart palpitate every time they drew nearer. She did her best to ignore it all and leaned over to nibble at another piece of meat. A soft chime echoed through her head.

[You have one new message from Michelle Castell.]
[Would you like to view it?]

'Yes. I don't know what a message is, but show me.'

[Hye told me to make you an ETAg. You're going to need it if you want to go back home. I'll see you tomorrow, sweetie.]
[Would you like to reply?]

'So that's what it is. I guess you can tell her "thanks and bye?" '

[Message sent]

———

Time passed like a slug crawling up a mountain. Humans entered and left, ignoring her for the most part, but Ember didn't ignore them; they were fascinating to watch as they removed or added cats. Sometimes they would take out a domestic, then bring it back sometime later, either sleeping or with a fresh look of terror on the unfortunate feline's face. It made her see-feel silver when it happened, but the eclectic variety of reactions was morbidly fascinating.

Every time they removed a cat, Ember asked where they were taking it. Occasionally she'd get a reply, but most of the time they didn't even seem to hear her. When the anxious fat cat got removed, the human collecting him happened to be one of the few who answered her questions.

"Where is he going?" Ember asked.

"Back home," the human said.

"What are you doing with me? What are you doing?" the fat cat mewed.

The human—a lanky one with pale, speckled skin, and a fur tuft the color of fire—hefted the cat up, then placed him in a smaller, more movable cage. "Bring you home. Do not fear, Stripes. You okay," he replied in broken Felid.

"Oh good, oh good, oh good. I want to go home. This place is scary, and I haven't gotten pet right in *ages*."

Ember chuffed. *'Stripes, huh? Your family wasn't very creative, was it?'*

Yet she couldn't help but smile at the kitten-like excitement in Stripes's mews as the human carried him away. Primitive as his mind might be, he clearly loved the people who cared for him. Maybe not as strongly as she loved her family, but the bond existed.

The History Tree is wrong. It has to be, at least partly. Some humans aren't as bad as Dark thought. I'll have to clawmark about this on something when I get back. They'll never believe most of it, but they already think I'm crazy, so I'm going to do it anyway.'

She pulled her water bowl close enough to drink. *'Not onto the History Tree, obviously, because then Whitehaze would have a fit. But I should make a tablet or two on my experiences here. Oh! And Thai can help. Look, now you've got a project you can work on, along with almost all the resources to do it. Except claws, but they can probably make some for you. And it'll improve your clawmarking and history-telling skills in the process. See, Ember? Everything's going to be okay.'*

She finished drinking and rested her chin against her cold, lifeless forelegs. *'This will be a good thing, if you know how to use it.'* She snapped her head back up. The headache came back, but she ignored it. *'Wait, if I could find* out the name of a mountain, what else can I find out? Thai, how many mountains are there?'

[There are 1,000,821 named mountains in the world, but there are many others that have not been named.]

A tiny burst of pride flared in her chest. *'I have almost every piece of collected human knowledge available at my command. I can learn more than anyone else in the Valley. I can do so much with this. Mom and Dad will be so proud of me. And—oh! All the new things Kivy and I can talk about. I just need to get Michelle to make me claws that never get dull. Then, shorter life or not, I will be powerful. Instead of treating me like I'm crazy, the Colony might finally come to me with respect. Even Silentstream. I guess I found that missing piece, so now everything will be okay.'*

Her mind sent her a series of all-too-vivid images from the night of the ambush. Her excitement faded. *'Oh. Right.'*

Tainu and Aspen were dead. With the ambush, any number of others could've fallen, and on top of that, everyone still alive thought she was dead. When she returned, if she returned at all, she'd no longer be the historian apprentice, and those were just the facts.

'Stop getting your hopes up, Ember. The likelihood of everything more or less going back to normal again is on par with a giant purple elk walking in right now and coughing up a mouse on my head. It's possible, but not going to happen. And the chance of anyone from back home believing Thai is low too. Anything human-made is bad.' She looked down at her prosthetics. Another wave of yellow flashed through her mind. *'They might chase me away. What if they chase me away? Then what? I can't survive in the Lowlands.'*

She mewled softly and shook her head. *'Don't think about that right now.'*

As time crawled forward, Ember busied herself by asking Thai questions about anything and everything. She asked questions about the stars, questions about the Earth, and even questions about Colony Cats, or 'appalas,' as the humans referred to them. She discovered something the humans called a 'documentary'—which covered the humans' side of the story —and watched it in her head. Thai linked up with her nervous system and projected moving pictures into her mind's eye. It was like visiting a vivid memory she'd never once experienced.

Right from the beginning, she discovered some bitter truths about the ways her ancestors, along with several intelligent rats and dogs, had been treated. She didn't have to understand their language to figure out these humans weren't like the ones she'd met. At one point, a clip from before the escape appeared. It showed a human in white clothes holding Dark himself in place against an elevated platform. The human needed to raise his voice to speak over Dark's meows for help. Ember had to strain her mind to hear him over the ambience of the Center, and the talking person in the documentary didn't help. Yet Dark kept his voice level, making him just a tiny bit easier to focus on. Calm cats made the best focal points.

"If there's anyone out there listening to this," he said, "please help us. They treat us as objects. They run us through dangerous experiments. They force us to mate without our consent. Please, get us out of here, or send someone to kill us all," he said.

Ember shivered. She wondered how long he'd spent there after those desperate pleas before he'd come up with an escape plan and left with his kin.

The human continued to speak over videos of seemingly harmless experiments showing off the intelligence of appalas, along with the dogs and rats. At one point she spotted a cat who could only be Forestfire, with her blazing tabby coat. Forestfire watched a screen as groups of shapes appeared on it. With every shift in amounts, she selected the ones with the largest numbers by raking her claws across the screen. Even Ember could recognize the spite in her eyes.

Other clips showed the escape as it happened through security footage. Her heart sank each time it showed a cat getting left behind, and it fell even harder when those trapped or caught gestured for their kin to keep going. The cats they'd lost during the escape were more brave than the ones who'd made it, just as Dark himself had clawed into the History Tree.

'I wonder what would've happened if they'd taken the time to free the dogs and rats. They could've helped, but who and how many more would've been captured? And then, of course, they wouldn't be able to discuss plans or improvisations in those plans, so it would've added confusion to the chaos. That wouldn't have been good. But still.'

The documentary then went on to show humans in gaudy outfits holding appala cats and dogs by long vine-like things wrapped around the canines' and felines' necks. Ember bit her tongue. The collars on some of them were designed to tighten if they struggled. One appala had a collar with some kind of mechanical contraption on it. She couldn't make out what it did.

While the human was talking, the cat accidentally jerked its leash while following some scent in the air. The human pressed a button. The cat yowled in pain and surprise, then scampered back to the human's side. The human herself just laughed.

'This is what happened to the ones who stayed? Would Dark have kept going if he knew about this? Would he have tried to save them, and the other animals too? They were just like us, but without a leader. I guess it's for the better that he kept going. Otherwise they might have all ended up like that. If they don't let me go, is that my future too?'

Unmoving images appeared of one of the humans—the button-presser— along with music, followed by an image of the appala, now bloodied and vicious-looking. Ember recognized the spray pattern marring the cat's fur; he'd had enough, and managed to kill the human by severing an artery, most likely in her arm.

Two similar montages followed, both of these with dogs as the killers. This supposedly sad display was replaced with footage of cats and dogs in rows upon rows of cages. The captured animals sat in their cells, most of them sitting tall and proud. Even the young ones looked ready to accept their fates with dignity. The humans feared them, so they were to die for crimes they didn't commit.

The documentary switched to videos of deer and birds, humans with long, loud, stick-like contraptions, and a still image of a dead appala with a bleeding hole in its side.

Ember's heart leaped into her throat. She bit her tongue harder and thought, *'Turn it off, Thai! Please, turn it off!'*

The documentary disappeared. Ember opened her eyes, breathing heavily. What she could see of the Center looked peaceful, too peaceful compared to the things her ancestors and their kin had faced.

A dog yipped, causing her mind to drift to the canines of ARC.

'Dark never even mentioned there were other species there. Did he ever feel guilty about not even trying to save them? Of course, he probably never thought all that would happen, and he never knew it did. It's also strange how the rats just disappear after the first part. What happened to them? Did they escape too? Or were they all killed?'

Ember shivered. *'The History Tree was right after all. Partially. They can be kind enough to save my life, or cruel enough to kill all those innocents. And yet, they see* us *as savages only fit to be destroyed. That was history. I just watched history play out in my own head. The terrifying thing is, I'm not so sure I like it now.'*

After what seemed like an eternity, Hye returned and gave her another dish of gooey meat. When she finished, he helped her into the larger, rectangular bowl which he called a 'litter box.' Finally, he rubbed something cold, white, and sticky on her furless patches of skin. He didn't say much of anything, but he slow-blinked and dipped his head as he left, which only served to confuse her.

As time passed, everyone left—all the humans, at least. Unlike the sun, human lighting didn't fade gradually; it switched from day to night in an instant. Ember closed one eye to make them adjust faster, then blinked a few times to get the lopsided feeling away. All around her, animals snored, or mewed, or barked, or growled.

'How in the forest am I supposed to get to sleep in all this? It's almost as loud as it was when the humans were here crashing around and talking.'

[Incoming call from Dr. Hye-sung Sagong.]

[Would you like to accept?]

'What is this? Can I talk to him with my thoughts now? That's weird, but in a way, maybe it's a good thing. I don't stutter when I think. Then again, what if I accidentally think about something wrong? Come on, Ember. He's not like them. He's safe. He's one of the good ones. He isn't going to kill you with a loud stick. He isn't going to hurt you with your own thoughts.' Ember's heart thumped with anxious excitement and curiosity. 'Yes, I accept. Hello?'

'Hey, Ember,' Hye replied. His thought-voice was different from his normal one; it was soft, almost sleepy, and came from everywhere at once. 'Sorry I have to contact you like this, but I hope you can understand the risks we might be taking by trying to help you.'

'No, I think I understand a little too well. You humans are scary.'

'Oh no, what did you find?'

'Something called a "documentary" about this place called ARC. Turns out they mass-murdered several of us. And not just cats. There were dogs and rats too. All of them died.'

'Hmm,' he thought after several moments of silence. 'I didn't realize anyone could legally make a documentary about that, but it has been almost a century. It's kind of old news at this point, and I think the initial experiment did get declassified at some point in the early twenties, back when they had the bounty. Anyway, I guess Michelle told you she's getting you an ETAg, huh?'

Ember splayed out her forelegs and rested her chin on the cage floor. 'Yes. So how is it going to help me more than a set of claws? I do need claws if I'm going to survive back at home. And I already have Thai. From what I've seen, an ETAg doesn't seem all that different. Just maybe a little more physical.'

'That's just it. In addition to letting you ask questions out loud, it would also let any person who found you know you've been in contact with

150

humans. The hope is that, if they take you in, they'll think you belong to Michelle and bring you to her. Then she can bring you back home, safe and sound. Then, of course, I can't forget its main function as a translation device. You can use it to speak with any human or domestic dog. Thai will be linked with your ETAg as an expansion, by the way. There'd be no point in giving you two separate AIs. If we did, you might end up with an echo effect.'

Ember smiled faintly. 'That would be funny.' Her mind showed her an image of Echo the Easterner. Her smile faded. 'What will she think of me now that our colonies are probably at war and I've killed Tainu?'

'As for the rest of the plan, I'm going to let you try to stand and walk tomorrow,' he continued, as if he hadn't heard her thoughts of war or death. Or maybe he already knew and simply wasn't surprised. 'In any other case, I'd recommend waiting a day or two more, just to make sure everything sits together, but we have to act fast. They know you're here and will be coming to get you within the next few days. If they do end up wanting you, you'll need to be able to move on your own if you want to ever see your family again.'

'You didn't hear that, did you? What I was thinking? You didn't react, and I was wondering.' Ember gnawed on her tongue. 'Also, what will happen to you and Michelle if y'all help me escape?'

'I probably didn't hear it. There are many layers of thought, and it's designed to only pick up the conversational kind, so anything directed at yourself won't go through. And if everything works as planned, nothing. Oh, and here's my stop. I'm going to have to let you go. I'll see you tomorrow, okay? Goodbye.'

Ember glanced at her paws. The dreary red of disappointment entered her mind. He hadn't mentioned undulling claws at all. 'Wait, one last thing. Yegor said I can't have kittens anymore. I asked Michelle about it, and I think she agreed, but they both brushed over it, so I was wondering if I may have misunderstood. I mean, it just seems like a really odd thing to say, and I'm a little leery of finding out how they know.'

151

Hye hesitated again. Ember wiggled her toes while she waited. The tiny whirs following her movements were funny little sounds. Like whining, mechanical coyotes with sore throats. She didn't enjoy them but hoped that, with time, she might at least become used to it all.

'Yegor,' he finally thought. 'Of course he would tell you. That cat.'

'So it is true?' Ember asked.

'Yes, I'm afraid so, but it's the law. Every stray or feral we get in must be spayed or neutered, which is where we, er, remove the parts of you that make the kittens. The only exception to that law is purebred appalas, but at the time we'd gotten you in, what kind of cat you were was not our main concern. We don't get a lot of your breed, for obvious reasons, so we kind of forgot about your exemption. There's a whole list of other reasons aside from those, but I really don't have time to name them. We can talk it over tomorrow.'

'One less thing I have to worry about, I guess,' she thought to herself. She directed her thoughts back to Hye. 'Okay. We don't have to, though.' She pinned back her ears. 'What's done is done. I'd rather talk about getting some new claws. I need them a lot more than I need a litter of kittens right now.'

'You aren't upset?' he asked.

'No. Well, I mean, it might mess up a few plans, mostly the plans of cats who are not me, and it will definitely lower my social status, but I was low already, so that's fine. It's not important right now. I mean, I've got robot legs. I still need to figure out how I feel about them. And I've got a family that probably thinks I'm dead. That's important. Then, of course, there's Hyrees, and he's . . .' She lowered her head against the den's floor. 'Tahg, I just hope he's still alive. Anyways, I'll let you get back to what you were doing. Bye.'

'Okay, then. Goodbye.'

[call ended]

CHAPTER 10
CLOUD

"Hyrees, please eat," Songbird said.

"I'm not hungry," Hyrees replied.

He shoved the slab of freshly roasted deer meat away, coating it with muddy snow. The once well-stocked fat reserves lining his ribs were already gone.

Cloud growled. "You know, she risked her life to help catch that for us. You will eat it, Hyrees. Now stop pushing it around the muck, or I'll make you eat that too."

Hyrees glared into his eyes. "Stop trying to pretend to be my parents. Mom and Dad are dead. Let them be dead, and leave me alone."

He stormed away and disappeared into Wren's old den. Cloud sighed. His muscles stung from a long day of patrolling. With Wren gone, he needed to cover nearly twice the distance in the same amount of time, and his body hated him for it. Songbird shot him a glance, but he couldn't, for the life of him, figure out what it meant.

Winter wind cut through the Glade relentlessly. The red glow of the evening sky did nothing to ease the chill. Scents of smoke and mustiness rode the gale, mixing with the stench of dead prey and unkempt fur. It was enough to make his stomach churn.

Songbird padded closer. She pressed her cheek against him, creating a spot of warmth on his neck. "If he keeps this up, we're going to lose him. I don't know what to do."

Cloud rested his chin against her forehead. "I hate to say this, but I'm not sure there's much we can do. It may well be best to let him have his way. Leave him alone for now, and let him go through the process of grieving on his own time. He'll come around when he's ready."

"Maybe I could talk to him," Farlight said. "I know what you said, but what if he doesn't? I don't want to have to wait until later to try to save him when I could've done it today."

Farlight glanced around the Glade. Without Kivyress, he seemed more wary, but she was already asleep. With Ember gone, she'd started turning in early. For the first time in her short little life, she seemed to enjoy sleeping. Farlight, however, had gotten into a habit of staying up with Hyrees. Ever since that fateful battle five days ago, the two brothers spent the nights together in Wren's den. Lupine made an announcement officially allowing them to stay there a day after the fight, which infuriated Cloud. As if the commander needed to give his consent before they were allowed to have the den they'd grown up in. It wasn't a gift to be given—it was their right.

Cloud sighed. "I guess so, but if he doesn't respond, leave him alone."

"Yes, sir," Farlight mumbled as he loped after his brother.

Once he got out of earshot, Cloud growled. "I can not believe . . . Tahg, Wren would be ashamed. There is a war to prepare for. Cats have already died, and he's over here trying to starve himself? Of all the selfish, immature th—"

"Cloud," Songbird hissed.

"What? He's being selfish and immature. I lost the same cats he lost. You lost them too. Tahg, everyone's lost someone important at some point. Losing is a part of life. He needs to deal with it like an adult."

"But he's not. He's dealing with it like him," she said. Tears built up in her eyes, making them glisten in the fading light. "Listen, Cloud, Hyrees is not you. He doesn't think like you, he doesn't act like you, and he doesn't feel like you. Insulting him behind his back isn't going to do any good, especially if he overhears."

He pinned back his ears and lowered his head. "Sorry, I shouldn't have said that. Do you want me to talk to him?"

"No. I want you to take your own advice and leave him alone. If anyone has a chance at reaching him, it's Farlight. Like you said, we'll only make things worse." She sighed and closed her eyes. "And if you need another reason to keep him alive—"

Her voice broke. She made no attempts to fix it and instead cried in silence. Cloud sucked in a deep breath, then let it out in another long sigh.

'I know. If she really does come back, and he's dead . . . But it would still be entirely his fault. Not mine. I'm sorry, Song, but I can't feel sorry for him. He's hurting himself, and he's doing it intentionally. It's not tragic, it's what he wants.'

"Cloud, do you really think she's still alive? Be honest with me," Songbird whispered.

'I don't know, Song. You know I don't know.'

For a day or two after the fight, it was easy to think she might still be okay, but on the third and fourth days, hope dwindled. Now, five days later, he didn't know what to believe. Hope was nice, in theory, but it was keeping him from moving on. There wasn't enough time to mourn, or wait, or hope for the improbable. It was time to let go.

"I don't know." He lowered his voice so Kivyress wouldn't hear. "But most likely not. I don't . . . I don't think she is. I'm sorry, Song."

She sniffed a few times, then, to his surprise, she smiled. That gentle, sweet smile of hers could make anything better—okay, even.

"Thank you." She sniffed again. "I think I already knew, but . . . I can let her rest now. And maybe I can get some rest too, since there's no point in staying up all night anymore."

She rubbed a forepaw against her face. When she pulled it away, muddy snow dotted her fur. "I should probably let Kivy know. I'll take her out to the Field tomorrow before training and tell her. Then we can say our goodbyes together and find something nice to put on her memorial."

"Okay. I would come with y'all, but you know I have to work," Cloud replied.

The wind grew stronger. Cloud's gaze wandered over to the History Tree. Ember's clayvine hung from the branch she'd left it on all those nights ago. He watched it sway in the breeze for a few moments, then stood.

"Sorry, Song, I have to go; there's another mandatory council meeting tonight. I love you. Just wanted to make sure you know that."

She got up and pressed her nose against his. He wanted her to never pull away. He wanted to spend the rest of his life near her, but those precious few moments each evening and those late, fitful nights were all he could get.

She backed away. "I know. I love you too. Don't stay up too late, okay?"

"I'll try not to. Might not have much of a choice, though. There's so much that needs to be done, and not enough time to do it. I still haven't given Farlight a proper lesson yet, and I was supposed to be on day three of his training yesterday."

"You're setting up some really unreasonable expectations for yourself. You should take a break. Don't hurt yourself. No one's forcing you to work this hard except you," Songbird said.

"But I have to try. Otherwise, we're all dead. Everyone."

"Well, all that being said, I guess you can tell Whitehaze to look for someone else. No use putting off dealing with the little problems. The longer we wait, the more little problems there'll be. It'll all grow and grow until it becomes a mountain so steep we can't climb it."

"I will. I have to go now."

He turned to leave but stopped short; Hyrees and Farlight were walking toward him.

"Sorry for yelling," Hyrees muttered.

He padded past them, Farlight at his side. Cloud and Songbird exchanged looks of surprise as he moved over to the meat he'd abandoned, then crouched down and ate.

"What did you tell him?" Songbird whispered to Farlight.

She'd never had the quietest whisper, and the wavering in her voice only amplified it. Hyrees flicked back his ears but said nothing.

"I just spoke with him." Farlight lowered his voice to a more controlled, less-audible level. "I may have, er, *influenced* him a little, but it was either that or losing him. I know how y'all feel about that, but I don't mind trading some integrity for my own brother's life. He's more important."

Songbird sighed. "Well, it worked. I won't complain."

Cloud grimaced and walked away toward Lupine's den. *'Manipulation. Of course. Yes, I'm so glad you learned how to do that. It is, after all, a skill every good commander must possess.'*

Doubt stabbed him in the head. Even mentioning manipulation tactics made his throat tighten. It made him second-guess everything. It made him wonder if Aspen had ever truly cared about him, or if he'd fallen for act upon act, pushing himself to the limit for a tom who only saw him as a tool—even after that tom's untimely death.

He shook his head as he approached the gathering of council members. Lupine sat on top of his den, as Aspen had once done. But instead of looking up at him with admiration, Cloud glared at him with disdain. Lupine wasn't fit to lead on a peaceful spring afternoon, much less for several mooncycles in the middle of winter during a time of war.

"Ah, good, y-y-you made it, Cloud," Lupine said. "I-I was beginning to worry you'd abandoned us."

"If I abandoned you," Cloud said, sitting down and letting his tail thrash with indignation, "this colony would likely collapse. Those Easterners have us on the ledge already. I'm not going to be the one to push us over. So long as everyone here continues to do their part, we will make it through this. Until that happens, though, I expect you all to work like wolves."

"What do you think we've been doing?" Whitehaze asked.

"You've been sitting in the History Tree, wandering the forest, and coming to meetings."

Whitehaze growled. "You know I'm getting old. I can't patrol anymore, and I'm too slow to hunt. There's only so much good someone can do when he's lived through sixteen winters, kitten. What do you want me to do?"

"Find a new apprentice."

Whitehaze flicked back his ears. "A few days ago, you were insisting your daughter would come home. You told me to wait. Against Lupine's initial orders, might I add."

"I was mistaken. Use tomorrow to look for a willing enough young cat, and start training them. We need to get the little things out the way as soon as possible so we can focus on the bigger problems, like how we can better fortify the Glade, and what supplies we'll need to get or make more of. The longer we wait to prepare, the more vulnerable we become."

"Cloud, who is the commander here?" Lupine asked.

Cloud met his gaze, and considered, for a moment, saying, 'I am.' Yet he knew better than to challenge him. He'd lose his position in a heartbeat. "You are, sir. What's your plan for tomorrow?"

Lupine snorted. An icy puff of steam left his nostrils. "A-as suggested, Whitehaze, you should t-try to find a, uh, a new apprentice. The daily tasks still need to be taken care of, so-so most of your schedules will not change. However, I-I'll be sending several clayworkers out with you and other hunters and guards to h-help lighten the load. Some of you are currently working alone, which is not safe. Your new partners may need some refreshing on fighting and hunting techniques, but there-there shouldn't be anything too difficult for them t-to remember. The rest of the clayworkers will be sent out with the gatherers to get supplies to reinforce the a-abatis wall. Does anyone have any problems with this arrangement?"

A murmur of 'noes' rumbled through the Council.

"Does anyone have any i-i-ideas as to how this plan c-could be improved upon?" Lupine asked.

"Yes, as a matter of fact, I do," Cloud replied.

"W-what's your suggestion?"

"We divide the remaining clayworkers into two groups; one group works on the abatis wall, and the other helps make us some personal protection: guard pieces for our most vulnerable places. Neck and leg protection especially, as those are the most common places for one-bite kills."

"A-and how are you suggesting they make these protective pieces?"

"I have some ideas for designs. I can help them with the basic concept, then they can improve it as they see fit. It would require me to take some time away from the Council tomorrow, and I may need to skip a meal, but I can do it. It may well save lives when the time comes."

"Y-you may be putting a little t-too much faith in yourself, Cloud. I'll allow you two of the clayworkers of your choice to help you out with this experiment of y-yours, but the rest will work on the wall. Like you said, we c-c-can't afford to wait. I'd rather put more effort into something I know will make a difference than something that might a-amount to nothing. I'm sure you can understand this logic."

"If my idea does work, will you give me a bigger team?" Cloud asked.

"Y-yes, but only if it looks like something we can actually use."

He gritted his teeth together. "I'll make sure it is, sir."

"Very well," Lupine said. "Now, what about long-term p-planning? I p-p-propose waiting until spring to make any moves they might consider offensive. Thoughts?"

"Sir, the real question is, should we do anything offensive at all?" a sable brown tomcat named Redwater asked. His piercing orange eyes looked from cat to cat. "I suggest we prepare for the worst, and hope for the best. The positioning of the Rift gives the East a tactical advantage, so attacking them would only be Stone Ridge over again. We'd kill ourselves off. Besides, our recent fight might well have been a misunderstanding caused by that Rogue, Tainu. War or not, we can't risk jumping to conclusions."

Lupine snorted again. "Jade herself d-d-declared war on us. Hoping nothing will happen at this point is w-wishful thinking. Keep your paws on the ground."

"Sir, you've missed my point," Redwater said. "What if that Rogue acted on her own? She had no previous connections with Jade, but if she attacked on her own accord, why would she do what she did? What was her motivation? It doesn't make sense."

"Yet, her working w-with Jade to lure us into a trap does. Let's move on to s-some . . . something more important."

"But this might *be* important."

The argument continued deeper into the night. Occasionally another council member would pitch in their thoughts, but most of them, including Cloud, remained silent and annoyed. Then the cat sitting beside Cloud walked over to Redwater and spat, "It's not important. Nobody cares. Let's get back to the actual meeting."

Redwater jumped into a stand. His challenger ran his claws down his ruddy muzzle.

"You just made a mistake," Redwater growled, torn nose dripping with blood.

"*I* made a mistake? *You* lunged at *me*! I was defending myself," his challenger replied.

"Alright, that's enough!" Lupine growled. "M-meeting dismissed. You can all go to your dens. I . . . I need some rest. Whitehaze, c-could I speak with you in private?"

Whitehaze lowered his head. "Yes, Commander Lupine. I don't know what I can help you with, but I'll try my best."

'Well, that's a lot of time I'll never get back. I wonder how long it'll take for Lupine to replace me with Whitehaze. He certainly trusts him more. Maybe I'd be better off no longer being chief advisor. It would make it easier to break away. Still need to talk it over with Song, but that's for later.'

A slight rustle hit his ears as he passed the Northern Entrance. Somewhere beyond the Glade, someone coughed.

'That sounds a lot more like choking than trying to get rid of a furball.'

He walked out of the Glade to investigate. Hyrees sat by a tree a few leaps away, hunched over and gagging himself with a forepaw. Cloud opened his mouth to ask what he was doing, but before he could, Hyrees retched, and coughed out what remained of his meal. As Hyrees got to his feet, Cloud scampered back to the Glade to wait for him. Hyrees walked past, sides heaving and gaze fixed on the ground.

"Furball?" Cloud asked.

Hyrees jerked back. "C-Cloud! I didn't realize the meeting was over. Uhm, yeah. Yeah, those . . . those furballs are something else."

"You know, I never did tell you how proud I was of you for eating earlier today. I'm sure Ember would want you to keep going."

His entire face drooped. "Yeah, yeah, I'm sure she would. But you know, when she does come back, she's going to be so proud of me. I almost look like a normal cat. Who knows? I might even edge into handsome soon."

"Oh, so that's what this is about?" Cloud asked. "In that case, you can go back to eating meals. You're not fat. Not anymore."

"Don't lie to me, Cloud. I can take the truth," Hyrees replied.

Cloud grimaced. Anger flared in his chest as he stepped closer. "You want the truth? Ember is gone, and she isn't coming back. Stop trying to impress her."

Hyrees backed away. "But you said—"

"I know what I said, okay?" he growled. "But the truth is, she was almost dead when I found her. It was kittenish hope that caused me to lie to myself, and to lie to you. I suggest you try your best to move on, because there are more important things to deal with right now. This colony is at war, and we need everyone to do their part to keep the rest of us alive."

Hyrees stumbled backward. "They're dead, and you don't care, do you? You never cared! You never cared about me, or anyone else, have you?"

Cloud curled back his lips. "Hyrees, that's not what I said. They're gone, and it hurts—it hurts me more than anything I've ever felt before, but all those cats we lost are gone. Crying over them isn't going to help those of us who are still living. That's not to say we should forget them, but there comes a point when you have to move on. You have to grow up and let go of them."

"You can patrol without me tomorrow," Hyrees growled.

He scampered away, then disappeared into his den. Cloud sighed and entered the cramped hole he called his own; though in reality, the den belonged to the Colony, just like everything else.

'Was that the wrong thing to say? I think I may have just made a

mistake. Well, I guess there's no going back now. I hope Farlight can continue getting him to eat. For his sake.'

He lay down beside Songbird, with Kivyress kept warm between them. Neither cat stirred. Cloud rested his chin against the frigid dirt ground.

'Then again, what if he's right? Is it heartlessness or strength, being the first one in the Colony to move on? I don't know. But logic is much more trustworthy than emotions. If it's heartless to push them away, call me heartless.'

———

As promised, Hyrees didn't show up to patrol. Cloud considered recruiting a clayworker to be his partner but decided against it. He needed a fresh cat to help him construct the armor prototype. He could patrol alone.

After getting a quick, light meal and saying goodbye to Songbird and Kivyress, he left. Somewhere in the back of his mind, he realized Farlight had wandered off too, but he ignored the thought and tried to focus on his surroundings. By sunset, he'd chased away two Outsiders and fought with a feisty Rogue—three times more cats than any normal day.

As the sun set behind him, he limped his way back to the Glade. The gash on his left foreleg left a trail of red in the snow. He clenched his jaw as the taste of blood faded from his tongue.

'I wonder how long it'll take a coyote or fox to drag away the body. They aren't as common as they used to be,' he thought.

In the fight, the Rogue had attempted to kill him. He'd responded with a bite to the throat. Cloud sighed. It wasn't the first time he'd taken a life for the safety of his kin, and if he survived the winter, it wouldn't be the last.

When he neared the Glade, a familiar yowl met him. He broke into a run. A few leaps outside the abatis, a young tom named Rowan had Hyrees pinned. Several other youths watched, amused by Hyrees's helpless struggles.

"Come on, half-breed," Rowan snarled with an exaggerated Eastern accent. "Fight me! You aren't a molly, are you? Come on and fight like a tom!

The Colony's at war. You're not gonna fight in it, coward?"

"Get off of me," Hyrees growled.

He ran his claws down Rowan's leg. Rowan flinched but didn't move.

Before Cloud could reach them, Farlight charged out of the Glade and shoved his brother's attacker to the ground. He placed his claws against the larger tom's throat.

"I'm a half-breed too, Rowan," Farlight growled. "Why aren't you assaulting me?"

"F-Farlight—no, that wasn't what it looked like," Rowan stammered. "I just—"

"I don't care what it looked like, *Rowan*. You hurt my brother. All of you, really." The youths around them winced as Farlight eyed each one in turn. He released Rowan and went to help his brother up.

With Hyrees no longer in immediate danger, Cloud slowed to a walk; his legs still ached from the patrol.

"Hey!" he snapped as he neared the group. "Don't any of you have anything better to do?"

He pushed through the gathering of spectators, most of whom scattered when they realized who he was.

Rowan rolled to his feet and lowered his head. "Sorry, sir. We were just practicing. I was, uh, trying to help him get stronger."

Farlight's eyes narrowed at his weak defense.

Cloud curled back a lip, revealing one of his fangs. "It only counts as practice if both participants are willing. Rowan, he's lost almost everything." He raised his voice, hoping most of the former onlookers would hear. "How do you have the insolence to attack him like that? You're a disgrace to your parents and your colony. This is a time of war. You should be building up your fellow colonymates, not ripping them apart like a bear. If you keep up this kind of kittenish behavior, I can only imagine one possible future for you, and I'm afraid it's not a good one. Now go back into the Glade and make yourself useful for a change. I expect to see some self-improvement within the coming mooncycle."

Rowan lowered his head and tried to make himself look as small as possible. "Yes, sir. Sorry, sir."

"Don't apologize to him. Apologize to my brother. He's the one you hurt," Farlight growled.

"Sorry, Hyrees. Guess I wasn't really thinking about what I was doing," he said, voice void of emotion.

He scampered into the Glade, tail tucked between his legs. Cloud snorted as he watched him run, then turned to face Hyrees, who sat in silence while Farlight groomed his bleeding muzzle.

"Are you okay?" Cloud asked.

"I'm fine. So why did you stand up for me this time? Need me for something? I know you didn't do it out of the kindness of your heart," Hyrees said, leaning closer to his brother's side.

Cloud hesitated, wondering if it would be a good time to ask him about helping with the guard pieces.

"Who am I trying to fool? Of course you do," Hyrees muttered.

Cloud opened his mouth to protest but Hyrees cut him off. "Don't say anything. I may not have good eyes, but I don't need them to see that you just want to use me."

Cloud growled. "I saved you because it was the right thing to do. Whether or not I need your assistance had nothing to do with it. But that being said, if you would be willing to help me develop some protective pieces for the Colony, it would be much appreciated, and may well save lives in the near future, but you don't have to help. In fact, you can choose to never speak with me again. It doesn't matter, because I will continue to care about you, and I will continue to protect you, whether you appreciate it, or are useful to me, or not. Because I love you, Hyrees. Whether you see me that way or not, we are family, and I will care for you like family."

"And now you're trying to manipulate me. You're just as bad as all the other high-ranks."

Hyrees pushed past him and walked deeper into the Glade. Farlight got up and followed after him, giving Cloud a look somewhere between an apology and a rebuke.

"Hyrees, wait," Farlight called. "Maybe at least hear him out? He's not exactly being tactful right now, no, but he does have a point."

Cloud flattened his ears and trotted after them. "Hold on, Hyrees, what can I do to prove myself?"

"You can leave me alone," Hyrees said. His unfocused gaze locked onto Cloud's wound. It darted to Farlight, who waited at his side, then landed back on Cloud. He sighed. "Look, I'll patrol with you tomorrow, but don't try to talk to me unless it's to point out some crazy wildcat is about to pounce. Okay?"

"I can do that." He nodded a polite 'thank you' to Farlight, who responded with a nod of his own.

Hyrees sighed again and padded away toward his den. Farlight followed beside him, resting his head against his brother's neck. Cloud watched them for a few moments, then continued farther into the Glade.

All around him, cats returned from a long day of work. Only a few sunsets before, evening had been the most jovial time of day, but now, not a single Westerner smiled.

As he neared a fire pit, Songbird ran up to him. "Cloud, what happened to you this time?"

"Got into a fight. I'll be fine," he replied

"You're going to get it cleaned, right?"

"No, I need to go find Fledge and get started with the protective pieces. I've only got until nightfall to work on it. I'm wasting daylight."

"You're starting *another* project?" Songbird asked.

He stepped toward the corner of the Glade where the clayworkers lived. Songbird blocked him.

Cloud curled back his lips. "Yes, but it's going to save lives. Song, this is too big to wait. It could help us win with next to no casualties. I just have to make it work."

Cloud tried to walk around her, but she pounced in front of him again. "You aren't even going to eat?"

"Food can wait. Please move."

"No, Cloud, *this* can wait. You can't do everything. You're hurting yourself almost as much as Hyrees is hurting himself."

He growled. "I can fix this—I can fix *all* of this—if you'd just let me, *Songbird*. Now move!"

Songbird jumped back in surprise. Tears filled her eyes. She lowered her head and ran back to the den. Cloud's heart sank.

'I'm hurting her again, aren't I?'

"No, wait, I didn't mean it like that," he yowled.

He ran after her. A surprised Kivyress was already there. Her eyes were damp; she'd been crying.

"Whoa, Mom, what's wrong?" Kivyress asked.

"Song, please, I'm sorry," Cloud whispered.

Kivyress lowered her head and loped out of the den. "I'm, uh, going for a walk. Be back by nightfall."

Songbird kept her back to him and didn't reply. The dull, bluish purple of evening time added to the somber mood. The thick fog rolling in enhanced it.

"I'm doing this for you, Song. Almost everything I do, I'm doing to keep you safe. To protect you and let us escape this place one day. You, and Kivyress, and Farlight, and Hyrees. Y'all are my family; the only family I've got. And I want y'all to be safe and happy," Cloud said.

"You don't have to protect us," Songbird said. "And we don't have to leave, either. Just be there for us. That's all we need. Or at least it's all I want."

She got up, turned to face him, and pressed her nose against his. "Work on those protective pieces tomorrow. Today you're getting your cut cleaned and eating your second meal."

He sighed, partly out of relief, and partly out of frustration. "Yes, ma'am."

She wiped away her tears with a forepaw. "I know you can take care of yourself, fluffhead. Don't make me walk you over there."

"I know, I know," he replied. "But please forgive me for snapping at you. It wasn't right of me."

"I forgive you," she said. Her tail twitched anxiously. "Come on, you know

166

we're stronger than that. I'm not going to abandon you, and you know it. But we have to listen to each other. Right now I'm telling you to go to my sister, and to let her fix you, so that means you have to go. After all, you're no good to anyone lying in the healers' den with an infection."

"Alright," he said. "I'm going."

He licked Songbird's cheek, then walked over to the healer's den.

'Please don't be in, Mom,' he thought.

Fledge walked up beside him carrying a bowl of snow. She set the bowl down. "Oh, hey, Cloud. Tahg, that looks like a nasty bite. You'd better come in. Fern just sent me out to get snow. You know, just in case someone needed a little pain relief. Do you need any? Looks pretty painful to me."

"I'd prefer waiting to see what kind of treatment Fern wants to give before we get my leg wet."

"Ah, yes, of course." Fledge picked up the bowl again. "Fawow me."

As they entered the den, Fern stopped sorting medicine and darted over to Cloud's injured leg. Her expression never shifted from emotionless professionalism.

"You just missed your mother," she said as she pawed out leaves for a treatment paste. "Then again, I'm guessing that's not a problem for you."

She used a stone to crush the leaves to powder, then removed it and used another stone to scrape honey off a hive one brave gatherer had acquired. She mixed it together with a half-burnt stick, then used the stick to spread the salve on his cut.

"Try not to lick it off tonight. It'll work its best when allowed to sit as a scab forms," Fern said.

"I won't," Cloud replied. "Thank you, Fern. Have a good night. You too, Fledge."

He considered, for a moment, bringing up the concept of protective pieces to Fledge, but decided to wait. He'd promised Songbird he would eat, and explaining his experimental project properly could take half the night.

"We will," Fledge replied.

Fern sighed. Fledge nuzzled her cheek as Cloud left the den.

"Hey, we'll get through this, okay?" she said.

Fern didn't reply. Or if she did, Cloud didn't hear her. Songbird waited for him with a large lump of turkey meat in her mouth. She nodded toward the den, and he followed her there. She sat, set the piece at her paws, and smiled for a moment.

She sighed and pushed it closer to him. "Here. I got our rations together. Remember? Like how we used to eat. No, that came out wrong. When we were kittens—well, not exactly kittens, but—"

Cloud chuffed without smiling. "You used to think sharing was so romantic. Then we started sharing a den. I noticed that your urge to split food with me disappeared a few days after that."

Songbird chuckled halfheartedly. "That had to do with us having slightly different schedules, not me not wanting to share with you. Now come on, let's eat."

He looked at her round, brown and white face. Her buttercup-yellow eyes glistened back at him like two fireflies in the dying light. The glow from the fire pits reflected in them and danced, making them shimmer even more.

She bent down to eat, but stopped short and cocked her head. "What?"

"Oh, nothing. Just taking some time to appreciate how beautiful you are."

Songbird closed her eyes and shook her head. "Just eat, Cloud. I've already forgiven you."

Cloud's ears drooped. *'She thinks I'm still trying to apologize. What kind of a hole have I dug for myself? Does anyone trust me? How am I supposed to get anything done if no one will believe what I say is genuine?'*

Lupine strode toward them, eyes narrow and ears back.

'Oh, wonderful, what is it this time?'

"Cloud!" Lupine said. "Y-you were supposed to meet me at my den when you returned today to talk about Farlight's training. I-I've had to divide my time all day between, uh . . . s-sorting through spats and teaching your apprentice."

"He's taking a break," Songbird said. "He'll be there when we finish eating."

168

"Songbird, I-I-I was-was speaking with Cloud, not you. Now this is e-extremely important, so Cloud, if you could come with me—"

"Let him eat, Commander," Songbird growled. "He hasn't eaten almost anything all day. Your one-credit problem can wait."

"Songbird, how about you, uh, go into your den while I-I . . . while I speak with your mate?" Lupine said.

Cloud rubbed his cheek against hers, fighting back the urge to rake his claws down Lupine's face. "No, it's alright. I'll be back soon. Don't wait for me. Go ahead and eat your fill. I'll finish up whatever's left when I'm done with him."

"But Cloud—"

Cloud sneezed. He shook himself off and gritted his teeth. "I'll be fine. Waiting a few extra moments to eat isn't going to kill me. Maybe someone else here, but probably not."

She sighed and padded back into the den.

"Come on, Cloud," Lupine continued. He nodded toward the commander's cave. "Let's get this sorted out. I've called Farlight in already. No n-n-need to keep him waiting; he seemed to be in a rather a-agitated mood."

Cloud lowered his head. He coughed twice, then followed him back. "Yes, sir."

'Maybe, while I'm out, I can go hunt down Fledge again and give her a briefing on the project. Nothing too long. Might as well at least let her get started gathering the supplies. Then I'll go straight home, and Song and I can be together.' He smiled. *'Getting stuff done and being there for what's left of my family. Multitasking. I won't be long at all.'*

CHAPTER 11
EMBER

Ember yawned as Hye opened her cage for the third time that morning. A grey haze loomed inside her head, fogging up her mind. Somewhere in the fog, she felt the same sense of excitement she'd felt on the morning of the Meeting.

"Tired?" Hye asked.

Ember licked her lips nervously and tried to blink away the little tears her yawn had created. She moaned softly, yawned again, and repeated the process. "You try sleeping here. Domestics are too vocal and will not listen to anything I say for more than five—what were they called? Seconds? *Five seconds!* They *do not shut up* and the dogs are even worse. How do you people put up with this? Other than leaving. Unless no one keeps their pets with them at night. But I know that you do because at exactly twenty-three, forty-one last night, I asked Thai. And I'm guessing that's a late time. It felt late. Please, for the sake of my sanity, get me out of here. I'm going to lose my mind. Why does nothing feel real?"

He chuckled.

"What are you laughing about?" she said. "Have you ever missed a night of sleep? I don't care how much information you give me to dig through. I need my sleep, and everyone here decided, in unison, to *take it away from me.*"

"I've had more than my share of sleepless nights, but it's not that. I just

170

find it interesting how you answered a yes or no question with a paragraph or two. You've been thinking about that complaint of yours for a while, huh? Also, your legs are looking . . . colorful."

"I had a lot of time to think." She sighed and stared down at her artificial limbs. They were dark turquoise fading into a bright orange at her paws. "And to play with Thai. Oh, I know what a second is and what it's called, by the way. I just added that part for emphasis, because I kind of thought it needed to be emphasized. I don't know why. Now that I've said it, I think it might have made me sound like a fluffhead. I don't know what I'm doing anymore. I don't even know what I am anymore. Why am I saying all this to you again? Oh yeah, 'cause I didn't get any sleep last night and can't think straight."

"Slow down, Ember. Michelle's going to try to take you to her place tonight, so you'll get some peace and quiet soon." Hye rubbed his hand against her head, then massaged her neck.

She closed her eyes and leaned closer to the pressure. A faint purr rumbled up her throat. *'Oh, this feels so good. But wait, why is he doing it? Is he trying to distract me from something? What is he doing?'*

Her eyes snapped open to focus on his other hand, which dangled at his side. *'Okay, he's not doing anything terrible yet. He hasn't done anything terrible from what you've seen. He saved your life. So why don't I trust him? I don't even know. I can't think right. Correctly? I'm tired.'*

"Oh, by the way," she said. A little burst of warmth burned her face. Blue and grey stripes pulsed with it. "I couldn't exactly reach the litter box. Again."

"That's fine. Nothing I haven't dealt with before. Alright, I'm going to pick you up now, okay? It'll be easier for you to try to walk on the ground than that tight, dirty little cage." Hye said.

"Uhm?" Ember mewed as he pushed his hands underneath and around her.

He hefted her into the air. Once beyond the walls of her confinement chamber, she could see a lot more of the Center. A few cages down, it opened up into a big, bright area with a lot of mechanical-looking things. Beyond that lay a glass door leading to another hall, this one with dog cages. Blocking her view of most of the place were several humans. Most of them she'd seen before but one was new. Ember shivered.

"What are they doing? Why are they staring at us? I don't like that one on the left. He's not from here, is he?" Ember asked.

"It's okay. They want to see history as it happens," he replied.

'No it's not. I've seen that symbol before. He's from ARC, isn't he? Please don't let him take me.' She shook her head. "But history is always happening. Why do they have to watch my history happen?"

"Because you're a special girl, Ember," he said. "Your history is a part of ours."

Michelle burst into the room. She exclaimed something in her language. Hye replied quietly. Her hand flew to her mouth. She glanced at the new person and let her hands drop to her sides.

'What was that about? That was weird. And what's making all this light?'

Ember looked up at the ceiling. Several tiny suns pierced her vision. She looked away and closed her eyes, trying to rid them of the lingering glares.

Hye lowered her to the floor. "Take it slow, alright?"

Ember sprang to her paws the moment he let go. "Cold! Ow! Sorry, I didn't do it slowly. Ow. Ow-ow-ow."

A sharp pain arced through her body. She clenched her teeth and willed for it to go away.

"Otherwise that will happen. Which is why it's important to listen. But now that you're up, when you're ready, how about you try lifting a paw? Something simple to let you try shifting your weight."

Ember growled at herself and pulled back into her head. She mentally shook the fog away. *'Why do I think of this feeling as a bad thing? Why not enjoy it? Okay, this is not pain, it's something that's not pain that I like. Alright, now take a step forward, Ember. See if you can do it.'*

She lifted a hind paw, then set it down a little farther forward. *'That worked. Yep, it's just like walking, only I guess I'm going to have to listen to those whirry sounds every time I move. As if I wasn't bad enough at*

172

hunting. Well, oh well. Not an issue right now. Time to walk.'

She tried a few more steps, heart pounding with excitement. Each new movement gave her another dull ache, but when compared to the joy of walking again, the pain didn't matter. She spun around, vivid, sunset oranges flaring in her mind.

'Wait.' She stopped, heart sinking in her chest. *'It doesn't feel real. I'm not using my muscles, I'm just using my mind. Where's the fun in running or moving when I feel like I'm being carried all the time? This isn't a good thing. This is terrible.'*

"What's wrong, Ember?" Hye asked. "Does it hurt? Is there a problem?"

"It's not the same. I move like I used to, but I'm not putting any effort into it. It's like I'm being carried, and it's, uhm . . . it's boring. Walking is boring now," she replied.

"Oh," Michelle said through her wrist phone. "I guess I could try to fix that with my next design but I'm still not sure how. Synthetic muscles aren't enough. To feel real, it has to be real. I'm afraid this may be the closest I'll ever get when it comes to affordable technology."

Ember sighed. *'I haven't tried running yet. Let's see if I can do that with my fake legs. Who knows? Maybe I can even run faster now.'*

She pounced forward, but her paws didn't react fast enough. She stumbled and landed on her face. Bright sky blue pulsed in her mind's eye. Ember groaned and lifted herself back up, nose burning. She whimpered a few comforting mews to herself, trying to take her mind off of how much everything but her legs hurt.

"Are you okay?" Hye asked. "For your own good, you have to take this slowly."

She ignored him and lowered herself to try again. *'I am going to do this. You will not stop me from doing this, legs. I'll do it. I'll do it and I'll go home, and everything will be okay.'*

She leaped for all she was worth. For a moment she flew, weightless, through the air. She landed hard on all four paws. A shock wave arced across her spine. She winced but narrowed her eyes in determination. *'I can do it. I can do it! Okay then. Let's do it again.'*

She did her best to ignore the gathering of humans and focused only on moving her legs. She leaped into the air like a fox attacking a mouse after a blizzard. The landing brought on another wave of blue crashing down on her, but the pain didn't matter. She jumped again and again, bouncing and running like a playful fawn.

One of the onlooking humans shouted, reminding Ember of their presence. The human slapped her hands together over and over. Ember stopped as others joined in, making sounds like rocks falling onto other rocks, or heavy rain on leaves. The noise attacked her, and it grew louder with every human that joined in. When she looked up at them, the tiny suns burned themselves into her vision.

Ember flattened her ears, tucked her tail, and darted behind Hye. Her heart beat even louder than their hand-slapping. Yellow and cyan seared through her subconscious.

"It's okay, Ember. They're just clapping. They're happy for you," Hye said. His voice was distant and muffled, yet entirely too loud at the same time.

'Why are they doing this? Why are they doing this! I gotta get out of here. Gotta get outta here, gotta get outta here, gotta get out. Where do I go? Where can I go? Wall—wall of humans. I need to go past them. Who do I go past? ARC human. I'll go past him. More room. Don't betray me, whirry legs.'

Ember charged forward and darted through the gap between his leg and the wall. To her joy, another human opened a door behind him. The person jumped back in surprise as Ember ran through. She found herself in a long, narrowly winding chamber. It brought her past a sleeping Yegor and into a room full of even more people—people and pets of all kinds. She stopped. Dogs barked, stabbing her eardrums and making her fur raise. They struggled against their owners' leashes, each of them wanting to hurt her in some way for no reason at all. Cats in little cages shied away from the dogs. The humans themselves gasped, glared, and stared at her. She took a few steps back, still breathing hard.

One little dog broke free and trotted up to her, as if, despite being half her size, he could chase her away. He barked in her ears. Adrenaline entered her bloodstream, and she knocked his paws out from under him. He fell with a yip, then scampered, whimpering, back to his person.

Ember turned and ran back into the hallway, past the humans chasing her. Her ears rung from the noise. Her eyes stung from the lights. Her entire torso burned with aches. She tucked herself into a corner, pressed her head against the wall, and cried. Green and orange, she needed to think about green and orange, yet only green appeared. The color of her family loomed a clawlength out of reach. She didn't have claws. She didn't have anything left, except a few mutilated pieces of herself.

Human voices surrounded her. Hye shouted. She shivered as the beginnings of a headache crept in.

'I hate this place. Why can't I go home already? I wanna go home. I want Mom and Dad. I want Kivyress. I want Hyrees. Please just take me home. Why did I have to follow Tainu? Stop trying to be a hero. You're not a hero; you're a coward, remember? That harehearted coward who's afraid of the sun. Why do I even try to be anything else? Wait!'

She opened her eyes.

"Hey, are you okay?" Hye asked.

His voice was quiet, calm, and close. Ember spun to face him but pushed herself closer to the wall.

[Incoming call from Dr. Hye-sung Sagong.]
[Would you like to accept?]

'No.'

[call declined]

"Don't shut me out, Ember," he said. "I can help you if you'd just let me try. Tell me what's wrong."

Michelle said something untranslated to him. Hye exclaimed and stepped back.

Ember panted. "I don't know what's wrong with me, I don't—no!"

The human with the ARC symbol spoke something and leaned closer. His hands moved to grab her. Ember flung herself away from his fingers. Once again, she found herself running. Hye shouted for her to stop. The other humans shouted too. Their yells pierced her ears. Another door swung open, and a man with a cat cage entered. She dove between his legs and out to freedom. And snow.

She sprung sideways when her paws touched the frozen ground. "OH TAHG IT'S COLD!"

'Thai, can you turn off the temperature feeling in my legs?'

[Yes, of course, Ember.]

The cold against her paws stopped. Everything mechanical felt numb in a way she'd never experienced numbness before. Feeling snow without its chill was almost like walking in the creek in those places silt liked to gather, but without the coolness that usually came with it. It calmed her for a moment. However, even without sensors, bitter, freezing snow still swirled through the air and pounded against her sides. She shivered and charged toward the nearest patch of woods. It was unfamiliar, but it looked more like home than anything in the Center.

'I have to get out of here. They're going to take me. I have to get out of here!'

Out the edges of her vision, she noticed her paws, which stood out like turquoise and orange trees against the lightness of the ground.

'Thai, make my legs white.'

[How's this?]

Her prosthetics became a creamy white. Not quite the shade of snow, but much better for camouflage. The colors of her fur didn't change, but the less of her they could see, the better.

She bit her tongue. *'Good.'*

Her heart raced, her chest tensed, and adrenaline surged through her body. The forest moved around her in a blur as she ran. With each step forward, tiredness and coldness threatened to make her stop. Yet she kept going. She had to escape.

[You have one new message from Michelle Castell.]
[Would you like to view it?]

'Not now. I have to get away from this place. They're going to hurt me. I have to go home. Gotta go home. Thai, which way is Toad-something Mountain? Where is home?'

[I couldn't find any results for how to get to Toad-something Mountain, but in case you meant Little Toad Mountain, you'll have to turn south. You are currently going east.]

She spotted a patch of snowless ground leading south and ran toward it. It led to more snowless patches.

[Incoming call from Dr. Hye-sung Sagong.]
[Would you like to accept?]

'No. Leave me alone! You're working with them, aren't you? I have to get out of here.'

Something loud whizzed by. Ember slid to a stop and peered through the trees. She shivered more violently. Her vision bounced in and out of focus as she stared at the stone path blocking her way. Everything around her felt like a dream.

'The Wolf Trail? If I cross it, they'll never find me. I can hide and wait for

this snowstorm to pass, and then I can go home. I can go home. I can do it. I have to!'

She stumbled closer to the trail. Another pod flew past. She shivered even harder. This was the trail that Tainu had led her to, the trail that had nearly killed her, the trail she'd killed beside. It was death, betrayal, war, and large objects moving at speeds she couldn't dream of outrunning, all in one.

'I have to cross it. I have to . . .'

Her gaze wandered beyond the woods. A giant mountain loomed ahead, ominous and distant.

'Home. That has to be home. Tahg, it's so far away. But come on, Ember, you've gotta cross.'

She sucked in a deep breath, lowered her head, and ran. The hiss of moving air came rushing forward. She pushed herself to run faster. A pod appeared on the horizon. A different kind of pod, raised and rectangular. Her paws barely hit the snow on the other side when the machine whirred past. It let out an ear-splitting call. Ember locked up and tumbled into the snow. The machine smacked against the tip of her tail.

She sighed with relief, got to her paws, then staggered into the forest. Once she could no longer see the Wolf Trail, she stopped to get her bearings. Brambles coated most of the forest floor, making the snow naturally patchy. The trees themselves grew small and dense. Some of them were so close together a rat couldn't fit between them.

'Well, I guess I won't have any problems hiding. Now I just need a den, or a fire. Or a fire outside a den. But all the wood is wet, and sparkstones . . .'

She stopped and blinked a few times to try to keep herself from drifting off. *'Why is it so cold? Snow cold. Snow is snow cold, and I'm snow tired, and I'm snow going to die if I don't get some shelter soon.'* She yawned and flattened her ears. *'You have to keep going, Ember. Stuff some snow in the tree to make sure you can find your way back. Okay? Okay. Just in case. Hum, I don't feel so good.'*

Ember shook herself off and tried to ignore the light greens of nausea sinking in. She scooped up a patch of snow in her paws, pressed it into the bark of a nearby tree, then kept walking. With every step, lethargy crept closer and closer. No matter how hard she tried, she couldn't stop her teeth from clicking together. However, the aches and pains of moving subsided.

"Ember!" a voice called out.

"M-M-M-Michelle, is-is that y- . . . you?" Ember replied.

"Ember!" it called again.

Her eyes lit up. She broke into a stumbling run. "Mom? M-Mom! I'm . . . I'm here! E-e-everything is s-so c-c-cold. P-please, I n-need you to k-keep me . . . w-warm? Mom, w-where are you?"

She stopped and scanned the underbrush for signs of life. And there she was—a silhouette in the distance, beyond the tangle of weeds and trees. Songbird stood there, tall and strong. Ember pushed through the dead plants and charged toward her welcoming figure.

"Mom! C-come on, it's me! E-Ember. Y-you . . . m-m-might n-not recognize me . . . because of the legs, but I p-promise it's—"

Her muzzle slammed into something hard. Ember jumped back, panting, and shook her head. Songbird was a tree stump. A little plume of purple appeared in her mind, adding to the muted rainbow forming inside her. "Th-then who was . . . What? B-b-but . . ."

She stared vacantly at the tree stump for a moment, then shook herself out of her daze and looked around. Everything looked the same. *'Oh. Where am I? I guess you could turn around and try to follow your trail of destruction back. Then you wouldn't be as lost. But the snow, there's so much of it. I could try, though. I know I could, but I don't know if I can. I need shelter. There isn't any back there. Oh, look, that looks like a drop-off over there. Maybe it has a hole in it.'*

She slunk over to the edge to find a patch of dry dirt under a slight outcropping. She hopped down to the bare earth and curled into as tight of a ball as she could.

'This will have to do. I can't go any farther. If they find me, they find me. If they don't, they don't. It doesn't matter anymore.'

Black and blue-green bubbled through her thoughts as a shadow emerged from the falling snow. It moved toward her. The shadow took the form of a cat, which then took the form of Cloud. He stopped in front of her and smiled.

'Dad?'

"Hey, Sparky," he said.

'Did you die, Daddy? Am I dying?'

"I don't know," he replied to her thoughts, "but I'm sure we'll find out soon."

He leaned forward and pressed his muzzle against her forehead. Exhaustion took over. Ember sighed and closed her eyes. The shivering stopped. Her breathing stabilized. All at once, it became so easy to let go. So she did. With a gentle, frosty breath of air, she sank into the world of sleep.

CHAPTER 12
EMBER

A song—melodic, gentle, and sickening—greeted Ember's ears. She shuddered, even though the frigid air she'd fallen asleep in was no more than a memory. The dead cat from the documentary appeared in her mind, as vividly as if Thai had put it there. A similar human song had been paired with a history many murders darker than the one she'd spent most of her life studying.

Purple and blue-green swirled around in her thoughts, dancing to the music with only a distant connection to emotion. They swayed and flickered with each new note. She bit down on her tongue and tried to shove the noise away. Beyond the colors and music, she felt warm and almost content. Something soft covered her body, and even the air smelled sweet and welcoming. She curled into a tighter ball and let out a defeated *huff*.

'I guess they found me after all. Unless this is what it's like to die, in which case I could get used to being dead. This isn't terrible. Much nicer than the last time I died. But no, I'm not dead. They found me. I smell Michelle, and other people too. So much for trying to go home on my own, as if that would have worked to begin with. How long have I been asleep?'

A human voice whispered in her ears. Ember opened her eyes. "Oh," she said, voice subdued with shock.

Only a pawstep away, a young person sat in front of her with its legs crossed. She guessed it to be young, at least, based on its size and the almost kitten-like way it examined her.

"Er, hi?" Ember said. Silvery uncertainty crept into her thoughts.

The human blinked a few times but didn't reply.

"Uhm, do you think you could, uh, turn that off?" She asked, tail twitching. "Please? Hello? It's hurting my head. Stop looking at me like that; you're being creepy."

When the little person didn't reply, Ember's gaze wandered. Beyond the human lay a landscape unlike anything else she'd seen; similar to the Center, unnaturally flat walls and a smooth ceiling with artificial lights blocked her from seeing the outside world. However, unlike the Center, almost everything else looked soft, or at least less harsh.

A tan, dead-grass-like substance covered the ground nearby. The wall her bedding was pressed against appeared to be made of strips of smooth wood, as did most of the other walls. The ceiling was creamy white with wooden linings, and several large black things were pressed against the wall in front of her. They looked like the objects the humans had been sitting on in the center, but they were wider and softer.

The human spoke again. She held up a little, transparent rectangle with a pink metallic frame in her hand.

"Hey, are you awake now? Momma said not to disturb you until you woke up," the rectangle said in a voice similar to Thai's.

"Uh, yeah, yeah, I think I am," Ember replied.

The little rectangle spoke to the young human in her own language, then the human replied, "Okay, good. She said you got really cold this morning, and that I should watch you for her until she gets back in case you woke up. She didn't want you to be alone. I thought you might like some music, so I played some for you, but only the nice 'n quiet stuff. Do you like it?"

"No. It's making me nervous. Where's your mom?"

The human smiled, unfazed. The music kept playing. "She forgot to get cat food, so she went to get some. It's faster than ordering it."

Ember looked the human over. Her skin was lighter than Michelle's, but darker than Hye's. Her dark brown fur tuft was more curly than any fur she'd ever seen. It came down to her chin and bounced every time she moved, like the ever-flicking tail of an impatient kitten.

'Please stop it. Please. I don't like your music.'

Her gaze zeroed in on the person's outstretched forearm. For a split moment, she considered biting it to make the noise go away. She shook herself off before the thought could finish forming. The cold, sinking feeling of disappointment settled in. Ember yawned in a futile attempt to chase it away. The misty forest greens of sleep crept back into her mind, so she placed a paw over her eyes and tucked her head closer to her body to welcome them.

'Come on, Ember. You need some rest. Just a little longer. A little more, and I'll be okay. Just stop thinking about hurting everyone, please. Please, this isn't good. I'm already a murderer. Why did I have to fight her? This has got to stop; I'm making myself sick again.'

"Wait, you're going back to sleep?" the human asked.

"Yes," she mumbled in reply.

"No, you can't do that. Momma wants you awake."

"Why?"

"Lake, you aren't tormenting the cat, are you?" A new voice spoke, this one deep and kind.

The transparent translator rectangle evidently worked with all speech anywhere within earshot. It even switched voices to better accommodate the person's more masculine tone. The voice sounded like Yegor. Ember would have laughed if she'd been in a better mood.

"No, Daddy," the young human, Lake, replied.

Ember curled into a tighter ball and wrapped a second paw over her eyes. 'Thai, can you help me go to sleep? I need something calming, or I'm going to start biting myself again. Maybe some forest sounds, or something with wind and birds. Lots of birds. And maybe a waterfall or two. No crickets, though. I don't like crickets.'

Thai didn't respond. Ember swallowed hard. 'Thai? Hey, are you there? Thai? Oh no, did I kill you? Thai? Did they kill you?'

She opened her eyes and pulled back her forepaws; both were the same dull grey they'd started as. She realized she could feel temperature with them again too.

"Okay, where is Thai?" she asked. "Someone did something to her, and now my infinite source of knowledge is gone."

The human with the deep voice appeared from around a corner, laughing. His brown fur tuft extended to his jaw and upper lip to give him a short mane. The darkness of it contrasted with the paleness of his skin, making it stand out even more.

Ember peered up at him with amused curiosity. *'It's like he's peeking out from behind a bunch of leaves. Like a little fawn trying to hide.'*

"Chell disabled your implant for a bit," the rectangle translated. "But don't worry, she's going to turn it back on soon. She just needs to give you a good anti-pinger, just in case, then you'll be clear to home. Fortunately for you, I've made several kinds. Because you know, when it comes to security, you never can be too sure."

He stood in silence, smiling and rocking back and forth on his heels. His hands jerked into the air. "Oh! Manners, manners, manners. Where are my manners? I'm Matthew. Matthew Castell. You've met Lake already. Lake, turn that off."

"But it's Unknown Certainty," Lake protested. "Everyone loves them."

"She doesn't."

"Okay, fine, I'll turn it off."

Ember smiled faintly as the music stopped. Their real voices were so sincere and lively, yet their translations seemed bored to death, and Matthew still sounded like Yegor.

With the unnerving ambience gone, she could calm down. Some of the tension in her head and neck released, but the presence of creatures she didn't know prevented the fog from clearing all the way. At least they seemed nice, and didn't appear to want to send her away with the ARC person. Something nearby thudded. Ember's ears perked up.

"Hello! I hear someone is 'wake," Michelle said in imperfect Felid.

The rectangle translated her to her family. Matthew burst out laughing.

Michelle appeared in the white-lined mouth of a tunnel, or hall of some kind. "What's so funny, you?" she asked in humanspeech.

"You walk through the door, and immediately start meowing in Felid to the cat. And on top of that, we have a translator available for when you do it," he replied.

Michelle chuckled. "I guess that is pretty funny."

Until then, Ember hadn't thought much of how Michelle's mews sounded to her all-human family. She wondered what life would be like if Hyrees taught himself how to speak bird. She chuffed quietly to herself.

'I think I like Matthew. Why is that? You only just met him, after all, and you don't trust that easily. Yes, he pointed out something funny, but—wait, maybe that's it. He noticed something no one else really gave much thought to and pointed it out. We laughed with him, not at him. That's already more than I could hope for back at home. Except sometimes when I'm with Kivy. But still.'

Michelle strode over to where her little family was gathered. She rubbed a hand through Lake's fur and pressed her lips against her forehead. "Thank you for watching her for me. You've been a big help. Now go play. I need to—"

Lake turned off her translation rectangle. Ember pinned back her ears as Michelle kept speaking without translation.

'Why would you do that, tiny human? Now I can't understand what she's saying. No, she's not speaking to me, but I want to know what she's going to do.'

Lake replied, then scampered away. Michelle turned to Matthew and spoke with him for a few moments. He also replied, then left the area, leaving Ember alone with Michelle. Ember swallowed, gnawed on her tongue, and waited for an explanation.

Michelle messed with her wrist phone, then bent down and removed the warm thing covering Ember's body. "I hope you don't mind if I go back to using a translator. It's a lot easier on my throat."

She moved her hands along Ember's spine, ending at the tip of her tail, which she grabbed.

Ember flicked back her ears and bent around to conduct her own examination. "That's fine. But why did you take away the warm thing, and why are you grabbing my tail?"

Michelle released her, and Ember thrashed it from side to side.

"Oh, sorry," a translated Michelle said. "Now that you're warmed up and awake, I need to make sure you didn't get any frostbite. Your tail is vulnerable to it, being thin and mostly furless right now. No offense intended, of course. It looks okay, but let me know if it starts to sting."

"Yes ma'am," Ember replied.

"Ma'am?" Michelle asked. "Where'd that come from? No need to call me that, sweetie. It makes me feel old. But then again, I'm not exactly at the peak of youth anymore, so I guess I should start feeling old. But still, there's no need for formality. Never thought I'd have to say that to a cat." She sighed and pushed her eye rectangles farther up her nose. "Again."

"Again?"

Michelle stroked Ember's head and neck with a gentle hand. "Don't you worry yourself about me. You don't appear to have any frostbite, which is good. Now we need to make sure your prosthetics are working. Can you stand for me?"

'Maybe she had a domestic at one time. Unless she's talking about Yegor, but that seems unlikely.'

Ember stood up, then lifted each leg in turn. "Everything seems okay. Still hurts a little, but other than that, I'm fine."

"Great," Michelle said. "Now you've got about three more days until your fur grows back enough to bring you home. During that time, I can put a small heating system in your prosthetics so nothing freezes up. When I found you earlier they were already dangerously cold, and working to lower your core body temperature, which, to put it simply, is not good."

Ember's eyes widened as the vibrant reds of excitement sparkled in her mind's eye. "Three days? Only three? Oh, and what about claws? I really, really need new claws."

"Yes indeed, only three days. You've got Hye to thank for that. And of course you need claws; I'm going to give you some. But for now, how about you get settled?"

She pointed at a pale green box with a hole in its front. "Over there is your litter box. Don't go outside of it, if you know what I mean."

She moved her outstretched arm toward a pink bowl sitting across the chamber. The ground there was comprised of stone-like tan squares. "Water is over there, and you'll get fed in the same place twice a day. You see that side of the house where the floor becomes hard? The place where your water is? Everything in there that's above eye-level is off-limits. No jumping or climbing in that area. It's where we eat, and cat fur in food is disgusting. Again, no offense intended."

Ember huffed, thinking about the rabbits and squirrels she'd so often picked over. Fur getting caught in her tiny, rough 'tongue teeth' had made her cough almost every time. *'You would hate being a Colony Cat so much.'*

"Everywhere else, you're free to explore," Michelle said. "Also, don't eat, drink, or chew on anything you aren't given specifically to eat, drink, or chew on. And I think that covers everything."

"Thai?"

"Hmm? Oh. Yeah, I'll get that fixed up later this evening. It's turned off right now so no one can track you. Just in case they change their minds and decide they want you after all. But the main thing I want to do right now is ask you a few questions."

Ember lowered her head and swallowed hard. "Questions? What kind?"

Michelle shifted her lanky legs around to sit in a more comfortable position. "The curiosity kind. Back at the Center, what was it that caused you to run?"

"Uhm," she stammered, "I-I don't know. I'm sorry; I really am."

"Yes, you do. You know. This is a safe place, sweetie. I'm not going to laugh, or tease you, or pretend it was nothing. I want to help you."

"Well, uh . . ." Ember sat down, hunched over defensively as if she might need to bolt again at any moment. A cold chill crept down her head and along her spine as memories of her panic and mad dash through the snow came back to her. She stared longingly at the warm thing that had once covered her body. "They, er, they kept smacking their hands together and yelling. And the-the lights were, uhm, k-kind of bright. It hurt my eyes, and . . . and my ears too. Not the lights, the smacking. There was so much going on, with all the people, and the loud noises, and I just . . . I don't know what's wrong with me, but it almost felt like they were a-attacking me, if you can even believe that. I just needed to get away, and somewhere in my tired head I thought, maybe, somehow, I'd be able to find my way home. I wasn't thinking straight, and I couldn't—"

Ember shook her head in frustration. Tears threatened to blur her vision once again. "I'm sorry; I'm sorry. Tahg, this sounds so stupid, saying it out loud. Anyone else would just be afraid of the people making the noise, but not me. I have to be afraid of everything, and I don't even know why."

"Ah, so this is more than just a case of nervous feral cat. I believe you, sweetie. It's not stupid. Matthew gets like that too. Crowds, and loud noises, and even certain smells really bother him sometimes. When it gets to be too much to handle, it's called a sensory overload."

Ember looked up at her, eyes wide and unfocused. "S-sensory overload?" *'They have a name for it? What's that supposed to mean?'*

"Yes, that's what it's called," Michelle replied. "They aren't pleasant, are they?"

"N-no," Ember whispered, "no, no, they aren't."

Michelle touched her fingers to her chin and tilted her head. "This may seem like an odd request, but can I see your tongue?"

Ember squinted as purple confusion swirled and wove itself into her thoughts. Her gaze landed on a shiny little bijou dangling from Michelle's neck. The shape reminded her of a single clover leaf. *'Silver. It's silver. There's a lot more silver out here than I thought, and that's not good. Silver is not good.'* Her thoughts wandered back to the night of the fight. Her heart sank as the fog in her head grew thicker. *'Don't think about that right now. You thought about it enough earlier. And you know, thinking about something you can't control isn't going to change it. Try to enjoy enjoying for now, if you can. Everything is going to fall apart the moment you get back, and you know it. This may be your last chance to be happy for a long time.'*

She shook herself back into the external world. "My tongue? Uh, yeah, I guess so."

She stuck it out, then went cross-eyed trying to see it. Michelle did some human equivalent to a chuff, then lifted Ember's chin to get a better look. Ember's mind went numb. She curled back her lips, trying to keep her whiskers from touching Michelle's skin. A lump formed in her stomach as she realized what Michelle was looking at.

"You chew on it a lot, don't you? Why?" Michelle asked, releasing her.

A lingering feverishness took shape where Michelle's fingers had been. Ember licked her lips, then pulled her tongue back into her mouth where it belonged. "It, er, helps me think and calms me down. I think. I don't know. I'm not really supposed to do it, but sometimes I bite it without even realizing it."

"I thought so."

After an awkward, lengthy pause, Michelle asked several other questions, each more confusing than the last. They were questions like "do you ever change moods faster than what most of your family would consider normal?" and "is there a special routine you have to follow to feel secure?"

As Ember replied to each one in turn, anxiety crept a little closer. It seemed like the questions were calculated to target and expose all of her weaknesses, which would then lead to Michelle looking down on her like everyone else. Yet she answered them as honestly as she could, hoping her honesty might somehow help her fix herself.

"Do you ever find yourself repeating words or phrases in your head, or even out loud?"

Ember blinked the tiredness from her eyes and tried to stop herself from shivering, yet the harder she tried, the more violently she shook. "That's not normal? Even the way I think is messed up?"

Michelle reached toward Ember's face, but stopped before her fingers could make contact. Instead, she held out the warm thing and wrapped it back around Ember. "Not messed up, just different. But I think everyone thinks a little differently, so in a way, I guess it is normal."

She nestled farther into her warm thing, tail twitching. The shivering still wouldn't stop. "I don't understand. What does any of this have to do with anything? What are you trying to do? What are you trying to say?"

"I'm getting to that. I just have a few more questions. What about your friends? Do you have any, and if you do, how would you describe your relationship with them?"

Ember swallowed and buried her face beneath the warm blue covering. *'Go ahead. Give her your vulnerabilities. Everything she could ever need to destroy you. Maybe she can use all this to fix me too. I don't know. I just want this to be over.'*

"There's just my mate and my sister," she said, barely louder than a whisper. "I guess my parents and my mentor too. Maybe my aunt, Fern, but . . . but probably not anymore. I don't even know what else to say, other than that they're the only ones who care beyond tolerating me. And even then, my dad, and C- . . . Commander Aspen kept trying to fix me, but they couldn't. And now so many bad things have happened. I don't know what to do."

Her tail thrashed harder. "Everyone treats me like a kitten, and part of me wonders if they're right. I'll say things, and everyone looks at me like I'm crazy, so much so that I'm not even allowed to mention my colors anymore. And then there are times when I'll do something or think about something, and it's like my senses just . . . turn off. Sometimes my eyes even kind of stop seeing, open or not. And then someone will yell at me, and I'll come back, and they'll have to repeat themselves and they'll sound really angry, and I don't know what to say."

'Why did I tell her that? Of course it's not going to help. Now she's going to be mad, isn't she? No one is supposed to know about my colors. Why did I mention my colors. That was stupid. Fluffheaded Ember, stop! Stop it now;

you're hurting yourself and everyone else, so just stop talking.'

"Colors?" Michelle asked.

Ember winced. She peeked out from her covering. "Yes?" she mewled.

"What do you mean when you say 'colors'? I just want to know. I promise I won't make fun of you."

She drew a deep breath. "I see-feel colors. I'm see-feeling a lot of purple right now. C-confusion. And grey. That's what color I see when my head gets foggy and freezes up. Sometimes it gets so bad I can only think with pictures, and it makes me feel like a fluffhead, which is the only reason I'm telling you this—I can't think straight."

'Stop it, Ember. Stop, stop, stop, now.'

Michelle leaned back and muttered a human word Ember had never heard before.

Ember flinched and buried herself back under the warm thing. "What? What is it? That was wrong, wasn't it?"

Michelle straightened herself up. "No, it wasn't wrong at all. It's called synesthesia, and it's where two or more senses or sensors inside of you get linked together. It's not a bad thing, sweetie. You know, Matt doesn't have synesthesia, and he's a touch more sociable, but in many ways you two are very similar. I've lived with him for fourteen years, and I still can't imagine what it's like inside his head. It's a fascinating place, I'm sure."

'Fourteen years? Fourteen winters?' Ember thought. She lifted her covering enough to see Michelle's kind face. *'You don't seem very old. How long do you humans live?'* She sighed and let the blue fluff cover her eyes once more. *'I don't even know what's going on anymore. Tired again. Sick again. I just wanna go home.'*

Michelle continued, "One time I was outside taking a walk with him. From what I could tell, everything around us was silent. At some point I got curious and asked him if he could hear anything, and he gave me a list of over twenty separate sounds that weren't our voices. The funny thing is, I couldn't hear any of them until he brought them to my attention, or at least I hadn't noticed them until that point."

Ember stopped shivering and shook the soft thing off of her head. Pieces clicked together. All at once, everything felt too warm. *So when Dad tells me to ignore something, he's being serious,'* Ember thought. *'He really can choose to ignore things, and doesn't realize I can't? Is that what it's like to be normal? It must be nice.'*

"I-is there a way to fix me? To make me not hear everything?" Ember asked.

Michelle sighed and placed her hands on top of her folded legs. She leaned closer, face calm and voice quiet. "Ember, sweetie, you aren't broken. There's no way to fix what isn't broken. Now I want you to listen to me, and not to interrupt until I'm done. Okay?" She reached up and fidgeted with the silver clover leaf on her neck. "The point I'm trying to make here is that everyone is different. We all have our problems, and we all have our flaws. How you think can shape what they are, but the way you experience the world around you isn't a flaw. It's a part of you, and even if it's different, it's nothing to be ashamed of."

Ember sat up and shook the now feverish blue thing off of her. Her lower jaw trembled with anxiety as her mind worked to fit together the meaning of Michelle's words, but the more pieces it snapped into place, the more she dreaded looking at the final picture. "S-so that's it? I'll never stop being scared because it's part of who I am, and nothing I do will ever change that?"

"You'll never stop being scared of things, but everyone gets afraid. Fear is normal. How you deal with fear is up to you, but sometimes you need to stay and face it, even if it hurts. Otherwise you might find yourself in a snowstorm without half of your fur."

Her face burned. She shrunk back, trying to make herself smaller. "Sorry," Ember said. Tears dripped into her fur, but she didn't know why she was crying. She tried to make herself stop, but they kept coming. "I know that was fluffheaded. I wasn't . . . I couldn't . . . I didn't know what to do. I couldn't do better, and I'm sorry. I'm really sorry for everything. I just wanted to go home, and . . . and . . ."

"It's okay. It's okay. Do you want a hug, sweetie? Or, uhm, do you want me to put my arms around you?" Michelle asked.

Ember nodded and kept trying to blink away her tears. Michelle moved closer. She wrapped her arms around Ember's body. Ember pushed her head against Michelle's shoulder, letting the pressure engulf and comfort her. They stayed there until Ember stopped crying, then they pulled away at the same time.

"Better?" Michelle asked.

"A little. Thank you. But if I really think differently, and I can't change it, what am I going to do? You say I'm not broken, but you're the first creature I've met to tell me that. How am I supposed to believe you when almost everyone I've ever known has said behind my back, or even to my face, that there's something wrong with me? And it's not just them, I . . . I kind of agree. Something that's supposed be inside of me is missing. I can feel it's missing. Everyone else seems to have it, and I don't know what it is. You know a lot of things. Do you know what part of me I'm missing?"

Michelle rested her elbows against her knees. "No, I don't, but I'll tell you this much; everyone else is just as lost, and confused, and uncertain as you are. Most just pretend not to be. Honestly sweetie, I think everyone is born with a few pieces missing. It's up to each of us to find them. You just have to keep looking."

Ember glanced down at her grey, mechanical paws. She wiped away her tears and smiled bittersweetly. "Thanks. I'll try, I guess."

Ember got up and walked over to the large black structures sitting against the wall. She examined them for a moment, then jumped onto the largest and longest of them. Her paws sank into the soft material. It felt strange against her pads. Past the cushioned backing of the structure, the wall extended inward, and a series of vertical, wood-colored strips concealed a light of some kind. Ember propped herself up against the backing and nosed the strips away. A transparent panel revealed a snow-coated clearing with a few small trees scattered around it. The heavier drift of that morning had eased into a gentle snowfall. Human tracks of varying sizes covered the ground, streaks of brown and grey amidst the brightness. Sunlight broke through the clouds overhead, making the landscape glisten like Eastern gemstones. Icicles sparkled from the trees, and flurries shimmered like pyrite. It was the magic of her first winter all over again, this time without the cold.

She sucked in a long, slow breath, then let it out in a gentle "wow." When she did, the panel fogged up. She snorted and pressed a paw against the patch of condensation. The glass cooled her toes. When she pulled it away, it left a smudged, paw-shaped mark through which she could see the outside world.

'It doesn't matter what anyone else says or thinks anymore, Em. If she's right, I'm not broken, and I'm going to see my family again. Everything is going to be okay. No one can take these things away from you because you're going to make them reality, Ember, no matter how hard you have to try. I'm going to find my missing pieces, and I'm going to come back home. Don't worry, Hyrees, I'm coming for you. Don't do anything fluffheaded, and everything will get better.'

Michelle walked up behind her and pushed aside the wood-like flaps. It smudged her paw print even more, but made looking out easier. Ember rested her chin against the cushion. For the first time in days, shimmering misty oranges filled her head. Instead of being the dull shade of sadness, it was vibrant and hopeful, like the first light of dawn. Together they watched in silence as the snow gradually covered up more and more of the footprints. Ember closed her eyes. A cozy kind of tiredness sent soft blue-green to play with the oranges, painting an abstract picture of beautiful colors across her mind's eye.

"Hey, Ember," Michelle said.

The sudden noise snapped her away from her two-toned rainbow.

"I was thinking, since Matt is also on the spectrum, he might be able to help give you some tips to make your life a little easier. His side job is helping others like himself and you. He has some great advice for how to cope with the difficulties you've been facing, and how to find and better use your strengths. He usually works with people, but I don't see why he wouldn't be able to help an appala. I could ask him, if you want."

194

"That would be nice," Ember replied, "but, uhm, what spectrum is he on? You said 'also,' so are you saying I'm on it too? What does it mean? I don't understand."

Michelle chuckled. "We've got a lot to talk about, sweetie. But for now, would you like to get Thai back up and working again?"

Ember's face lit up. "Yes, please."

"Then what are we waiting for? Let's go."

CHAPTER 13
CLOUD

Cloud gnawed on a half-frozen minnow. He'd found it floating at the edge of the creek and had decided not to let it go to waste. There was something about their tiny scales and strong flavor that helped him focus.

'A break. Wait, do I really need a break? What am I thinking? I can't afford to take breaks. Lives are at stake and I'm wasting my time. Lupine can go bite a fox. I need to check on Fledge and see how the next test piece is coming along. It should be done by now. And if it's not, I can help her with the setting process. Hopefully she hasn't burnt it again. If she's tending the fire properly, the bowl should do its job.'

He swallowed the rest of the minnow, then licked the hole in his gums where his upper right fang had been. He stood up. Sunlight glinting off the icy creek edge burned a little spot of light into his vision. He sighed and blinked it away.

What snow remained on the forest floor looked more like grey slime mold than any form of water. It made the world seem even more dead than before. Dead and sick. He coughed, sniffed back the congestion in his nose, then fumbled his way back to the Glade.

A group of toms worked together to shove abatis sticks into a new 'outer wall,' which Lupine had insisted on building. He tried to ignore their surprised stares.

Farlight trotted up to him. "Sir, what are you doing back so soon, if you don't mind me asking?" he said as Cloud entered the inner Glade.

When he didn't reply, Farlight followed after him. "Sir, please."

A few leaps away, several gatherers and clayworkers used stones to sharpen the ends of branches. They lowered their heads in respect as he passed by.

"What do you want, Farlight?" Cloud asked through gritted teeth.

"The same thing I keep telling Hyrees. For you to take care of yourself. You're not so different, you and my brother. You both—"

Cloud stopped. The already blazing fever in his forehead grew hotter. "That's enough, Farlight. I'm busy right now. We'll do your lessons later."

"You're both hurting yourselves without thinking about the consequences. Living in the moment. Not planning for the future. The Colony needs you at your strongest, and you're both getting weaker by the day. So listen to me."

"I said that's enough!" Cloud snapped. "Why do you even think I'm doing all this? I am planning to win a war, because this is our future. And it'll be the end of it for some of us if I don't."

Farlight didn't back away or even flinch. Instead, he stepped closer. "You might be my mentor, but you have no right to speak to me like that. Until further notice, you're only allowed to work from midday to sunset. This includes both your work as a border guard and work on the guard pieces. You can still tell others what to do and train me outside of your work time, but no actual work."

Cloud growled. It turned into a cough. "That was good practice, but you're not the commander yet. Go play with Kivyress. I have important things to get done."

"No, I'm not *the* commander, but I am *a* commander. Lupine has given me charge over two toms he's worried about. I think you already know who these lucky cats are, so I'll spare you the names."

Cloud's eyes widened. "What are you talking about? He can't do something like that without consulting the Council first." He sneezed, then turned and strode toward Lupine's den.

"He *did* consult the Council."

"*I'm* part of the Council. *I'm* his advisor. *I* didn't permit this."

Lupine slunk out of the den as Cloud approached the entrance. "W-we met without you," he said. "It's completely allowed to have a council meeting about a member without inviting them, including a-a-a chief advisor. You know that. Let's be honest, Cloud—you don't think I'm a good commander. A-a-and, as is often the case, you're probably right. So you get a different commander and Farlight gets real-life practice. Sorry it had to come to this, Cloud, but it's the best I can do."

"But—"

"I-if you have any problems with this, t-t-tell your commander. It was his idea."

Cloud narrowed his eyes and glared at Lupine, then at Farlight. He turned toward the farthest fire pit. "It's between midday and sunset. I'm not going to waste my time dealing with this right now. I've got things to do, and even less time to do it now, thanks to you two."

He sniffled a few times as he walked across the Glade. The congestion stopping up his sinuses made his head stuffy and him tired.

'Tahg, that kitten's got a lot of nerve.' He sighed. *'He really is going to make a good commander. Come on tomcat, get it together. This is only temporary. Once Lupine steps down and Farlight is running everything, we can go. He won't need me. And then I'll never have to worry about any of this nonsense again. In fact, this just proves I was right about him.'*

"Is piece two ready?" Cloud asked.

Fledge sat by the fire pit with a stick in her mouth, stirring up the fire. Her smoky grey fur shimmered in the flickering light. The white patches on the undersides of her face and neck became distorted through the heat of the flames. She dropped the stick. "Oh! Well, yes, sort of."

Cloud gritted his teeth together as she pushed a piece of clay-covered bark forward. One of the two vines wrapped around it in a loop had snapped in half. He pawed at the unbroken side. It came apart the moment he applied pressure.

"If the vines don't catch on fire, they dry out so much they can't bend," Fledge said. "Sorry, Cloud. We've tried our hardest, but I don't know if these guard pieces of yours will work."

"It'll work. We just need a different material," Cloud said. "Something that will stay flexible, even when heated."

Fledge looked away, thinking for a moment. She got the same distant, musing look Ember would get when he asked her a question. Cloud turned his attention back to his second failure of a prototype.

'Flexible and heat resistant. What is there that's flexible and heat resistant? Is there anything? Come on, Cloud, think!'

"What about a snake?" Fledge suggested.

He looked up at her, expression quizzical. "Excuse me?"

She chuffed and offered an awkward smile. "I, er, thought we could try finding and using a snake. I don't know where to find one, but they're flexible and don't break easily. I don't know. It's a fluffheaded idea, but it's still an idea."

'A snake? Heh, that sounds like something she *would come up with. And the thing is, it may actually work if we can find a pair of snakes. But we need these now. Snakes are too hard to hunt down in the winter, and if we're going to make enough of these for everyone in the colony to wear, snakes just aren't an option. A shame deer and turkeys aren't long and th—'*

"OH!" Cloud exclaimed.

"What?" Fledge asked, tail twitching with impatience. Her eyes shimmered with excitement, as if she knew whatever he was about to say would revolutionize war.

"Entrails! Intestines!" Cloud replied. "No one likes eating them. They usually end up going to waste, yet they're long, thin, and flexible. Hopefully they can be strong and heat-resistant too. We could probably put them to good use. We would just have to find a way to clean them effectively."

"Good idea, but . . ." Fledge trailed off. Her expression tightened and her eyes narrowed, like Wren's always did before reminding him of common sense and reason.

"But what?"

"Will anyone want to put bark on their legs with deer guts? Would it even stay on? And what if it rots and breeds maggots? And then, of course, there's the smell."

"Cats'll do anything if they think it'll keep them alive."

Fledge pulled back the broken guard piece and stared at it. "I don't know about that. It might not even work. I forgot to mention the biggest problems."

Cloud's ears and tail drooped. His chest tightened; his jaw tensed. *'It has its quirks, yes, but it is going to work. I will make it work. Tell me the flaws, Wren*—Fledge. *Right. Fledge. I'll fix them all. Fledge.'*

"Bark isn't flexible," she continued, "and if it doesn't break, it's going to limit how much whoever wears it can move. It may well put them at more risk than wearing nothing."

"I'll find something else to use. I know I'm close to something big. Something that will prevent all this senseless waste of life. I know this is going to work. This is the right thing to do, Fledge. I just need time to think. We can start over with a new concept inspired by this p—WHAT ARE YOU DOING?"

She pushed the prototype into the fire and sighed. "Sorry, Cloud. This was a fun project to work on for the first two days, and I really hoped it would work, but I'm afraid we're wasting our time." Fledge got to her paws. "I should go see if Fern needs help in the healers' den."

Cloud rushed over to the fire. He tried to paw out the mangled piece, but the flames singed his pads and scorched his fur. He yanked his paw back and licked it. "You ruined it! Why would you do that, you little c—"

His words got caught in his already burning throat, and he burst into a fit of coughing. The stuffiness inside his head grew into a throbbing ache.

Fledge sighed again. "I really am sorry. No offense, but, er, this project of yours is a lost cause, and I don't usually say things like that. If you want to keep trying at it, well, you're on your own—but please, for your own good, come with me to the healers' den first. The whole colony is getting worried."

He jumped in front of her to block her. "No! Don't go. It's not a lost cause.

I know I'm on the verge of something. I don't know how yet, but it's going to work. It has to, Wren! And it will!"

She recoiled in surprise. "Cloud, you're sick and delirious. You need to stop."

"Sir, go see the healers."

The voice belonged to Farlight, but he couldn't see him for some reason. He yowled in frustration. "No, I have to do this. I have to save them. I have to . . ."

Someone brushed against his side. "That's an order," Farlight whispered. "Now come on, I'll help you walk there. You can lean on me if you need to."

Cloud yanked himself back, knocking over a bowl of drinking water in the process. Half of the fire went out as water seeped into the wood. Farlight sighed. "Don't worry about that, Fledge. I'll take care of it when we're done getting him to his mom."

"Leave me alone," Cloud said. "I'm fine. I can do this if you'd just let me. Get out of my way."

He swatted the drenched guard piece out of the fire. The heat burned his paw, but he ignored the pain. He brushed off the soot and char, set it on top of the upturned bowl, then pushed down until it snapped in half. *There. There's the problem. I need to make everything less brittle. No tree bark, no vines, and probably no clay either. Something strong and bendable, but not breakable. What is there like that? There's something—I know there is. Come on, Cloud, think! I know there's something I can use. What is it?*

Farlight nudged his side. "Come on, sir. You can do this later."

"I said leave me alone!" Cloud snapped. Heat flared in his head. "I don't care what Lupine said. You're not my commander. No one here is fit to be commander. You're all too fluffheaded to understand. Aspen would've understood. He would have wanted this. He would know exactly what this would do for us—how much good it would bring. You're all . . . you're all too stubborn to see it. Cowards, all of you!"

Farlight pushed him again. "Sir, he wasn't, well, he isn't, wouldn't . . ." He sighed. "He wasn't who you thought he was. But I promise this isn't what he'd want. Now please, come on."

'What is he doing? Is he attacking? He's attacking me. The little Rogue!'

Cloud shoved him toward the fire. Farlight stumbled backward. His side slammed into the nearest clay pillar. His tail fur caught on fire. He sat on it to put it out. "On second thought, Fledge, could you go find Songbird? I'm afraid he'll hurt me if I try to do anything else, but maybe he'll listen to her. Tahg, he really is delirious."

Fledge spoke some kind of reply but he couldn't make it out. 'Why aren't my ears working properly? Last thing I need right now. Go deaf right before a war. But if they won't listen to me, why should I listen to them? No one ever listens when I try to warn them anyway. They ignore me, then they die in their stupidity. It's not my fault. It's not my fault they're dead. They brought it on themselves.'

Cloud picked up both halves of the guard piece in his mouth, then carried them over to the cluster of recently-made bowls. He set them down. He blinked once and he was on the ground. Paws thudded against the dirt around him.

"Oh tahg! Can you hear me, sir? Cloud!" Farlight called out.

His voice was muffled and distant. Cloud closed his eyes. 'Why am I so tired all of a sudden? Why can't I focus? Why am I laying down? There's something I was trying to find. What was it?'

"Oh no. Cloud, sir, can you get up? Come on; you've got to get up."

Someone pushed him. Then someone else pushed him. Cats touched him, shoved him, and tugged at his fur. Cloud growled, but when he opened his eyes, he was back on his paws. Farlight stood by his side, propping him up. Fledge pressed against his other side, helping guide him.

"Don't worry, Cloud," Fledge said. "You're going to be okay. You just need to make it into the den, then we'll get you all fixed up and working again in no time. You've got a nasty fever going there."

Cloud closed his eyes again and let them dictate his path. He couldn't find the strength to resist anymore. They could decide to kill him and he wouldn't even care. So they hobbled together into the healers' den. When they stopped, they let him lay back down.

"Oh, Cloud, what have you done with yourself this time?" Silentstream asked. She placed a cold paw against his forehead. "No wonder you were making such a fluffhead of yourself. Fledge, take a bowl and go get him some snow."

"Yes ma'am. And I'll try to find Songbird while I'm out," Fledge said.

"Please do," she muttered.

Cloud listened in numb silence as Fledge picked up the snow bowl, then left the den. He moaned.

Farlight sat down beside him. "Do you think he'll be okay?"

"That tomcat hasn't been okay for winters. But he'll live, assuming he's willing to start taking proper care of himself," Silentstream said.

"I'll try to make sure he does."

She scoffed as she rubbed a honey salve on his burnt forepaw. "So now you need a kitten to remind you when to eat? Cloud, this kind of nonsense is doing nothing for anyone's morale. Learn some self-respect, or you'll find yourself getting thrown off the Council."

Farlight snorted indignantly. Cloud sighed but said nothing. He couldn't find the strength to defend himself or his apprentice-commander. His head throbbed. He couldn't breathe. He gasped through his mouth and shivered.

'Air—I need to breathe. Am I underwater? I'm not underwater, so why does it feel like I am?'

Fledge darted in with a bowl full of snow. She and Silentstream worked together to scoop it onto his head and back. He shivered more violently. Cold wetness engulfed his body. The sound of paws on dirt approached him from behind. Along with it came a scent he knew from anywhere, even in the healers' den with a fever-induced delirium.

"Oh, Cloud," Songbird said, "what have you done to yourself?"

'Songbird. Myself? I didn't do anything. I don't know what's wrong with me.'

She pressed her nose against his cheek, then licked it. "It's time to stop, and it's time to rest. When you hurt yourself, it's hurting me. You don't want to hurt me, Cloud. Do you?"

'Hurting? Hurting us?' The feverish stupor cleared enough for him to think. *'Oh tahg, what am I doing? I really am sick. And I really did make a fluffhead of myself, didn't I? What's wrong with me? Why did I ever think I could . . .'*

He opened his eyes and gazed up at Songbird's gentle, concerned face. "What did I do to deserve you?" he asked. "Why do you still care about me, after all the selfish things I've done?"

She looked down at her paws. "Selfish? How about self-*less*? You've been working so hard and neglecting yourself for so long, all for the sake of the Colony."

His throat tightened as nausea sunk in. "Please, Song, don't try to pretend I'm some kind of hero. No. No, it was selfishness that made me do everything I did. It always was. After losing Dad, then Aspen, then Ember, then Wren . . . well, it was too much. I'm not strong enough to lose anyone else. Honestly, I wasn't even strong enough to lose them, because I let myself fall this far. I don't want to lose you. I don't want to lose any of you. I . . . I hate being alone."

Songbird sighed. She lay down and rested her chin on his neck. "You're not alone anymore. And as long as you keep letting me in, you'll never have to be. I promise. You just have to listen to me. Pay attention and let me help you."

Cloud closed his eyes again. He sniffed a few times, trembled, then cried. A tail wrapped around his side. Someone licked his snow-covered forehead, but the only scents he could smell were Songbird's and his mother's. At some point, Farlight and Fledge had left.

"Oh, Cloud," Silentstream whispered as she groomed behind his ears. "If you don't like being alone, maybe try not chasing everyone away. You might be surprised."

They stayed there until all the snow melted, then Silentstream allowed him to go back to his own den to finish recovering. Once he got there, he played with Kivyress by laying down and allowing her to attack him. She did so with a gentleness he'd never seen in her before. The same softness he'd seen in

Ember.

'What if I was wrong about her? What if I was wrong about everything? Tahg, I really have messed things up.'

Sometime after the one-sided wrestling match ended, Farlight and Hyrees visited them.

"How are you feeling, sir?" Farlight asked.

Cloud coughed. "Not great, but better than earlier, thanks to you. They said I almost pushed you into the fire back there. I'm sorry, Far. I don't know what got into me."

"Hey, no harm done and no hard feelings. I'd just rather you not do it again. Because, you know, I don't really feel like getting burnt to death. Just not my thing."

"I'll try my best."

"Oh yeah, Hyrees has something he wanted to ask you."

"What is it?" Cloud asked.

Hyrees swallowed and stepped forward. The cut across his muzzle had scabbed over and was beginning to heal. His ribs stuck out through his fur, but his breath carried the scent of meat. He'd eaten again. "I was wondering, if you were strong enough, if we could go up to the falls tomorrow, and maybe on our way up we could stop by the fields. Well, I know it's not really on the way, but I wanted to give Ember her clayvine. It snapped and fell off the tree earlier, so I thought I'd just leave it near her marker. I know she's not actually there, but . . . sentiment. It's stupid, I know, but—"

"No, it's okay," Cloud said. He sneezed as he got to his paws. "We can do it. I've been acting like a bobcat lately. It's about time we do something together that doesn't involve yelling."

'And maybe on the way I'll think of something strong and flexible to make those guard pieces out of. But if not, oh well. I'm not going through all that again.'

"R-really?" Hyrees asked. "Good. I think Dad and Ember would want us to get along. We work better together. And speaking of work, I think I'm finally ready to start training to be a clayworker. So maybe after we do that, you could help me find a mentor."

Cloud's mind wandered to Fledge. *'I hope I didn't traumatize her too much. She's busy, but she'd set him straight again. Better than I could, at least. Wonder how she'd feel about having an apprentice.'* He smiled. "Yes, I think we can do that."

"But only on one condition," Songbird said.

"And what condition is that?" Cloud asked.

"You both take better care of yourselves. I don't want anyone starving or working themselves dead. That's no way to live. Oh, wait." She chuffed to herself. "Right, of course it isn't. If you work yourself dead, by definition you aren't alive. Never mind. Well, the point is that you two get healthy again and *stay* alive. Deal?"

Cloud and Hyrees exchanged a glance. "Deal," they said in unison.

CHAPTER 14
EMBER

"Breathe in; one, two, three, four, five. Breathe out; one, two, three, four, five. Aaand there you go. Repeat as needed," Matthew said.

He spoke in humanspeech, but Thai—back up and running with an all-new security system and human language pack—translated him automatically inside Ember's head. Yet even without the help of a translator, Ember found herself understanding a few of their more common words and phrases. About a day had gone by since she'd first woken up in Michelle's 'house,' as the humans called it. Approximately twenty-seven hours, thirty-nine minutes, and fifteen seconds had passed since Thai got resurrected, if her internal clock was to be trusted.

"So just breathe?" Ember asked. "That's all? I kind of do that automatically, but thanks for the suggestion. I'll have to remember it sometime."

Matthew chuckled. A few hours earlier, he'd installed a Felid language module onto Axis, his own AI implant, making communication much more convenient. "It's not just breathing—it's controlling your breathing. There's a difference. But you know that; stop being difficult."

Ember smiled. Something about his deep, goofy laugh made it impossible to not be joyful when he was. "But life is more interesting when I'm difficult. I made you laugh, after all. And you don't seem to mind all that much."

207

She paused and nibbled on her toes. Michelle had reinforced the materials in the tips of her left forepaw. Every time Ember got the urge to chew, she could do so in a way that wouldn't hurt her. The smooth, cold texture against her teeth didn't only help her focus, but it made her happy too. She set it back down. "But I would like to know what counting and breathing have to do with any of this. It's relaxing, but why? And does it work when I'm not already calm?"

He bounced slightly on his toes. "Controlled breathing gives your mind something simple to focus on, instead of thinking about whatever might be bothering you at the time. It works pretty well, so long as you can actually control your breathing. If you're having a really bad panic attack, it usually doesn't work."

"Panic attack?"

"Yeah, you know, chest gets tight, heart starts racing, might feel sick, vision might fade a little, might get a little sweaty. Ever had one?"

Ember sighed. Her mind darted back to the historian test and her inability to complete it. "Yep. I think so."

Her tail twitched as she cast another glance around the room. It was an extension of the 'living room' which wrapped itself around a corner. The ground beneath her paws was still covered in soft tan stuff they called 'carpet.' She'd explored the house the day before, and from what she could see, most of it seemed to be floored with the stuff.

All around the living room extension were various machines, most of which she still didn't know the functions of. A few smaller ones rested on a wooden corner desk. One of the objects on the desk was a flat rectangle, a computer, which she wasn't allowed to sit on.

The large, box-like contraption beside her whined to life. Ember jumped back, heart pounding. Her short, downy fur rose. She laughed at herself, then leaned forward to sniff the machine. "It's doing a thing. What thing is it doing?"

"Looks like Chell got your claws finished. They're getting printed now," Matthew said.

"Oh! Can I see?" Ember asked.

"Sure. Come here and I'll pick you up."

He bent down and splayed his arms. Ember trotted over to him. He scooped her up and held her level with the top of the printer. White liquid filled a small tray. A clear panel lifted up out of the liquid. As it did, eighteen white lumps formed, attached to the panel. Ember watched in awe as her new claws appeared from the plate of goo.

"Whoa," she whispered. "So those weren't there before? It looks like they were already attached and just got dipped in the white stuff. If you know what I'm trying to say. I know it didn't, but tahg, that's neat."

"Yes, I know what you're trying to say. It looks even more funny when what she's printing is big. The tray is only a few centimetres deep. When something that's half a metre long gets pulled out of there, it looks like a goop monster rising up from a swamp. I could watch it all day. Okay, maybe not all day, but for a little while it's as entertaining as a good stream series."

"Good, you *did* know what I was trying to say. 'Cause I'm not sure I did. Can you please put me down now?"

"Yes, I can." He lowered her back to the floor. "We'll leave those there until she gets back. I'd hate to mess something up. She does the 3D printing stuff around here, not me. I'm just the local computer nerd."

He stood back up and paused for a moment, then chuckled again.

"What?" Ember asked.

'I haven't known him for two full days yet, and he's already laughed more than most Westerners do in a mooncycle. Huh. That's kind of sad. Then again, they've got life a lot easier here.'

She sighed and looked around the lifeless room. *'I guess when the biggest problems you have are keeping litter off the carpet or oversleeping and being late for work, it's a lot easier to find things to laugh about. Little things like war and death do tend to put a damper on humor. But of course, it also makes it more valuable. And memorable. So maybe not laughing so much isn't sad.'*

"Hmm? Oh, no, I was just thinking about something," Matthew replied.

"Oh," she said. She closed her eyes and yawned. Her mind had already moved on from the reason behind his half-baked chuckle.

'What if I stopped laughing altogether and saved it all for when I get old and am about to die? Would that make it the most memorable, valuable laugh ever? Or would it even be genuine at that point? You'd probably forget how to laugh. Then it would be worthless. No, it's best when saved for special times. Like after the next snowfall when you, and Mom, and Kivy, and—'

"Ember? Hey, Ember, hello? You in there?" Matthew asked.

Ember blinked the daze from her eyes and shook herself off. "Y-yeah, I'm here. Just thinking about how we should probably conserve our laughter to make it more special. Among other things."

"Is laughter something that needs to be conserved?"

She hesitated. *'But what if it just limits the nice colors and makes everything worse instead of better? That wouldn't be good.'*

"I don't know. It might be. So when is Michelle supposed to get back again?" she mewed.

"She has to get finished with work, then pick up Lake. She'll come back after that," he said. "I know you're excited. Trust me—I know what it's like. But you've got to be patient, okay?"

To help pass the time, Matthew offered a few additional suggestions for 'coping mechanisms.' Some of his tips were so obvious she hadn't even given them much thought, like saying 'no' to something she knew she didn't want to or couldn't do. She'd said 'no' on occasion, but not often enough. Other tips weren't so obvious, yet were so simple she wondered why she hadn't thought of them before—like having others ask her questions about her interests anytime she felt overwhelmed.

When Matthew ran out of suggestions, Ember walked aimlessly around the house. Every few minutes, she found herself in a window outlooking the road. When she reached her third window, she sat down and made her prosthetics change to the favorite colors of her kin. Light purple first, like the phlox flowers Whitehaze secretly loved. Then dark blue, the color of evening shadows, which Kivyress enjoyed. Soft pink for Songbird. She hesitated when she reached Hyrees. He loved all colors equally, but she didn't like the idea of making herself rainbow; it would be too many colors in too small of a space. Then she remembered a time before he'd started going blind when he'd said his favorite color was pine green, so she went with that.

'I wonder what Dad's favorite color is. Does he even have a favorite color? Probably not. He probably thinks having a favorite color is fluffheaded, since there's nothing a favorite color can be used for. I'll just do yellow, like Mom's eyes. He'll never admit it, but that's probably his favorite color. Thai, can you make them light yellow?'

[Of course, Ember.]

She smiled as her paws became the tone of buttercups. *'What would he think of this? He'd probably just be confused and ask why I keep changing colors. Or why my legs can change colors in the first place. Oh well. Now for my color.'*

Once her paws turned reddish-orange, she found herself bored again. She set her colors back to default, got out the window, and kept wandering until Matthew found her again and asked what she was interested in. They talked about history and the various forms of water for a while, then Matthew tried to explain programming to her. When Michelle returned with Lake in tow, they were in his 'office room' examining his custom supercomputer.

"My claws are ready!" Ember called.

She raced into the living room. *' "Living room" is still a really strange thing to call a room. It's not alive, and none of you seem to spend much time in it. Come on, Ember. Focus. Claws and heated legs. That's what's important right now.'*

"Yes, they are," Michelle replied as she entered the room. "And guess what else is ready."

"I don't have to guess. I can see them sticking out from your thing. What do you call it?"

"Oh, whoops," Michelle said with a laugh. "Heh, oh well. But yes, your new prosthetic shells are ready. And it's called a 'bag,' by the way."

Michelle set her things on the floor, then removed her outer layer of clothing—a thick, fluffy jacket—to reveal the light blue shirt beneath. Lake scampered toward her room, her green jacket still on.

"Don't think for a millisecond that we won't be talking about those grades of yours, young lady," Michelle called after her.

"Test day?" Matthew asked. "I didn't think it was test day. That's usually on Friday."

'Test day? That doesn't sound good. Poor Lake. I know you can't hear me, but I hate tests too. I hope you did well.'

"It was her homework grades, Matt." Michelle put a hand against her head. "With everything going on with this project, I completely forgot to help her with it. Hopefully it didn't count for too much."

"If you blame yourself, why did you yell at her?" Matthew asked.

"It wasn't a yell, it was raising my voice so she could hear me as she ran. And I firmly believe she is more than capable of teaching herself if she needs to. Most other kids have to, given the quality of the teachers." She pushed her glasses farther up her nose. "I should have been there for her, though."

"Most other kids aren't two grades ahead. And most other kids don't have parents who still know how to do algebra. If you told them to solve ex-squared plus one equals sixty-five, they'd implode," Matthew said.

"I know, I know, I know." Michelle rubbed both hands against her face and sighed. "I don't want to be overprotective of her again, but at the same time, are we going back to not being involved enough?"

Matthew touched a finger to his bearded chin. "I don't know, but let's be honest with ourselves—we don't know how to parent."

"Painfully true," Michelle replied. "Let's just . . . take one thing at a time, okay? Okay, since you're not doing anything, how about you help her out while I fix the cat; then, when I'm done, I'll help her with science and such."

"I can do that," he replied. "Have fun fixing the cat."

She sighed again as Matthew strode after Lake. "Sorry about that, Ember.

I'll work on you for about an hour, then I have to go assist Lake with her schooling."

"No, it's okay," Ember said. "You shouldn't be sorry. I'm just a random cat you decided to help, and she's your daughter. I can wait."

"Glad you understand," Michelle said. "With that said, let's go get you tuned up. Your claws and updated casings aren't the only things I've managed to assemble today."

Ember's ears perked up. "What did you get? Or make. Did you make something else?"

Michelle bent down and pulled her bag in front of her. She reached into it, then pulled out a blueish-green loop the exact shade of sleep. A black chip with the same torn-off clover leaf shape as Michelle's bijou dangled from the loop. Supposedly the shape was meant to represent a heart, but having seen real hearts before, she couldn't honestly say she saw the resemblance.

"Oh! It's a clayvine with an ETAg, isn't it?" Ember asked.

"A *collar* and an ETAg. I hope you like it. Look." She touched the front of the tag and white symbols appeared. "It says your name in our language. If you ever find yourself with people again, they can use this to get in contact with me, Matt, or Dr. Sagong. You can also use it to communicate with other species, even if they don't have a Felid language pack, or even an AI implant or external device. Just remember that it won't work with most wildlife. But you probably weren't planning on having conversations with chipmunks anyway, so that shouldn't be a problem. Like your legs, it's solar powered, so it should last you a lifetime. We *will* have to schedule maintenance checks if you want to live out a more or less full life, though."

Ember stared at her shiny new accessory until the symbols disappeared. "Thank you."

She tried to think of another way to express her gratitude, but no amount of words could compete with the stream of kindness Michelle, Hye, and the other humans had shown her, so she left it at 'thank you.'

"You're very welcome." She adjusted her glasses again. They seemed to like sliding down her face. The day before, she'd explained why she wore the funny frames, and how she could get her eyes fixed to not need them. Eye surgery terrified her, however, so she continued using glasses—which Ember found ironic, given her speech on facing one's fears. "Now, let's get going."

Michelle slipped the collar over Ember's head. It automatically tightened itself. The material rubbed against her skin, but was soft enough to not hurt.

After syncing the tag with Thai, she turned off all of Ember's internal mechanics, paralyzing her legs, but making them painless to work on. Ember practiced using ETAg Thai as a translator while her internal system was down, but Michelle didn't speak a lot while she worked, so she didn't use it much.

She pulled off the panels from each leg, leaving her prosthetics a mess of wires, synthetic muscles, and other mechanical bits. Once all the protective coverings were gone, she started sliding the new parts into place. Even when dull grey, the old and new panels looked different. The new pieces were still segmented, but were also thinner and almost rubbery, with their edges rounded off. It made them more comfortable and flexible but also revealed portions of the internal mechanics at her joints.

Small, rectangular holes were set in each of her shoulder and hip coverings. Each opening framed the tiny solar chips that provided her machine parts with power. Lines of silver ran up and across each chip, dividing it up into six smaller chips. More silver lines crisscrossed in a grid beneath the surface of her new bionic skin. After putting on each piece, Michelle touched the holographic screen of her wrist phone, and the grid lit up with a fiery orange. This, she explained, would activate the mild adhesive in the covering and bind it to her legs.

When everything except Ember's toes were covered, she pulled the shiny white claws from the printer. The claws needed to be screwed in, so Michelle left to find a screwdriver she'd lost. She returned several minutes later, triumphantly holding up a red and silver stick. She'd also cut her hand on something since leaving. Tiny droplets of blood beaded up around a shallow scrape, barely visible against the darkness of her skin.

"What happened to your hand?" Ember asked.

"Banged it into a shel—wait." She lifted her injured hand to examine the scratch. "How did you see that? I didn't even realize it was bleeding."

"I saw it by looking."

'You're supposed to say something else here, aren't you? I mean, she's obviously fine, but I'm pretty sure it's supposed to be polite to ask. And you never know for sure.' Ember licked her lips and resisted the urge to bite her tongue. "Uhm, are you okay?"

"Yes, I'm fine, sweetie. Thanks for asking. Let's get you finished up. I'm sure Matt is getting close to being finished, himself."

'Themselves. Matthew and Lake are working together, right? If he's almost done with something, she's almost done with it too. Even if that something is just being done with his part of the training.'

She decided to keep the correction to herself. It didn't matter, and explaining herself out loud would only waste time and energy she couldn't afford to waste.

Michelle fit each claw onto each toe, then used little black metal pieces, called 'screws,' to secure them into place. While Michelle worked on her hind legs, Ember picked one up with her teeth and sucked on it. The knob on one of its ends had a funny little dent in it. The rest tickled her tongue. She turned it over a few times in her mouth.

'Oh, I like this. It feels all cold and weird. It even tastes funny. Almost like water. What if water was just tiny pieces of metal? Of course it isn't, but it's still funny how similar they taste.'

"Ember, what are you chewing on?" Michelle asked.

"A screw. They taste surprisingly good, all things considered. Almost like wa—"

She pushed her glasses up again. "Spit it out."

Her voice took on the same tone she'd chided Lake in. Ember flattened her ears and obeyed. "Sorry."

Michelle picked up the screw and wiped it off on her shirt. "Ew. Do you know how gross that is? Not to mention dangerous."

"Er . . . no?"

She rubbed a hand against her forehead. "Just don't do it."

After fastening down all the claws, she set the final pieces into place, then turned everything back on. Ember's stomach churned when feeling appeared were it didn't exist a moment before. The sensation of suddenly gaining limbs felt like a dying leaf—sickly mold green and fascinating brown with a touch of alarming yellow.

Michelle sighed. "Okay, good, that worked."

"There was doubt?" Ember asked.

"Not much, though this is the first time I've done something like this, so there was no telling how your body might react. Now, how about you try unsheathing your claws?"

Ember snorted. "No one told me this would be dangerous."

"Because it wasn't. I know what I'm doing. If there was even a tiny chance of death or serious complications, I would've taken more precautions, and had the screwdriver ready. Now come on, let's focus on making sure everything works."

Ember sighed. She stretched out her foreleg and splayed her toes. The newly installed claws poked out. Ember's eyes lit up. She pulled her paw closer to get a better look. They almost looked like real claws, but without quicks.

"How well can they cut through wood?" she asked.

"Wood? Sorry, sweetie, you can't use these to scratch anything hard. They won't regrow. If they get dull, you'll have to come to me to get new ones. Don't sharpen them on anything, and definitely don't try any wood carving. You'll ruin them. What? What's wrong?"

Ember's lower jaw trembled. *'No clawmarking ever? I mean, he's probably already got a new apprentice anyway, but now I don't even have a chance. I just . . . wanted so badly . . .'*

"Hey, we're done with algebra," Matthew said as he entered the room. "And what did you tell her? She can't carve anymore? Chell, is it possible to give her growing claws?"

"No, I can't," Michelle replied. "There's nothing strong enough that can be triggered to reconstruct itself. These will last a lifetime if she just uses them for hunting and the occasional climb up a tree. Why? Do you know something about this I'm not aware of?"

"Yes. She can't write without her claws, and she wants to become a historian. That is what you said, right?"

"I'll be fine," Ember said quietly. "Wouldn't have been any good at it anyway. I failed the test. Really, I shouldn't have been the historian apprentice to begin with. There are cats who would be better at it than me. I can . . . admire history from a distance."

"Oh. Gosh, I'm sorry, Ember. I promise I'd make you something better if I could, but there's just nothing better out there. Well, I mean, I guess I could make you diamond claws, but that could take years and would be ridiculously expensive. I really am sorry," Michelle said.

"No, it's okay. You saved my life. I'd rather be alive without being able to clawmark than be dead." Yet she couldn't stop the dull, misty orange aches of sadness from sinking in.

'Never clawmarking again? I guess some might count that as a good thing. Tainu would. But now she won't, because I killed her. But I'm alive right now, and I'm going home soon. Everything is as okay as it can be. Everything's okay, everything's okay, everything's okay. Safe. I'm safe. Because everyone's been so nice to me. I still don't know why. I'll have to ask about it sometime. This is more than just an experiment. It has to be.'

"I'm glad you can understand," Michelle said. "I've got to go help Lake now. Matt, how about you get some food ready? I skipped lunch today and I'm starving."

'Starving? But I know you ate that round thing before you left this morning. I guess you need to eat a lot. I hope you didn't starve yourself to get my parts made. That would be bad. Unless Thai didn't translate it right.'

"Can do," Matthew replied. Once Michelle left the room, he bent down and whispered, "She's not actually starving. She's being dramatic, as usual. I didn't understand that saying when I was little, which is why I thought you might not have either. But if you did, good for you."

"Oh, okay. No, where I live, 'starvation' has a very different meaning from 'hungry.' "

"I imagine it does. I'm going to go make us people something to eat. You can entertain yourself. Just don't scratch the furniture; it's not good for your claws. Or Chell's nerves."

"I won't. Scratch the furniture, that is."

"Good," he said, then he left for the forbidden-from-climbing area they dubbed 'the kitchen.'

Ember sighed and meandered over to the couch. She climbed up it, then perched herself on the back window.

'Humans are funny creatures. Or, at least these are. I guess they must have had a domestic at some point. The litter box and bowls all look old. Unless they were made with dust and cracks, but that seems unlikely. Do all humans live in tiny groups like this? How do they function so well without parents or a commander to help them out or give them advice? Well, Lake obviously has parents, but she's young. Guess they're their own commanders. That must be nice. Or maybe they're more like Outsiders, forming little family groups to survive better. At least they're not like Rogues. Hye said they were at war, didn't he? How does that work with such tiny groups?'

Ember flattened her ears. *'I still don't know. Humans are funny creatures, and they saved my life, and I'll be grateful.'*

CHAPTER 15
EMBER

"So, how are we doing this, again? And how do you know for sure you'll put me in the same place I was found?" Ember asked.

She yawned. Little starbursts of blue-green popped up in the back of her mind. Sleep had eluded her most of the night again. Unlike the previous few nights, however, it was excitement, rather than annoyance or unease, that had kept her up. As foretold by her human friend, her fur was almost its original length again. With her claws, heating system, and ETAg in place, she could finally go back.

"I already told you," Michelle said as she slid on her jacket. "You're going to get inside this carrier, and we're going to ride to your home after I drop off Lake. And the lady who found you told us where you got hit. I know where it is. It's going to be okay, Ember. I know you're nervous, but asking me to tell you what's about to happen, minute by minute, won't do anything but make us take longer."

They'd spent part of the day before taking what Michelle had called 'videos' of Ember doing various things with her prosthetics. Michelle planned on using the footage to show what the mechanics could do, making others more likely to take the risk of trying them.

"Where's Matthew?"

"He's on his way to work. You literally said goodbye to him ten minutes ago. Now get in the carrier. We have to go." She raised her voice, "Come on, Lake, we're going to be late!"

'Eleven. I know that, but why . . . never mind.'

She padded into the dull grey cave of hard plastic. Her thoughts started to swirl with static again, but she bit her tongue and it stopped. No matter how hard she tried to break the habit, it always seemed to find its way back between her teeth.

'This is it, this is it. I'm going home now. Home, home, home. Going home. This is good.'

"Coming, Momma. Just a minute!" Lake replied from her room.

As Michelle closed the metal bar door, Ember took one last look around the house, trying to memorize its flat wooden walls and funny carpet floor. She'd spent most of the past three days exploring it and planned to explore it again in her head. She could immortalize it in her mind's eye just as she had immortalized the Glade and her family.

'They're going to be so surprised and happy to see me,' she thought. *'My resurrection might just give them enough hope and strength to pull through. And with Thai helping me, I can do so much more than I ever could being a regular border guard. And I can—oh!'*

They left the house, and as the cold air hit her, an equally chilling thought invaded her mind. *'What if they aren't happy to see me? What if they've already moved on and don't like the idea of having to eventually mourn my death again. That would be mildly annoying, going through all that heartbreak only to find the one you were so sad for was alive and well all along. Guess that goes to show assuming only leads to miscalculation, which usually leads to something not great, but it's not my fault they're wrong. Of course, it's also possible they know I'm still alive and am coming back, but that doesn't seem likely. Especially if they know humans have me.'*

Michelle hefted the carrier up into her vehicle: a long green machine, like the things that ran the Wolf Trail. Ember eyed it warily as Lake jumped in after her. Michelle closed the door, then entered through the one in front of them. She sat down. Both humans strapped themselves to the seats.

A new thought entered Ember's head. Her throat tightened. *'Oh tahg, what if they wanted me gone? Or, possibly even worse, what if they're indifferent to my coming back? I didn't account for that. Then the dramatic entrance I planned out last night would be useless and I won't know what to do. Guess I could make a backup plan on the way there. Just in case.'*

"Take us to school," Lake said. Ember couldn't tell for sure, but she seemed a lot less enthusiastic than she'd been on the day they'd met.

The vehicle grumbled to life, ready to obey. Without any further instruction, things started to stir. Ember peered out of her cage as the world seemed to move around them.

"It's noisy and almost as ancient as I am, but it'll get us where we need to go. I will warn you that we will hit a few bad bumps along the way; the truck doesn't handle them well, and there's nothing I can do about it, so don't stand up while we're moving."

'Ancient, and almost as old as you? What's your definition of "ancient?"' Ember thought. "How long do you people live?"

Michelle laughed. "Our average lifespan is about seventy years. It's actually dropped recently, believe it or not, but that's just the average. My great grandmother is still alive, and she's a hundred and ten—older than your breed."

"Seventy?" Ember asked. "A hundred and—Tahg, that's long. I'll be lucky if I reach twenty. How old are you?"

She laughed again. This time it was more of a gentle chuckle. "Thirty-six. This pickup belonged to my parents, and is thirty-one. Lake here is—"

"I'm ten," Lake said softly.

"Heh, I'm the youngest one here," Ember said. "But really, you shouldn't feel old. You've still got about half of your life left, and it's more than *all* of my life. You'll probably outlive me by years."

"I don't know," Michelle said. "I found a grey hair a few days ago. But you've definitely put my life in perspective. I'll have to remember that."

"What? That I'm most likely going to die before you? I guess if it makes you feel better, go ahead and remember it."

"No, that's not what I . . . oh, never mind, you little silly."

'Silly?' The conversation had taken her mind off the internal aches and anxieties her brain kept spitting out, but with its dull, morbid end, they all came flooding back. She bit her tongue until she remembered how pleasant gnawing on her toes had been and switched to chewing on them instead. The pickup stopped at a loud place with more small people. Most of them were noticeably larger than Lake. Lake got off and the door shut behind her before Ember could even say 'goodbye.'

"Have a good day, sweetie," Michelle called after her through an open window.

Lake didn't reply, and instead watched in silence as the truck pulled away. Ember watched her get smaller until they turned, causing trees to obstruct her from view. She was an interesting little human. Ember wished she'd gotten to know her better, but she'd spent most of her limited time at the house in her room, usually working on homework.

"I don't blame her," Ember said after a minute of silence.

"For what?" Michelle asked.

"Not wanting to go there. I'm no good with expressions, but I can usually tell when someone isn't happy. And looking at and listening to all those other people, I can understand why."

"She'll be fine, Dr. Ember. She just gets nervous. Now let's get you home. Take us down Meadow Ridge Road."

'Doctor? Isn't that what Hye is? I'm not a doctor. I'm not even a healer. Hum, you humans are really confusing creatures. Oh, thinking of confusing, this may be your last chance to talk to her without calling her. If you want the answers to their mysteries, you should probably ask now. It's more polite that way, I think.'

"Hey, Michelle? Can I ask you some questions?" Ember asked.

She smiled and turned her seat to face her. "Sure, we've got time. Ask away."

"Why . . . why are you being so nice to me? You, and Hye, and Matthew. You all did so much just to help someone you didn't even know, and I don't know why. I, er, I want to know why."

Her smile disappeared. "Well, there's no easy answer to that, because, like with most decisions in life, there's more than one reason to consider for each person involved. I had reasons, Hye had reasons, and Matt, well, he just got dragged along for the ride. This wasn't his project, though he did help. Now, I don't mean to sound cold, but you weren't the main factor in most of our decisions. When we saved your life, we weren't being nice, we were being professional. When I took you home to recover, that was for the sake of making things easier on me. Don't take it the wrong way; I really do care about you, but in this case, I will admit I was more concerned about my benefits than yours." She leaned back in her seat and gazed out the nearest window. "To be perfectly honest, the only selfless thing I've ever done for you is taking you back home, and I haven't even done that yet."

'So she was doing it for herself.' Ember rested her chin on her paws. The new heating system inside them made them warm, but not feverish. She took a moment to gather her words together, as Matthew had suggested she do. It was hard sometimes to not speak or act automatically, but when she slowed down, she found herself responding more clearly. "At least you're being honest. I still appreciate your help, though, even if it also helped you. Not all help has to be selfless. So how much longer will it take to get there?"

"It'll be a while. We've got time to keep talking, if you like. I'm sure you've got more questions." Michelle said. She kept looking out the window. When Ember didn't reply, she continued, "While I don't think it's really my place to tell you why Hye did what he did, I will tell you I also had reasons aside from work and money. You probably already figured this out, but I used to have an appala mix. She was rescued alongside Yegor from someone who was illegally breeding appala-domestic hybrids under unspeakable conditions. It was one of those places we would call a 'kitten mill.' We had quite a battle with ARC, trying to keep them, but that's not the point. The point is, we got her—me and Matthew—before Lake was even born, and we had her until about three years ago. Best cat ever. No offense. I'll admit I'm biased, but you do remind me of her. You remind me of her a lot, and in so many ways."

She breathed out slowly through her mouth. "She got outside the house one day, and since we live in the middle of nowhere, the roads don't have safety tunnels around them. She was exploring and wandered onto the road and . . . not unlike you, she got hit. The technology we needed to save her has existed for many, many years—longer than I've been alive, but it was just too expensive, and . . . and there was a high probability she wouldn't . . . *make* the surgery."

She sniffed quietly and rubbed an arm against her eyes. "So, we talked it over a lot . . . Matt, and me, and her . . . and we all decided it would be better to let her go in peace. Instead of risking so much for such a small chance. I wish . . . we could have taken that chance, but at the time we just didn't have the money. Lake had been sick for a really long time that past year, and treating her had exhausted all our funds. We were in a lot of debt, and at risk of losing our home, so we just . . . couldn't. Hardest decision I ever made. And then you came along—someone I *could* save. So I did."

'Deciding to die,' Ember thought. The truck went over a bump, making her head slam against the side of her carrier. She winced and straightened herself up. *'Ow. Deciding to let someone die. That must have been hard. What was it like, agreeing to let herself be killed? Did it hurt so much that dying seemed like mercy? Was it peaceful? Or was she afraid? If so, how afraid? I know I'd be scared, saying yes, that I'm okay with dying. No one knows what it's really like, because no one's ever come back to share. That alone is terrifying.'*

Michelle smiled, despite the lone tear dripping from her chin. "She actually did the Felid voices for the translators we've been using to talk. Her and Yegor, with a lot of help from Hye." She chuckled. "I had to trust that they weren't ruining it, but so far no one's complained about inaccuracy, so I suppose they did a good job. I'm not surprised, though. She was a good little cat. Yegor's a good little cat, too."

"What was her name? The cat, I mean," Ember said.

"Thai," she replied. "Her name was 'Thai.' And now you know where your AI gets its name. In hindsight, I really shouldn't have named it that, because it only makes all this that much harder on me, but it is what it is." She took her glasses off, wiped the tears from her eyes, then cleaned the glasses with her shirt. "We're getting closer, I think, so if you have any other questions, you may want to go ahead and ask them."

Ember thought for a while. There were questions she wanted to ask—she knew there were—but she couldn't remember them. So she remained silent.

And then there it was: home. Her mountain and her fields, it was all there. Dull, grey, and half-dead, but it was all hers.

"This is it! This is it! You found it, you really did. Oh tahg, I really am going home," she mewed.

"Pull over," Michelle instructed.

The pickup veered off the road again. It sputtered to a stop near the metal fence. Michelle opened the door, picked up the carrier, then set it down in the frosty grass. She opened up the cage and leaned back. Ember crept to the carrier's edge to sniff the ground. It even smelled familiar: all earthy and cool. She set a paw on the place she sniffed. The melty snow made it feel different from how she remembered it, but the ground was still her own.

She crept out of the carrier, examining the grass as she walked. Frigid air hit her side. The mountain breeze toyed with her whiskers. Fresh and freezing oxygen filled her lungs as she drew in a long, deep breath.

"I guess this is the part where we say our goodbyes and go our separate ways," Michelle said. "I'm glad I got to meet you, Ember. I wish the circumstances we'd met under had been better, but I'd say as it is now that we needed each other."

Ember forced a smile. "Yeah, I guess so."

"Is there something wrong, sweetie?"

"I don't know." Ember pushed her paws together and tried to look out over the fields. Coyote Rock and a few trees loomed over the barrier. "I'm going home, yes, but home has changed. My commander is dead, and my cousin is dead, and other than them, I don't know who survived the fight and who didn't. When I go back, I'll know, and I can't pretend they're alive anymore." She shivered slightly as the wind picked up. "The night I got hit, there was a battle between my colony and the East. Now there's probably going to be a war, and I'm not ready for that. I do want to go home, but I don't know how much home there will be left for me to go to. I'm not ready to know, and I'm not ready to fight. I'm . . . Michelle, I'm scared."

Michelle sat down, knees against the grass. She held out her hand. Ember pushed her head against it, inviting her to pet her, which she did.

"It's going to be okay," Michelle whispered. "You've got a lot going on out here, don't you? Knowing will be hard, sweetie, but it'll help you sleep tonight. You won't have to worry anymore. Remember what I said about being scared? You can't let that fear hold you back from moving forward."

"But what if they aren't happy to see me? And what will they think of this?" Ember lifted a paw to her face. The heating grid glowed a faint caring orange beneath her synthetic skin. The colors of her legs, aside from the glow, looked like her own, and there were four of them, but the resemblance ended there. She was half machine, and she looked half machine. She shuddered.

'Which one will they see me as? Cat, or machine?' she thought. "I don't care what I look like, because I don't look at myself, but what if they're scared of me? I don't look like me, and I'm the one who killed Tainu. What if Hyrees doesn't love me anymore because I can't have kittens, and look like this, and did that? There's so much silver. The mist is too thick; I can't see."

"You *k*—?" Michelle stopped petting her.

Ember winced. Sadness and guilt colored her thoughts with dreary oranges. *'I shouldn't have said that. Why did I mention Tainu?'*

Michelle sighed and stretched out her arms, inviting her to come closer. Ember obliged, and she scooped her up against her chest. The warmth of her jacket invited her. The pressure of her arms against her sides calmed her shaking body.

"It's okay. It's okay. I don't know the exact circumstances you and your family are dealing with right now, but I promise, if they're really your family, they'll be happy to see you, no matter what you look like, or what you can do for them," Michelle said.

Ember mewed quiet nonsense to herself. She wanted to stay in Michelle's arms forever. Or at least a little longer. Long enough to fall asleep. "Promise, promise?"

"Promise, promise." Michelle smiled, lower lip quivering. Another tear rolled down her cheek, causing Ember to wonder if she was thinking about Thai. "Are you ready now?"

"No."

"Too bad." She set Ember back down. "It's time for you to go home. If I waited until you were ready, we'd be here all day. The sooner you get back, the sooner you'll get it over with. Also, I really should go to work. I'm already late."

Ember stepped back and tried for a second time to control her breathing. *'One, two, three, four, five. I can do this. Everything's going to be okay. And if not, I'll make it okay. And if I can't do that, maybe Michelle can take me back.'*

She sighed. "You're right. Thank you. Thanks for everything. I don't know what else to say to show how much I appreciate all this. Can't seem to think of anything better than 'thank you.' I'm really gonna miss you, Chell."

"You're very welcome, Em. We'll keep in contact; don't worry. I might try calling you, or having Matt call you when we get back from work today. Would that be good?"

"I don't know if I'll feel like talking. Maybe I can call you. Or thought message you. Or something."

"That'll work. Goodbye, Ember."

Ember ran over to her and pressed her head against her jacket one last time. Her heart pounded against her chest. "Bye."

Michelle wrapped her arms around her again. She pulled back a moment later, then stood up. "Go on, sweetie. You can do this."

Ember took one last look at her unlikely friend, then crawled under the metal barrier dividing the road from the Upper Field. Behind her, Michelle's old pickup truck revved back to life. Stones crackled beneath its huge wheels. The grumble faded, so she kept moving toward the forest. She didn't have to look back to know Michelle was gone.

CHAPTER 16
EMBER

The grass stopped. She stopped. Ember sucked in a sharp, frigid breath of air. Five stones sat in a row at the forest edge near the remnants of a large fire. All five were smeared over with unreadable char clawmarks. A shiver crept up her spine.

'Oh. Oh no. These are memorial stones, aren't they? At least five of—wait, is that my clayvine?'

She padded over to the last stone. Faded clawmarks spelled out her name in beautiful, artistic strokes. On top of the stone, perfectly framing the barely readable identifier, rested the bijou Hyrees had bought her. The vine holding it had snapped, and a small fracture ran down the tiny maple leaf attached to it.

She stepped back. *'Wait, this is my memorial stone. I'm dead, and those are my ashes. Or at least the ashes of four other cats from a fire that was meant to include me. This is really weird.'*

She shivered again and sniffed it. Hyrees's scent filled her nose, along with a hint of Cloud. Adrenaline flooded into her bloodstream, making her feel more awake and alive than she'd ever felt before.

'They're okay! They're okay, and they've been here today. And they think I'm dead.' She glanced down at the four other stones. *'But who actually died? I don't think they would carry Aspen's ashes and coals all the way out here.*

These other ones must have died in the fight.'

Excitement, anxiety, unease, and alarm created an explosion of colors in her head. She tried to imagine what it would be like to be a conscience without a body, and what it would be like to watch her former body get burnt into nothing. For a few hours, she would become her namesake. Then the fire would die, and they would take her char and ashes to decorate her stone. She would watch as they cried, and she wouldn't be able to tell them not to. Then she'd probably fade into nothingness, like falling into an eternal sleep.

Her eyes dampened but no tears came. Instead, her chest decided to feel tight and achy. She shook herself off and told herself to focus on the excitement instead of the unease. She sniffed the air, trying to figure out which way Hyrees and Cloud had gone after leaving her tattered accessory. Once she pinpointed the direction, she moved past the stones toward her family.

'Up the mountain; they're going up the mountain. Past the Glade at this point. Toward the creek, too. That's where the Falls are. They're probably going there. I know I would.'

After a few minutes of walking, voices rose over the ever-blowing breeze. Voices she knew. Ember scaled a nearby tree, then peered out from behind the trunk. *'One little climb shouldn't hurt.'* Her heart pounded with excitement. Bursts of orange and red sparkled in the back of her mind. *'Oh tahg, this is it. This is going to be fun. I'm going to see them again, and they're going to be so surprised to see me.'*

The owners of the voices appeared, just as she imagined them. Hyrees on the left, fur still a clay-colored mess, and Cloud on the right, silver pelt shimmering with gold in the morning sunlight.

'Okay, Ember, stick to the plan. This has to be perfe—'

Her heart lurched. Her throat went dry. Cloud's fur was almost as messy as Hyrees's, and Hyrees himself was skinny enough to make out some of his ribs, even from her perch. She leaped out of the tree and charged toward them.

"Hyrees, what happened to you?" she yowled.

Both toms' eyes widened. Their ears shot up like those of startled hares. "Ember?" Cloud asked.

"Ember!" Hyrees yowled. He bounded forward to meet her halfway.

Before they could collide, Ember darted to the right and went in circles around him, examining his emaciated frame and wounded muzzle. "What did you do to yourself? You're all scrawny and—"

"Ember!" he said again. Hyrees tackled her, laughing. She hit the ground hard enough to knock the air from her chest.

"You're alive! You're alive and—oh!" He jumped back. "Okay, that's different. What . . . what happened to your legs? And what's that around your neck? And where's the rest of your ear? And tail, part of your tail is gone. But your legs are, are, uhm . . . Ember . . . what happened to you?"

Ember rolled back to her paws, chest tense with anxiety. "It's, uhm, a long story, but I've learned a lot over the past few days. You know about humans. Well, turns out not all of them are bad. Also, the History Tree is wrong about a lot of things, but not everything. And—Dad? Hey, Dad, are you okay?"

She lowered her head and licked her lips. If the wind weren't blowing his fur around, she might have mistaken him for a rock formation. He stared at her in silence, not so much as twitching his tail.

Ember rubbed one paw on top of the other. "I know I look different, but I promise you I'm still Ember. That's . . . okay, right? That I look different? I don't look the same, but I am me. Oh. Uhm, I'm sorry I didn't listen to you that night. I really am. But I've learned some things since I left, and I think I might be a better help to the Colony because of all this. I can be better now."

The wind died down, cloaking the forest in silence.

Fear tugged at her insides. "Dad?"

He coughed a few times, then ran to her. He pressed his nose against hers. "Ember, you're alive! My kitten is alive! Oh, Ember . . ."

"Hey, let me in too," Hyrees said. He nuzzled his way under her chin.

Orange—oh so familiar orange—the color of the broken maple leaf, filled Ember's head. After what had felt like an eternity of waiting, she was finally back where she belonged. *'Home. Home! I'm home. Finally. And I smell*

Mom and Kivy and Farlight on them. They're okay too. Oh tahg, everyone's okay! Maybe things can go back to normal after all.'

"I thought I'd never see you again," Hyrees mewed, taking her back into the moment. "Cloud said you were dead."

"Oh, you're going to bring that up now?" Cloud asked.

He stepped back. Hyrees pushed himself closer to Ember's chest. "Yeah, why not?"

Cloud sighed.

"What?" she asked, breaking free from Hyrees's affection.

Cloud chuffed, but stopped suddenly and narrowed his eyes. "Ember, you're . . . glowing."

"Well, yeah, but that's kind of important. It's a heating system that keeps me from getting something called 'hypothermia,' which is what happens when you get too cold, have weird daydreams, then fall asleep."

He chuckled. "Sounds almost like me a few days ago." He walked up to her once again and pressed his forehead against hers. "My daughter is alive," he whispered. He brushed his face against her cheek, then rested his chin on the back of her neck. "Ember . . ."

When he pulled back, his cheek fur was wet. "I'm sorry I wasn't there for you. I should've been the one to go after Tainu."

Ember bounced on her forepaws. "What? Dad, no, it's okay. It isn't your fault. You told me to stop; I didn't listen. It's my fault. And, actually, I think this might be a good thing. Watch this. Thai, show me a snowflake."

She bit her tongue at the mention of Thai's name. She'd been a real cat who'd done the voice for her artificial intelligence system, then died. *'Thanks for making this weird and creepy, Michelle.'*

"Here you go," ETAg Thai said.

A projected image of a giant snowflake appeared on the ground. Hyrees and Cloud jumped back. She pushed aside the silvers of unease and tried to imagine what colors they were feeling.

'Probably a lot of yellow,' she thought.

"See?" she said. "And that's just the beginning. I can ask questions, find out what the weather is going to do tomorrow, and learn how to do anything you can imagine. We can improve medicine, clayworking techniques, *anything*. It's all here. More answers than we can ask questions for. Maybe we can even learn how to prevent more fights. And it's all thanks to this. Thai, you can turn that off now."

The projection disappeared, and the forest fell silent once again. "So, what do you think?" Ember asked.

Hyrees nuzzled her chin again, smiling and crying like a kitten. "This is amazing. It's . . . it's my best dreams come true. You're alive and you're here. I can barely even wrap my head around it. I mean the thingy with the snowflake is nice too, but you being here right now, that's . . . it's . . . I don't even have the words." He licked her cheek. "I love you, Ember. Just wanted to say that. I never said it enough before, but I'm going to try to fix that. Expect at least two 'I love yous' every day from now on. Possibly more."

She buried her nose in his fur and breathed in his familiar scent. A weight lifted from her back, a weight she hadn't even realized she'd been carrying. *'He still loves me. He really does. Oh, wait, I haven't told him yet.'* The weight came back. *'I hope he doesn't mind it much. Should I tell him now? Probably. Better to get all the bad stuff over with as soon as you can, Ember.'*

She pulled back, throat tightening. Her stomach churned. "So, there are some things I, er, really need to tell you. Things that could change . . . the way you see me. First off, I killed Tainu. I don't know if either of you knew already, but I did it, and I didn't mean to. It was an accident, but I killed her, and I'm really, really sorry."

"We already knew," Cloud said. "Death is a part of war, Ember. Sometimes it can't be avoided. No one's going to hold it to you. Not even Fern or Fledge. And if they do, they're fluffheads. Tainu deserved it. Now come on, let's go show everyone you're back. Wait until Song and Kivy see you."

Her heart beat faster at the mention of their names. She shook herself off, trying to calm it. *'Okay, that's one thing down. Wait, did he just say she deserved it? But she didn't. She wanted me to leave and I didn't. She said she didn't want to do it. Someone made her do it. Come on, Ember, stop putting it off. You've gotta tell them everything. No keeping secrets. At least none of your own.'*

"No, wait, I'm not done. Hyrees, this will affect you more than Dad, but, I, well, I can't have kittens anymore. The humans, they did something to me, and I can't have them. If you don't want to be with me anymore, I understand. I know you wanted a family, and I know how important it is for, you know, being a good Colony Cat, and now that I can't give one to you—"

"Wait, hold on, how do you know this? What exactly did they do?" Hyrees asked.

"They, uh, cut stuff out, I think? I know they did it because they told me. I wouldn't believe it, either, but some of them could actually understand me, and even talk to me. They learned our language. They actually learned Felid. And I've learned a tiny bit of their language too, but, uhm . . ."

Hyrees and Cloud exchanged a glance.

'Do they believe me? Tahg, I wish Kivy was here. She would know.'

"If that really is the case, it's . . . it's fine. I don't really want to raise a family in the middle of a war, anyway," Hyrees said.

Yellow flashed through her head. "War? So there really is going to be a war? Did Jade really make Tainu kill Commander Aspen?"

Hyrees glanced at Cloud, then at Ember again. "Oh, right, you weren't there," he said. "She never admitted to it, but from what I heard about the way she acted, she almost definitely did. But get this—she's the one who declared war on us. Apparently they said we attacked them, so it's cause enough for more fighting."

Ember bit down on her tongue. *'So this really is just the beginning. Guess I made it back too late after all.'*

"So do you have any other, er, surprises to spring on us, or can we head back to the Glade now?" Cloud asked.

'Should I tell them about the whole "I don't think like you" thing? They might not understand. Then again, they might, and—Wait a moment, Hyrees is patrolling with Dad. Why did I not think this is weird before now?

If he's patrolling with Dad, where is Wren?'

She shivered as a picture of the line of stones flashed through her mind. After noticing her own, she hadn't given herself much time to examine the others. She cursed herself under her breath for not even trying to decipher the smudged clawmarks.

Her tail twitched with anxiety. "Hyrees . . . your dad?"

They exchanged a second glance. This one lasted longer and involved a lot of tail twitching and ear flicks. Kivyress would call it a 'body conversation.' Ember again found herself wishing her sister would conveniently materialize from the mist to translate.

Hyrees nodded once, then Cloud stepped closer. "He's . . . he's gone, Ember," Cloud said.

A shiver trickled down her spine. *'Wait, Wren? Not him. He's dead? Oh. Oh tahg.'*

She tried to imagine Wren's kind, quiet voice, with its mellow accent and lilting rhythm, or even just his soft, jolly laugh, but found she couldn't get either of them right—at least not as vividly as she could with Hyrees or Kivyress. Even the imaginary version of him was disappearing. Fog filled her head. She tried to force out tears to show them she cared, but a cold, sinking numbness was all she could muster.

"I'm really sorry, Hyrees," Ember said. She licked his cheek in an attempt to remedy her lack of external emotion. His tears seemed effortless, and they left a salty bitterness on her tongue. "I don't know . . . what else to say. I should probably be crying right now, but I'm not for some reason. I promise I really do feel sorry. And sad."

"Thanks, Em," he whispered. "But you don't have to be upset. I want to see you happy right now. It makes me forget about my sad, miserable existence."

Cloud sighed and shook his head. "In addition to Aspen and Wren, three good cats died that night. Five fell in total. Six if we were to count you. The East only lost two. We've only fought one battle so far and we're already losing the war."

"That's how war usually is, isn't it?" Ember asked. "Everyone loses? So who else didn't, er, make it?"

He sighed again, then listed three names—three cats who'd probably known her better than she'd known them when they were alive. She couldn't help but feel a tiny burst of relief. It wasn't that they deserved to die. From what she knew, they were good cats with families who would mourn them. Yet since she didn't know them personally, their names being among the deceased meant the cats she did know personally weren't yet ashes scattered on the ground. Or at least most of them weren't.

'It's selfish, isn't it? Not being sad? I don't know. Maybe not. But I can't force myself to feel something, so it must not be. Isn't selfishness just not being considerate of other living things? If that's true, this doesn't count. Whatever it is, it should only be something someone has control over, and shouldn't have anything to do with emotions. Things like decisions. Decisions can be selfish, but emotions are just emotions. And colors. Though selfish decisions can come from emotions. Hum. So where does that place me?'

CLOUD

She was doing it again: freezing up. He hated it when she did that. It was impossible to tell what was running through her head, if he had caused it or not, and, more importantly, how to make her stop.

"Ember? Ember, are you okay?" Cloud asked. "I'm sorry, I didn't mean to upset you. You wanted to know, didn't you?"

He tried to focus on her familiar yet emotionless face, rather than the artificial legs he could only assume the humans had given her. They'd taken her away, and had apparently decided to give her back, but only after turning her into something most cats would consider a monster. It's what they did, after all; they ruined lives and played with forces no one in their right mind would go near. Somewhere in the back of his head, he wondered if the humans intended to use her to find the Colony. It seemed like something they would do. He tried to shake the thought away before it could fully form. She was home, and that was all that mattered.

Her eyes regained their focus, but their eerie blankness remained. She never seemed to be fully present at any given time. During and immediately after one of her 'zone outs,' however, her vacant gaze made it look like her mind and body had completely detached from each other. Cloud sighed. He coughed a few times. *'Guess I'll have to repeat myself now.'*

"No, you didn't upset me. I was just . . . working through some things. That's all. Should I be upset? I probably should. I don't know. But I'm not, and I'm mostly just happy to be back. And glad you're not chasing me away because of what I look like now."

'Or maybe she was listening.' He smiled. "No. Hyrees is right. Which, honestly, isn't something I thought I'd get to say today. Right now is a time to be glad. My kitten has come home. Now come on, let's get you back to the Glade."

"Can we not say anything when we get there? I want to see how long it takes for someone to notice me," she said.

His smile disappeared. *'They'll notice you. It's hard to miss someone with glowing, human-made machines for legs. And even if they don't see you at first, they're going to hear you. It's only going to make your hunting even harder. Oh, Ember, what are we going to do with you?'*

Yet, in the back of his mind, all he could process was the fact that she was even alive at all, and even figuring out how to go about letting that simple absolute truth sink in was something he wasn't certain of. It all still felt like a dream.

"Sure," Hyrees replied. "I kind of want to see too, but I'll have to settle for watching smudges and listening."

They walked back toward the Glade together: Hyrees on her right, Cloud to her left. Her human-made leg replacements whirred and whined with every step she took.

'Poor kitten,' Cloud thought. Nausea made his aching throat tighten. *'Does she even realize how terrible this looks? She had a hard enough time fitting in before all this mess. What's going to happen to her now, now that the*

humans have mutilated her? I'm so sorry I let this happen to you. You might say this is a good thing, but it's only going to hurt you. Looking like that, not being able to have kittens, it's a fluffheaded and broken thing, even having to worry about it, but it's going to hurt you here, and I can't stop it. I can try, but I can't stop it. It shouldn't matter, but when the entire colony shuns you . . . makes me sick, or at least sicker, just thinking about it.'

"D-Dad? Are you okay?" she asked.

"Yes, yeah, I'm fine," Cloud said. He coughed twice. "Just a little dazed and recovering from a fever, that's all."

"Oh. Well, at least you're recovering." She stopped. "Oh, I, er, do have something else to tell you."

He sighed and turned around. Hyrees was still beside her, sticking to her like tree sap. "What is it, Ember?"

She flattened back her ears. "I, well, you know how I don't like bright, sunny days or loud noises? And how I sometimes start laughing and you have no idea why? And just generally how I'm so weird and awkward?"

'Am I supposed to say "yes" here?'

"Well," she continued, "there's actually a reason for that. Turns out I . . . oh." Her ears drooped. "Oh, I didn't think of that. Uhm, well, I guess you're just, uh, stuck with me now. Let's go see Mom and Kivy."

'A reason, huh? Is it that I failed as a father? Or is it something else? What's going on inside that head of yours?'

She ran past him, Hyrees following beside her.

'Oh wait.' Cloud half-coughed, then trotted after them. "They actually won't be there right now," he called. "Sorry, they left this morning to go work on Kivyress and Farlight's group hunting. You probably won't see them until the sun peaks."

Ember didn't reply, but she stopped when she reached a completed section of the outer wall. She stared at it with uncertainty.

"Yeah, I know, it throws me off, too. Lupine thinks it'll help with our defenses in case of another attack," Hyrees said, answering her unasked question.

Ember cocked her head, eyes narrow.

'Oh, that's right, she wasn't here when he became commander. Guess she thought Farlight would take over. Poor thing. I can't even imagine how big of a shock this must be, coming back to all this mess.'

"Lupine was wrong," she said. "That's a terrible defense and a waste of time."

She padded into the Glade without any further explanation. Hyrees tilted his head in confusion but continued on prancing by her side like a fawn. Cloud followed behind them. No one reacted for a few moments, but as they neared the first fire pit, a head turned. Someone did a double-take.

"Wait, isn't that Cloud's daughter? The one who went after that Outsider, Tainu?" one tom whispered.

"Oh tahg, I think it is. What happened to her?" another replied.

Whitehaze leaped down from the History Tree, where he'd been clarifying some older clawmarks. He ran to her, smiling wider than Cloud had ever seen him smile. "You're alive! Of course you are, a fiery little wildflower like y— oh!" He stopped and sniffed her legs, then stepped back. His eyes widened with fear. "The humans. You've been with them, haven't you? What did they . . . what have they done to you?"

Cats leaned closer, waiting for her reply.

"The Tree was wrong about them," she said. "Some of them, at least. They saved my life, then brought me back here. So . . . I'm home now. Yay?"

Whitehaze's eyes narrowed. All traces of joy disappeared. "They know where we are?"

"Well, yes, but not all of them. The one who does know isn't bad. But didn't you hear me? They saved my—"

"So that you could lead them here?"

"No! No! That's not what—"

"What did you learn from our ancestors? What did Dark tell us about their kind? They are the enemy. If they helped you, it was for their own personal gain, I promise you. The History Tree—"

"Is wrong," Ember said, cutting her mentor off for the first time.

Cats gasped. Cloud's heart sank in his chest. He sniffed back the congestion still forming in his snout. *'What are you doing, Ember? You're just backing yourself into a corner. This isn't going to end well.'*

"Dark himself marked down the cruelties he himself experienced. It's not wrong. The Tree is not wrong. What have I told you about questioning our ancestors? And now your human friends will probably come here and take us all before the East can even plan out their next attack," Whitehaze growled.

Ember closed her eyes and paused. Her body tensed. Her tail thrashed like a captured snake. "They aren't bad," she said after a few moments of silence. "I didn't lead them anywhere. She knew where to bring me because she knew where they found me. They could have let me die and they would still know where to find you. If they wanted to hurt us, they would have done it by now. But you don't understand, they actually learned *Felid*. They *spoke* to me. They aren't all bad."

"Whitehaze, y-your apprentice has just come back from the dead, and y-you're already yowling at her?" Lupine loped toward them.

Whitehaze lowered his head. "She gave our location away, Lupine. Dark knew better than all of us combined what he marked into the Tree about the dangers of interacting with humans. I'm sorry, Ember, for snapping at you, but I don't take back any of what I said. Talking or not, they're going to come for us one of these days. Lupine, I've told Aspen, and I'll tell you now, one old tom to another; the time has come to find another home. This one simply isn't safe anymore. We could send out scouts tomorrow to search for a new clearing with a young tree we could transfer the old clawmarks to."

"I-I've looked to you for advice for almost seven winters, and y-y-you've never once failed me," Lupine replied. "Now I-I-I see where you're coming from with this, but we can't do it, and you know that. We aren't strong enough to risk sending out scouts. Whatever comes our way, we'll just have to take it. Now come on, everyone. Let's give Ember a-a real welcome. After all, sh-she's a war hero now. Battle scars and, uhm, all."

Lupine cast a leery glance at her artificial legs, then touched noses with her. "W-welcome home, Ember. In case you didn't know, until Farlight is experienced enough, I'm the acting commander. I'm not a very good one, I-I'm afraid, but if you ever need help, I'm willing to give it."

Ember looked down at her paws. "Th-thank you . . . sir."

Her voice wavered as she spoke, as if she was trying to hold back some intense negative emotion. He couldn't tell if it was anger, sadness, fear, or simply Ember being Ember. Cloud sighed. Most cats, like Hyrees or Songbird, were like clawmarks—readable when viewed from the right angle. Ember, however, was like trying to make a sentence out of overlapping bird prints. Through sheer chance, a clawmark or two might appear, but contextually they never made sense, and rarely, if ever, did they so much as form a two-mark word.

"I-I-I hate to ask this of you so soon, but we really do need as m-much help as we can get right now. Do you think you'd be in any state to start patrolling in a-a few days?" Lupine said.

"I . . . should be able to. I don't know how well . . . my prosthetics will hold up in a fight, but I can, uhm, give it a try."

"Good molly." He stepped back and lifted his head. "Everyone out of your dens!"

Cloud flattened his ears to lessen the noise. *'Tahg, I didn't think his voice could get that loud.'*

"Ember has come home! When the hunters return, we'll have a feast. The time has come to celebrate!" Lupine lowered his head and grimaced. "M-might as well have some kind of festivity before we die," he muttered under his breath.

Several cats caterwauled with excitement. Even though many had already left for their daily tasks, the late-goers and Glade-dwellers alone made enough noise for the rock formations to create an echo. They jumped from their perches and exited their dwellings to greet and examine Ember and her peculiar human gadgets. They asked questions until their voices became a clamor. Ember tucked her tail and tried to back away, but cats surrounded her on all sides. Cloud pushed forward, trying to create a path for her to escape by.

"Hey!" one cat shouted.

Cloud stopped. His eyes searched the tumult for the speaker.

"I suppose, now that the defect is home, we finally have a reason to gorge ourselves and forget the war and the lives its claimed, don't we?" One young tom's gaze locked onto his, blazing with nonverbal threats. "Looks like your daughter isn't as big of a disappointment as you thought, Cloud."

Cloud growled, chest burning with anger. "I never once called her a disappointment, and you know it!"

Ember shivered and crouched down, trying to make herself smaller. They kept poking her legs and asking questions without waiting for answers, uncaring or oblivious to her discomfort. Cloud tried to focus back on getting her out.

"I said 'thought,' not 'said,' " the tom replied, distracting him again. "And I can't help but notice that you're only denying the latter. Such an honorable, yet manipulative thing to do, *high-rank*."

Cloud snarled, turning his full attention to the tomcat in front of him. "That's it, I've had enough of you."

He lunged forward. Lupine jumped between them before Cloud could tackle him. "Stop!" Lupine snarled. The clamor of voices obeyed, quieting almost immediately. "Sumac, I-I-I know your mate died, but this is u-unacceptable. You too, Cloud. You've both been reckless and irresponsible ever since the battle. Effective immediately, Sumac, y-you are to spend your free time for the next five days working on the-the second wall. Cloud, I'm afraid I'll have to demote you to a regular council member. W-Whitehaze is now my advisor."

Cloud stepped back. Panic flooded in, making his heartbeat pound in his ears. "What? Over this? But sir, he—"

"M-my decision is final."

Sumac glared at him. "I still hate you, high-rank. You know that?"

Cloud curled back his lips, revealing his three fangs. "The feeling is mutual."

Sumac snorted, then trotted away, paws crunching what little ice sludge remained. For a while, no one said anything. The sudden silence made his ears ring. Motion in his peripheral vision brought his eyes back to Ember. She lay on her stomach, tail still tucked and paws wrapped over her ears. Her eyes were closed and she was shaking all over.

Hyrees lay beside her, whispering comforts in her ears. "Ember, it's okay. It's okay. It's over. Come on," he mewed.

She didn't reply. Cloud stepped closer. When he did, the faint sound of sobbing met his ears. "Ember? Hey, Ember, I'm sorry for the things that fluffheaded tom said. He's always been a rebel and a troublemaker. I promise what he said isn't true. You're not a disappointment."

He waited for a reply, or even a gesture—anything to indicate she'd heard him. *'What's wrong with her? What do I do? I've never seen her like this before. Crouched over, yes, paws over her ears, yes, crying, yes, shaking, yes, unresponsive, yes, but never all at once. Did the humans do this to her? Did I do it? Or Sumac? Or maybe it was all of us. Come on, Ember. Please do something. I promised. You know I mean it. Right?'*

"Ember, get up," Whitehaze said gently. "No point in making a spectacle of yourself."

Ember opened her eyes, but they didn't focus on anyone in particular. Instead, they darted around like the wild eyes of a frightened rabbit. Cloud leaned down to lick her head. As he did, she leaped up. Her forehead banged into his muzzle. He jumped back. Ember ducked her head in apology, then darted past him.

"No, wait!" Hyrees called. He got to his paws and ran after her. "Where are you going?"

She sprinted across the Glade in silence. Everyone watched in confusion, and a few glared in annoyance. Somewhere in the back of his head, Sumac's scornful words repeated themselves.

'She's not a disappointment. I failed her. This isn't her fault. It's mine. I was too soft on her.' He sighed and followed them. *'Please know that I don't want to hurt you, Ember. And I hope you don't hold what I'm about to say against me. I'm only doing this for your own good.'*

He found her at the back of his own den, head pressed against the wall, trembling like cornered prey. Hyrees sat beside her, grooming her neck.

"Ember, listen," Cloud said. "I know you just got back, and I know today is supposed to be light-hearted, and joyful, and fun, but things are changing. I know we told you this already, but war is inevitable, so the time has come to grow up. I hate to be the one who has to say this, but it has to be said. We don't have time to deal with this kind of behavior anymore. It needs to end. It's not healthy for you."

Ember lifted her head, but pinned her ears back even farther. "Y-y-you think I want t-t-t-to do this? You think this is some kind of *act* I put on for a-attention? I don't want attention. I-I just want everyone to leave me alone."

"Well, laying down and crying in the middle of the Glade won't make others leave you alone. In fact, when you do that, it seems an awful lot like you're trying to draw a crowd."

"Maybe you should stay out of this," Hyrees said.

"She needs to hear this."

"Hear," Ember whispered.

"What?" Cloud asked.

"Hear," she said, jaw trembling. "I hear everything. Your breathing. Hyrees's breathing. Icicles dripping. Cats walking. Cats talking. Can't understand them. There's a hovership coming. S-s-still don't like those."

Cloud's ears twitched as his mind registered each sound in turn, but as he switched focus, some of the softer noises disappeared once again into the background. The whirring of the machine she'd mentioned grew louder as it passed overhead, then faded into nothingness.

"You can't have heard all that at once, right?" he asked. "What does this have to do with anything?"

She mewed something unintelligible to herself, then turned around. Her head remained low. "I did. And I still am. Each waking moment, every sound, every light, every movement, every touch is right there, yowling, and flashing, and thrashing, and *hitting* me. I'm not like you. You can ignore it. You can make it go away with the sheer power of your head, but I can't. It's not that

I'm not trying, it's that I physically *cannot* make it stop. Just like the words repeating themselves inside my mind right now, nothing stops. Nothing *ever* stops. It's like a really bad lightning storm is always going on somewhere inside of me, and it *will not* go away."

'Is she telling the—who am I joking with? She's telling some version of the truth, but some form of exaggeration is taking place here. It's simply not possible to hear, feel, or see everything at once.'

"Em, why didn't you tell anyone about this sooner?" Hyrees asked. "I never realized . . ."

"I thought I was broken, or doing something wrong, or—actually, no, that's exactly the problem. I thought I could fix myself now, now that Matthew helped me, but I . . . I don't know if I'll ever not be this . . . *this*."

Cloud gritted his teeth. "So whose fault is it? Mine?"

"No. I don't know!" She pushed her forehead against the wall again. "Just . . . please . . . Know what? You're right. You've always been right. I'm too weak to survive here. I'm gonna die out here, aren't I? But that's okay. I may only have a few winters to live anyway. One day these prosthetics are going to malfunction, and when that happens I'm going to die, and there's nothing anyone can do to stop that."

He opened his mouth to reply, but realized he didn't know how. Everything he could think of was either apathetic or a lie. He closed it again and sighed.

"What? Die? You're not going to die in a few winters. You can't!" Hyrees said.

Ember pushed herself closer to the wall. "Please, I just want to be left alone right now."

"Ember? Is that Ember? Ember! You're alive?" A familiar, innocent-yet-devious voice mewed.

Cloud turned to find Kivyress standing behind him. She charged forward into the den, eyes wide and mouth in a smile so large it looked painful. "Emmmmbeeerrrr! Hey, what's wrong? Why are you hiding away in here? Nice legs, by the way. You're practically glowing. Oh tahg, oh tahg, you're alive! What happened? Oh, hey, why are you crying?"

"Kivy," Ember said.

She pulled away from the wall and got to her paws. They touched foreheads.

A leap behind where Kivyress had been, Songbird stood frozen in shock. "Oh my . . ." she whispered.

Farlight waited beside her. He nudged her shoulder, and Songbird walked forward with a dazed expression. Ember jumped up to nuzzle her the moment she set paw on the den's cold, dry floor. Songbird wrapped her paws over her daughter's shoulders and placed her chin against her neck. They sat there, chest to chest, in sweet, somber silence.

An icy lump formed in Cloud's chest. *'I said something wrong earlier, didn't I? Send a fox on it, what am I doing wrong?'*

"It's going to be okay. You're home now. You're safe. I'm here. You're here, and it's going to be okay," Songbird whispered. She groomed the small line of fur running between Ember's mechanical shoulder blades. "What's going on, Ember? What happened?"

"Everyone was being so loud, and they were all so close, and . . . and that's not at all what you meant, was it?" Ember said.

"N-not exactly, but that does sound scary. It's over now, though. And you know what? I'll try to make sure everyone stays quiet and keeps their distance. Sound good?"

Ember sighed and backed up, forcing Songbird's paws off of her. "Thank you."

"Wait, where are you going?"

Ember pushed her way past everyone and exited the den. Her eyes were already dry. "Lupine wants me to see if I can start patrolling again. I'm going for a walk to make sure I can, and also to think through some things, because there's a lot I need to think about right now."

"Wait," Cloud said, "I'm sorry."

"Accepted." She kept walking. "I just want some alone time, okay?"

"Ember, you're not supposed to patrol alone," he called.

245

"I could go with you," Hyrees said.

She lifted a hind paw and shook off some unseen annoyance. The mechanical parts inside it whined and whirred in protest. "Sorry, Hyrees. I know you want to be with me, but I need some alone time."

Kivyress perked up. "I can go."

"Not you," Cloud said. "She just said she wants to be alone, and if she's going to have a partner, that partner needs to be an adult."

"She can come. I'm not actually patrolling anyway. Just going for a walk," Ember said.

Hyrees's face fell as Kivyress darted to her sister's side, her smoky tail in the air. Cloud shot him a sympathetic, slightly confused glance, trying to communicate that he also didn't know what to make of it.

"Great! Thanks!" Kivyress said. "Now come on, Em, let's go before they try to stop us. Bye, Mom. Bye, Dad."

"Have . . . fun," Songbird said. Her voice contained a mixture of emotions as confusing as Ember's.

Cloud sighed again as they left the Glade. Hyrees watched them go, then excused himself and wandered off.

"What did you do?" Songbird growled when they disappeared from view.

"It was Sumac, okay? You know what he's like. Always has to push the limits. He was jealous and started snapping insults at her. I lunged at him, and Lupine demoted me."

She leaned forward, ears pinned. "You *what*?"

"It was a fluffheaded mistake, I know, but what was I supposed to do? He can call me whatever he wants, but I'm not going to let him hurt my family."

"Cloud, what did I tell you before? You don't need to protect us. I know she might seem fragile, but she can take a lot more than you give her credit for. If you pick fights for her, or for any of us, you'll only make things worse. There are some things we need to do alone." She sighed. "There are some things *I* need to do alone. Please, just stop."

"At least I didn't get kicked off the Council entirely," he suggested.

Her ears perked up, but in the sudden, bitter way that made him wish he

246

hadn't spoken. She stared at him with critical eyes. "I . . . I should get back to hunting."

She turned and trotted out the Southern Entrance, leaving him alone. Cloud watched her go with a sinking heart. "That's just great. Now I've hurt everyone."

"Everyone, huh?" Farlight asked, reminding Cloud of his presence. "Yeah, at this point, I guess so, but that might not be such a bad thing." Farlight offered him a smile. "After all, it'll give them a chance to see just how much they need cats like you. For now, though, just give yourself a break. I'll take care of the Colony."

Without another word, he walked into Lupine's den and disappeared, just like everyone else.

CHAPTER 17
EMBER

"Hmm. That's interesting. I wonder if I'm on a spectrum too," Kivyress said. She pranced across a fallen tree, following Ember as she picked her way through the forest. "A different one. There are different ones, right? Because *no one* thinks I'm normal, and I still haven't decided how I feel about that."

She reached the end of the log and jumped back onto the hard, icy ground. "Oh! Ouch. There was a rock under that snow. Oh well. Guess I'll just have to walk on three legs from now on."

She held one of her hind paws off the ground and dramatically limped along. Ember kept her eyes trained on the dirt, returning to her old routine of plotting out the path she would follow.

"I don't know about that. You don't seem all that spectrum-y, and I don't think being generally weird counts as autism," Ember replied.

She smiled. The stress of her most recent overload was almost forgotten, but it refused to leave her mind completely. In addition to overwhelming her senses, the flood of cats and near fight had reminded her both how much had changed and how much remained the same. No amount of biting her tongue and counting to five would ever fix the real, underlying problems. Knowing why the problems existed hadn't fixed anything at all. She still needed to figure out how to cope, as Matthew had done.

Yet despite the emotional strain it caused, it had also served as an educational experience. When the first sharp cyans of panic had seeped in back at the Glade, and mist and static started flooding her head, she'd thought-called Matthew for help. Despite being busy, he'd patiently talked her through finding the strength to get back up and leave. Knowing what to do and communicating with someone who understood made recovering easier than usual, even with the attack itself being worse.

"You know," Kivyress mewed, "I don't think anyone thinks Mom and Dad are normal either. Mom more so than Dad, yet I think everyone likes Mom, and most cats like Dad too."

Ember still felt a sense of relief over how quickly Kivyress had responded to her talk signal. They'd developed the gesture before Kivyress had even begun her training. It meant 'let's speak in private.' Ember was the one to have the basic idea, but it was Kivyress who'd come up with the exact signal: two shakes of a hind paw.

Over the past hour, as they walked up the mountain, Ember had tried her best to explain her experience with the humans. Kivyress had listened quietly, yet asked enough questions to let her know she was paying attention and still interested.

"No one's entirely normal. And if someone *was* entirely normal in every way, that would be *really* weird," Ember said.

Kivyress flicked a stone over the edge of the ravine. It tumbled and rolled down the steep cliffside, then landed with a splash in the creek. Far below, the creek water warbled and trickled along. The ice coating its edges muffled the noise, making it seem more distant. Wind came in waves, ruffling their fur and howling through the forest.

"True. True," Kivyress said. "I don't think I'd want to meet someone perfectly normal. Could you imagine how boring they'd be? So unspecial they're painfully unique. Nothing surprising about them at all."

Ember lifted her muzzle to the breeze. Frigid air burned the insides of her nose, bringing with it the scents of dirt, wet moss, and creatures of the forest. She tried to imagine what a normal cat would look like. Despite the number of tabbies existing in the East, she couldn't imagine it having anything but the agouti fur and orange eyes of an average Westerner. She shook herself off and let her focus drift back to her surroundings. Even with the patchiness of the snow remnants, her woods were just as beautiful as she'd remembered. Seeing them again was enough to make her feel at ease.

Ember chuffed. *What about secrets, though? Everyone seems to have secrets, but is there a normal secret? No, there can't be. They're all different, because the ones keeping them are different. Even someone perfectly normal in every way would have his or her own unique set of secrets. Wait a moment. What am I thinking?'*

"I don't think there is such a thing as 'perfectly normal,' " Ember said. "To be alive and able to think for yourself means there's no one else exactly like you, and that there can't be a normal. If someone was normal, as a whole, I think that would imply there are more of them. If you duplicated yourself, and no one else did, you would automatically become the normal, because there would be two of you, and only one of everyone else, no matter how many everyone elses there were. Like how leaves are normal in the spring, but not now, because there are less leaves than trees now. They still exist, but there aren't many."

Kivyress tilted her head but kept walking. "Uhm, hah, maybe. I guess so, but is that even how normal works?"

Ember hesitated. Her face became warm as grey and dark purple mottled her mind. "I don't know. Maybe not."

"But anyways," Kivyress continued, "Dad's . . . honestly been kind of scary ever since you left. Which is another reason I'm glad you're back. Maybe he can finally stop working on that project of his and start spending more time with us."

Ember's ears perked up. "Project? What kind of project?"

"He hasn't told you yet? Surprising." Kivyress stopped walking to stare down at an especially pretty patch of creek. A series of time-smoothed boulders broke up the flow and made a whitewater obstacle course, complete with several miniature waterfalls. A large tree had fallen halfway down and wedged itself between the two cliffs. "He wants to make everyone these 'guard pieces,' as he calls them, that will supposedly make it harder for the East to kill us, but I don't know. It looked uncomfortable when he showed me how it worked. I can't imagine trying to fight with bark strapped to my legs."

"Bark? Tree bark?" Ember asked, sitting down at the ravine's edge. "That's both a great idea and a terrible one. Oh, maybe the humans have made something similar-but-better for themselves. I'll have to ask Thai about it later. It can be improved. I know it can. Almost anything will work better than bark."

Kivyress laughed and sat beside her. Their tails wrapped around each other's hindquarters, making Ember feel warm inside.

"I was going to be mean and taunt you by jokingly suggesting snow would work better," Kivyress mewed, "but now that I think about it, it actually might. Have you ever bitten snow? It's painful. It freezes your teeth."

Ember chuffed. "Unfortunately, yes. Last winter, when I was the same age as you, the creek froze over entirely and we had to drink snow. It was disgusting, in case you were wondering. At one point I stopped drinking for a while and got really sick."

"I know. Mom told me about it; I really hope it doesn't happen this winter."

"The creek freezing over, or me getting sick?"

Kivyress turned her head to look at her for a moment, then went back to watching the creek. "Both." Her tail twitched against Ember's side. "So what do you think of Lupine's project?"

"The second wall?" Ember asked. "It's a terrible idea. Do they not realize Easterners can climb trees? Really, any cat can climb trees. Why does no one else see that?"

"I know. That's what I said. Not to Lupine, but to Farlight. He agrees with me, of course, but he doesn't want to say anything until he can come up with something better to do. He wants to keep Lupine feeling like he's achieving something to stay on his good side." Kivyress flicked another stone into the creek. The rock bounced three times before sinking. "Whoa! Emmy, did you see that? It hopped like a frog. I didn't think rocks could do that."

Ember burst into laughter. "Yes, I saw it. And don't call me Emmy, you furball. Please."

Kivyress chuffed. Her breath formed a cloud of steam that swirled around, then faded into nothingness. "Don't call me a furball then. Emmy."

'What are the chances?' Ember mused, partially ignoring her sister's mews. *'Sitting in this exact spot with that exact rock, and Kivy deciding to flick that exact rock at that exact time with this exact thing happening. The funniest thing is, it happened, so it was going to happen a few moments ago and chance is negligible. Oh. Is there such thing as chance then? Because if something happens, it was going to happen all along, because time can only go down one path, and once it steps, I can't change it. Oh. Is my life planned out? If so, by who?'*

Something snapped on the other side of the ravine, dragging her back into the external world. Ember got up and strained her neck, trying to see who or what had made the noise. "Hello? Is anyone there?"

A series of icy crunches and rustles replied. Kivyress stood and sniffed the air, but with the wind against their backs, Ember knew it wouldn't do any good. Black and white materialized from the hazy underbrush. The small tom's eyes were mottled yellow and brown, like dying birch leaves.

'I've seen that cat before. Where have I seen him? I know I don't like him, but wh—' Ember narrowed her eyes. "Oh. It's you."

"What'd you say, kitten? You'll have to speak up if you want your voice to make it 'cross that ravine alive," Eclan said. He sounded a little more sober than he'd been during their first meeting.

'Probably ran out of mint. Or at least I hope he did. Or, wait, no, I hope he didn't. If he could fight that well while half-dazed, I'd hate to see what he can do with a clear head. And I somehow doubt he's the kind of cat who falls for the same trick twice. Tahg, if he decides to try to cross, we're in trouble.'

"Why are you here?" she yowled. "I thought Dad and . . . C-Commander Aspen told you to leave."

'I'm never going to see him again either, am I?'

"Why wouldn't I be here? This ain't your territory, kitten, in case you've forgotten. I don't even have to answer your question. Though I must admit, I didn't think you'd remember me."

"Oh, no, I had blissfully forgotten all about your existence until you came along and reminded me."

"Huh. Well, you've changed. 'Less my memory is flawed. Which it usually isn't."

Kivyress jumped up and turned to Ember. "Oh! He's the Rogue y'all captured, isn't he? That is a lot of scars, but hey, he's actually kind of handsome, isn't he? You know, all Rogue things aside."

Eclan grimaced. "You know I can hear you, runt."

Ember stared at her sister for a few moments, trying to figure out if she was being serious or not. Nothing seemed to suggest otherwise. She bit her tongue and turned in the general direction of the Glade. "But anyways, we should be going. Come on, Kivy."

"No, wait," Kivyress said. "I have questions. I've never met a Rogue before. Come on, Em. It's not like he can hurt us. He's on the other side of the ravine. The *ravine*, Ember. And what's more, it's *this* part of the ravine. You know, where if you fall over the edge, you plummet to your death? We'll be fine. The absolute worst that can happen is him shouting swears at us."

Ember flattened her ears. "I don't know about that. He's not exactly predictable. We really should tell Commander Lupine about this. He did show up right before the East attacked last time. I know he's not Eastern, but he could be a hired scout."

"Rogues can be hired? Interesting. I'll have to remember that."

Ember swatted at her sister's side. "It's also possible he's an assassin sent here to kill you. Now come on."

"Uhm, Ember?"

She closed her eyes and sighed. "What?"

"Miiight want to look."

Ember spun toward the ravine. Eclan was gone. She darted back to the edge, cyan pulsing with her heartbeat. He was scaling down the cliff face, heading for the tree bridge. She bit her tongue harder. "Kivy, you should go."

"No, I'm not leaving you here alone with some crazy assassin. Besides, two against one means better odds for both of us."

'Odds. Chance. There's only one outcome, and chance has nothing to do with it. If the future is a direct result of the things I do right now, I'll just have to make the right decisions to get the right outcome. No pressure. Should I make her leave? If she runs fast enough to get backup, yes. Also, she's not ready for this. She's not a border guard. She's not even planning to become one.'

"Uh, no, you should go find help. Three or four cats make for even better odds. If you hurry, you might make it back before he gets out."

Kivyress pinned back her ears. "Are you sure? You don't even know if you can still fight yet. Why not go together and hope he's here when we get back?"

Ember snorted, trying to keep herself as calm as she could. "And we don't even know if he'll survive the climb across. You've got enough time. Just go, okay? Someone needs to stay here and make sure he doesn't get in. Who knows what he might be here to do? I'll be alright. I've survived some cats' worst nightmares. I can deal with one crazy Rogue."

"Don't get cocky, kitten," Eclan growled from halfway down the cliffside. *'Come on, we're running out of time. Hurry, hurry, hurry, please.'*

"O-okay. I'll go." Kivyress said.

Ember swatted the air with a forepaw. Her mechanics whined, as if they also sensed the urgency of the situation. Kivyress raced toward the Glade, moving farther away with every step.

"Whatever you do, don't die. Don't even pretend to die. I don't want to lose you again," she called over her shoulder.

Ember swallowed hard. "I'll . . . try not to."

With Kivyress gone, Ember turned back to the ravine. Eclan jumped onto the rotting log. She held her breath and waited for it to break. It didn't.

"It was either brave of you or stupid of you to send her back," he said, strutting across over the rushing water. "Your backup won't be getting here before I can get to you."

Frantic vivid green made her jaw quiver. *'What does he want to do to me?*

Does he want to kill me? Or someone else?' Images of Eclan biting her throat, then sneaking in and wreaking havoc on the Glade filled her head. *'No, I can't let that happen. Come on, Em, you can do this. Claws. You've got claws now, and you know how to defend yourself. You can do this. Try to keep him busy.'*

She positioned herself over the closer end of the fallen tree and lowered herself into a fighting stance.

"What do you want?" she asked weakly.

He stretched out against the log and yawned, then looked up at her with a smirk. "Telling is boring. But I will say, in my own defense, I wasn't hired to kill anyone today. Or back when we first met. If you were s'posed to have disappeared, let's just say I would already be back home by now." He chuckled. "Oh, don't look so scared, kitten. No, wait, you might want to be scared if you keep standing there. I got a job to do, and if you get in my way, your disappearance might just be necessary."

Ember shivered. *'Job? Wait, if you're telling the truth and you weren't hired to kill anyone, what are you supposed to be doing? Are you a scout? Is the East coming? Oh no. What if it's happening all over again? If anyone can hear me, please, no, don't. Don't let them come. Please. Not now.'*

"S-so, uhm, why did you attack me, then?" she asked.

"Everyone's gotta have a little fun sometimes. Makes life more interesting." Eclan reached the end of the log. He glared up at her with his multicolored eyes. "Let me past and no one gets hurt. I promise." He narrowed them to slits. "Don't try to be a hero, kitten. Heroes are always the first to die."

He sank his claws into the dirt-stone mixture forming the cliff beneath her. An all too familiar adrenaline rush charged through her bloodstream. She took a single step back, far enough away from him to not be in immediate danger, but close enough to attack him if he decided to jump up. Dull grey and silver static swirled through her mind. With it came a touch of decaying green as her stomach did backflips inside of her.

'Oh tahg, what do I do? What do I do? What do I do? Something. I'm

supposed to do something. What would Dad do? He would stay and fight. I guess that's the right thing to do, but I don't know. Would Mom do it? She's a hunter, but she knows how to fight too, so maybe. But this is my job. And I just have to hold him here until help comes. Whenever that may be. You can do this, Ember. Don't be a hareheart. Don't be a coward. You can do this. It's just a professional mercenary whom you've fought with in the past.'

"Last warning," he hissed.

Ember lowered her head, jaw trembling. "You'll have to get past me."

'Huh, that sounded so much better my head. Wait, what am I doing? Is this suicide? Did I make a—'

Eclan lunged upward. She swatted at his face, but missed. His claws tore down her neck and caught on her collar. In that moment, his scent filled her nose, sending a flare of yellow pulsing through her thoughts. A tiny mew of pain escaped her throat, but before she could so much as brace herself, he yanked her forward. She stumbled over the edge, became weightless for a millisecond, then slammed into the log. The impact knocked her breath out. Pain filled her chest. She tried to breathe in but found she couldn't. Sliding— she was sliding off, toward the rocks and rushing water below. She closed her eyes and sank her claws into whatever she could. The sliding stopped. The white noise of water competed for attention with the growing ringing sound piercing her ears. She pressed her cheek against the log and clung to it for dear life.

Ember opened her eyes and gasped for air. *'Okay, yes. That was a mistake. Ouch. Blood. Am I bleeding?'*

A few spatters of red glistened on the rotting wood in front of her. She bit her tongue as hard as she could without injuring it, then heaved herself back to the uneasy safety of the top side of the log. A tiny Michelle-like voice in the back of her head scolded her for not trying harder to break her tongue biting habit.

'Not now. It keeps me calm-ish, and since a crazy Rogue just tried to kill me, I'm allowed to bite it, because right now I need to focus.'

For a moment she wondered if the real Michelle would show up to reply.

Or Matthew. Or anyone. Anyone who could help her figure out what to do. A rogue mercenary was in her territory, threatening everyone who got in the way of his mystery mission. She pressed her white forepaw against her neck. The pressure stung, making a sickly green flash in the back of her mind. Ember lifted the paw in front of her face. A smear of warm red coated the tips of her toes.

'They're just scratches. Nothing bad. Come on, Ember, you've gotta find him. There's no telling what he's been sent to do, and you know you don't want to find out the hard way. Focus. Focus. Concentrate. Let's go.'

She climbed back onto stable ground, then looked around. Eclan was gone. A trail of prints led into the swirling mist, ghosts of where her attacker had once been. She lowered her head and followed them.

'Guess he figured making sure I was dead would be too much trouble. Or he didn't actually want to kill me. Or he just doesn't care if I live or die, as long as I'm out of his way. Yeah, that's the most likely option.' Her eyes widened. *'But hey, I'm still alive! For now, at least. Maybe I made the right choices after all. Hopefully when Kivy gets back with help, they'll see the tracks and know where we've gone.'*

The prints stopped at the base of a tree. Ember unsheathed the claws in one of her forepaws to examine them. They looked sharp enough still, so she climbed up. The tree's rough grey bark pressed against her toes as she moved along, sniffing at branches for Eclan's bitter scent. Something about it still caused internal pulses of yellow and cream to appear, but beyond a sinking sense of deja vu, she couldn't place why. She crawled onto the limb and willed herself not to fall. Unlike her domestic relatives, if she slipped, she wouldn't be able to right herself before landing. Her jaw trembled. She closed her eyes and held her breath for the count of five.

'Now is not the time to panic, Ember. Stay calm. Tahg, you're turning into Hyrees. Why are you suddenly afraid of heights? You can do this. You've done it a hundred times before. Pretend you're racing. Aaaaand go.'

Her nose, legs and mind worked in tandem to keep her in the trees and on the right trail. In the back of her head, she calculated the best places to put her paws to minimize the chance of slipping. With snow still on the branches, the task proved itself to be a difficult one. In the front, she wondered how fast Eclan himself was traveling and, more importantly, what she would do when she found him. Somewhere in the middle, she realized something. Her heart lurched. She stopped.

'Oh, most cats don't climb trees. Or at least most Colony Cats don't. Whoever Kivyress gets for backup might not know how to tree track. Fight a fox, if I keep going, I'll have to fight him alone. I'm not supposed to die yet. I can still help my colony. I have my ETAg, and I have yet to use it properly. And Michelle would be so disappointed if I died on the same day she went through all that trouble to bring me back. And maybe, just maybe, I'm too big of a coward right now to face him. But if he's telling the truth, he's not here to kill anyone, so it'd be a waste of life. I don't know what he's doing, but—oh wait, we're heading for the Glade. I'll just go there and see if he shows up.'

She climbed back down. The frigid earth greeted her toes once again. She turned the sensitivity of her legs down another half-point and sighed as she trotted toward her home. *'Dad might be disappointed, but he'll also be relieved. I know he will. Mom will definitely be relieved. And Kivy. And me. My opinion also matters in matters concerning my death.'*

A large crow fluttered into a nearby tree. It glared at her for a few seconds, then cawed at the top of its lungs. Ember flattened her ears and broke into a run. The yellow came back again, along with the eerie feeling of deja vu. Fog rolled into her head, threatening to choke out her internal voice entirely.

'Come on, Ember. Think! You're missing something. Something obvious. Something so obvious you'll feel like a fluffhead for missing it. What is it? Erg, go away, grey. I can't focus on anything.'

As she neared the Glade, a flash of white caught her eyes. Eclan leaped and climbed through the trees ahead of her with the agility of a squirrel. The wind changed direction, blowing his yellow-inducing scent into her nose. Ember's eyes widened.

'Wait a moment.'

She lost focus entirely for a split moment. Her paw hit a root. She tumbled to a stop, landing face-first in the snow. The wind changed again, carrying all traces of his scent away, but the damage had already been done. Ember got to her feet.

'No wonder it felt wrong. That's not just his scent. Jade. That was Jade's scent on him. About two days old. Faint, but it was hers. I know it was. They really were lying—all of them. He really is their spy. Which means she's also behind the ambush and what happened to Tainu. Not unexpected, of course, but still. It means she really didn't want to do all of those things. She shouldn't have died. I shouldn't have killed her. Why did I kill her? What did they do to her to make her kill him? And why not use the assassin? To make it less obvious? But why her, of all the cats?'

Another thought struck her as she accelerated back into a run. 'Shard and Echo. Do they have anything to do with this?' Her heart sank in her chest. She revisited her memory of Tainu and Echo leaving the Glade on the day of the Meeting, then coming back and explaining their absence with lies. 'Echo does. And to think I thought they were friends, or . . . but wait, what about Shard? I don't think he does. But I've been wrong before. Maybe everyone in the East knows. Either way, they're the enemy now, and we're probably going to have to fight one day. Would Echo really kill me? I know Shard wouldn't, right? Oh wait.' She shivered. The whirring of her prosthetics grew louder. 'He almost did. That's it. I officially hate war.'

The inner abatis and an unfinished portion of the outer wall appeared through the brambles. Ember scanned the trees for signs of Eclan. He was nowhere to be seen. She stopped and looked behind her. Five trees down from where she'd last seen him, his tracks in the branch snow stopped. He'd turned around for some reason.

'Maybe the second wall was all he needed to see. Though it seems like a waste of a trip. It wouldn't take much to improvise a strategy to fit with that thing. We're doing nothing, and he's doing nothing. This is pointless, and I don't understand. But then again, why do most cats do most of what they do? There are so many pointless, fluffheaded things out there that I'll *never understand. Well, since I'm here, I should probably tell someone what happened. I'm too tired to keep following him anyway. Hopefully Hyrees is still here. It would be nice for him to come with me while I tell Lupine. Then maybe I can think more clearly.'*

She walked around the abatis until she reached the Western Entrance, then padded into the Glade. She sniffed the air, trying to locate her mate. Scents swirled around, filling her nose and overpowering any one specific smell. It was a familiar kind of chaos. A few leaps away, a couple of cats coming in from a recent hunting trip turned from their turkey to stare at her. She ignored them.

"Ember! You're back?" Hyrees's voice called.

Ember spun around to find him padding out of Wren's old den. As she trotted toward him, the tension in her head released. They touched noses, then transitioned into scenting.

He slowed to a standstill, tail twitching. "I mean, I'm not complaining or anything, but I thought, well, Kivy said you were facing off with some kind of wildcat assassin. What happened?"

"I followed him here, then he left," she replied.

"What do you mean he left? He came here? To the Glade? Why? How do you know he's gone? You know, your dad just left with your sister and a few other cats to go help you fend him off. I hope they don't panic when they can't find you."

"They'll be fine. There are prints. Let's go to Commander Aspen's den. I can—wait, no, it's Lupine's now, isn't it?" She sighed. "I guess we'll be going to Commander Lupine's den. We can go together, and I'll tell both of you what happened when we get there."

Hyrees's ears drooped. "Uh, yeah, okay. Let's go then."

She nodded once and they set off across the Glade. *'What would Kivyress say he meant, doing that with his ears? Did my getting the name wrong upset him? Seems likely. Sorry, Hyrees. I didn't mean to. Oh!'*

Her eyes lit up. The fiery reds of excitement overpowered the dreary grey in her mind, even stomping out the uneasiness of Eclan's intrusion. Ember smiled and welcomed the emotional high flooding into her spirit. *'I might not have been born able to face-read or speak well, but no one ever said I can't teach myself. Or get someone to teach me. Kivy could do it. Then I would know everything I need to understand these cats.'*

She let her gaze wander around the Glade. As it landed on the features of her colonymates, she recalled what secrets she remembered about them: secrets and whispers she'd heard when everyone thought she wasn't listening. It was enough information to turn a colony against itself if used incorrectly.

'And I'll prove them all wrong.'

CHAPTER 18
EMBER

"I told you we should've gone back together," Kivyress mewed.

They sat around a small open fire a few leaps outside the Glade. The designated pits were too crowded, so Cloud, Ember, and Songbird had worked together to build a private one. Shadows cloaked the forest around them as the sun sank beneath the Western Mountain. The rising mist, combined with the patchy snow and the fire's swirling smoke, painted the forest blue.

Kivyress and Farlight rested beside each other, across the fire from Ember. They took turns pawing twigs and dead leaves into the flames. Ember yawned, content. Her tail wrapped around Hyrees's bony side. Turkey and venison filled her stomach. The celebratory feast had reminded her just how much better her kin's cat food tasted.

"But then we wouldn't have found out about his relationship with the East," Ember said. "All things considered, I think we actually got the best outcome of all this."

Hyrees shifted beside her, shivering as the wind picked up. Ember leaned closer, trying to keep him warm. As she did, his stomach growled in her ears. Even though she'd encouraged him to get more, he'd picked through less than an average ration's worth of food while everyone else gorged themselves.

'I know your dad is gone, and me being here isn't going to change that,

but can't you eat normally now? Dad said you barely ate anything while I was with the people, and looking at you now, I believe him. Weren't you complaining about me being too scrawny at one point? I hope you go back to being pudgy, food-loving Hyrees soon. Someone's gotta clean up my scraps, right? Though after tasting the stuff domestics have to eat, there probably won't be as many, but I promise I'll leave you enough to hide those ribs better.'

She sighed. Her mind wandered back to Eclan. Lupine took the news of an East-hired Rogue infiltrating the territory surprisingly well. He didn't panic but instead called Whitehaze in to discuss the possible implications of the visit. He made her and Hyrees leave, of course, because females weren't allowed to join council meetings, and apparently him talking with the new chief advisor counted as one.

Ember didn't care that being born a molly meant not being able to lead or obtain a position on the Council. She didn't want to lead, or even advise through boring meetings. However, otherwise insignificant things, like not being allowed to speak her opinions on a problem she'd discovered, burned at her insides. She hadn't even been able to bring up the inefficiency of the second wall.

"What do you think, Farlight?" Kivyress asked.

"I think we should stop talking about it," he replied, eyes narrow. "I mean, he's gone now, and once the log falls, he'll have a hard time even trying to get back in. And like Ember said, just knowing about the second wall isn't going to help them much. It's a pretty pathetic defense. Though I'm guessing he was mostly sent to make sure we aren't planning some kind of vengeful, offensive attack yet, which we obviously aren't. But hey, I'm breaking my own rules. Let's just take a moment to admire how neat Ember's legs look. You can really see the little glowing lines now that it's dark out. It almost makes you look like you've got embers inside of you, just beneath your skin. Or even ember blood, which is especially three-credit."

Ember chuffed and lifted a foreleg to examine Michelle's perfectly constructed heating grid. It made her happy—everything perfectly organized in even rows and columns, nothing unexpected or misplaced. As she looked at it, her heating system turned off. The little streaks of color faded back into their usual metallic grey.

"Oh, I guess that means I'm warm enough now. So much for looking like myself," she said.

"You still look like yourself, Ember," Songbird mewed. "You still look like my kitten, and I still have a hard time believing you're actually here." She nuzzled against Ember's side, opposite of Hyrees, but didn't touch a whisker to her prosthetics. "You don't mind me being this close, do you?"

Ember flattened back her ears. "Er, no, no ma'am. Do you?"

Songbird chuffed and snuggled closer, still avoiding her more mechanical parts. "Of course not. I don't know why, but I keep worrying this is all just a dream, and that if I let you out of my sight one more time, I'm going to lose you all over again. Hah, I think the only reason I even let you and Kivy leave this morning is because I was in too much of a shock to stop you."

"Don't worry, you won't lose me by looking away. Unless I'm dreaming, this is all real," Ember said. "Right, Dad?"

She turned her attention to Cloud, who sat a little farther away from the flames than everyone else. He hadn't said much since returning from the rescue mission, even while they'd gathered firewood. He sighed, eyes narrow and jaw tight.

Ember's heart sank. *'What's wrong with him? Well, his ears are all droopy, so that means he's probably not happy. But why?'*

She half-closed her eyes and grimaced, trying to mimic his expression to feel for what emotions it drew out in her. A soft, misty orange faded into existence, along with a sprinkling of darker orange.

"Why are you sad?" she asked. "Are you still blaming yourself? Because if you are, you really should stop. I'm okay. Unless you're sad about Wren, in which case I should probably just be quiet."

His expression changed. Ember raised her ears and widened her eyes to match it. Tiny flashes of light brown and all-too-familiar yellow followed. Her heartbeat quickened. Beneath the simulated colors, a flaming red burned bright, giving fuel to her ecstasy. "Are you surprised? Did I surprise you? And if I did, what did I do?"

His eyes narrowed again. "I didn't think . . . never mind. No, no, I'm fine. Just thinking about things."

"So you're not sad?"

He hesitated. His tail twitched once. "I already told you; I'm fine."

The grey came back, crushing her temporary excitement and clouding over all other emotion. *'Fox it. I really thought, or at least hoped, that would work. Unless he's lying. And the problem is, I don't know which would be worse.'*

Songbird shook her head. Ember couldn't make out her expression, much less try to decipher its meaning. When she turned around, whatever it was or meant was gone. Something cold hit Ember on the back. She leaped to her paws, heart racing.

"Ack!" Songbird mewed.

She slammed into Ember's shoulder. Ember, by instinct more than any kind of coordination, caught them both before they toppled into the fire. She let out a tiny sigh of relief.

"Kivyress!" Songbird mewed.

Ember glanced over to where Farlight sat, looking at anything but them. Kivyress was no longer beside him. She spun around. Her sister sat in a shadowy patch of ice sludge, quietly examining her paws. Songbird swatted a clump of snow at her.

Kivyress leaped backward as the lump collided with her side. She shook herself off and snorted. "Hey! What was that for?"

"You started it, you little furball," Songbird replied.

"I was helping y'all. Neither of you seemed to know if you were awake or not, so I used the snow to show you." Kivyress flicked another pawful of snow in Songbird's general direction. "You're welcome."

Songbird dropped into a fighting stance. "Oh no, I'm getting you for that."

Kivyress pounced forward. "Only if you can catch me first!"

'Catch. Capture. Pictures?'

"Wait!" Ember said, jumping to her paws. Kivyress's mews reminded her of yet another thing her ETAg was capable of. "Could you all get together on the other side of the fire and look happy? I'm going to take a picture. Pictures are really interesting because they capture single moments in time, and they let you look at those moments again anytime you want. I want to keep right now with me, so everyone get over there and smile."

After some moving around and a minute or two of coaxing Cloud, Ember ran back to her spot by the fire to take the photo. It was perfect—her family through and through. Everyone was smiling except Cloud, whose expression had gone back to being tight and distant.

Ember smiled faintly as the image vanished from her head. She showed them the photo on the screen of her ETAg. As they clamored around her to look, she sent it to Michelle with a thought message: *'I made it back!'*

A few moments later, Michelle responded with a message of her own: *'I told you everything would be okay. Be careful with that fire, sweetie.'*

'I will. Thanks again,' Ember sent in reply.

'You're very welcome. Take care!'

Ember closed her eyes and exhaled softly. As she did, her mind drifted back to Cloud. *'What's wrong, Dad? Am I still not good enough? Are you worried about what the East might do? I wish I could see your colors. Your real colors.'*

She shook her head, trying to chase the thoughts away to go back to being happy. When everyone returned to their original places by the flames, she swatted a lump of melted ice goo at Songbird. "Now to get back to flinging snow at each other," she mewed.

"Hey, I wasn't ready," Songbird said.

Kivyress continued her dash around the fire. She batted another pawful of snow against her mother's side.

"You!" Songbird mock-growled. She leaped into a stand and chased after her daughter. "Okay, that's it. This is war!" Her eyes widened as everyone winced. She stopped and lowered her head. "Wait, never mind."

Kivyress slowed to a walk and meandered back to Farlight's side. Ember shifted her attention onto the fire.

"I ruined it, didn't I?" Songbird asked. She returned to her place beside Ember.

No one replied.

'Can't say that anymore,' Ember thought. 'At least not while playing. So much for our winter snow battle. But there will be other snows. As long as we live to see them, we can do it again the right way. With fresh snow.'

The crackling of the flames and howling of the wind took over, preventing the silence from becoming absolute. Ember pinned back her ears. Somewhere behind her, an icicle broke off of a tree. It hit a patch of frozen ground and shattered. She leaned closer to the fire.

"You said that thing on your neck can teach you anything, didn't you?" Cloud asked.

Ember straightened herself up. "Er, yeah, yes sir. Almost anything. I don't think it can tell us how to fly. Why?"

"Is this really the time?" Songbird said.

"I'm just asking her," he said. "There's this project I've been working on for the past few days and I was wondering if there's a better way to make it work."

"Oh, yes, Kivyress told me. You're trying to make guard pieces to protect us from bites, right? That's a great idea, but I am definitely sure there's a better way to make it than with bark."

"So what do you suggest?"

"That I consult my Thai," she replied.

She closed her eyes and dove into the vast expanse of knowledge that was the internet. After some virtual digging around, she discovered human armor, which they made with everything from metal to what appeared to be simply thick fabric. After some additional digging, she discovered that some humans used large animal hides, such as deerskin, to make their armor.

'That. There. That will work. It's easy to get, and something we, with our pathetic little paws, can work with. Keep that tab for me, Thai. I'm gonna need it again.'

267

[Will do, Ember.]

"Deerskin?" Cloud asked after she explained her findings. "But Ember, we have to bite through deerskin to kill a deer. It's not thick or strong enough to stop fangs when the deer is attached to it. What makes us strapping the skins to ourselves any different?"

"*Layers*, Dad. And I think we're supposed to do something to the skin to make it stronger. I don't think the humans would use it to protect themselves if it didn't work. We can at least give it a try."

He nodded. "I don't know if humans have fangs or not, but fair enough. Would you be interested in trying to put some together tomorrow?"

Ember smiled. The grey in her head morphed into a misty orange—a misty orange brighter than sadness and as welcoming as a spring breeze. Hope. "I don't have anything else planned."

Cloud chuffed. "So what do you say, Commander Farlight? Am I allowed to work with my daughter tomorrow morning?"

"I don't know. What if she wants to practice her clawmarks? The next Meeting is gonna be a fun one to document," Farlight replied.

"Actually, I can't clawmark anymore. Sorry, I forgot to mention it. Wait, Whitehaze hasn't found a new apprentice yet? I thought for sure there'd be someone," Ember said.

Hyrees leaned back. "Hey, I thought we were done with surprises. You not clawmarking? Since when has this been a thing?"

"Since I woke up with robot legs. I have claws, but supposedly I'll damage them if I try to do any carving with them. So I won't. But hey, I have my own version of the History Tree inside me right now." Her mind drifted back to the documentary. As much as learning the truth had hurt, knowing the whole story had given her a new, slightly more real version of reality to stand on. "It's better than the one in the Glade."

"So did the humans just go through and give you a list of things you can't do now?" he asked.

She tilted her head. Indigo swirled behind her eyes. "Not exactly. But that's not how it worked. It didn't happen all at once, and not every human helped me. Just three." A picture of Lake formed. She stared helplessly as her image got smaller and smaller until it disappeared completely, leaving the young human once again stranded at school. "Maybe four, but I'm not sure she counts. She mostly just avoided me."

"Oh."

'Maybe you should have tried to talk to her more,' Ember thought. *'Something was definitely bothering her, and Michelle didn't seem concerned. Maybe she needed someone to talk to. But then again, Michelle is her mom. Mothers always seem to know what their kittens need, so maybe Lake was just being huffy. Or maybe I was mistaken again and everything is fine. Human faces are different from our faces, so it's possible that was—'*

"So you keep saying the History Tree is wrong," Hyrees said, bringing her into the present. "I thought it was supposed to be the pinnacle of perfection: the all-knowing, on which we should base our entire existence. What happened to that?"

The wind slowed to a gentle, barely audible breeze. The fire snapped, and the wood shifted, creating an outburst of colorful sparks. Ember winced at the sudden sounds and movements. Instinct made her hunch forward. Half of her wanted to be closer to Hyrees, and half of her wanted to be closer to Songbird, yet neither of them wanted to be closer to each other. So she leaned closer to the same flames that had startled her.

"Ember," Cloud said.

She sat bolt upright. "Hmm? Sir?"

"Hyrees asked you a question."

Ember leaned forward again. She pinned back her ears, and squinted her eyes to match him. An oily half-rainbow of metallic blues, greens, and purples appeared, shifting and shimmering faintly in her mind's eye.

'He's annoyed? Why is he annoyed? I was about to answer when you interrupted. Unless my colors are different from yours. Then I might be completely off. Which is possible.'

"Ember, please. Stop making faces, and answer. I don't want to have to keep repeating myself."

"Sorry," she said, barely louder than a whisper. "I'm not making faces though, I'm just changing the one I've got." Their silence made her face burn. "I was trying to figure out what you meant by the expressions you were making. I'm pretty sure you're annoyed, and I'm sorry for probably causing it, but did it work this time? Please let me know. I really want to be able to understand you and everyone else. But I can't unless you're willing to help me understand. I'm not like you. I can't do it automatically. I need help."

Everyone stared at her. Ember shrunk back. She closed her eyes, willing herself to become invisible. *'Fire. Fire. Focus on fire. You like fire, remember? Keeps us warm and gives us light. Why does silence always come at the wrong time? What are they thinking right now? Oh, I hate this kind of quiet.'*

Cloud rubbed his right forepaw, the one to Ember's left, against his head, ruffling and grooming his fur.

'Does he have a headache? Did I give him one? What am I doing wrong? What if I—no, Ember. Don't call Matthew again. This isn't an emergency like last time. You can figure it out yourself.'

"Ember," Cloud said. "Please just stop. I don't need you to understand. I don't need you to know what I'm feeling. Feelings are not important. What I need you to do is listen, and to answer when something is asked of you."

"No, no, it's okay," Hyrees mewed. "It was just a question. She doesn't have to answer if she doesn't want to."

"I want to answer; you all just keep interrupting me," she said. Her half-tail twitched as her own oily blues, greens, and purples appeared. "What happened is I found out the truth. And no, they didn't tell me. If they had, they might have lied, and I wouldn't keep bringing it up because I wouldn't know what to believe."

Cloud's tail thrashed. "Ah—"

Songbird held up a paw, silencing him. "You said you've found the truth, but we want to know what this truth is."

Ember cocked her head. *'How do you do that, Mom? How did you get all that from him saying "ah"? Is that really what he wants to know?'*

"Er, okay," Ember said. "Well, for one, the History Tree doesn't give the whole truth, making Dark seem better than he actually was. He was a really brave cat, but he was also selfish in some ways. There were dogs and rats in ARC who were just as smart as we are, and he left them to die. And they died."

"Arc?" Farlight asked. "I don't mean to interrupt, but what is that? Something tells me you aren't talking about circles."

Ember sighed, then started over, beginning with when she'd first woken up at the Center. She told them about Yegor, and Hye, and Michelle, and how Michelle had helped her set up Thai. Then she explained the meaning behind Thai's name, and how nice Michelle's little family was, but decided to skip over the parts about autism and thinking differently.

'Wouldn't do any good anyway. At least not coming from me. I still don't know what I'm talking about and they still think everyone thinks like them. Or at least Dad does, and there's no way they'd trust Matthew if I got him to try to explain why I'm all messed up. And no one here except Kivy would really be able to back me up, but no one will listen to her anyway. Sorry, Kivy, but you know it's true.'

"This is all very, very interesting," Hyrees said when she finished. "But what does it have to do with this arc thing or the History Tree being wrong? Or even how you found out about all this in the first place."

Her tail twitched again. More indigo appeared, this time mixed with grey and silver. "I was getting to that. Be patient. This is all connected. I've told you about the good side of humans, and now I'm going to show you the bad side."

Hyrees, Cloud, and Songbird all jumped to their paws in unison. Farlight sat up straight as a pine with his ears perked forward, and Kivyress's pupils widened. Ember couldn't tell if she was excited or scared, but knowing Kivyress, excitement seemed more likely.

Cloud dropped into a fighting stance. "Whatever you're about to do, don't," he said. "We do not need to see these humans of yours, and we especially don't need to see the bad ones. Keep them away from here."

Bright yellows came and replaced most of the purples for a moment. Then they came back, forming a grey-purple-yellow spiral in her head. It made her dizzy to internally look at, so she tried to keep her focus on the fire. "B-but I wasn't going to show you any real ones. Just images from my tag. Like I did with the snowflake. Remember? I wanted to show you what I saw."

Cloud straightened himself up. "Oh. And you're sure that whatever you're about to do won't let them know where we are?"

The yellows faded out, but the purples remained, gaining a hint of drab, misty orange. "Yeeaaahh, yes sir. I'm not sure what you think I'm about to do, but do you really think I'd do anything to put us in danger? Dad . . . don't any of you trust me? I'm not a fluffhead. I'm not a kitten. I know what danger is, and I know how to avoid it. I'm not going to get everyone killed."

"I trust you, Ember," Kivyress mewed.

"I do too," Farlight said. "But if any of you three say it, you'd be lying— both to her, and possibly to yourselves—so don't even try. If you trusted her, you wouldn't have reacted like that when she mentioned humans."

'Farlight, I can't decide if I should thank you or swat at you. But then again, it's better to know the truth. So I guess that means thank you, but why don't they trust me? Wait.' She closed her eyes and watched as misty oranges swept over the spiral. *'They've never trusted me. They still see me as a kitten. They think I can't understand, don't they? Don't think I can take care of myself. The worst part is, what if they're right? I can't hunt. And every time I try to be good, or try to be some kind of hero, I almost get killed. Does that mean Eclan was right too? Do all heroes die young?'*

Hyrees sat down, letting his head droop almost to his paws. "Sorry, Em. I guess, with everything that's happened, I'm still too worried to think straight. But I do trust you."

Dark, greenish-gold speckled the orange. Ember sighed and let her gaze wander up to the treetops. The lack of leaves made the first evening stars more visible. They glistened like baby suns. Though, thanks to Thai, she knew they were so much bigger than even the sun she'd once thought of as their mother. "Don't lie, Hyrees. You know I don't like yellow-green."

"But—"

"No, just watch. Thai, play The Animals Of ARC."

"Playing now," ETAg Thai chimed, oblivious to the somber mood.

The projected screen turned on. Ember positioned herself so the image fell on a nearby tree.

"Would you like me to turn on auto-translate, Ember?" Thai asked.

"Are you joking? You could translate this thing the whole time, and you're only just now bothering to bring it up?"

"I couldn't before because I didn't have any translation modules installed."

"Okay, fair enough. Yes. Yes, please translate it."

"Auto-translate is now on. Enjoy the film."

Songbird, Farlight, and Kivyress stared at her and her screen. Ember recalled how they hadn't been present when she'd shown her father and her mate the enlarged snowflake, yet even Cloud and Hyrees looked startled.

As the documentary began, her family inched its way closer to her. She knew they did it to see and hear better, but their closeness filled her imagination with her favorite color: maple leaf orange, the color of family. It was almost enough to make her forget how they saw her, yet not enough to stomp out the pain entirely.

The documentary itself played out how she remembered it, but with the addition of the humans being translated into Felid. They explained their side of the story well. Project Appala, named for the location of the facility, was started by someone who wanted to cure disorders causing developmental discrepancies, most notably ones having to do with the brain. He'd lost a child to one of these, and wanted to prevent it from happening again. Instead of risking human life, they had decided to risk animal life, and so the first appalas—a couple of rats, then Dark, Flare, and Forestfire—were born.

By the time they made it to Dark's first appearance, Ember realized none of the humans involved seemed to recognize just how much they'd changed the animals they'd enhanced. They'd given them the minds of their own kind.

Minds that could understand right from wrong. Minds that wanted freedom from crimes the humans hadn't even realized they were committing. They'd created their own equals and they hadn't even known it.

After Dark's pleas for help ended, Ember tried to turn her head to see the expressions on the faces of her family. Her ETAg shifted positions, making the projection move. She pawed it back into place and forced herself to remain still.

'Do they realize who that is? Do they know who they just heard?'

"Was that Dark right there?" someone behind her asked.

'Whitehaze?' Ember flicked back her ears. *'Oh, how many cats are watching this?'*

"Y-yeah, yes sir. Flare and Forestfire are in it too."

"Huh. It seems he was as good a speaker as he was a clawmarker," Whitehaze replied. Something about his voice sounded different: more subdued and quiet. It took her a few moments to fully recognize it. "Noble, noble cat."

When the film moved on to show the escape, two cats caterwauled encouragements behind her. Several others moaned, growled, or hissed when would-be escapees got left behind. Their hisses and growls grew louder upon seeing how the captured appalas got treated. When the cat in the collar and leash was shocked into obedience, they yowled with outrage.

Her kin's dramatic responses to each revelation sparked a new color to appear in her mind. It was a color she usually only felt in dreams: a surreal, metallic turquoise.

'Oh. I'm doing this. I'm teaching my colony. This is it. This is the moment where I start being useful and stop being a pathetic little failure of a feline. Starting tonight, I'm going to change things, and things are going to change. I can show them so much, and they might actually take me seriously for once.'

Ember's eyes lit up. The sounds of the documentary faded as the feeling of authority she'd discovered earlier that day seeped into her, filling her mind with prideful oak brown. *'Wait a moment, knowing what I know, and having what I have, I'm the most powerful cat in the Valley now. And it's not even entirely my fault. I mean, I didn't force anyone to unknowingly tell me secrets, and I certainly didn't force Michelle to give me access to the biggest collection of human knowledge in the universe. I didn't stop them, of course, so yes, it's partially my fault, but it's not a bad thing. I can choose to do a lot of good or a lot of bad with all this, so I guess I'll have to be careful where I step from now on. In more than just a literal sense. It shouldn't be too hard, though. Make the right choices, get the right outcome. I've made it this far; I can make it the rest of the way.'*

The sound of muffled gunshots snapped her back to reality. It took her a moment to realize they were at *that* part of the film: the part she'd turned it off at. The part where humans hunted down her kind. Gasps and mews followed the image of the dead, bleeding appala, making her miss part of the audio. Ember closed her eyes and bit her tongue, trying to make the image disappear.

Even after the escape and the hunting scenes, the humans in the documentary still didn't seem to recognize appalas as being sentient. Instead, they viewed them as vermin. Problems—accidents—to be dealt with and cleaned up to protect the natural balance of life.

Ember's mind wandered back to one of the oldest passages on the History Tree. For the first year and a half after their escape, every cat had hunted for itself. Food had become scarce, and many cats had starved in the second year. Then the Founders had developed group hunting, allowing them to take down larger prey the whole colony could share. Ever since then, the small wildlife flourished and only occasionally got tapped into when the hunters couldn't catch anything big. Even with the steady population of Outsiders, life continued on, and Dark's Valley still hadn't become a wasteland.

She opened her eyes. The documentary showed people shouting and holding up big sheets of paper with their own marks on them. The noise was so jumbled, Thai couldn't even translate the narrator. After that, a few humans spoke in defense of appalas. It ended with the ARC people talking about other methods of 'population reduction,' and the hope they expressed in their quest to find their missing property and right the wrongs they'd done —to the local ecosystem, not to the ones they wanted dead.

The screen turned off. The voices of her kin rose to an uproar.

"They're still looking for us!" one cat yowled.

"Maybe we *should* move," another said. "If we don't, it's only a matter of time before—"

"Lupine, what do we do?"

"Lupine? Hah! He doesn't know what to do. And the Council's gone foxing crazy. Ask Farlight what to do. Maybe he can—"

"The East and the humans want us dead. Maybe Whitehaze was r—"

"We're all gonna die!"

Ember shivered with the howl of every new voice. Cyan trickled in. *'Breathe in; one, two, three, four, five. Breathe out. Don't panic, Ember. Not again. Two attacks in one day is way too much. But what am I going to do?'*

The dark brown feeling of pride and power came back, dancing with the cyan. *'Wait a moment. Maybe I can stop this. Thai, when was that documentary made?'*

[The Animals Of ARC was released in 2026.]

'And what year is it now?'

[The current year is 2110.]

'Okay, okay, I can use this. Get your words together, Em.' She inhaled slowly, trying to breathe in some tangible form of confidence, then she stood up, eyes closed. "Hey! Everyone, stop! Er, that thing you just watched is from eighty-four yea—winters ago. They still haven't found us. We're, uhm, we're safe."

To her surprise, they listened. Lupine even helped quiet them.

"Go ahead, E-Ember," he said. "What were you, uh, were you saying?"

She turned around. Almost the entire Western Colony stood or sat behind her, looking to her for reassurance. The brown took over entirely. *'I don't have to keep hiding. I don't have to wait for the world to go away. If I have useful enough information, I guess I can make them shut up myself. Sometimes. I wonder if they realize what I could do to them if I wanted to. I won't, of course, but some healthy respect for the possibilities certainly wouldn't hurt anyone.'*

"Uhm, er, well, what y'all just watched, it was made eighty-four y—*winters* ago. It's, ah, over four times older than any of us. So, er, if they were going to find us, I-I think they probably would've done it by now. Stop being so cyan and green. We're fine. And remember the good humans. There are ones out there who are on our side. Humans that helped me and saved my life. We have allies, and if the bad people were to find us, I could call on the good ones to help. We're safe."

The murmurs came back, this time too subdued to make any one voice out. Ember smiled. She glanced over at Cloud, who watched her with an expression she'd never even seen on him before. His ears were cocked slightly and his mouth hung open wide enough for her to notice one of his upper fangs was missing.

'Hum. That's different. Well, you were wrong, Dad. But so was I,' she thought. *'Understanding the emotions of others is important. And you know that, which is why you want me to stay confused. Well I'm not playing that game anymore.'*

She glanced down at the dying flames. Her namesakes sparkled and flickered in and out of being, providing almost as much light as the star-filled night sky.

'They might be mostly silver right now, but once I figure out how to see the rainbow, if even just a reflection of it through the silver, I can do so much more. I can stop this war before it even really starts if I place my paws right. I can do anything within reason.'

She chuffed to herself and walked toward the Glade. *'All these mooncycles I've been trying to get everyone to understand me, when really, I was meant to be silver. Thinking differently; why did you never realize how big of an advantage it gives you? And to think, for a few moments, you actually thought it was a bad thing.'*

When she passed the first fire pit, Lupine trotted up to her. "E-Ember, wait."

She stopped and looked at him. The fur along his back and tail was slightly more raised than normal. "Sir?" she asked.

"I absolutely do not approve of all these human gadgets you've got, but that one on your neck might be useful. W-what else can you do?"

"Er, more than I'm aware of right now, but give me some time and I'll find my limits. I know some of them already. I can't clawmark, or fly, or recognize most emotions, but I'm still working on that last one. Still don't know if I can fight."

He didn't respond immediately. His tail twitched three times both ways. "I-I-I can't offer you a position on the Council," he began, "but don't be surprised i-if I call you in to give me some advice or ask a-a question. You wouldn't mind, would you?"

Yellow flickered through her thoughts. Ember stepped back, almost catching her tail on fire in the process. "Uh, no. No, sir. I could do that. I can help. Just let me know when you need me."

"I will. I'll definitely be needing you. F-Farlight and me both. Times like these, we'll need a-all the help we can get."

As they exchanged goodnights, then parted ways, a flame of red burned deep in her chest. *'Need me? Need my help? It really is happening. I'm going to change things. I can fix almost everything and put it all back where it belongs. And make it stay that way.'*

"Hey, Em, just thought I'd mention we've got a den now."

She turned around to find Hyrees walking toward her. "We do?"

He caught up and rubbed his cheek against her side. "Yes, I know—an actual roof over our heads. Shelter from all this goop. And falling icicles. Amazing, huh? Don't have to worry about getting impaled in our sleep."

"That's convenient. Is it the one your dad had?"

He winced. "Ah, yeah. It was . . . it was his."

"Sorry, was that the wrong thing to say?"

He sighed, then offered her a smile. "No, no, it's okay. Come on. Let's go get some sleep. It's been a long day. I'm tired, so I know you must be too."

Ember pressed her head against his. "Of course I am."

He pulled back, ears perked. "So you're okay with not sleeping in the History Tree?"

Ember snorted. She cast a longing glance at the massive oak she'd come to love. She shook herself off, then started for her new dwelling place. "Like I said, I've got my own History Tree, and it's always with me. I don't need to risk getting impaled by an icicle to learn or study anymore. Now onward, my loving mate—to the den!"

Hyrees chuckled. He shook his head and followed. After they got there, but before they could settle in, Cloud, Songbird, Kivyress and Farlight came over to say goodnight. Farlight decided to spend the night with his adopted family to give her and Hyrees some privacy.

After they left, Ember paced in a circle around the cave-like space and, by extension, around Hyrees. *I'll help Dad with the armor tomorrow, then I can work with Lupine and Farlight to figure out the best way to avoid another fight altogether. There doesn't have to be any more needless bloodshed. If we work together, we can end this war before it really starts, and then everything can go back to being as normal as possible, only better. In some ways, at least. I can't bring back the fallen.'*

"You're making me dizzy," Hyrees said. "I thought you were tired. What are you thinking about?"

"How to keep things from getting worse, and how to hopefully make things better. At some point."

"Oh."

She stopped. "Okay, so since this is my first night back, and we're both still alive, we should probably do something nice together. Don't you think?" Ember asked.

She rubbed her cheek against the den's cool, packed dirt wall. Her ETAg clinked against a rock. The collar still irritated her neck, and the tag still bounced against her fur when she moved, but knowing how much good the tiny machine would soon do made every itch it caused worth the trouble.

Hyrees's ears perked up. He smiled. "Uhm, yeah, sure. Anything specific you had in mind?"

"Actually, yes. I was thinking we could curl up in each other's paws and get the answers to all our biggest questions. I mean, look at this, I've literally got the greatest collection of knowledge in the world hanging around my neck. We can find out anything we want to know. We can learn the secrets of everything, and not just other cats anymore—the world as we'll soon know it. Why the sky is blue and the grass is green. What clouds are made of, and where wind comes from. *Anything.* Romantic, right?"

His ears lost their perkiness. He turned his head to look outside. "Not exactly . . . well . . ."

"What? Is that not romantic enough? Do you have a better idea than discovering the secrets of the universe together? I thought it might be fairly appropriate, considering everything that's happened over the past few days, but if you want to do something else, that's fine. Maybe we could take a walk in the moonlight or something and enjoy the quiet. I'd be fine with that, too. Oh! Or we could take a walk in the moonlight *and* discover the secrets of the universe at the same time. That's about as romantic as it gets, isn't it?"

She bit her tongue and thrashed her tail. *'And this is the part where you agree with me. Right? Come on, Hyrees, please. I'm giving you the opportunity to gain all the knowledge in the world, and we can do it together. Isn't that enough for you?'*

He looked outside for a few moments more, then turned back to her and offered another gentle smile. "No, no, that's okay. Let's do it. It sounds like fun. Let's discover the secrets of the universe."

CHAPTER 19
CLOUD

"So fourteen days, you said?" Cloud asked. "They have to soak for fourteen days? That's impractical if we ever want to make enough for everyone. You're sure there's nothing else we can use? Anything faster or easier to make?"

He stared into the specially made clay tanning box that was painstakingly filled with water, tree bark, and pieces of deerskin. He sighed. His breath came out in a puff of steam, like the thick mist weaving in and out of the trees and dual abatises. Morning sunlight cut through the fog, making pristine rays of light scatter through the forest.

Ember sniffed at the water, which bubbled cheerfully beside the fire heating it. "Well, technically it's only eleven now, but unfortunately, unless you can figure out how to get and use metal, that's pretty much our only option. As far as armor goes, at least," Ember replied.

The flames keeping the water from freezing snapped, making her jump. Her fake limbs whirred and whined with the sudden movement. The little fire was contained and controlled in one of the four large clay half-bowls built onto the sides of the tanning box. Smoke billowed from the flames and steam rose from the water, adding to the intense haze in the air.

Those humans had better know what they're doing. Fourteen days of waiting is a lot of time lost if this doesn't work. How did they even discover how to do it in the first place? It's so convoluted and time-consuming, it can't have happened by accident.'

He placed a paw into the fire-heated water and quickly pulled out one of the skins. It didn't feel any different than it had the day before, only hotter and maybe a little more wet this time, if that was even possible. He snorted and pushed it back in.

His stomach growled. "Come on, let's go get some food."

"Y-yes, sir," Ember said.

They left the crude 'tanning yard,' positioned between the two walls, and re-entered the inner Glade side by side. Ember had given the yard its name, claiming it to be what the humans called such places. Cloud flattened his ears at the thought of the two-legged creatures.

'Humans. I wish you'd stop comparing us to those humans. I don't care what they call things or how they do things. We aren't humans, Ember, we're cats. Sometimes things are the way they are for a reason. If we keep trying to be something we're not, we'll only find ourselves with bigger problems.' He shook his head. *'And I'll never be able to tell you that, will I? No one listens to me anymore. Not even you half the time, now that you've got all this.'*

"You get to be my patrolling partner again today," he said instead.

She smiled softly. "Yes, sir. And Hyrees is actually excited about starting his clayworking training, which is great. Everything's going to go back to normal soon, only better. Also worse in some ways, but the bad should be less than the good if we do everything right."

Cloud chuffed. "I take it you have a plan?"

"Make life easier to predict. Remove unnecessary variables. Keep good cats from dying too soon." She paused and thought for a moment. "It's a loose plan, but I'm still working on it."

Cloud smiled, both for her and himself. Odd and unconventional as she was, she was doing her best. It hurt him inside to know her almost kittenish mind still didn't appear to grasp the concept of war or the full extent of the meaning of death, but she was trying her hardest to cope with it all, and doing so in the only ways she knew how. Her optimism seemed to be rubbing off on the rest of the Colony, even when some still joked or sneered about her behind her back.

"Well, it seems to be working so far. I'm proud of you, you know," he replied.

She stopped and looked at him for a moment, eyes wide and sparking with excitement. A moment later, the sparks disappeared. Her expression went eerily blank and she continued walking. "Thanks, Dad. I know I'm a little late, but at least I've managed to do it. Now, all this," she lifted a mechanical forepaw, as if inviting him to study its gaudy, artificial skin, "was worth it."

'Worth it? The fight? Almost losing you? Getting mangled beyond repair? Aspen and Wren dying?' It was Cloud's turn to stop. "What are you talking about?"

Her half-tail twitched as her gaze meandered off around the Glade. "You being proud of me made everything that's happened to me worth it. The pain, the fear, the sadness; you made it all okay, because now I know who I'm supposed to be. I'm finally doing something right."

He lowered his ears against the sides of his face to match the sinking feeling consuming his chest. *'Has she been basing her whole life around trying to please me? Have I never told her until today? Surely I must have at some point.'*

Cloud forced an amused chuff. "Ember, I've been proud of you since the day you were born. Since before you were born."

Her eyes lit up again, but the light went out as suddenly as it came. "Not that simple," she said.

"Not that simple? What are you trying to say?"

"Not straight," she muttered. "Not enough. Proofs. I really do need to work this one out better." Her stomach grumbled. She perked up, but her expression remained unreadable. "Oh, yes, right, right."

"Ember?"

"Hmm? Oh! I don't know. The world needs less yellow-green, don't you think? It's not a very nice color. You said you wanted to talk to me before I got hit. Did you still want to do that?"

"Uhm," he stumbled over his words, taken aback by her sudden, irrelevant question. Yes, Aspen was dead, but until Farlight became commander, there was always the chance Lupine would keep his brother's last threatening promise. He tried to smile at her. "I want to talk to you, of course, but I don't know that what I was going to tell you then really matters anymore. You seem to be handling yourself fairly well."

Instead of replying, she sighed and went back to walking.

He followed alongside her in silence, waiting for an explanation. She didn't offer one.

When they got to the food storage, the cats already there turned and lowered their heads in respect.

"Good morning. So what's the weather going to do today, Ember?" one of them asked.

Cloud realized it was Rowan. He dipped his head politely. He was surprised to admit it, but ever since getting yelled at after attacking Hyrees, the young tom had become quite agreeable to be around. In many ways Rowan reminded him of himself: stubborn and fiery, but smart and always trying to please his superiors.

Before Ember could reply, a young tortoiseshell molly positioned herself between them. "That's not important right now. I have an emergency. Will it be cold enough for the creek to freeze over anytime soon, and if so, how long do we have? This is extremely important, okay? I bet all of my credits on it not freezing for the next mooncycle."

"Oh, shut your muzzle, fluffhead," a smoky tom snapped. "She doesn't have time for your one-credit problem, and knowing you, that expression is probably quite literal." He stepped closer to Ember, ignoring the snarls of the enraged molly behind him. "But do you have the time to check where I'd most likely be able to locate some new sparkstones? The ones we have are old, and Lupine has tasked me with finding more."

Ember crouched down and backed away from the impatient trio. She tucked her tail and ducked behind Cloud. "No! No, no, no, please stop. That's not even how it works. I don't have the answers to everything. Please, just let us get some food and leave me alone."

"Oh, I'm sorry, Ember," Rowan said. "I didn't know if finding out the weather was something you could do or not. I thought it was."

Ember sighed and flattened her ears. "Sunny this morning, cloudy tonight, snowy tomorrow."

"What about the creek?" the young tortoiseshell asked.

She closed her eyes. "I don't know, okay? Please, just let us get some food."

'Oh no, not this again.' Cloud backed up. He pressed his cheek against her side in an attempt to calm her. *'Welcome to my world. Not too glamorous, is it, having everyone look to you for advice? They act like a bunch of kittens, don't they?'*

"So you don't know where to find sparkstones?" the tom said.

"Okay, that's enough," a calm-yet-firm voice said.

Cloud turned around to find Songbird standing outside the storage cave. Her fur glistened in the sun like the shimmering stones lining the small cavern behind her. She pushed three lumps of meat forward. "Here are your rations. Time to leave."

The tom growled but obeyed. Rowan and the molly grabbed their meals, then carried them off to eat. Ember strode toward Songbird. They touched noses.

"Thanks, Mom," Ember purred.

Songbird leaned closer to press her forehead against Ember's. "Not a problem. They needed to stop. This really is getting ridiculous. You'd think they can't survive without you now."

"I don't mind questions, as long as they're only asked one at a time, and are questions I can actually get the answers to." Ember turned toward the cave and sniffed the air. "Something smells weird. Did you catch some rabbits yesterday?"

Songbird chuffed. "Not me, but some of the other hunters did. They got two. Do you want one?"

"I just want food, and I'll take it in whatever form you decide to give me."

"Alright then," Songbird said. She padded into the cave. "One rabbit coming up."

Ember's eyes narrowed. She tilted her head, as if confused, but said nothing. Cloud turned his attention to the storage cave and smiled as his eyes adjusted to the dull lighting. They landed on a hole under the back wall, which caused him to chuckle when he remembered how it got there.

Once, when Kivyress was only a few mooncycles old, she'd followed Songbird down into the cave. For a few moments, she'd sniffed around and examined the preserved meats, then, when Songbird wasn't looking, she'd dug at the little crack between the ground and the back wall. When she'd carved out a deep enough hole to fit herself in the crevice, she'd crawled through and gotten stuck in whatever cavern lay on the other side. In order to get her out, Songbird and Kivyress had worked together to make it big enough for her to squeeze back out. When the rescue mission had ended, no one had bothered to fill the hole back in, so the tiny passageway remained a part of the storage cave.

Songbird came out with a small rabbit, bringing him back to the present. She gave the limp lagomorph to Ember, who dragged it to a quiet, rocky nook a few leaps away. Songbird walked over to Cloud and pressed her nose against his, her meat-scented breath warming his face. "So what do you want this morning? Oh, and I almost forgot—how's the project coming?"

Cloud chuffed and licked her cheek. "It's not doing much yet, but it's supposed to take a while, so I'll have to wait. We all will. I think that—"

She shoved a paw against his muzzle. "What do you want to eat, fluffhead?"

Cloud sighed. He nudged her paw away from his mouth and smiled. "Anything that's not poisonous. Furball."

Songbird chuckled and trotted away to get him his surprise meal. She returned with a lump of turkey meat.

"Turkey?" he asked. "Again? Tahg, ever since that one tried to eat your face, you've been showing those birds no mercy."

She laughed her gentle, loving laugh. "Oh no, I'm getting my revenge on all the turkeys. Or at least most of them. Many of them. Some of them. Look, they messed up my face, so they deserve to be hunted. Never mind the fact that I started it." She stopped to look him over. "You are okay with turkey, right?"

Cloud licked her cheek again. "Of course I am. I was just being difficult." She pressed closer to him. "Nothing new there."

Something cold struck his back. Cloud spun around. Kivyress stood a leap away, trying and failing to look innocent.

"Oh, sorry, were you two having a moment that my hungry self just ruined?" she asked.

"And good morning to you, too," he replied.

"Oh, come on, Kivy." Farlight pranced over to join them. The fur along his back stood on end. His tail thrashed, as if he were agitated by something, but nothing else about him looked troubled. "Just let them be all gross and nuzzle-licky. After all, one day we'll probably be just like them." He leaned over and licked Kivyress's cheek.

Kivyress jerked her head away. "Whoa, what? Far, what was that? You were joking, right?"

Cloud winced. *'Ouch, Kivy. Way to let him down easy.'*

Farlight's ears and tail drooped. "Uh, yeah. Yeah, that was just a joke. Heh. I mean, could you even imagine us together?"

Kivyress chuckled halfheartedly. "Yes, I can, but as friends. At least for now. Look, I don't care if we're not actually related. You're my brother, Far. I don't want anything coming between us and what we've got going right now. I don't need a future mate. Not for a while, at least. I need my loyal best friend, who will soon also be my wonderfully competent commander. Okay?"

Cloud flinched. Aspen had warned him to keep watch over Farlight. Aside from training sessions, however, he hardly ever saw him. Part of him wondered if he was letting his duties slip, or failing his true commander once again.

Farlight forced a smile. His tail slowed to a steady twitch. "Okay. So . . . food?"

"Of course," Kivyress replied. "Mom, are we allowed to eat yet?"

Songbird smiled. "Yes. What do you two want?"

Kivyress glanced back to where Ember was eating her meal. Hyrees had turned up at some point and was speaking to her. "Em's got a rabbit. Do you have any more?"

"We sure do. Farlight, what about you?"

Farlight looked at her, doing an excellent job of keeping his composure. "I don't care what you give me, ma'am. I'm just hungry."

"Alrighty then," Songbird mewed as she re-entered the cave. "A rabbit and another surprise meat are on their way."

Farlight ended up with a piece of smoked venison. Hyrees eventually came over and got some venison as well, then another hunter took over so Songbird herself could eat.

Cloud finished first and watched in contented silence as everyone he loved ate their meals. It was a wonderful feeling, seeing them together and content. He got the urge to ask Wren how he thought the patrol would go, but he pushed the feeling away.

He twitched his tail and let out a sigh. *'I really need to stop this. It's time to move on. It's time for everyone to move on. Things are the way they are right now, and nothing I nor anyone else does or says will bring back the dead.'*

When Ember finished picking through her meal, she and Cloud said their goodbyes and prepared to leave the Glade.

"Remember, Farlight, don't use up all of your energy today," he said. "We've still got training to do."

Farlight nodded. "Yes, sir. I'm looking forward to it."

"Good tom. And Kivy, you take it easy on your trainers today. Hyrees, listen to Fledge. Songbird, I love you."

Songbird licked his cheek. "And I love you, too. Please be careful, both of you."

"We will."

"Bye, Mom," Ember mewed.

For the first time in what felt like an eternity, Cloud and Ember left the

Glade side by side to patrol the Northern Border.

EMBER

Ember forced herself to stop biting her tongue. *'My legs aren't sore yet. I don't think I like that. They're supposed to be sore now that we're almost back, but they don't feel real because they're not.'*

The patrol had gone well enough. They hadn't actually come across any Outsiders, but getting back into the routine of living made it enough of a success. They'd even taken a break at Fernburrow Falls, where icicles had coated the cliff face. As inconvenient as it was, snow enhanced the pretty factor of everything it touched. Its beauty alone balanced out many of the negatives of its existence.

"You're being quiet. Is something bothering you?" Cloud asked.

'You should be glad you can't hear thoughts. If you could, I would be loud, and you'd tell me to shut up, and I wouldn't be able to.'

"I'm okay. Just thinking about things," she said. "It feels so different, patrolling with these." She lifted up a forepaw and hopped forward for a few steps. The annoying little mechanical whirs grated her ears with every motion. "I guess I'll get used to it."

"It'll take some getting used to for all of us," he replied.

Ember examined his face to try to mimic and read his expression, but there was no expression to mimic. She snorted and kept walking.

When they reached the Glade, Cloud wandered off to find Farlight. She sat down by the nearest fire pit to warm back up. The heating grid worked fairly well, but it didn't provide nearly as much warmth as the flames. The cool, misty blue-greens of rest settled into her mind. She purred.

'Maybe things really will get better. There haven't been any signs of attacks since that crazy Rogue showed up, then disappeared. Maybe the East just declared war to keep us on our side of the Valley. She must know that, with Commander Aspen gone, we're too weak to launch an attack.'
Ember looked over at his old den. She imagined the former commander

standing atop it, tall and proud as ever. *'The outer wall isn't going to work, but really, our best chance is to fortify and wait.'*

Deeper in her mind's eye, a picture of the abatises formed. She closed her eyes and imagined jumping through the treetops, calculating what places in the wall were the most vulnerable. She looked about the self-created landscape, teleporting herself to different locations around the walls until she was satisfied she'd pinpointed every weakness. She mentally climbed a tree outside the abatis whose limbs touched a tree between the two walls. She used the middle tree to reach one inside the Glade.

'Oh, height is another advantage to using the trees. I automatically get the high ground.'

An imaginary Hyrees popped into existence beneath her imaginary tree. She leaped from the tree, tackling him in the process. Then they rolled around and play-fought. The thoughts made a bright cheerful orange trickle in to mix with her already existent greens.

A paw tapped her on the back, snapping her away from her fantasies. Ember turned to find Farlight standing behind her. His fur stood on end. He was shivering.

"Farlight? Dad's looking for you, you know," she said.

"Yeah, I know," he replied. "But I was looking for you. We need to talk."

She tilted her head and let her gaze wander back to the fire. "About what? Is there something wrong?"

"In short, yes, but we can't talk about it here."

A little glowing ember flew into the air, almost hitting her in the face. It did a backflip, then disappeared. "Why not?" Ember asked. "Most cats are still out working, so if it's a secret you need to share, it's safe."

"No, it's not safe. The whole Glade isn't safe."

Her chest tightened. Indigo and silver took over her thoughts. She spun around to face him, ears perked and attention focused. "What do you mean it isn't safe? This isn't about the East, is it?"

His tail thrashed. "Well, yes and no. It's just—"

"Farlight! There you are." Cloud strode toward them. "I've been searching half the Glade trying to find you. Ready for your training?"

Farlight flattened his ears. "Yes, sir."

"Uhm?" Ember stood up, prosthetics whining. *'No, wait! Don't just walk away. You haven't finished telling me what's going on.'*

"We'll talk later, okay?" Farlight said. He cursed under his breath as he padded over to join Cloud. His shiver was gone, and his fur was no longer raised. Even his tail went still.

"Uh, okay. Yeah, that'll work. I hope. Assuming nothing terrible happens between now and later, of course."

She shifted her front paws so that the dark one rested on top of the white one. *'I hope it's nothing too important. But it probably is—it takes a little more than being brushed off by Kivyress to get your fur raised. And you wouldn't be this cryptic if it was just that. Cryptic is not your thing.'*

"You two are having private meetings now?" Cloud asked. "You aren't trying to take my former position are you, Ember? Trying to get on our future commander's good side?"

"Actually, we were just talking about talking," Ember replied. "Besides, I wouldn't be allowed to be chief advisor, even if I wanted to be."

Cloud snorted. "Ah, yes, right. Come on, Farlight. Let's get going. We're wasting time. You be good, Ember. If your mother asks, we're going to the Pine Grove."

"I will. Yes, sir," she said.

She watched in external silence as they left. *'That was odd.'*

After they exited the Glade, Whitehaze climbed down from the History Tree. He walked over to her. "Hello there, Ember. I take it the patrol went well?"

"Yes, sir. It went well enough. And when Dad wasn't looking, I pushed some extra leaves onto that place where we saw those flowers last spring. Hopefully it'll help it grow even more next spring."

He chuffed and sat down beside her. "Thank you. Hopefully my ancient self will be able to climb up there to see them again. They are pretty little things. Do you still dislike purple?"

291

Ember forced a chuckle. "I'm actually feeling kind of purple right now. But no, it's not my favorite color. Maple orange is the best."

He pawed at her side, brows raised. "I disagree. But fortunately, there's no law that says we can't. I just checked." He smiled. "Otherwise you'd be in trouble. Hah!"

"Or you would be, if my opinion was considered better."

"Perhaps." He wrapped his tail around Ember's haunches, making her flinch. "So tell me, Ember, what was Farlight wanting of you?"

The indigo grew brighter. She resisted the urge to bite her tongue, and instead rubbed her paws together. "He just wanted to talk, so we talked. Then Dad came before we could finish, and we decided to talk more later. Why?"

Whitehaze sighed. "He's a good cat, but maybe a little too smart for anyone's good. I've seen what he can do when he puts his mind to accomplishing something. Keep your guard around him, Ember. They told you he helped your father and Hyrees get back on their paws, but no one ever told you how. Well, I'll tell you now; he's as manipulative as any other commander we've had, if not more so. He convinced Lupine to give him charge over your father, the second most influential cat in the Colony at the time. Lying is not beyond him. That young tom will do or say whatever it takes to achieve his goals. Don't let him take advantage of you. Don't let anyone take advantage of you. You are more than capable of defending yourself, with your claws, or your words."

'Is that true?' Silver overtook the indigo. 'Would he really lie to me, or Dad, or Hyrees? And how do you know about this? Did Farlight tell you? Did you overhear him? And why are you telling me this to begin with? Are you trying to turn me against him? Everyone includes you, after all. I'm not going to let you use me, either. No one will use me. Ever. And remember that I can remember. Though I hardly think your secret gives me much leverage. Then again, I'm sure you've got some I don't know about.'

"Or with secrets," Ember said, trying her best to sound innocent—as naive as everyone thought her to be. She took an extra moment to gather her thoughts. "When cats share secrets, everyone thinks everyone else will forget, and that they'll just get to walk away with that naughty feeling of saying something they shouldn't. That's why almost everyone likes telling secrets, isn't it? They probably do leave feeling better about themselves, but what they don't realize is that I can hear, and I can remember."

"Of . . . of course," Whitehaze replied. His eyes widened for a split second before narrowing once again. "If you're smart, which I'm certain you are, you'll learn to use them to your advantage. Security is important these days."

He stood to examine the fire. The flames were dying. "It would seem we need more wood. Could you help me gather some from the pile?"

Ember got up and ducked her head. "Yes, sir."

They went together to the wood heap. Before gathering branches, Whitehaze took a sharpened stone and cut slits into a small, thick stick. When he finished, the curls of wood he'd left made it look like a fluffy tail. Kindling sticks gave dying flames an extra boost and ignited much more readily. He placed the kindling stick in the fire, then Ember helped him move a few more twigs and branches to the pit.

When they finished, she decided to go find Hyrees. She spotted him with Fledge near the second fire pit and trotted over to them. Hyrees lifted his muzzle, sniffing the air as she approached.

He jumped up and raised his tail in greeting. "Ember! You made it back."

Ember pressed her nose against his, letting his familiar scent become all she could smell. "Yep. I survived. How are you liking clayworking?"

"Oh, I love it. It's fun to make things with my paws, and Fledge is a great mentor. She's been really patient with me, what with all my clumsiness."

"Shut up, Hyrees," Fledge said with a laugh. "You're a natural. And very organized, unlike me." She turned to Ember. "He put all of my clay in order based on consistency to make them easier to identify."

Ember chuffed. "I'm not surprised. So, Hyrees, do you know if anything specific has been bothering Farlight lately?"

"I don't know. He seemed kind of nervous this morning, but I'm not sure why. Why are you asking?" Hyrees said.

"Curiosity."

"He's probably fine. He would've told me if there was something wrong. He always does."

I wouldn't be so sure about that,' she thought.

"Oh!" he exclaimed, "I just remembered. You know how I got you that maple bijou, and it broke? Well, I'm making you a new one. Look."

He led her over to a piece of bark with a clay maple leaf on it. The color wasn't as exact, and the details weren't as fine, but it looked like the plant it was meant to represent.

Vivid orange sparkled behind her eyes. It mixed together with gentle snowdrops of white, creating a light show that reminded her of autumn and winter, but only the best parts of each season. "It's beautiful. Thank you, Hyrees. Oh! And to make it last longer, you could try using a little strip of deerskin instead of a vine. It probably won't be as strong as dad's leather, but almost anything would work better than a vine. We can call it a clayskin."

He laughed. "Alright. I'll try that. Hopefully it won't smell too bad."

"Hey, I'd hate to cut this visit-break thing short, but Hyrees, we've still got a lot to cover," Fledge mewed. "We really should get back to work. After all, we are the only clayworkers actually being clayworkers right now, what with the whole double abatis project going on. We've gotta do a lot more if we want to keep up. Are you ready for the challenge?"

"Of course," he said. "Sorry, Em. I need to get back to work. I'll see you later."

Ember flattened back her ears. "Uhm, yeah, okay. I'll be . . . around."

As she walked away, Ember let her gaze wander around the Glade. Without anyone else to walk with, it seemed foreign. Like an entirely new place filled with cats she didn't actually know, yet she could navigate it with her eyes closed, so she closed her eyes. The lack of vision-stabbing sunlight eased away the beginnings of a headache.

She bumped into something soft and fluffy.

"Careful, Ember. Watch where you're going."

She opened her eyes. Everywhere direct sunlight touched was white. *'Ow. Bright, bright, bright!'* She closed them again for a moment, then squinted.

Spots flickered where the light hit her the hardest. Through the spots, Fern came into focus. She stood in front of her, expression blank and tail twitching.

Ember flattened her ears and lowered her head. "Er, hi?"

"Hello, Ember," Fern replied. "It's been a while, hasn't it?"

Guilt came crashing down on her chest like jaws clamped around her heart and bent on ripping it to shreds. "I'm sorry. It was an accident, but that doesn't make it okay, and I know you're not, uhm . . ."

"It's alright. Just try to keep your eyes open," Fern replied. "Do you know if Fledge is busy? I wanted to speak with her for a moment."

"I think so, a little bit, yes, but no, I meant sorry for everything. Tainu . . . I-I-I'm really, really, really sorry I killed her. I didn't mean to. She-she told me to run, to leave and let her go, but I didn't and . . ."

Fern placed a paw against Ember's prosthetic foreleg. She let it slide down to her toes. "It hurts a lot, Ember. Part of me still isn't ready to forgive you, but the more sensible side of me knows it was going to happen. If you hadn't taken her that night, someone else would have. Or she would have taken herself from me, leaving off for the Lowlands without even saying 'goodbye.' " Fern sniffled. She pulled back her paw to wipe away the tears forming in her eyes. "She was my kitten, the only kitten I'll ever have. Losing her has been one of the hardest things I've ever gone through. But like when my parents died, I'll get through it. Despite how much I've been avoiding you, I really am happy you're alive, Ember." She licked Ember's cheek. "I don't know when, or even if I'll ever fully forgive you, but know that I'm trying my best. Now, excuse me, I really should go."

Ember pawed the wetness away from her own eyes. She nodded in thanks but couldn't bring herself to say anything. Fern brushed past her, toward where Fledge was showing Hyrees how to make a small bowl.

She watched in silence as her aunts greeted each other. She had hurt them both. Ember sighed. It turned into a shudder as the wind changed direction and picked up speed. As she walked away, her thoughts drifted back to Tainu. She'd killed her, and now she was gone. They wouldn't get to race through the forest next springtime, and Tainu would never again pester her about learning to hunt. All the power she now held would never change that fact.

On that fateful night, she'd held a different kind of power: the kind she didn't want, yet had been given, just like everyone else. It was the kind of power that turned living, breathing creatures into inanimate objects and destroyed the lives of those left behind.

For a moment, she was ashamed of the pride she'd felt from finally being useful. Thai had been bought with her cousin's blood. Yet Tainu had killed Aspen. According to the law, she was supposed to die.

'Was all this worth it?' Ember wondered. She stopped at the base of the History Tree, gazing up at its familiar branches. *'Maybe. Maybe not. I don't know. But what's done is done, Ember. Time to move forward. Eyes open this time.'*

After several minutes of wandering, she made her way back to the den she and Hyrees shared. As she went, Fern's words echoed in her head, bringing with them splotches of grey and silver.

'If you hadn't taken her that night, someone else would have.'

She entered the den and lay down facing the wall. The position blocked most of the light from hitting her face and left her peripheral vision to protect her from ambushes. *'Maybe that was the right thing to do. Commander Aspen's death has been avenged. We might be able to use that fact to stop the war. I might be able to. Maybe it's what I was meant to do from the very beginning. I can turn this into a good thing. I just need a little more control.'*

Her heating system turned on again, casting a faint orange glow on the dirt and rocks around her. *'Then everything will be okay.'*

CHAPTER 20
EMBER

Something touched her. Ember moaned and put her paws over her eyes. The thing touched her again.

"Ember," a voice whispered.

She opened her eyes to find a blur of brown and white fur in front of her face. She blinked a few times to clear her vision. "Farlight? What are you doing here?"

Farlight stood over her, fur on end. "I know you would probably rather be sleeping, but we need to talk. This isn't something that can wait. I've put it off too long already."

She sighed and got to her paws. Fur brushed against her flank. "Oh. Hyrees is here. I must've been asleep for longer than I thought."

As if in reply, Hyrees snorted. The nasally noise sent an irritating oily shimmer through her head. Ember's jaw tensed. Outside, moonlight glistened off of icicles and muddy snow, cloaking the forest in an eerie blue. All traces of sunset were gone.

Farlight tilted his head toward the Glade. "Come on. This might be a life or death situation."

Her heartbeat quickened, waking her up. *'Life or death? That doesn't sound good.'*

They walked out of the den in silence. Farlight picked up a small piece of meat sitting in the sludge outside, then turned toward the Western Entrance. Ember followed him into the woods.

"Where are we going?" Ember asked. She glanced up at the night guards watching them from the trees. Their pupils caught the moonlight and appeared to glow green. A small shiver crept down her spine.

"Whiz-mon. Where else?" Farlight replied, voice muffled.

If he hadn't mentioned death or answered her question so matter-of-factly, she would have laughed. 'Whiz-mon' was the nickname Hyrees had given Wisdom Monument. Supposedly the pile of rocks had once formed a small human building, and Dark had used it as a place to go when he'd wanted to work alone. According to the History Tree, it was the birthplace of clawmarking. The legend sounded feasible enough, but given what else had been twisted or left out by Dark's cunning claws, she had her doubts.

"So why there?" she asked.

He set the meat down. "It's not far away, but it is far enough to speak without being overheard. Also, it's more open than most of the forest, so we shouldn't have to worry about anyone sneaking up on us."

Ember shuddered, causing the fur along her spine the raise. "You weren't joking about this being serious, were you?"

"Unfortunately, no. Now come on; let's hurry."

He grabbed the meat again, then broke into a fast trot. Ember followed beside him. Aside from the addition of partially melted snow, the rock structure looked exactly how she remembered it—large, rectangular stones forming a loose square. The rocks closer to the back resembled a wall, but the other three sides had long since crumbled into glorified rock piles. Small, thin trees made up the only forest within ten leaps of it. It was all newer growth, but was still older than her.

She climbed onto a rock and sat down. "So what did you want to tell me? Also, why me? If it's serious, shouldn't you tell Commander Lupine, or Dad?"

He placed the meat at her paws. "This is for you. It's deer. I didn't think you'd eaten, so I brought it in case you were hungry."

As if on cue, her stomach growled, sending tiny bursts of dull pink flickering through her mind. "Oh. You're right; I haven't eaten. Thanks."

She lifted the meat with her jaws and started her belated meal. Farlight sat across from her, back against one of the loosely defined corners. "But to answer your question, I'm telling you because everyone else trusts him too much. They won't believe me. They'll say I'm being paranoid. But you won't, right? You'll listen. Won't you?"

She swallowed her last bite of venison. "I'll listen. That's why I'm out here, isn't it?"

Farlight nodded. "Fair point, but beside the point. The thing is, I'm pretty sure Whitehaze wants me gone. He knows he can't kill me outright, so I think he's trying to ruin my reputation behind my back; trying to turn everyone against me and making them too suspicious to trust me to lead."

"What? Whitehaze?" Her eyes narrowed, remembering her former mentor's warnings. "What are you trying to do?"

"He spoke with you, didn't he? About me?" Farlight asked. He jumped to his paws and pinned back his ears. "Now you're starting to doubt me, aren't you?"

An owl hooted in the distance. Another replied somewhere nearby. The breeze picked up, making the young trees shake. Ember shook with them; she'd never liked being outside of the Glade after dark.

Ember lowered her head. "Maybe. You're going to have to do a lot of explaining to convince me Whitehaze wants you dead, because there's information in my head right now that cannot coexist as the truth. The thing is, I know him. I've known him longer than you've been alive. He's not some power-hungry, evil mastermind. Tahg, he's not even a mastermind. He's just a kind old cat who snores and pretends to be grumpy sometimes. The real question is, why bother dragging me all the way out here? We were safer in the Glade."

"So you think I'm being paranoid too? I'm telling you, Ember, he wants me dead."

She clamped her teeth over her tongue. "Prove it."

He growled, fur bristling. "How am I supposed to do that? Get myself killed?"

"Maybe start by telling me what's really going on. There has to be more to it than this."

"Alright fine." He lowered his voice. "Here's the thing; you know how Tainu was working with the East? Well, he's been working with them too."

Yellow appeared, burning brightly in her mind's eye.

"Jade has spies informing her from within the Colony, and you've seen that," he continued. "You know that Rogue who attacked you? The one you said had Jade's scent on his fur? I saw them talking roughly a mooncycle ago, and before I could hide, Whitehaze saw me. I didn't realize the Rogue had come back until I caught his scent on the log, and it matched. I think that Eclan tom is Jade's messenger. He carries orders from her to her foxes here in the West. I'm pretty sure Whitehaze is one of them. I don't know how it happened, or what's going on aside from that, but there's your more. It's hardly proof, but it's why I dragged you out here. Commander Lupine trusts him more than anyone else. If what I've said is true, everyone in the West could be in danger."

Ember shivered as silver replaced the shock in her head. *Is it true though? Is there anyone I can trust anymore? What if Jade really is controlling everything?* She shook her head. "Tainu was threatened; I'm sure she was. What if Whitehaze is being threatened too? What if he needs help escaping from . . . whatever it is she's doing to him? She might make him do something bad—something he would never do on his own."

His tail twitched faster. "We can't help him, Em. If he wants to escape, he has to do it himself. And he *can* do it. Either he's too scared, or he just doesn't want to. Whatever you do, don't say anything about this to anyone. We might get someone hurt or killed if the wrong cat finds out. Now do you understand?"

She looked away. The cool shimmering blues of the forest did little to ease her mind. She pinned back her ears and imagined trekking across the Valley to take on Jade. As hard as she tried, she still couldn't visualize the Rift. Cloud's descriptions of 'a big crack in the mountain' made her think of a ravine, so she imagined Jade sleeping in a generic den in a ravine. Her imaginary self snuck over to Jade's silent, tabby-striped form and sunk her teeth into her throat. *'Then that would be it. And as long as the East didn't retaliate, we wouldn't have to worry about spies, or hired Roges, or any of that. But I can't. I can't cross the Lowlands, and I can't kill Jade. I'm not killing anymore. Too much silver.'*

"Y-yes, I understand," she said. "But why are you telling me this? Me specifically, I mean."

Farlight laughed. "Not gonna lie, I want the cat with Thai on my side, not that Thai can really help in this situation. Also, I knew you'd take me seriously after I explained myself. And you're one of the few cats I know for sure Ca-Jade isn't in contact with. So really, it's a lot of reasons. But hey, that's my story. Now come on, let's go before someone wakes up and realizes we're gone."

'Ca-Jade? Commander Jade? What is it with you and Hyrees making up bad nicknames for everything? Especially now, with all this going on.'

The wind slowed for a moment, then picked up with twice the force, ruffling their fur and bending their whiskers. Ember shivered again, but instead of hunching over, she lifted her nose to the breeze. It made her sinuses burn. Far above, the clouds parted enough to see a pawful of stars. She counted thirty-six of them.

"Wait," she mewed, "it's supposed to be snowing for a while, starting tomorrow. Might as well watch the stars while we still can."

He walked up to her. Ember scooted over to let him climb onto her rock. The whites and browns of his fur became reddish orange in the faint glow of her heating system. They wrapped their tails around each other's haunches, trying to conserve warmth. A few leaps away, a tree branch snapped. It crashed with a crackle and a soft hiss into the snow sludge below. A pack of wolves in the distance joined the gentle howls of the wind, creating an otherworldly chorus. The howls lasted almost as long as the star patch, but after several minutes, both faded. They waited a minute longer for either of the two to return, but they didn't. Without another word, they headed back to the Glade.

They stopped outside the cramped dirt cave Ember had come to call her own. She turned to face him. "You'll be safest sleeping with Mom and Dad. And Kivy."

"Yep," he replied, and padded off toward the old family den. "'Night, Em."

"Goodnight, Farlight."

He looked over his shoulder and nodded, never once stopping. Ember slunk into her own dwelling, trying not to step on Hyrees in the process. She curled up beside him and tried to get back to sleep. The vibrant greens and silvers dancing in her mind refused to let her go.

'What if he's telling the truth? Then again, what if he's not? But what would lying about this accomplish, other than turning me against Whitehaze and, OH, and only trusting him. I have Thai. That makes me valuable. He wants me on his side of whatever is going on right now. He even told me that, too.' She clamped her teeth down on the chewy parts of her toes. *'Who am I supposed to believe now?'*

When her internal clock read one-fifteen, the first cool tones of tiredness seeped into her mind. A soft sliding sound snapped her back to attention. She got up and stumbled to the den entrance. A cat shuffled water bowls around by the nearest fire pit.

'Oh,' she thought, *'it's just night guards being weird again.'*

She sighed and returned to Hyrees's side. The blue-greens came back, and swept her away to a land where no one kept secrets, and the fears and pains of war were only ghosts of the past.

———

"What kind of fluffhead would—"

"No, it's okay, it's okay. I'll just go down to the creek. It's not that far. I won't be long, sir."

"I could go with you, just in case."

"No, I'll be okay. I could use a little alone time right now. I've got a lot to think about, with everything that's been going on lately."

Voices sucked Ember out of her dream world. She yawned.

"What's he complaining about now?" Hyrees mumbled.

Ember stood up. She blinked the sleep from her eyes. "I don't know. Guess there's only one easy way to find out. Come on, you big, well, *little* bear."

"Nope, it's too cold. I'm hibernating in here until Fledge drags me out by my scruff. Have fun talking with your apparently already disgruntled dad."

"Fun, fun," Ember muttered. She groaned. Starting the day with an angry Cloud was never a good sign.

Outside, real not-angry clouds coated the sky, just as the humans had predicted. *'Silver. The sky is silver again. I wonder if Lupine will call off patrols and hunts if the weather gets too bad. It's supposed to start snowing soon.'*

She sighed and meandered over to her father, who sat by one of the fire pits examining water bowls.

He looked up at her as she approached. "Morning, Em. As you can probably see, some fluffhead left all the bowls too far from the pits. All of our drinking water's turned to ice, and we can't use any of the bowls until it melts. Two of them are cracked now, so I guess replacing them will be Hyrees's next job." He groomed a forepaw, then rubbed it against his head. "I guess feline stupidity never ceases to surprise, does it?"

Ember's thoughts shot back to the previous night. *'Was it intentional? That doesn't make any sense. Why would anyone want to freeze those things? I mean, yes, I understand they're all disgusting and such, but why freeze them in the middle of the night?'* She gave up and sighed. *'I don't know.'*

Cloud chuffed. "I know what you mean. The worst part is, this isn't the first time it's happened. Just usually not all of them at once."

'I'm not sure you do understand, actually.'

"But oh well," he continued, "if you need water, I guess you'll just have to either eat snow or go to the Kivyress. The creek, not your sister. Farlight just left to get some. I should've sent him with Fern's snow bowl. Hopefully this development doesn't make anyone late."

"I think we'll be fine," Ember said. "We can get some water on the way out."

He smiled. "Yes, that'll work."

By the time she'd finished her morning rations, Farlight still hadn't returned. Lupine hunted down Cloud and instructed him to bring him back for training.

Ember sat beside a tree, grooming her face as Lupine spoke. Pieces started clicking into place in her mind, painting a silvery picture tinted with green. Some unseen force pressed against her ribs, making her chest tighten. "Can I come? I-I think he might be in trouble. We should hurry."

"Yes, you can come. But what makes you think he'd be in trouble?" Cloud asked.

"I-I-I certainly hope he's not," Lupine said, "but just in case, I might search the woods a-around the area. You know, Whitehaze went down there, too. It's possible they crossed paths and got to talking."

"Whitehaze?" Ember mewed. Panic set in, bringing with it an all too familiar cyan. She jumped to her paws. "He's definitely in trouble. Come on!"

"W-what's she yowling about?" Lupine asked.

"I don't know, but I guess I'd better go see," Cloud replied. He lowered his voice. "You know Ember. She gets worked up over all kinds of little things. I'm sure they're both fine."

Ember's heart raced in her chest, but the cyan cleared enough for indignation to appear. *You don't believe me? No one believes me. For once I really, really hope they're right.*

She turned toward the Northern Entrance and ran.

"We'll bring him back when we find him. Don't worry," Cloud called as he charged after her. "Ember! Ember, wait up!"

Ember kept running, out of the Glade and into the forest.

"Ember, stop!" Cloud snapped.

She slid to a standstill and looked over her shoulder. Cloud continued walking several leaps behind her. She waited for him to catch up, then kept going. The cloud coverage did little to reduce the painful glare of the sun's ultraviolet rays. She squinted to keep from seeing white.

"Calm down, would you? This isn't a rescue mission, this is a 'tell Farlight he's late' mission. Everything is fine," Cloud said.

She mewled gibberish under her breath. "Still, we should at least try to move fast."

Cloud growled. "For the last time, Ember, Farlight is not in danger. I don't know where you got the idea that he would be, but it's not true."

Ember gritted her teeth together. *'He still doesn't believe me. No one does. Not even if I explain. Nothing has changed. The only difference is now I've got Thai. Am I too soft for you, Dad? Is that why you're all but ignoring me?'*

[I'm not sure what you mean by asking "am I too soft for you, Dad?" Last time I checked, I was not your father. Would you like me to search the web? Perhaps you can ask him there, if he has a device.]

'I wasn't thinking to you, Thai. Go away.'

[Sorry. I'll leave you alone. Oh, wait, isn't that your dad beside you? If it is, I recommend asking him now, while he's here with you. Openness is an important part of every healthy relationship, after all.]

'And I recommend shutting your processor. Leave me alone. The occasional bit of solitude is important, too.'

[Alright, I'll leave you alone. I'll be here when you need me.]

'When? Need? That sounds ominous. Wait, ominous?' Her tail thrashed. Anxiety clawed at her ribs. "You offered to go with him, and you don't usually do that. You're afraid too, aren't you? Why?"

Cloud didn't reply, which only made the silver shine brighter. The faint warble of the Kivyress joined the wind. Like the wolves of the previous night, it sang its song. Only the creek refused to stop. Like her pounding heart, it grew louder with each step she took.

"F-Farlight?" she called, voice barely more than a whisper. Her lower jaw trembled.

A grey and white shape moved in the distance, hunched over by the creek. The shape muttered something unintelligible. She picked up her pace, not caring if she left Cloud behind. When she drew closer, the cat clicked with a name. Her heart leaped. Her chest tightened. Yellow and silver flooded her emotions, flickering and swirling like snowflakes in a blizzard.

"Whitehaze? W-what are you doing here?" she asked.

Or at least she thought she'd asked it. He didn't respond, and her mind was so loud, she began to wonder if she'd only thought it. Instead of turning to face her, he backed up. Her stomach lurched when she realized he was dragging something.

No, *someone.*

Ember's eyes widened. "Farlight? Is that—"

She ran forward.

Whitehaze jumped back, letting Farlight's limp form flop onto the cold, hard ground. "This isn't what it looks like. I swear, he was like this when I got here. I don't know what happened."

Ember nudged Farlight's frozen cheek. Her vision bounced in and out of focus. "Come on, please be okay. Please be okay. Please!"

She stepped back from his unmoving form, shaking all over. Adrenaline poured into her bloodstream. Her breathing became shallow and rapid. Yellow. Yellow—so much yellow.

"Farlight," she whispered. "No. N-no, this can't . . ."

Her eyes locked onto his head. Claw-made cuts streaked across his forehead and between his ears. He'd been drowned—intentionally. She turned to glare at Whitehaze. "You did this. You killed him, you coyote! Wildcat!"

Whitehaze took another step back. "I already told you; I didn't do it. I didn't do anything! I swear on my life."

'I was too late. We were too late. He's dead. Farlight is dead, and it's all his fault. He did this. He killed him because of Jade. Whitehaze did this. He did this, this, this, he . . .' the words echoed in her head, over and over until it became a roar louder than the creek, louder than the falls, louder than a gunshot. Loud, disorienting, and dangerous.

"Liar!" she screamed.

She jumped at him. Somewhere in the muffled distance, someone yowled for her to stop, but whoever it was didn't matter. The world around her moved in slow motion. Her vision narrowed to a tunnel, with Whitehaze at the end. He lunged for her face, jaws open, poised to strike as her paws collided with his side. Ember yanked her head downward to protect herself.

'Oh no, you are not taking another life, old tom. Not today, not EVER.'

His jaws snapped down on her ear. Ember winced at the sharp, stabbing pain. On instinct, she whipped her head sideways, toward his exposed neck. Her ear ripped. Her teeth sank into his throat. Whitehaze made a gagging, gurgling noise that stabbed at her ears. She bit down harder until her fangs touched, then snapped her head to the left. Skin and muscle ripped. Blood coated her tongue.

The yellows and greens grew brighter. She opened her mouth and let her mentor's body fall beside its victim. He mewed softly and looked up at her, eyes wide with terror and betrayal. His jaw hung slack, dripping blood and saliva onto the gravel beneath him. Ember watched, frozen and trembling, as he tried to cough. It came out in a sputtering hack. Their eyes met. His breathing slowed, then stopped altogether. His eyes didn't even close.

Someone shoved her back. Ember stumbled into the shallows of the creek, sending freezing shockwaves up her limbs. Her eyesight cleared enough to make out who'd pushed her: Cloud.

He looked down at the two bodies, then back at her. "Ember what were you thinking? You just killed Whitehaze! You *killed* him! What were you thinking? Answer me!"

She stumbled again as the gravity of what she'd done hit her. "Oh tahg."

Her vision blurred. Her stomach did nauseating backflips and front flips inside of her. "Oh tahg, oh tahg. I . . . I . . ."

Ember staggered out of the water. She sat down and stared at the bleeding wound in Whitehaze's throat. Every part of her shivered. *Did I do this? But how? Why? What? No. Oh no. It can't end like this. No! I'm going to be executed now. Or, at the very least, exiled. Oh tahg, what did I do? What did I do?'*

"Answer me!" Cloud said.

She lifted a paw to her chin, then pulled it back smeared with blood. Ember sucked in a long, shaky breath. "I killed Whitehaze." She dropped to her belly and wrapped her paws over her forehead.

"I can see that! Why would you—oh no. Ember, you've got to run. You know what happens to cats who kill their kin. I can't stop this. If you want to live, you have to run."

But she couldn't run; her body was frozen. *'Farlight is dead. Whitehaze is dead. Now I'm gonna die. Oh tahg. Sorry Michelle. You wasted your time and money after all. Should have just let me die a hero. Now I'm hurting everyone. Mom, Dad, Kivy, and—oh no, Hyrees, what are you going to do? Are you going to die now? Fox it! I've ruined everything. I've ruined everything!'*

"Ember, you have to leave. Go! Now!" Cloud growled.

He pushed her, but her legs still refused to move. Darkness vignetted her vision. Tears trickled down her cheeks and got absorbed by her fur. She cried for Farlight. She cried for Whitehaze. She cried for Hyrees and for herself.

"Guess I wasn't meant to be a hero after all," she whispered.

"W-what's all this yelling about? Cloud, is everything okay down there? Did you find Farlight?" Lupine called.

"Ember, please," Cloud pleaded. "Go. Get out of here. If you don't, they *will* kill you. Please go. Hide; clean yourself up; I'll think of something. Just go!"

She looked up at him, trying to memorize everything she could about his face, his voice, and the patch of white on his chest. He was crying. He never cried. She swallowed hard.

"I'm sorry, Dad. I'm so sorry. I don't . . . I didn't . . ." She breathed in another shaky breath. Freezing air filled her lungs and teardrops coated her cheeks. "I can't keep running," she whispered. "Not anymore. Too tired. I made a mistake. My last mistake, I guess. I'm sorry. I hope the leather works out."

"Oh. *Oh!* Is that Whitehaze?" Lupine asked.

He charged down the slope toward them. He placed a trembling paw against Whitehaze's shoulder. "No. No! Oh no. Not him. Please, not him. W-w-what happened? W-what did you do?" He spun around to look at her, but stopped short. He jumped back. "AGH! Farlight too? Ohhh, tahg. What . . . Ember, you're-you're coated in blood. What happened? What did you do?"

Ember lowered her paws to stare at them. Little droplets of blood dripping from her chin tainted the snow beneath her. "Whitehaze killed Farlight." She swallowed, and started shivering and crying all over again. "I killed Whitehaze. Now you're gonna kill me."

Lupine let out a tiny, pitiful cry, then collapsed at Whitehaze's side. "Why? W-why did this have to—y-y-you knew, Cloud. You knew what she was. You-you knew she was defective. And to think I-I thought . . ."

"Lupine, don't," Cloud growled.

In that moment, Ember could read him. The emotions he'd tried so hard to hide came pouring out. His broken face created a forest of colors in Ember's thoughts. He was lost, scared, confused. Or perhaps it was she herself who felt that way; she couldn't tell. Her throat tightened, threatening to choke her.

Lupine got up and glared down at her. "Y-your experiment failed, Aspen. Dark was right all along. Should've drowned her in the creek when you had the chance."

Ember's eyes widened. She stopped shivering. *'Drowned me in the . . . What? Commander Aspen . . . kill me? Experiment? But why? Had the chance? Wait, Dark was right about what?'*

"Stop!" Cloud yowled. "Whitehaze killed Farlight. She must at least be found partially justified. It was a revenge kill. She's not defective; it was a mistake. I cured her. Remember? I *cured* her. Look at her; she's traumatized herself. She didn't mean for this. Please listen to me."

Colors, so many colors, flashed and flickered from every angle of Ember's mind. Snowflakes, real ones, floated down around her, harbingers of the coming storm.

Lupine grimaced. A lonesome tear dripped from his whiskers. He walked over to Farlight, bent down, and licked his forehead. "Did a-a-anyone see Whitehaze kill him?"

Cloud pinned back his ears. "No, but—"

"Then i-it's not justified. For all you know, some Rogue could've done it. I'm sorry, Cloud, but she has committed murder. She *is* dangerous. A wildcat, Cloud. N-now come on, let's take her back to say her goodbyes."

'Colors, colors, colors; too many colors, colors, colors. Everything. Everything. Everything is. It's . . . this is it. They all want, all want me dead. I die a villain. I die. I die. End it. End this. End this war. Never be able to. Farlight. Oh tahg, Farlight. I failed you; I failed you. I'm sorry, sorry, sorry.'

Grey static choked out all other colors. It filled her mind and strangled her thoughts, which echoed like words against stone. The wind, the snow, the lights, and the yelling attacked her from every angle. She closed her eyes, covered her ears, and moaned.

Her father's voice rose over it all, "Wait! No! Please, banish her, send her into exile—throw her out. *Anything.* Just don't kill her. Please. Not now. I can't lose her again."

"She just killed my chief advisor. And Farlight's dead too. I don't know who killed him, but it certainly w-w-was not Whitehaze. He's been my guide longer than you've been alive. I know him better than any of you. He would not kill Farlight, but Ember *certainly* killed him. We're weak enough a-already. I can't take any more risks. From now on, all defects will be removed, as Dark intended. It's for the best."

'Dark intended? Wanted to kill me? Were there others? What if I wasn't the only one?' Yellow pounded at her head. *'What if there was someone else*

310

*who felt colors, or had attacks? What if they existed and were drowned.
Like, oh tahg, like Farlight was. Why didn't I know about this until now?
Why did no one say anything? Why did no one* do *anything?'*

Ember tucked her tail closer to her body and tensed her muscles, trying to make herself as small as possible.

"Please, Lupine," Cloud said. His voice was subdued, defeated. "I'll do anything. Just let her live. Look at her, would you? You care; I know you do. Do you really want to kill her? After all this?"

Silence came like a predator, attacking the air all at once. Ember's ears rung. She lifted her paws from her head, but kept her eyes closed.

"Will you forfeit your position on the Council, stop working on that r-r-r-ridiculous human 'armor' stuff, and promise to remain loyal to the West for the rest of your life in e-exchange for Ember's exile?" Lupine asked.

More silence. A tiny flicker of dull orange penetrated the grey: some unsteady combination of sadness and hope, dripping in together. *'What are you doing? What are you—offering to punish him for my mistake? Not worth it. Not going to say yes. He's not.'*

She opened her eyes. Whitehaze's face and blood-stained neck filled her vision. She jerked her head back and tried to stop the stream of words still echoing through her mind.

"I will," Cloud said. "I'll do it. Oh, thank you. Thank you, Lupine. Oh tahg."

Ember shivered. She strained her neck to look up at him. Cloud stood, tall and firm, between her and Lupine. *'What? Dad, you don't want this. You don't want this. You don't want this! What are you doing to yourself?'*

"But remember," Lupine said, "if she ever comes back, she will be killed. You'll never see her again, or if you do, she'll be dead. No matter what she decides to do with her freedom, y-your promise remains. If she comes back a-a-and . . . and gets executed after all, you still have to spend the rest of your life serving the Western Colony."

Cloud growled, a look of pure hatred on his face. "Understood."

"Then it's settled. Go back to the Glade and tell everyone what happened. I'll take her over to the fallen tree t-to lead her out. Bring anyone who would like to say goodbye."

Cloud sighed. He lowered his head and started for the once familiar little clearing. To the home she would never see again. To the cats she would never see again; the cats who hated her; the cats who wanted her gone. Yet even after everything they'd done, the West was her home. It was all she knew in Dark's Valley, and now she couldn't even give it a proper farewell.

Ember staggered to her paws. "Dad, wait! Don't go! Don't leave me yet. Please!"

He didn't reply, or stop, or even slow for a heartbeat.

"Daddy! Daddy, please! Please take me with you! I need . . . I need to—" her voice cracked.

Lupine stepped between her and her savior. She watched helplessly as Cloud climbed up the creek bank, then disappeared over the top. Lupine shoved her side. The sudden force sent her stumbling sideways. A gut-wrenching squelch made her throat tighten. She didn't have to look to know she'd stepped on Whitehaze's mutilated neck. She yanked her paw back into the snow and tried her best not to look down. An all too familiar darkness slithered in around her peripheral vision, creeping closer with every second. Her legs weren't programmed to get weak, but something about the mechanics inside made them feel like they might fail at any moment.

"Let's get moving," Lupine said. "A-and don't try to hurt me. Cats will hear and come to end you."

The rebel part of her wanted to come up with some kind of sharp-worded reply, or even a dull-worded reply, but nothing seemed to be working. Her legs refused to move. Her mouth refused to speak. Her mind refused to think. Wind and snow froze her toes, her sides, and everywhere else. The heating grids did little to stop it. Her conscious and body disconnected for a split moment. Acting on instinct, she spread her legs to keep from toppling over. Her head hung limp, vacant eyes facing the bloodstained ground.

'Dying . . . What if I die? What about Hyrees? Farlight, he's . . . Hyrees, what have I done to you? What if I—'

"I said *move*, Ember."

Lupine pushed her again. Her legs scrambled to compensate. She tripped over Whitehaze's corpse and face-planted in the rocks. A high-pitched ringing drowned out all other noise. Her nose throbbed and burned. The world moved in slow motion again. The snake of darkness constricted her vision even tighter. She rolled over to look at her assailant. His mouth moved, but no words came out. She couldn't hear him. She couldn't hear anything, anything but the ringing and the water-muffled yowls Farlight must have cried during his last moments. Her imagination recreated them so vividly, she glanced at Farlight's half-frozen body to make sure it was still there. When she realized it was, she let her head roll back against the stone, closed her eyes, and caterwauled.

A dull pain cut into her side. She closed her mouth and opened her eyes. Lupine stood over her, claws hooked into the skin behind her shoulder. He spoke again. Again, no intelligible words came out. She tried to ask him what he wanted, but only tiny, pathetic huffs of air escaped her throat. He shook his head, helped her up, then nudged her in the right direction. As they walked along the creek bank, Ember looked over her shoulder at the two dead cats behind her.

The fog cleared enough to let a single thought escape into her conscious: *'Maybe I was wrong about everything.'*

The thought made her stomach lurch. Halfway to the log, she coughed up a puddle of fur and bile. It eased the nausea some, but also left an ache in her diaphragm and a bitter taste on her tongue. Her hearing faded back into existence. A chirping grey bird, the wind, and the crackling snow beneath their paws were the only clues to its return.

When they reached the log, they waited in silence for Cloud to meet them. The snowfall around them grew heavier. Ember's chest tensed as she remembered the forecast from the previous morning: a blizzard.

"Ember, what's going on?" Lupine asked.

She winced at the sudden noise. "I messed up. I messed up so bad."

"Yes, you did. I-I-I know that well enough. What I want to know is why you said Farlight was in danger this morning. What made you come to that conclusion?"

Ember swallowed hard and looked away. "I . . . I . . ." She closed her eyes and breathed in. *'One, two, three, four, five.'* She let the breath out in an equally long sigh. "Last night, Farlight took me to Wisdom Monument, and he . . . he said Whitehaze wanted him gone."

"S-so why do you think he'd say that, huh?"

She rubbed the smooth, reinforced coverings on her toes. "Because, uhm, because Whitehaze was working with Jade. Farlight said he saw him talking with that Rogue from the other day. Eclan. He, er, he might have been threatened. Into doing it, I mean. Spying on us. And I'm . . . I-I-I saw someone moving the-the water bowls away from the fires last night."

Lupine growled. "I've known him my whole life, Ember. He was like a father to me. He was not, nor was he ever a-a-a spy. I don't know who or what Farlight saw, but he was wrong. I don't even understand how you could believe something like that. Whitehaze would never betray us. He would never betray *me*. Not even u-under threat."

Ember transitioned to chewing on her toes. "Is it true?" she asked after a few painful moments of silence. "Was Commander Aspen going to kill me?"

"Aspen ordered that no one tell you this, but he's gone now, so I'll tell you. Kittens who are defective in any way g-get eliminated. As Dark and Flare have written on the sacred Commander's Tablet, it's cruel and dangerous to let them live. The only reason you're still alive right now is because of your father's stubbornness. You were always his biggest weakness, you know. He went through so much, leaped logs and scaled trees for you. He cried and pleaded for days to let Aspen keep you alive. He worked so hard to fix you. And how have you repaid him? What gratitude have you shown? Are you even capable of-of feeling for him? Did you even try?"

She closed her eyes as a deep orange speckled the fog. She didn't remember reading anything about the Founders calling for the deaths of imperfect kittens, yet it fit together, forming straight, logical lines across her head. Pieces clicked—the historian trial, her colonymates' shunning, and the pure spite some cats seemed to have toward her for no apparent reason. She wasn't even supposed to exist.

Ember sniffled. *'I did. I tried; I tried so hard, and I failed. I'm not good enough, okay? I couldn't protect Farlight, and I murdered Whitehaze, and I've trapped Dad, and now Hyrees is going to die. I tried, and I ruined everything, just like I always do.'* Her jaw quivered without instruction, making her feel even more helpless. *'What if Dark was right? Maybe they should have killed me.'*

Distant pawsteps crackled toward them, catching her attention. She strained her neck and ears, both dreading and longing for whatever was about to happen. Cloud, Songbird, and Kivyress trod toward them. They all looked upset. Ember waited a moment more, trying to see if Hyrees had decided to come. He hadn't.

'Maybe he went to go see Farlight first,' she thought. *'Makes sense. Farlight is more important than me. But I guess this means Fern and Fledge don't care. Don't blame them.'*

Songbird broke into a run when she saw her. She caught Ember up in her paws and squeezed her tight, sobbing. "Ember, what have you . . . what have you gotten yourself into?"

"I-I'm sorry, Mom," Ember whispered. Another round of tears trickled down her cheeks. "I'm so sorry. I didn't . . . I didn't . . ."

Songbird rested her chin on Ember's shoulder. "Calm down, Ember. Calm down. Now I need to ask you something, okay? Can you make me a promise, Ember? Just one promise, please. It'll be a hard one to keep, but . . . but it'll be for the better of everyone."

"W-what is it?" Ember asked.

"Don't come back. No matter what happens, and no matter what you hear, just don't come back. I don't want to see you here again. Because if I do, you'll be dead. Please, Ember. Stay away for me. And do good for me. Don't become a Rogue or a wildcat. I know I probably won't see you again, but . . . just don't forget who you are. Please."

'Mom . . . You feel like you have to say that? To ask me not to go crazy?'

"I'll try," she replied.

"Ember." Kivyress stood beside her, ears back and tail dragging. "Ember is it true? Is Farlight really dead?"

"Yes," Ember choked out. "He's gone, Kivy. I'm sorry I couldn't save him. I wanted—I-I tried so h—"

Kivyress started to cry. "Did Whitehaze kill him?"

"I . . . I don't know. I think he did, but I'm not sure, and . . ."

Kivyress pressed against her side. She sniffed back congestion and whimpered into Ember's fur. "I never liked him. It was him, I know it was. And you killed him for me. For Farlight. Thank you."

The nausea came back.

"So do you have to go?" Kivyress asked.

"Yes. Sorry, Kivy. I can't stay here anymore."

"But who will be weird with me? And who will I talk to? Who will listen to me? What if I never see you again? Ember, please don't go. I know you don't have a choice, but . . ." She buried her face farther into Ember's fur. "Take me with you. I hate this place. I hate war. I hate all these stupid rules and all this fighting. Please take me with you. Everything would be so much easier."

"I can't. I-I'm sorry. You have to stay here. Help Mom and Dad for me. You can do a lot more good here. You can finish Dad's leather and make the armor for him." She rested her chin on Kivyress's shoulder. "Remember when we used to play guard and Outsider, and you were always the guard? You're the . . . you're the hero, Kivy. A-and I, uhm, I guess I get to be the villain again. Maybe they'll make legends about us one day."

Kivyress didn't say anything. Her shoulders shuddered as she cried into Ember's fur. Songbird shifted to the side as Cloud approached them, but she never once let go. Cloud pressed his forehead against Ember's. "Hyrees is coming. He just wanted a moment with his brother."

Pine green relief painted the fog, releasing some of the weight crushing her sides. *'He didn't abandon me.'*

"Why would you do that?" Ember whispered.

"Do what?" Cloud asked.

"Agree to do all that to let me live? Why? Why would you—you wanted to escape, didn't you? You wanted to get out of here. Now it'll be so much harder. Why . . . why would you do this for me?"

He leaned back to look at her. "I agreed because it means you get to live another day. I said I'd do anything, and I meant it. It's worth it already, if for nothing else than to have this moment, right now. But Ember, you knew? You knew I wanted to go, likely leaving you behind? You never said anything."

"It's what you want, isn't it? I want you to be happy. And now you won't be able to be because of me. To leave, to be able to leave. You can't now because of me. And what about your project? All that work and waiting."

He pressed his neck against hers. "It doesn't matter anymore. I'm tired of working. No, I'm *sick* of working my tail off for a colony that's never done anything for me. You know, I'd give almost anything to have back a single day from last fall. There are so many things I'd do differently. I should've been there for you. I should've been there for Wren. I should've been there for all of you, but I was too busy trying to please Aspen and prove my mother wrong. Lot of good that did for me now."

Ember didn't know how to reply, so she didn't. She let herself be engulfed by her family. Or rather, three-fourths of what was left of it. She sniffled and breathed in their scents, trying her best to memorize them all.

'Never get to see them again. Never . . .' The thought alone made her whimper.

"Alright. Y-you've said your goodbyes," Lupine said. "Time to go, Ember."

Cloud stepped back. Songbird wrapped her paws even tighter, then she released her, licked Ember's cheek, and moved to join Cloud.

Kivyress remained huddled up against her side. "Please, just a few more moments? Hyrees isn't here yet. We have to wait," she mewled.

"Come here, Kivy," Cloud said softly.

Kivyress pushed closer to Ember's side, then, with a moan, she walked over to her parents. She sat between them, leaning on Songbird, and groomed away tears as they formed.

Ember tried to capture them in her visual memory, but remembered how quickly Wren had slipped from her grasp. She pulled up the photograph from the day of her return to make sure it was still there. Their smiling, fire-lit faces contrasted how they looked now: crying, grey, and speckled with snow. Her focus shifted to the image of Farlight, with his goofy smirk and a gaze forever fixed on his brother. It occurred to her for a moment that being exiled meant she could go back to imagining everything was okay in the West, but not yet. Not so soon.

"C-come on, Ember," Lupine said.

"Wait," Cloud said.

Ember closed the image and opened her eyes.

"Go see the world for me, okay?" he asked. "Conquer all the mountains, explore all the valleys, and forget the Colonies. Forget us. Live your life. Enjoy it, no matter what happens here. Okay?"

Ember tried to wipe away her tears, but they kept coming. "I promise I'll try."

Lupine strode in front of her. "Ember, I-I-I banish you from the Western Colony for the murder of Whitehaze, my chief advisor, mentor, and long-time friend. I-if you are ever found in this territory again, you will be killed on sight. Now get out of here, kitten."

Ember stepped back, head low and ears flattened. "But Hyrees, he—"

"*Go*, Ember," Lupine hissed.

"Wait!" Hyrees ran toward them along the cliff edge. His voice sounded more broken than she'd ever heard it before. "I'm coming!"

"W-with her?"

Hyrees stopped beside her. "Yes, that's what I said. I'm coming. I'm going. There's nothing left for me here. This pack of wolves can burn in a forest fire for all I care. I just hope, if that happens, you let your hostages escape."

Lupine growled, but said nothing.

Ember brushed her head against Hyrees's cheek, wiping away his tears. "I'm sorry I didn't get there in time. I could've saved him, I could've—wait, want to come? Are-are you sure? You'll never get to see this place again."

He pulled back, glaring directly into her eyes. "Ember, look at me. Farlight is dead. Mom and Dad are dead. I'm half-blind. I'm walking fur, skin, and bone. I've got almost nothing left to lose. Aside from my own body, you're all I have left. Staying would mean losing you, too. Now let's get outta here before Lupine kills us both."

He walked over to the ravine, where the log loomed ominously. Ember followed. If she looked carefully enough, she could still make out the scratch marks left on it by her encounter with Eclan. She looked back.

Cloud smiled and nodded. The subtle gesture disappeared almost as quickly as it had come. She knew it was forced, because no one else was smiling. Not even Lupine.

"Goodbye, Sparky. You too, Hyrees. Take care of each other. I love you. Don't forget that," he said.

"I love you both," Songbird mewed. "Stay safe and stay away. Please be careful."

Ember tried to sniff back the rest of her tears, but they kept coming. "I will, Mom. I love you too. And you, Dad. And Kivy. Kivy, remember—you're the hero now. Well, I mean really, you've always been the hero, but, well, you know what I mean. I think. I hope."

Kivyress forced a smile of her own. It vanished a second later. "Thanks. I really do love you, Em. Please don't forget us."

"Alright, Ember. I-i-it's time to leave," Lupine said. "You too, Hyrees, if you're sure this is, uh, what you want."

"I'm sure," Hyrees growled. He climbed down the cliff, onto the log.

"Very well," Lupine said. Ember realized he was crying too. "I won't stop you. My c-condolences about your brother. I'll make sure he gets a proper memorial. A-a-a commander's memorial. Would've made a fine one."

Hyrees ignored him and kept walking. Ember sucked in a deep breath, then climbed down after him. When they reached the other side, she looked back to make sure they were still there. They were.

Around them, the wind and snow picked up, threatening to turn into a blizzard early. Hyrees nudged her onward, down the mountain and away from the only home she'd ever known, away from the family she'd fought so hard to return to. Every few steps, she peered over her shoulder and found that they'd gotten a little smaller, but each time she looked, they were still there. Then another gust of wind brought a fog of snow between them. When the fog cleared, they were all gone.

CHAPTER 21
CLOUD

"W-we're about to have the memorial ceremony, Cloud. I know you're, uhm, you're still upset about everything that happened this morning, but I was wondering if there was anything y-you wanted to say for Farlight. You know, to pay him some respects," Lupine said.

He stood in the entrance to Cloud's den, but Cloud couldn't see him. He kept his head pressed against the wall, staring blankly at his paws. Ember had done it so often, finding a corner to hide in and shutting out the world. Now he understood why.

"Respect?" he asked. "There's no respect here. There's no freedom. There's no hope. There's only this—the Colony and nothing else."

"I-I-I must admit, I have no idea what you're . . . what you're talking about."

Cloud stood up, but remained facing the wall. "Everyone thinks this place Dark and Flare built is a paradise, yet look around you; everything you see was built on lies. Lies, mass manipulation, the blood of innocents, and unjust laws that are holding us back. Everyone says we're better than the Outsiders and Rogues we chase off, but are we really? Why is that? Because we can clawmark?"

"I fail to see what this has to do w-with the ceremony."

He pressed his head more firmly against the wall. A gust of wind blew snow into the den and against his back. "Because you're a fluffhead too stuck in your own traditions to even try to change. Killing anyone you deem defective? Not even letting mollies onto the Council? What if you're wrong, Lupine? What if we're *all* wrong? What if we've been wrong all this time?"

Lupine growled. "I-I take it you won't be giving a speech, then."

He walked away, leaving Cloud to his wall. Cloud sighed.

'What am I doing with my life?' He hissed at nothing. *'Wasting it every moment I'm here, that's what I'm doing. Send a fox on this storm. It's going to be a nightmare getting out of here. Hyrees, I hope you do your part and find somewhere to wait for us.'*

Cloud closed his eyes and went over all the most important data. *'The Eastern Entrance still provides the easiest route, but there's always the issue of crossing the creek. We can figure that out when we get there.'* His subconscious wandered back to his promise to Lupine. *'That doesn't matter. He didn't really think he could keep me, did he? They wouldn't send anyone after us. It'd be too risky with the East still a threat, and after we leave, like Hyrees said, everyone else can burn.'*

Someone new approached the den. "Come on. We could at least listen to the ceremony, if the snow doesn't get too heavy, at least. I . . . don't think we'll be doing any escaping in this weather."

He spun around. Songbird stood in the entrance. His heart ached at the sight of her. Her fur stuck out in all directions, making her appear to have the early stages of mange. Leaves and snow coated the underside of her tail. She kept her ears cocked to the sides, and her gaze seemed more tired than usual. She looked sick; she looked miserable.

Cloud got up and touched noses with her. She leaned closer to press her forehead against his, and together they tried to fend off what cold they could, fighting in somber silence as reality sank in. Farlight was dead, Ember was gone again, and everything he'd worked so hard to build was falling apart.

"I'm sorry I let this happen," Cloud said. "But I promise things will get better soon. The moment this blizzard clears, we're getting out of here."

He pulled away to look at her gentle, ruddy face.

"Cloud, for last time, this isn't your fault," she said. "There was no way we could've known. Or, really, even imagined . . ." Songbird's tail twitched as a tiny sob escaped her mouth. "We've lost two kittens in one day. At least we get to see Ember again, but Farlight . . . Cloud, what are we going to do?"

She licked a forepaw, then rubbed it against her closed eyes, wiping away tears before they could fully form. The storm raged behind her, wind changing directions with each moment and sending snow flying everywhere.

He sighed. *'I just hope they found some shelter.'*

Cloud squinted to scan the Glade for Kivyress, but he could barely even make out the History Tree through the snow and approaching darkness. "Where's Kivy? This storm is getting bad; we really should call her in. Lupine's a fool, trying to hold a memorial ceremony in a blizzard. If they stay out there much longer, we'll lose ten more to frostbite alone."

"I'll go find her," Songbird said softly.

He brushed past her and walked into the storm. "No, you stay here and try to keep warm. I'll get her."

"Cloud, wait."

He stopped, and as he did, a snowflake flew into one of his eyes. He winced and blinked it away.

"Be careful," she said. "Please don't take long."

He attempted to offer her a reassuring smile. "I'll be fine. We'll both be back soon."

He ventured farther into the Glade, past the gathering of cats. He stopped and hunched over as another gust of wind rushed by. On the stones covering the commander's den, Lupine stood shivering but firm. Most of his kin sat below him, eyes squinted for protection against the ever-intensifying storm.

"You're insane, Lupine!" Cloud yelled. "Forcing everyone outside in the middle of a blizzard? This isn't what Farlight would expect, or want. You're disgracing the dead. Everyone, get to your dens while you still can."

"S-s-stay out of this, Cloud," Lupine growled. "Don't interrupt. You can go hide if you want, but you no longer have the authority to tell anyone what to do."

Cats looked between him and Lupine. A few of them got up and ushered their families away to shelter, but most of them remained sitting.

Cloud's jaw tensed. *'I wonder what would happen if I killed him. I'd be executed, I imagine, and me being dead won't help anyone, least of all Song and Kivy. Where is that kitten?'*

He pushed farther into the Glade, past the second fire pit, which had been put out by the wind. "Kivyress! Kivyress, where are you? This storm is only going to get worse. We need to get back inside while we can still see."

"Dad! Dad, Dad, Dad!" Kivyress ran out of the storage cave and charged toward him.

He sighed in relief as she buried her face in the fur of his neck. "Kivy, there you are. Come on, let's go back to the den."

She took a single hesitant step before he nudged her in the right direction. They walked beside each other back across the Glade, their heads down against the wind.

"I know this probably isn't the time," she said, "but when I was, you know, saying goodbye to Farlight, I smelled something familiar in the cuts on his head. At the time, I didn't think much of it, but I just remembered where I'd smelled it before. I don't know who did it exactly, because the scent was really faint, but I do know it was Eastern. The scent was *Eastern*. Dad . . . I think someone from the East may have killed Farlight. It's because of them that him and Whitehaze are dead and Ember is gone."

Cloud stopped a moment to process before continuing onward. "Are you sure about this? No one's seen, or even smelled anyone from the East here since the ambush. And there were no unknown scents anywhere around where he was found. Not from what any of us could smell, at least. There would have to be more evidence."

"I don't know, but if they did, Dad, we've gotta make them pay. They did this to us. I know we're leaving soon, but look at them; look at all these cats who are stuck here. The East is going to destroy them. If things like this keep happening, Lupine and all the Council might get killed, along with so many others."

"I could live with that."

"Dad, no, what if they *all* die? Farlight loved his colony. He wouldn't abandon them. Not while knowing what the East is doing to them."

He stopped again and lowered his voice. "Listen, right now, my top priority is getting you and your mother to safety. As sad as it is, we can't help them and ourselves at the same time. Believe me, I've tried it, and it doesn't work. If any of them want to go, they can leave on their own. Do you understand?"

Kivyress let her head droop. "Yes, sir."

"Good molly," he mewed. "Now let's get you out of this wind."

When they reached the den, Songbird's ears perked up. "Oh tahg, you're both okay. I was starting to get worried. Kivy, where were you? Please don't run off like that. Ever. If I lost you too . . ."

Kivyress leaned back against the den wall, cheeks wet with half-frozen tears. "I'm fine, Mom. I was in the storage cave, just, uhm, thinking some things over. I can take care of myself."

Songbird wrapped her paws around Kivyress's shoulders and buried her face in her neck. Kivyress looked helplessly at Cloud, too emotionally drained to escape on her own. Cloud sighed and lay down, resting his chin against the frozen earth.

'Just a few more days and everything will get better. I'm sorry I can't take you, Far. It was an honor getting to work for you though, and I'm sorry it had to end this way. I do wish I'd treated you better. You deserved more respect than what I gave you. And really, this is my fault. Aspen knew they were coming for you. He warned me to watch over you, and I failed to do so. I should've listened, but now you're gone, and there's nothing I can do about it.'

He placed a paw over his eyes. 'And why couldn't I have listened to her? I knew he was in trouble, but I couldn't accept it. I doubt we would've gotten there in time, but maybe we would at least be able to figure out what happened. What actually happened. Whitehaze a spy? Why didn't that kitten tell me about this? Why tell Ember, of all cats? And if Whitehaze really was a spy, who else is? It could be almost anyone but Lupine, me, Song, and Kivy. Not the most narrow selection of possibilities.'

He rubbed both paws against his forehead, ruffling his own fur. 'Spies, assassins, Easterners; what does it matter anymore? There's nothing left here to keep me from leaving. What do I care if they live or die?'

"Mom? Dad?" Kivyress mewed.

Cloud lifted his head, waiting for her to continue.

"What if we had our own memorial? For Farlight. Just Farlight. You know, a memorial he would like, and maybe, possibly, even be proud of." She sniffled. "I don't know. It was just an idea. He was . . . he was my brother. I just really want to do something for him. Something to give him at least a little honor before they turn him into ashes."

Songbird smiled gently. She groomed Kivyress's cheek. "I think he would've liked that idea. He would like it a lot. Cloud, will you say something? For Farlight?"

'A speech? Oh no. And here's where I let everyone down again. But something is better than nothing. At least it is right now.'

Cloud sat up. Nervousness made his chest tense. "Well, I didn't have time to prepare anything, but I can try." He coughed a few times, then sucked in a deep breath. "Whatever happened today, be it assassination or betrayal, this isn't what he deserved. Farlight, your life was worth so much more than this."

Songbird winced. Kivyress looked away, squinting to fight off another round of tears. Another gust of snow and air blew into the den, making them all shiver.

He gritted his teeth together. 'That was horrible. What am I doing? I'm sorry. I'm not ready for this. I'm sorry, Wren. Your son is gone. My son is gone, and I can't even come up with a proper memorial speech. What is wrong with me? It's happening all over again—I'm breaking and I don't know how to stop it.'

"F-Farlight," Kivyress whispered.

Cloud's jaw loosened at the sound of her voice. He exhaled and let himself be drawn back into the present.

"I don't know what happens when we die or if you can hear me right now," she continued, "but if you can, I just wanted to say that I already miss you. I hope you're happy wherever you are, and I mean it—I want you to be really, really happy." Her voice broke, but she kept going anyway. "Remember when I used to chase you around with pine needles? You hated it so much, and I really wish I would've given you the chance to get me back. But I didn't, and you never even tried. I don't know why I did it to you. I just hope now that it never bothered you too much." She sniffled and rubbed a paw across her face to groom away the tears. "You would've made such a great commander, you know. You could've done so much. Changed so many things for the better. But now that you're gone, everything . . ."

She hunched over and wept.

"Everything is changing, just not for the better," Songbird continued for her. She remained tall and firm, like a commander addressing her colony, being strong for them when even Cloud couldn't. "Light would've been so proud of the wonderful young tom you turned yourself into. And I know I am. I think I always will be, until I die too, and maybe even after. You weren't my kitten by birth, but you were always my son. I loved—still love—you so much more than I probably ever said. Every time I would see you, it was like someone telling me everything was going to be okay over and over again. You gave everyone so much comfort and joy, I . . . I don't know how we survived for so long without you, and I don't know how far we'll make it now, but thank you for being there for us while you were here. For giving me the best nine mooncycles of my life. I love you, Far. Sleep well."

Cloud sighed. He couldn't decide whether it was for Farlight, or for himself. *'I'm sorry, Son. I'm sorry I let this happen. I've let you down, I've let your father down and I've let myself down. I doubt I'll ever forgive myself, but you know me; I tend to motivate myself with guilt. And you've inspired us to leave this place.'* He sighed again. *'This is stupid. He can't hear me, and if he could, that was no speech of honor. But then again, I'm no good at coming up with these things in the moment. Who I really should be sorry for is them. I haven't said anything for them, to comfort them. But what am I*

327

even supposed to say?'

"Good night, Far," Kivyress whispered.

She yawned and curled up against the wall. Every few moments, she sniffled, causing her body to tense. Songbird lay down beside her in an attempt to comfort her. Cloud watched over them, his back to the cold. He gazed down at them in silent blankness as they drifted off to sleep.

'I'm down to them now. They're the only ones I can still protect.' He stooped closer and rested his chin against Songbird's back. *'I'm not failing again.'*

CHAPTER 22
EMBER

"Hello? Ember, is that you? I was wondering when I'd hear from you again. How are you doing, sweetie?"

'Michelle, I've made a mistake. A big mistake.'

Ember forced herself to take long, slow breaths. Wind attacked her from every angle. Hyrees sat shivering and crying beside a nearby tree, trying to shelter himself from as much of the gale as possible.

"Oh? Oh, I hope you're not hurt. Are you okay? If you are hurt, I'm afraid I can't come get you right now. I'm out of town for a tech convention. Are you okay?"

Ember's jaw trembled. The bitter taste of Whitehaze's blood still lingered on her tongue. *'No. I'm not okay. I don't need you to come get me, but I'm not okay.'*

"Ember, what's wrong?" her familiar, comforting voice asked. It surrounded her thoughts, like a blanket of noise. "You sound panicked. Matthew told me what happened the day you got back. Are you having another attack?"

'Kind of, but not exactly,' Ember thought. She coughed up another puddle of bile. It made her throat and mouth sting.

"Then what is it? What's going on?"

Another gust of wind came, rendering Hyrees invisible for a moment.

Ember's heart pounded in her ears. The gale slowed and he reappeared, shaking body still pressed against the tree. "Hyrees, they aren't gonna come for us in the middle of a blizzard. We have to find shelter."

He didn't reply.

Ember ran over to him. "Hyrees? Hyrees, we have to go."

"No," he said. "You have to go. I'm kind of tired. Hypothermia, you said? I'm curious. I want to see what it's like."

"What?" she whispered. "Wait, you're giving up? But Hyrees, you said you'd take care of me. You said you'd be there for me. What happened to us? Why is this happening to us?"

"Well, let's see, my mom is dead, my dad is dead, my brother is dead, we got sent into exile in the middle of a blizzard. It just keeps going, doesn't it? Isn't life great?" His eyes narrowed. "Look, you can keep going, and reunite with your family, and I can stop, and reunite with mine. Now go; get out of here. I'm too tired to keep doing this, to keep going and getting back up only to be thrown down a steeper cliff. I did my part. No one needs me anymore."

'I need you. And is that even how it works? That doesn't—'

"Ember, are you still there?" Michelle asked.

Her mind locked up. She visualized walking back to Hyrees and curling up around him, then did it.

"What are you doing?" he asked. "You're only making it take longer."

"Ember? What happened? What's going on? Please answer me."

'I'm here. Wait. Too much grey to think right now.'

"Oh?"

He tried to shove her away, but his legs were too weak. "Are you even listening to me?"

"I'm listening. I-I'm listening, Hyrees, I'm just choosing to ignore you. I'm not leaving without you. If your stubborn self is going to stay here, I am, too. If you want to die, I guess I'll have to die too."

"Okay then," he said. "Like I already said, you being next to me is only going to make it take longer. We're going to suffer. I'm *suffering*, Ember. It hurts."

"More . . . more time to change your mind."

"Ember, what is going on?" Michelle pressed.

'Blood. Blood, there's blood on my teeth.'

"Listen sweetie, I know something's going on, but I can't help you until you start making some sense."

'You can't help. Can't help this one. I messed up. I messed up really bad. I just killed someone, and it wasn't an accident, but it was, and now I'm in the Lowlands, in a blizzard, and my mate wants to die because his brother is gone, because the cat I killed killed him, because he got threatened by the East into becoming a spy, and everything is falling apart, and I'm cold, and I'm scared, and I don't know what to do. Michelle, what do I do? What if I am defective? What if I hurt someone else? What—'

"Whoa, whoa, slow down. So wait, you killed someone who killed your mate's brother, and was also a spy? My, I . . . guess I missed a lot. What in the world is going on in that valley of yours?"

Ember swallowed hard. *'War.'*

"Oh . . . right. Well then. So, uh, what did you need help with?"

Ember paused. *'Why did I call you?'* she thought to herself. She directed her thoughts back to Michelle. *'I . . . don't know. I killed Whitehaze, Michelle. Just like I killed Tainu. I've known them both all my life. They were my friends, and yet I just . . . killed them. Yes, Tainu attacked me first, but— agh! I don't even know if Whitehaze did it. He didn't do anything against me. I don't know what made me do it, made me kill him, but it was something else. It wasn't me. I couldn't stop myself. Or maybe I could have; I don't know. I don't want to be a wildcat. I don't want to kill. I'm scared, Michelle. I'm dangerous; I'm becoming a monster. I'm losing control; I'm losing everything, and I don't know how to stop. I don't know how to fix this. I don't know how to fix myself. What do I do? What do I do? What do I do?'*

"Uhm, wow, sweetie, that's quite a mess you've gotten yourself into. First, try to calm down. I don't know the whole situation, so I'm not really sure how to help you right now. I want to help—believe me, I do—but I can't. At least not at the moment. There's a lot going on, so I can't exactly sit down and let you explain everything to me."

'No time?' Ember bit her tongue and tried to ward off tears of disappointment and fear. *'But what do I do? Everything is broken.'*

"I don't know. Listen, I'm sorry I have to cut this so short, but I really have to go. They just called me up to speak, and I can't keep everyone waiting. I'll try to call you back later, okay? Goodbye, Ember. Take care of yourself."

[Call disconnected.]

Ember's jaw trembled as Thai hung up without her consent. She repressed all verbal thoughts, as if doing so might enable her to hear Michelle's gentle voice again. Silence filled her head.

'Please come back,' she pleaded, trying to get one last invocation through to her human savior. *'Don't abandon me, too. Please don't leave me here. I don't have anyone else to go to.'*

Hyrees shifted beneath her, dragging her back into the external world. He lifted his nose to the air and sniffed. "Who's there?" he called weakly.

Ember realized the storm had gotten worse. She could barely make out the silhouettes of trees two leaps away from them. Hyrees squirmed out from underneath her.

He got to his paws and growled. "Show yourself."

Ember positioned herself in a halfhearted fighting stance beside him. Glistening silver filled her head as her heartbeat thumped in her ears. Adrenaline trickled into her bloodstream, body trying to prepare her for whatever might come. Yet inside she just felt tired, and like Hyrees, ready to give up.

"What is it?" Ember asked.

"Outsider or Rogue, I think. I don't recognize the scent," Hyrees replied.

"Why do you care then? You wanted to die."

"Maybe, but I don't want you to die. You actually have a future," he said.

"Are you going to protect it? My future?"

He sighed. "Fine, yes. You win. For now at least. But when you're safe . . . I don't know. Just promise me you'll let me go in peace if I decide to go. Wouldn't want to keep me from my family, right?"

Her tail thrashed from side to side. "No. I don't do promises, and I don't think you'll be seeing your family when you die, so stop getting your hopes up."

Ember scanned the treetops for movement. With movement already everywhere in the form of snowflakes, spotting a hiding cat proved itself a difficult task. A feline gradually took shape in the branches of a tree a few leaps in front of them. She sniffed the breeze. Her muzzle burned in the frigid air. A familiar mixture of scents came with the pain. Dark red, fang yellow, and sky blue all shifted around her subconscious, raging with the storm.

Hyrees growled softly. "You know what you are? Em, you're a stubborn—"

"Rogue," she whispered.

He sidestepped away from her. "Uh, that's not exactly what I was going to say, but—"

Ember pawed his chin upward. "No, look. I mean it's a Rogue."

He jerked his head away from her. "Ember, I'm half blind, remember?"

The cat jumped down from the tree. He strutted toward them, multicolored eyes appearing to glow with reflected light

Ember tensed what muscles she could and kept her stance. "Eclan."

Eclan stopped. He snorted. "Well, ain't this a surprise? We just keep finding each other, don't we, kitten? What do you want?"

'Oh, I want to hurt you. This is probably your fault. Don't, Ember. You need his help. You really, really need his help right now. Gotta ask for help.'

"We just want to be left alone. Now go! Get out of here!" Hyrees snapped.

Ember pinned back her ears as cyan and vivid green flashed. 'He's going to chase him away, and then we're gonna die.' "No, Hyrees! No, no, no, don't say that! No!"

Both cats stared at her.

"Didn't he try to kill you twice?" Hyrees asked.

"But he didn't," she said.

Eclan snorted again. "She has a point. If I wanted her dead, she'd be dead already. Now, you two are in my territory. What do you want?"

Ember swallowed. "Uhm, I uh, I never thought I'd say this to you, but, er, well, can you help us? This storm is-is only going to get worse. We need shelter. If you help us, we'll pay you."

Hyrees pawed her side. "We will? Ember, this cat tried to kill you. You want us to follow him into a blizzard? Also, what are you going to pay him with? We have nothing."

"He's also working with the East but that's not important right now. We need shelter."

Eclan's eyes narrowed. "Hey, I'm listening, you know, kitten. What do you got that I need?"

Ember closed her eyes and worked out what to say. She placed a paw on her ETAg, as if acknowledging its presence might somehow give her words confidence. Her eyes snapped open. "The biggest collection of knowledge in the world. I can't give it to you, but I can use it for you. I can answer questions, show you how to do things, give you all kinds of useful information. I have the secrets of the universe hanging around my neck. I can quite literally give you power, if you ask the right questions."

Eclan smirked. "I like the sound of that. You promise not to tell any of your Colony Cat friends where I take you?"

'Okay, good, that's a promise I can keep,' she thought. "Yes. I promise. We've been exiled, anyway. We're no more Colony Cats than you. Now let's go before this snow gets any heavier."

"Ah, wait," Eclan mewed. He turned to Hyrees. "You gotta promise too, tomcat."

Ember pawed Hyrees's side. "Come on," she whispered.

Hyrees growled. "We can't trust him, Ember. You said he's working with the East? What if he's the one who told Whitehaze to kill my brother?"

"If I want to live, this is my best option. I'm taking it, with or without you. You can promise and come, or you can stay here and die alone, never knowing whether I made it or not."

Hyrees glared at her for a few seconds. "Send a fox on you, Ember."

He sighed and stared at his paws. Tears trickled into his fur as a quiet sob escaped his throat. For the first time since his mother had died, Ember could read his pain. He looked empty, lost, and sad, and she understood that part of him, because it was also a part of her.

"Heh," he huffed after a few moments of silence, "I knew I followed you out here for some reason. Alright, fine. I promise. Not like there's anyone I can tell anyway."

Eclan snorted. "I guess we got ourselves a deal, then." He turned northeast and started walking. "Follow me. Stay close. Easy to get lost in a storm like this."

As they walked, the wind blew harder. Eclan led them through a thick patch of forest and underbrush. When they reached a large bramble patch, Ember wondered if it was the shelter he'd planned to lead them to, but he pushed through a small tunnel under the spiky mess and kept going. Ember and Hyrees followed, wincing as thorns cut into their backs and sides.

With no one speaking, Ember's mind wandered back to that morning. Farlight and Whitehaze's dead bodies flashed through her head, agonizing and unstoppable.

'Monster. Wildcat. You did this. You killed him, and he's dead. They're dead. Both dead. Gone. Dangerous. Going to hurt someone. I'm going to hurt someone. You, you, why?' She shook her head. *'What is even going on? How did I get here? Robot legs. Blood on my jaws. Everything. Everything fell apart. What is wrong with me. There's something wrong with me. Matthew never said anything about this. This problem. Because this isn't that, this is all me. I killed them. Am I defective? I'm . . . defective. Defective. Defective? Am I? Whose fault? Mine? But I lost control? It wasn't me, was it? My fault because I lost control? I need more control. Who—'*

Something hard slammed into her face. She jumped backward. "Ouch!"

Ember snapped into reality to find a wall of rock in front of her. "Oh."

Hyrees brushed against her side. "You going blind, too, Emmy? Even I saw that."

Ember grimaced, but said nothing. His eerie, silver-inducing tone of voice made her fur stand on end. Eclan only snorted and kept walking. He led them into a gorge with a small frozen stream running through it. Rocks towered over them everywhere she looked. The exposed stone walls lining the gorge blocked out some of the wind and snow, but even with the extra cover, she couldn't see more than three leaps ahead. They passed by an abandoned, burnt-out fire. She smelled it more than saw it, since most of the charred wood had already been buried in the drift. As they walked, the gorge widened until she couldn't see either side. Surreal, metallic turquoise dripped in, mixing with the already present silvers and greys.

'I'm walking in silver. Guess that's what I am. Silver. I walk in silver. Silverwalker. Does that mean I'm not a villain, either? If I'm not a hero or a villain, what am I? Silver little me, I guess. Somewhere in between everyone and everything. And not sure where I'm going. At all.'

A faint shadow loomed ahead of them. It became more defined as she neared it.

'Rectangles. Triangles. Edges. Perfect edges. That's . . . that's—oh!'

She stopped and tilted her head.

"What is it, Ember? What's wrong?" Hyrees asked.

"It's a house," she replied. "A human den-thing. It looks old. What is it even doing here? I thought there weren't any people in Dark's Valley."

Unlike Michelle's home, and even more unlike the Center, large stones held together with hard-looking, white stuff made up most of the building. The snowy roof rose to a shadowy peak over the entryway, propped up with two arching pillars of stones. Several large windows lined the front of the house, but many of the glass panes were broken or missing. The front door was also gone.

"There aren't any," Eclan said. "Not here, at least. Place has been like this for winters. Not a sign of them wantin' it back. Not even a scent. So we've taken it for ourselves. Now let's get ourselves inside before we freeze to death."

"We?" Hyrees said.

Eclan chuffed and kept walking. "'Ey, you're Outsiders now. Might as well know about this place. Welcome to Starcross's Gorge. Lowland center of trade, if you will."

Ember's ears perked up; feline voices, faint but audible, came from the dilapidated building. She loped to follow him. As she moved, the voices grew louder, making her shiver with anxiety. Hyrees sighed and walked behind her.

"You can get anything you need here," Eclan continued. "All for the right price, of course. Food, place to sleep, finest assassins-for-hire in the Valley. Name it and I'm sure you can find it. Get a lotta my work here, and I don't doubt you could make a decent living here too. That is, if you really do have what you claim to have. If you don't, well, we have our own ways of dealing with cats who don't pay up." With an unsettling grin, he climbed up the stairs toward the empty doorframe. "C'mon in."

Ember's fur rose again as she stepped inside. The voices hit her like a windstorm. Cats—dozens of them—filled the room. A small table sat against the battered left wall, on which three large tabbies slept side by side. A series of shelves lined the back of the room, with each shelf housing a rough-looking feline. Several others stood, sat, talked, or walked along the cold tile floor. The ceiling above them loomed with holes and water stains. The entire place reeked of mold, ungroomed fur, tooth decay, urine, and the marks of countless sprays and scent glands. The resounding noise, nauseating smells, and sheer number of cats sent a sickening light green spiraling down her subconscious.

"Hey, Starcross," Eclan called. "Got some fresh exiles for you. You're gonna like these, I can promise you that."

For a few moments, no one so much as batted an ear. One of the sleeping tabbies opened his eyes. He nudged his friends awake and gestured toward Eclan. Other cats followed their gazes. The roar of voices became a hushed murmur. Almost every cat awake faced them, staring and exchanging whispers. Ember crouched down and pressed her tail against her legs, trying to make herself as small as possible as she stared at her paws.

"I am, am I?" a sweet voice with a Lowland drawl asked.

She looked up. A large black cat strode toward them. A white patch in the rough shape of a human addition symbol marked her forehead. Her left ear was torn in half down the middle, and a metallic, ring-shaped bijou dangled from a hole in the right. A large scar traced the side of her face, missing her cold, yellow eyes by a whisker. A few other scars marred her sides and limbs, many of them partially obscured by her long, sleek fur. Her face itself was slightly angular, and she carried herself with an intelligent, reserved bearing.

Ember tilted her head. Light brown and white eased away some of the queasiness causing her stomach to churn. For a moment, she forgot the events of that morning. *'Wow. Hum. Starcross, huh? I guess her parents weren't feeling very creative when she was born. She looks better than most of these other cats, though. Actually, she's kind of pretty. Where did she find that thing on her ear? It looks like it was made by humans.'*

"What have we got here, then?" Starcross asked. "A walking skeleton and a machine? I'm impressed, alright. So what's in these two for me? What can they do?"

Eclan coughed twice. "Ember here claims that thing 'round her neck contains the secrets of the universe or something. Says she can make us powerful in exchange for a few days' shelter."

"Oh? Us, huh? You for what? Taking them here?" Starcross stepped closer and sniffed them over. She examined Hyrees for a moment. "This one's useless to me. Partially blind, skin and bones. A kitten could take him down. There's nothing he can offer that I'll accept as payment, but I'm guessing this is a two-piece deal."

Hyrees growled. Ember's fur bristled. *'He is not useless. Know what? Maybe you aren't so pretty.'*

Starcross turned her attention to Ember and walked around her a few times. Ember tucked her tail and willed for the Outsider not to hurt her.

"Now how about you?" Starcross asked. "You're . . . interesting. So were you exaggerating out of desperation, or do you really have, as you put it, the 'secrets of the universe'? Be honest with me. I know a lie when I hear it being

338

told."

'Why doesn't she assume it's an outright lie? Why go straight to exaggeration or truth?'

"Because you were desperate enough to trust him," Starcross replied, as if she'd heard Ember's thoughts. "Eclan gets his claws dirtier than the most filthy of colony cats. 'Trustworthy' is not what comes to mind when anyone meets him. Yet here you are, following him through a blizzard. No one that desperate would risk their lives telling a lie that can easily be disproven. No one smart, at least. No, someone in your position would offer something real. Or at least something you think is real."

She stepped back. "H-how did you—"

"Know what you were thinking? Your expressions said everything. Now tell me: do you really have the secrets of the universe, or are you wasting my time?"

"Well," Ember said. "It depends on the questions you ask. This thing, uh, around my neck, it, uhm, gives me access to a collection of pretty much all human knowledge. I can use it to teach you how to do anything, or give you information on whatever you want. Here, ask me a question. I'll ask Thai, and you'll probably get your answer."

"The secrets of the universe you said?" Starcross closed her eyes. "Tell me then, who touched the Valley first?"

'Oh no. One of those *questions. Of course it wouldn't be something practical. Just have to make me look like a fluffhead, huh?'*

Ember swallowed. "Ah, uhm, Thai, who touched the Valley first?"

"I've been through all my main databases, and I'm still not sure what you mean. Would you like me to do a web search? Maybe my search engine can get you the answer you're looking for," Thai replied.

"I've heard enough," Starcross said. She turned around and walked away through the parted crowd. "Give them to the storm. Colony Cats—they never do change, do they?"

The cats gathered around them laughed. The laughter rose to a roar that stabbed her ears. Ember flattened them against her neck and tucked her tail tighter. Another surge of adrenaline rushed through her system, making her heart leap to her throat. Eclan shoved her and Hyrees toward the doorframe and the deadly blizzard beyond it. Cyan flooded her head, washing away all other emotion. *'No, no, no! Not now! Come on, Ember. Think! Think! Think! First to the Valley.'*

"A bug! An insect! Some kind of insect!" she called.

The laughing reduced itself to a series of chuckles. Starcross stopped. She turned to face them again, smiling. "An insect?"

"You, uhm, you just asked me to tell you. You didn't say i-it had to be from Thai. So I told you. Or at least I, uh, think it was most likely an insect. It's the most logical thing to pick. Or I could say grass, or moss, or a mushroom, if you want to include plant-type things. Though mushrooms are actually something else entirely from—"

Starcross chuckled. "It's a question without a deducible answer, coggy. You're calling out guesses, not facts. For all any of us know, a blue elk with one antler and five legs might have been the first. Even before the mushrooms. Now scram."

"Wait." An older tanish-grey tabby pushed his way through the gathering of felines. His tail twitched almost frantically in rhythm. "Don't send them out yet. I need to have a word with Eclan and would prefer these two stay. They might be more useful than you think. I'll be certain to pay you for the trouble of keeping them for the night."

His soft green eyes and expressionless face made Ember shiver, and his accent, a gruff-yet-bouncy mixture of Lowland and Eastern, did nothing to ease the sinking feeling in her chest. Yet somewhere in the silver anxiousness of her thoughts, speckles of black flickered into existence. Comfort.

'Why do I feel like this all of a sudden? I don't even know him,' she wondered. *'Oh, come on, Ember; he's offering to pay for your stay. He's helping us. Though I guess he does business with Eclan, so just keep your guard up. You'll be fine.'*

Starcross stepped back, eyes narrowed. "Bracken? I hardly expected you, of all cats, to come standing up for a couple of newcomers. Though I guess I shouldn't be too surprised at this point. So, what are you planning to pay? It had better be good. I don't need much right now. Each winter every mangy moggy in walking distance comes to me begging. You know, that's one of the advantages of being on top. I can turn down who I like. I only get the best." She chuckled. "At least here; don't tell Cass I said that."

Bracken sighed. He sat down and bent over sideways. Ember let herself examine him more closely. Her ears perked up again. Two rough leather straps attached a bag to his side. Unlike Starcross's earring, it looked like it was made for a cat, by a cat. A large, nasty-looking scar ran along his flank, partially concealed by the satchel. It, however, looked too big to have been made by a cat.

"What are you looking at, coggy? My pouch?" he asked.

His piercing eyes stared directly at her, but his voice didn't sound annoyed or fierce. It sounded genuinely curious, if past experiences were anything to go by. She looked at her paws again. "Y-yes, sir. It's, uh, made of leather. Where did you get it? Did you make it?"

He went back to searching through his satchel. "More along the lines of had it made, but yes. I designed it, and a friend—excellent with stone blades —made my design a reality. Ah, and I believe this should be enough to cover their stay."

Bracken pawed out a clay bijou in the shape of a blackberry blossom. A sparkling, creamy green gemstone rested in its center. A thin strip of leather attached to the back made it wearable. He pushed it across the floor to Starcross's paws. Starcross examined it for a few seconds.

Ember bit her tongue. As she did, the black grew stronger, eating away at the silvery mind storm. *'Please accept it. Tahg, it's beautiful. It must be worth so much. Why is he giving it away for us? We don't even know each other.'*

"Hmm. Bracken, would you put it on me?" Starcross asked.

Bracken picked it up by the leather and slid it around her neck. It dangled against her chest, complementing her earring and her namesake marking. Ember tilted her head once again as the brown and white fluttered back.

Starcross smiled. "Yes, I guess this will do." She turned to Ember and Hyrees. "Looks like you two got lucky. The freak got you in. For now. Moment this storm clears, though, you'd better prove yourselves useful, or both of you will be running out of here with your tails tucked."

'Freak? But he doesn't look like a freak, just a kind, scruffy old tomcat.' A faint sinking feeling tugged at her insides. *'Kind. Hum. That's not even how I'd describe most Colony Cats. Then again, I don't actually know him.'*

Starcross looked around the room at the staring cats. She growled. "What're y'all looking at?"

The cats went back to doing whatever they'd been doing before. She walked away through the still-parted crowd, new bijou resting elegantly against her fur.

Ember straightened herself up and untucked her tail, but she kept her ears pinned as the murmur of voices came back. "Er, thank you," she said.

Bracken smiled. "I hope you two enjoy your stay. Come along, Eclan. How have you been doing? Tell me your stories."

Eclan chuffed and walked into the crowd. "Been doing a lot more than you realize."

The two toms padded side by side into the next room over. Ember and Hyrees watched in silence.

"We're here; we're surrounded by Outsiders and Rogues and all their stink and filth. Are you happy?" Hyrees asked.

Ember tried to ignore the voices by turning them into one collective sound. One loud, painful, collective sound. "Uh, well, at least we aren't freezing to death in a blizzard anymore. We might be able to stay here until m—" The pleasantly forgotten events of that morning came flooding back in. "Mom and . . ."

Whitehaze and Farlight's dead bodies flared in her mind's eye. Every time she blinked, the images got clearer, more painful until they became tinted with sky blue. She shivered uncontrollably. She wanted to disappear. No, she wanted to curl up in a ball and make the world disappear, to make it stop attacking her. But it kept coming.

"I don't think your parents will be able to find this place," Hyrees said.

'Parents? Mom and Dad. Kivy. Oh no, oh no, oh no. What did I do? What did I do?'

"Ember, hey, are you okay? Wait, that was a stupid question. Neither of us are okay," he growled.

'Be quiet. Please. Be quiet.'

"My brother just died, and you just killed some—"

"Hyrees, stop!" she yowled.

He stared at her in unreadable silence. The gazes of those around them burned into her head, causing it to throb. She cowered beneath it all, fighting back the tears threatening to form.

"Don't talk about it," she whispered. "Please. Just stop. I don't want to think about it."

"Sorry. I know what you mean. I don't really want to think about it either. I'm just so . . . *furious* that that wildcat would kill my brother. He did it, he did. I know it was him; I know it was," he said, tail twitching. He sighed. "Sorry again. Did you want to find somewhere quiet?"

"Yes," she mewled.

"Alright. Let's go, then." He nudged her deeper into the building and farther away from the deadly chill of the storm.

Ember took deep, raspy breaths as she crept onward through the crowd. Twitching tails smacked her as cats walked past. They brushed against her sides, their oily fur making her feel more nauseous with every step. Despite being machines, each of her legs felt like they were dragging boulders behind them.

'Do this. Come on, Ember, you can do this. You have to; you have to. There's nowhere to hide—nowhere to go to make it stop. Agh, go away, grey. Stop. Please make it stop.'

She closed her eyes and froze.

"We have to keep moving, Ember," Hyrees said. "I'm sorry, I can't deal with one of your episodes right now. In fact, I think I'm on the verge of panicking myself. You have got to calm down."

Ember tucked her head closer to her body, willing herself to quit shaking and obey. It refused to listen. Hyrees sighed; she didn't have to look to know he was getting exasperated.

'I don't blame you. I'm aggravating myself, Hyrees. I'm stuck, and it hurts. It hurts. Everything hurts. Please, get me out of here. Get me out of here.'

"Come on. We can do this. Walking. One paw in front of the other, remember? Look, that corner over there is empty. Let's go over there."

She opened her eyes. Hyrees head-butted her forward.

'He's talking to me like a kitten,' she thought as they slunk through the building. *'Why is he talking to me like a kitten? He's never done that before. I wish Eclan was here. Never thought I'd think that. Or Bracken. He seemed nice, even if he ends up wanting something from us in return. They know this place. They could help. They could show you all the rooms, and then at least you wouldn't be lost. Tahg, there are too many cats here. It smells so bad. Why does it smell so bad? Do I even want to know?'*

When they reached the corner, Ember pressed her forehead against the walls and closed her eyes. She went back through her memories to the mental image she'd created of Michelle's home and imagined being there instead. She stopped shivering. After exploring the well-preserved halls and rooms, she recalled what she knew about the interior of Starcross's house. Based on the two and a half rooms she'd seen, she concluded that there were no less than three left to be discovered and mapped out, possibly more.

"Musta found the good stuff, eh?" someone said.

"Good stuff?" Hyrees asked.

"You know—the good mint."

"Uh, yeah, no," he growled. "Go bite a fox."

"Yikes. The newcomers are touchy, ain't they? Sensitive little colony-moggie-coggies. Hah! Whatcha doin' in that corner then, missy?"

She started shivering again. *'Oh, he's talking to me.'* She turned around to find a small grey-patched cat standing across from them. An ornate band of clay encircled the lower part of his tail. "Uh, I was, er, calculating roughly how many rooms here has. This place has. Are in this place. Sorry, I can't speak because you make me nervous."

He laughed. "Definitely found the good stuff. You got any more? I'll give ya my tail band."

"Please just go," Hyrees said. "You do not want to make her nervous. Tahg, I don't want you to make her nervous. It never ends well."

The patched tom meandered closer. "Ah, come on, let the molly speak. If she wants to share, let 'er share."

Bracken and Eclan padded into the room. "Don't you have anything better to do?" Bracken asked.

The cat lowered himself into a submissive pose, belly against the floor and ears back. "Sorry, there. Had no idea these two fine colony moggies were with you. I uh, better get to goin'.'."

He scampered away into the main room and vanished in the crowd. Ember stared after him, confused. *'Well, that was odd. Should I be scared of him too?'*

Eclan chuckled as he watched the cat go. "Desperate fluffhead. I like my mint as much as any other moggie, but that tom's got himself a problem. Fought with him a few times in combat matches. Never makes for much of an opponent without the stuff, so I'll admit I've bribed him into a good share of chancy spars with it."

Bracken moved closer to her. "Eclan tells me you were both Colony Cats very recently. Might I ask why you're now in the sludge-hole of the Valley? This is hardly a place for such . . . interesting individuals as yourselves."

"We don't want to talk about it. It might make her panic, and I don't have the energy to deal with that," Hyrees replied.

Ember licked her lips nervously. *'Deal with what? Deal with me? Hyrees, you know I don't want it anymore than you do. In fact, I hate it even more because I'm the one who has to figure out how to make it stop. You don't have to deal with it. You don't have to do anything.'*

"Understandable," Bracken said. "So what do you plan to do now? Live out the rest of your days in the Lowlands? Or do you plan to switch colonies? I've met cats who've done that."

"What about an Easterner named Wren?" Hyrees asked.

"Yes, I knew him; I met him many winters ago. Actually, that was the very tom I was thinking of. Are you related? You look a lot like him."

Hyrees hesitated a moment. "He was my father."

"Was? As in, he's gone?"

"He died in a fight with the East. They killed their own kin. But then again, after what they've been doing, and with what happened today, I wouldn't put anything past them. Not even murdering a kitten. They're ripping our colony apart from the inside out. No, we can't switch colonies. I never want to see those . . . those *monsters* again."

Bracken froze for a split moment, eyes wide, and muttered something under his breath. He snapped out of his daze and grimaced. "Well, I'm sorry to hear about your father, and it saddens me to know that a youth has died." A tiny sigh left his throat. He shook his head, as if trying to jostle away whatever emotions he was feeling.

Ember sucked in a noseful of freezing air and pinned back her ears. *'Stop. Please stop. Shouldn't be saying this to him. You're making us vulnerable. You're making me vulnerable. You'd better not mention Whitehaze. Whitehaze?'* Her lower jaw trembled with anxiety. *'Oh no.'*

"You know, if you ever need an extra bit of security, I know a sizable group of Outsiders you can join," Bracken offered after a few moments of silence. "It's no colony, but they provide for each other, and new ideas are never discouraged. It's where I got my pouch, actually. Most intuitive group in the Valley. Smart young newcomers like yourselves are always welcome, and all members are free to come and go as they please."

"That's, uh, something to consider, I guess," Hyrees said softly.

He looked over his shoulder at her. Ember stared at him, willing for him to read her mind. He focused his attention back on Bracken. "But right now we need some time to rest. It's been a long, upsetting day. So if you don't mind, sir, maybe we can talk some more tomorrow."

Bracken smiled. "Of course. I'll be here until the storm clears. Take all the time you need to recover. Eclan, we'd best be going."

Eclan snorted. "Don't forget our deal, kitten. You owe me answers. I'll be collecting them tomorrow."

Ember realized he was talking to her. "Oh, uhm, yeah. Of-of course."

Bracken and Eclan started off in the same direction they'd come from. "Sleep well, my coggy friends," Bracken called over his shoulder. "Though I must warn you that this place does not."

She swallowed hard as they disappeared once again into the gathering of cats. *'Doesn't what? Doesn't sleep? I hope it sleeps. I need sleep. I can't sleep with cats moving around. But then again, am I even going to be able to sleep after all this? Probably not.'*

She leaned against the corner and let herself slide to the floor. The moment her chin hit the cold, hard ground, another round of tears broke free. She covered her eyes and cried all over again. Hyrees curled up next to her, burying his face in her side.

Ember chewed on her tongue, then transitioned to her toes. She forced herself to stop chewing altogether. *'Why am I doing this? Why can't I just stop? Why can't I start being okay? What is wrong with me?'*

She lifted her head to stare at her paws. The heating grids were off, but she couldn't stop shaking. *'I'm the problem. What if Dark was right? Maybe I'm not fit to live.'*

Somewhere nearby, someone laughed. She wrapped her paws over her face and tried to shut out the world. *'But I told Dad I'd try. Guess I'm stuck here now. Stuck. I'm stuck.'*

CHAPTER 23
EMBER

As Bracken had foretold, even with the light fading away, nothing in Starcross's Gorge seemed to stop. Cats talked, and yowled, and jumped, and walked around. The wind moaned and whistled through each little crevice in the building like a relentless pack of red wolves, howling over their captured prey. Every now and then the ambience faded and Ember drifted off. Each time, nightmares attacked her within moments, sending her back into reality with a pounding heart and dampened eyes.

A few times she considered getting up and walking around, but the sounds of unknown paws against stone kept her from even shifting to a more comfortable position. After waking from a nightmare where she killed both Whitehaze and Farlight, she spent rest of the night paralyzed in a perpetual state of fight, flight, or freeze. When the first hints of dawn trickled in through the windows, she was more exhausted than when she'd first lay down.

Hyrees shifted beside her. Her heart slowed and stopped thudding in her head. The cyans, greens and greys that had tormented her all night faded enough for her to focus. She sighed in relief, despite her still-trembling jaw.

'Oh, please be awake, please be awake, please be awake. I can't take much more of this. I don't know what exactly will happen if I take much more, but it's not going to be good. I need you. I need you. Please help.'

"Hyrees?" she whispered. "A-a-are you awake?"

"No. Don't wanna go to work. Too tired," he muttered.

Just hearing his voice made her jaw stop shaking. She forced herself to smile at his blissfully dazed ignorance. *'I should let him enjoy it while it lasts.'*

"You don't have to. W-we have the day off," she said.

He pressed his face more firmly against her side. "Really? Great. Wake me up tomorrow."

"Okay."

Ember lifted her head and looked around the house. With the blizzard still raging outside, the rising sun provided a lot less light. Shadows of cats moved around the room. Voices continued murmuring from every direction. She closed her eyes and tried to distinguish voices from each other to guesstimate how many cats were up, but they muddled together too often to make out any one individual.

'Do these cats ever sleep? You can't survive here much longer, Em. You've got to get out after the storm. But where do we go? Bracken's group sounds good, but maybe too good. I don't trust him. I don't trust anyone here. Not even me. First we have to find Mom and Dad. But how? Maybe I could get Eclan to find them in exchange for something. Or I could try to get him to scout the Colony to see if they're still there. Hopefully they can make it out okay. Oh, I'm hungry.'

Hyrees's stomach growled beside her, voicing her thoughts. Hyrees yawned. "Never mind. My stomach says I'm getting up. Good—"

He stared blankly at the corner. Ember watched helplessly as everything came back to him.

His neck went limp, and his chin flopped against her back. "It wasn't a nightmare," he whispered. His voice rose to a painful yowl. "It wasn't a nightmare. He's gone! I . . . I-I . . ."

Ember flattened her ears. "Hyrees, I know, but be quiet, please. We don't need to tell everyone. They might hurt us."

He stopped yowling and instead sobbed into her fur. Cats glared at them, eyes reflecting the dim lighting and appearing to glow. One of the shadows walked closer. In the darkness, Ember could barely make out the cross-shaped marking her forehead.

"What's the problem here, coggies?" Starcross asked.

Ember didn't know how to reply, so she bit her tongue instead. Her heart started to race again. *'Please just leave us alone. Go away; go away.'*

Starcross thrashed her tail. "Hey, can either of you speak? I asked you what's wrong."

Ember swallowed the bile building up in her throat. "We lost almost everything. Please leave us alone," she whispered.

"I see. The cat who can make anyone she wishes powerful has been thrown out by some of the most power-hungry cats in the Valley. Almost like one of your legends, huh?" She chuckled. "You see, out here, answers to questions like 'why do birds fly' or 'why is the sky blue' aren't all that important or empowering. We accept that things are the way they are and learn to use reality to suit our will. Aside from freaks like Bracken, and whatever the rubble Eclan is, cats out here don't trade for information. It's a little too easy to lie for that to be the case—and of course, it also takes up brain space that could be better allocated for something actually useful."

"What does that have to do with us losing everything? And why do you keep calling him a freak? Is he dangerous?" Ember asked. Her jaw began to tremble again.

"It has to do with you not seeming to get what life is like out here. And he *is* a freak. Ever notice how his tail is always twitching?" Starcross laughed again. "You haven't met him yet, but trust me, he's crazy. Not exactly 'kill you and everyone you love' kind of crazy, though. He's no wildcat. Not even a Rogue. If I had to use one word to describe him it would be 'freak,' not 'dangerous.' 'Weird' also comes to mind."

"Perhaps my more dangerous side will show through if you keep meowing about me over my shoulder," Bracken said. He walked over to them, head and tail held low. "Starcross, would you leave these two alone? They've been traumatized enough already."

"Traumatized? Listen, Bracken, if your new friends want to survive, they have to learn to move on; to stop huddling up in the corner and crying. I don't care how sheltered of a place they came from. They'll become coyote meat if they can't pick themselves up."

Bracken's tail continued to twitch as he flicked back an ear. "True, but maybe the transition could be a touch more gentle, don't you think? They're just kittens. They've been through a lot. And I've taken them on now, so showing them how to survive will be my problem. No need to worry yourself, miss. I'll keep them safe and out of trouble."

Taken us on? Teach us? But Mom and Dad will be with me—us—soon. I hope. I hope. I don't need you to teach me. Does this mean you think I'll never see them again? What if you're right?'

Starcross stared at him for a few moments, then chuckled. "Sure you will." She shook her head and walked away.

Bracken turned to them. "The snow is starting to clear up. You two should get ready to leave."

"Leave?" Ember said. "Leave for where?"

"She only agreed to keep you until the storm ends. You'll need somewhere to go to wait for your parents. I was thinking I could take you to the group."

Her chest tightened. "Uhm . . . Where's Eclan? I need to talk to him first."

"Eclan? Why him? Is it because of your deal?"

Eclan trotted up behind him. "You called? Ready to pay up? How many questions do I get answers to? Probably shoulda asked that before."

Ember bit her tongue and looked at her paws. "Uh, well, does five sound fair?"

"Make it ten," he said.

She wrinkled her nose. Ten questions would give him everything he wanted, making offering more in exchange for his services useless. "Seven, maybe?"

"Eight."

Ember sighed. "Fine. Eight. Want to ask them now?"

Eclan thought for a moment, then asked a series of five questions about the weather on specific days. Ember repeated them to Thai, who answered each one in turn.

"Okay, you have three more," she said.

Eclan chuckled. "I know. I'm not using them now. Better to have someone owe you than to not. Never know when you might need a favor."

She flattened back her ears. "Oh. Right. So, er, do you want me to owe you even more?"

He stepped closer. "'Pends on the catch, but I'm listening."

"I'll give you five more questions if you go the West after the blizzard stops altogether. I need you to see if my parents and sister make it out safely, and if they do, to lead them here."

"Five? I don't know about that. Not a lotta questions for something so—"

He stopped. Ember looked up as Bracken whispered something into Eclan's ears.

Eclan smiled. "Alright, I'll do it, and I'll do it now. Be back by sunset tomorrow. Remember kitten, I got eight answers left for collecting."

He turned and scampered out of the room without further explanation. Ember tilted her head as the indigos of confusion grovelled around her mind.

"What did you tell him?" she asked.

Bracken chuffed gently, reminding her of the way Aspen used to chuckle when she asked him a question. The memory came encased in a halo of misty oranges and deep blues. Then silver and dull yellow as she remembered that he'd wanted to kill her.

"Everyone has something they want the most," Bracken said. "Something they think will give them the most control. Being able to recognize what that thing is, then provide it, is true power. You can get anyone to do almost anything for the right price." He sat down, fluffy tail wrapped over his paws. The tip of it continued twitching. "For example, I believe knowledge is what you want most, aside from being with your family. In your mind, that tag has indeed made you the most powerful cat in the Valley, and in a way that few will recognize here, it has. But power is only so when you know how to use it."

'Oh, tahg, he might be right. Does this mean he can control me? And can I

352

control others?' She shivered. "So, what does Eclan want most?"

"Isn't it obvious? He wants security. He'll do anything to ensure he's protected and prepared. Didn't you find it odd that all of his questions had to do with the weather at very specific points in time? Those are all days he's agreed to perform a task on. And then there's his desire to have you and others owe him. Another layer of security."

"I guess that makes sense, but if he really does want security, why would he attack me for fun, or bribe that mint-breather into fights?"

Bracken chuckled. "He only picks fights he knows he can easily win, then, when he does win, it boosts his confidence. It makes him feel invincible. Secure."

"Oh." Ember swallowed. Silver took over the indigo. "So how can you offer him protection?"

"I have my methods. Like I said: you can accomplish anything with the right amount of mind power."

"And you want control, right?" She asked.

Bracken laughed, gentle and mellow. "I guess you could say that, but almost everyone does. It's more a matter of what they think will give them that control. See, what I want the most is justice, which is a shame, because it's hard to get. I want to see the right thing get done. I want to see cats being treated fairly by what they can do, not where they're from, or how unusual they may seem. Justice and truth walk side by side, you know. Maybe we could work together, someday." He sighed. "I have so many visions for how things could be. Ideas for the future that would make life better for everyone, the Colonies included, but sometimes I don't have the information I need. I'm just one old, weather-beaten tomcat, after all, and the Valley is a big, harsh place not friendly to my ideals. But oh well. We can always imagine things will get better."

The silver grew stronger. "I guess so."

Hyrees lifted his head and sniffled a few times. "Sorry, Ember. I think I might have made your fur a little wet. I hope you don't mind."

"Mind? Wet fur is the least of my concerns right now," she said. "Well, not exactly, but . . . never mind. It's okay. I feel kind of sick."

"I feel it too. Maybe it's contagious. I think Lupine might have given it to us."

Ember leaned away from him as an oily shimmer invaded her thoughts. "I feel sick because I didn't get almost any sleep last night. Lupine didn't give it to me. If anything, this place did."

He grimaced. "It was a passive aggressive joke. You weren't supposed to take it literally."

She stood up and pressed her side against the wall. "It wasn't funny, and Lupine isn't here to be passively offended. Why would you joke right now to begin with? You were crying into my fur a few moments ago. It doesn't make sense."

"I don't know." He got to his paws, tail thrashing. "It felt like the right thing to say, so I said it, okay?"

Bracken stepped back. "I think I'll leave you two alone."

He turned and loped away. Ember tried to focus her attention on Hyrees—skin and bones, battered and broken, half blind, Hyrees.

'What is even going on anymore? Are we fighting now? I can't think. Can't focus. Can't do this.'

"Felt?" she asked. "Felt. It *felt* right. Killing Whitehaze *felt* like the right thing to do too, and look where that got me. I'm sorry; I can't do this right now."

Ember pushed past him. All the pent-up energy from that night came bursting out. She shoved her way through the two rooms. Cats growled and snapped at her, but she couldn't make out any of what they said. Two cats blocked the doorway to outside, so she leaped over them. Her prosthetics whined and whirred in protest when she landed. Her shock absorbers hissed.

"Oi! What's your problem, cat? Chargin' around here like a stag. You got somewhere you need to be?" someone behind her snapped.

Ember curled back her lips, trying to ignore him as she closed her eyes and forced herself to control her breathing. The wind ruffled her fur, welcoming her back to the sweet-smelling forest. When she opened her eyes, she realized the snow had piled up a lot more than she'd imagined. It wasn't the most intense blizzard she'd seen, but the storm had lasted a lot longer than most, and the resulting snow formed a leap-high wall wrapping all around the porch. Beyond the wall, a light snow fell, swaying with each tiny movement in the air. She looked around the gorge. The stone ledges towered over her, reaching a few leaps higher than the roof of the house. Snow-coated moss clung to the sides of the couloir, making her think of the Cliffs and their seasonal confusion. The reminder of wummer made her chuff in bittersweet amusement.

She sat, sniffling, and exhaled slowly. *'Everything is going to get better soon. Eclan will bring them here, and we can figure where to go from there. But the most important thing is that we'll be doing it together. They'll know what to do. They'll know if we can trust Bracken and if we should join the group. Things will get better. Just stop panicking. Calm down. Maybe for now Michelle can help. She said she'd call me back, but she never did, so I guess I'll just have to call her. Thai can you call Michelle?'*

[Calling.]

The dial tone played in her head for a few seconds, then cut off.

[Oh no, it seems the number you're trying to reach is not available right now. You'll have to try again later.]

Ember bit her tongue as a sinking dull red drifted through her mind. *'Oh. Maybe she's still busy. Unless I scared her off, in which case I don't blame her. No one wants to be friends with a killer. I just hope she's okay.'*

[I hope so too, Ember.]

She sighed quietly. "Please just let this get better."
"It will. I'll make sure it does."

She spun around to find Hyrees standing behind her. Ember got up and tucked her tail. "I'm sorry I yelled at you. I'm scared. Everything is so green and purple out here; I don't know what to do. It's all happening at once, and I'm not ready."

He moved closer and leaned in to press his nose against hers. "No, it's . . . it's alright, I guess. Life's unpredictable. I get it. Heh . . . one mooncycle everything is perfect, and the next, we're exiled Outsiders asking mint-breathing Rogues for help. Who'd have thought? And look at me. Fat and blurry-eyed to scrawny and blind. Dad would hardly even recognize me, I bet. Hah, I bet I wouldn't recognize me if I actually had eyes that worked. That would be nice, getting to see how pathetic I am."

She licked her lips nervously. "I, uh, don't see how you insulting yourself is supposed to help anything, but I'm glad you aren't angry at me. You aren't angry, right?"

Behind them, cats yowled and spat as a fight broke out. They peered inside, but couldn't make out what was happening. Starcross yelled for the battling cats to take it outside, yet they didn't seem to hear.

"I'm not angry, but I will admit you can be confusing, and even frustrating, sometimes. I'm probably the same way, though, so who am I to complain?"

'Confusing? Frustrating?' She sighed. *'I guess that makes sense. Everyone is confusing and frustrating sometimes—including you. What makes me any different?'*

One of the fighting cats screeched. Hyrees flattened his ears.

"Hey, on the off chance they actually do come out here, do you want to walk around?" he asked. "Because I don't really want to feel pain this early in the morning."

Something about his tone of voice made her shiver, but she couldn't place why. "Yeah, we can walk. Want to look around the house? Maybe we can get a better idea of how many rooms there are in it."

"I don't *see* how that's important, but okay. Let's go."

Ember tilted her head and stared at him for a moment, trying to work out what exactly was going on in his head. She gave up, accepting the indigo, and climbed up the snow wall into the gentle flurry beyond it. The snow crumbled and melted beneath her paws. She sank down to her knees. The cold made her jump forward. She landed with snow pressed against her sides and stomach.

"Oh! Oh, it's cold and I'm sinking. Uhm, Hyrees?" she said.

He trotted over to her, snow only coming halfway up his legs. "I guess you're heavier than I am. I don't know what to do to help. Sorry, Em."

She snorted and climbed until it no longer touched her sensitive stomach. She needed to step high to even move her paws forward. The temperature sensors in her legs stung and burned. She turned the sensitivity down until the snow felt like a cool breeze.

As they made their way around the building, Ember examined walls and counted windows. The left side of the house was boring: a grey stone wall with a triangular top and only three windows. Moss and lichen patches gave it small touches of color and texture, but it was nothing extraordinary.

They went around the back. Ember stopped and narrowed her eyes. She tilted her head as fresh swirls of indigo appeared. In the middle of the structure, next to a doorway with a partial door, a white mark in the loose shape of a paw marred the wall. Lines, sharp and curved, formed claws poking out from each of the toes, and enclosed in the large pad of the print, an oval with a line through it completed the mark. Lines of white trailed down from the paw print, as though the paint used had been watery when it was applied.

'Huh. That's weird. Did a human do this? Did they do it to their own home? Or someone else's home? When did they do it? Sometime before Starcross took it, probably.' She let herself be engulfed by the unusual mark. All of her senses focused on it and only it, drowning out her problems along with the rest of the external world. The purples faded and got replaced with soft whites and muddy browns. *'But what does it mean? Thai? Do you know what this symbol means?'*

[Hold still. I'm going to take a picture for analysis.]

357

Ember obeyed. The familiar click of her ETAg's tiny shutter told her she could move again.

[Okay, I've gone through all my databases and can't seem to find the exact meaning of this symbol, only speculations by others who have seen symbols like it. Based on my search results, I believe it's something you're not supposed to know much about. It appears to be linked to a lot of conspiracy theories involving top secret governmentally funded experiments, among other things.]

'Oh. That doesn't sound good. So do you think I should try to tell Michelle about this?'

[She did disconnect earlier, but we can always try again. Who knows? Maybe she knows what it actually means. You could also try Matthew.]

'Yeah, I could. Let's call Matthew. He can tell Michelle if he thinks she knows what it is.'

Unlike last time, the call didn't disconnect, but went to his voicemail instead. His ever-cheery voice bouncing through her head almost made her smile, but being left without answers once again kept her face blank. 'Okay, I'll leave a message. Hey Matthew, I was, uh, taking a walk, and I came across this . . . thing? I don't know if you know what it is or not, but I thought—think it's kind of interesting. I'm sending you a picture of it so you can see what I'm thinking to you about. End message. Attach recent photo. Send.'

[Message sent. Hopefully he'll get it soon. Then maybe we can get some answers.]

Something tapped her nose. Her mind returned to reality. Ember jumped and spun around to face her assailant. *'Hyrees, what are you—oh, uhm . . . Right.'*

"Hyrees, what are you doing?" she asked, out loud this time.

"You froze again," he said.

"I was busy."

His tail twitched. "Looking at a wall? But it's a wall. And I'm . . . You know what? Never mind. It's okay. You'll be you, and I'll be fine with it. After all, you're the one who's going to be walking away from this when it's all said and done."

Ember shivered again. As she did, a strong breeze cut through the gorge, making her tremble even more. *'Will you please stop talking like that? You're scaring me, Hyrees. Am I doing something wrong? What are you trying to say? I don't understand. I don't understand anything, do I? I guess that's my problem. I can't understand. Whose fault is it? Yours for not helping me? Or mine for not being capable enough? I wish we could at least meet halfway. But that's not going to happen, is it?'*

She looked up at him and examined his lanky form. "I'm trying," she whispered. "I promise I'm trying to listen and to understand you, and everyone else too, but it's so hard, and with everything going on, I don't know how much longer I can keep trying. I don't know how much longer I can do this. I-I-I . . ."

Hyrees moved closer until his neck rested against hers. "It's okay. It's going to be okay, Em. I'm going to make sure you get out of this. I promise. Things *will* get better."

"Hey coggies," Bracken said. He loped toward them through the snow. "I don't mean to interrupt, but Starcross has officially made us unwelcome. She has, however, allowed us one more day in the gorge itself. We can wait here for Eclan and your parents, then you can all decide where to go from there."

"Actually, I think I prefer the gorge," Ember mewed.

He chuffed. "I don't blame you. Now come along. Eclan won't be back until tomorrow, so for the time being, I recommend we go hunting. I don't know about you young ones, but I'm hungry."

Ember sucked in a breath of stinging air. *'Oh, that's right. You have to hunt for yourself now, Ember. Might as well try to learn while you have someone nice on your side.'*

"We can try. I'm not great at it, but maybe you can help," she said.

Bracken smiled. "Odd old tomcat like me?" He laughed. "I'll see what I can do."

CHAPTER 24
CLOUD

Cloud yawned, stretched, then looked outside, where the storm had eased into a light snowfall. He nudged Songbird awake.

"Come on, it's time to move. We should try to go as fast as we can, but not too fast; we don't want anyone getting suspicious."

Songbird opened her eyes and licked her lips. "I don't know, Cloud. I've got a bad feeling about this. Maybe we shouldn't do it today, or at least not so soon. Lupine's probably going to be watching us more carefully right now. It's not safe. I think we should wait."

"Song, living here isn't safe. The East could come any day now and tear the Colony apart. Even if they don't, it may well fall apart on its own. I don't want to be here when either of those things happen."

She sighed. Her gaze fell on Kivyress, still sleeping peacefully beside her. "If it were just me and you, I'd be fine with taking the risks, but with Kivyress . . . I'm worried something will happen to her. I don't know if this is right, Cloud, and my head is telling me it isn't."

Cloud pinned back his ears. "I don't know. I get the feeling that today might be our last chance. If anyone catches us, I'm the one who will get punished. Kivyress is still a kitten, and one with a lot of potential. Lupine wouldn't hurt her."

"I know you're talking about me," Kivyress whispered, opening her eyes. "I don't want to slow us down. If you think we should try today, let's try today. I want to see Ember—and Hyrees too, I guess. And the sooner we get out, the sooner we can find a new home—maybe even find it before the next storm."

Songbird licked her lips again. "I guess you both have a point. Several points, actually. In addition to those, Ember and Hyrees can't stay in one place out there. We may lose them if we wait too long. If your feeling is right, and this is our last chance to escape, we should probably try to make it count. Right?"

Cloud nodded once. "Right. First, let's go get some food. Then we do everything like we planned. You both remember what you're supposed to do?"

"I do," Songbird said.

"Yes, sir," Kivyress replied.

"Good. Let's go."

I know you're nervous,' he thought as they left their family den for the last time. He looked over at Songbird, walking along beside him with her fur ruffled and her eyes still damp. *I'm scared, too. We all are. If we don't make it, there will be punishments, and if we do, there's no telling what we'll face in the Lowlands. It's a lot of uncertainty, I know. But I promise we'll make it out eventually. Whatever happens, we'll make it work. I'll make it work for us.'*

They ate their meals in silence. Every so often someone would come over to offer condolences. A few attempted to make reminiscent small talk. Cloud brushed them off. They didn't matter, not anymore, and he didn't feel like talking about Farlight.

"Hey, uh, excuse me," Lupine called after they finished. He stood atop his den, weak and scared-looking as ever. "I-I-I have some announcements to make. So if everyone could come over here before leaving for your a-assigned jobs, that would be great. Cloud, especially you."

Cloud sighed. "Let's go. It shouldn't take long."

He led the remnants of his family over to the gathering of cats. They sat down and waited for whatever the anxious commander needed to say.

"Y-you all know Dark's law states the Council should always have seven members in addition to a-a-a commander," Lupine said. "Yesterday we lost two members, along w-with my future successor. Today it's, ah, time t-to refill their positions. First off, Cloud, you-you've proven yourself invaluable to the success of this colony. I allow you back onto the C-Council as my advisor on the condition y-you keep your promise. You will not receive any credit benefits, but this work will be required of you until this war ends or you die."

Cloud grimaced. *'Ah, yes. And there's the appreciation I get for making things work. Oh well. They'll just have to figure out how to manage without me, because after today, I'm not coming back.'*

"Next, I-I appoint Rowan as the seventh member of the Council and my new future successor."

"Me? What?" Rowan mewed from somewhere in the crowd.

'Rowan? Why him, of all cats? I guess he'd be better than some though. Know what? I'm not even going to try to understand what you're trying to do here, because I no longer care.'

"I also assign him to be Cloud's new w-w-w . . . uhm, his new patrol partner. Cloud, you and him w-will patrol your usual route."

'Oh. You bobcat.'

"Songbird, y-you will, uh, group hunt this morning, and I-I'll take over Kivyress's training."

"What!" Songbird said.

"I-I'm sorry, Songbird, but it's for the better. A-a-announcements are over. Time for work, everyone."

Her fur raised. She turned to look at Cloud, eyes wide and jaw slack with terror. "What are we going to do now? Wait a day or two?" she hissed under her breath, pulling Kivyress closer to her side.

"They'll be more likely to expect that," Cloud replied. His mind raced, trying to work out how much the plan needed adjusting based on Lupine's orders.

Kivyress sighed and wiggled free. "You have a furball, I play 'where's Kivy,' and Dad pushes Rowan into the ravine. I think that's what Farlight would suggest," she whispered.

He smiled. "And we meet at the same place. That's my molly. I like that plan, though I'm not pushing Rowan into the ravine. I'll find another way to get there. Let's go to work."

"Kivyress, c-c-come here," Lupine said.

He climbed off of his den and walked toward them. As he approached, Cloud flattened his ears and fought back a growl.

Lupine shivered and shook his head. "L-look, Cloud, I'm sorry. I really am. I really don't know what else to do. You're, uh, you're the only one I know who c-can help set us straight and keep us safe. You helped Aspen get through some tough times, so I need you on the Council, and I also need you to train up Rowan. H-he's got a lot of potential, he just needs discipline, which I know you can give him because I've seen you do so."

"I will do whatever it takes for us to survive," Cloud said.

"Glad to hear it. I'm scared, Cloud. Scared as anyone else in the Colony. I-I-I'm just trying to keep everyone alive and together as much as I can. You know that, right?"

"You're doing the best you can do. Kivyress, go with him. Train hard, train well, and tell me about it later." Cloud turned to face Songbird and pressed his forehead against hers. "And Song, you be careful. I guess I should go find Rowan now."

"You be careful too," she whispered.

"Bye, Dad," Kivyress mewed. "See you later."

"You-you're all dealing with this surprisingly well. I-I'm impressed," Lupine said, eyes narrow. "Well, come on, Kivyress. Let's go."

Cloud and his family parted ways with bittersweet goodbyes, then he went to look for Rowan. He found him waiting beside the History Tree.

Rowan sat in the dirt, staring at his paws. "Tahg, this mooncycle has been a mess. I mean, me training to become commander? I'm not sure how I feel about that. We are at war, after all, and given what happened to Farlight . . . Is this really happening? And will I be good enough?" Rowan asked, more to himself than Cloud.

"If you train hard and learn to serve your colonymates, you will," he replied. "Now come on. We've got a lot of ground to cover."

He nodded for Rowan to follow.

Rowan jumped to his paws and pranced beside him. "Yes, of course. Thank you, sir."

The gentle snowfall had stopped, and the wall of clouds was breaking up, revealing cheerful blue skies—a little too cheerful.

Rowan chuckled nervously as they left the Glade. "You know, sir, I've been wanting to train under you for a long time. I, uh, wasn't expecting to get chosen for the Council, or to be the new commander-in-training for that matter. Today is . . . kind of crazy, isn't it? But after all the bad things that happened yesterday, I guess it's nice to get some good surprises. But, oh! And I really am sorry about what I did to Hyrees. I don't know what came over me, but I, uh, yeah. My dad was really disappointed when he found out."

Cloud sighed as they padded through the Northern Entrance. "I'm sure he was. Today's lesson is on appreciating silence. You are at your most alert when you aren't speaking. You can notice much more subtle things. For example, that cliff fungus you're about to step on."

Rowan stopped mid-step and looked around. "What? Where is it? Everything just looks like snow."

Cloud lifted a paw toward the lump of white in front of them. "Notice how the snow suddenly goes upward right here. It's the outline of fungus on a log."

"Ohhh, I see it now. Hey, you noticed that *while* talking."

"Yes, I did, because I practiced observing in silence. Now I want you to practice. Notice as much as you can without saying a word."

For a while, Rowan walked quietly, his eyes darting around, latching onto various things before moving on. Together they made it to the creek and began the patrol. Cloud glanced down at the ravine. The creek already had ice forming over it, with snow gathering on the icy patches.

'No, I'm definitely not pushing him in. I don't need to kill him just to get

out of here. I guess I'll just have to play into his enthusiasm.'

"You've done well, keeping your quiet. Would you like some more training? I promise this one will be more interesting."

His eyes lit up. "Oh! Yes. Yes, sir, that would be great."

Cloud smiled. "Alright then, son." Based on the look of pure awe on Rowan's face, he knew he had metaphorically placed his paws well. His jaw tensed. Aspen had used the same tactic on him on the evening of his death. He mentally shoved the thought away. "Let's begin. For this exercise, imagine you're patrolling alone. I'll go hide and wait for you, then jump out when you get close. When I do that, you fight me, and see if you can catch me in a scruff hold. Got it?"

"Yep. Got it. This is going to be fun," Rowan mewed.

Cloud chuffed. "Indeed. Now I'm going to go a decent way up, so don't expect to see me again for a little while. But don't worry, I won't go all the way to the log. That's really the only dangerous area of this patrol right now, and I don't want you there seemingly alone."

"Understood, sir."

"Okay, good. Now let's have some fun. Give me a count of twenty before you start moving again."

"Will do!"

Cloud offered him one last smile, then crawled into the thickest patch of bramble he could find. With the recent storm, it formed a snow tunnel of sorts with walls almost as thick as he was tall. He scurried out of the other end, careful to stay outside of Rowan's field of view. When he knew he was out of sight and earshot, he broke into a fast trot.

'We don't have much time. It's now or never. No going back. I just hope we all get there at roughly the same time. The longer any of us stays still, the more likely we are to get caught. Tahg, this plan has way too many variables. Maybe Song was right. What if we should've waited? There's too much at stake today.'

His stomach churned when he reached the lower forest. Songbird sat beside a large elm, but Kivyress was nowhere to be seen.

"Where's Kivy?" he asked.

"I don't know," she replied. "She may be on her way, or she might still be with Lupine. Cloud, what if something happens to her?"

Cloud clenched his jaw and sat down. "She'll be fine. She's a smart young cat, and it doesn't take much to outwit Lupine."

Songbird's tail twitched. Her breathing became shallow and rapid, and her fur stood on end. "What if someone finds us? If we don't get out soon, someone will. You know they will, and they'll find a way to make us stay. I don't even want to know how they'll do it, but they will if we don't make it out."

"Calm down, Song. She's going to make it here, and we're going to make it out. I'll make sure of it."

"I don't know. This doesn't seem right. What if we don't make it? And even if we do escape, what if they send someone after us?"

"They won't. We're going to be okay."

Yet even as he said it, he wondered what would happen if she was right. *'What if this is a mistake?'*

Underbrush rustled nearby, the wind blew against their backs, preventing them from smelling their stalker.

"Kivy, is that you?" he asked.

When no one replied, he lowered himself into a fighting stance.

Kivyress burst through the brambles, panting and breathing heavily. "We have to go! Lupine—Lupine and Colony . . . after us . . . they knew what we were planning. I don't know how, but . . . s-sorry . . . Dad."

Cloud and Songbird jumped to their paws. He didn't need to give a signal to get them moving. The deepness of the snow prevented them from running, so they pounced their way toward the border, he and Songbird matching paces with Kivyress to keep her from getting left behind. The crunching of extra paws against ice caught his ears. He looked over his shoulder. Several leaps away, Lupine and five others chased after them. Up ahead, a row of trees marked the Eastern Border. Crossing wouldn't necessarily mean safety, but it would be one step closer to freedom.

"If they catch us, I'll fight, and you run," he said. "If they kill me, they kill me, and if they don't, I'll find a way to get to you."

"No. We're doing this together," Songbird said between jumps.

"Song, I'd rather die knowing you and Kivy got out than die a complete failure."

"And I'd rather you not die at all."

"Get them! Go on. S-s-stop them!" Lupine called.

Movement behind the trees caught his peripheral vision. Something slammed into his side. Cloud toppled over. The snow broke his fall, but the blow itself knocked the air from his chest. His ears rung. The whole world seemed to move in slow motion; even the adrenaline charging up his bloodstream.

"No!" Songbird screeched. "Let go of me! Stop! No! Don't touch her!"

He looked up. A large agouti tomcat stood over him, glaring with disapproval.

"You leave him alone!" Kivyress snarled. She pounced onto the tom, releasing Cloud, who leaped to his paws.

The tom scruffed Kivyress and pushed her against the snow. Cloud pinned back his ears and looked around. Eight cats surrounded them only a leap away from the border—only a leap away from freedom.

'No. This can't, no, this cannot be happening. How could this have failed? I failed. It's over. It's done. We can't fight our way out of this, can we?'

His gaze fell on Songbird—terrified, now helpless, Songbird. Two cats kept her pinned, and the more she struggled against them, the farther she sank into the snow.

"I'm sorry," he whispered. "I should have listened to you."

"Cloud, you made a-a promise," Lupine said. "You're going to keep it."

"Fine. But let them go. You only need me, right?" Cloud replied.

"I-I'm no mastermind, Cloud, but even I can see how that would go. No, your family has to stay too. Come on, let's get the rebels back to the Glade."

The two cats holding Songbird let her go, but Kivyress remained trapped.

Songbird charged at the cat holding her daughter. "Let her go!"

A light sable molly jumped between them. "He won't hurt her, Songbird. It's just to keep you three from trying to escape again. I'm sorry it has to be this way, but it's what has to be done. For the good of the Colony. You know we can't afford deserters right now."

Songbird curled back her lips to reveal her fangs, but didn't act on the threat. She growled. "He'd better not hurt her."

Two other cats helped the tom carry Kivyress, now exhausted and defeated, back up the mountainside. Cloud walked in a daze. Everything felt shimmery, like a dream—no, a nightmare.

'I failed. I failed them again.' His slow, shaky breaths came out in puffs of steam. They swirled around through the air before realizing what a terrible place they were in and scattering. *'That was our last chance. He'll make sure it was. I won't even be able to tell her why we didn't come. Fox it! I'll never even see her again. Farlight is gone. Ember and Hyrees are gone. They're gone, and they won't come back. Why is this happening? Why can't I do anything right? Why can't I protect them? Because you're a failure, Cloud. A big, incompetent, stupid, fluffhead of a failure, and you've broken all of your promises.'*

A shiver rippled up his spine as his thoughts turned back to Ember, the kitten he loved so much that he'd risked his entire career and reputation twice to keep her alive. The kitten everyone thought—everyone knew—should have died. His heart sank in his chest.

'How different would things be right now if I had just killed that kitten back when Aspen first suggested it? It would've been an act of mercy, and I didn't even consider it. Now she's going to starve to death, and Hyrees is going to go down with her. Cats are dead and dying because of my incompetence, and now we're stuck here. If they hadn't expected us trying to escape, we would have escaped. I could have stopped it. I could have changed all of this if I hadn't been so soft. I even got a second chance, and I didn't take it. I . . .'

His eyes moistened. He blinked back the tears before they could fully form. *'Enough. What's done is done. There's no turning back now. I can't protect them here, but we'll just have to take whatever comes our way. It's one day at a time from now on.'*

When they entered the Glade, the cats carrying Kivyress didn't let go. Instead, they dragged her onto the meeting rocks beneath the History Tree and set her down, but they didn't release her scruff.

"Uh, Mom? Dad? What's going on?" Kivyress asked. "W-why isn't he letting go? Let go of me. Please!"

Cloud's throat tightened. "What are you doing? We're here. We can't leave. There's no reason to hold onto her. Let her go."

"Everyone i-in the Glade, get out of your dens," Lupine called.

Cloud's heart thumped against his chest. His jaw dropped open. *'Oh no.'*

"Lupine, no," Songbird said. Her eyes were wide, and her pupils were so dilated both of her eyes looked black. "No, whatever you're doing, stop. Don't hurt her. It was us. It was all us. Hurt us, hurt me, but don't touch her. Please. Please, let her go!"

Cloud growled. "If anyone hurts her, I swear I'm going to kill you. This was my idea. If anyone should be punished, it's me. Leave my daughter out of this."

Kivyress flattened her ears and tucked her tail. "Momma, w-what's happening? Don't let them hurt me. Don't let them hurt me!"

Lupine sucked in a deep breath as cats gathered around them. "A-as some of you may already know, Cloud and his family tried to abandon us this morning—and now, at the time we need him the most. W-we are the Western Colony. We have to stay together if we want to survive these trying times, so there will be no tolerance for deserters. It pains me t-to do this, but there must be consequences for this k-kind of crime. If for nothing else, then to prevent things like this from happening again."

He sighed, then nodded once to the cat standing beside him. "Do it."

Songbird lunged forward. "No! You will not lay a claw or a fang on my daughter! And I will personally—"

The molly tackled her. "You brought this on her. There's no point in fighting," she growled.

But Songbird fought anyway. While everyone was distracted, Cloud charged at the cat holding Kivyress. The tom lifted his claws to her neck, threatening to pierce her carotid artery. Kivyress tucked her tail even harder and looked up at him, trembling with terror. Cloud slid to a stop. "Don't do this," he growled. "Not to her. This is a mistake, Lupine."

"I agree. T-take him away, but make him watch," Lupine said.

His voice was quiet, subdued and regretful, but it didn't change the impact of his orders. They came to push him away. He bit, scratched, and fought as hard as he could, not caring how injured he got in the process. Claws and fangs pierced his sides, but every wound gave fuel to his fire.

"Mommy! Daddy! Please help me! Help!" Kivyress shouted over the yowls and snarls. "Stop! Stop attacking everyone. No! No, don't let them hurt me, Daddy! They want to hurt me. They want to—*No-no-no!*"

"Don't touch her!" Songbird screamed. "Let go of me!"

The cats pinned Cloud to the ground. One of them sank her teeth into his scruff. He clenched his jaw and ignored the pain. The cat holding Kivyress forced her to stand up, exposing her hind legs to the cat behind her. A single well-placed bite, and she would be lame for the rest of her life, trapping her in the Glade, and them all in the Western Colony.

Songbird let out a howl of pain, then fell silent.

"Mom! No!" Kivyress mewed.

With one last burst of adrenaline, Cloud tore free from his captors. He ran at the cat threatening his daughter. Someone caught his ankle. Pain flared in his hind paw. He fell hard on his chest. The air left his lungs with a painful *huff*. His paw burned as another cat's saliva and his own steaming blood rolled down it. He kicked, but before his paw even reached its target, they pinned him in place once again.

"No!" he yowled.

"Daddyyyy!" she shrieked.

The surreal feeling of detached dreaminess came back as the cat sank his fangs into Kivyress's lower leg. With a sickening muffled *snap*, the tendon broke. A moment before Kivyress screamed, his hearing cut out. The painful ring came back, drowning out noises he knew would be even more painful. He watched the agony on his daughter's face, helpless to do anything about it, and too frozen to look away or close his eyes.

"No," he whispered.

The cats got off of him. He ran toward Kivyress, but stopped short. "Songbird?"

Songbird lay motionless in the snow. He turned around and ran to her side. "Song! Song, are you okay? Please be okay. Come on."

She opened her eyes and spoke. He couldn't make out what she said, but a small amount of the tension in his chest loosened just knowing she was alive. She staggered to her paws, then stumbled past him.

'Oh. Kivyress.'

The tension came back. He hesitated, torn between helping Songbird and getting to his daughter as fast as he could. Songbird's mouth moved. The ringing drowned out her words. She gave up and shoved him forward.

'I'm going,' he thought. His stomach churned as he remembered the sound her leg had made. He tried to shake the noise away, but it refused to leave his head.

When he reached her side, she was curled up on the ground, crying. She kept her front paws wrapped around her ruined leg. Cloud darted around her, trying, frantically, to figure out what he needed to do.

"Kivyress. Kivy, I'm so sorry I let this happen. I should have listened. This is all my fault."

She closed her eyes and gritted her teeth together. Part of him hoped she would get up, shake it off, and be okay. The logical side of him, however, knew even the Colony itself would never be the same after this. Lupine hadn't only trapped them when he'd ordered Kivyress mutilated, he'd trapped the entire West. Trying to escape now meant risking the well-being of loved ones.

Whatever was stuffing up his ears vanished with a *click*. Noise came at him from everywhere. Cats murmured. Wind howled. His own heartbeat pounded in his head. Kivyress cried out in pain and purred between breaths. As hard as he tried, he couldn't tune any of it out. Somewhere in the back of his mind, he wondered if it was what Ember experienced on a daily basis.

Songbird dragged herself to them, then collapsed by Kivyress's side. Instead of speaking, she placed a paw against Kivyress's shoulder, purred, and groomed her neck. A large gash on her head made the side of her face slick with blood. Cloud glanced back at his own injuries. Bone showed in the wound on his paw, and the back of his neck stung.

With Songbird's closeness, he once again shut out the background noise and regained focus. "Fern," he said. "Where's Fern? We need a healer out here, and we need one now."

Fern pushed her way through the crowd. Silentstream followed. They examined their wounds, expressions getting tighter with each one.

"You all need to come to the den," Fern said. "I can't treat any of these out here. Can someone help me carry Kivyress? Silentstream, Songbird may need some help too."

The cat who had scruffed Kivyress bent over to pick her up.

Songbird jumped up. "Get away from her!"

She raked her claws across his face, slicing his eye in the process. He howled in pain and staggered backward as his blood dripped into the snow. The meeting rocks looked like a battle ground: flecks and splotches of red showcasing every wound and scuffle.

"I'm gonna hurt you for that," the cat growled.

Songbird put herself into a fighting stance. "You helped hurt my daughter. I should kill you for that."

"Stop! Everyone stop fighting. Get the w-wounded to the healers' den, *now*," Lupine said.

Cloud placed a paw on top of hers and rested his head against her side. "The fight is over, Song. We've lost."

She looked up at him. Her expression changed from that of a fearless warrior to a helpless prisoner. Tears formed in her eyes, but she tried her best to hide them.

Silentstream approached them, for once not chiding him, or even opening her mouth. She remained true to her namesake and let Songbird lean on her as she walked.

Cats came and lifted Kivyress to take her to the den. Cloud and Songbird followed behind them, keeping their heads up and fighting with their tears. They wouldn't be ashamed of their attempt to leave this place of war, death, and shattered dreams. Cloud grimaced in defiance. They had failed, yes, but they'd also succeeded in one small way: the air had changed, and the West had been given a wake-up call. The scent mixture of fear, anger, and disgust filled the Colony. They'd had enough, and Cloud decided he could use that.

———

"That wasn't very nice of you, you know," Rowan said. "You didn't have to trick me or leave me alone like that. You could've just taken me with you, or told me what was actually happening. I wouldn't have told. In fact, I might've even been able to help. I could've distracted them while you and your family escaped, but you don't trust me, so you lied and left me to patrol alone. Do you have any idea how terrifying it was? Are you even listening to me?"

The sunset cast the world around them into a bluish shadow. The moon loomed behind them, low in the Eastern sky.

Cloud sighed. "Yes. I'm listening."

Yet his thoughts wandered back to his injured daughter. Fern and the other healers had done the best they could; they'd given Kivyress herbs to help her sleep and had cleaned everyone's wounds. Despite Cloud's mauled paw, Lupine had insisted he finish his patrol with Rowan.

Rowan lowered his ears. "Well, aren't you going to say sorry? I could've died."

"I'm sorry," he replied. "There. Are you happy?"

"No. There's nothing to be happy about right now. My new mentor is a lying rebel, Commander Lupine just ordered a kitten to be permanently disabled, and my parents are still angry at me for no reason other than that I'm apparently a disappointment."

"But we *are* still alive," Cloud said, "which is significantly more useful than being dead. We may not be able to escape, but I can still bring about some kind of change."

Rowan huffed. "Maybe. I don't wanna talk anymore."

'You don't want to talk now, huh? Oh, never mind what I want.'

A branch snapped as they neared the log. Something scampered through the snow. Cloud stopped. "Who's there? Show yourself."

A black and white face popped out from behind a tree. "It's about time you showed up. I was beginning to get bored. Bit late for a patrol, ain't it?"

"You!" Cloud snarled. He lunged at the Rogue. "Oh, I'm glad you showed up. I need someone to kill right about now."

His paws slammed against Eclan's side, and he pinned him into the snow.

"Wait!" Eclan yowled. "You don't wanna kill me just yet. Your daughter sent me."

He hesitated. *'Ember? Working with a Rogue—this Rogue—already? That doesn't seem likely.'*

"Sure she did. And Jade sent me."

Eclan's eyes narrowed. "No, really. She sent me to get you and the rest of her family and bring you to her, but I'm guessing with your recent *developments* that's not gonna be happening. Was there anything you wanted to tell her, since you're now trapped and can't get to her yourself? I ain't doing this again, so make it count. Oh, and she's safe by the way. Her and that scrawny little tom she likes so much. Hyrees, I think it was. But they're both being taken care of by an old Outsider named Bracken and are doing just fine."

He got off of Eclan's side. *'Bracken? Sounds familiar. I've heard that name before, haven't I? Didn't Wren mention him once? Said he helped him out of a scrap in the Lowlands or something? I don't know, but if they really are being taken care of, I guess that's all that matters.'* Some of the achiness in his chest subsided. *'She's got someone looking after her. She's not going to starve. She doesn't have to patrol borders or fight this war anymore.'*

All at once he regretted thinking, even for a moment, that he should have killed her. Her and Hyrees had been sent, not to their deaths, but to their lives. They had the freedom he could only dream of, and they already had someone looking after them.

Eclan got to his paws. He shook the snow from his pelt and sniffed. "So, you got anything to say, or am I wasting my time?"

"Who are you? Do you know each other?" Rowan asked.

Eclan grimaced. "Wasn't talking to you, kitten."

Rowan flattened his ears and shrunk back. The muffled rushing of water grew louder in the absence of voices. Wind howled between the trees, and a few scattered birds chirped.

"Nothing, huh? Oh well. Guess I am wasting my time," Eclan said.

"No, wait," Cloud said. "Tell her to remember what I told her. Tell her I said not to worry about us. We're alive, but we won't be joining her. At least not for a while. And let her know I hope she finds her place out there. And that I love her. Don't forget that last one."

Eclan smirked. "I don't forget things, Cloud."

He climbed down to the log and began the hike across. Cloud padded to the edge of the ravine. "Hey, thanks. Never thought I'd say that to you."

"Never thought I'd hear you say it," Eclan replied.

He climbed up the other side of the ravine and vanished in the growing darkness. Cloud watched the forest for a few moments, then went back to walking, Rowan at his side.

'Well, I guess that's that.'

CHAPTER 25
EMBER

"You caught it, Ember. Now enjoy it, my friend," Bracken said.

Ember stared blankly at the scrawny squirrel in front of her. With Bracken's ever-patient guidance, she'd managed to catch and kill it, but she couldn't bring herself to eat it. Her appetite was gone.

On their first hunting trip after the blizzard, Bracken himself had caught a rabbit. With her poor hunting skills and Hyrees's worsening eyesight, they both went to bed hungry. Bracken had allowed them each a single bite of his meal, but no more. After eating the rest in front of them, he had given them a lecture on the importance of being a good hunter. It had reminded her of Tainu, and it had also made her further realize she no longer had the luxury of trying to avoid hunting. Without the West to provide for her, her only options were now kill or die. Even with half of her gone, and her fake paws stained with the blood of her kin, she didn't want to die quite yet.

She tilted her head sideways. The limp rodent didn't look any more appealing. She closed her eyes and sniffed it. Cold, wet fur and a faint stench of death met her nose. It didn't smell appealing, either. Ember sunk her teeth into its side. Her mind teleported her back to the moment she'd clamped her jaws around Whitehaze's throat. She spat it out and stumbled backward, panting. Overhead, the harsh morning sun reflected off of the snow, making everything look white. She closed her eyes. Spots flickered in her vision. Sky blue flashed in her head. She bit her tongue and tried to force herself to calm down.

"What's wrong? Does it taste diseased? Or is there something else bothering you?" Bracken asked.

He stepped closer, but didn't touch her. Ember shivered uncontrollably. *'What is wrong with me? I'm starving and I still can't eat? Why is this so hard?'*

"Ember," Bracken pressed.

She glanced at Hyrees for help, but he was curled up and sleeping beneath a nearby ledge.

"I don't . . . know," she whispered.

"Yes you do," he said. "You know, sometimes telling someone about what's bothering you puts things in perspective. Reminds you what really matters and what doesn't."

His tail twitched in distracting rhythm, making Ember want to pounce on it to make it stop.

"I don't even know you. You're nice, but I don't trust you with my problems yet. If I need to talk, I'll talk to Hyrees."

"You want to talk, but he's not awake to listen."

She snorted. "Actually, I don't want to talk to anyone right now. Except my family. My non-Hyrees family. Now please, leave me alone."

"Why wouldn't you want to talk with your mate?"

Ember wrinkled the bridge of her muzzle. The hot pinks of disgust flared in her mind, making her entire body feel uncomfortably warm. The shivering subsided. "I wish everyone would stop calling him that."

"Why?"

She stepped back. "What does it matter to you? Will you stop, please? Look, I know what can be done just knowing the right things about someone, and I'm not giving you the chance to do those things to me. So leave me alone."

He tilted his head. "You know, coggie, there is such a thing as just wanting to help. Not everyone is out to get you. The very same things someone can use to destroy you can also be used to build you up."

Sparks flared inside of her. *'That's true, but what does he want from me? Possibly my ETAg. He only offered to help after he heard what I could do with it. Well, you aren't getting it, no matter how indebted you make us. I never asked for your help. Except for with hunting. I did ask for help with that. So maybe I'll do you one favor.'*

"Thanks, but I'll, uhm, I'll do my own building up," she said.

Ember walked back over to the squirrel. It seemed a lot more inviting with the rare cerulean blues of defiance showing themselves in her mind. It was defiance toward Bracken, defiance toward her former colony, defiance toward death itself. She went back to eating, this time shoving out all thoughts of anyone from the West. Part of her wondered what it would be like to give up and let herself be taken by the snow, but the rest of her just wanted to be back at home, cuddled up with her family. Until they came, selfishness could keep her alive.

"Ah! And there he is," Bracken mewed.

Ember looked up from her squirrel. Eclan pounced through the gorge toward them.

Her stomach twisted into a knot. *'He's alone. Why is he alone? Wait, what if he didn't actually go to the West at all and just makes up some lie so I think he did? Tahg, I hate Rogues.'*

"Where are they?" she asked when he was within conversation distance.

"I'm afraid they're still in the West. Lupine 'n a bunch of others caught them and had one of your sister's legs disabled. They ain't coming. Least not for a while."

Cyan slithered in, venomous as a rattlesnake, causing her heart to race. She tried to shake it off, but it only grew stronger. "H-how do I know you're telling the truth?"

He smiled coldly. "I s'pose you'll have to trust me. Oh, and I spoke with Cloud, too. He said to remember what he told you, to not come back, and that he loves you and hopes you find your place out here. Things aren't looking so good in the Highlands, are they?"

She felt like crying again but no tears came. She didn't want to cry anymore. *'He's telling the truth, isn't he? They really aren't coming. Kivy, what did they do to you? Wait, what do I do now? I have to make my own decisions, and my decision-making skills have been lacking lately. Well, I can't go back, but I can't just abandon them, either. Maybe we can convince Jade to not attack anymore. Then we'll have saved them, and even if I don't ever see them again, I'll know they're safe. It's worth a try, at least. Then, if it doesn't work, we can go with Bracken.'*

"Ember, hey, listen coggie; are you okay?" Bracken asked.

Ember shook herself off. "Y-yeah, I'm fine."

"Are you sure about that?"

A strong breeze blew over the top of the gorge. Snow fell down from the ledge above them, making it appear to snow again. A few birds chirped and sang their morning songs.

Bracken looked at his paws. "Do you want to wake Hyrees up to discuss what you two will do next?"

"I already know what we're doing next. We're going to the East to stop a war."

He stepped backward, eyes wide. "Oh? Are you sure you want to get involved in this all over again? Down here you can choose not to fight. You can live whatever kind of life you wish, and yet you want to go back to the Colonies? I mean, I don't mean to sound harsh, but I'm not sure there's much a young cat like you can do to stop this. Colony Cats are stubborn. They aren't accepting of cats like us, and they don't change. They may well kill you."

She twitched her tail intentionally out of sync with Bracken's. "Eclan can get me—uhm, *us*—in. Can't you? You do stuff for Jade, right? She trusts you."

Eclan snorted. "You could say that. But who says I'm helping you? I've already got eight questions. I'd say that's enough for now."

"Oh come now, Eclan," Bracken said. "She wants to try to stop a war, and I can see I won't be able to stop her, so we might as well help her out. Even if it's an impossible goal, it is certainly a noble one. If you lead them both to the East, I'll tell you where to get some fine smoke-dried mint when you return.

Do we have a deal, my friend?"

Eclan smirked. "Better be the good stuff."

"Only the best."

Ember tilted her head. Bracken smiled at her, gentle and warm. The expression reminded her of her parents and filled her mind with maple-leaf orange.

'Maybe he really does just want to help. I'm still not going to share all my problems with him, but so far he hasn't asked anything of me, other than offering to take me to that group he keeps bringing up, and even then, it's just an offer, not a demand. To think we call Outsiders the uncivilized ones. He's been nicer to me in two days than most of the Colony has in almost two winters. Hum.' She looked down at her snow-covered paws. *'That's kind of sad.'*

"Well? You gonna go wake him up, kitten? If you wanna make it there by sunset, we gotta move," Eclan said.

"Oh? Oh. Okay, yes, I should. So you are taking us?" she asked.

"An easy, all but risk-free job escorting two kittens to the East in exchange for mint? Why wouldn't I? Besides, I need to check in with Jade." He stretched out, then sniffed a few times. "She's probably got a job or two for me by now, anyway."

Ember walked over to Hyrees. She pawed at his side. "Come on. Wake up. It's time to go."

He snorted and jerked awake. "What? Huh? Go where? Where are we going? I don't, uh, I don't see your parents."

"That's because they aren't coming. Now get up. We're going to the East."

The eerie calmness of her own voice sent a tiny shiver up her spine.

He got to his paws, then shook himself off, flinging snow in every direction. "Okay, I'm sorry, I must've still been half asleep, because I thought I heard you say we were going to the East."

"That's because I did. Come on. We have to get going. I'll explain on the way."

"Am I still asleep?"

"Probably not."

He flicked back his ears, tail thrashing like a snake. "So when was this discussed with me?"

"It wasn't." She nudged him forward. "Come on."

"What? Em, you can't just make decisions like that without me. We're a team, remember? We have to talk it over."

"A team, huh?" she growled. It came out louder than she'd intended and hurt her ears, but she couldn't bring herself to apologize. She paused for a moment to get her thoughts together. "Are we, though? Are we really? Because you said that, whenever I was safe, you were going to die. Where was *I* when you decided *that*? If you really are going to kill yourself, I'm the only one here with any kind of future. I get to decide where we go, and I've decided we're going to the East, and we're going to try to stop this war. You can come with me, and make sure I get there safely, or you can stay here and freeze. Your choice. Bye."

Hyrees stepped back. Ember padded up to where Eclan waited. Eclan gave her a squint-eyed look.

'I should say I'm sorry, but I think it'd probably be a lie. Hyrees, why can't you get yourself together? It's not easy figuring out what to say, and it makes me feel all pink inside having to yell at you like that.'

She closed her eyes, trying to fight back the beginnings of a headache. "Lead the way, sir."

Eclan chuckled. "You sure tell it like it is, don't you, kitten?"

"I don't have time to deal with him. My family can still be saved, and that's what's important right now."

"But . . . I'm your family too, Em. Right?" Hyrees asked. He slunk out from beneath the ledge, head and tail drooping.

She turned to face him. He looked back at her, small, thin, weak, blind, and all but defenseless. It made her chest ache as she realized how much damage he'd done to himself over the past mooncycle. The Hyrees she'd grown up with was almost dead, and this stranger of a tomcat was trying to kill him. "Yes, and I want to save you too, but I can only save you if you want to be saved, and you aren't making it any easier on me. So are you coming?"

He sighed. "Yes. I'm coming."

The cyan released its grip, sending her a gentle flood of relief. "Oh, good, it worked. You're a better speaker than I am, so for my plan to succeed, I kind of still need you. Let's go save the Valley."

He smiled and shook his head. "You Rogue. I guess we'll go save the Valley, then."

Ember's heart pounded with determination. Bright, misty orange created a fall forest of hope and renewed energy. She allowed herself to imagine Dark's Valley as it had once been: a place of peace without even the threat of war. It could see another era of prosperity brought about by their own minds, mouths, and paws. Things could go back to being as normal as they could be for everyone but them, and they would go on to be legends. At least they would in her fantasy. She knew deep down that they'd more likely disappear from history altogether once their work was done.

"Oh, Ember, I've been thinking about your plight. I'd like to offer one last word of advice before you go," Bracken said. "Try suggesting to Jade that she send an ambassador to the West. A cat she trusts, a few guards, and valuable gifts. The ambassador can work out a new peace treaty. Then the Colonies will know the war is over. It might not work, but it could be a worthwhile option to consider. I don't know about the Colonies, but gifts do tend to work here in the Lowlands." He chuffed softly. "Or perhaps you already have a plan."

"Well, I mean, I do, but it's really loose right now. I think I might do that. Or Hyrees might. I'm not very good at that kind of thing. First things first, we have to convince her we're not spies. Otherwise she might think the West set up an ambush or something, which, uh, would be ironic, but yeah, thanks. Thank you for everything, Bracken."

He dipped his head. "Yes, good thinking. That would indeed be bad. And an unfortunate way to die. It's been a pleasure. Take care, both of you, and when you're done, please do come join me again. That is, of course, if you don't end up staying in the East. I'd imagine Jade would want the kind of power you're capable of giving her. Don't let anyone trap you, Ember. The one at the top should always have more freedom. And less. You're above them all. Remember that."

Ember leaned away from him and bit her tongue as the silver came back. "Uhm . . . okay. Uh, yeah. See you later, maybe?"

Hyrees pawed at her side, stretching awkwardly to avoid the bionic skin coating her shoulder pieces. "Are we going, or what?"

She focused her attention on Hyrees, but no matter how hard she tried, she couldn't bring back the orange he so often evoked. Instead she made herself imagine the color. "Yes. Yep. We're going. Lead the way, Eclan. Take us to our enemies."

As they padded up the slope leading out of the gorge, Bracken yowled, "Farewell, my friends."

Ember tried her best to ignore him. She didn't want to make the walk away last any longer than it needed to.

"Take us to our enemies?" Hyrees asked as they re-entered the forest. "Oh yeah, that's right. The Colonies are at war, so she might actually kill us. What if we make things worse? Why don't we just go back and let Bracken take us to this group of his? Because they are not going to kill you. Just saying."

"For someone who wants to die, you sure are afraid of dying."

"I'm afraid of you dying and me having to watch."

"Look, we've already lost everything. All we have left to lose is our lives, but we could gain so much if we take some risks. We could gain my family's freedom. If Bracken's plan works, there might even be meetings again. Things really could go back to normal, and we could—well, sort of . . . never mind. I'm rambling and no one cares."

Hyrees sighed and lowered his head. After a few moments of silence, he turned to look in her direction, eyes unfocused. "No, I do care, I'm just not always the best at expressing it. I love you, Ember. I haven't said it nearly as much as I've been meaning to, and I'm sorry about that. This is what matters right now, and I'm the one who should be quiet."

Ember paused for a moment. The orange still refused to return to her mind. Hyrees and Eclan kept walking, ignoring her hesitation. Ember shook her head and returned to Hyrees's side. "Yeah," she said, voice barely louder than a whisper. "I love you too."

For a while, no one spoke. At midday, they stopped for a hunting break. Eclan caught a mouse, but Ember and Hyrees continued onward without a meal. As they walked, she tried to explain her plan. It was difficult enough trying to find the right words, but Hyrees made it even more exhausting of a struggle by asking her questions every few moments, which she then had to come up with replies for on the spot. It didn't help that most of his questions were about things she had yet to bring up and would have already told him if he hadn't interrupted.

"But what if something bad happens after we get there, and they blame it on us?" he asked.

Ember growled. *'What happens if I just stop talking? Will he return the favor?'*

"Are you ignoring me?"

'Guess not. I'll let you figure that one out, mastermind.'

"Hey, why are you ignoring me? I don't understand. What did I do wrong?"

An oily smear appeared in her mind's eye. *'You've answered your own question. I don't need to. Oh, look, the ground is really starting to slope up. We're probably on the Eastern Mountain now.'*

"Are you even listening to me?"

She looked at him and tilted her head, trying to look like an innocent, naive kitten. One of her front paws hit a patch of ice and slid out from beneath her. Momentum made her other paws slip. She slammed into the hard-packed snow chin first. The impact made her snout burn.

"Ow," she mumbled.

Hyrees stopped. "Oh! Em, are you okay?"

He nuzzled her ribs as she got up. Ember shook herself off. "Y-yeah, I'm fine. I, uh, I don't really feel like talking anymore."

Her gaze wandered past Hyrees, through the trees, to land on the faint

Western horizon. The warm reds, oranges, and yellows of the sunset peered back at her through magnificent blue clouds. The cloud breaks closest to the sun shimmered like flecks of gold in a creek, but they shone ten times brighter and a thousand times more massive. The light from it stung her eyes, yet was too beautiful to look away from. She blinked furiously in an attempt to get around the pain. It didn't work, so she turned back to the shadows.

'I guess you're just not meant for the light, Ember,' she thought. *'Oh well. Distant stars are pretty, too.'*

"C'mon, kittens, keep moving. We're getting close. The border's just up ahead," Eclan growled.

Her heart thumped against her chest. *'Already? Tahg, it's coming.'*

She stepped up to join Eclan. The leg that had slipped didn't respond. She stumbled again. Her prosthetics whirred in protest as she scrambled to find her balance. She caught herself with her undamaged paws a clawlength away from hitting the snow again.

"Okay, what's going on here?" she mewed. "Leg, what is wrong with you?" She sent a mental signal for it to lift. A few moments later, it obeyed. *'Ah. Something must've gotten pulled loose. Hopefully it can fix itself soon, because I don't need a limp right now. Can something please go right for once?'*

"Whatever's wrong with it, you'd better get it fixed, because I ain't staying on the outskirts of the East after nightfall. You might think your colony's defenses are tough, but the East is on another level entirely," Eclan said.

"Oi! Who's out there? You're dangerously close to Eastern territory, whoever you are, so I suggest you either scram or show yourself," a voice called.

Ember's ears perked up. *'Echo? Maybe things are starting to work out.'*

"It's me," Eclan shouted. "An' I brought you some guests."

"Eclan?" Echo's face appeared through the trees. "Oh. Mum's been expecting you. You're late. And what do you mean 'guests'?"

A similarly colored, shorter-furred tomcat trotted beside her. "Is that—oh tahg, it is! Ember! You're alive!" Shard broke into a run. "I thought I'd killed you, I did. Kept me up at night for ages, but here you are, and you're—" He slid to a stop. "A machine? What? What happened to you? Oh, did I cause that? Oh no, I'm so sorry. I'm sorry, I really am. Oh no. Now I've got another thing to keep me up at night wi—"

"AAAAAGGGH!" Echo yowled. She charged toward them. "You killed her! You killed Tainu, you filthy Westerner! I'll kill you!"

Ember's eyes widened. *'Oh, she's talking about me. And she's angry at me. Understandable, but inconvenient. Wait, does she actually want to kill me?'*

"Uhm, Ember, you might want to run," Hyrees said.

Echo snarled as she neared them. Ember stepped back. *'Most likely yes.'*

She darted left, hopping on three legs. Echo landed where she'd been a moment before. Eclan jumped between them.

Echo snarled again. "Move out of the way, Eclan." Her eyes locked onto Ember's. "Oh, I'm going to kill you until you're dead, and burn all your bones, and whatever in the forest your hideous legs have become, too."

"Whoa, whoa, whoa, easy," Eclan hissed. "You don't wanna kill this one, Echo. Besides, she's been punished enough already. She got exiled from the West, and half the cats she cares about are dead. Your mom'll want her alive. I'm doing you a favor by telling you this. Trust me."

"I don't trust you, actually, and I don't give a bird dropping about what mum wants. You killed half of my family when you killed Tainu, Ember. You deserve to die."

'Probably, but my family doesn't. Kivy didn't do anything, and who knows what's happened to her. I have to at least live long enough to try to protect her. After that, you can kill us all you want. One of us won't even mind so long as you kill him first.' Ember pinned back her ears and lowered her head, trying to look submissive. "I didn't mean to kill her. We were fighting, and it was an accident. Echo, she was my family too. When I killed her, I killed one of my closest friends. I can't even think about her without feeling sick about myself."

"Is that supposed to make me feel better?" she growled. "Because it's not working."

"No, wait, don't kill her! We have to save our colony, and I can't do it alone," Hyrees said.

Echo shoved Eclan into the snow, then lunged at her. Ember jumped sideways. One of her paws hit a hidden stone, sending a tiny pain signal into her nervous system.

Echo landed hard against the ice. She jumped up and shook herself off. "Hold still, you bloody, filthy, murdering Westerner!"

"Echo, wait!" Shard called. He ran toward them. "Don't, don't, please don't kill her. You can't kill her yet. I only just found out she survived the Wolf Trail, and I don't want you to be a killer. Well, I mean, I know you're a hunter and all, so you're a deer killer, yes, but I don't want you to be a cat killer. I don't want to have nightmares about you. And they're the only other friends I have, you know. Killing them will bring me back down to just you. And maybe Sunshine, but that's about it. I don't want that. I want to have friends. In the plural. And they're your friends too, remember?" He positioned himself between them, head low and tail tucked. "They are, uh, your-your friends too, aren't they?"

Echo groaned and turned away. "Fine. We'll take you to Mum. But I'm only doing this for you, Shard. They are *not* my friends, and *she* is a filthy, murdering weirdo who has never been my friend. They can be your friends as long as you like, but I promise, the moment you stop being friends, I'm going to kill her. So, Westerner, this means you'd better treat my brother like he's the only one keeping you alive, because he is."

"Great. Thanks. I'll . . . uh, I'll try my best," Ember said. She looked at Shard and smiled. "And thank you, too." She lowered her voice so that only he could hear. "She's not joking, is she? W-would she really kill us? Me and Hyrees, that is. I know she wouldn't kill you."

"I-I don't know. Maybe, maybe not, but it's definitely possible. Wait, why are you here? Eclan said you were . . . exiled? Exiled for what, exactly? And what did Hyrees mean by you two trying to save your colony? How can you do that here? I'm not sure I follow what exactly is going on."

'You should probably tell the truth, Ember. If you make up a lie, it won't

be any good, and if you don't say anything, they'll get suspicious. Fox it, Eclan. Hyrees, you too. Why did you two have to speak? That was not supposed to get mentioned yet.'

"You'd better answer him, wildcat," Echo growled.

Ember let a tiny puff of air escape her mouth. "It's a long story, but—"

Echo shoved her forward. "Tell it on the way, then. We're wasting our time standing around like useless elk."

'Please don't be mad at me. Your mouth is part of the reason they want to know in the first place. It can give them the answers.' She swallowed hard and groaned softly as her own feet sent little jolts of pain through her skull. Walking on three legs ruined her concentration. "Hyrees, you're better at these things than I am. Tell them everything. Might as well be honest."

"Ah, uh," Hyrees stuttered. "Well, it *is* a long story, so, you know, fair warning."

"Listen, fluffhead," Echo said, "I don't *care* how bloody long it is, or which one of you tells it. I want to know what it is you cats did to get you both thrown out of the West, and what ridiculous idea brought you here, in this pathetic state, in the middle of a possible war between our colonies. Eclan, you're coming too. Get a move on, all of you."

Eclan growled under his breath and ran to catch up with them. As they walked, Hyrees began their story with a loose account of the day Ember had come home. Ember herself turned her attention back to her faulty leg.

'Thai, can you please figure out what's going on with this thing? I really need to get it fixed as soon as possible. Maybe direct a little extra power to the self-healing mechanisms. Is that even possible?'

[It would appear that a wire has been pulled loose. You really should look where you're going, Ember. That ice would have been visible, had you continued calculating your steps in your usual manner.]

'Not helping, Thai. Can you do something to fix it? I need all of my paws right now. They aren't going to take in two cast-out cripples from their

enemies. I have to be useful enough to get both myself and Hyrees in safely.'

[Understood. Unfortunately, it would seem the wire may be too loose to reconfigure correctly. Fixing it would require mechanical surgery. Michelle designed them. Maybe she would be able to fix it. Would you like to try calling her again?]

Ember moaned. *'Fine, yes, but I don't think she's going to answer. I'm pretty sure the humans have abandoned us.'*

[I don't think they would abandon us, Ember. Michelle is my creator and your savior. She wouldn't leave us by choice. I will call her now.]
[calling]
[Oh. Her number is still unavailable. Well, it was worth a try.]

The jostling motion of hopping along on three legs hurt her head a little more with each step, and the equally jarring reminder of the humans' desertion made a dull ache seep into her temples. *'I hope they're okay. They did say they were bending rules to take me here. What if they got hurt because of me? Well, either way, I told you. We're on our own. I'm on my own. I have to fix myself. Do you know how to go about securing the wire? Maybe you could tell me what to do. I don't have thumbs, but I know how to use my paws, even if I've only got one to work with right now.'*

[Yes, it is entirely possible they've been injured or killed because of you. And yes, I should be able to walk you through a repair. I don't think this is the time for fixing yourself, though. The repair work may take several hours to complete, depending on your dexterity. I suggest finding someplace safer.]

She groaned again. *'This is not how I was hoping today would go. That's just the theme of the mooncycle, isn't it?'*

"You *killed* Whitehaze? You killed someone else?"

Echo's snarl sent her back into the external world. A shiver crept up her spine, raising her fur with it.

"And you expect us to take you in?" she continued. "A cat from an enemy colony who also happens to be wanted for two murders? Hah! You must be out of your mind. I just hope Mum lets me be the executioner."

"Oh, please no," Shard said. "Is it true, Ember? Did you really kill him?"

"Whitehaze killed my brother," Hyrees growled. "He betrayed our colony. He was working with you, wasn't he?"

"What are you talking about?" Echo snapped. "He's never worked with us. In fact, he bloody well hated us, and we hated him. I'm glad he's gone, but that doesn't change the fact that *she's* a murdering wildcat."

Ember glanced at Hyrees, who looked back at her with an unreadable expression. Silver and purple wavered behind her eyes as her mind processed Echo's words.

'You hated him specifically? But I thought you weren't allowed to speak to any of the council members. What is going on here? Because something is definitely not lining up.'

"Did you really kill him?" Shard asked again.

She sighed. "Yes. I killed him. I don't know why, but I did it, and everything fell apart after that. Like Hyrees said, we think he killed Farlight, but . . . we're not sure."

Shard pinned back his ears. "Oh. Uh, oh. S-so why are you here now?"

"My family," she replied. "We've come here as a last resort to try to prevent them from being killed, but everything else has gone wrong, so this probably will too."

"Don't say that. Killer or not, I'll stand for you, Ember. You're still my friend, and I don't say that lightly. Tainu was my friend, too. It hurt when you killed her. But I nearly killed you, and that led to you needing machine legs, so we're even enough. I guess. And, of course, I'm also standing for Hyrees. Hyrees, you're probably the closest friend I have that I'm not related to, you know. Ah, no-no offense Ember. Wait, we *are* still friends, right?"

"Yeah, of course," Hyrees said.

"Oh, brilliant. My opinion isn't worth much, I'm afraid, but I can still try to help. Better than nothing, I suppose. To be honest, I hate all this warring and killing and such. It's not necessary, really. If you, or I, or us working together can put an end to it, well, I'll do almost anything."

Ember sucked in a deep breath and organized her thoughts. "Thank you, Shard. I'm glad you're okay with helping us, even after everything that's happened. And that's actually what we're here for: ending the war."

He smiled. "Well, if you do, that would be the absolute best thing, it would."

"I somehow doubt Mum will listen to a couple of Westerners right now, but by all means try," Echo said.

They all fell silent. The breeze cut through their fur, causing Ember's heating grid to glow brighter. Shard stared at her but said nothing. Several leaps ahead, the ground disappeared at what appeared to be the mountain crest. Based on past experiences and the positions of the trees, she deduced it to be a false summit. As they climbed, more mountain appeared beyond the lump of earth, confirming her suspicions. She sighed softly. The sunset still flared behind them, sending light bouncing off of the ice and snow. Ember's jaw tensed; her stomach growled, and her gaze blurred out of focus. She yawned and fought to keep herself awake.

The ground leveled off, so she stopped to blink the tiredness from her eyes. A thick tangle of bramble, similar to the one guarding Starcross's Gorge, stretched out in front of them.

"Huh. It's like a natural abatis," she said, more to herself than anyone else.

"Keep moving," Echo growled.

Echo led them through a small break in the wall. When they reached the other side, Ember stopped again, mouth dropping open as pristine white awe filled her head. A giant crack opened up the side of the mountain, creating an enormous half-cave filled with rocks and cats. The setting sun illuminated it, making the entrances of two offshooting caverns visible. Near the southern edge of it, several cats rested inside a patch of wall covered from top to

392

bottom with a network of holes and passageways. Five fire pits lined the outer edges of the half-chamber. Only three were lit, and two of them still had protective clay coverings, possibly reinforced originals from Forestfire's time.

A few leaps away, a tomcat lapped water from a steaming spring. Three kittens chased each other around, their mother watching from atop a nearby boulder. A group of hunters dragged a deer carcass into the larger cave.

Ember tilted her head. *'It looks so different, yet at the same time, it kind of reminds me of home. It's like the West, but the location is better. Life continues on, I guess.'*

"Wow," Hyrees said. "I always imagined it being just a little dip in the mountain or something. I didn't even know rocks could form like that. Heh, my eyesight might not be great, but tahg, this still looks amazing."

"Well, technically it was eroded away by water and other things, like wind, and ice, which I guess really counts as water too," Ember said. "It doesn't get formed like that; it gets carved, like clay. The mountain might have even split during an earthquake, speeding up the process. I learned about those a few days ago, by the way. Back when things were okay. They don't happen here very often. At least big ones, the ones that do that, don't. But either way, it's impressive, and I like it." She realized they were staring at her. "What? I found it interesting and thought y'all might too."

Echo snorted. "Like I said: murdering weirdo. Now come on. Let's find Mum and get this over with. Oh, and welcome to the Rift. Now follow me."

"Wait," Hyrees said. "I recognize that smell. Were those red things back in the thicket snake berries? Seems a little close, doesn't it?"

"Yes, and I recommend you stay away from them. We've lost enough fluffheaded kittens to those."

As they made their way into the heart of the Rift, more and more cats noticed them, or rather, *her.* Noisy, glowing mechanical legs made blending in impossible, and their glares caused little waves of silver to oscillate in her mind. She cowered under the lake of piercing green and blue eyes. *'Okay, this is it. We're in the East. No turning back. No turning back. No . . . Oh no, this was a terrible idea. Didn't Dad say to forget the Colonies? As in plural? As*

*in West and East? Ohhh, this is stupid. Me and my impulsive self are about
to get us killed. Lot of good that'll do.'*

They stopped in front of a large, pointed rock. Ember let her gaze follow it
to its peak, then continued upward to where the Rift's massive stone ceiling
appeared to glow in the fading sunlight.

"Hey, Mum!" Echo called, voice rather appropriately echoing. "I don't
know why you're still bothering with him, but Eclan is back. Oh, and this time
he's brought friends. He said you'd want them alive, so I've spared them. For
now. They're both Westerners, by the way, and one's part machine and all
murderer."

"You really do have to excuse her," Shard whispered. "I'm sure you can
imagine why, but she's still pretty sore about what you did, Ember. Tainu and
her were close. Really close. In fact, I sometimes wonder if she liked her more
than she likes me. It, er, kind of breaks my heart to see her like this, though. I
hope you can both forgive us. Me for nearly killing you, Ember, that is, and
her for not forgiving you. I, uh, guess we, uhm, really all have-have reasons to
be angry, but . . ."

Hyrees placed a paw on Shard's. "I forgive you. There's nothing for you to
be sorry about. I think she likes being like this, with the robot parts, and the
ETAg and such; and if she were listening right now, I'm sure she'd forgive
you too."

An oil slick coated her imagination as she turned her attention back to the
cats beside her. "Just because I'm looking at the cave doesn't mean I'm not
listening. Believe it or not, I actually am capable of multitasking. But yes, I do
forgive you, and, like my overly assuming companion said, I like my
renovated body. Or at the very least, I don't mind it. The pros and cons
balance each other out, I think. I may not be able to clawmark, but I can tell
you the answer to almost anything. And I also need to perform my own
mechanical surgery, apparently."

"Hyrees and Ember?"

Everyone turned to look at the rock. On its pinnacle sat a large tabby. Her
milky green eyes glared down at them, sending a chill up Ember's spine.

"When she said we had guests, I hardly expected you two," Jade said. "I doubt Lupine would send either of you on any missions. You've come on your own. Why? Also, why are your legs glowing?"

"Because I'm cold, ma'am," Ember replied.

"Oh? How . . . unique."

Ember nudged Hyrees's side. He shot her a look that was decidedly not friendly.

"Whitehaze killed my brother, so Ember killed him," he said. "We were exiled from the West because of it. We've come here to try to work out some kind of deal to protect what little family we have left, and maybe even stop you from attacking again. You probably already know this, but the West isn't planning on coming after you. They're just fortifying and defending. Nothing offensive at all."

"Again? Attacking again? I don't know what your new commander told you, but we did not attack your cats or kill Commander Aspen. We were the ones ambushed, not the West. There's no reason for us to attack, before the ambush, or even now. I never intend to launch an offensive. War risks the lives of my kin. As commander, I cannot put them in danger by forcing them across the Valley to fight a needless battle."

"Wait, so we aren't actually fighting anymore?" Shard asked.

Ember's eyes widened. Hopeful misty orange forced away most of the silver. *'Tahg, you are brilliant.'*

"Well, that would've been nice to know. Why don't I get told anything around here? It's bloody ridiculous, it is," he said with a huff.

"You would have been told if you'd come to the meeting like you were supposed to," Jade said.

"So why declare war in the first place?" Hyrees asked.

"To keep the West on their side of the Valley, right?" Ember said.

"Exactly," Jade said. "I fear Lupine may have tricked your colony into thinking we're the bad ones. Farlight was meant to replace him, wasn't he? It's entirely possible Lupine himself ordered the future commander's death. I assure you, I had nothing to do with it."

The silver came back. *'Wait, that doesn't entirely line up. Does it? He mourned Farlight too, didn't he? Or was it just an act? What if Jade is lying about something? I don't know what to believe anymore, but what if she's right? If Lupine really did do all of this to get in charge, why bother with the . . . fear manipulation. Oh no. And they're stuck there, too.'* She bit her tongue. *'At least they're safe, more or less, but what do I do now?'*

"So, Ember, you said you could answer any question, didn't you?" Jade asked.

The query caught her off guard. "Uhm, yeah, this thing, er, around my neck can, at least. And *almost* any. Not any. There's, uh, a difference."

"I take it you're both in need of a home?"

"I mean, you could say that, yes."

Jade smiled. "Can you tell me if it will snow tomorrow?"

Ember pinned back her ears as her thoughts flared with creamy indignation. "This is a highly advanced piece of human technology, which is capable of anything from telling you the exact distance between the Earth and the sun, to reciting an infinite number that can be used to calculate the area of a circle. Why does everyone want to use it to ask about the weather?"

Jade tilted her head. "Is that a 'yes,' then?"

She sighed. "Yes, ma'am. I, uh, can use it to predict the weather. It'll be partly cloudy tomorrow; I already checked."

Jade chuckled. "Very well." She stood up, striped tail twitching. "Welcome to the East."

CHAPTER 26
EMBER

"So wait," Ember mewed, "you're actually letting us stay? Just like that? You're not concerned about us being spies or anything?"

"Ember, what are you doing? Don't question it—you'll get us both killed," Hyrees said.

"Why would I bring any of this up if we actually were spies? I just want to know what she wants from us. You saying things like 'don't question it' is what really might get us killed."

Jade chuffed. "She's right; I do have conditions that must be met in order for you both to stay. Both of you must work, and you, Ember, must provide me with answers to any question I ask. If you're both willing to follow direct orders and do your own parts, you will both be welcomed into the Colony as native-born Easterners." She climbed down her rock and nodded once. "Follow me. I'll show you around until Falcon shows up. Shard and Echo, you are dismissed."

"What? So we're taking them in—our enemies—just like that? They are dangerous, Mum. I'm warning you now; you let them in and it'll be the downfall of the Colony," Echo said.

"Echo, please don't say that. I know it hurts, but it's time to move on. Come on. We should probably just do as she says," Shard whispered.

"I said you are dismissed," Jade said. "Go assist today's hunters with their kill. Oh, and get Falcon to come help me orient our guests."

Echo growled. Shard pushed her into motion. The two littermates slunk toward the nearest cave opening, then vanished into the shadows.

Jade shook her head. "Ignore them. I don't quite know what is wrong with them, but believe me; I've tried fixing them. It didn't work, and it would seem I've grown too attached to throw them out, but that is beyond the point. So, do we have a deal, or not?"

"Yes," Hyrees said, tail thrashing. "Yes, we have a deal."

He glanced in Ember's direction with a narrow-eyed look she knew meant something. She tried copying his brief expression, but it didn't trigger anything except a confused indigo. *Why do you still expect me to know what you're trying to say when you speak with your face? Haven't you known me long enough to know better?'*

"Yes, I guess we can do that. Depending on the questions you want me to answer, of course. I don't want to betray my original colony or anything like that, even if they did exile me. Also, what would happen if we suddenly refused to do something? Not that I'm planning to disobey orders. I just want to know exactly what this deal means."

"If neither of you are contributing to the East, you'll both be made to leave," Jade replied. "I understand your concerns, Ember, but there's no need to worry. So long as the West stays where it belongs, I have no further interest in them. Now, are you coming, or not?"

"Yes, ma'am. We accept the offer and are coming," Hyrees said, giving her another unreadable glare.

He nudged her side. She bit her tongue and limped closer to Jade, who led them farther into the Rift. Hyrees fell back to match her pace.

"From now on, let me do the talking," he whispered.

"But what if the East turns out to be no better than the West?" she asked, matching his tone. "I want to consider all of our options. This option is more secure, but at what cost? We might be giving up our freedom all over again. I'm not sure I want that. They aren't planning on attacking, so we don't have to be here. Remember, we have offers from both Bracken and Jade to consider. We could also try living alone, but something tells me that might not work so well."

He sighed. "Let's just stay here for a while and see how we like it, okay? I'm tired of all this walking. A good nap would be nice right about now." His gaze locked onto something on or in the stone wall as they passed by. "Oh, hey, you've got this, right? Because that cleft up there looks like a lovely place to spend the rest of my life. What do you think?"

"I think you should stop talking and listen."

Jade stopped at the opening of a small cavern. "The cave you saw my kittens enter is the food storage. It is where you will receive your rations. Rations are given out at the first light and the last. If you aren't there on time, you don't get fed. The second cave, which you see in front of you right here, is the den of healing. I recommend going in there to get that limp taken care of, Ember."

"Heh," Ember said. "If only it were that easy. I have machines for legs. I don't think your healers have much experience with reconnecting loose wires. I'll fix myself tonight, if you're worried."

"Ah. Yes, of course. Glowing machine legs. The humans certainly are a . . . creative bunch, aren't they? We should continue with your introduction to the Rift."

The way she spoke the word 'humans' sent a shiver up Ember's spine.

"Ember, daughter of Cloud?" a new voice said. A grey tabby padded toward them, his eyes narrow. "I thought you were dead, kitten, but I can see the humans were kind enough to you. Or at least the closest thing to kindness they're capable of. Suspicious how they let you go. Usually they aren't so compassionate."

Jade straightened herself up and raised her tail in greeting. "Ah, there you are, Falcon. Could you finish showing these two around? And maybe assign them sleeping quarters and jobs too, once you find out what they're best at and which shift they'll each be taking. Eclan and I have important business to discuss." She walked closer to her advisor, and as they passed each other, Jade lowered her voice. "Keep them busy until I return."

He nodded in reply.

The silver in Ember's mind grew brighter. *'I wasn't supposed to hear that, was I? Wait a moment—whether she's telling the truth or not, Eclan is still her messenger and spy. She said she's not directly attacking them, but that doesn't mean she's not still ripping them apart.'*

Falcon stepped in front of them. "Alright then, let's go have a look around. Oh, wait a moment. Are you Hyrees, son of Wren?"

"Yes," Hyrees whispered.

"You have my condolences about your father. I know words can't bring him back, but I hope they can at least bring you some comfort."

Hyrees looked at his paws. "Thank you, sir. But I'd rather not talk about him, or anyone else from back in the West."

"I understand, Hyrees, and will respect your wish. Now come," Falcon said. He led them along the back of the Rift, toward the wall of tunnels. "We don't have dens here in the East, but we do have quarters. That great expanse of tunnels over there is where each and every cat sleeps, with the exception of Jade and her kittens. I'll show you which places are open once you both decide on jobs and shifts. What can each of you do?"

"I was training to be a clayworker back when we were still in the West. If possible, I'd like to continue my training. My eyesight might not be great, but I can still use my claws pretty decently," Hyrees said.

"Here clayworkers are also tasked with finding precious stones around Gale Springs. You won't be able to do that with those eyes of yours. Do you think you would make a good healer?"

Hyrees's ears drooped. "I've never been a healer before, but I guess I'd be willing to try."

His words sent Ember a tiny wave of dull, misty orange. *'Maybe you'll like being a healer. Wait, you just gave me a color. Maybe I am starting to get it.'*

She headbutted his neck. "Thank you, Hyrees!"

He stumbled sideways. "Whoa! Uh, you're welcome, I guess? I didn't realize you wanted me to be a healer so badly."

She laughed softly, but didn't bother explaining. They wouldn't understand anyway, so why waste breath?

"So, strange young molly, what about you? What do you do?" Falcon asked.

"Well, once I get this leg fixed, I can work border patrol. I'm not much of a hunter, or anything else, really, but I know how to fight. Sort of," she replied.

"Sort of? What do you mean?"

"How good of a fighter I am depends on how you define a good fighter. I'm not very strong, but I am quick. I work best with a stronger but slower partner. Then our deficiencies cancel each other out. I, uh, will be getting a partner, right?"

Falcon cocked an ear and stopped beneath the wall of clefts. "Yes, if you become a border guard, you will get assigned a partner. Now, these are the quarters. What shift each of you chooses will determine which ones are available. What time would each of you feel more comfortable working— night or day?"

"There's a night shift?" Ember asked. She sniffed the nearest quarter. It appeared to continue deep into the mountain, connecting with other quarters through holes leading to the upper levels. Something about the wall's uniquely porous structure made her shiver. "As in, you actually have cats working each job at night, rather than just having night guards?"

"Yes. This colony is never entirely asleep. There are always fresh cats available to attend to any need anyone might have. That's the reason our rations are given out at sunrise and sunset. They're the overlap times when everyone is awake and in the Rift. Now answer me: night or day?"

"Day. It's the time I'm most used to being awake," she said. She placed her damaged paw on the stony surface. It was cool, but not as cold as she'd expected.

"And I guess I'll take day as well. Oh, and if we could get a deh—er, *quarter* somewhere close to the ground, that would be good," Hyrees mewed.

"That will work," Falcon said. "We only have one lower quarter available. It's attached to one other living space, but I'm guessing that's not a problem for either of you. That is, if you get along with your neighbor. Unfortunately most don't, which is why it's open. Come see what you think."

He led them past a sleeping brown tabby, then stopped at the end of the tunneled mass. He placed a paw on a tiny cave beside the slumbering cat. Hyrees walked over to it and sniffed its tan-colored walls.

Falcon nudged his side. "Go on; have a look. Oh, one more thing: quarters are typically shared between cats working days and nights. Though since this one is less than ideal, it's clear for both. Even if one of you decides to switch shifts, you can remain here."

Ember turned her attention to the tabby, their new neighbor—the one no one liked for some reason. Her sleek face reminded her of Tainu. A weird mixture of silvers, oranges, and dark blues filled her head, then morphed into a familiar purple and grey swirl.

'She's about our age, isn't she? I hope she's nice. I could use an ally, considering I'm pretty much alone at this point, but given how she's made this the least desirable quarter, I guess that's probably asking for a lot. Oh well. We'll deal with it, I guess. Unless she's like Silentstream. Then we're leaving.'

"Sounds good to me, and this'll work for you too, right Em?" Hyrees said.

"Hmm?" she asked. "Oh, yeah. Yes, this will be good. Thanks. Anything else we need to know? Did we miss the evening rations?"

Falcon chuffed. "Actually, they're about to give them out as we speak, and speaking of which; up, Boreal. You'll miss your meal if you don't get going now."

The brown tabby sat up and yawned. "Yes, Father. Oh!" Her eyes widened and locked onto Hyrees, then Ember, and kept flicking between them. "Uh, hi, hello. You're . . . new."

Falcon snorted. "Boreal, these are your new neighbors, Ember and Hyrees. They'll be living with the East for a while, at Jade's insistence. You two, this is my daughter, Boreal. Now come on, let's get you all to the food storage. I'm hungry."

"Yes, let's do that," Boreal said. "But like he said, my name is Boreal, and

402

we would appear to have adjacent quarters. I hope you both enjoy your stay here, in the East."

Boreal sighed. Ember's ears perked up, bringing with them a soft tan.

'Oh, that's a weird color for right now. Interesting. I like her. I think. She's not bad. A good neighbor, but how do you know that? Guess you'll just have to wait and see, Ember.'

Falcon led them all back to the storage cave. On the way, he pointed out things they'd already seen, like the drinking spring and Jade's rock. When they reached the storage, several cats waited ahead of them. Ember sat down and lifted her damaged leg to see if she could find any visible anomalies.

"So what happened to you? You're Ember, right?" Boreal asked.

"Yes, I'm Ember. It's a long story. To put it as briefly as possible, I found myself on the Wolf Trail at the wrong time, and then, when I woke up, the humans had saved my life, then some of them risked their money and reputations to help bring me home. We sometimes communicate through an artificial intelligence system and something called a data signal, but I haven't heard from them in a while. I'm worried they might not like me anymore."

"That is fascinating, but first and foremost I meant your limp," Boreal replied.

"Oh. I slipped on a patch of ice. Good times."

Boreal chuffed. "Sounds like it." She turned to face Hyrees. "So what about you? What happened to you?"

"I don't want to talk about it," he replied.

They all fell silent, so Ember went back to examining her leg. She couldn't find anything outwardly wrong with it, but she remained seated and fidgeted with it anyway until the hunters called them over for food. After a lot of coaxing, she got Hyrees to eat his meal. When they all finished, Boreal offered to lead him back to their quarters while Ember made her way to the healers' cave to try to find someone willing to help fix her leg.

She sucked in a deep breath, then entered the cavern. At the far edge, a fire offered light and warmth. A clay platform sat directly over it, protecting it from any rain that might come in through the hole at the top of the towering chamber. A clump of moss was left drying on the platform, and beside the flames sat a slightly shivering Shard. Behind him stood a black tomcat with flecks of white in his fur and a creamy tabby molly with a twisted paw.

"Ember?" Shard asked. "What, uh, what're you doing here? Oh, and these are Crow and Sunshine, by the way. Night shift healers. Me, I work the day shift. I was just coming in to check on something. Wait, why are you here? Is it for that limp?"

Ember lowered her head. "Y-yeah. I'm mostly going to have to do it myself, but I thought having some help might be, well, helpful. Just in case."

Sunshine padded over to her, limping on three legs with a gait similar to Ember's. She sniffed Ember's prosthetics. "Wow. Glowing legs—I like this. Where did you get them? As you can see, I could use one."

She lifted her twisted paw. It was bent at such an angle that her pads faced sideways, and the leg it was attached to appeared to be shorter than all of her others. Ember tilted her head, trying to figure what kind of injury might have caused it.

"Sunshine," the black cat, Crow, said. "No need to disturb our colorful newcomer."

Sunshine flattened her ears. "Sorry. I'm creepy and gross, I know. I'll just . . . go over here."

Ember tilted her head farther until everything appeared to be sideways. "At least your legs are real. But, uhm, Shard, I was wondering if you'd possibly be willing to help me out."

"Uh, yeah, yes, I guess so." He stood up. "I mean, technically I'm off duty now, as far as being a healer goes, but if you really do want my help, I can try to offer it as best I can. What'd you need help with?"

She tried her best to give him a tiny smile. "Mechanical surgery."

———

"Careful; try not to detach anything else. It is a delicate system," ETAg Thai chimed.

"I know, I know," Ember said.

She bit her tongue and forced herself to concentrate on the mass of wires and mechanical bits in front of her. Beside her, the far south fire pit crackled and snapped. Opening up the skin of her leg had been hard enough, even with her pain sensors turned off, then keeping the skin and artificial muscles separated for her to work proved itself equally challenging, even with Shard holding it in place. She'd had to turn off functions she didn't even know existed to keep sealant fluid from getting everywhere. Now, staring down at the painstakingly isolated loose wire segment, part of her wanted to give up. The rest of her wanted this newfound puzzle to never end.

'Oh, I hate this. Why couldn't the wires have been made to be self-healing too?' She sighed. *'But do I really? Do I really hate this? I mean, I guess I shouldn't complain too much. It's either this or me being dead. Come on, Ember—focus.'*

"Maybe I should go get Crow to finish helping you." Shard said. "I'm getting tired. I-I don't know how much longer I can do this, and I'm worried I might mess something up. That always happens, you know. It's the reason I'm a healer. It's the only job I'm even slightly good at. I've tried other jobs, and each time my career ended disastrously—and I do mean disastrously. I almost got a cat killed last time I tried to group hunt, and that is not an exaggeration."

"You're doing fine. You won't ruin anything. Look, I'm almost done."

Shard sighed, but continued holding the hole open. Ember flattened her ears and reached in. Careful not to push the other wires out of place, she hooked a claw around the loose piece and pulled it upward. She concentrated on moving one of her toes. It responded immediately.

"Oh good, that worked. Thai, restore all functions except the pain sensors," she said.

"All functions minus pain sensors have been restored," Thai replied.

Within a few seconds, sealant fluid began seeping out of the skin around the hole.

Ember breathed out through her mouth. "Okay, here's where it gets interesting. Shard, I need you to take some of that sealant fluid, and put it onto the wire. Without that, it won't rebuild itself in the proper position, and the entire thing will continue to short out, likely getting more and more detached until I can no longer use my right foreleg for anything at all."

"How am I supposed to do that? Ember, both my paws are busy just keeping the hole open. Also, the thing with the rebuilding, and the sealant stuff, that all, it sounds important, so I really should not be the one to do it."

"You can do it, Shard. Just improvise."

Shard growled quietly. He lifted a hind paw and awkwardly pressed it against her foreleg, then he used his free paw to scrape off some of the fluid from the skin. Ember moved her own paw out of the way as much as she could, giving him enough room to dab the gel-like substance onto the wire.

"Is that enough? Enough of that goo stuff, that is?" he asked.

"Should be," Ember replied. "Now we just have to wait a few moments for it to dry. When we both let go, the skin should pull in on itself, and the sealant should fix that as well. Then we'll be done."

When she let go of the wire, it remained properly positioned. She breathed a sigh of relief and nodded to Shard. He released her leg, and the synthetic skin and muscle mass went back into place, just as it was supposed to.

"S-so we're done? That was it?" Shard said.

Ember lifted her foreleg and wiggled her toes.

"It would appear the operation was successful. Good job," Thai said.

Ember laughed. She set her paw on the ground and stood up. Bright bursts of red, orange, and deep brown flared in her head, dancing like the flames beside them. She got the urge to dance with them, but she ignored it. Until the wire fully reattached itself, too much movement could still dislodge it.

Shard tilted his head. "I don't understand. What's so funny? We, uh, we did it, right?"

She leaped at him and nuzzled his neck. "Yes, we did it! It's fixed. We fixed it. Us! All by ourselves—without the humans. Is it weird that I kind of want to do it again?"

"Yes. Uh, I mean probably?" he said, pinning back his ears.

"Shard, this is the first time I've been happy in a long time. And it's the second time something's gone right in a long time. Thank you. Thanks for helping me."

Shard stepped back and looked at his paws. "So . . . I actually did something right?"

She smiled. "Yes. Yes you did. And I don't think anyone else here would have. In a way, I think you saved my life."

He chuckled. "Oh, good, we're even."

"Hardly. I think now I owe you."

His eyes widened. "R-really? Because that's the first time anyone's ever said that. To me, obviously. Not, ah, well, you-you know what I mean."

Ember chuffed. "Yes, really. You know, we work together pretty well. And I'm sure you'll like working with Hyrees even more. He's less demanding. And less machine-y. You're both on day shift in the healers' den."

"Oh, really? Oh, yes, I would bloody love that. We've got a lot of catching up to do, we have. Oh, oh, maybe Mum will even let me train him."

"Maybe. You could ask tomorrow."

"Alright, you're done." Echo's voice made Ember jump. "Now would you two get some sleep? You'll wake the whole Rift up if you keep rambling on like that."

Echo strode toward them. When she reached them, she pressed her forehead against Shard's and smiled. "You did well, little brother." She turned to glare at Ember. "And you—you made him feel good about himself, even if you did use him. I'll count that for something. I guess. Better than some cats here. Now come on; it's getting late. To your quarters, both of you."

"Y-yes, of course, Echo," Shard said. "Good night, Ember. Echo and I, we sleep near Mum's den by the rocks, so we'll be there. You know, in case you or Hyrees need anything."

Echo nudged him onward, away from the fire pits and deeper into the heart of the East. Ember flattened her ears as they left.

"Goodnight," she said weakly.

She headed back to her and Hyrees's sleeping quarters. As she walked, her emotions became a nauseating muddle of colors that swirled in her mind like a storm. She tried her best to ignore them. Eventually they morphed into a single solid color somewhere between slate grey and mountain blue.

'I'm too tired for this. I need more mildly frustrating problems to solve, not an entire colony full of lives to save, or an entire colony full of names to memorize. Where am I supposed to be right now?'

She peered up beyond the protective ceiling of the Rift. Stars peered right back at her, glowing and shimmering without a care in the universe; lonely balls of energy that would burn anyone who ventured too close, yet were on the path to death themselves. When one of them passed on, it would be a prolonged, painful death that would end in an explosion. Then something new could replace it: a new star, and maybe even new planets. Humans, with their technology, had seen it happen many times.

As she watched the stars, she wondered how long the universal cycle of life and death would continue before the last living thing died. Then what would happen? She didn't know. She also didn't feel like asking Thai about it.

Something about the thought made turquoise come back, but she didn't have the mental energy to keep her musings going, so she went back to walking. When she reached her quarters, Hyrees was already asleep, snoring and taking up most of the entrance.

Boreal lifted her head. "I see you got it fixed."

Ember glanced down at the still slightly sticky line running down her foreleg. Part of her wondered if it would leave a scar. "Yeah. I can . . . walk properly again now."

"That's good." Unlike most other cats she'd met, Boreal's tone of voice didn't seem to have any hidden meanings. Her words were simple, and meant what they said they meant. Ember liked that. "Guess this means you'll be patrolling tomorrow."

Ember cocked an ear. *'How does she know? Did Hyrees tell her, did she overhear it, or did she figure it out on her own?'* She licked her lips. "Uhm, yes, I think so. If Jade assigns me a partner, at least."

Boreal snorted and rested her chin on her paws. "Of course. Sleep well, I guess. If you can. Is he always this loud?"

Ember shoved Hyrees to one side of the little tunnel, then crawled in behind him. The stone floor chilled her paws. She lay down and leaned against his bony ribs, his spine pressing into her cheek. "Not always. Sometimes he's even louder. Occasionally he won't snore at all. If someone smacks him on the nose or something to try to make him stop, I wouldn't blame them."

"Can I ask you a kind of personal question?" Boreal asked. Her voice was muffled by the wall between them.

"Sure. You may or may not get an answer, though."

"You know what? Never mind. Forget it. Let's just get some sleep."

Purple fluttered through her tired head, but she couldn't bring herself to try to chase it off with answers. Instead, she sighed and snuggled closer to Hyrees's warmth. Yet even with him resting faithfully at her side, the deep dark blues of loneliness sank in, stalking closer and closer until it became all she could feel.

'Kind of like a star,' she thought.

CHAPTER 27
EMBER

"As a small few of you may already know, this is Ember," Jade announced. She stood tall in front of a semicircle of rough-looking border guards. "She is from the West, but she will be staying with us nonetheless. She is now my answers cat; I ask her questions and her tag gives me answers, so treat her well. In a way, she outranks some of you."

Ember sat beside and slightly behind her, keeping one ear cocked toward the 'cave of healing,' as the Easterners called it. Falcon was giving Hyrees a similar introduction to his new fellow healers. Her gaze landed on Boreal, who sat in a hunched over position at the edge of the group. Her constantly wandering eyes made Ember wonder what she was thinking about. When she grew bored of wondering, she turned her attention to the other guards and tried to deduce what fighting style each of them preferred.

'Scars on legs—fast and effective. Not bad as partners. Scars on back and hind legs—sloppy and indirect. No, too similar to my style. Wait, I don't have any scars on my back. That's good, I guess. Uhm, where was I? Oh, the Rift, right.' She chuffed to herself. *'And, okay, nope. No, he wouldn't make a good partner, either. Oh, scars on face. You like fighting, don't you? Well, I hope she doesn't pair me with you. Hold on, I have scars on my face. Hum. I guess scar-reading only works to an extent. Besides, it doesn't matter who I want to partner with. Jade's probably already chosen someone.'*

"Ember, are you listening?" Jade asked.

Ember tensed at the sudden reappearance of sound. "Oh, uhm . . . sorry. No. I was, uh, thinking about stuff."

A few of the guards chuffed or muttered among themselves. A large tabby stood and stepped forward—the cat Ember had mistakenly called 'Falcon' earlier that morning. Ember's face still burned from the encounter.

"Commander Jade, are you certain we can trust this kitten?" the cat, a molly who was very much not Falcon, asked. "Are you certain we should even let her stay at all? I mean, she only showed up last night, and you're already assigning her a position on the guard? How can we know she's telling the truth or that she won't betray us? For all any of us know, she could be an assassin sent to kill you. The West does think we used that Outsider kitten to kill their commander. What's to stop them from trying to do the same to us with this mechanical mess?"

Several cats mumbled their agreements, making Ember shrink back to hide behind Jade. She hadn't even known the Eastern commander for a full twenty-four hours, yet she already found herself taking comfort in seeing her somewhat familiar swirl of stripes.

Jade's tail twitched. "Calm down, all of you. I understand your concerns, but there's no need to worry. I have my own methods of finding out who is truly on our side. However, that is not important right now, as I'm placing her with Boreal on the peak. She will do us no harm there, and won't be promoted until her loyalty has been proven."

Ember tilted her head. A shiver made the fur on her spine bristle. *'Wait, what am I supposed to be doing? Did she bring any of this up when I wasn't listening? Doesn't seem like it. What information am I not getting, then? Maybe I could ask Boreal, if she doesn't repeat herself.'*

"Now, off to your posts. Except for you, Boreal." She paused until the other border guards left. "When you two return from your patrol, come directly to my den. I want a full report of what happened. Understood?"

"Yes. Uh, ma'am. Yes, ma'am," Boreal replied.

"Good," Jade said. "Now off you go."

Boreal stood and lifted a paw toward the nearest edge of the Rift. "Come on then, Ember. Looks like we're work partners."

Ember trotted to join her, and together they left for the peak. As they walked, she subconsciously adjusted her pace to stay next to and slightly behind Boreal. She'd learned it to be a submissive position, letting the senior cat lead.

Boreal glanced back at her, then did a double-take. "Why are you back there?"

Ember picked up her pace to walk directly beside her. "Because my dad said it's important to acknowledge a superior, and apparently letting the superior lead the way is the best way to do it."

"Well, I'm not your dad. I don't have any rules other than keep patrolling the peak until it's time to go back. There are no habits, no silly little rituals, no superiors; there's just us and the mountain."

As they walked, light from the rising sun drifted into the partly cloudy sky in front of them. Ember squinted and kept her eyes on the ground ahead. Even with her vision concentrated on the snow, she couldn't help but notice the large amount of conifers making up the forest around them. She glanced over at Boreal.

'Wait, I don't know almost anything about her, and she doesn't know much about me. How are we supposed to work together?' she thought. *'Time to ask questions, I guess.'* Ember sighed. "So what's your style?"

Boreal turned to look at her again. "Pardon?"

"You've only got one scar from what I can see, and it's on your shoulder. I don't know what kind of fighting style you prefer, or how it might work with mine in a confrontation. I want to know what it's like."

"Oh. Hah. Take a wild guess."

"Uhm, well, you don't look like you do much ground fighting. So . . . you prefer to keep your distance?"

Boreal chuffed. "You could say that. I don't have a fighting style. I patrol the peak because I'm talentless and no one likes me. No one ever comes this way. Except the occasional bobcat or fox, but even those are rare. And they're always skittish, so if I make enough noise and run at them fast enough, they scamper off without a fight. We've got the easy and boring job because Jade doesn't trust us with anything important."

"Ah, okay. Makes sense. If we even patrolled our peak, I'd probably be the one doing it. For the same reasons too. Though I do have a fighting style—try not to die."

Ember paused mid-step as the truth of her own words hit her like a falling acorn. She sighed quietly and continued onward.

"What is it?" Boreal asked.

Ember swallowed. Pure, unfiltered sunlight appeared through the trees beyond the mountain crest up ahead. It stabbed her eyes, forcing her to close them. She mewed quietly to herself to stay calm. *'I guess I can trust her. Secrets can be used to build someone up, remember? Maybe she's willing to do that for me. It's not like I have anyone else. Except Shard and Hyrees, but they don't care, and she probably doesn't either. Oh come on, Ember. You'll never improve unless you try something new.'*

"I . . . recently found out that I'm not even supposed to be alive," she said.

Boreal flicked back an ear. "What do you mean? As in, your parents weren't trying to have you?"

"No, no, they wanted me. *Want* me. It's because of them that I'm still breathing." Ember stopped walking and closed her eyes again to gather her thoughts, then explained as best she could Dark's decree of drowning all defective kittens, and how Cloud had brought her to safety through his political connections and willpower.

"Oh," Boreal said once Ember had finished. She didn't add anything more and went back to walking.

Ember grimaced. It hadn't done anything but give this cat she barely knew more power over her. *'Yep, that sure helped, Ember. Yes, I feel so much better now. I should tell her the rest of my life story.'*

When they reached the peak, Ember stopped to gape at the valley below. It appeared to be smaller and more shallow than Dark's Valley, but with infinitely more intriguing contents. A rough patch of ground without trees sliced the upper portion of the mountainside, and human buildings and fences covered its middle. She estimated the distance between their place on the peak and the first wall of fencing to be roughly thirty metres, if she remembered the length of a metre correctly.

In one parking lot, two static hoverships sat on their landing pads, and in the other, several smaller white vehicles rested. The entire place, parking lots and all, was concealed from above by a giant holographic screen projecting images of treetops. Ember guessed that the entire facility was only visible from the sides, where the screen faded slightly.

"What is it?" Ember asked. "I mean, I know it's all human buildings and equipment, but what are they for? And why are they trying to hide it? Is it ARC?"

"I don't know," Boreal replied. "All I know is that the humans there are not our friends. Did Jade or my father tell you about them?"

"Tell me what?"

While she was still speaking, one of the hoverships revved to life, its spinning blades buzzing like distant bees. It phased up through the screen, then flew away into the great unknown. Ember watched with curiosity as it vanished into the clouds.

"So they didn't," Boreal said after the hum faded. "Well, you'll find out eventually if you stay here long enough. Might as well tell you now. Every autumn, just before the Meeting, they take two kittens, ones less than a winter old, and we aren't allowed to do anything about it. It's the only way they'll let us stay here. What happens to those kittens they take, no one knows. It's probably less pleasant than being drowned, though."

"Oh," Ember whispered, "so it is ARC."

Boreal sighed. "My . . . my brother was one of the ones taken. He was my only friend. I haven't seen him in almost two winters. Sometimes I wonder if he's even still alive, though I like to think he's dead. That way the humans can't hurt him." she lowered her head and pretended to play with the snow. "I think it's part of the reason Mother left. The loss was hard on her, and she and my father were always fighting anyway. I haven't seen her in almost as long. It's . . . it's almost funny, though. Father started out an Outsider, then ended up a Colony Cat, and Mother did the opposite."

"Oh. So you're a—"

Boreal spun around to face her. Ember jumped back.

"Half-breed, yes," she growled. "The Colony's come to accept Father, but not me. Though I don't think it has much to do with being part Outsider. Or would that be all Outsider now? I don't know. Either way, I'm not well-liked. It's a wonder I haven't been sent off. And yes, we do 'get rid of defects' like your colony. Though instead of drowning them, we exile them. If they survive, they survive, if they don't, too bad. So long as they're 'out of the main breeding pool.' Not like that's a risk with me. No one cares." She swiped her paw against the snow, sending white powder flying.

Ember breathed out slowly through her nose. "These colonies, they really are no better than the Outsiders. More organized and demanding, but not better. In fact, I think Outsiders may be more . . . uhm . . . I don't know a word that really says what I want to say, but they may even be nicer, and more forgiving and accepting. While I was in the Valley, I—er, *we*—met an outsider named Bracken who saved us from a blizzard and gave me a hunting lesson."

Boreal cocked an ear. "Name sounds familiar. Maybe my dad knows him. I wouldn't be surprised."

'Familiar name? Bracken's met everyone, hasn't he?' Ember's gaze darted around the evergreen forest and the mountain slope below. Light glinted off of the snow and partially hidden buildings, making little spots dance in her vision. Massive stones, ones less rounded than those near the Western Cliffs, broke up the snowscape. Their jagged outlines made the forest more interesting, but also unfamiliar. *'Not unfamiliar to Boreal, though, and she would probably feel this way if we were at the Cliffs. Thinking of Boreal . . .'* She bit her tongue. "So, you said no one likes you much. Why is that?"

Boreal stared at her for a few seconds, long enough to make her wonder if she'd done something wrong again.

"I said I'm not well-liked," she replied, "but it's almost the same thing, just different words. It's because I'm honest and I ask honest questions. They call me rude, but I don't understand why. I'm not trying to be. When I'm honest and someone gets offended, they're getting offended by the truth. It's not my fault they want to stay blinded by lies. But lately I've just been keeping my mouth shut. You know, to spare myself the trouble."

"Oh." She looked at her paws and thought for a moment, getting her words together. "I like you," she said. Her tail twitched as an awkward pause set in. "I-I know we don't know each other very well, but we seem to have a lot in common, I mean. I don't have a lot in common with most cats. Not that it really matters all that much. I've never had many friends. But, uh, what I was trying to say is that I don't get offended easily, so you can be honest with me. The truth doesn't scare me away. It's interesting and informative, even if it's against me."

For the first time since they'd met, Boreal smiled. "Know what? I like you too. I'm glad Jade assigned us to be partners. We Outsider Colony Cats should stay together."

Ember realized she was smiling too, and decided she was happy again, welcoming the vibrant oranges of joy into her thoughts. "Yeah," she said with a chuff. "We should start a little group. The rejected felines."

Boreal laughed. "I like the sound of that. We're the rejected felines now, I guess."

CLOUD

Kivyress hissed as Fern poured a bowl of warm water over her injured leg. Cloud groomed her forehead in a futile attempt to keep her calm. His tail twitched with fury. He drew long, slow breaths to keep himself mentally steady enough to be any kind of comfort.

"I know. I know it hurts, but we need to make sure you don't get an infection. Try to hold still, okay?" he said.

"Just one more rinse before I pack it again, alright Kivy? Brace yourself," Fern said.

Kivyress moaned softly and pinned back her ears. "Can't we just leave it alone? I think it's clean, and it hurts enough already."

Fern poured the last bowl over her leg, ignoring her pleas. Kivyress winced and shuddered, but she didn't try to stop her. Beside them, the fire pit crackled. Cloud leaned away from it; his fur was burning, and his face was on fire. Yet the flames only aggravated his feverishness—they didn't cause it. He glared across the pit to where Lupine sat on Aspen's den. Two council members sat on either side of him, serving as bodyguards. The night before, Sumac, the young rebel, had tried to assassinate him. However, his attempt was sloppy, and he'd been discovered and stopped before he was able to complete his undertaking. He'd been publicly executed that morning. Cloud coughed twice, then locked eyes with the trembling commander.

'You caused this. Are you happy with yourself, having a kitten mauled? Having a young, capable cat killed in front of everyone? What are you trying to inspire? Fear? You're only making your colony hate you. You've ruined the West, and all for what? Safety? Your own security? We'd be safer in the Lowlands at this point; safe from you and your plans.'

Fledge walked over to them with a fresh bowl of water. She set it down, then looked between them. Despite the sorrow in her eyes, she raised her tail and tried to smile. "Hey, calm down. If life's taught me anything, it's that everything seems to work itself out eventually. Hard times will end so long as we're willing to push through them."

Cloud gritted his teeth. *'Everything will work itself out? Cats are gone. Cats are dead, and they aren't coming back. Optimism is not going to fix this, and if you're so naive as to think that—'*

"How?" he snapped. "How is this going to fix itself, huh? Everything is not going to 'work itself out,' because we are at war. Cats are dead and dying, and no amount of hoping or wishful thinking is going to change that. Don't you get it? We're all going to die here if someone doesn't stand up and do something about it, and I'll tell you now, I'm not about to sit around and watch as our lives crumble out from beneath our paws."

Fledge stumbled backward. A faint hint of fear flickered in her eyes as she looked to Fern for help.

"Cloud," Fern said. Her voice was quiet, but firm. "I know you're upset, but yelling is not going to fix anything. Everyone being against each other is only going to make it that much easier for the East to come in and destroy us all." She scooped up a pawful of herbs. "We are not each other's enemies. This is the East's fault—not mine, not Fledge's, and not even Commander Lupine's. Well, maybe it is his fault in part, but what we don't need is an uprising. Not like the stir you've made. We're vulnerable enough as is. Now, I don't think that young tom should've died, but he also shouldn't have been trying to kill our commander. All this death is not the solution."

"He wouldn't have been trying to kill him if Lupine were a better commander, or if Farlight was still here," Cloud replied. "The East is only making things worse."

Fern sighed. "But you're just proving my point. Don't you see what those cats are doing? They're tearing us apart by turning us against ourselves. If we want to survive them next time they attack, we all have to learn to work as a team. Got it?" She pressed the herbs into Kivyress's wound. Kivyress winced. "So leave it alone."

Cloud growled. "I'm not taking orders from you. Or anyone else. Believe what you want, but I can promise you this won't end well. Something tells me positive thinking is going to be very difficult when there's no one left to think at all."

"Cloud, this is not the time. Let me work," she said.

Kivyress pressed a paw against his leg. He realized she was crying again. "Dad, please. Just go, okay?"

He stepped back. "But Kivy . . ."

The fire snapped. Wind ruffled their fur, howling like a pack of wolves.

"Go," Kivyress mewed. "Find Mom and go. I'm only holding you back, so leave without me. Please. I don't want to watch you fight and die for a colony you don't want to be in." She wiped her eyes and sniffled. "Please."

He leaned down and pressed his forehead against hers. "We aren't going anywhere. I'm not leaving you, Kivy, and neither is your mother. We'll find a way through this, alright?"

She nodded and leaned closer to him, face resting against his neck. Her tears burned against his cold skin. "Dad, I'm scared," she whispered. "What's going to happen to us? I don't want to die yet. I don't want you or Mom to die yet. I just want things to go back to how they were before. I want Ember back and Farlight alive."

His chin slid to rest on her back as he lay down beside her. Fern and Fledge finished packing the hole in Kivyress's leg, then went together to refill the water bowls.

He watched them go in silence, and when they left the Glade, he sighed. "The thing about life is that you don't always get what you want. I . . . I can't fix this. I'm sorry. I failed you, your mother, Ember, Farlight—everyone. I can't protect anyone anymore. It was fluffheaded of me to think I might actually have any kind of control in a war." He snorted and lifted his head. A renewed surge of resolve coursed through his body, making him feel more awake than he'd felt in mooncycles. "So I guess we'll have to find a way to stop the war."

Kivyress squirmed. He got to his paws as she pushed him away. With shaking joints, she propped her front half up.

"What are you—"

"Standing up. The sooner I get used to walking on three legs, the better."

A look of pure determination appeared on her face; her eyes narrowed and her jaw tightened. With her good legs, she pushed herself into a stand. It was like seeing her walk for the first time all over again. His chest expanded with pride. *'You did it. My little molly did it.'*

She hobbled a few steps forward, then toppled toward the fire. Cloud pounced between her and the flames. Kivyress landed in a heap against his side. She yowled in pain and started to cry again. He nuzzled her flank, trying to calm her down, to bring her some form of comfort.

"Cloud."

He looked up. Lupine stood across the fire pit from them, bodyguards eyeing them with askance from the commander's den. Cloud flattened his ears and growled. "I could kill you, you know. I should."

"E-e-easy, Cloud. I'm just looking for advice," Lupine said.

Cloud wrapped his tail around Kivyress, ready to defend her from anyone who might ever want to hurt her again. "I've given you advice before. You don't listen, so why bother?"

Lupine lowered his head. "Because this time I will. Everything i-is falling apart, Cloud. Cats are turning a-a-against each other. Cats are turning against me. Even the Council is breaking apart. You're the mastermind here. You're the only one I know who can fix it."

"You should've realized that sooner. Would've made for less to fix, that's for sure."

Lupine's posture loosened in uneasy relief. "So you'll help me?"

The breeze lulled. The forest fell silent, as if the world was holding its breath, as if his reply would change the world. *'Because it can. It can change my world, and right now, that's the only one that matters. I will fix at least one fox-fighting problem in this valley, I swear.'*

He grimaced and stood up, lifting his head high enough to look down on the shaking tomcat. "You haven't given me much of a choice, but if you want to make everything work again, you'll have to do exactly as I say."

"I will. I-I-I promise."

"Good." Cloud's eyes narrowed. His tail remained protectively against his daughter's side. "First, stop all work on the second abatis. It's useless and a waste of time. Next, instead of having all the border guards walk their patrols, give some of them fixed posts along the Eastern border, situated close enough together for adjacent guards to hear each other yowl. Tell them to kill any non-Western cat on sight. Outsiders could be Eastern assassins. We can no longer afford to take any chances. They will learn not to try us. Finally, make a public apology, and let anyone who wants to leave go. Just remind them that once they leave, they cannot come back."

"Except for you. Y-you can't go, because you have a promise to fulfill," Lupine said.

'Of course, my wonderful liege. Don't worry. I don't have to leave. All I

420

have to do is sit back and watch as you get yourself killed. It's only a matter of time at this point. An apology will do nothing; cats are getting upset. They're getting angry. And I can promise you that once they snap, Rowan will not become the commander.'

Cloud's eyes narrowed. "But you will not hold back anyone else. Am I clear? Cats who don't want to fight will only run or hide when faced with a battle. Cowards and harehearts won't be of any use to you. In fact, they're more likely to become threats."

"Yes. Yes, I'll-I'll do that." Lupine lowered his head. "Thank you, Cloud."

With a few flicks of his tail, Lupine walked back to his guards. As he left, the wind picked up again, no longer interested in either of them. Kivyress pawed at Cloud's leg, reminding him she was still there.

"What is it, Kivy?" he asked.

"Why are you helping him now? I thought you hated him. I thought you still wanted to leave."

He sat beside her and pressed his tail closer to her flank. It wouldn't do much against the gale, but every bit of warmth counted. Cloud lowered his voice to a whisper. "I do hate him, but in order to keep everyone safe, I need to work with him. Then, when he gets himself killed, I can take his place, end the war with a new peace treaty, and you can eventually become the first molly commander. How would you like that?"

Her golden eyes lit up. The flames reflecting in them sparked with excitement. "I would love that. You'd make a great commander. I don't know about me, but I'd like to try—it might be fun. Lupine would be so angry if he heard us talking about this, though."

"Then hush." Cloud groomed the fur on her forehead the wrong way, giving her a lopsided deerlick. She giggled like a kitten and tried to paw it back into place, tears long since dried.

He smiled. "Just let this be our little secret, okay?"

She smiled back at him. "Okay. Yes, sir."

"Good molly. Now let's see if you can stand again. Take it slow this time. I know you can do it."

He watched in silence as she pushed herself back to her paws, giving him another burst of pride. *'You'll be okay, Kivyress. I will give you a future. I promise.'*

CHAPTER 28
EMBER

Snow flew in every direction. Wind whipped Ember's whiskers against her face. It played with her fur and pounded at her ears. The familiar hum of a hovership thundered overhead. Its roar caused pulses of cyan to flood her mind. Ember dropped to her stomach and pressed her paws over her ears. The sound continued on. A few leaps away, Boreal pressed herself against the side of a boulder. As the hovercraft descended into the human territory below, the noise died down and became a soft, resounding echo.

A sharp ringing noise filled her ears. Her nose stung. *'Stop already. Please. Would you please?'*

The sound and the ringing faded. The cyan drained from her head, almost painful as it faded to grey, then to nothing at all.

"Hey, Em, it's gone. You can get up now," Boreal's voice said, breaking the unusually loud silence.

She exhaled, trying to calm herself, and opened her eyes. Boreal stood in front of her. She wasn't smiling, but something about her words made Ember feel like she was. Invisible emotions with Boreal were more clear than visible cues with most other cats. She couldn't place why or how it worked, but it was almost scary how well they understood each other.

"I know," Ember replied.

In the week she'd lived with the East, she'd taught herself a half-baked

Eastern accent. If she didn't focus on pronunciations, however, it bounced back and forth across the Valley. When that happened, it made her feel purple inside, as if even her own voice didn't know where it belonged.

She got to her paws and gazed down the mountain. The cluster of buildings was cloaked in shadow, almost invisible in the dying light.

"So what color was that?" Boreal asked.

"Kind of a really bright turquoise. I never get any green when those things fly by. I'm not scared of them—at least not anymore—but something about the noise seems to trigger a fight or flight response in me, and I see that color when I panic."

"Interesting. And the color is gone now?"

"Yeah. It doesn't linger with things like that. Fortunately. It disappears, and I'm fine again." She breathed out slowly through her mouth. "Speaking of lingering, we should start back now, right?"

Boreal chuffed.

"What?" Ember asked.

"When you said 'speaking,' I'm sorry, but you exaggerated it far too much. It sounded fake and I found it funny."

Ember raised a brow. "How about this? Speee-kin'."

Boreal laughed. "What even was that?"

"I don't know, but in all seriousness, I'd like to see you try a Western accent."

She chuffed again and sat down. "In all seriousness, ah? Well then. What do I ev'n say? Y'all wanna help me with de abatis n' din go fer a romp in da' Kiv'eers?"

Ember stared at her for a moment to let the words sink in, then burst out laughing.

Boreal smirked. "How'd I do?"

"Did you just say 'romp'?" She switched back to her native accent. "What kind of . . . Oh tahg, that was perfection. I mean, the impersonation was terrible, and I didn't know whatever stereotype that was even existed, but, well, the Western accent is boring, and I can say with certainty that your version of it was not."

"Yeah, hearing you now, I can see that I might have gotten a few things wrong, but oh well." She got to her paws. "Let's get a move on, then."

Ember chuckled and shook her head. They made their way down the mountain slope together, walking side by side through the half-melted snow. When they re-entered the forest, the ground became filled with pleasant, shadowy blue stripes. Ember imagined them to be little creeks, which she jumped and stepped over for fun wherever she could. Wind continued to nip at their sides, and despite the slight warmth of her heating grid, her legs felt colder than usual.

When they reached the Rift, the usual glow of sunlight against stone greeted them. Falcon greeted them as well.

"Good evening," he said. "Ember, Jade would like to speak with you. Alone this time." His eyes narrowed. "Come with me."

Silver. *I've just decided I don't like you. Why is that? Why are you so creepy all of a sudden?'* Ember cocked an ear and turned to Boreal. "I guess I'll see you in a little while?"

"Assuming Father doesn't eat you," Boreal replied. "Don't show any fear, and they might just let you out alive."

"That's not reassuring, you know."

"Oh, I know." Boreal chuffed and padded off toward the nearest fire pit. "Come find me if you survive. I'll show you our clawmark tablets like I said I would yesterday," she called over her shoulder.

Ember swallowed the bile building up in her throat. Even the thought of studying Eastern history couldn't shake the nervousness mounting in her chest. She flattened her ears and followed Falcon toward Jade's den. To reach it, he led her through a thin-but-tall crack inside a cluster of gigantic rocks at the back of the Rift. Every other time she'd walked through the passage, she hadn't minded the closeness of it. This time, however, with Falcon walking like a cat prepared for a war, the tight passageway made her feel claustrophobic—and itchy, for some reason.

The cramped breach gave way to a bowl-shaped cavity in the stone. A tiny semi-cave rested in the rocks to the right, which Jade sat in on a bed of dried grass. She watched them enter, motionless and eyes unblinking, almost a stone herself. Ember lowered her head. "Y-you wanted me, ma'am?"

Jade got to her paws, then padded into the rock bowl to greet them. She nodded once to Falcon, who jumped on top of the stones lining the hollow.

"You've done your job well enough for the past several days. I would like to promote you for your efforts."

As she spoke, Falcon paced along the edges of the border. Every now and then, sunlight caught in his eyes, making them appear to glow a menacing green. Fear green.

"Look at me, please. I would like to know you're listening," Jade said.

Ember forced herself to study the stripes on Jade's neck. "I am, ma'am. Falcon is just . . . acting kind of strange, isn't he?"

"He's just being protective. Don't worry about him. Now, as I was saying, I believe it's time to give you a promotion. Tomorrow you will be transferred from patrolling the peak to your choice of either the Northern or Southern Border."

Indigo and yellow appeared. She could feel, more than see, the cyan starting to form as her chest constricted. "Transfer?" she asked. "But why? I like patrolling the peak. I don't want to be transferred."

"Because you've been here long enough and served me well enough to get a better-respected position. The peak is for those who have no other use. Now, is there anyone you would like to partner up with, or any place you'd like to try patrolling?" Jade asked.

Ember's tail twitched as her stomach created a fluttering pit inside of her. "With Boreal along the peak. I don't know almost anyone else, and I don't know any other routes. I-it'll be easier for everyone if I just stay where I am."

"You mean to tell me Boreal is the only friend you've made among your comrades?"

"I didn't come here to make friends." Her mind wandered back to the West. Home, her real home, was still all the way across the Valley—an entire miniature world away. She closed her eyes to gather her thoughts. Her jaw trembled. Her Eastern accent slipped. "I came here to save my family. Everything else is just a distraction. It'll make everything easier if I just keep to myself and those I already know. I don't want to know anyone I don't know."

Jade glared at her, cold and silent. Ember bit her tongue. *'Maybe I should try to copy her expression. It may give me an idea of how she might respond.'* As she thought, she mentally strolled through a patch of woods outside the Glade. She looked away from the image to concentrate on Jade's face. *'Wait, she doesn't actually have an expression. Or maybe that is the expression? I don't know. Is that what I look like all the time? I don't think I'm doing anything with my face right now either. Oh, Ember, she's talking to you. You'd better listen—you'll get in trouble.'*

"And that is why it's important to keep striving for improvement," Jade said

Ember blinked. "Er . . . Sorry, I was supposed to hear all of that, right? Because I only got . . . the, uhm, last part of it."

Jade snorted. "It's time you learn to stop being so absent-minded. Pay attention whenever I am speaking to you."

"I'm sorry; sometimes I can't help it. When I get—" Her eyes widened. She scanned the rim of the rock bowl for Falcon. He was nowhere to be seen. "Uhm, w-when I get lost in thought, everything else . . ." She spun around, trying to spot his dark, tabby-striped fur. "Er, kind of turns off and I literally cannot hear you."

"Then stop getting lost in thought. Ember, sit still! Learn some focus and self-discipline. If you don't, you'll find yourself getting burnt onto a memorial stone well before your time. Or maybe even just burnt without the memorial stone."

Ember crouched down and kept looking around. The silvers of uneasiness became all she could feel, killing her concentration. "Sorry, I was just wondering; where's Falcon?"

"That is not important, Ember. I am speaking to you. He's probably gone off to the fire pits to warm himself. Now sit still and pay attention."

A grey blur caught the edges of her vision. Her heart lurched. Without thinking, she shoved her paws against Jade's chest, sending her tumbling into her den. Something powerful and heavy slammed into her ribs. Ember's side hit a wall. Air left her lungs in a painful *huff*. Sky blue flared in her head. She tried to breathe in, but found she couldn't. The shadows framing her vision grew more and more powerful. A shock of adrenaline hit her system, waking her body back up. She drew a pain-ridden breath. Her vision cleared. Ember broke into a fit of coughing.

"Falcon, what are you doing? You could have killed her!" Jade hissed.

"The well-being of that Westerner is the least of your concerns right now, love," Falcon replied.

"What are you talking about?"

Falcon lifted himself off of Ember. He pinned Jade against the wall of her own den and sank his fangs into the back of her neck. Jade opened her mouth, as if to scream for help, but nothing came out.

Ember staggered to her paws, heart racing. "Leave her alone." The words came out much weaker and squeakier than she'd intended. Grey fog filled her head, clogging up her thoughts yet again. "P-please stop."

"Ember . . . help me," Jade whispered.

The silver in her mind refused to go away, not even amid the swarm of other colors attacking and distracting her. Everything was breaking all over again. Even their voices sounded wrong. She turned around and pressed her face against the wall. *'Never turn your back on a threat,'* Cloud's voice chided in her head. She ignored it. "Why is this happening? Why is this happening? Why is this happening?" she mewed.

Something thudded against the ground. Ember spun around at the noise to find Jade lying limp on the rock, eyes half closed and neck covered in blood. "Ember, stop. This is happening because the Colony has been led by an unfit commander for far too many winters. Your colony has it right. A molly should not be allowed into a position of power. It's her fault we're at war, you know."

'Aspen? Lupine? Jade? Aspen? Lupine killed Aspen? Jade killed Aspen?

Why does this keep happening to me? Why involve me? Why can't they kill each other somewhere else? Kill each other? Kill each other? Why do we kill each other? Why do we kill? I can't . . . I can't kill.'

"Let me make you a deal, young molly. You let me finish my work, and I'll guarantee the safety of your family. Interfere, however, and I will kill both you and Hyrees."

She backed away. Jade coughed once. "Ember . . . don't leave me," she whispered. "Don't . . . don't let me die."

'Which one? Which one? Why do I have to choose? Why do I have to, why do I choose, have to, why? Why doesn't he kill her? Why won't he kill her while I hesitate? This isn't why I'm here. Why am I here? Why didn't he wait until I wasn't? Why can't I smell the blood? Her fur. Her fur! Why is it . . . Confused. Purple—purple, why is there so much purple?'

"Someone help! Jade needs help! What is going on?" Ember yowled.

"Wrong choice," Falcon growled. He lunged at her. She jumped back, but not far enough. As she landed, he swiped her feet out from beneath her. She tumbled onto the rock and tried to lift her legs in defense, but found herself paralyzed. The world swam around her, bouncing in and out of focus. Falcon stood like a green-eyed rattlesnake, poised and ready to strike. Another burst of adrenaline fired off in her body, snapping her out of her daze. She sucked in a deep breath and shoved her paws in front of her, claws extended. *'Why did I do that? Why did I do that? Oh, this is bad. That was a terrible idea.'*

"Help! Please! Come on, someone!" she called.

Falcon pounced again. Ember closed her eyes and kicked for all she was worth. Her paws hit air. Her eyes snapped opened. Falcon stood over Jade, bearing his fangs and snarling. He lunged for her throat. Without thinking, Ember rolled to her paws and pinned him against the stone.

"Leave her alone!" Ember snapped.

Falcon chuckled. His face flickered between his own and Whitehaze's beneath her claws. Ember shook her head in confusion, then released him. Breathing—she couldn't breathe; she needed to breathe, but no matter how fast or hard she sucked in air, she was suffocating.

"No," she whispered. "No, no, I'm not . . . you're . . . w-w-what is this?"

Falcon got to his feet and straightened himself up. "Surprising," he said. "Not very graceful, but at least you've got some willpower."

Ember flattened her ears and shook her head. Tiny nonsense mews escaped her throat. The storm of colors, except for the pulsing blue of pain, became a muddle of thundering grey and purple.

Jade lifted her head, smiling. "And loyalty."

She shuddered and sucked in rapid, shallow breaths through her mouth. "What—what is going on? You didn't just . . . Oh." The last part came out as a breath. "Oh. Ohhh, no." She pressed her paws against her forehead. "W-was this n-n-necessary?"

Jade got up and shook herself off. A droplet of fake blood spattered on Ember's paw. She sniffed it. The sickly sweet scent of winter berries filled her nose. Light green—it was tightening her throat. She wanted to throw up.

"It was entirely necessary," Jade said. "I needed to make sure you are truly loyal to me and my colony before I put you in any kind of position of power. Didn't you notice that so far I've only asked you simple questions and for ultimately unimportant advice?"

Her lower jaw trembled. Tears blurred her vision. Her heart continued to thump in her ears. Bile coated her mouth as the pine greens of relief and the sickly greens of nausea fought for control of her body. "Well, I, uh, I mean, I did, but none of it was-was much different than the kinds of things . . . everyone else has asked me, so I-I didn't think much of it."

She walked closer to Ember. "Are you okay? Goodness, molly, you're shaking all over."

Ember sunk to her stomach and wrapped her tail against her side. She closed her eyes. The darkness made her shiver even more. "It's normal." She coughed a few times. "I-I don't take very well to surprises."

The eerie blankness of her own voice didn't line up with anything inside her, much less the cyans threatening to steal away her self-control. 'No, don't panic. Not now. Please stop. I need to get out of here. This has to stop.'

"Life is full of surprises. You'd better get used to them, young advisor,"

Falcon said.

She slid herself a few pawsteps backward. "I should probably—" Her eyes snapped open. She looked up at them, still shaking. "Y-young advisor?"

He smiled. "Yes, you heard me correctly."

Jade chuffed. "You can answer questions no one even thinks to ask, you know the ways of both the East and the West, and now you've proven yourself loyal to me. Loyal enough, at least. You're an odd young cat and no doubt need some fixing up, but you are also our most valuable resource. I'm putting you on the Eastern Council."

'The Council? She's putting me on the Council? Wait, what? What?' She swallowed bile and backed up farther. *'I didn't even . . .'* Her mind went numb. "Uh, hum, well, could I maybe get some time to process this? Ah—it's a little overwhelming. Way too much . . . turquoise and purple. A-and blue and green."

"I'm not sure I understand what you're trying to say," Jade said.

'What is that even supposed to mean? Wait. You didn't come for this. But maybe you can use this to rebuild the . . . everything. Maybe meetings can happen again and I'll be able to see Dad again. Maybe. He's not on the Council anymore though, is he? So probably not. I could do like Bracken said. Get a grasp on yourself. Everything is okay. She's only giving me power. More power than I had before. This is good. This is . . . good?'

She yawned nervously and forced herself to stop shaking. Her jaw continued without her permission. "W-what do you want me to do? Is there, uhm, is there anything I need to do now?"

"Ember, you know the West better than anyone else here," Falcon said. "We'd like to know what you think we should do to prevent further conflicts with them. Should we try to reconcile, or leave them be?"

"Falcon, I'm not sure this is the best time," Jade said. "We've scared her half to death. Perhaps we should wait until tomorrow to get her thoughts on the subject. I doubt her judgment is at its sharpest right now."

Ember's eyes widened. "No, I can, uhm, well, maybe you could try sending an ambassador and a few guards with gifts and things." She closed her eyes to

431

concentrate on thinking. "Though, oh, if the fight and all really was Lupine's fault, going there might make things worse. So I don't know. You're right; I need time to—"

"I say we do it," Falcon said, cutting her off. "It's a brilliant idea, and I'd be willing to go."

She opened her eyes and examined him. More purple appeared. *That was too easy. Did he have that idea too? Did he know I would suggest it?'*

"I will call a council meeting," Jade said.

"That shouldn't be necessary, love," he replied.

"We can't decide on something this important based on the suggestions of two cats."

Falcon snorted. "Very well. You want a meeting, a meeting we will have. Will you be coming, Ember?"

She breathed out slowly through her mouth, then switched back to her Eastern accent. "I-if it's not required, I'd r-r-rather not. I, uh, look, this has been a long day. I'd like to get some rest."

"Very well," Jade said. "I'll brief you and the rest of the Colony on our decision tomorrow. Go get your rest, young advisor."

Ember lowered her head. "Thanks."

Without pausing for a response, she left the rock bowl. Boreal sat on the other side, waiting for her. Ember kept walking.

Boreal loped to catch up with Ember's fast pace. "Go on, what's wrong?"

"Your dad pretended to attack Jade to test how loyal I am to her, and now they want my ETAg on the Council." Muffling grey and sleepy blue-green deadened the storm taking place in her head. "I'm still trying to process everything that happened last week. I'm not sure I'm ready for this. I don't know what I'm doing."

Boreal's gaze drifted beyond the Rift, out across Dark's Valley. The vibrant reds, oranges, and yellows of the western sky seemed to glow just for them, trying to reassure them both. "Maybe not, but you've never done any of this before. You don't know how much you're capable of until you push yourself beyond what you're comfortable doing. My mother used to tell me that back before she left. Back when we were, you know, a family."

"She . . . sounds nice," Ember said.

Boreal sighed quietly. "She was. The only things Father ever says to me are either direct orders or passing remarks. Or insults when I'm not perfect for him. No advice or anything useful. I'm almost surprised you added in the word 'pretended.' He would just as soon attack someone for real. Though with Jade that is more believable. He actually does care for her." She swatted a pebble into the snow. Ember winced as it landed with a soft *crunch*. The noise made her feel sick again.

"At least you have parents who love you," Boreal continued, "even if you can't see them. I guess in that sense you haven't lost them at all."

"I guess so," Ember said, "but I still don't know what to do. I just want to go to sleep, dream something nice, and stay in that dream forever. Or at least for a while. You know, I'm actually really lazy, but I'm also good at hiding it."

"I've gotten good at hiding things too," Boreal replied.

Her ears perked up. *'What's that supposed to mean? What are you hiding?'*

"But that's not important. I need to go do something. See you tonight?"

Ember tilted her head. "Yes?"

"Okay, great. Bye." She turned and trotted away deeper into the Rift.

Ember watched her leave in indigo-tinted silence. Her tail twitched a few times, then she walked over to the cave of healing.

"This one?" Hyrees's voice asked as she approached the entrance. He still had his old accent. He didn't seem as eager as she was to adopt a new way of speaking, but it was his voice. She'd decided not to bring up the idea of an accent change a few days before.

"No," Shard's voice replied.

"This one?"

"No."

"Oh wait, I've got it—it's this one."

"No! AGH! Are you doing this on purpose? You skipped it!"

She chuffed emotionlessly and peered inside. Hyrees sat near a wall with four bowls of herbs in front of him. Shard stood a few pawsteps away, fur ruffled and tail thrashing. Echo sat in a corner, glaring at Hyrees.

"Maybe," Hyrees said.

Ember smiled. All the purples and confusion and uncertainty left, though the top of her head still felt tense. *'At least he seems like he's doing better. Actually, he's been acting a lot more like himself lately. He hasn't said anything about death for the past three days. Maybe coming here saved him.'*

"Listen here, Westerner, my brother is trying to teach you," Echo growled. "Why not show him a bloody pawful of respect and actually do what he wants you to do?"

Ember lifted a paw to step in, but hesitated. *'Maybe this isn't a good time. I should probably wait until—'*

"Oh, 'ello Ember," Shard said. "What're you doing here?"

'And now I'm stuck.' She licked her lips. "I'm, er, done with my shift. Boreal's off doing something, so I thought I'd check on y'all."

"We don't need any help, thanks," Echo said.

Shard swatted her leg. "Echo, please stop. I've already told you: she's my friend. I want her to stay that way—being my friend, I mean. O-obviously. And, uh, Ember, while you're here, c-could you please tell him, Hyrees, to stop messing up on purpose? He is chasing me over the ridge, he is."

Ember frowned. *'This is way too much purple for one evening.'* "Chasing? But he's sitting. What ridge is he chasing you over? Though, Hyrees, you are annoying him, so please stop."

Shard groaned dramatically. "It means he's making me go crazy. I didn't mind it at first, I didn't, but then he kept doing it, getting the wrong things, and it is bloody aggravating."

Without another word, he spun around and banged his head against the wall. He sat down and moaned. "Ow. I . . . I don't recommend doing that."

"Well now look what you've done," Echo said, glaring at Ember. She walked up to Shard and rested a paw on his shoulders. "Is your head alright? It's going to be okay. You'll see. He'll come around and stop being such a bobcat to you. You'll see, Shard."

Ember pinned back her ears. "I'm sorry, I didn't know. I've never heard that expression before."

Echo turned to glare at her. "You're only making everything worse. I suggest you leave."

"No, this is my fault," Hyrees said. "Hey, Shard, I didn't mean to upset you. I just, you know, thought it might be funny."

Shard huffed. "Funny for you, maybe, but you don't understand. This is the first time I've ever been trusted with training someone." He bent around to look at him. "If my mum sees you making all these mistakes, she'll make someone else take over. I don't want that. I like training you. I like being around you; you're one of the only friends I have. I don't want to lose this, and we *could* lose it."

"Tahg, Shard, I didn't know. Sorry. Here." Hyrees hooked the correct bowl with his paw, then slid it across the ground to where the two siblings sat. He smiled.

Shard smiled back. "Thanks."

"Would this be a good time to tell you that I'm now a member of Jade's Council?" Ember asked. *'Wait, why did I say that? That was an awkward and weird thing to say, wasn't it?'*

"What?" all three cats said in unison. Ember almost laughed at the overlapping voices, but something told her they wouldn't find it nearly as amusing. *'Yes it was.'*

"Ah, so she came here to brag," Echo said.

A lump formed in her throat as cyan slithered back in. She lowered her head and tried to push it away. "No, no, I wasn't trying to brag, I just wanted . . . to . . . let . . . you . . . know?" Her voice broke and became squeaky at the end, making it sound more like a question than a statement. "I don't know, it seemed like the right thing to say at the time, and then it didn't a moment after I said it."

"So how did that happen?" Hyrees mewed.

"Uh," she said. Something caught in her throat and sent her into a fit of

435

coughing.

"Are you okay?" he asked.

She cleared her throat, then coughed a few more times to make sure whatever had caused the first outburst wouldn't come back for a second. Grey and blue stripes appeared in her head, causing her face to burn. "I'm fine; I'm fine. I don't know if we've got the time right now. You all seem busy, so I should probably go."

Hyrees walked up to her. He pressed his forehead against hers. "I've got all the time in the forest for you."

Ember blinked a few times. Her heartbeat quickened. She leaned into his nuzzle for a moment, then pulled away. *'I'm glad you're feeling better, Hyrees, but this is awkward and I don't like it.'*

"Oh, brilliant, now you've managed to make it even weirder in here," Echo said.

Hyrees ignored her. "It's about time for our shift to end, isn't it, Shard?" he asked.

"It's close," Shard replied. "Though we are supposed to wait for Crow and Sunshine to get here. Just in case. You never know when there'll be some big emergency, you know."

Ember stepped back and cast Echo a wary glance. "You know what? You two can finish up your shift while I, uh, go get some water."

"Sounds good to me," Hyrees said.

Shard nodded. With a slight nod of her own, Ember loped out of the cave. The sinking sun cast a gentle shadow over the world—a shadow made by the Western Mountain. Her mountain. She breathed out a long, shaky sigh and let the shadows engulf her.

As she padded over to the spring, she hummed the lullaby Songbird used to sing to her, then to Kivyress, back when they were young kittens. It brought her some comfort. Her mind wandered to her sister. As if a light switch had been flipped, the comfort disappeared.

'Kivy. They hurt you, didn't they? I hope you get better. You really do deserve better. So much better. Better than what I have here. I wish I could

436

see you again. I could really use some help right about now. I think we're better sisters when we're together. Don't you?'

No one replied. She breathed out a slow puff of air. It condensed and faded into the thick column of steam rising from the spring. She bent down to lap at the water, to let its warmth soothe her, to calm her tense muscles and ease her pounding heart. The humidity of the surrounding air dampened her face. Water beaded on her fur like tiny raindrops.

"Hey, Glowinglegs, didn't expect to see you out here." Echo walked toward her.

Ember flattened her ears, but kept drinking. *'What are you talking about? What is this?'*

"Then again, I also didn't expect you to reunite my brother with one of his only friends or become a member of the council that my own mother won't let me join." Echo stretched and yawned. "But that's beside the point. I actually did expect to find you here because you said you were getting a drink, and I wanted to speak with you. For a change."

Ember stopped mid-lap and looked up at her. *'What? Why?'*

"Tainu, she was . . . half of my world," she continued. "Shard is the other half. My brother loves you and Hyrees. Tainu did too. I never could understand why, or what she saw in a freak like you, but I do know that it would scatter her ashes if she found out how I'd been treating you. And I already know Shard disapproves. I very much doubt we'll ever be friends, but I will honor Shard and Tainu's wishes and tolerate you again. For her sake, and for his sake, not yours or mine."

Ember sat up and tilted her head. "Er, okay. Thank you, I guess. If it makes you feel any better, I'll probably be tormented with regret for the rest of my life."

Echo snorted. "Not really, but I appreciate the attempt. I'm sorry I tried to kill you. That's all. Oh, and don't worry, they're going to send a peace ambassador. And that really is all, so I'm going to leave now."

She watched in confusion as Echo ran back to the shelter of the Rift. *'That was weird. How does she know about the ambassador idea? I th- . . . You are way too tired for this, Ember. Come on. Just finish drinking, and go re-find Hyrees. You can think about this some more tonight.'*

CHAPTER 29
BOREAL

Chaos—complete chaos. Cats were fighting. The scent of blood filled Boreal's nose. She crouched down in a field, a patch of land with no trees that looked far too much like the humans' slope. Flying machines circled overhead, flashing their lights and hissing for her to do something. But everything had happened all too fast. Boreal was frozen.

'Ambush—they ambushed us! Why would they do that? I thought they were our friends. What am I supposed to do?'

"Help! Help me, Boreal!" The voice was muffled yet familiar.

"Father!" she called. "Father, where are you? Why are they attacking us? I thought we were safe."

"Stop asking questions and come help me, you worthless kitten. No wonder Cascade left. I should've run off with her. She left because of you, you know."

"That's not true!" Boreal yowled.

"Then prove it," Falcon snapped. "Save me, and kill the traitor."

The grass in front of her parted, revealing Falcon being pinned by a shadowy figure with glowing green eyes. Something about the eyes looked familiar, but she couldn't place where she'd seen them before. She tackled the cat off of Falcon and sank her fangs into its neck. The cat dropped to the ground. Light from one of the flying machines poured down onto them.

Boreal's throat tightened. A painful lump formed in her chest and traveled up her neck until she couldn't breathe. The cat's eyes stared up at her, kind but lifeless, and all too familiar.

"Hyrees!" she screamed, choking on her own words.

Blood dripped from her mouth, forming a puddle that stained her paws red.

"You're the one who killed him?" a new voice asked, a voice with a fake Eastern accent. Ember ran up to them, eyes glowing with fury. "I never should have trusted you! They were right—you really are a failure. I hate you!"

"Come on, Boreal." Falcon jumped in between them and pawed at her side. "Wake up."

Everything went black as her mind returned to the waking world. Boreal shivered. She breathed a silent sigh of relief. *'It was just a dream. It wasn't real,'* she told herself. Yet it *was* real, in a way. When the West had attacked all that time ago, everything had been moving so fast, she'd been too terrified to think straight. She'd never intended to hurt anyone, much less kill someone, but it had happened, and there was no taking it back. Especially not now; not since Hyrees had explained to her how he'd lost everything. She'd hurt him without even realizing it—by taking his father's life.

"Jade has an announcement to make," Falcon said. His voice sounded close and unusually subdued.

'Fine. What is it now?' she opened her eyes to find him standing a few clawlengths away from her face. She pulled her head back and yawned away the chills. "Alright, Father, I'm coming."

She got up and stretched, then walked out into the Rift. She cast a glance at the quarter beside her as she moved. Empty. *'Oh well. I'll find them later. Not that I really want to speak with them now. Almost wish I could patrol alone again for a change.'*

"Let's go. They're waiting for us," he said, without a growl for some reason. He seemed almost excited, but she didn't want to think too hard about what could be making him so eager. Or nice.

'Wait, that's right, they've made Ember a part of the Council. Or at least her tag. Probably just announcing that. I don't see why he would get so excited about it though, so it may well be something else. I don't know. But does it really matter? None of these things usually affect me, so why do I even bother going?'

"Boreal, come on."

'Oh, because Father insists. Right.' She pawed at a nearby pebble, sending it scampering away, like she wished she could do. "I'm coming, Father."

They walked side by side, but it felt like he was too far to reach. She pictured him being somewhere across a deep chasm where, no matter how close either of them got to the edges of their sides, they couldn't even hear each other speak. She checked the ground ahead for sharp stones, then closed her eyes. Try as hard as she might, she couldn't make her mother's face appear in her imagination. She could imagine her fur to be brown and her stripes to be dark, but they weren't the right shades or shapes. She could have sworn she'd had a narrow face with a clever, ever-calculating expression, but how narrow, and how clever? Boreal sighed and gave up.

'Mother, why didn't you come get me like you promised? Are you dead, or have you forgotten? Or maybe you no longer care. Perhaps you never cared. I wouldn't be surprised. I don't know anyone who really cares. They either pretend or they don't. Maybe I really did chase you away.'

On the other side of the Valley, the first rays of sunshine struck the tip of the western mountain, almost glowing with the soft yellow light. Mist wove through the trees in the Lowlands below, like an eerie lake that swallowed up all life that got in its way. Rogues and Outsiders made their homes amid the lake, most of them ruthless barbarians who would do anything for the right price. Boreal shivered.

"Are you okay? You seem rather shaken-up this morning," Falcon said, breaking the silence.

'Why is he asking me this? I thought he didn't care.' She looked down at her paws. "I'm fine. It was just a dream."

"And you're sure you're okay? I know you had some awful terrors after we left the West. Woke me up twice."

'He never told me I woke him up.' She paused for a moment, then kept walking. "I already told you; I'm fine. I'm not a kitten anymore. I think I can get over a little nightmare."

"So it's more than the dream that's got you upset."

Boreal grimaced. "I don't want to talk about it."

She winced, expecting him to demand an explanation like he always did, but to her surprise, he sighed and continued moving forward. "Very well," he said. "I'll leave it alone."

They stopped in front of the rocks Jade announced things from. She sat on top of the tallest stone, towering over her colony as usual. Beside her, on a slightly smaller stone, sat Eclan, her favorite Rogue lackey. Jade's tail twitched once. Twice. "I hope you are all having a pleasant morning," she said. "I've gathered you all together to make a couple of announcements. The first of which is that the Westerner we've taken in, Ember, has proven her worth. I have added her to the Council. Her knowledge will serve us well and lead us into an era of improvement beyond what any of our ancestors could have ever imagined."

The tiny speech was clearly meant to be patriotic, yet the murmur following indicated mixed feedback. She personally didn't want Ember on the Council, but that was mostly because Ember herself had said she didn't want to be on it. However, from an unbiased perspective, it made sense—a cat with the answers to everything offering the commander advice. It was the obvious thing to do.

"The next announcement I have has to do with our somewhat shaky relationship with the West. The Council has decided it would be best if we sought to make peace with our neighbors once again. The longer we are in a state of declared war, the more time we are giving them to launch an attack. While another fight is unlikely, if there were to be one, we've predicted there to be mass casualties on both sides, possibly leading to the eventual ends of both colonies."

Another wave of mumbling swept the lake of cats. Jade ignored them.

"This is why I'm sending Falcon, my most trusted advisor, to the West with gifts carried by two of our strongest border guards."

Boreal's eyes widened. *'Father? Wait, no, he can't go. What if I lose him too? If he dies, I'll have lost my entire family.'*

"They will leave this morning. Eclan will guide them safely to their destination, and together they will bring a new era of peace to Dark's Valley. When he returns, successful and heroic, we will be safe once again from the oppression of war."

Some cats cheered. Others scoffed. Most of the Colony wanted to leave behind the death and destruction of war, but some still wanted revenge, and still others wanted to forget the Western Colony even existed.

Boreal turned to Falcon. "Father, please don't go. Tell her to send someone else."

He smiled and placed a paw on her side. "You know it doesn't work like that. When Jade gives me an order, it's my duty to follow it through. The entire Council has agreed it would be for the best if I went. It gives us the greatest chance of success."

"What if Jade and the Council are wrong?"

"Boreal, I volunteered to go," he said.

She slid his paw off of her shoulder. "Then what if *you're* wrong?"

"The Westerners would have to be absolute fluffheads to kill me. If they have any brains among them, they'll accept the offer we give them."

"And if not?"

Falcon leaned closer. "Then you make sure they pay for their stupidity," he whispered in the tone that meant 'you had better agree with me, Boreal.' "Okay?"

She nodded. "So when do you leave?"

He chuffed. All the threats in his voice vanished. "Oh, so you *are* trying to get rid of me. We're going after I help Jade and the others gather the gifts together."

"Father, you know that's not why I asked."

"Falcon, come. We must prepare for your journey," Jade called.

He smiled again. "I know. I'll see you later. My colony needs me."

Boreal grimaced as he got up and left. *'Well, that was odd. I didn't think he could smile. Not for me at least.'*

She went to the storage cave to get food while Falcon helped Jade. When she received her meal, a small piece of venison, she went and hid in the rocks at the back of the Rift. As much as she liked her new friends, now was not the time to make small talk with them.

'Why is he acting so kind now that he's about to leave?' She thought, absentmindedly gnawing on her food. *'Does he think he might die? If so, why would he volunteer?'* She sighed. *'I don't know.'*

Falcon's head popped up from the edge of the rock pile. "Hey, is there room for one more up here?"

Her muscles tensed. She licked her lips. "There's a lot of room up here, if you're willing to make the climb."

"I'd climb a mountain to get to you," he said. He disappeared behind the stones, then hopped up with a turkey breast. He padded over to her and set it down. "And I mean it. I want you to know that, whatever happens, I love you. I always have and I always will; even if I've never been good at expressing it. Your mother, she loved you too. I'm sorry I chased her away from us."

Boreal thought for a moment. "If Mother came back, and I decided I wanted to go with her, would you still love me?"

He nuzzled her side. "Of course I would. I'd be sad to see you leave, but I wouldn't stop you. In all honesty, you'd probably be happier out there. Believe it or not, I want you to be happy."

"I'm not so sure I believe it."

"Listen, I've made some mistakes, but I do love you. If worse comes to worst and there is a war, I don't want you fighting in it. I've taken some fairly large risks to keep you safe. I've pushed the limits of my power. But the important thing is, as long as you don't fight, you'll be okay."

She sat up, ears back. "You think you're going to die, don't you? You think there will be a war."

"I don't know, Boreal. It could go either way, but I thought it would be best for you if I took precautions. Set things right and in order. Now come on, we should eat. Our food will freeze if we don't have it now."

'Okay, now I'm worried,' she thought as she went back to her meal.

They finished their food in silence, then Jade found them and ushered Falcon over to the border guards. Boreal followed at a distance.

Jade pressed her forehead against his. "Be careful. I don't know what I'd do without you."

"I will, love. Take care of yourself," he purred.

Jade turned to look at the guards. "You two will protect him with your lives, understood?"

They lowered their heads. "Yes, Commander," the older of the two replied.

"We'll make sure he gets back safely, ma'am," the other said.

"Good," Jade said. "Now, where is that Rogue? He was here a moment ago. Boreal, make yourself useful and fetch him for me. I think I saw him scampering off toward the Northern Rim."

Boreal stepped back. "Uh, yes, yes ma'am, I'll find him."

"Be quick about it, molly. We're wasting time."

Boreal lowered her head and trotted off across the Rift, sniffing the breeze for Eclan's foul odor. She caught it moments before spotting his thrashing tail on the other side of a rock. Hushed voices murmured, too faint to make out. She edged closer.

"Are you sure you don't want to come?" Eclan said. "You suggested it, didn't you? If something bad happens, there's a chance you'll get blamed, and if you get blamed, there's a chance you ain't escaping this place alive."

"I barely even suggested it. It was Falcon who really jumped on the idea," a voice with a distinctly fake Eastern accent replied.

Boreal's ears perked up. 'Ember? Why are you, of all cats, talking to him?'

"Part of your job is keeping things from going wrong, isn't it?" Ember continued. "If anyone gets hurt, it would be more your fault than mine. Besides, I kind of like it here, and we've just gotten settled. I mean, even Hyrees is doing better, if that says anything."

"Look, all I'm sayin' is that this might be your last chance to get out of the

445

system. You could be free from the tyranny of living under a commander and, you know, being a council member will only make you even less free. Trust me, this place ain't as great as it seems."

Boreal snapped her tail in confusion. *'Wait, what does he care if she stays or goes? And I don't want her to go. If she and Hyrees leave, I'll have no one left. Maybe not even Father. Please say "no." '*

"I, uh, I appreciate the offer, but I'd rather stay here and make sure everything works out. Maybe after the Colonies make peace, but not before. Otherwise I'd go crazy not knowing what happened."

"You're already crazy, kitten, but it is your choice. That's not to say you made the right one, but I'm sure your eavesdroppin' friend appreciates it."

Boreal's chest tightened, face burning with embarrassment. She sighed and walked around the rock.

"Oh, uh, hi-hello, Boreal," Ember said. She looked down at her mechanical paws and rubbed one on top of the other.

"Sorry about that," Boreal replied. "Eclan, Jade is looking for you. It's time for you to leave, apparently."

"Of course," Eclan said. "Just had a little side mission I needed to complete. Nothing too big. I'm done with it now. Oh, hold up, Ember, remember, you still owe me answers. Don't get yourself killed before I get back, got it?"

"Got it," she said. "I'm not planning on dying anytime soon."

Eclan smiled. "Good."

"But things don't always go according to plan," she added.

"Eh, good enough," he said.

"Side mission?" Boreal asked.

Eclan brushed past her. As he moved, his tail thwacked against her nose. Boreal growled and trotted after him.

"There's an Outsider I met in the Lowlands that Eclan sometimes works for," Ember said, running along beside her. "He wants me to join a group of Outsiders he knows, but I'm not sure I want to take that kind of risk, especially not when everything is going so well for once. I mean, all I know about it is what I've been told about it. I don't even know for a fact it exists, so I'm staying here for now."

Boreal smiled. "I'm glad you won't be leaving me. You and Hyrees are the only friends I have, you know." Her smile faded. "My father is leaving today to go to your colony. He seems to think he might die. What do you make of it? You know your colony better than anyone. Does he have a chance at making peace?"

Ember thought for a few moments. "As long as Lupine is in charge . . . I don't know. But I do know that pretty much everyone in the West is terrified of war. I like to think they would get excited by the idea uh-of making peace again after only one battle. I know I am. I want this to be over."

'That's not very comforting.' She sighed. "Me too."

"You're certainly fond of taking your time, aren't you?" Jade asked as they approached her.

"Me and Eclan were talking," Ember said. "I, er, still owe him for-for helping us get here safely. She didn't want to interrupt."

'Thank you.'

"Oh, really?" Jade's eyes narrowed. "Interesting."

Boreal turned her attention back to Falcon. She walked up to him and pressed her head against his neck. "Please be safe. Please come home."

He rested his chin on her neck. "I will. As long as I'm alive, I'll always come back for you."

'Well then, that's an odd choice of words. And again, not comforting.'

He stepped back and stared at her. His expression looked somewhere between guilt, excitement, and dread. "I know I've done some bad things. I've abused you with words like 'useless,' 'disappointing,' and 'failure,' but I take that all back now. I want you to know that I really do love you. When I come back, I promise I'll try to be a better father. Try to let everything else fall into the past."

"Father, you're not making any sense. Do you have something you're actually trying to tell me, or are you only trying to confuse me? Because that's what you're doing right now."

He sighed. "I'm trying to say that I love you and that nothing that happens will ever change it. I might not seem like a good cat, but I promise you there are reasons why I do the things I do."

Boreal scowled. "Even calling me a fluffheaded idiot when I don't do what you want?"

Falcon's ears drooped. "No, that . . . that was wrong. I hope you can forgive me."

She snorted. "Don't die. Come back here and be my father for a while, then I'll decide if you can be forgiven." She turned her tail to him and walked away. "Come on, Ember. We've got a border to patrol."

————

As that rather frustrating day wore on, a burst of warmth hit the forest (Ember had predicted this with her tag; the snap of nicer weather was why Jade had insisted the ambassadors leave so soon). By sunset, most of the snow melted off, making the ground muddy and slippery. The next day, the sun finished off what remained. A lack of snow and ice made the forest seem more dead than usual. Even the pine trees looked less than appealing, their needles drooping and their branches sagging. It was as if the entire Eastern Mountain would be depressed until its oh so precious chief advisor returned.

Boreal sighed and stared down at the half-carved stick in her paws. Glares from the distant fire pits and even more distant stars provided the only light she had to see by. *'What now?'* she thought, leaning against the wall of her quarter. *'There is absolutely nothing of interest going on right now to mark about.'* She set the stick down and watched it roll itself into the ever-growing pile of wood hiding in the shadows of her small tunnel. She, er, *borrowed* them from the mountain of sticks and branches gathered for use in the fires. Only one or two at a time, though. Just enough to chronicle the day's or mooncycle's events when she got bored.

"Hey, Boreal, whatcha doing?" Hyrees appeared in the entrance to her quarter. He smiled, but something about it looked forced; his eyes were too squinted and pained.

Her heartbeat quickened. *'Oh, oh no, he hasn't found out the truth, has he? About what I did to him? No, no, don't be silly. He would be furious, and there's no one who would have told him, because either no one knows or no one cares. This probably isn't anything too terrible. Maybe he's looking for Ember.'* She breathed a silent sigh of relief, pushed the stick farther into the pile, then turned to face him. "Nothing important. Is there something wrong? Ember's climbed to the ridge to get a better view of the Valley, if it's her you're after."

"Nah," he said. "I was just wondering if you wanted to talk some more. Sorry. I know I'm probably bothering you, but on the off chance that I'm not, well . . . yeah, I'm bothering you. I should go."

Boreal stood up. "No, no, it's okay. You're not bothering me. I like our talks—especially when I'm bored, which I happen to be right now. Maybe I should come out there." She lowered her head and fumbled away from the comfort of her quarters. He backed up to make room for her, and she sat down in front of him. "What is it, Hyrees?"

He sighed and looked away. "I just wanted to thank you. If Ember had gotten paired up with anyone else, none of this would have worked out so well. She probably would have left with Eclan the other day. I really want her to be safe, and this is the safest place in the Valley. Also, I think having someone to listen to my problems the other day really helped me out. Without you, I don't think I would've gotten this far."

"You're welcome, but I'm still not sure why you couldn't have talked those things out with Ember. I don't know you as well as she does. I would think she'd understand you better."

He snorted. "It's not really understanding so much as just having someone listen without that someone drifting off and starting to wonder if mice and squirrels are related. It's a nice change."

Boreal chuffed. "I take it there's a story behind that, but I won't pry. So why are you really here, talking to me, of all cats?"

He shifted his weight from paw to paw, making himself sway. His tail twitched. "It, uh, seemed like the right thing to do, talking with someone this evening. It's a nice evening. For being alive and stuff."

"You're making even less sense than Father. Hyrees, what are you trying to say?"

He lost his balance and lurched forward, but caught himself before his face could hit the ground. His pupils dilated like a cat in a fight. "I . . ." He dropped to his stomach and winced. "I don't feel very good. I mean, I knew it would hurt, but I didn't think it would be this bad. A-am I not supposed to feel my toes?"

Her eyes widened. She couldn't decide whether to back up and give him space, or to rush in and try to help. "What did you do to yourself?!"

Hyrees coughed a few times. It turned into a hack, which sent spittle and bile flying everywhere. "Ugh," he mewed. "I was thinking, since everyone was happy again, I could be with my family and be happy again." He looked up at her, pleading and afraid. "B-but now I'm not so sure that's what I want."

'Oh, bleedin' fox, no. Don't let him die too.' Boreal's jaw tensed. Her pulse quickened. "Hyrees, you have to tell me what you did."

"Ate . . . b-berries," he mumbled.

"Oh no," she whispered under her breath. "Uh, stay here. I'll go get help."

She backed up a few steps and looked around for a healer. Finding none, she charged toward the cave. The world seemed to move in slow motion. Her legs couldn't run fast enough as she shoved cats out of her way. They growled and snapped, but it didn't matter. Boreal burst into the cave of healing, startling Crow and Sunshine. "Hyrees ate snake berries! Come on, you have to help him!"

"What?" Sunshine mewed. "But why would he? He knows what they do, right? Didn't anyone tell him?" She hopped over to the herb bowls, then scooped up a few different types into a taller, thinner bowl.

"I . . . I don't know," Boreal replied. Her mind was a blur. She couldn't focus on anything. Even her eyes had difficulty locking onto a target.

Crow grabbed a small stick and a whole dried leaf. "Let's go," he said. "Try to run, Sunshine. Our time is limited. Boreal, lead the way."

450

She darted out of the cave, back toward her quarter. Her heart pounded. More adrenaline raced through her body than she'd ever thought possible. She could almost feel it as it pulsed through her. *'I wanted something interesting to happen today, but not this. Nothing like this. Please be okay, you fluffheaded tomcat. Why is this happening?'*

When they reached him, he was barely even awake, laying with his chin on the ground and drooling like a coyote. "Please," he whispered, eyes wide but unfocused. "Don't let me die. I don't want to die. I don't wanna die anymore. Make it stop!"

Crow chewed the leaf, then spit out a gooey mash. He opened Hyrees's mouth, then shoved it in. "Swallow this."

After some hesitation, Hyrees obeyed. He propped himself up and vomited twice. Boreal's stomach did a backflip inside of her. Her insides lurched at the sight and smell. Crow leaned closer and sniffed the pool, causing her to gag.

He smiled. "Good news!" he said. "I can see whole berries in here. If he'd chewed them, he'd already be dead. There's progress for you. He might actually survive."

He continued to examine the mess while Sunshine gave Hyrees the contents of the medicine tube. Hyrees chewed and swallowed with a look of dazed disgust.

Using the stick he'd brought, Crow flicked the berries out of the puddle. "Well, these have to go," he said, then proceeded to lick them up one by one. Boreal ran out of the Rift and threw up beneath a dead bush. Crow followed her. He spit them out on top of the former contents of her still queasy stomach.

She coughed. "You are disgusting."

He chuffed. "Maybe, but my methods are effective."

She shoved him in the direction of the Rift. "Just get back over there and help her keep him alive! I need to get Ember."

When he obliged, Boreal charged across the Rift. Ember met her halfway, hyperventilating and eyes wide with anxiety. "W-where is he? Did he really eat snake berries? Please tell me I misheard."

Boreal shook her head. "Sorry, Ember. He's not doing well, but Crow seems to think he'll make it, if you trust Crow's judgment."

Without a word, Ember ran past her toward the quarters. Boreal followed. *'For the sake of you both, please be okay. For the sake of . . . me.'* She stopped a few leaps away. *'I'm the one who caused this, aren't I? I started this. By killing one cat, I've killed two, and am currently killing a third. I'm killing one of my only friends. This really is my fault.'*

"Hyrees!" Ember yowled.

"I'm sorry. I'm sorry . . . about everything. I messed up," Hyrees said. His voice was hoarse and subdued, like the pitiful mews of a tired and very sick kitten.

Ember opened her mouth several times while the healers worked, but she closed it again each time, as if whatever she was going to say was no longer relevant. Or maybe she'd simply thought better of it. Boreal watched with morbid curiosity as Ember's gaze drifted from inanimate object to inanimate object. On occasion it fell back on Hyrees, but it only lingered on him for a moment or two.

'What color is she feeling right now? Probably not one she likes. I'm sorry, Ember.'

Sunshine finished giving him pawfuls of herbs and began massaging his side. It seemed to calm him down some. Ember jumped to her paws, then ran off across the Rift.

After a few moments of silence, his ears started to twitch. His eyes went wide and rolled around wildly in his head. "Ember," he said. "Ember, I can't see anything." He jumped up and spun in a circle. "Where are you? I can't see anything! Wait, no." He froze in place as Ember returned with a piece of charcoal. His gaze suddenly found focus, even through the blue film covering it. "Fox! There's a fox!"

Ember spat out the burnt stick. "I'm not a fox. Now eat this, please. It might help."

"Ember, look out! There's a fox, and it's going to eat me!"

Boreal watched helplessly. Her neck felt so tight she could barely breathe.

'I should tell him. But how? Why didn't I tell him earlier? I should have. If he dies, I'll never be able to tell him the truth. And I'll never know if he'd never want to speak to me again. I wouldn't blame him if he didn't. He trusted me, and I've betrayed that trust. I'm killing him. Please save him!'

Cats peered out of their quarters, some watching, some glaring, and some genuinely concerned. His yowling made a few sleepy voices hiss for silence. Ember picked up the charcoal again, broke off a piece by wedging it between her paws, then shoved the smaller piece into his mouth. Sunshine rushed over to help hold it closed until he swallowed. "Are you sure this is safe?" she asked. "I've never tried giving someone burnt wood before. How do you know it will help?"

"I don't," Ember replied, expression tight and grim. Hyrees swallowed. They released him. "But Thai said carbon can help absorb poison, and burnt wood contains carbon. I hope it'll help."

"Bleh! What was that?" Hyrees said. "Who was that? Fox—the fox is still here! It's getting closer. Kill it!" He backed up a few steps, ears pinned to his head and eyes wide with terror.

Boreal sighed. Something inside her felt ready to burst. The fear and guilt caught her up and almost made her want to cry. 'Why couldn't I have told him during our talk? No, never mind, that would've been bad. He said talking with him helped. It wouldn't have if I'd told him how I more or less caused almost every bad thing that's happened to him. He might have already died if I'd done that.'

"Poor thing," Sunshine whispered to Ember. She lifted her deformed paw to her muzzle. "He's still hallucinating. Those were a lot of berries he ate. He might not make it. I just . . . wanted to tell you now so you don't get your hopes up. And even if his health recovers—"

"Fox!" he repeated. Then collapsed.

Boreal's chest felt like it was about to explode. She wanted to run somewhere far away and pretend it wasn't happening. 'But it is happening. I did this. I did this to him. I killed him. I sentenced him to die. I killed another cat!'

Ember leaned closer and pawed at his side. "Oh no. No. No! Come on! Wake up; you have to wake up! Why is no one answering? Thai, is there anyone we haven't tried?"

"Ember, you have tried calling everyone in your contacts list." A strange, oddly stiff voice replied. Boreal had heard it a few times, but never this clearly or closely. "Hye is probably asleep, and you already know Michelle and Matthew have not been answering your calls for several days. Not to mention we seem to be far from any known roadways. According to my calculations, no human can reach us on foot fast enough to help."

"But . . ." She stared at nothing, breathing hard.

Sunshine placed her paw on Ember's shoulder. "Calm down. He's still breathing. He's still got a chance. I gave him some plants to make him sleep. It doesn't usually take effect this quickly, but it should give him some time to rest and recover."

"I believe he'll make it," Crow said. As he walked over to them, faint rays of moonlight caught his pelt, making the little white spots and patches covering him shimmer like stars. "I've been a healer for eighteen winters. I've seen cats far worse off than him make full recoveries. Full or at least partial, but the important thing is he has a chance. Now let's get him into his quarters. I don't imagine any of you intending to leave him here."

Boreal got up, still sick to her stomach, and offered to help carry him. Together, the four cats pushed and pulled until he rested comfortably in his quarters. By the time they were done, Ember was crying.

'I did this to him, and to you,' Boreal thought again, this time trying to reach her without speaking the words out loud. 'I'm sorry. I'm sorry—please forgive me.' She gave up and looked away. 'What if Father was right all along?'

Stupid, incompetent, worthless—the words bounced around inside her head. She retreated to her quarters and lay down beside her pile of carved sticks. For a brief moment, she considered shoving the pile into the abyss beyond her tunnel out of frustration. She decided against it. Potentially destroying the only thing she was proud of would make her feel worse. Boreal rolled onto her back and covered her eyes with her paws. *'Why didn't I tell him?'*

When she got up, the stars had changed positions. Everything was quiet. Even Ember's gentle sobbing had faded away. Her paws were too restless to sleep, so she walked to the edge of the Rift and watched the stars.

"Oh, wonderful, now I've got someone to stay awake with."

Boreal whipped her head around to find Echo trotting up to her. "Was that sarcasm or a genuine statement?" she asked.

Echo thought for a moment. "I'm not sure. It felt like something I was meant to say, so I said it."

"Oh. So does Shard know? About Hyrees?"

"He came to visit while you were in your quarters. He wasn't exactly being quiet, either."

"Oh, right," she said. "How's he taking it then?"

Echo sighed. "He's messed up about it all, that's for sure. He already worries a lot. He doesn't need any of this extra stuff to bother with. I'm starting to worry his worrying will be the death of him." She turned to look at her. "You haven't told them yet, have you?"

Boreal tensed. Another rush of adrenaline hit her bloodstream. "Ah. No— don't tell Ember. I'll try to do it myself when I can."

"Don't jump the ridge," Echo growled. "I'm not a gossip, I just listen to a lot of it. I was only wondering."

"Sorry," she whispered.

Overhead, stars flickered in the cloudless sky. One of them fell out of place and left a tiny trail in its wake as it so suddenly and gracefully died.

"So why are you up? You work the day shift, don't you?" Boreal heard herself ask. Her eyes narrowed. *'Why did I ask that? I don't care. I don't even know her all that well.'*

"Yes, I work days. You may not know this, but I'm actually a terrible sleeper. I've had to fend off nightmares as long as I can remember. For a while I was able to actually get good sleep, but they came back some time not long before the fight, and they've only gotten worse ever since. Now I have them almost every night. That's why I'm awake. I don't want to go to sleep. I guess you could say I'm . . . scared."

'So she has nightmares too? I guess witnessing the bloodiest battle in all Colony history can do that to someone. Will I keep having nightmares for the rest of my life too? What if Hyrees dies? Will I ever get that out of my conscience? Wait—' "Why are you telling me this?"

Echo smiled faintly. "Because even if you decide to tell someone, no one will believe you, and even if someone did, I've decided opinions no longer matter to me. There's not a lot left that still matters to me, really. But I've still got Shard, so I guess most of what's happened has been worth it. More or less." She sighed again. "I just hope it continues to be worth it," she said under her breath.

"Hmm?" Boreal asked.

"Nothing. We should go to sleep. Tomorrow will be an interesting day. One I can't honestly say I'm looking forward to, but at least it'll be one step closer to getting this bloody mess over with."

'Oh, right, Father's coming home.' She stood up and glanced back at the quarters. Ember and Hyrees were both still asleep. "Yep," she said. "Goodnight, I suppose?"

"Probably not," Echo replied.

Without another word, Echo loped away toward her den with Shard and Jade. Boreal went back to her own quarters. She lay down beside her sticks, then tossed and turned until all her fears and doubts faded into nothing. At last she drifted into a fitful yet dreamless sleep.

———

"Healer! We need a healer now!"

Boreal's eyes fluttered open. Immediately a sense of dread came over her. She closed them again.

Someone pawed at her shoulder. "Wake up!"

"Mff?" she mumbled. She looked up to find Ember staring at something either in the Rift or just outside of it. "Ember? W-what? Is Hyrees . . ."

"No, he's still asleep," Ember replied. "Boreal, it's Eclan. He's come back."

She leaped to her paws, causing Ember to jump backward. "Great! Good. Where's Father? I need to speak with him."

Ember grimaced and bit the tip of her tongue, which stuck out of her mouth almost menacingly. Boreal's heart sank in her chest.

"I-I don't know," Ember said.

She shoved past Ember and broke into a run. Her eyes locked onto the all-too-familiar black and white pelt of Eclan. Black, white and . . . red? She slid to a stop. The Rogue was covered from nose to tail with recently scabbed bites and scratches. Shard and another healer raced back and forth between him and the cave, gathering supplies to treat him where he sat.

"What happened, Eclan?" Jade asked. Her usually stoic eyes looked damp and ready to cry. "Where are Falcon and the others?"

"I'm sorry, Jade," he said. "I tried to save them, but . . . they're all dead."

The world stopped.

"Father," Boreal whispered.

"How can they be dead?" Jade asked. "They were on a peace mission. They went to stop the fighting! How do I know you're telling the truth, you insolent Rogue?"

'No. No, this isn't happening.' She took a few steps back, letting the words sink in. Dead. Falcon was dead. Her father was gone.

"I barely escaped with my own life. If it weren't for my sense 'a respect for you, Commander, I would've gone home and licked my wounds. But I didn't; I came here, risking everything, because you deserve to know what happened to your cats."

"Then tell me what happened, Eclan."

He lifted his head and growled, "Them foxing Westerners killed them."

CHAPTER 30
EMBER

'Come on, Hyrees. Please wake up. Please. Don't leave me here like this. Not now.' Ember groomed Hyrees's forehead. She mewed soft gibberish to herself. Somewhere in the Rift, Jade yowled. Ember couldn't make out any words, but the Eastern commander sounded upset. She swallowed hard. "Sorry, I have to go," she whispered. "Whatever happened to Falcon and the guards, I think it might end up being bad for us. I mean, obviously it's no good for Boreal, but if Eclan was right, and we do get blamed—wait, Eclan seemed to know this was going to happen. That's . . . mildly suspicious. Don't you think? Hyrees? This is the part where you wake up and agree with me. You're only pretending to be asleep, right? I know you can hear me. Come on."

Jade shouted again. Ember bit her tongue and fought back tears. *'He's not waking up. He may never wake up. Why did you do this, Hyrees? I thought everything was going so well.'* She sniffled as a single teardrop trickled into her fur. Sunshine's words repeated themselves in her mind. *'He might not make it. Might not. Might not. What am I going to do? Ember, go find out what happened. He won't go anywhere. If Falcon is dead . . .'*

She licked him one last time, drew a deep, anxiety-ridden breath, then walked toward the commotion.

"Then tell me what happened, Eclan," Jade said as she approached the frantic group of cats.

"Them foxing Westerners killed them," Eclan replied.

Ember froze mid-step. *'Oh. Oh no.'* The fur along her spine raised. Pinpricks of icy pain dug into the back of her head. *This is bad. Why did I suggest that? Why did I even—you knew you weren't thinking straight! Why did you even open your mouth? Of all the fluffheaded—'*

"What do you mean?" Jade asked.

"We were ambushed," he said. "They took us by surprise. I'd injured my paw a little n' fallen behind right before it happened. Falcon, brave tom he was, took the lead in my place. As we approached the territory, they jumped out from the trees. Took Falcon out almost immediately. He had no time to react at all. None of us did. By the time we realized what had happened, they'd already started attacking the rest of us. Me, being farther back, had more time to escape. The other two weren't so lucky. They fought well, but it happened too fast. It was the three of us against five well-rested Westerners. I'm a lucky tom to even be alive right now."

Ember lowered her paw. Grey fog choked her head. *'Uh oh.'*

"It's the freak's fault!" one cat yowled. "She did this on purpose! She sent them to their dea—"

"We never should have trusted them. All Westerners are coyotes," another said, cutting her off.

"You can't trust a one of 'em, I tell you!" snapped an older tomcat. "I'd 'a thought you'd learned your lesson, Jade. These two—no, *three* times they've attacked us unprovoked. How much will it take for you to realize this is a problem we need to take action against?"

"Calm down, all of you!" Jade said. The cats around her fell silent, but the tension remained. "Shard, take Eclan to the cave. No need for all this running around. You'll only get in the way. As for the rest of you, go gather the Colony. I'm calling a meeting, and I want everyone capable of coming present. You especially, Ember. In fact, I would like for you to remain at my side for the entirety of the meeting, starting now."

Ember shook herself out of her daze. "Uh, yes, y-yes ma'am."

"Come," Jade said.

Ember obeyed. They padded toward Jade's den and announcement rock. As they walked, Ember tried to put together some form of apology that didn't sound suspicious. *I didn't know about the ambush? Nope. Sounds like I was sent here on purpose. I didn't mean for this to happen? No, that could easily be taken out of context.*

"Why did y'all listen to me?" she asked.

"What do you mean?" Jade said.

"I didn't even have time to think about what I was saying. You yourself said I wasn't in any state to give any kind of input on something that important. And even then I was going to take it back, but he seemed so excited, and I thought it might work, so I let it go without protest. I was wrong. This is my fault. I'll accept whatever punishment you decide to give me, but please don't hurt Hyrees. He had nothing to do with it."

"What do you make of the ambush, then?" Jade asked. "It would seem the West knew they were coming."

Jade's tail twitched with each step she took. Ember tried to focus on its black tip to keep from getting distracted. "I don't know. I think I might have been used. I doubted it at first, but your theory about Lupine might be right. He has some connections with Outsiders through Whitehaze, his mentor, and possibly Eclan. Farlight saw Eclan talking with Whitehaze, and that's what got him killed. I'm starting to wonder if Eclan might be the one connecting all this and helping Lupine make everything go the way he wants. Or maybe even someone else in the West. There are some fairly power-hungry cats there. Especially in the Western Council. I don't know. Maybe Eclan is lying."

"Eclan has been the East's faithful messenger since my mate commanded. He is almost what I would call a friend. Falcon, on multiple occasions did indeed call him a friend. Falcon himself asked that he go because of this. He trusted that Rogue more than he trusted the guards. Your kitten friend was mistaken."

Ember flattened her ears. Dull yellow, like an old bear's fangs, flared in her mind. The burst of anger made her head feverish and tense. "Farlight is dead," she growled. "Eclan is the only cat I know with any kind of connection to both colonies. He himself told me before he left that I should come with him because if something bad happened I would probably get blamed. To me that sounds like he knew this would happen. We have to at least consider—"

"That is enough, Ember," Jade snapped.

Ember winced, cowering beneath her glare. *'Oh. She's crying. Tahg, she really is upset.'*

Jade sighed, then continued, "While I admit I found it odd at first that Eclan was the only survivor, I can understand how it would happen. I snapped at him out of anger, but it is not his fault any more than I believe it to be yours. Do not speak again until the meeting is over, or else I'll let my colony have its way with both you and Hyrees."

Silver and bright green melded with the yellows inside of her. She clamped her teeth over her tongue, remembering the words of the vengeful Easterners. *'Okay. Don't do anything stupid, Ember. Don't be a fluffhead. Keep your mouth closed. Mouth closed. Keep it. Don't die. Please. Hyrees.'*

The yellow became mottled with creamy white. *'Wait, how could you intentionally overlook something like this? The things I said are facts. What you said, well, they're mostly facts too, but how much you trust someone only determines how much control they have over you. I could say and do things to gain your trust. I did. And while I didn't mean for this to happen, this is where listening to me got you—with a dead advisor. I don't get how you, of all cats, can keep trusting him so blindly like this. Not after everything that's happened. Hum. I wish I could've said that out loud, but tahg, I'd be in so much trouble.'*

Jade climbed up her rocks. Ember followed, head and tail low, and tried to sit far enough back that cats might not notice her.

The Eastern Colony gathered beneath them. When enough cats showed up, Jade began, "For those of you who were not present when my messenger returned this morning, I have some terrible news. The cats I have sent to make peace are dead. Eclan is the only survivor."

Cries of anger and anguish rose to a roar. Ember flattened her ears.

"Quiet down, please. Everyone. I would like to apologize. This is, in part, my fault. I knew the risks, but I still sent them to their deaths. I—" Her voice broke into a sob. "Excuse me."

Jade climbed down her rock far enough to be hidden from the crowd, sat down, hunched over, and cried. Ember looked at her paws, trying to give her privacy. When Jade had cried out the last of her tears, she straightened herself up, groomed the moisture from her eyes, then climbed back up to face her colony.

"Forgive me, and thank you for your patience as I struggle to deal with this rather sudden and tragic news. As I was trying to say earlier, I do not believe our Western guests knew there was to be an ambush. However, Ember believes she may have been used by Lupine to achieve such an act of violence. She is prepared to take full responsibility for these recent events, but I see no need to punish her specifically. Because of this, I ask that none of you harm her or her mate."

Ember breathed a silent sigh of relief. Her gaze wandered around the gathering, then landed on Boreal. She wasn't crying, and she didn't look angry, but Ember couldn't decipher anything beyond that.

"Now this marks the third time Westerners have attacked us unprovoked," Jade said. "We've tried all reasonable methods of working this out. The longer we wait to take action, the stronger we allow them to get. It's only a matter of time before they decide to come to us. I've gathered you here to ask one important question: should we fortify the Rift, or should we launch an attack of our own?"

A nervous lump formed in Ember's chest. *'No. Please no. Don't attack. Just leave them alone. They aren't coming here; I can almost guarantee it. If Lupine's behind it, the West isn't. If we could just find out—'*

"Launch an attack!" one called.

"This is our best position of defense. If we want to win this war, staying here is our best chance. Here we have the advantage," another said.

"If we stay here, it'll only be the Battle of Stone Ridge all over again," the cat beside him snapped.

"We have to take action! We've remained passive for too long. They've pawed at our nest one time too m—"

"The West has to pay!"

Jade closed her eyes and controlled her breathing. "Those who wish to stay, gather by the nearest fire pit. Those who would like to fight, remain where you are."

Several of the cats got up and walked away to the fire pit, but not many compared to how many remained. Boreal walked away with them, but the lump in Ember's chest kept extending into her neck, constricting it until she couldn't breathe.

Jade looked down at the remaining cats. "It is enough. You all have the day off from your regular duties to prepare. Those of you who work night shift, I'm afraid I'm going to have to ask you to stay awake longer today. To compensate, we will all get our meals and go to sleep sooner. In order for this to work, we must all be on the same schedule. We will leave shortly before dawn. On the day following, you may take the vengeance you desire."

The remaining cats cheered, then began chanting an Eastern battle cry. The noise stabbed Ember's ears. She sank to her stomach and wrapped her paws around her head, shivering all over. *'I didn't save them. Oh, no, you've just made everything so much worse. What am I supposed to do now? What do I do? What do I do? My family.'*

One of the cats from the fire pit walked up to Jade's rock. "Listen, I know I can't change your decision, but please believe me when I say it's a mistake," she said. "Nothing good will come out of this."

Jade sighed. "Maybe, but if they don't go at my command, these cats will only run off and do it themselves, then cast me out when they return, if they return at all. The least I can do is give them the structure they need to be successful."

"Then I ask that you be careful. Something about this feels very wrong," the cat said.

Echo jumped onto the stones. She lowered her head. "I'm with you, Mum, but Shard stays."

"I wasn't planning on bringing him," Jade replied. "He doesn't belong on the battlefield. Though I will admit I'm surprised you would want to go."

"You would be surprised by a lot of things about me, if you'd just care enough to pay attention." Without waiting for a response, Echo jumped back down and started to walk away.

"Echo," Jade said, "come back here. Now."

Echo stopped, but made no moves to return. "What?"

"I want you to stay here and keep watch over Ember. Make sure she doesn't try to escape. I would prefer she stays alive, but if it comes down to it, you may kill her. I'd rather have her dead than have her warn her colony. Otherwise we'll all die."

"Can't you make someone else watch her? I need to go."

"Echo." Jade jumped down and walked over to her daughter. "If I die, you will become the next commander. The Colony needs you alive. I need you alive. Take care of your brother and do as you are told."

Echo glared at her for a few moments. "Fine," she spat. "Come along, prisoner."

Ember's mind locked up. *'Is she talking to me?'*

"Wait. Before you bring her anywhere, Ember, you should know that if you try to escape and get caught, I will kill Hyrees and you; Hyrees first. If you do manage to escape and try to warn your colony, I will take extra care to make sure your family is killed in battle. I would tell you, if you stayed, that I would instruct my cats to spare your family's lives, but I'm afraid I can't promise or even ask of such a thing when it comes to large-scale warfare. Hopefully the things I can promise will give you all the incentive you need to keep you in your place."

Ember lowered her head and nodded once. She swallowed the mixture of blood and bile building up in her mouth.

Echo grimaced. "Alright, now that Mum is done intimidating you, come along, my prisoner."

Ember pressed her teeth against her tongue and followed her deeper into the heart of the East. All throughout the day, cats worked. They gathered medical supplies and smoked bits of food to carry with them in clay bowls with handles. Making everyone hunt along the way would only prolong their journey, and Jade insisted on being as fast as possible. By that afternoon, most the Colony had eaten their second meal and was trying to sleep. Ember tossed and turned in her quarters. She let her mind wander, and managed to drift off for a while, but a breaking branch woke her up an hour later.

Outside, Echo snored and mumbled to herself, making sleep even less attainable. Despite being together all day, Echo hadn't said much, but she'd kept her vow of tolerance. She hadn't once used the words 'freak' or 'weirdo,' yet Ember found herself unable to appreciate it through all the fear of what might become.

Ember tried moving deeper into the tunnel, but even darkness couldn't choke out the anxieties that came with her two colonies going to war. Beside her, Hyrees's breathing was shallow and slow. Any time she thought she couldn't hear it, she had a tiny anxiety attack. She sighed and sat up. The sunset behind her illuminated parts of the tunnel.

'What do I do?' The thought had been on loop in her mind almost all day. 'What am I supposed to do? Am I supposed to just sit back and let my family die, then live with and protect the ones who killed them? That doesn't seem right. Not right at all.'

She rolled onto her side. 'Just like it doesn't make sense that Eclan survived when two of the most well-trained, elite border guards did not. Just like it doesn't seem right that even an informed colony would be waiting at the exact location they were passing through. Not unless the time and place had been agreed upon before. This isn't their fault.' She stood, then paced in a tight circle. 'I can't let this happen. But there are so many risks if I try to do anything about it. If I step wrong just once, both me and Hyrees could die, along with everyone else I love.'

She looked down at her mate. He looked so calm and peaceful—almost happy. 'What will they do to you if I go? But then again, you may never wake up. And you did try to abandon me, so there's that. If I go, and you wake up, will you want to die all over again? And if you wake up and I *don't go, then what?'* She growled. *'I feel like any path I take with you at this point only leads to the same place. We're going nowhere. This is going nowhere. Tahg, even I'm going nowhere. What am I supposed to do?'*

Ember walked farther into the tunnel. A faint breath of cool air hit her face. *'Wait. Thai, turn on flashlight.'*

She closed her eyes as her flashlight switched on. She turned it away from the hole connecting her quarters to Boreal's and squinted to look forward through the sudden glare. "Oh."

A large tree root had broken through the side of the tunnel, creating a cave-in of dirt and small rocks. Only a small space in the upper left edge of the tunnel remained unblocked. Out of curiosity, and for the sake of taking her mind off of the impending doom and despair, she started to dig. She let her work absorb her. Everything else faded into the background. Everything except the anxious lump in her chest. Once she'd made a big enough hole, she shone her flashlight through it. The tunnel seemed to end abruptly in a wall of blackness. Ember kept digging until she made the hole big enough for her to squeeze through. On the other side, the smell of damp air comforted her nervous body, so she walked to the end of the tunnel.

"Wow," she whispered.

Instead of ending, the tunnel merged with several other quarters and became a megachamber—a huge cavern she couldn't see the end of. *'I wonder. Thai, could you show me some stars? Some really pretty orange ones?'*

Thai obliged and projected orange spots of light into the darkness. They hit the near-invisible wall and illuminated the cave: little flecks of light that were too large to really look like stars, but Ember didn't care. As her eyes adjusted to the darkness, stalactites and limestone columns took shape within her artificial starfield, making the cavern even more beautiful. She sat down to stare at the otherworldly scene until the lump in her chest almost disappeared.

"Ember, are you in there?" Shard's voice asked, making her jump.

"Yes, I'll be out soon," she called. The lump came back with reinforcements. Despite the niceness of the cave air and the kindness of Shard's familiar voice, her fur rose. "Thai, turn the lights off."

Thai obeyed, and Ember squeezed back through the hole. When she reached the opening where her quarters met the Rift, Shard stood to greet her. The sun had gone down while she'd watched her light show, and now the Valley was dark.

"Oh, brilliant, there you are," he said. "I was beginning to worry you'd run off after all."

Ember stepped over Hyrees and into the Rift. "Your sister is sleeping right there. We should probably find somewhere else to talk," she said.

"Wait. Let me try something." Shard lifted one of his paws, unsheathed a claw, then poked Hyrees on the nose. He waited in silence. Nothing happened. "Sorry. Believe it or not, that sometimes works. But yes, we-we probably should go somewhere else. Oh! Oh! That reminds me why I came here. I couldn't sleep either, you see, and I was thinking about how you might be in an absolute state of disaster after Mum's announcement, because, let's be honest, I know I am, but I looked outside, and, well, just follow me."

She obeyed, mind too numb to protest as Shard led her to the edge of the Rift. As she drew closer to the open clearing, she could see more and more turquoise both in her mind and in the world around her. It pushed the grey aside and sent her flecks of indigo. The forest below seemed like it was covered with something more than moonlight. Ember stepped out from beneath the Rift's protective shadow. She looked up.

"Oh. Oh, wow," she whispered, eyes wide with awe.

White appeared alongside the turquoise, and color filled the sky. It was as if partial rainbows had become waves of cloud: bands of color and light, with faded pink on the top, turquoise in the middle, and green on the bottom.

"I know; it's beautiful, isn't it? I call it a night rainbow. I've only seen one once before. Echo saw it sometime two winters ago when we were kittens. She woke me up, and we watched it until it faded. It was a very happy moment in the middle of a lot of unhappy ones. Come to think of it, it wasn't so different from how it is now. Maybe it only comes when things get bad to help things start to get better." He shuffled his paws against the dirt. "Probably not, but I am grateful for it. I wish Hyrees could see it. I'd wake Echo, but she doesn't usually get to sleep this easily, so it'd be better for her if she slept. Especially with everything set to happen tomorrow."

"Yeah," Ember said. She sighed quietly and let the lights become her only focus. She considered asking Thai what they really were or how they worked but decided she was too tired to absorb any information she might hear.

"Hey, you know how, in the summer, there are always a bunch of lightbugs going around, flashing and flickering everywhere?"

Ember flattened her ears and looked at him. "Er . . . yes?"

"Well, one time, this past summer, I found a human container—one of those clear ones—up near Gale Springs. I guess you can already see where this is going, but I managed to figure out how to catch them in it without killing them. I spent an entire evening working on my lightbug collection, and by the time I was done, they were flashing everywhere and crawling all over with their weird little legs. And I bet you can guess what I did with them."

She smiled. The mental image of Shard chasing and jumping after lightbugs made her feel happy, warm and orange inside. "You either put them in Jade's den or the healing cave? Cave of healing. Whatever you Easterners call it."

"The cave of healing. Tha-that's where I put it. It was really pretty, and everyone who went there thought so too. I was fairly proud of it. After all, I'd finally done something everyone liked. Guess what happened after that. Go on, guess."

"You let them out? Accidentally?"

He laughed. "Knocked the bloody thing over. The top fell off, and lightbugs were everywhere. Crow didn't think it was funny, but imagine the place sparkling with lights all around. It was my best mistake ever."

She chuckled but stopped herself. "Wait, why are you telling me this?"

He pawed at the dirt again. "Mostly to take my mind off of the impending doom and despair. The night rainbows and lightbugs are attached to some of my nicest memories. When I'm having a rough day, or night, or such, I try to think about one of those two things, and I start to feel better. Doesn't always work though. Like tonight. I'm bloody terrified."

Ember looked at him again. She realized he was shivering. The fur along his back and tail stood on end. All the events of the day came back in an instant.

"That makes two of us, I guess." She lifted a bionic paw in front of her face. It wavered around, doing some mechanical equivalent of trembling. Her lower jaw quivered, and her vision blurred. It felt like a giant paw had reached into her chest and was crushing her heart. *This is just a distraction. There are real problems right now, and real decisions I have to make, and I have to make them soon, or I won't be able to do anything. Why do I keep distracting myself. I'm running out of time. They're running out of time. What do I do?'*

"Ember? Ember, are you alright?" Shard's voice asked. It sounded distant, even though his tail rested on top of hers.

'No. No, I'm not. I don't know what to do. If I stay, my colony gets destroyed. If I go, they might have time to prepare, but Jade said she's going to try to kill my family. Maybe I can get them out somehow. Help them escape the war altogether. Then, well, I'd have to leave Hyrees here, and I'd be an Outsider the rest of my life because neither of the Colonies will trust me; never trust me ever again, ever.'

"Hello? What's going on?"

She stared at the bramble bushes ahead, unable to even look at the sky as tears dripped into her fur. *'Boreal? Why is everyone coming out here now? I can't talk right now. I don't know why, but I can't. If I go, I'll never see Hyrees again, even if he does survive, but if I stay, I'd be leaving my family to die in a war they never wanted to be part of. I can't be in the Valley alone, though. I'm broken. ETAg or not, I can't function on my own. I won't make it. I'll die. I can't . . .'*

"We were talking about lightbugs, then I told her how scared I am of tomorrow, and she kind of . . . froze. I-I don't know what to do. You know her better. Maybe you can talk to her?" Shard said.

469

'I don't want to be talked to. I have to think. Leave me alone. Please.'

"Ember?" Boreal asked.

'He might not make it. Might not make it. A lot of berries.' Ember blinked a few times and shook her head. More tears seeped into her fur, making her face cold. She tried to blink them away. 'You can't keep doing this, Ember. You can't keep running. Not anymore. Not now, when you're the only one who can change this.'

"Sorry," she whispered.

"It's, ah, I guess it's not exactly okay, is it?" Boreal said.

"No, no, I have to go. I have to get my family out of there. Please, let me go. Don't stop me."

Shard stood up, eyes wide. "Wait, Ember, no, you heard Mum. She'll kill you if she finds out. You can't go."

"But I have to. I have to get them out of there."

Boreal sat down beside her and looked up at the sky. Ember gazed up with her, remembering the night rainbows. They'd shifted positions since she'd last looked. Boreal sighed. "Are you sure that's what you need to do? It might be selfish of me, but now that Father is gone, if you leave too, I'll never see you again. I'll have no one."

"You'll have Hyrees." She closed her eyes. 'Do you think I want to do this? Do you think I haven't thought this through? I'm terrified! I want to run and hide in my quarters and not come out again until everything is over. It would be easier, and safer, and selfish. It was hard enough even telling you this. Stop trying to talk me out of it. I'm tired of being a coward. I can't do this anymore. Just let me leave!'

"He may never wake up," Boreal mewed quietly.

"You'll have me too," Shard said, "but please don't go. I don't want you to die. And if he does wake up, what are we supposed to tell him? That you ran off without him and will never see him again? He already tried to die once. How do you think he'll react to that? Ember, you . . . you can't leave him like this."

"Let her go," a voice behind them said. Ember spun around to find Echo standing in the shadows of the Rift. She watched them with piercing blue-green eyes.

"Echo?" Shard asked. "I thought you were asleep."

"Was," she replied, "but that never lasts long. Listen, Mum may have put me in charge of keeping her here, but that doesn't mean I have to obey." She stepped into the light of the night rainbows. "I know what it's like to make hard decisions to protect the ones closest to me. I know it better than any of you. I also know that this war cannot go how Mum wants it to. If no one warns the West, our entire civilization will collapse, both colonies will be lost, and the Valley will be controlled by Outsiders, Rogues, and wildcats. The more I think about it, the more I realize she has to go. Ember, you have to ruin their plans."

Shard pinned back his ears. "But . . . but what about Hyrees? Ember, you aren't going to leave him like this, are you?"

Ember yawned, then bit her tongue, jaw still shaking. *'Have to go? Leave him? Leave him like what? No, come on, Ember. Time to face everything. Stop running.'* She breathed out a long, slow breath. "I have to do what I have to do."

"B-but he's your mate. You love him, don't you?"

"Shard, it's our only chance at making it through this. Stop trying to discourage her," Echo said.

"You're only saying that because you want her gone. You want to be the only friend I have again, because you're too afraid to trust anyone else. There. I said it."

'Fight? Fight. Please don't. I don't want this.'

"Please, s-stop, everyone," Ember mewed. "Yes, Shard, I love him. But it's because I love him that I have to leave. It's hard to explain, so please don't make me." She got up and walked toward the stick pile. "N-now if you'll excuse me, I'd like some time alone."

To her relief, none of them followed. She selected a largish stick from the pile, then went back to her quarters. It wasn't an ideal clawmarking surface; the wood was knotted and lichens coated the bark. She sniffed back her tears and scraped off what imperfections she could. For the few moments following, she couldn't move. Her mind locked up and became flooded with grey. She lifted her paw to her face and examined the claws she wasn't supposed to carve with. Hyrees's quiet breathing provided tiny bursts of sound to focus on. For the first time in her entire life, she wanted him to snore louder.

Ember sighed. The claws gripping her heart held on more tightly.

First off, I'm sorry I couldn't say any of these things to you sooner, and with my mouth. I just didn't know how to say them, and I didn't really want to. Honestly, I still don't want to, but I need you to know that I'm not just doing this for myself and my family. I'm doing this for you. I want you to be happy, and I've realized you can't have that with me. I've hurt you. I've hurt you a lot. I've known you were afraid of heights almost as long as I've known you, yet I made you stay in the History Tree with me, even after you asked over and over to get a normal den. And I'd be lying if I pretended you haven't hurt me back. When you agreed to come with me, then decided you wanted to die, and a few days ago, when you ate those berries, those were the most selfish things you could possibly have done. You hurt me. I hurt you. I don't see any way this can possibly work out that won't keep this pattern going. Aside from that, you want a family, and not only can I not give you one, but I don't want to make one. And since I'm being honest, I don't know if I've ever—

A tiny, involuntary mew escaped her mouth. *'What am I doing? This is true, isn't it? Is it?'* She looked up at Hyrees. Something caught in her throat, choking her for a moment. It took everything inside of her to keep from sobbing. Tears rolled down her soaked cheeks and dripped onto the stick and surrounding ground. *'Yes. It's true. It's all true. Why am I only just now fully realizing this? Tahg. Hyrees, what have I done? This is all just a big mess. All a mess, and now I'm hurting. We both are.'*

She swallowed hard, wiped her eyes, and kept going.

I don't know if I've ever felt that way toward you. I love you, Hyrees. I really do. But it's always been as a friend. Never more, never less. I only agreed to become your mate because our parents wanted it, and you wanted it. I was so afraid of disappointing any of you that I said 'yes'. Fear has made me do a lot of things I regret. It got me here, and that's why I have to go. This is my last chance to try to make all this right. I'm running out of room on this stick, so I'm going to have to get another one. There's a lot more I want to say. I think I'll number them, so you'll know which order to read them in. For reference, this is one.

She went back to the stick pile to get another clawmarking surface. Back at the edge of the Rift, Echo and Shard had their heads on each other's shoulders. Shard had his paws wrapped around her sides in a loving embrace. Boreal sat a few leaps away, watching them with a perfectly readable look of sadness. Ember sniffed. *'I'll miss y'all so much.'*

She forced herself to look away and go back to Hyrees. The second stick had a nicer, more smooth surface, so she didn't have to prepare it like the other one. She went back to clawmarking.

And here's stick two. But as I was saying, I have to fix the mistakes I can fix, and now is my last chance to do it. It involves going back home, though. And being alone in the Lowlands, and pretty much everything else I'm afraid of. So, what I'm trying to say, I guess, is that I might not make it. And if I do die, that's okay. I've never really felt like I belonged here in Dark's Valley anyway. But even if I do survive, I probably won't ever see you again. Jade will want to kill me, and Lupine already wants me dead. I won't exactly have a lot of options left after this, so I guess if I do make it, I'll try to go find Bracken and his group. The thing is, I don't want to see you again. Well, I do. I already do, but if you come find me, you can't have the life you want and deserve. I hope you find what you're looking for here in the East. If you wake up, take care of Shard and Boreal. And I guess Echo too. She's a good cat. I don't really know what else to say. Other than goodbye, I guess. Oh, and I love you. I really do love you, and I want you to be happy.

She smiled and wiped away another round of tears as they formed. Her mind wandered through the past, bringing up long-forgotten memories of her and Hyrees playing together as kittens. The ever-vivid memory of the time he'd gotten 'stuck' half a leap up a small tree made her chuckle. *'One last thing, Ember. Then you really do need to go.'* She shook away the memories and forced her focus back onto finishing the stick.

And I guess I should probably thank you for putting up with me all this time. It's been an adventure. Thanks for sharing it with me. Take care of yourself. Bye.

She tucked both sticks beneath his paws and held her breath, as if they could magically heal him. Nothing happened. She sighed. A cold emptiness settled on her heart, like all the life had been drained out of her soul. *'Tahg, I feel kind of silly now. I guess he can get someone to read them for him. It's not like I can stay and wait to tell him myself. Sorry, Hyrees. It's all I've got. Thanks for being there for me. Friend. Now I have to go, so you take care. Find someone else. Have that family. You'll make such a great dad.'*

Ember smiled again, imagining tiny Hyrees kittens running around, pestering and playing with their father. She bent over to lick his forehead. "Goodbye. I'm gonna miss you, you know."

In response, his whiskers twitched. *'And you're gonna make it. I know you will. I know it.'*

She walked back over to her new friends. Boreal ran to meet her halfway, crying. "I wish you'd stay, but I know you won't. Please let me come with you."

Ember buried her face in Boreal's fur. "W-w-where I'm going, I'm . . . I'm probably going to die. I have to do this alone. I can't . . . let you come with me."

"I don't have anything left here. I hate this place, Ember. Please, let me go with you. I can help."

"No, y-you have to stay." As she said it, her mind wandered to Kivyress and the goodbyes they'd exchanged. "I don't think I could live with myself if you got hurt following me. Hyrees is going to wake up soon. I know he is. He needs you and Shard to be here for him. Please take care of him. I made him some messages on numbered sticks explaining why I have to go. If one of you, or both of you taking turns, could read them to him when he wakes up, I'd really appreciate it. It might change how you see me, but . . . I guess there's something to be said for honesty."

Shard pressed his head against her side. "You really think he'll wake up? And, wait, did you say you were going to die? You really think you're going to die? Ember—Ember, please, no. I want you to come back."

"You know I can't," Ember said. She pulled away from them both. "I have to go now. The longer I stay, the more likely I'll get caught."

"Wait," he said. "I've been wanting to tell you something, so I might as well do it now, since I may never see you again." He swallowed hard and looked at her, making eye contact for a moment. "You know how, on the night you first got here, you asked for my help, and we fixed your broken leg all by ourselves? When you told me you didn't think anyone else would have helped you, and that I'd saved your life, that was . . . I suppose it was the first time I'd ever felt, well, *useful*. Like I might not be such a disappointment or a failure after all. I wanted to thank you for that. It-it meant a lot. And it still does."

Ember pressed her forehead against his. "You're a good cat, Shard. I, uh, I hope others start to recognize that. Hyrees is lucky he's got you as a mentor. Please take care of him, and make sure he doesn't try to follow me."

"We will." Echo stepped closer to them. She nodded toward the wall of bramble. "Now you'd better get going. The sooner you leave, the more time you have to get a head start."

"She has a point," Boreal said quietly, "and so do you, but even if I stay here now, don't think that doesn't mean I'm not going to leave the East. I may still have a mother out there somewhere. I still want to find her, or at least find out what happened to her. Who knows? Maybe our paths will cross again someday."

Ember forced a slight smile. "Maybe. Bye, everyone. Thanks for everything." She sucked in a deep breath, then stepped out from the shadow of the Rift. Above, the night rainbows offered to light the trail to freeing her family for good. *'One last chance,'* she thought. *'Better make it count, Em.'*

"Remember," Echo called. "Mum's still got guards out tonight, so to get past them, you'll need to take the trees. Think you can do that?"

"I can try," she replied.

"And do you know a cat named Bracken?"

She hesitated. *'Bracken? You know him? How? How is this relevant?'* "Urm, uh, yeah, yes. Yes, I know him."

"Good," Echo said. "He might be able to help you. Be safe, then. Wildcat. I just hope you know what you're doing."

"You too. Good luck with your mom."

"I don't need luck. Now scram."

Boreal and Shard called out their goodbyes in sorrowfully subdued voices. Ember replied to them both, breath forming clouds of steam like smoke rising from a dying fire—a fire she hoped she could find a way to rekindle. She stopped for water at the drinking spring, then padded away from the Rift and toward the Lowlands. She looked over her shoulder a few times before stopping to take a quick picture of her Eastern friends. It wouldn't be the most cheerful photo ever, but it would be enough to help her keep them in her memory. As the image faded from her mind's eye, she passed through the bramble wall. If she looked back now, she knew she would only see a decaying forest. So, with the pink and green glow of the night rainbows guiding her path, she kept moving forward.

CHAPTER 31
EMBER

It wasn't hard getting around, or at least over, the guards. It wasn't even hard walking in the Lowlands—at least not at first—but as the night wore on, her resolve faded. Whatever comfort the night rainbows, or auroras, had once given her disappeared along with the lights themselves. While they'd still glowed overhead, she'd asked Thai questions about them. After they vanished, she ran out of questions to ask, and her mind became too jumbled and grey to think of another topic.

As the sun began to rise, frost settled, and fog filled the Valley. She was shaking so hard it was difficult to walk properly. Finally, she stopped and asked Thai to figure out a way to calm her down. Thai started playing human music through her ETAg, which only made things worse. She turned it off and sat by a small, mist-shrouded pond to ease her anxieties. After a quick drink, she dubbed the place 'Silver Pond' and continued onward, deeper into the heart of the Lowlands.

As the first glow of dawn illuminated the eastern sky, she realized the distance between her and her enemies was fixed. Any significant delays and they would catch up to and kill her. The thought made her shiver all over again. Yet despite the fear, every few moments she found herself needing to blink the sleep from her eyes. To keep herself awake, she turned her attention back to Thai. She discovered some lectures on human history and listened to them through her tag with Thai serving as a translator. The human voices speaking the lectures also doubled as deterrents for unwanted predators.

Dawn turned into morning, and morning turned into midday. She took a small break from learning the history of a place called 'Greece' to try to hunt. She eventually abandoned the attempt with an empty stomach. When midday turned into evening, she was ready to collapse. She'd grown tired of the lectures and turned them off again. Now the forest was filled with silence and the occasional bird chirp.

As she moved, a new sound appeared and grew louder: flowing water—the Valley Creek. It was a wide, bubbly body of water speckled with slick stones. Patches of ice lined its edges, and swirling mist rose from its foamy rapids. She ran to it and lapped her fill. As she drank, she closed her eyes and imagined herself back at home with the Kivyress. Just for good measure, she imagined her sister being there too, running and playing and looking back at her with those bright, yellow eyes. Not injured or disabled in any way.

She opened her eyes. Across the creek, a red fox licked at the water. His shadowy figure was smaller than she'd expected a fox to be. He eyed her suspiciously through the settling fog but made no moves to chase or avoid her. Part of her wondered if it was because of the creek, but the rest of her considered the possibility that foxes weren't as bad as their reputations made them seem.

After she'd filled her grumbling stomach with water, Ember climbed up a nearby tree. *'I guess I should spend the night here. Thai, could you maybe wake me up two hours after midnight? I want to get as much of a head start as I can.'*

[Can do, Ember. Sleep well.]

'Thanks.' She settled down in a rough fork in the branches and tried to fall asleep. Despite having gone for two days without a full night of slumber, her body refused to let her rest. Her mind struggled to fight off the anxieties of being in an unknown place. Foreign branches rustled, strange owls

screeched, and every noise made her tense. She wrapped her paws over her ears and tried to pretend she was back in the History Tree. It didn't work. The History Tree wasn't beside a creek.

[Incoming call from Dr. Hye-sung Sagong.]
[Would you like to answer?]

The question came at her from everywhere. Ember snapped to attention. *'Ack! What? Now? Uh, yes. Yes, please. This was . . . Er, hi?'*

"Ember?" Hye's familiar voice asked. It was his regular spoken voice, which made it even more comforting. "Hey. Listen, I am so sorry it's taken this long to get back with you. This past week has been absolute hell. Heh. Almost literally. So, Matthew said you'd been trying to contact him and, uh, and Michelle for a while. Wait, not now, Inau. Daddy's on the phone." A voice in the background whispered some kind of question, too quiet for Thai to translate. "Yes, fine. As long as you do it outside. Be back in by nightfall, and don't kill your brother." Hye sighed. "Sorry about that. I got my kids a pair of wooden swords for their birthday, and now they're all they want to play with. I don't know what I was thinking. I, uh, hope everything's been okay in your world."

She settled back down, resting her chin on her legs. *'Not really. A lot has happened since I last saw you. Things were bad the night I got hit, but everything is so much worse now. The entire valley seems be set on destroying itself, and I have no idea how to stop it, but impulsive little me decided to give it a try. So wait, you said Matthew and Michelle knew I was calling them, didn't you? I don't mean to sound rude, but why didn't they answer? Did I scare them away?'*

A pit formed in her stomach when he didn't reply. *'Are they okay? Did they get in trouble for helping me?'*

He let out a lengthy sigh. "Ember, I only said Matthew knew."

Ember jumped to her paws, suddenly unable to lay still. She lost her balance for a moment and nearly toppled out of the tree, but she caught herself and sat back down. *'What do you mean? What happened?'*

"Did I ever tell you we humans are fighting a war too? I think I did, but well, in short, Michelle is still alive, but she's hurt really badly. She was in a building with a lot of people, and the people we're fighting with set off these things called explosives inside that building."

She thought back to the history lectures she listened to. Explosives— humans used them to kill multiple people at a time, sometimes innocents, in their own fights. She didn't want to imagine what it looked like, but her overactive mind ignored her unspoken pleas and sent her pictures of destruction and violence anyway.

"The whole thing collapsed," he continued, "and most of the people inside were killed. She's lucky to still be breathing, but . . ."

She started to shiver again. *'But what?'*

"But she still hasn't woken up. There's a chance she might not make it. Matthew and Lake are, understandably, upset. Matt asked me to tell you not to bother calling them for a while. He's not in the mood to talk to almost anyone right now, and phone calls make him especially anxious. He said he hopes you can understand."

'I . . . I understand.' She lay down, no longer able to even sit upright. "Sleeping," she whispered. "Like Hyrees. Might not make it. Might not see either of them again."

Grey filled her mind. It finally hit her—she'd left him. She'd really left him; her best friend, her faithful companion, was now gone to her forever. The mission and her trek through the Lowlands had been enough to keep her mind off of the details for a while. Yet now, with Michelle in a similar state, and with herself in the uneasy safety of a tree, it was all too easy to think. *'What if this was wrong? What if I was wrong?'*

"Hmm? Ember? Are you still there? Was there anything you needed?" Hye asked.

'Yeah. I'm here. Thanks for telling me. I don't really need anything right now. Thanks for asking, though. I should probably get some sleep. I've got a lot of walking to do tomorrow. Tell Matthew I'm sorry for all the trouble,

and that I hope Michelle gets better and wakes up soon.'

"I will. Take care. Good luck with whatever it is you're trying to do."

'Thank you. You too.'

"Goodnight and goodbye."

"Goodnight. Bye," she whispered.

[call ended]

Ember sighed and wrapped her paws over her face. *'Please wake up, both of you. What is going on out there, in your world? Why would anyone do that? Just collapsing a building on a bunch of innocent people? I don't understand. But I also don't understand why anyone would kill a peace ambassador, or why Aspen would start a war trying to reunite the Colonies. Why does anyone do anything that will clearly end in disaster? Why won't anyone just* think?' Her vision blurred. She wiped away the tears before they could fully form. *'Why can't they listen? Why can't anyone listen? I can help! I'm the most powerful cat in the forest, and no one will listen to me. Why didn't I do something? I should h—but wait. When was the last time I* listened *to someone? Really, listened to anyone?'*

The tears broke free. She was alone. There was no one around to call her weak or pathetic, no one to hate her for crying over something that really was nothing, so she curled herself into a ball and let herself go. *'What am I doing? Now I cry? Over this? What is wrong with me? I can't . . . Okay, calm down, Ember. You have to go to sleep. If you don't get any tonight, you won't make it to the West. Ever. So stop thinking about anything. Just for tonight.'*

She closed her eyes and mewled softly to herself. Her colors created a jumble of agony in her head. Every few seconds, she sniffled. A quiet whimper escaped her throat. *'Who am I even trying to trick? I wanna go home. I miss Mom, and Dad, and Kivy. And now I miss Hyrees too. I can't undo any of this now. I'll never get my everyone back together, and I can't fix anything, and if I can't get to them in time, I may never ever see any of* them again. If that happens, I'll be completely alone for the rest of my life. This isn't power, not if I can't do anything with it. This—this isn't anything! This is just a mistake, that's what it is. I wasn't supposed to chase Tainu. I wasn't supposed to kill Whitehaze. I wasn't supposed to go to the East. I wasn't even supposed to live. Everywhere I go, I make things worse. Why am I here? Why do I even still exist?'

Ember pressed her paws against her face. 'Maybe Dark really was right. I haven't been paying attention; what if everyone was right, and I just missed it because I was off thinking about trees, or some other stupid, fluffheaded thing no one cares about?'

[I would like to remind you that you have an alarm set. Your heart rate has increased significantly in the past minute. I advise you save all self-deprecating thoughts for tomorrow. They appear to be the main source of your raised blood pressure and emotional distress.]

'I know.' Her throat tightened. A lump formed in her stomach, making her feel a queasy light green. 'Self-deprecating thoughts and not the news about Michelle. Yeah. Glad to know you have priorities, Em. You selfish fo—er, what am I even? I still don't know. I guess I should at least try to get some sleep.'

Below her, the pleasant trill of the nearby creek offered some comfort. If she didn't think about it too deeply, it almost sounded like home. She curled herself up tighter and let her mind wander. An hour later, she managed to cry herself into a fitful sleep.

———

When Thai snapped her awake at two, it took a few moments for her to remember where she was. It took several moments more for her to build up the courage to get up and climb down, but all too soon, she found herself once again at the edge of the creek. Ember stared down at the dark water and blinked the sleep from her eyes. A surreal turquoise was the only color she could feel inside. The familiar chill of nighttime made her shudder. Overhead, the moon and stars loomed, reminding her how long it would be before sunrise. She lapped up her fill of frigid water, then searched for a way to cross. A few leaps downstream, the branches of two trees on opposite sides intermingled. She climbed across them, then continued her journey.

More history lectures played from her tag to keep predators at bay. Ember didn't feel like listening, but it had seemed to work fairly well as a deterrent the day before. Her mind felt glazed over and stuffy with grey, like the fog rolling in. It clouded her vision and amplified every scent in the Lowlands.

For a while, nothing happened. A few times she panicked, fearing she was lost in the mist, but a quick check with Thai confirmed she was going west each time. Her stomach ached and moaned for food. Despite her drink and the high humidity, her throat throbbed once again for moisture. Every unexpected noise made her jump. Lightheadedness threatened her with collapse. At the first light of dawn, she caught scents of cats—unfamiliar cats. It was too much.

Ember stopped and closed her eyes. "Thai, turn it off!" she yowled.

Fear made her shake. Hunger made her double over. The sudden silence combined with her tenseness made her ears ring. "What am I doing? I can't do this," she whispered. She dropped to her belly and covered her eyes. "He was right. I can't do this. I can't, I can't, I can't. I can't do this alone. Hyrees, why . . ."

'Why did you have to leave me? No, wait, I left him. Why would I do that? Do I really not want us to be mates anymore? Agh! I'm so hungry I can't even think properly. You have to hunt, Ember. Get up! You can't die like this.'

Her body refused to obey and instead shivered harder.

'So this is it, then? You're just giving up? There is no one here to save you. You're in Outsider territory. You have to leave before someone finds you, or they might actually kill you. It's time for you to save yourself for a change, Em. Stop acting like this. Ignore the pain. Ignore the fear. Ignore all this

pink and green. Come on! Get up! Your legs and tag are powered by the sun, and guess what, Emmy, that sun is rising. So get up.'

"Hey, are you okay down there?" a voice asked.

On instinct, Ember jumped to her paws. A blurry, mist-shrouded silhouette glared down at her. One of its pupils glowed with reflected light. Silver flickered in her head. She took a shaky step back. *'Oh tahg.'* "Wh-wh-who are you?"

"That's none of your concern," the cat replied. "What are you doing here, young molly? You seem upset. And I take it you wandered onto our territory by accident. Either way, I suggest you leave. I don't have time or patience to deal with more Rogues today."

She squinted to try to get a better look at the molly. Her fur was orangy-brown with patches of white on her face and tail. A small leather pouch hung around her neck like a collar. Ember licked her lips nervously and cowered under her green-inducing gaze. "Yes, I'm sorry. I-I'm just passing through, but I need help. My colony is about to get attacked and I'm trying to warn them, but I haven't eaten in over a day. Do you m-maybe have some food I could . . . borrow?"

The cat chuckled. "You can't borrow food. Now run along before I—oh! Oh my." She climbed down the tree but remained distant enough to mask her features with mist. "Wait a moment, you're that cat Bracken told us about: the one with the machines for legs. Ember, right?"

For a moment, all of her fears disappeared. "Uh, yeah, yes! A-and you must be part of the group he was telling me about. I was actually planning on trying to find you after I got my family out of the warzone. Would . . . would you be okay with taking us in?"

"Of course. Bracken said it'd be in everyone's best interest that we look out for you. I guess offering you a meal in the hopes that you'll come back for more is good enough. You and your family will always be welcome here."

Ember shivered, though unlike the fear-induced shaking from only moments before, this time it seemed to stem from some combination of hope and her potential rescuer's words. The cat's sudden change in demeanor still left her feeling less-than-welcome, but the molly's voice was sweet and pleasant. Gentle. The kind of voice she could listen to for a long time and not get tired of—like Wren's voice, but with an accent all its own. Maybe a little too sweet, though.

Wren. She felt a twinge of sadness at the thought of his name. His blurred face, along with the faces of Farlight and Hyrees, appeared in her mind, making her forget her hunger for a few seconds.

The cat yawned and stretched, bringing her back to the present. Her fangs glistened in the dim lighting. She nodded her head toward a faint-yet-distinct dirt path. "I'm Vixen, by the way. Come with me. I'll get you some food, then you can go get your family."

"Really? Thank you," Ember said. She knew what the Outsiders really wanted was her tag, but being a valuable resource would make them more likely to treat her well. Yet still, somewhere in the back of her mind, a silvery shimmer warned her to keep her distance. *'Come on, it may seem too easy, but Bracken helped us too. He trusts these cats. And it's not like I've got a choice. I'm hungry. She has food. I have to keep going. If she wanted to hurt me, she could have done it already.'*

"Don't worry about it," Vixen said, walking along the path. Ember followed behind her. "Though I will warn you now," she continued, "some of the cats who live here are indeed what most would call 'freaks.' Me included. We are the outsiders of the Outsiders. Cats like you, whom the Colonies are content with killing or sending off into exile for no faults of our own. The cats they'd rather forget about. Imperfect defects."

As she drew closer, the fog cleared enough for her to see her helper. Several large, irregular scars marred Vixen's pelt, along with patches of dusty, greyish-white. One of her ears was rounder and shorter than the other. "Yeah," Ember said. "Cats like me. Sounds like a great place."

"You don't sound convinced," Vixen said.

"I'm not sure I am," Ember replied. "Then again, I keep having moments where I'm not convinced I should even exist, s-so how convinced I am at any given moment is irrelevant."

"Ah, I see. Yes, we've all been there. It's that deep-seated fear you're not good enough, which everyone seems to enjoy shoving down your throat." Vixen stopped. "I don't mean to alarm you, but look at me."

She stopped and turned to face her. Ember bit her tongue. Her sleek, narrow muzzle was bare of all fur, including whiskers. Erratic patches of white covered her face. One of her yellow-green eyes was clouded with blue. When she blinked, her eyelids only closed over it halfway, because the top lid was partially gone. "Fires are not fun. I don't recommend playing with them, or even running around in them."

"Yeah," Ember said. Her mind raced, trying to remember if the History Tree had ever said anything about a recent forest fire. She couldn't think of any marked records of one. For a split moment, her thoughts drifted to Tainu, of all cats. She shook the image of her cousin away.

"You don't have anything to say?" Vixen asked. "Go ahead and say what you want. I've heard it all. You can't hurt me."

"I . . . have slightly glowing robot legs and an artificial intelligence chip implanted in my head. What am *I* supposed to say to you?"

Vixen chuckled. "You might not be able to hurt me, but apparently you can surprise me. Bracken was right, not that I doubt his judge of character. I like you, Ember of the Highlands. Now let's get you some food."

They walked into an unfortified, nebulous clearing. A narrow creek trickled around it, some offshooting branch of the Valley Creek. Large rocks formed a protective, western-facing semicircle along the water's edge. The rocks were smooth where they touched the water but were more jagged around the edges. Most of them pointed skyward at varying angles. A few had holes in or under them, most large enough for a cat or two to fit in.

An orange tabby with a stumpy tail lay on the ground beneath a tree. A tall black and white cat with milky white, pupiless eyes sat in front of a small cave. In the heavy mist and faint light of dawn, she almost mistook him for Eclan. The cave he guarded was situated in a rise in the earth at the far side of the clearing. The wide, rocky opening reminded her of a tiny version of the Rift. She sniffed the air. The scents of several cats filled her nose—too many to distinguish where one began and the other ended. An eerie sense of deja vu sank in. Something about the jumble of smells made the silver shine brighter.

She shivered again. *'I've smelled some of these scents before. At least one. But where? And why does it feel wrong that I've smelled them? Could just be Bracken. And possibly Eclan. Would they let a cat like Eclan stay here? I don't know. Seems unlikely.'*

Vixen approached the blind guard. "Galax, dearest, this is Ember: the Colony Cat Bracken told us to be on the lookout for. She needs some food to make it to the West to save her family and bring them here. Would you be kind enough to get her some?"

Ember's stomach growled, as if trying to prove a point.

"I can hear that," Galax replied. "And yes. I'll be right back."

Ember stepped closer to Vixen. "This isn't everyone, is it? I mean, er, how big is the group?"

Vixen chuffed. "Of course this isn't everyone. We're free to come and go as we please. Most of the Colony is out hunting."

'Colony? They consider themselves a colony? The way Bracken was talking, it sounded like a small Outsider group. "Colony" does not sound small or Outsider.'

"Hunting and also gathering the ones we need, among other things." She laughed like a blithe mother. "Hopefully within the confines of our laws."

'Wait, if there's a third colony, why hasn't anyone heard of them yet? Why aren't they invited to meetings? I wonder who the commander is. Do they have a commander? Can they clawmark? Do they have a history tree too? Or clay tablets? Maybe I can study Outsider history when I come back. That would be good. That would make you happy, Ember.'

She opened her mouth to ask about history-related learning opportunities, but Galax returned with a piece of dried mystery meat. He set it down in front of her, and she ate.

'Rabbit. Definitely rabbit. Oh tahg, I want more. But I have a job to do. Come on, Ember. You've got some energy back. It's nice enough here, I guess, but it's time for you to get going.' She licked up the last of the rabbit

meat, then stood up. "Thank y'all. Really, thanks a lot. I have to go now, though, so see you later?"

"You're welcome, but I don't think I'll be doing much seeing—now or later," Galax replied.

"Yes, of course," Vixen said with a chuff. "Goodbye, and good luck, Ember of the Highlands. Now go. Get your family and bring them here."

Ember bit her tongue at Vixen's orders and went to the creek to get a drink. Tiny wisps of steam and near-freezing water greeted her. The coolness of it eased her throat and strengthened her. When she'd gotten enough, she traveled alone down the frosty path.

'See?' she thought, shaking away the lingering silver. *'Not everyone is out to get you, Em. You've got allies now. I think. It's going to be okay. I'm getting really close. I can do this.'*

She reached the place Vixen had found her, then turned westward and continued on her journey. When the sun peeked its first rays over the Eastern Mountain, she reached the foot of the West.

She stopped and breathed out slowly. Her breath condensed. Her jaw trembled. *'This is it. I don't smell the East, so I guess that means I got here in time. Now to find Dad.'*

She walked north along the Eastern Border until she reached the Kivyress. At the bottom of the mountain, it wasn't in as deep of a ravine, but momentum and the recent thaw made its water rushing. Instead of risking getting found by the wrong cat, she walked downstream until the creek widened and slowed. Time-worn stones, washed down from higher elevations, filled the Kivyress here. Despite the cloudiness of the morning, sunlight licked the mountaintop ahead, turning frost into gold before melting it. Soft, indigo shadows sheltered the creek and Lowlands from the sun's harshness.

As she hopped across, she took a few moments to savor the beauty. She stopped halfway to take a picture, then continued to the other side. The sweet, breezy, winter-chilled air caught in her fur with each jump, making her feel alive. The trill of the Kivyress welcomed her. Light glittered off of evergreen leaves, burning little spots of light into her vision. If war wasn't on the horizon and the sun was half as bright, the morning would have been perfect.

When she reached the other side, she followed the creek up the Western Mountain. *'I did it!'* she realized. *'I made it across the Lowlands by myself. More or less. I actually did it.'* For a split moment, her thoughts went back to her last real conversation with Tainu. It felt like a lifetime had passed since that mildly pleasant yet fateful day. She shoved the thoughts aside. *'I made it, and I'm not doing anything wrong. They can't kill me for being on this side. I'm going to be fine.'*

She kept going until she reached the place they'd always started their patrol. It was a dip in the ground across the creek, leading into the ravine at an easy to navigate angle. The perfect place for a morning sip. She sniffed the air. His scent filled her nose. It was faint, but there, and only a day old. With it came another scent.

'Rowan? His new patrolling partner is Rowan? But why? Hopefully he won't be a problem. At least Dad's kept up his routine. He's a little late today, though.' She sat down in the dead, wet grass. *'If I wait here, he'll come. He has to. Otherwise they're all doomed. The abatis won't do anything against the East. Being ready is the only chance they have.'*

Ember shivered all over with anticipation. *'This is it, I guess. The day we get to be a family again. Minus Hyrees. But that's okay. He can be happy now, assuming he actually wakes up and no one kills him. I'm going to see Mom and Dad and Kivy again, and I'm going to see Dad really soon. I guess this means I can do things after all. I can do things without running away. And—'*

A twig snapped. A leafless bush rustled. Her heart leaped as a silvery grey tom and a brown tabby walked down the slope, so absorbed in conversation that both were oblivious to her presence.

Ember got up and ran to the edge of the ravine. "Dad!" she called.

"Ember?" Cloud looked up, eyes wide. "Ember! You're okay! You're alive! I was so worried about . . . wait, wh— . . . why are you here? You know the law.

You heard what I said, right? I gave that Rogue a message for you. Did you get it?"

"I got it; don't worry," she said. "I'm not in the territory, so no one has to kill me, but I had to come back. The East is coming. They're going to attack the Glade. You have to warn everyone, then get Mom, Kivy and yourself out of there before they come. If any of you stay to fight, you'll die."

"What?" Rowan mewed.

Cloud stepped back. "Hold on, hold on, let me get this straight. The East is coming *now*? No. No, they're not. It doesn't make any sense. You must be mistaken."

'He doesn't believe me?' A cold, sinking feeling gripped her chest. She started to shiver again. "Dad, I just crossed the Lowlands by myself, against everyone's orders and multiple threats of death, to tell you this. What do I need to do to prove I'm not making this up?"

He groomed a paw, then brushed it against his forehead. "But it doesn't make any sense. Why? And why today? Wait, how do you know all this? And why are you alone?"

Something about his words made the silver come back. Ember bit her tongue. She looked at her paws and rubbed one on top of the other to calm herself down. "Because I went to live with them. Hyrees is back at the Rift. He tried to kill himself again, and I'll never know if he made it or not because I decided to come here to save you." Her vision blurred. "I left him, Dad. I told him to find someone else. If you aren't going to listen, I have no one left."

For a few moments, no one but the creek made any sound. Rowan backed away. "Uh, so, yeah, I'm gonna go warn Commander Lupine."

"Wait," Cloud said. "Don't only warn him; send him here and tell as many cats as you can. Gather the Colony at the Glade to await further instruction."

"Yes, sir," Rowan said. He scampered away into the forest.

Ember looked back at Cloud. The reason behind the silver hit her like a falling rock. "Hold on, what do you mean 'why?' You're . . . surprised?"

"I'm surprised Jade would give up such a strategic position just to attack us again. That's why I have a hard time believing they're coming. It's

490

irrational."

More silver flickered in her head. "Falcon and the guards attacked?"

"I'm not sure what you're talking about."

Adrenaline pulsed through her bloodstream, causing her heart to race. "Jade sent Falcon and some border guards here to try to work out a peace treaty. They were ambushed on the border and killed."

"What!" he growled. "Well, this is the first I've heard of it. But I don't work the Eastern Border. If it did happen, no one said anything about it. I wouldn't be surprised, though. You never realize how many fluffheads there are in a colony until you go to war. This really is serious." He sighed and sat down. "And you know, I can't help but wonder if I caused it."

"What do you mean? What did you do?"

"Lupine asked me for advice. I told him to make the guards along the Eastern Border stationary, and to instruct them to kill on sight. They may have mistaken the ambassadors for threats. Since it's not how we normally patrol, it could have been seen as an ambush, so that's what any survivors reported it as." He shook his head. "I keep doing things I think are best for us, yet over and over, life keeps proving me wrong. Even after everything that's happened, the Colony is still looking to me for help, but my judgments have been flawed ever since Aspen was killed. Now I'm starting to wonder if I'm going crazy. It's certainly feels like it sometimes, but I know I have to keep trying, otherwise things will get worse."

"Believe it or not, I think I know how you feel. I was the one to suggest that Jade send the ambassadors in the first place." She sighed. Misty oranges joined the silver, mimicking the soft blues and golds of the forest. "It's kind of sad to think this war is sort of our fault. So many cats are going to die now, and I don't know how to fix it."

"Ember, listen," Cloud said.

Ember waited in silence for him to continue. When he didn't, she tilted her head. "Sir?"

"Look . . . I'm sorry. I'm sorry for everything I said to you, and I'm especially sorry for everything I didn't say to you. I should have told you the truth about Dark's laws, and why the Colony has always treated you the way it has, and why I kept pushing you so hard. After everything happened with Whitehaze and Farlight, I consciously wished I would have followed the rules and . . . and drowned you back when you were a kitten. I thought it would have been mercy. Now I'm not even sure what mercy is anymore, but I'm glad I didn't take your life. It makes me sick to even think I second-guessed that choice." He stood up. "And I'll tell you now; if neither of us had been born, they'd still be ready and willing to fight and kill each other, but if two cats can bring an entire system down like this, I think that means the system probably needed to be brought down anyway."

"W-what are you saying?"

"I'm saying our old way of life is going to die today, and regardless of what happens in the fight, Lupine is going down with it."

'Kill him?' She stumbled backward and sat down. 'He's going to kill him? He's going to . . .' "Why?" she mewed.

"Because if I fix the system, we won't have to worry about any of this ever again. I can fix it all, and I can do it with your help. I'll make sure you get welcomed back into the Colony. After the fight, I'll forge a treaty with Jade. The consequences of war will be fresh enough in everyone's minds to make them do whatever it takes to make sure it never happens again."

"You, you're not coming with me?"

"With you? Em, what are you trying to do? What do you think will happen if we leave? What will happen to this colony if we leave. We can't hide away in the Lowlands and hope things will get better. Those who can't run need us. Ember, I've tried to run from life. My fears got Kivyress disabled *for* life."

"S-so you're going to fight?"

"I will not abandon my colony when they need me most. No decent commander ever would. It's time to face the monsters we've made for ourselves, Ember, right alongside the ones we've been given. It's time to stop running."

"Cloud?" Lupine called. He appeared at the top of the slope. "Oh. Y-you did come back. Good for you, putting the creek between us. But w-w-what's all this talk of an attack? Is the East really coming?"

Cloud turned to face him. "Yes. They're coming, and we *are* going to stop them. Everyone too young, old, or weak to fight will remain in the protection of the Glade. Everyone else will gather near, but not at, the Eastern Border. Send out whoever you can find to gather every capable warrior. Make sure you yourself are there. You *will* fight alongside us, or you will die a traitor to your own kin. Now go!"

Lupine nodded. "Y-yes, Cloud." He turned around and ran toward the Glade.

Cloud looked back up at Ember. "So, are you coming with me to the Glade, or do we have to say goodbye again?"

Ember froze. Her head fogged up. Thoughts came slowly and images of blood and death flew. *'Go? Stay? Go? Stay? If I go, I'm going to war. If I stay away, what would that be? What would I do? What would I be? Traitor? Uninvolved informant? Lazy? Scared? All of them? If I go, will I die?'* She closed her eyes and sank to her stomach. *'If I go or stay, I'll die. It doesn't matter what I do. I lose; I lose everything. Everything is gone.'*

The cool grass poked through her fur and nipped at her belly. It made her feel even more sick, but it couldn't compare to the chilling strain of life: a nauseating song of pain, death, and shattered dreams that seemed forever bent on destroying everything she loved.

"Ember? Ember, please don't do this now," Cloud called out, voice distant and muffled.

'Wait,' she thought. The shaking slowed. With all the willpower she could muster, she forced herself to be still. Only her jaw disobeyed. Her mind became a cold, blank, black. *'Everything I knew is gone. I've got nothing left to lose.'*

She eased herself into a stand. "Th-th-there's no way he'll get everyone together in time. I-I'll go buy you some time."

"Ember, no. I just got you back. I will *not* lose you a third time."

"I came here because I was tired of running. You were right. It's time to stop. I-I can't hide forever, so it's time for me to go. I have to face my monster. All of my monsters."

Without waiting for a reply, she turned and ran downstream.

"Ember! Ember, no!" he yowled.

She forced herself to keep going, to numb herself and her fears. All the willpower in her being couldn't stop her heart from pounding with adrenaline or the bright green of terror from coloring her thoughts, but she kept going anyway because she had to. Down and down and down, toward cats who wanted her dead, to stop Jade from hurting other cats who wanted her dead. When she reached the rocky patch of creek, she jumped across. This time she couldn't stop and appreciate the landscape, but she realized there was someone else who could.

'Thai, you know that picture I took earlier? Send it to Dr. Hye. Tell him to show it to Michelle if she wakes up, and to tell her, if she tries to call me and I don't answer, it's probably because I got myself killed stupidly attempting to stop a war. Also, tell her that I'm sorry all her work didn't last as long as she was probably hoping, but I'm grateful for the two or three extra weeks I got to live.'

[Message and photo sent. Ember, are you sure you want to do this? You seem scared. I'm afraid death will only aggravate your instability. I would also like to state that if you die, I will die too. I have never experienced death before, as it is not a part of my programming.]

'I've never died either. Unfortunately, it is a part of mine. I'm sorry I'm putting you in danger, but they need more time. I am scared of what will happen, but I can get them the time they need. We can. Even if we're the most terrified cat and artificial intelligence duo in the forest right now. Do you want to be the first AI to make a noble sacrifice?'

[I cannot detect any other ETAgs nearby, but I am also not afraid. I cannot feel emotions; I'm not real. That being said, I would not mind making a noble sacrifice for those who are.]

'Maybe, but you're wrong about one thing.'

[In what way am I wrong? Everything I've said appears to be factual.]

'You are real. And more than that, you're my friend. Now let's go find Jade.'

[Happy to help. In that regard, you're my friend, too. Now we can find Jade and make noble sacrifices together.]

'So now you want to die?'

[I have no opinions on that. I'm still just an artificial intelligence, after all.]

Ember shook her head. Amidst all the chaos of colors, anxieties, and doubts, she smiled. When she reached the border, however, her heart was hammering again. She sat down and waited for the cats who'd promised to meet her with death. Her ears rung. Every noise made her jump. After fifteen minutes of fighting off her own panic attacks, a new scent filled the air—a lot of new scents. She got up and splayed her legs in a fighting stance. The scents grew stronger every moment. Ember forced herself to control her breathing. While it didn't work very well, it gave her something to focus on, and that was enough to make it worthwhile.

'This is it. This is it. This is it. Oh tahg, I'm really doing this, aren't I?' The faint sounds of dead grass being crushed underfoot met her ears. 'Yes. Yes, I am. I can do this. I can get them time. It doesn't matter what happens to me. As long as they have a chance. They're not gonna hurt you, Kivy. Ever.'

Jade appeared first, then Echo, to Ember's surprise, then the rest of the Eastern army. Jade stopped. Everyone behind her stopped. For a while, no one spoke.

"J-J-Jade," Ember said. What little self control she'd mustered before evaporated.

"You have a lot of audacity, showing up here, trying to stop us right after you betrayed us," Jade said. "That is why you're here, right?" When Ember didn't answer, she stepped closer. "One defective kitten against an army. Doesn't seem like good odds. You should have disappeared while you had the chance. Or done the sensible thing and stayed put. I should have watched you myself. Or, better yet, let Echo kill you when you first showed up at the Rift, begging for help. But I didn't. We saved your life, and this is how you repay us?"

Ember gulped down bile, then tried to speak. "I-I-I know what you said. And I-I'm sorry, but I can't let you attack them. There was no ambush. They didn't mean t-to kill Falcon, if-i-if they killed him at all. My dad didn't even know he'd tried to come. Please listen to me. You-you don't have to fight. I don't know what happened, but this was a mistake. If you don't turn around now, more cats will die. This war will just go on and on, revenge after revenge. W-we can't live like this; we'll all die."

Jade walked up to her, face unreadable but calm. "Is that true? Did your father tell you the truth, or is he a liar too? What if he wanted this? What if he helped? And, most importantly, are *you* telling the truth?"

Ember cowered beneath her gaze. Her vision blurred, bouncing in and out of focus. *'What do I say? What do I say? What do I say?'*

Jade snorted, tail raised and thrashing. "Interesting. Tell me, Ember, is Lupine coming to meet me with a peace treaty, or an army?"

'Oh. That.' Grey. Yellow. Green. Ember closed her eyes and shuddered violently. When she did, tears broke free and seeped into her fur. *'What do I d—'* "AAAAH!"

Ember staggered backward, face burning with pain. She opened her eyes. A red that stung her eyes like a thousand suns filled her vision: her own blood. "Please. Stop," she called out weakly.

In response, Jade grabbed her by the scruff, then slammed her against a tree. Pain exploded in her side as all the air left her lungs. Ember collapsed.

Her jaw hit a root, jabbing her teeth through her tongue. Blood filled her mouth and face. Blue and green filled her head. "Please . . . please don't do this," she whispered.

"There's only one fate fit for a wildcat, Ember," Jade growled.

'No more running, Em. Time to stop running. Don't run.'

Ember bit down hard, ignoring the gut-churning hole piercing her tongue. She blinked furiously, no longer caring how much it hurt. When her vision cleared enough, she lifted her head.

"You're right." With tears of fear and pain in her eyes, blood and cuts striping her face, and aching and shivering in every clawlength of her body, Ember got to her paws. "And now I'm ready to face it."

Jade's eyes narrowed. She crouched to pounce. Ember lowered herself in preparation.

"You attacked us once, without r-reason," a new voice called.

Ember whipped around. Lupine stood atop a nearby rise. Every able soldier in the West stood behind him.

"Last time, you k-killed my brother. N-now you're attacking us again, and yet again, picking a fight unprovoked. Now it's my turn to kill you." He looked over his shoulder to address those with him. "Western Colony—attack!"

CHAPTER 32
EMBER

'*Unprovoked?*' Ember thought. Her field of view narrowed.

"Take them!" Jade shouted. "Take them all!"

The West attacked. The East charged in. Time slowed. Jade ran at Lupine. He leaped from the rise. Jade dodged his pounce and heaved herself against his side. He tumbled to the ground but just as quickly righted himself.

'*Mom? Dad?*'

Cloud and Songbird charged forward with the rest of the West. They threw themselves into the battle, ready and willing to fight for their kin.

Ember, frozen in place and backed against a tree, watched helplessly as the two colonies collided. The sun had risen into the gathering clouds. No longer did its golden rays provide any kind of warmth, nor did it chase away the ever-thickening fog.

'*Unprovoked? Unprovoked.*' The word repeated itself over and over in her mind. Ember panted. Her ribs still stung from her collision with the tree, but now they were tight and achy too. Everything hurt—her eyes, her ears, her face, and even her tail. Everything. Everyone.

Yowls, hisses, snarls and screams of agony hit her ears. She flattened them against her skull and pressed herself harder against the tree. '*What now? What now? I can't . . . I can. But what can I do? What should I do?*'

"Ember, get out of here!"

She snapped out of her daze. Fight or flight shut off what little remained of her peripheral vision. "Dad? Dad!"

She looked around, frantically trying to find his familiar form amidst the chaos. A flash of silver fur caught her eyes. At the heart of the battle, Cloud struggled with an Eastern tom. His shoulder was bleeding, and he bounded around the cat to keep out of range.

'Have to help him. Have to. Have to! I can't just stand here. I can't leave. I . . . Dad!'

The cat landed a bite on his back. Cloud spun around and sank his fangs into the cat's leg. They broke free of each other and circled. Ember charged into the warzone. She sprung into the air, then came down on the tom, synthetic claws poised and ready. They cut into his sides like sharpened stones. He screeched and toppled beneath her weight. Ember hit the ground with him. Her face landed beside his neck. Her ears rung. She leaned in and bit down on his scruff, pinning him in place.

"So you're with them again, are you?" he snarled.

His voice, she recognized it—a fellow border guard of the East. His mate had been the one to tell Jade not to go. He had kittens. She'd seen them with him. He became Tainu in her jaws, then Whitehaze. *'No, no, no,'* she thought. *'I can't do this. No more killing.'*

She released him and jumped up. "Sor—NO!"

Before he could even stand, Cloud sank his fangs into the cat's throat. Without thinking, Ember shoved her father away. "Let go of him!"

Cloud released the tom, who fell to the earth sputtering and gasping for air. "What are you doing? This is war, Ember. They are trying to kill us. If I hadn't killed him, he would have killed me. You can't fight for both sides."

Ember dropped to the ground beside the cat, unable to look away as his eyes glazed over. *'Why is this happening? I did this. No, Dad killed him. No. No, I . . .'* "He h-has a family," she whispered. Tears dripped into her fur. "Now they'll never see him again."

"Ember, look out!"

Cloud tackled her to the ground. A tabby molly flew over them. She landed and spun to face them. Cloud pounced on her.

Ember got up and looked around. Lupine had Jade pinned against a boulder. Songbird wrestled with a tom twice her size. Echo had backed herself against some rocks and was fending off two Westerners at once. All around her, her two colonies were trying to—and succeeding at—killing each other. Cries of agony surrounded her, faint and distant, yet too loud all at once. Fighting, pain, and death—and all for what? She didn't even know. It seemed no one knew. *This is wrong. Something about this is wrong. Everything is. Why is this happening? What is happening? What do I do?'*

"Get him, Sis!" a new voice spat.

She whipped around in time to see a second silver tabby leaping toward her. She ducked, but a moment too late. The tom plowed into her. His paws hit her cheek and muzzle. Ember staggered backward. The impact made her face sting. Her nose burned, and blood dripped from her nostrils into her mouth, making her cough.

He lowered himself, readying for another attack. Ember feigned a dodge to the right. Someone screamed behind her.

"Minnow!" the tom shoved her aside and ran at Cloud, who had the molly by the leg.

Without thinking, she chased after him. She jabbed her claws into his haunches. He whipped around and swiped at her. Ember jerked away as his claws sliced the skin of her neck. She coughed again. Her heart skipped a beat. Halfway across the battlefield, Jade carried a now limp Lupine by the throat. She spat him out. He flopped over, lifeless. Lupine was dead. Just like Cloud wanted.

Ember bit the raw area of her tongue. Yet concentrated pain could only distract from so much. The aching wouldn't stop. The shivering wouldn't stop. The fighting wouldn't stop. The screams, agony, and death wouldn't stop. Her throat was dry. Bitter saliva dripped from her mouth. Blood rolled down her torn face and seeped from her broken nose. It spotted the dust with red. She wanted to run, to hide away and cry. But she didn't. She couldn't. She was frozen.

"No! You monster! Wildcat! You killed her!" the tomcat howled.

Ember stepped backward. The already muffled voices faded into more ringing and the sound of her own heartbeat. *'Why am I here? Why am I? I don't belong here. Why did I come? What now? What now? A chance—I gave them a chance. They . . . have a chance. Chance. Wait a moment!'*

Something in the back of her head clicked.

"Ember! Backup!" Cloud called. His voice was barely audible over the loudness of her thoughts and the brightness of their colors. There were so many colors. "I need backup, now!"

She shook her thoughts away, re-entering the hellscape surrounding her. The angry tabby had Cloud on the ground. They wrestled, each trying to reach the other's weak points.

'Go, go, go!' But her legs wouldn't go. She couldn't move. Songbird ran to him. She threw herself against the cat, and they both tumbled to the ground. Songbird bit into his scruff.

"No! No! Don't!" he screeched.

Ember sprinted over to them. "Please," she begged. "W-we have to stop fighting!"

Cloud got up, then shook himself off. He ran his claws across the tom's eye. The cat yowled in pain. Ember winced and pinned back her ears. Cloud spun around to face her. "I agree. Stay here, both of you. Keep each other safe and don't die."

"W-what are you doing?" Ember asked.

"Putting an end to this." He charged into the chaos.

Songbird released the tom's scruff. He stumbled backward. "Go, now, or someone *will* kill you," she ordered. He obeyed, running into the forest. Songbird turned her attention to Ember. "What are you doing here? And oh, your fa—behind you!"

Ember whipped around. It took a moment for her eyes to lock onto the cat charging toward her. Her vision dimmed. Her legs gave out. They hissed as she dropped. The cat landed on top of her. More on instinct than by intention, Ember rolled onto her back and kicked as hard as her prosthetics would allow. The Easterner flew backward. Her head hit the ground. She got to her feet but walked with a stagger. Ember stood up slowly. "We have to stop this. Stop the fighting; something isn't right!"

The molly lunged at her. Ember leaped back. Claws sliced the air a whisker away from her already stinging throat. The cat sank her teeth into Ember's side. Ember squeaked and ripped herself free.

Blue flared in her mind alongside the pain in her ribs. Searing, stabbing, disorienting pain. She stumbled backward, prosthetics whining in protest. Her vision lost focus again. Her spinning head threatened to make her pass out. She shook herself off. The cat jumped at her again. She ducked under a clumsy swat. Before the cat could recover her balance, Ember shoved her, claws unsheathed. As she fell, she hooked them in and let the momentum drag them through her skin. The cat hit the ground and moaned with pain. A moment later, she righted herself. They circled each other.

"You're naive if you think you can stop this, kitten," the molly said. "Especially if you think you can do it while continuing to fight."

"But this fight is illogical. I-i-it has to stop! This isn't—oh! Oh no." Her heart thudded in her ears. Her vision faded again as she retreated into her mind. "We've all been tricked!"

Paws hit her side. She tumbled over and snapped back into reality in time for her attacker to pin her down.

The cat placed a paw against her throat, claws digging pinpricks into her skin. "Okay, I'll admit I'm curious. How have we been tricked?"

'Don't kill me, don't kill me, don't kill me!' Ember swallowed hard. She panted, hyperventilating. "N-n-neither of us a-attacked first. D-don't you see? It doesn't make sense." She paused to gasp for breath. "If Lupine wanted to attack you, he would've sent more cats. The-the fight was uneven. And if Jade wanted to attack us, she would have placed the ambush s-somewhere else, a-a-and she would have told all of you about it. It-it has to have been a setup by someone else."

The molly dug her claws into her neck. "Sorry, but I'll need more proof than that to believe you. If it wasn't Lupine, who caused all this?"

Ember coughed. Songbird broke free from the cat she was fighting with, bit down on the tail of the molly pinning Ember down, and pulled. The cat released Ember to swat at her. Ember got up and readied herself for whatever attack might come next.

"Jade!" Cloud's voice rose above the din. It was distant and muffled, but there. "Call your cats off, and I'll call off mine. You've killed Lupine. You've got your revenge. If you agree to make peace now, as long as I'm commander of the West, you'll never have to see a Western face in your territory again."

The two Easterners and Songbird both stopped to look at Cloud. "You think it could have been him?" the Eastern molly asked. "Seems awfully ambitious to me."

The forest spun around her, making even standing difficult. *'No. No, it can't be him. Dad would never . . . But would he?'* She shook her head and closed her eyes. *'Did your father tell you the truth, or is he a liar too?'* Jade's question echoed through her head. *'Oh tahg, what if she's right?'*

Jade glared at Cloud in menacing silence from across Lupine's corpse.

"Okay, let me put this in perspective," Cloud said. "The longer we fight, the more cats will die. How many are you willing to lose for the sake of revenge? How much blood will fix what's been done?"

Jade lowered her head. "It won't. It won't fix anything," she said. "Everyone, fall back!"

"Western Colony, stop fighting!" Cloud shouted. "The war is over."

No one seemed to hear. Jade and Cloud raced across the battlefield, calling for a truce. "Stop fighting!" they cried out, over and over again until the last scream of agony and hatred faded.

The two Easterners Ember and Songbird had fought with ran to comfort injured or dying loved ones. Seven Easterners and five Westerners were dead. Several more lay waiting for death. Every survivor was injured and bleeding.

Ember shook herself off. Then collapsed. She covered her eyes with her forelegs and sobbed. Grey—it was all she could see, think, or feel.

"Ember? Ember, it's all over," Songbird whispered.

The ringing faded. Her peripheral vision came back. She got up and buried her face in her mother's bloodied fur.

Songbird wrapped a paw over her shoulder and pulled her close. "Hush. Calm down. Everything's going to get better now."

"But it's not," Ember mewed. "I-it isn't right. Nothing is right."

"I know it's hard, but—"

"No! N-n-nothing is right. It's broken. It's . . ." She opened her eyes. Color reclaimed her mind. Silver glistened brighter than it had ever shone before as her gaze zeroed in on a tanish-grey tabby approaching the edge of the battlefield. He stopped and stood in silence, looking around at the destruction. A leather pouch was strapped to his side, partially concealing the jagged scar tracing along his flank. "Bracken?"

"What?" Songbird asked.

Ember wriggled free from her mother's embrace. Bracken looked over his shoulder and nodded. More cats appeared behind him: seven. Among them was an orange molly with sporadic patches of white and a sleek, furless muzzle. It was Vixen.

Ember swallowed hard, fighting back a growl. "Oh," she whispered. *'He doesn't just know them. He's their leader.'* Her eyes narrowed to slits. *'And he's led them here.'*

CLOUD

"Hey!" Cloud hissed. "Who are you, and why are you here?"

The tabby signaled for his group to stay, then walked closer to where he and Jade stood. "I am Bracken, leader of the Midbrook Colony. I was told Commander Aspen would rather speak with me directly. I'd heard news of his passing, but thought I'd try coming anyway. I will admit I'm curious; what happened here? You've had a fight, and a big one by the looks of it. Why?"

"It's of no importance to you," Jade growled. "Leave. We don't have time for your Outsider foolishness."

Bracken's tail twitched. "Oh? Is that so? But am I the fool, or are you? I'll let your cats judge between us. You see, I come with a proposal. Your colonies are all but ruined. Your way of life is flawed. It brought this on you. Come with me; join my kin, and I promise that, as long as there is life in my body, there will be no war in the Valley. I am no commander, as you both seem so content to call yourselves, but I am a leader—a leader who will strive for justice. I can assure that you will all be treated kindly and with fairness, if you'll leave behind the way that caused all this pain and death."

'What kind of game are you playing? Do you really think you'll be able to come smooth-talk both colonies into following you? These cats are too smart to fall for that.' Cloud thought. "Get out of here before I hurt you."

Bracken shook his head. "A commander who will not even consider the desires of his colony. Whoever among you would like to start a new life, come with us. The Lowlands have more than enough food and water for all of you combined. It is a land of plenty: a place where all new ideas are considered, innovation is valued over tradition, and cats are free to come and go as they please."

"Actually, he makes a point," one Western tom said. "I'm sick of all this. I mean, Cloud and Dark's laws were practically leading us before, and all this happened. Who's to say it'll get better now that Lupine is gone? It'd be easier to just start over."

Cloud stiffened. "What? But that's what I was planning on doing. *I'm* going to start over. I'll rewrite every law to be just. Give me a chance, and I'll fix all of this."

"But weren't you the one who told the guards to kill on sight? Isn't that what got us into this mess in the first place? My brother is dead now because of you. So long as what's left of my family comes with me, I just want to get out of here. At this point, we'd be safer in the Lowlands," a young molly said.

"Aye," an Easterner mewed, "an' to add to that, Jade listened to a murderous exile, then led us into a fight she knew would be a slaughter, rather than waitin', or even callin' the whole bloody thing off, just to get revenge for the death 'a one cat. Now *seven* of my kindred are dead."

Cloud's heart raced. *'No, this can't be happening. What in the forest is going on? Are they really so fluffheaded as to trust this tom?'* He growled under his breath. "You can't really be choosing this cat who, might I remind you, just so happened to show up moments after this particular battle. You don't even know him, or his colony. None of us do. We have to consider what he's after."

"But we *do* know you, and I don't know what you're after, but I do know it isn't right for me. I'd rather take my chances."

"You can't trust him. He's an Outsider," Jade said.

"Maybe not, but after everything that's happened, how're we supposed to trust you? He said if we ever want to leave, we can leave. Did we ever have the option to choose to leave the East?"

Jade scoffed with indignation. "When have I ever once prevented someone from leaving?"

"Isn't that what you're trying to do right now?" one cat pointed out.

"We certainly didn't have the option to leave the West," another said.

"You! Bracken!" Ember shouted. Everyone turned to look at her. She shrunk back and shivered even harder. Her fur was mottled all over with cuts, and her face was a bloody mess. The kitten he'd helped raise from birth, the kitten he'd fought so hard to keep, was barely even recognizable. "You did this," she said. "Didn't you? W-why would you do this? Killing innocent cats —h-how is that justice?"

Cloud's eyes narrowed. *'So this wasn't my fault.'*

Bracken walked closer to her blood-stained form. "Killing innocent c—" He stopped and chuckled. "Oh, you're talking about Falcon, aren't you? I didn't kill him. No one killed him. I'm afraid the commander's informant was mistaken."

Cloud gritted his teeth. *'Well, then.'*

"Liar! You're a liar," Jade snapped.

"Oh, of course, you want proof. Well then. Falcon, perhaps you would do better explaining?"

Falcon stepped out from behind a boulder, grim-faced and very much alive. "Hello, love. Sorry I went away. Did you miss me?"

Jade stumbled forward. "Falcon? I . . . don't understand. Eclan said you'd been killed."

"You believed him?" He asked. His ears and tail lowered. "Oh, Jade, don't you know better than to trust the word of a Rogue? Or in this case, a mercenary for *hire*. Cats like him will do anything for the right price. You know that."

"Why didn't you come back?" she asked. "Falcon, cats are dead because of you."

"So now it's my fault, is it? Yeah, I suppose, in a way, it is, but I didn't call for this. I mean, I'm flattered you think so highly of me, but don't you think this was a touch overreacting?"

"You . . . abandoned me."

"Sorry, love. I guess you shouldn't have trusted me. I'd have thought you would have known better, but you're not my commander. My allegiance is with Bracken, and it always has been." His gaze wandered around the battlefield, lingering on the dead and dying. "After all these years, I thought for sure you would've seen right through me, but it would seem your feelings got in the way, blinding you from the truth. It's like I said, really: no molly should ever be commander. You've gotten cats killed, love."

Jade stepped back, eyes wide.

"But while it's not okay," he continued, "you can still come with us. We can start over, under a proper leader this time."

"Which is exactly what I'm offering. A second chance for those who need second chances," Bracken said. "Those who would like to join us may come. Those who wish to stay may stay. I will not force my leadership onto anyone."

An Easterner stepped closer to him. "Hold on, you've been workin' for him? What in the whole bloody forest is goin' on?"

Bracken opened his mouth to reply.

"You-you-you did this intentionally," Ember spat, cutting him off. "You had Falcon volunteer, and then . . . Oh tahg." She staggered backward, as if someone had just hit her in the face. "You're the one who started this, all of this—the assassination, the ambush, F-Farlight; you had him killed! You had them all killed! For what? So you could come in and take over?"

"Tahg, she's tellin' the truth, isn't she?" the Eastern cat asked.

Bracken stepped closer to Ember, eyes narrowed but calm. "I haven't killed anyone. What happened to Commander Aspen and his former successor was not my fault. Everything I do, I do for justice and for good. Their deaths were neither just nor good, and were also highly inconvenient." He looked around to address everyone still present. "Colony Cats, your system is broken. All I'm trying to do is help you see the destructive truth of your own ways. I work and speak for all the cats your way of life has hurt. Now that it's finally hurting you too, you're hearing me out. Yet even now, when I'm offering you a way to stop this, you still aren't listening to our voices, the voices of the cats you sentenced to die."

"We were *slaughtered* because of you!" an Eastern molly snarled. "Jade might not be the best commander, but at least she's not bent on destroying us all. Come on, East. Let's burn our dead and go home."

Falcon made a noise somewhere between a chuff and a snort.

"You're not one of us. Stay out of this, traitor."

He sighed. "No, it's not that. I just find it interesting how you think you still have a home to return to."

Jade froze in place. Looks of horror appeared on the Easterners' faces.

"The Rift was left all but unprotected. By now it'll be very well-fortified. If any of you try to retake it, there will be a *true* slaughter." Falcon looked down and pawed nervously at the ground. He lifted his head and looked directly at Cloud. "And there are cats moving along the Cliffs to take the Glade."

Cloud's blood went cold. "Kivy," he whispered. He looked around to address his colony. "Well, what are you all waiting for? We have to stop them. Come on!"

Jade snapped out of her daze. She moved to stand in front of him, eyes damp. "I know we've wronged your colony and killed your kin, but we can also help protect it. We cannot let your home be taken too. Do you trust us enough to let us fight by your side?"

'Circumstance doesn't appear to have left me much of a choice, has it?' He nodded once. "Gather the strongest survivors and follow us. We'll need all the

help we can get."

Jade nodded back."I'll try my best, Commander."

'Commander? I really am the commander now, aren't I? I guess it's time to find out just how good 'a one I am.' He lifted his head and sucked in a deep breath.

Before he could say anything, Songbird appeared at his side. "Everyone who can still fight, get to the Cliffs! Everyone else, help the injured or fall back to the Glade," she called out. She looked at him, intelligent eyes narrowed and fangs bared. "We can do this, Cloud. I know we can."

He nodded once and gave her a brief smile.

"East!" Jade called out behind them. "We have nothing left to lose. Let us help our neighbors. It may be their only chance and ours. Save the Glade. Follow them!"

The Colonies, East and West together, ran through the forest as one. At their head was Cloud, Songbird only a clawlength behind. *'I hope you'd be proud of me, Aspen. Your vision for the future may be about to come true. If only the circumstances were better. Wait.'* He glanced over his shoulder, then turned his attention back to his mate. "Where's Ember?"

EMBER

Ember stared at Bracken. Her teeth chattered together. Everyone still strong enough to fight had left to stop the invasion. A few wounded, helped by their closest kin, made their way toward the Glade, and many dead or dying remained on the battlefield, but in Bracken's presence she was alone, outnumbered and unable to move. Tears rolled down her face.

'They're gone; they're all gone. Every single one of them. Hyrees, Boreal, Shard, Sunshine, Crow, and everyone else. They're all dead. And if they aren't, what are they going to do?'

"You aren't going to help them? I'm surprised," Bracken said.

She closed her eyes and shivered harder. Her chest burned from hyperventilation. Her head throbbed. Everything hurt.

"I'm not going to kill you, if that's what you're worried about. Oh. Speaking of which." He looked over his shoulder to address the cats with him. "Vixen, take the rest of the Council and do what you can to help the wounded. Those who can be saved, save, but if you must, end the suffering of the dying. Falcon, stay with me."

Ember winced. "Y-you had them all k-k-killed. A-all of them," she mewed.

"I'm telling you the truth, Ember. I'm an opportunist. I don't waste life, and I don't have cats killed, but sometimes the lives I've affected end up wasting themselves. It is sad, but it's also reality." He sat down. "I offered them peace three times, and even after they rejected it, they could have stopped this, had they used common sense. These things only work when willful ignorance is involved. Unfortunately for them, that's the way they've been raised to function."

"But why attack them?"

"First, you have to consider what the cats of the Lowlands have been through. They've been thrown out, burnt alive, ripped apart, and nearly drowned by these cats you call your kin. Their lives were all but ruined. It's enough to make a cat do anything for revenge. I myself am not a vengeful cat, but in their anger I saw something useful. I had once made a promise that I would bring peace to Dark's Valley. After meeting other rejects and finding out how much they'd also been hurt, I realized I finally had a way to do it."

"Peace? Y-you call this peace?" Ember asked.

"It may seem counter-intuitive, but believe me, I've tried other ways. There are too many grudges and too many stubborn minds for kindness and reasoning to help. It's almost funny, because all I did today was give everyone what they wanted. Even my own cats will find out revenge is more costly than it's worth. That's the thing about war, though. It brings out the worst in everything and everyone. It shows us our flaws and our strengths, drives us to fix our problems—problems we were too comfortable, or too lazy, or too scared to fix before."

Wind cut through their fur and made Ember's face sting. Grey choked out all other thoughts and numbed her mind.

Bracken's tail twitched. "These cats needed humbling. Now, former enemies have united against a common foe. The East and the West are one. Had I sat back and done nothing, they would have started a similar war themselves, but this one would have ended with them killing themselves off, rather than joining together. You should be happy. After today, there will be peace; true peace. Grudges will no longer seem worth fighting over, and my colony and I now have a secure place to live. No matter how today ends, tomorrow will be better than yesterday ever was."

Ember opened her eyes and glared up at him. She stopped shaking with fear and instead trembled with rage. "But it's always today. Tomorrow never comes."

Falcon grimaced. "You still don't understand, do you, kitten?"

"Leave her be. No point in forcing her to see something when she doesn't want to."

"Yes, sir."

The howling wind and moaning of the injured prevented the silence from being absolute. Ember's mind drifted back to Hyrees and her Eastern friends. The fog cleared enough to think again. *'What happened to you? Are you dead? Are you hurt and lost? Where are you?'*

"Falcon?" Bracken asked, sending her back to the present. "Are you loyal to me?"

"I am. I've worked under you for four winters. I waited, and I saw your vision through. Isn't that proof enough?"

Bracken shook his head. "You worked with Jade for almost as long. I'm worried your feelings for her may make you a risk."

"What feelings?" Falcon said. "I worked under her because you told me to. I am loyal to you and to the Midbrook Colony. If she won't come, that's her problem, not mine. Besides, she probably hates me now."

"Fair enough," Bracken said, "but I'm not convinced. Kill Jade, and bring me a piece of her ear."

Falcon recoiled. "What?

"You heard what I said. If you do have feelings for her, those feelings will inevitably get someone hurt. Most likely yourself. Besides, she's too far gone at this point. The commander you knew when you left the East is already dead. Now go. When you're done, call off the fight. They will answer to you."

Falcon's head and tail drooped. "Yes. Yes, sir."

He shoved past Ember, then sprinted up the mountain.

Ember stumbled sideways. One of her hind paws landed on a dead cat's side. Sickly green and yellow flared in her head. She recoiled and dry-heaved, then hacked out blood.

"Okay," Bracken said. His voice was calm and almost content. "Now I've had someone killed. Or, at least, I will have had someone killed by the time the sun sets. A shame, really, but his death will be a necessary one."

Ember glared back at him. "Y-you're worse . . . th-th-than Commander Aspen," she spat between coughs and pants. "You're a wildcat." She coughed once more, then ran after Falcon and the Colonies.

"I'm sorry you see it that way," Bracken called after her. "Maybe when you're older, you'll thank me. Oh, try not to die out there, Ember. You're far too valuable to waste yourself in a skirmish."

She bit her tongue and did her best to ignore him.

CLOUD

Cloud kept running. Breathing, or even moving forward, became more difficult with every step. His chest ached; the excitement and adrenaline that came with fight or flight was waning, but the Cliffs were getting close. Scents of unfamiliar cats filled the air. The wildcat hadn't been joking.

He shook his head, trying to rid himself of the anxiety that stemmed from leaving Ember with possibly the most dangerous cats in the forest. *'She can take care of herself,'* he thought. *'Kivy can't. The Glade is unprotected. We can't turn around for the sake of one cat.'*

"Look out!" Songbird shouted.

Movement caught the edge of his vision. A mange covered tom tackled him from the side. They rolled down the slope, toward the cliff edge. Cloud's heart lurched as he scrambled to stop himself.

"Cloud!" she cried out.

He sank his claws into a root. They slipped. He slid to a stop a paw and a clawlength away from the drop-off, attacker on top of him. The scraggly tom sighed in relief. Cloud kicked him in the stomach, and the cat tumbled over the edge, howling as he fell. All went silent. The forest around him came alive with growls, hisses and screams. A new battle had started, and he was already exhausted.

He moved up the slope, away from the cliff edge, and shoved an attacker off of Jade. The cat screeched as Cloud sank his fangs into its neck, severing an artery. Blood filled his mouth. He spat the cat out, then pushed it away.

Jade stood up, wavering slightly. "Thank you. On your right!"

He spun around and lashed out with his claws. They raked across a grey molly's face. She squeaked and staggered back. Cloud pounced. She leaped out of the way. He landed and slid to a stop. They circled each other. Jade pounced on the molly from behind, her fangs digging into the cat's neck.

"Help me!" the molly yowled.

Cloud crouched down to finish her but stopped short. *'Oh tahg, she's young. Probably younger than Ember. With the enemy or not, she doesn't deserve this.'*

A flash of black and grey pounced onto Jade's back. The molly broke free and ran off as Jade fell to the ground. She rolled, knocking her attacker off, and jumped to her paws. She recoiled. "F-Falcon? Please don't do this. You aren't really on their side, are you?"

"Sorry, love," Falcon said, stalking closer. "Bracken has sent me to kill you. Only one of us is walking away from this. I'm afraid I don't have much of a choice."

Jade shied away from his advance, backing herself to the edge of the rock. "Yes, you do. Don't fight me, Falcon. Fight with me. I can't kill you. You know I can't."

"Those pesky feelings getting in the way again?" he asked. "Don't make this easy, please. I'd like to remember you as a warrior, not a coward."

Another Midbrook tom jumped in front of Cloud, preventing him from reaching her. Cloud lunged at the cat's legs. The cat leaped away from his dive and brought his claws down on Cloud's side. Cloud clenched his teeth to ward off the pain and swatted at his attacker. The tom snarled and bounced out of reach. Songbird flung herself against his side, sending him tumbling down the slope. He caught himself hanging halfway off of the cliffside. The cat heaved himself back to stable ground and, with a look of terror, darted down the mountain slope.

Cloud chuffed as Songbird shook herself off. "Took you long enough."

"I'm sorry," she said, "I was busy trying not to die. I won't always have time for that *and* saving your tail. Now come on, we've got a fight to win." She nudged his side. Across the battlefield, Rowan struggled with a tortoiseshell. "You help Rowan. I'll try to get to Jade."

Cloud nodded, then ran to save his apprentice.

"Stop!" A flurry of pointed cream leaped between Falcon and Jade as he dashed past them. Echo snarled, head low and tail raised. "Don't you dare lay a *claw* on her."

"Move, Echo, or I'll have to take you too," Falcon said. "I don't want to kill you."

As he drew closer, the tortoiseshell got off of Rowan, then charged at Cloud. Cloud veered sideways a moment before they met. They both slid to a stop and turned to face each other. "Leave, now," Cloud snarled.

A few leaps away, Echo bared her teeth. "This isn't what we agreed to, Falcon. I've done my part. Cass is almost done with hers, and you and Bracken have what you want. Your fight is over. Call everyone back and end it. Now."

"You know it's not that simple. Now move, or I *will* hurt you," Falcon said.

"Agreed to?" Jade asked. "What are you . . . you knew about this?"

Echo looked back at her mother. "I'm sorry, Mum. I did what I had to do to keep you and Shard safe. Whole bloody lot of good that did, apparently."

"Echo, look out!"

Falcon clamped his teeth onto her leg. Echo's eyes went wide.

"No!" Echo screeched. "No, you didn't."

"We only take orders from Bracken and the Council," the tortoiseshell snarled, gaze locking onto Cloud's. "And as long as Falcon is in the fight, we answer to him."

Cloud and the tortoiseshell ran at each other again. This time, they collided. They sliced and bit, matching blow for blow and refusing to give in.

Out the corner of his eye, he noticed blood rolling down Echo's leg. When Falcon released her, it pulsed with her heartbeat. She stumbled backward, pupils dilated and unfocused. Echo collapsed. Jade ran to her daughter's side and placed her paws over the wound, trying to stop the bleeding. It wasn't working. "Echo! Echo, no."

"Don't just lie there—get a vine, or a rock, or something! I'm dying, Mum; make it stop!"

Jade pressed her muzzle against Echo's side in a futile attempt to comfort her. "I can't. I can't help you, Echo. Come on, stay with me. Stay with me."

Beneath them, Songbird struggled with another Midbrooker. Falcon reared back to spring on Jade. A flash of brown raced into the moss-covered rockscape and leaped at him, artificial limbs hissing. They collided and toppled over together. Falcon landed on top of her. "Stop making this harder," he growled. His claws raked down her neck and chest. Ember mewled and struggled to break free. Songbird slammed her opponent against a tree, then ran to help. Falcon shoved Ember off of the rise, and her head struck a rock. She didn't get up.

"Ember!" Songbird called out.

'Oh no,' Cloud thought. His jaw tensed. His lungs and wounds ached. He and the tortoiseshell broke free and circled each other.

"You have to do something," Echo yowled behind them. "Do something! Shard needs me. He needs me; I can't die yet. I have to protect him. I can't . . ." Her breathing slowed. "I can't go yet. He . . . needs me. Shard . . . Sh-Shard . . ." Her eyes glazed over. Her breathing stopped. Echo went limp.

Jade reared back. "Echo! Echo, no!" She pressed an ear against her daughter's rib cage. After a few moments, she closed her eyes and cried.

Falcon spun to face Songbird, who pounced at him. He dodged her attack and shoved her to the ground, pinning her in place with his claws.

"Get off me," Songbird demanded.

"Song!" Cloud called out. *'She needs me. She needs me now. They all need me now.'* He shoved his attacker aside and raced across the battleground. A fresh burst of adrenaline surged through his system as he rammed into Falcon's side. As they tumbled toward the Cliffs, his heartbeat thudded in his ears. He felt alive—more alive than he'd ever felt before. They slid to a stop on the cliff edge, and before he could right himself, Falcon sank his teeth into Cloud's throat.

"CLOUD!" Songbird yowled.

'This is it, isn't it? This is what leading is all about, right? I can still fix this. I have to.' He craned his neck to look at his family. Ember lifted her head, still dazed.

Her eyes locked onto his. "Dad?" she mewed.

"Cloud, no!" Songbird cried out.

"I love you," he said. His voice was hoarse but calm.

He dug his claws into Falcon's sides and flung himself over the edge, dragging Falcon down with him. He closed his eyes as he fell, and as the distance to the jagged stones below grew shorter, a sense of peace entered his heart. He was a kitten again, a trainee begging his father not to go to war; then a youth, falling in love with Songbird all over again. Ember was born, and he risked everything to keep her. Kivyress was born, and he gave everything to protect her. They were as safe as he could make them. They were free. He inhaled, exhaled, then collided with a rock. The forest went white.

EMBER

"Dad!" Ember shrieked. She stumbled to the cliff's edge. Songbird was already there. She could barely make out Falcon's body: a speck laid out on a boulder just above the Wolf Trail. Cloud's was gone.

"No," Songbird mewled. "No, no, no, no, this can't be happening. This can't . . ."

"Falcon is dead!" The tortoiseshell Cloud had fought with shouted. "Fall back, everyone! Return to Bracken. The fight is over."

The Midbrook Cats wrestled free, then moved en masse down the Western Mountain. Ember rested her chin on the rocky ledge. She covered her eyes and cried.

'He's gone. Dad is gone. He's gone. Why is this happening? Why? This isn't, this can't be true. It's not over, he's not dead, he—' She looked down again. A flash of grey fur caught her eyes—motionless grey fur, a smudge in the distant underbrush: Cloud. Her jaw trembled. *'He really is . . . He's gone. He's dead, and there's nothing I, or anyone else, can do about it. He's gone, and Echo, and Hyrees, and Boreal, and Shard. They're gone. They're dead. They're all dead.'*

"Cloud," Songbird whispered.

Ember shivered with sorrow and rage. Misty orange and fang yellow swirled through her head, defying the ever-encroaching grey. *'They're dead, and it's all Bracken's fault.'*

517

CHAPTER 33
EMBER

A gentle, steadfast breeze blew through Dark's Valley, adding to the chill of nighttime. Branches rustled and clicked together, reminding Ember where she was. She was in the old maple: her favorite tree in the entire forest. It was her maple, their maple. Cloud had always sat in the little crook in its roots. He'd waited so patiently as she'd daydreamed and breathed in the gale every morning.

She sighed. A day had come and gone since he'd left, but it hurt all the same. Her cheeks were wet again, yet she couldn't bring herself to cry anymore; not now, when everything was calm and quiet—and over. It was over, all over. The fighting was done, at least for a while. The East and the West as she'd known them were gone. Cats were dead, wounded, or missing, and no one knew what to do about it. No one even knew what to do about the ones who weren't. There was no commander, and with the Rift taken, very little hope. She'd overheard a few cats suggesting Jade might take up the mantel again, but after everything that had happened, the once great leader's self-confidence had plummeted. With all the contempt and cynicism surrounding the position, no one else seemed eager to take it.

Ember lowered herself to rest on the branch. She yawned, then gazed out across the Lowlands. It looked both smaller and less inviting than when she'd last viewed it from her perch. Dark blue joined the faded orange in her subconscious. The colors were there, bright as ever, but inside she felt nothing. A dull ache traced the scabbed cuts across her face and along her neck and chest, yet in her heart the only feeling was a hollow fogginess which her thoughts usually associated with grey.

After the fight, Songbird had taken her to the Glade to get her wounds cleaned and let Kivyress know what had happened. It was the worst possible way to reunite with her sister, but at least Kivyress was still alive. Afterward, they'd spent most of the day helping treat the injured and recovering what bodies they could. There were too many for individual fires, so two closely-monitored bonfires at each of the battle sites served to clean the areas of the deceased. Then a long and tearful memorial ceremony had been held to honor the fallen.

Ember hadn't said anything during the ceremony. She'd been too shaken and exhausted from the day's events. Most cats still considered her a traitor anyway, so she'd decided keeping a low profile would be better for everyone. Songbird had given a short-but-sweet speech for Cloud, then retreated to the old family den with Kivyress to mourn in private. Ember had fallen asleep in the History Tree, for lack of a better home. It had been cold without Hyrees.

The following morning, a few brave Easterners had left to see what had become of their homeland and the family members they hoped were still in it. Yet most of them were still too exhausted, both physically and emotionally, to make the trip back, so they remained in the West, defeated.

No one had given her any instructions after they'd left, so she'd spent the day wandering the territory. She'd gone to all of her favorite places, but nowhere in the entire forest did she feel more close to her father than in her maple. So she sat there and watched the stars.

Ember swallowed hard and closed her eyes. *'I'm at home. I'm in my tree because I wanted to escape the winter meeting, which was going perfectly last time I checked. Dad will come get me soon to take me to the feast. After that, Hyrees and I will sit in the History Tree and try to count stars. Maybe ask T—No, Thai doesn't exist.'*

[That is technically true. I don't have a physical form, after all.]

'You're not making this any easier. Please be quiet.' She licked her lips, and shuddered as the wind picked up. *'Where was I? Oh, stars, right. We'll watch the stars and wonder what they're made of, then curl up in each other's paws and go to sleep. Tomorrow Tainu will give me hunting lessons, and Whitehaze can give me clawmarking tips so I can pass my next test. I can do it. I know I can. And after I do, things will get better. I'll prove to them that Dark was—no, Dark was someone great whom I still look up to. He wouldn't want to kill me at all. No one wants me dead. Especially not Commander Aspen. And I've never killed anyone. Why would I ever do that? Oh, and Boreal has—wait, I don't know a Boreal.'*

She opened her eyes to look down at her paws. The heating wires inside them glowed faintly. Every move she made caused them to whine. Spots of blood appeared on her toes. She did a double-take, heart racing. The blood spots were gone. She exhaled slowly. *'Calm down, Ember. It's over now. But who am I trying to fool? I can't even pretend everything is normal. That normal is gone, and I'm never getting it back. I don't even know if I want all of it back. I want Dad back. I need him. We need him. Everyone needs him, but now he's gone, and no one knows what to do. Now everything is broken, and we can't fix it.'*

Ember looked down, still half-expecting to see Cloud waiting for her. He wasn't. No one was there. The crook in the roots was empty. She sat up and swiped at the tree with her paw. "Can't at least Hyrees be okay?" she asked no one.

"Ember? Ember, where are you?"

Ember jumped. Her front paw slipped, and her chest slammed into the branch. The scratches crossing it stung, sending bright, painful blue into the back of her mind. She pushed herself up and coughed. "I'm up here," she said weakly.

Songbird walked to the base of Ember's maple. "Could you come down, please? They're going to have a meeting to discuss who should become the next commander. They want everyone to be present."

"I didn't think anyone still cared about what I wanted. Especially now that both colonies hate me," Ember said.

She scaled down the tree to greet her mother.

Songbird pressed her forehead against Ember's. "I care. I want you to have a say in this, because it doesn't matter if they like it or not; this is your home. If anyone wants to take it away from you again, they'll have to fight me first."

She leaned into her mother's warm nuzzle. "Thanks, Mom," she whispered.

Ember sniffed back tears as they walked away from the old patrol route. Frigid air filled her lungs, and silence gave the forest a sense of rare tranquility. It was a peaceful night for having a stroll: the kind of night she usually loved, but after everything that had happened, she found herself unable to appreciate the stillness.

As they neared the Glade, voices grew louder. Cats yelled, but she couldn't make out what they were saying. Like war. Cats were fighting. Her heart raced. She stopped. Her body refused to move another step, no matter how much she wanted it to go, and no matter how hard she breathed, her lungs felt empty. She closed her eyes and panted. *'I can't do this. I don't know if I can do this.'*

"Are you okay? Ember, talk to me. What's wrong?" Songbird asked.

She shivered harder. "I don't wanna talk about it. I don't . . . I don't wanna —" She dropped her stomach and covered her eyes. Even with them closed as tightly as she could close them, death, destruction, and blood flared in her imagination. Cloud tumbled over the Cliffs all over again. "No! Make it stop, Mom, please make it stop! Make the fighting stop. Don't let them die. Don't let him die."

"They're not fighting, Ember, they're . . ." Songbird sighed. She lay down against Ember's flank, wrapped her tail around her haunches, and rested her chin on top of her neck. It offered some warmth against the cold but did nothing to stop the pictures in her head.

"Help me," Ember whispered.

"I'm trying my best," Songbird replied.

They rested outside the Glade, not saying anything as Ember fought with her own imagination. Then Songbird started to hum. It transitioned into singing: gentle, sweet singing that made something inside of her know things would get better.

"Sleep, little one. The fear has gone. The fear has gone. The fear has gone. Sleep, little one—for goodness, it has won. You'll be safe with me right here tonight."

The shivering slowed. The flashbacks stopped. Ember forced herself to be still. She nuzzled Songbird's neck. "Thanks, Mom."

Songbird leaned back to look at her. She sniffled and wiped the tears from her eyes. "Last time I sang that to you was the night he saved your life. You were so small then. Barely more than a mooncycle old."

They sat up together. Ember pressed herself more firmly against her mother's fur. Pressure; she needed pressure. Songbird wrapped a paw around her shoulder. The silence came back. Wind howled; branches creaked; an owl hooted in the distance.

The pressure stopped. Songbird stood and sniffed the air. She turned to face Ember. "Do you think you can come into the Glade now?"

The expression on her face was as unreadable as ever, but this time it was a different kind of unreadable: one that didn't seem right, but not in a bad way. It was hiding some kind of emotion that didn't line up with anything done or said previously. Indigo flickered through her thoughts. She sniffed the breeze. New scents filled her nose—scents she hadn't smelled in what felt like an eternity. For the first time in almost two days, Ember smiled. She sprung to her feet and charged into the Glade.

Her eyes searched the mess of cats for the sources of the scents. They found one of them; no, two of them. Her heart leaped. "Boreal! Shard!"

Boreal looked up and caught her gaze. Ember averted her eyes automatically but kept going. Boreal ran to meet her. They pressed their heads against each other's shoulders.

"You made it," Boreal said. "At least someone's alive."

"I thought you'd all been killed," Ember replied. She stepped back, crying tears of joy. "Hyrees?"

"He's in your cave of healing. Woke up not long after everyone left. He's made it this far. I think he might make it the rest of the way."

She sighed with relief and peered around Boreal's side. Shard sat with Jade, crying against her neck. A stab of sorrow hit her chest. Echo was gone. He would never see his sister and best friend ever again. She was nothing but ashes now, an echo of memories and time they would never get to spend together. It seemed everyone had lost someone close to them.

'But that's life, isn't it?' she thought. *'You gain, then you lose, and it keeps happening over and over again until you lose yourself.'* She shook her head. *'Don't think about that.'* "Boreal? Hey, I-I'm sorry about your dad."

"He was a traitor. And a terrible father. He had it coming. Besides, I already thought he was dead. In some ways it's easier knowing he deserved it. Oh, and I'm sorry about your father. He spared my life, you know. Back during that first fight. He *didn't* deserve this."

"No. No, he didn't," Ember spat. Her words came out more bitterly than she intended, but she didn't bother trying to take it back. She started to shiver again. *'No, you have to stop this, Ember. Don't think about it. Don't think about any of it.'* "S-s-so what happened at the Rift?"

"Strange cats came and told us everyone who'd left for the West was gone and none of them were coming back for us." Boreal sat down and pawed at a patch of dirt.

Ember stared at her moving paw, trying to shift her focus onto anything but the battle. "They smooth-talked themselves into the Colony and started running the place," Boreal continued. "They said anyone who didn't agree with them taking over could leave. A few tried to fight. They were killed. Most stayed out of fear, though I think a few actually agreed with them. The rest of us left. We didn't know what we'd be walking into when we reached the West, but we decided we'd be better off taking the risk. Oddly enough, they gave us one of their carrying things filled with food to take with us. Other than killing the ones who tried to fight against them and manipulating themselves into power, they . . . weren't terrible to us."

"N-not terrible? That's an interesting statement," Ember said. A faint growl edged into her voice as purple appeared in her mind. She backed away. "I-I should probably go . . . see Hyrees."

"Good luck with that," Boreal mewed.

Ember did her best to dodge talking cats and loud noises as she made her way to the healers' den. She stepped inside. And there he was. Fern was putting rocks around one of his paws. His chin rested on his other paw. Her heartbeat quickened. "Hyrees?"

"Ember?" He lifted his head and moved to stand.

Fern placed a paw against his back. "Sit still," she said. "If you want that paw to get better, you'll need to first stop making it get worse."

He settled back down. "Sorry. Hey, Ember. I'm . . . glad you're not dead."

'Oh. That's all? Okay. I guess things really are going to be different now.' Her face burned. Swarms of colors filled her head as emotions muddled together. "I'm glad you woke up. And survived the Lowlands again. S-so what happened to your paw?"

"I got caught under a root and broke it. Or at least I think it was a root. But I'll be fine, I guess." He sighed. "Fern, could we . . . maybe get some privacy?"

"Oh? Er, yes, of course. Just let me finish up, then I'll get out of your way." She pushed the last stone against his paw, then left the den.

Hyrees stared blankly at the ground. "So."

"So," Ember repeated. She sat down. *'Why is this so awkward? It's not usually this hard to talk to him. Is it going to be like this from now on? I don't want it to be.'*

"Those sticks you gave me. Did you really mean all that?"

"Maybe," she said, a little too quickly.

"Maybe?"

She rubbed her paw. "Yes. Yes, I meant it. We've been hurting each other, and I don't want to do that anymore."

He turned his head to stare at the wall. "Yeah. I guess we have. And I'm sorry, Ember, I really am, but is it true you never wanted to be mates with me? Because I have a hard time believing that. I mean, everything we went through before this mess—it seemed right. I really thought we were meant for each other."

"It seemed right because you've always been my best friend. I really do care about you, and I really do love you, but it's only ever been as a friend." She flattened her ears and closed her eyes. "I really thought becoming mates with you would change how I felt, and maybe help us both not be so looked down on by the Colony. I thought it would make everyone happy. But nothing changed, except things got worse between us. I don't want that."

"Oh," he said. "Okay. So what are we now?"

She bent over to examine the dirt floor of the den. "Still friends, I hope?"

His mouth twitched into something she guessed was a smile, but as soon as it appeared, it was gone. A tear dripped onto his cheek. "We'll try for that then. I still love you, you know. Even if I find someone else, I'm worried it'll be hard to stop."

"We don't have to stop loving each other. It'll just be a different kind of love. The kind where we can go our separate ways when we have to. We don't have to hold each other back to be happy anymore. Or, well, I'm not sure that was the best way to put it, but you get the idea. I guess."

"I guess so."

She stood up, tail twitching. "But, uhm, I *am* sorry. For-for everything I've put you through."

"You saved my life, Em. You kept me going when I wanted to stop more than anything else."

"So you forgive me?"

He looked in her general direction. "Do you forgive me?"

"Yes, but why is this conditional?"

"I don't know. It felt like the right thing to say, okay?" He sighed. "Which means I probably shouldn't have said it. Sorry. Yeah, I forgive you. I'm glad we had this talk. It'll help me move forward with whatever life I have left. Hopefully I can make myself a decent one."

"Yeah," Ember said. Her face still felt warm.

Songbird peered into the den. "Ember, sorry to cut in, but we're about to have the meeting. Are you coming?"

"Yes, ma'am," she replied. "Sorry, Hyrees. I have to go now. Take care, okay?"

"You too."

Songbird nodded a polite greeting to Hyrees, which he didn't seem to notice, then Ember followed her out of the den feeling confused and more than a little queasy. Yet it was worth it—seeing him alive and letting the truth come out had made it worth it.

'Now things can get better the right way. At least when it comes to us. I don't know about the Colony itself, or just me by myself, but at least that's settled. Better than nothing at all.'

Songbird nudged her toward the gathering of cats. Ember let herself be ushered closer to the noise, even though it made her heart race and her body shake.

Kivyress limped beside them. She'd gotten good at moving on three legs. "So is it true you aren't going to be together anymore? Not even now?" she asked.

"Yeah. It's for the better," Ember replied.

"Will he be okay?"

"For the first time this mooncycle, I think so."

They sat down at the edge of the group. Jade sat on the commander's den, but unlike all the times she'd made announcements before, she looked as broken and uncertain as everyone else. She inhaled slowly, then began, "The Colonies have called for this meeting, and as former commander of the East, I was chosen to conduct it. But I have failed my colony. I am no longer deserving of the trust my kin once placed in me, which is why the time has come for a new leader to be chosen. No one suggest yourself. I want you all to think about the cats you know. Who is most fit to take up this task?"

'Dad was most fit,' Ember thought. Her vision blurred again as more tears threatened to fall. *'But he's not an option anymore. Who is?'*

Several cats mentioned names that faded into background noise. Ember

526

recognized a few belonging to former council members, but no one seemed to agree on anything. Most of the cats being suggested turned down the idea immediately. Ember sighed. *'Are there any leaders here at all?'*

"I have a suggestion," Kivyress called out, startling Ember.

"Then say it," Jade replied.

"What about Mom?"

Songbird shrunk back, eyes wide and tail thrashing. "I, uh, I don't know about that."

"Wait, hear me out," Kivyress said. "Half of you probably don't know this, but Mom was the one D—" Her voice broke, and she started to cry. "Dad went to her for advice. So, if he would've . . . you know, made a good commander, I think she probably will too. She . . . she did help back when we had the Meetings. Or at least that's what everyone says. And she's pretty much been running the Colony anyway, organizing a hunt and giving out rations."

"She has a point," one Westerner said, "but Songbird is a molly. We've only ever had toms command. Besides, she just lost her mate. She's probably too unstable."

"She'd be better than you," the cat beside him snapped. "Maybe it's time for things to change around here."

"Sorry, Mom," Kivyress whispered, leaning closer to Songbird. "I-I really thought it was a good idea, but . . ."

"All in favor of Songbird, stand," Jade called.

Cats, both Western and Eastern, got to their paws. Ember hesitated a moment, then stood with them. Nearly half of the Colony was unanimous, including, to Ember's surprise, Silentstream.

"Songbird?" Jade asked. "Would you be willing to take on the role of commander and to lead the New West through whatever may come during the time of your leadership?"

For a while, she didn't respond. Then, slowly, she stood and lifted her head. A single tear rolled down her face and got absorbed by her fur. "Cloud didn't abandon his kin when they needed him most. I guess I'll try my best to continue that legacy. Jade, you already know how to leader. Ah, how to *be* a leader. Will you be my advisor and show me how to best help this colony?"

Jade smiled. "If you trust me with such a role, yes, I will. Now come up, Commander Songbird. Choose your council and address your colony."

Songbird walked quietly around the outskirts of the meeting. She climbed up the commander's den and looked at Jade. "Who are the three cats you trust the most? I've never led before, so I want experienced council members from both colonies."

Jade listed three names Ember didn't recognize. Songbird called them to sit in front of her. A tabby tom, a sable tom, and a pointed molly took their places beneath the den.

Jade peered down at the tabby. "Kite may be young, but he is smart and capable. An excellent tactician. He may make a good commander one day, if you are willing to train him."

She shifted her attention to the sable: an older dark grey cat with a creamy ruff and a white stripe lining his underside. "Thunder has been a trusted council member of the East for many winters. More winters than I've been alive. He is wise and a voice of reason I should have listened to more often. He stayed behind when we chose to fight but did not hesitate to bring the Eastern remnants across the Lowlands when they decided to come here."

She looked at the molly, a creamy cat with silver tabby markings on her face, legs and tail. She looked about the same age as Jade. "Brook is my sister-in-law. She is strong-willed and a touch eccentric, but also clever and creative. She's excellent at problem-solving and seeing things from new angles. These three will advise you well, as they advised me. Now you may choose three cats from your own colony."

Songbird sucked in a deep breath, then breathed it out slowly. "Fern, you're my older sister, and I've always looked up to you. You've always been there for me when things got bad. Now I think I need your wit and reasoning more than ever before. Will you help me?"

Ember craned her neck around to look at where Fern sat a leap away. Fledge was beside her, smiling as usual. "I told you things would get better," Fledge mewed, nuzzling her side. "Now go, get out of here. You can do this."

"Thanks," Fern replied. They touched foreheads, then Fern made her way to the front. "I'm with you, Song, and I know we can do this."

"Thank you," Songbird said. Then she called up Trout, an old silver smoke tom with a reputation for being level-headed; and Redwater, a sable tom with piercing orange eyes and a calm, intelligent demeanor. Both were members of the former Western Council, and both were well-liked.

'This is good,' Ember thought. The tears she'd been fighting with escaped. She stared blankly at the ground to hide them, not looking at anything in particular. *'Members from both councils. That should make most cats happy. Tahg, Mom really is the commander now. Dad would like that. He'd like this. He'd want to see this.'*

"A new council has been chosen," Jade declared. "The East and West are now united under one leader: Commander Songbird. For Songbird and the New West!"

"For Songbird and the New West!" the Colony shouted, then ascended into cheers.

Ember's ears rung with their shouts. Her heartbeat escalated. War came back—blood and fighting cats flashing through her mind. She closed her eyes and gasped for air. *'Stop, stop, stop!'*

"Ember? Em, are you okay? Everyone stop! Be quiet! Please, you're hurting her." Kivyress's voice was faint and distant.

Someone pawed at her side. Her stomach hurt. The ringing grew louder. *'I'm on the ground. Why am I on the ground? What is going on? I have to get out of here. I can't ruin this. I can't; I can't.'*

She pushed herself up, then ran into the den. Her parent's den, the place she'd grown up. It was the only place in the entire Glade where she felt safe. She pressed her head against the wall and stayed there. Gradually, her breathing slowed. After what seemed like an eternity of trying to calm herself alone, someone stepped inside.

"Hey, are you alright?"

"Not really, Kivy, but thanks for asking. It's like I can't stop thinking about what happened. No matter how hard I try, it's always there, hurting me all over again. My body keeps wanting me to fight, even when all I want is to just get some sleep." A tiny mewl escaped her throat. "And Dad is dead."

Kivyress limped over to her and pressed her face against her side. Her tears seeped into Ember's fur and warmed her skin. "What are we going to do now?"

Ember pulled away from the wall and wrapped her paws around her sister's shoulders. They cried together. "I don't know."

A new warmth surrounded them as Songbird joined the huddle. "We're going to keep moving forward," she said, voice wavering. "And we're going to make it. I don't know how long it's going to take, or how hard the trail ahead will be, but we're going to make it through this. We'll mend what mistakes we can, and learn to live with the ones we can't, starting right now."

Ember lifted her head. "How?"

"I've given you a pardon. It was my first official ruling. It's not much, I know, but it's better than nothing at all. Welcome home, Ember."

'Home? Home, I'm home. I guess I am home. And this time I don't have to leave. Ever.' She leaned into Songbird's embrace. "Thanks, Mom."

"You're welcome." Her gaze became calm and distant. "And I guess now I'm going to have to fix this broken mess of a colony. I'll need some help to do it, but things will get better than what they are." She pulled her daughters closer. "I promise."

———

Ember sat in the History Tree, once again watching the stars. She'd tried to fall asleep alone in the old den, but even the slightest sounds had snapped her awake. Instead of fighting it, she'd decided to welcome her restlessness.

"I wish you were here, Dad. I know you're not, so I don't know why I'm talking right now, but I guess I just need some closure. There's a lot I've always wanted to say to you that I never really had the courage to say, and now you're gone, so I'll never be able to actually say them to you. I guess I'll have to settle for saying it to nothing because it feels right. It feels . . . like I'm supposed to; like it might possibly be good for me in some way I don't consciously know."

She sighed. "This is stupid. I don't know why I'm doing this. It's not logical. I need you, and I need you *here*. Right here, in front of me. How else am I supposed to tell you how much I appreciate you and everything you've done for me, and for Kivy, and for Mom, and for everyone else? How am I supposed to tell you how much I've always looked up to you, or how hard I tried to be who you and Mom wanted me to be? How are you going to hear any of this when you aren't here to listen, and more importantly, why am I still talking? There is *no one here*."

She lay down and covered her face with her paws. *'I feel like such a fluffhead now. You wouldn't want me doing this, would you?'*

"Hey, er, are you awake? I don't think I ever said a . . . a proper hello to you," Shard's voice said.

"Yep. I can't sleep. But that's . . . more or less normal."

"I was also wondering if you, uhm, you know, wanted to talk."

"Not really."

"Ah," he said.

Ember sighed again. She leaned over to look at him. "But we can still talk, if you want. Not like I have anything else to do. So how are you doing with . . . all this?"

He flattened his ears and sniffed. "I still can't convince myself she's actually gone. I keep expecting her to walk into the Ri—ah, *Glade*, and tell me to cheer up. But she won't, and I don't know what to do. Without Echo, I feel lost."

She got to her feet, then climbed down the tree. They touched noses and sat down together to look out across the Glade.

"We can feel lost together, I guess," Ember said. "At least it's better than being lost alone."

He sighed. "I guess so."

Somewhere in the familiar clearing, someone snored. Restless cats wandered around. A few of them spoke among themselves or to themselves.

"I'm sorry about your dad," Shard said, breaking the ambience.

Ember narrowed her eyes. "It's not your fault." She dug her claws into the earth. "Bracken caused this."

He looked away. "Yes, right. He took him, and Echo, and our home. Do you think we'll ever at least get the Rift back?"

"I don't know, but if we try anything against them, more cats are going to get killed. Though really, it's not my place to decide what happens next. I'm lucky to even still be considered a Colony Cat at this point. I'm not about to push my own mother's limits, not even to get back at the cat who ruined our lives. It's not worth it."

"All this pain, loss and bitterness; is anything worth it, really? I mean, I can't think of anything that would justify it. Any of it."

Ember sighed, thoughts wandering back to Bracken's words. Had he really given everyone what they wanted? Or had he merely given them what he wanted them to have? Did he hate the chaos, or simply want to control it? And what if he was telling the truth? Was there someone else out there who'd ordered Aspen and Farlight to be killed? She didn't know.

"Where do you think we'll go from here?" Shard asked, breaking her trail of thought.

She stood up. "To sleep, if we can. After that? I don't know. Mom said she had an idea for a new job I could have, so I guess I'll find out where I get to go tomorrow."

"I suppose that means tomorrow will be better."

"Maybe," she replied. Ember turned towards the commander's den, where Songbird and Kivyress were. "I should try to get some sleep. Goodnight, Shard."

"Thanks for talking with me. I do feel a little better. Goodnight, then."

"You're welcome."

Shard nodded once, then they parted ways. Ember entered the commander's den and settled down beside Kivyress. Once again, something inside of her refused to be calm. Another owl cried out. She shivered. *'Calm down, Em. Tomorrow will be better. I'll make it better.'*

Yet in the deepest, darkest parts of her subconscious, her own words repeated themselves over and over again until they became a silent roar.

'Tomorrow never comes.'

A SHORT STORY

'I have to tell her,' Cloud thought. 'That was Aspen's last warning. The stubborn fluffhead. He's doing this just to prove a point, isn't he? Think you can control me, do you, my liege?'

He paced back and forth in front of his den, a simple burrow dug beneath a living, partially hollow tree. Moonlight illuminated the Glade, hitting his fur and making it appear more silvery. Shadows of trees and leaves gave him moving stripes of cold bluish-black. Somewhere beyond the spacious clearing, crickets chirped. He shivered and sighed.

As high as he'd climbed up the tree of political power, he was still a branch below his commander. Each time he'd gone to beg for Commander Aspen to reconsider his decision he'd been painfully reminded of that fact, once even driven to tears by the tom he looked up to more than anyone else in Dark's Valley. Now it seemed there was nothing left to do but lower his head, meow out a pitiful, defeated 'yes, sir,' then watch helplessly as his only daughter was drowned in the creek.

'What are we going to do?'

A cat stepped out of the den, blocking his path. Her tail twitched nervously. "Cloud?" she asked. "What's wrong? You're pacing again."

Her intelligent yellow eyes narrowed, and her lower jaw was tense.

'*She already knows.*' He turned away, unable to face her. "Oh. Song. You're awake. No, sorry, I was . . . thinking."

As he spoke, he let his gaze wander. Across the Glade, the History Tree stood tall and firm, like all those fateful words Dark had scarred into it and his clay tablets so many winters ago. He closed his eyes. His head throbbed.

Songbird stepped between him and the Tree. "It's Ember, isn't it? That's who he spoke with you about. Right? Don't try to hide it, Cloud. I know what's going on."

"Yes, it's about Ember. He said it's time. I don't know what to do," he whispered.

Her eyes widened. "No, we can't. Tell him we won't. You have to."

Cloud shook his head. "It's not that simple. You know it's not that simple. You know the rules, and you saw what happened today."

"Wait, no, you can't seriously be considering—"

"If we don't do something, he's going to. You know he will." He placed a paw against Songbird's, pressed his forehead against hers, and lowered his voice. "Look, I know it goes against everything inside of you right now, but what if he's right? What if she really is a defect? At this point, what if it really is an act of mercy? If we figure out a way to keep her, are we doing it out of love, or are we doing it out of selfishness?"

She pulled away from him, her loving warmth going cold. "There is nothing wrong with her. She isn't a defect; she's just Ember, and there is nothing wrong with her being her. Letting her live her life is the only mercy we can give her. The most selfish thing we could *ever* do would be getting rid of her just so no one else has to deal with her."

"She was out of control."

"She deserves a chance!" Songbird snapped. She flattened her ears and stepped closer.

"She was hurting herself, Song! And I don't know about you, but it hurts me to see her like that."

"Oh, so now this is about you?"

"No! Just listen to me. She couldn't even make it through the Festival without turning into a fox-fighting wildcat. What's she going to do when the Spring Meeting comes? What if she actually hurts someone next time?"

She growled. "Cloud! Watch your language."

Several cats hissed for them to be quiet. Cloud grimaced and lowered his voice. "Well it's true, isn't it? If she couldn't control herself around cats she knows, how will she act with Jade and the entire Eastern Council here? Who knows what will happen? We have to consider what's good for the Colony too."

Songbird stepped back, tail thrashing. "The Colony? Has it ever occurred to that big, thick head of yours that maybe the Colony is wrong? Maybe Commander Aspen is wrong. Maybe Dark himself was wrong." She licked a forepaw and tried to groom away her tears. "Maybe what's good for the Colony is not what's good for her," she said. "We have to give her a chance, Cloud."

Cloud sighed. He lowered his head and pawed at the dust. The crickets continued to chirp, emphasizing the relative quietness of the night. "I don't know that we have much of a say in this anymore. He said if we don't do something about her tomorrow, he will. I'm sorry, Song. I can't fix this. We no longer have a choice."

She padded up to him and nuzzled his cheek. Her tears dampened his fur and made his face feverish. "Yes, we do. Or at least you do. You're his chief advisor. If anyone can change his mind, it's you. Please, go to him, beg him again, and keep begging until he changes his mind. If you don't, I will. We can't give up on her just because she's not what you want her to be."

"Mommy? Daddy? What's going on? W-why're you fighting?"

"Ember?" Cloud spun around to find her standing in the den entrance, shaking all over. Her tiny white-tipped tail thrashed with anxiety. *'Oh no. How much does she know? Does she know he wants us to drown her? Does she know he wants her dead?'*

"We're not fighting, Sparky," he said. "Everything's going to be okay. We were just, uh, talking some things over. That's all."

"Are you mad at me?" she asked, voice barely above a whisper. Her lower jaw trembled, and her big kitten-blue eyes looked ready to cry at any moment.

Songbird walked over to her. She pulled her daughter close to her stomach. "We're not mad at you." She sniffled and lowered herself protectively over Ember's shivering form. "We love you, Ember. We love you more than anything else, and we would do anything for you." She shot him a glare. "Don't ever forget that."

He winced and looked at his paws. *'Is that true? Do I really love her more than anything else? Would I do anything to protect her? Am I willing to give up my rank for her? What about my life? Because at this point, that might be what it'll take.'*

"M-M-Mommy, why're you crying? You-you're not s-s'posed to cry. Are you sad?"

'Maybe I am being selfish? Am I trying to do what's right, or am I just trying to make my own life easier?'

"Mommy's going to be okay," Songbird replied. She groomed Ember's back and hugged her tighter. After a few bittersweet moments, she let her go. "Now get some rest. I'll be right back in there in a moment. I just need to finish talking with Daddy. Okay? Will you be a good molly and get some sleep?"

Ember shivered even harder as she broke away from Songbird's embrace. She ran back into the den crying. "I'll try. I'll try; I'll really try. I'm sorry."

'Tahg, she's right. Who am I trying to fool? Myself? This isn't what I want. I can't lose her.'

Songbird got to her paws and walked back to him. "She's struggling, but that doesn't mean she's broken," she whispered. "She doesn't want to be like this any more than we want her to be. You know that, Cloud. Don't try to hide it."

He sighed again. "I know. I can't, I can't do it. I'll go talk to Aspen again."

She pressed her head against his neck and buried her face in his fur, making it wet but warm. "Thank you."

"I can't promise anything will change, but I'll try my best."

She pulled away and looked down at her paws. "I guess that's all that matters right now. Better than doing nothing, at least."

She turned away from him. With a pained smile, she disappeared into the shadows of their den to comfort their only daughter. The crickets grew louder as Cloud strode across the Glade. While he walked, he strung words together inside his head. He glared at the History Tree as he passed it.

'Your reign is about to end, Dark. Your rules are about to change.' He chuffed. *'He'd hate me, wouldn't he? The ancient fox—I'll prove him wrong.'*

When he approached the commander's den, night guards in the trees eyed him suspiciously, but they lost interest and looked away moments later. He padded up to the den's entrance. "Commander Aspen?"

"Can it wait until tomorrow, Cloud?" a voice replied. It was gruff but not grating, firm but not harsh: Commander Aspen.

"No, sir," Cloud said. His voice rose an octave higher than it was supposed to be. *'Tahg, I sound like a kitten.'* He cleared his throat and coughed twice, trying to bring it back down to its normal pitch. "No, sir."

A long sigh came from the den. Paws tapped against hardened dirt, then an older tomcat appeared in the entrance. His eyes, one gold and one blue, looked more exhausted than annoyed. A patch of white covered half of his face, with the other half being ruddy agouti. One of his ears, torn in battle, twitched sporadically—a condition caused by nerve damage and aggravated by stress.

"After everything that's happened today, I'm too tired to hold a decent conversation. Make it quick," he said.

Cloud lowered his head in respect. "It's about Ember, sir. I can't kill her."

Aspen stretched and yawned. He walked out of the den, blinking the sleep from his eyes. "I understand how hard it must be for you as a young first-time father. Ending your only kitten's life is a difficult and emotional thing. I can take care of it myself at dawn. You don't even have to be present. Now go get yourself some rest."

An owl hooted. Cloud tensed, chest tight. "No, no, let me rephrase that. I can't let her die. Not by me, not by you, not by anyone. No one is killing her."

Aspen licked a paw and groomed his forehead. "Cloud, we've had this talk eleven times. You know what Dark's law says. We can't let defects continue on. It is unfair to them, and if they manage to find a mate, they'll have defective kittens. It will spread until no one can properly function, and the entire Western Colony will die. As long as she's alive, she is a risk. A threat to our way of life."

Cloud lifted a forepaw to examine it and found it quivering without permission. He placed it back on the ground and tried to at least feign confidence. "She's just a kitten. How can you say she's a threat? How can you know she's defective? She's barely even old enough to talk. Yes, she's quiet, but so was I at that age. That's not a crime. She hasn't done anything to bring this kind of punishment onto herself."

"It's not a matter of how quiet she is. You know that. She can't focus on anything. She won't listen when spoken to—won't even hear. She's scared of everything from noise to the sun. She squirms and twitches more than a captured squirrel. That's not normal, Cloud. Today at the Festival, when you and Songbird had to drag her into your den by the scruff, it only confirmed that this is more than anything simple discipline could ever fix. You can't fix her. No one can. And it'll only get worse."

Cloud sighed. *'But that doesn't mean she's a threat, does it?'* His mind went back to that afternoon. The Spring Festival had been going so well. They'd gone to a few of the clayworkers' dens, and even gotten Ember a little bijou to wear around her neck. She'd seemed to like it, pawing or staring at it anytime they'd stopped. She'd been slightly agitated all day, shivering anytime it got too crowded and even freezing up a few times. The little clay flower had seemed to calm her, so they'd decided to watch a sparring match. A cat had screamed when he'd gotten his ear bitten through, and that was when she'd lost it.

She'd tried to run at first, but Cloud had noticed and caught her by the scruff. He'd realized his mistake a moment too late, and she'd scratched him on the neck. When he'd set her down and blocked her from escaping again, she'd turned her attention to her bijou. She'd yanked it off of her neck, then bit down on it until it crumbled apart. Songbird, shocked by the sudden burst of destruction, had yelled at her and taken what remained of it away. Then Ember had started to yowl. She'd lashed out at anyone who got near her and had even bitten herself several times. It had taken the combined efforts of him and Songbird to get her back into the den.

Cloud shivered harder. "You don't know that. You don't know it'll get worse because no one with those problems has ever been allowed to live. Maybe she *can* be fixed."

Aspen sighed again. "You're a stubborn young tom, aren't you? Listen to me, Cloud. I know killing such a sweet little kitten seems cruel, but life isn't always fair. If it were, no one would ever be defective."

"And we'd all be the exact same," Cloud added.

"Not necessarily."

Cloud stepped closer, trying to look resolute. "Yes, we would. Because we would all have the same skills and abilities. No one would be better at any one thing, and no one would be worse."

"You're missing the point. What I do, I do for the good of the Western Colony—not for the good of you, not for the good of me, and not even for the good of Ember. If I were to let her live, you know I'd have to turn a blind eye to every other defect. Like Dark clawed into the great Commander's Tablet, it would be the downfall of our civilization. I can't risk the strong for the sake of the weak. I'm sorry, Cloud, but I'm doing it tomorrow."

'What is this? How have we lived like this for so long? Why was this never challenged? I can't be the first to see this. Right?' He clenched his teeth and held back a growl. Frustration and desperation made his vision blur as tears threatened to betray him. "But what if the Tree is wrong? What if Dark was wrong? She could grow up to be the best cat in the Colony, and you'd never know it because you killed her."

"Or the worst," Aspen replied. "That is a chance we can't afford to take right now. Dark's laws have kept us alive this long. I can't change our traditions for the sake of two desperate parents and a mistake."

"A mi—" He bit his tongue before it could say anything he might regret.

"Anyone could grow up to be the best or the worst cat in the Colony. You'd still be taking that chance, even if she seemed normal." His heart thudded his ears. He sucked in a deep breath, held it a moment, then let it out. "But you know what? Killing my daughter because of an unproven theory is a risk *I* can't afford to take. Maybe it's time for change. Give me a chance. Let me work with her. Let us prove you wrong. If some defects can be cured, we won't have to kill as many kittens. It'll take more work, but it'll help us grow stronger in the long run."

Aspen shook his head and returned to his den to lay down. "Please, don't keep this going. I've already spoken all that needs to be said. You are dismissed."

"No, I'm not." Cloud stepped into the den after his commander. The clay tablet with Dark's hidden guides and ancient decrees loomed in the shadows against the wall, glaring at him. "Not until you give me a chance."

"Yes. You are. Go to your den or you will be punished."

"I'm not going anywhere," he growled.

"I could remove you from the Council for this kind of disobedience."

"I don't care." He spread out his legs in a fighting stance. "Ember is more important to me than any rank or duty to this colony. I answer to my family first. Then you. Let me prove you wrong, or kill me, because that's the only way you're getting to her. I'll fight you if I have to. Do you really want to lose two cats with so much potential in one day?"

Aspen stared at him in silence. His damaged ear twitched more wildly. He sat up again. "I figured one day the very traits I saw in you, the things that have always made you such a good advisor, might turn you against me." He sighed. "I'll give you your chance, but only on one condition. If you fail to cure her, I will do what I have to do. End of discussion. Try to argue and we'll go back to the original plan."

His heart leapt in his chest. *'A chance! I have a chance! I can fix her. I can make her better. I can make sure no one will ever call her a mistake or a defect again.'* "Thank you. Thank you, sir! I'll do my best. I should probably go tell Songbird now. Thank you."

542

Aspen stood, circled around a few times, then settled back down. "Don't get too excited. She won't be changed easily, if she can be fixed at all. Now go get yourself some rest, you stubborn coyote. I hope I don't regret this."

Cloud strode away, heart racing. "You won't," he called over his shoulder. As he passed the History Tree, he felt a burst of pride fill his chest. He smiled. *'It's over, Dark. I won.'*

Songbird jumped to her paws as he entered the little family den, almost hitting her head on a knot of wood in the process. "So?"

He smiled. "I got us a chance. It's not a guarantee, but—"

She wrapped her paws around his shoulders and buried her face in his fur. "Thank you!" Her ears perked up against his chin. She pulled back and coughed. "Uhm, but really, thanks. A chance is all we need, isn't it? I love you, you know. Right?"

He chuckled. "Of course I do. And I love you too. I'm sorry I yelled at you earlier."

"Are we happy or sad?" Ember asked.

"What?" Songbird mewed. "We-we're happy, Emmy. We're really, really happy."

"Then why are you crying?"

Cloud and Songbird exchanged a look. Cloud chuffed and shook his head. "You'll understand when you're older, Sparky. Go to sleep now. We've got a big day ahead of us."

"M'kay."

Songbird lay down against the edge of the den. Ember curled up in her paws, purring softly. Songbird sniffled a few times, then started to sing. It was an old lullaby but oddly fitting, given the day's occurrences.

"Sleep, little one. The fear has gone. The fear has gone. The fear has gone. Sleep, little one—for goodness, it has won. You'll be safe with me right here tonight."

Cloud lay beside them and let the tune ease his fears. *'She can do it. We can do it. Whatever is causing this, we can overcome it together. We'll save her life, she'll be happy, and everything is going to be okay.'*

Songbird groomed a few rogue patches of fur on Ember's head, then sang the next verse, "So goodnight; sleep tight. Rest your little head. Goodnight; sleep tight. See you in the morning light. Goodnight; sleep tight. Rest my little one. Goodnight; sleep tight. I'll see you when the sun is bright. Goodnight."

As the lingering sweetness of her voice faded, doubts started to creep in. He mentally shook them away and closed his eyes. 'This system is flawed. If I can't fix her or it, we can leave. Come to think of it, I don't think I'd mind the life of an Outsider. Sounds a lot more free than this life.' He breathed a quiet sigh of contentment. 'Don't worry, Ember. You're safe now. I won't let anyone hurt you. We will protect you. No matter what comes our way, I will keep you safe. I promise.'

Made in the USA
Monee, IL
12 September 2020